HEAVENLY DESCENT

He descended from the sky.

Virtually all of the witnesses said that he left a glowing track through the air as he came down, but none claimed to have seen any sort of vehicle. Unless the laws of falling bodies have been repealed, Vornan-19 was traveling at a velocity of several thousand feet per second at the moment of impact, based on the assumption that he was released from some hovering vehicle just out of sight above the church. Yet he landed upright, on both feet, with no visible sign of discomfort.

He was naked. Three of the witnesses asserted that a glittering nimbus or aura enfolded him, exposing the contours of his body but opaque enough in the genital region to shield his nakedness. A loinhalo, so to speak.

It happens that these three witnesses were nuns on the steps of the church. The remaining ninety-six witnesses insisted on Vornan-19's total nudity. Problem: Did the nuns collectively hallucinate the nimbus that supposedly protected Vornan's modesty? Did the nuns deliberately invent the existence of the nimbus to protect their own modesty? Or did Vornan arrange things so that most of the witnesses saw him entire, while those who might suffer emotional distress from the sight had a different view of him?

I don't know. But I refuse to underestimate his deviousness. Nor do I think it would have been technically impossible for Vornan to appear one way to ninety-six onlookers and another way to the other three.

THE MASKS OF TIME
BORN WITH THE DEAD
DYING INSIDE

Robert Silverberg

BANTAM BOOKS
TORONTO • NEW YORK • LONDON • SYDNEY • AUCKLAND

THE MASKS OF TIME
BORN WITH THE DEAD
DYING INSIDE

A Bantam Book / April 1988

PRINTING HISTORY
THE MASKS OF TIME copyright © 1968 by Robert Silverberg.
BORN WITH THE DEAD copyright © 1971, 1972, 1974
by Robert Silverberg.
DYING INSIDE copyright © 1972 by Robert Silverberg.
From BORN WITH THE DEAD
Excerpts from "Little Gidding" in FOUR QUARTETS
by T.S. Eliot are reprinted by permission of Harcourt Brace
Jovanovich, Inc. and Faber and Faber Publishers.
Copyright 1943 by T.S. Eliot; renewed © 1971 by
Esme Valerie Eliot.

ISBN 0-553-27286-1

Published simultaneously in the United States and Canada

Bantam Books are published by Bantam Books, a division
of Bantam Doubleday Dell Publishing Group, Inc. Its trademark, consisting of the words "Bantam Books" and the por-
trayal of a rooster, is Registered in U.S. Patent and Trademark
Office and in other countries. Marca Registrada. Bantam
Books, 666 Fifth Avenue, New York, New York 10103.

PRINTED IN THE UNITED STATES OF AMERICA

O   0 9 8 7 6 5 4 3 2 1

INTRODUCTION

"Science Fiction" is a term that can be stretched to cover a great many widely differing kinds of story. Consider the biting social satire of *Gulliver's Travels*, the flamboyant spoofing of history and myth in *A Connecticut Yankee at King Arthur's Court*, the visionary power of *The Time Machine*, the harsh political insights of *1984*, and the technological cleverness, so advanced for its time, of *20,000 Leagues Under the Sea*. All these books are science fiction—that is, they develop in a logical and plausible way the consequences of a single fantastic premise—and yet each differs radically from the others in the manner of its telling, the effect it creates in the reader, and, unless I am greatly mistaken, in the primary intention of its author. They are not only great works of science fiction, of course: all five are classics of literature which have won permanent places in our collective imagination. You will note that I see nothing that is necessarily mutually exclusive about the terms "great science fiction" and "classics of literature."

Neither Swift, Twain, nor Orwell was what anyone would call a science fiction writer: they were writers, non-categorized and non-categorizable, who made use of science fictional themes in unforgettable ways when using such themes was appropriate to their purposes. Wells, though he spent ten or fifteen years producing some of the greatest science fiction anyone has ever written, would have balked at calling himself a science fiction writer. During those productive years Wells regarded himself as a philosopher, a journalist, a social historian, and a polemicist; his science fiction was only one of the many ways he expressed his view of the world. Verne, perhaps, was a different item, a professional writer of fantastic romances through much of his life: very likely if he were writing today he'd be showing up at science fiction conventions, trading shoptalk with the gang, and walking away with his share of Hugo and Nebula awards. More than any of the other writers I've mentioned, he had the specific "science fiction" way of viewing the world that is so typical of Robert A. Heinlein, Isaac Asimov, Theodore Sturgeon, and the other great s-f writers of modern times.

Though those three writers, and many more that you or I could name, have done creditable work worthy of the mantle of Wells or Verne, science fiction in the modern United States has generally moved away from the mainstream literary tradition and placed itself firmly in the category of popular, commercial entertainment. For a long time the only place it was published in this country was in magazines with names like *Astounding Science Fiction* and *Thrilling Wonder Stories*, presented in gaudy formats designed to win adolescent readers away from comic books; and when it became a staple of paperback publishing in the 1950's it was (and still is) usually offered to the public behind lively poster-like cover paintings of writhing monsters, brawny swordsmen, and slinky seductive temptresses. Though the fiction within those often crass packages tended to be more complex and thoughtful than a casual glance would indicate, the conventions of pulp magazine writing came to dominate even the best work in the field. A fast narrative pace, a strong plot, a neat and usually positive resolution of conflicts: these were the underlying requirements of the magazine and paperback editors, because they were the requirements of the newsstand audience. The writers who deviated significantly from these requirements (Ray Bradbury is the first who comes to my mind, but also Sturgeon, C.M. Kornbluth, C.L. Moore, and Fritz Leiber) were few and far between.

As science fiction as a commercial publishing category evolved toward its maturity in the United States, we saw it subdivide into a number of distinct subcategories. There was s-f of Wellsian visionary power—I cite Arthur C. Clarke here—and s-f as social satire—Frederik Pohl and Robert Sheckley come to mind—and s-f as technological speculation—here I cite Hal Clement and Poul Anderson—and s-f as black humor, exemplified by Philip K. Dick or Thomas M. Disch.

There was the s-f of Philip Jose Farmer, in which biology shaded into eroticism. There was the s-f of rip-snorting unabashed adventure, pioneered by E.E. "Doc" Smith. There was s-f that clung so close to the present day that it was almost indistinguishable from the political thriller, and s-f that ventured so far into the remote future that it operated in a barely comprehensible realm of private imagination.

In my own career as a writer, which began some 35 years ago, I have tackled just about all of these variants, some with rather more success than others. But as my own career developed I found one mode of science fiction more congenial than any other: one that derives, perhaps, from H.G. Wells, in which the central focus of the writer's attention— beyond, of course, the development of the overriding science fictional *idea* that must infuse itself into every line of a good science fiction book—is the exploration of character. This drew me inevitably in the direction of what we in science fiction call "mainstream" literature: back toward the world of "real" novels, where a concern with human reality and with questions of literary expressivity are at least as important to the writer as a book's underlying ideational structure.

I'm not telling you that I produced great literature in that period, or even that I set out to produce great literature. A writer who claims to have achieved great literature is a braggart, and one who embarks on a book with the *a priori* idea of creating great literature is a fool: I hope I am neither. A sensible writer, giving as little thought to posterity as he can, conceives a story and attempts to write it with all the skill and conviction at his disposal, making use of whatever richness of perception his life's experience has provided him with and all the technical resources he can muster. If all goes well, he may achieve greatness, but that's for others to determine, usually at some remove in time. The writer's job is to serve the story, and thereby to serve the reader; the making of literature is a by-product of those goals, not a primary intention.

What I tried to do at the time when I wrote the two novels and three long stories that this book contains, between 1967 and 1973, was to approach the *material* of science fiction with the same sort of high seriousness of purpose that the "mainstream" writers I most respected—Conrad, say, or Faulkner, or Hemingway, or Joyce—would have applied to their material. That is, I tried to step away from the pulp magazine traditions in which science fiction had too long been encased, and to deal with such well-worn science fictional subjects as telepathy, immortality, and time-travel as if they were new, handling my themes as intensely and as honestly as the authors of *Lord Jim* or *Portrait of the Artist* or *The Sun Also Rises* or *Absalom, Absalom* had dealt with theirs.

It was a chancy thing to do in a field where writers are dependent for their livelihoods on their popularity with readers in search of light entertainment. Someone who had just gone to see *Star Wars* and now wanted to find a science fiction book that would provide the same sort of easy good-natured fun was not likely to be pleased with *Dying Inside* or *Born with the Dead*. I suppose that I alienated many new readers who were looking for something simpler and less demanding than I was trying to provide, and even some older readers for whom science fiction had never been more than a light diversion. What they wanted to read was not what I wanted to write, but they had no way of telling that until they had bought the book.

Well, there are readers and readers, there are writers and writers, there is science fiction and science fiction. Such stories as *The Masks of Time*, *Dying Inside*, and *Born with the Dead*, which also includes "Going" and "Thomas the Proclaimer," may alienate some readers, but evidently they offer rewards to others, as is shown by the awards they have collected over the years and their continued popularity with readers of serious science fiction in a dozen countries. There are no slimy monsters here, no spaceships, no glamorous princesses, no sword-swinging heroes, and if those are the things you want science fiction to provide for you, I recommend in all kindness that you put this book back in the rack and search for something else. On the other hand, if those are the very aspects of science fiction that put you off but you are nevertheless open to the sort of imaginative thinking that only science fiction can provide, there may well be something here for you. So I have been told by others, often enough so that I tend to believe it.

At any rate, these are stories in which I tried to reach beyond pulp magazine traditions toward the highest levels of narrative art. How far I may have climbed toward those levels is not for me to say, and nothing you have just read is meant to stake out a claim for me in the pantheon of letters next to

Joyce and Faulkner, or Twain or Swift, or any other writer whose name I've invoked here. What I will assert—and here no one may dispute me—is that in these stories I've written as well as I know how, and that I feel the pride of an honest craftsman in the results. There are many sorts of science fiction. Those readers who are pleased by the sort of science fiction of which this book is a representative will, I hope and believe, be pleased by this book. I know that that verges on tautology; but one indisputable and comforting thing about tautologies is that they're true. I wrote these stories for myself, but also for you: and you know who you are.

—Robert Silverberg
September, 1987

THE MASKS
OF
TIME

for A. J. and Eddie

One

A memoir of this sort should begin with some kind of statement of personal involvement, I suppose: I was the man, I was there, I suffered. And in fact my involvement with the improbable events of the past twelve months was great, I knew the man from the future. I followed him on his nightmare orbit around our world. I was with him at the end.

But not at the beginning. And so, if I am to tell a complete tale of *him*, it must be a more-than-complete tale of *me*. When Vornan-19 arrived in our era, I was so far removed from even the most extraordinary current matters that I did not find out about it for several weeks. Yet eventually I was drawn into the whirlpool he created... as were you, all of you, as was each of us everywhere.

I am Leo Garfield. My age is fifty-two as of tonight, the fifth of December, 1999. I am unmarried—by choice—and in excellent health. I live in Irvine, California, and hold the Schultz Chair of Physics at the University of California. My work concerns the time-reversal of sub-atomic particles. I have never taught in the classroom. I have several young graduate students whom I regard, as does the University, as my pupils, but there is no formal instruction in the usual sense in our laboratory. I have devoted most of my adult life to time-reversal physics, and I have succeeded mainly in inducing a few electrons to turn on their tails and flee into the past. I once thought that a considerable achievement.

At the time of Vornan-19's arrival, a little less than one year ago, I had reached an impasse in my work and had gone into the desert to scowl myself past the blockage point. I don't offer that as an excuse for my failure to be in on the news of his coming. I was staying at the home of friends some fifty miles south of Tucson, in a thoroughly modern dwelling equipped with wallscreens, dataphones, and the other expectable communications channels, and I suppose I could have followed the events right from the first bulletins. If I did not, it was because I was not in the habit of following current events very closely, and not because I was in any state of isolation. My long walks in the desert each day were spiritually quite useful, but at nightfall I rejoined the human race.

When I retell the story of how Vornan-19 came among us, then, you must understand that I am doing it at several removes. By the time I became involved in it, the story was as old as the fall of Byzantium or the triumphs of Attila, and I learned of it as I would have learned of any historical event.

He materialized in Rome on the afternoon of December 25, 1998.

Rome? On Christmas Day? Surely he chose it for deliberate effect. A new Messiah, dropping from heaven on that day in that city? How obvious! How cheap!

But in fact he insisted it had been accidental. He smiled in that irresistible way, drew his thumbs across the soft skin just beneath his eyelids, and said softly, "I had one chance in three hundred sixty-five to land on any given day. I let the probabilities fall where they chose. What is the significance of this Christmas Day, again?"

"The birthday of the Savior," I said. "A long time ago."

"The savior of what, please?"

"Of mankind. He who came to redeem us from sin."

Vornan-19 peered into that sphere of emptiness that always seemed to lurk a few feet before his face. I suppose he was meditating on the concepts of salvation and redemption and sin, attempting to stuff some content into the sounds. At length he said, "This redeemer of mankind was born at Rome?"

"Bethlehem."

"A suburb of Rome?"

"Not exactly," I said. "As long as you showed up on Christmas Day, you should have arrived in Bethlehem, though."

"I would have," Vornan replied, "if I had planned it for its effect. But I knew nothing of your holy one, Leo. Neither his birthday nor his birthplace nor his name."

"Is Jesus forgotten in your time, Vornan?"

"I am a very ignorant man, as I must keep reminding you. I have never studied ancient religions. It was chance that brought me to that place at that time." And mischief flickered like playful lightning across his elegant features.

Perhaps he was telling the truth. Bethlehem might have been more effective if he had wanted to manipulate the Messiah effect. At the very least, choosing Rome, he might have come down in the piazza in front of St. Peter's, say at the moment that Pope Sixtus was delivering his blessing to the multitudes. A silvery shimmer, a figure drifting downward, hundreds of thousands of the devout on their knees in awe, the messenger from the future alighting gently, smiling, making the sign of the Cross, sending across the multitude the silent current of good will and repose best befitting this day of celebration. But he did not. He appeared instead at the foot of the Spanish Stairs, by the fountain, in that street usually choked by prosperous shoppers surging toward the boutiques of the Via Condotti. At noon on Christmas Day the Piazza di Spagna was all but empty, the shops of Via Condotti were closed, the Stairs themselves were cleared of their traditional loungers. On the top steps were a few worshippers heading for the church of Trinità dei Monti. It was a cold wintry day, with flecks of snow circling in the gray sky; a sour wind was blowing off the Tiber. Rome was uneasy that day. The Apocalyptists had rioted only the night before; rampaging mobs with painted faces had gone streaming through the Forum, had danced an out-of-season Walpurgisnacht ballet around the tattered walls of the Colosseum, had scrambled up the hideous bulk of the Victor Emmanuel Monument to desecrate its whiteness with fierce copulations. It was the worst of the outbreaks of unreason that had swept through Rome that year, although it was not as violent as the customary Apocalyptist outburst in London, say, or for that matter in New York. Yet it had been quelled only with great difficulties by *carabinieri* wielding neural whips and wading into the screaming, gesticulating cultists in complete ruthlessness. Toward dawn, they say, the Eternal City still echoed with the saturnalian cries. Then came the morning of the Christ Child, and at noon, while I still slept in Arizona's winter warmth, there appeared out of the iron-hard sky the glowing figure of Vornan-19, the man from the future.

There were ninety-nine witnesses. They agreed in all the fundamental details.

He descended from the sky. Everyone interviewed reported that he appeared on an arc coming in over Trinità dei Monti, soared past the Spanish Stairs, and alighted in the Piazza di Spagna a few yards beyond the boat-shaped fountain. Virtually all of the witnesses said that he left a glowing track through the air as he came down, but none claimed to have seen any sort of vehicle. Unless the laws of falling bodies have been repealed, Vornan-19 was traveling at a velocity of several thousand feet per second at the moment of impact, based on the assumption that he was released from some hovering vehicle just out of sight above the church.

Yet he landed upright, on both feet, with no visible sign of discomfort. He later spoke vaguely of a "gravity neutralizer" that had cushioned his descent, but he gave no details, and now we are not likely to discover any.

He was naked. Three of the witnesses asserted that a glittering nimbus or aura enfolded him, exposing the contours of his body but opaque enough in the genital region to shield his nakedness. A loin-halo, so to speak. It happens that these three witnesses were nuns on the steps of the church. The remaining ninety-six witnesses insisted on Vornan-19's total nudity. Most of them were able to describe the anatomy of his external reproductive system in explicit detail. Vornan was an exceptionally masculine man, as we all came to know, but those revelations were still in the future when the eyewitnesses described how well hung he was.

Problem: Did the nuns collectively hallucinate the nimbus that supposedly protected Vornan's modesty? Did the nuns deliberately invent the existence of the nimbus to protect their own modesty? Or did Vornan arrange things so that most of the witnesses saw him entire, while those who might suffer emotional distress from the sight had a different view of him?

I don't know. The cult of the Apocalypse has given us ample evidence that collective hallucinations are possible, so I don't discount the first suggestion. Nor the second, for organized religion has provided us with two thousand years of precedent for the cold statement that its functionaries don't always tell the truth. As for the idea that Vornan would go out of his way to spare the nuns from looking upon his nakedness, I'm skeptical. It was never his style to protect anyone from any kind of jolt, nor did he really seem aware that human beings needed to be shielded from anything so astonishing as the body of a fellow human. Besides, if he hadn't even heard of Christ, how would he have known anything about nuns and their vows? But I refuse to underestimate his deviousness. Nor do I think it would have been technically impossible for Vornan to appear one way to ninety-six onlookers and another way to the other three.

We do know that the nuns fled into the church within moments after his arrival. Some of the others assumed that Vornan was some kind of Apocalyptist maniac and ceased to pay attention to him. But a good many watched in fascination as the nude stranger, having made his dramatic appearance, wandered about the Piazza di Spagna, inspecting first the fountain, then the shop windows on the far side, and then the row of parked automobiles at the curb. The wintry chill had no apparent effect on him. When he had seen all he wished to see at that side of the piazza, he sauntered across and began to mount the stairs. He was on the fifth step and moving without hurry when a frenzied-looking policeman rushed up and shouted at him to come down and get into the wagon.

Vornan-19 replied, "I will not do as you say."

Those were his first words to us—the opening lines of his Epistle to the Barbarians. He spoke in English. Many of the witnesses heard and understood what he had said. The policeman did not, and continued to harangue him in Italian.

Vornan-19 said, "I am a traveler from a distant era. I am here to inspect your world."

Still in English. The policeman sputtered. He believed that Vornan was an Apocalyptist, and an American Apocalyptist at that, the worst kind. The policeman's duty was to defend the decency of Rome and the sanctity of Christmas Day against this madman's exhibitionist vulgarities. He shouted at the visitor to come down the steps. Ignoring him, Vornan-19 turned and serenely continued upward. The sight of those pale, slender retreating buttocks maddened the officer of the law. He removed his own cloak and rushed up the steps, determined to wrap it around the stranger.

Witnesses declare that Vornan-19 did not look at the policeman or touch him in any way. The officer, holding the cloak in his left hand, reached out with his right to seize Vornan's shoulder. There was a faint gleaming yellowish-blue discharge, and a slight popping sound, and the policeman tumbled backward as though he had been struck by an electric bolt. Crumpling as he fell, he rolled to the bottom of the stairs and lay in a heap, twitching faintly. The onlookers drew back. Vornan-19 proceeded up the steps to the top, halting there to tell one of the witnesses a bit about himself.

The witness was a German Apocalyptist named Horst Klein, nineteen years old, who had taken part in the revelry at the Forum between midnight and dawn and now, too keyed up to go to sleep, was wandering the city in a mood of *post coitum* depression. Young Klein, fluent in English, became a familiar television personality in the days that followed, repeating his story for the benefit of global networks. Then he slipped into oblivion, but his place in history is assured. I don't doubt that somewhere in Mecklenburg or Schleswig today he's repeating the conversation yet.

As Vornan-19 approached him, Klein said, "You shouldn't kill *carabinieri*. They won't forgive you."

"He isn't dead. merely stunned a bit."

"You don't talk like an American," said Klein.

"I'm not. I come from the Centrality. That's a thousand years from now, you understand."

Klein laughed. "The world ends in three hundred seventy-two days."

"Do you believe that? What year is this, anyway?"

"1998. December twenty-fifth."

"The world has at least a thousand more years. Of that I'm certain. I am Vornan-19, and I am here as a visitor. I am in need of hospitality. I would like to sample your food and your wine. I wish to wear clothing of the period. I am interested in ancient sexual practices. Where may I find a house of intercourse?"

"That gray building there," said Klein, pointing toward the church of Trinità dei Monti. "They'll take care of all your needs inside. Just tell them you come from a thousand years from now. 2998, is it?"

"2999 by your system."

"Good. They'll love you for that. Just prove to them that the world isn't going to end a year from New Year's Day, and they'll give you whatever you want."

"The world will not end quite so soon," said Vornan-19 gravely. "I thank you, my friend."

He began to move toward the church.

Breathless *carabinieri* rushed at him from several directions at once. They did not dare come within five yards of him, but they formed a phalanx barring him from access to the church. They were armed with neural whips. One of them flung his cloak at Vornan's feet.

"Put that on."

"I do not speak your language."

Horst Klein said, "They want you to cover your body. The sight of it offends them."

"My body is undeformed," said Vornan-19. "Why should I cover it?"

"They want you to, and they have neural whips. They can hurt you with them. See? Those gray rods in their hands."

"My I examine your weapon?" The visitor said affably to the nearest officer. He reached for it. The man shrank back. Vornan moved with implausible swiftness and wrenched the whip from the policeman's hand. He took it business end first, and should have received a stunning near-lethal burst, but somehow he did not. The policemen gaped as Vornan studied the whip, casually triggering it and rubbing his hand across the metal prod to feel the effects it produced. They stepped back, crossing themselves fervently.

Horst Klein broke through the crumbling phalanx and flung himself at Vornan's feet. "You really *are* from the future, aren't you?"

"Of course."

"How do you do it—touch the whip?"

"These mild forces can be absorbed and transformed," said Vornan. "Don't you have the energy rituals yet?"

The German boy, trembling, shook his head. He scooped up the policeman's cloak and offered it to the naked man. "Put this over yourself," he whispered. "Please. Make things easier for us. You can't walk around naked."

Surprisingly, Vornan consented. After some fumbling he managed to don the cloak.

Klein said, "The world doesn't end in a year?"

"No. Certainly not."

"I've been a fool!"

"Perhaps."

Tears ran down the broad, unlined Teutonic cheeks. The frayed laughter of exhaustion ripped through Horst Klein's lips. He groveled on the cold stone slab, slapping his palms against the ground in an improvised salaam before Vornan-19. Shivering, sobbing, gasping, Horst Klein recanted his faith in the Apocalyptist movement.

The man from the future had gained his first disciple.

Two

In Arizona I knew nothing of this. If I had known, I would have dismissed it as folly. But I was at a dead end in my life, sterile and stale from overwork and underachievement, and I paid no attention to anything that took place beyond the confines of my own skull. My mood was ascetic, and among the things I denied myself that month was an awareness of world events.

My hosts were kind. They had seen me through these crises before, and they knew how to handle me. What I needed was a delicate combination of attention and solitude, and only persons of a certain sensibility could provide the necessary atmosphere. It would not be improper to say that Jack and Shirley Bryant had saved my sanity several times.

Jack had worked with me at Irvine for several years, late in the 1980's. He had come to me straight from M.I.T., where he had captured most of the available honors, and like most refugees from that institution he had something pallid and cramped about his soul, the stigmata of too much eastern living, too many harsh winters and airless summers. It was a pleasure to watch him open like a sturdy flower in our sunlight. He was in his very early twenties when I met him: tall but hollow-chested, with thick unkempt curling hair, cheeks perpetually stubbled, sunken eyes, thin restless lips. He had all the stereotyped traits and tics and habits of the young genius. I had read his papers in particle physics, and they were brilliant. You must realize that in physics one works by following sudden lancing insights—inspirations, perhaps—and so it is not necessary to be old and wise before one can be brilliant. Newton reshaped the universe while only a lad. Einstein, Schrödinger, Heisenberg, Pauli, and the rest of that crew of pioneers did their finest work before they were thirty. One may, like Bohr, get shrewder and deeper with age, but Bohr was still young when he peered within the atom's heart. So when I say that Jack Bryant's work was brilliant, I do not mean merely that he was an exceptionally promising young man. I mean that he was brilliant on an absolute scale and that he had achieved greatness while still an undergraduate.

During the first two years he was with me, I thought he was genuinely destined to remake physics. He had that strange power, that gift of the shattering intuition that pierces all doubt; and, too, he had the mathematical ability and persistence to follow up his intuition and wrest firm truth from the unknown. His work was only marginally connected with mine. My time-reversal project had become more experimental than theoretical by this time, since I had moved through the stages of early hypotheses and now was spending most of my time at the giant particle accelerator, trying to build up the forces that I hoped would send fragments of atoms flying pastwards. Jack, on the contrary, was still the pure theoretician. His concern was the binding force of the atom. There was nothing new about that, of course. But Jack had doubled back to reexamine some overlooked implications of Yukawa's 1935 work on mesons, and in the course of reviewing the old literature, had generally reshuffed everything that supposedly was known about the glue that holds the atom together. It seemed to me that Jack was on his way to one of the revolutionary discoveries of mankind: an understanding of the fundamental energy relationships out of which the universe is constructed. Which is, of course, what we all ultimately seek.

Since I was Jack's sponsor, I kept an eye on his studies, looking over the successive drafts of his doctoral thesis while devoting most of my energies to my own work. Only gradually did the larger implications of Jack's research dawn on me. I had been looking at it within the self-enclosed sphere of pure physics, but I now saw that the final outcome of Jack's work had to be highly practical. He was heading toward a means of tapping the binding force of the atom and liberating that energy not through a sudden explosion but in a controlled flow.

Jack himself did not seem to see it. Applications of physical theory were of no interest to him. Working within his airless environment of equations, he paid no more heed to such possibilities than he did to the fluctuations of the stock market. Yet I saw it. Rutherford's work at the beginning of the twentieth century had been pure theory too, yet it led unerringly to the sunburst over Hiroshima. Lesser men could search within the core of Jack's thesis and find there the means for total liberation of atomic energy. Neither fission nor fusion would be necessary. *Any* atom could be opened and drained. A cup of soil would run a million-kilowatt generator. A few drops of water would send a ship to the moon. This was the atomic energy of fantasy. It was all there, implicit in Jack's work.

But Jack's work was incomplete.

In his third year at Irvine he came to me, looking haggard and depleted, and said he was halting work on his thesis. He was at a point, he told me, where he needed to pause and consider. Meanwhile he asked for permission to engage in certain experimental work, simply as a change of air. Naturally, I agreed.

I said nothing whatever to him about the potential practical applications of his work. That was not my place. I confess a sense of relief mingled with the disappointment when he interrupted his research. I had been reflecting on the economic upheaval that would come to society in another ten or fifteen years, when every home might run on its own inexhaustible power source, when transportation and communication would cease to depend on the traditional energy inputs, when the entire network of labor relationships on which our society is based would utterly collapse. Strictly as an amateur sociologist, I was disturbed by the conclusions I drew. If I had been an executive of any of the major corporations, I would have had Jack Bryant assassinated at once. As it was, I merely worried. It was not very distinguished of me, I admit. The true man of science forges ahead heedless of the economic consequences. He seeks truth even if the truth should bring society tumbling down. Those are tenets of virtue.

I kept my own counsel. If Jack had wished at any time to return to his work, I would not have attempted to prevent it. I would not even have asked him to consider the long-range possibilities. He did not realize that any moral dilemma existed, and I was not going to be the one to tell him about it.

By my silence, of course, I was making myself an accomplice in the destruction of the human economy. I might have pointed out to Jack that his work, extended to the extreme, would give each human being an unlimited access to an infinite energy source, demolishing the foundation of every human society and creating an instant decentralization of mankind. Through my interference I might have caused Jack to hesitate. But I said nothing. Give me no medals of honor, though; my anguish remained in suspension so long as Jack remained idle. He was making no further progress on his research, so I had no need to fret over the chances of its successful outcome. Once he got back to it, the moral problem would face me again: whether to support the free play of scientific inquiry, or to intervene for the sake of maintaining the economic status quo.

It was a villainous choice. But I was spared making it.

During his third year with me Jack pottered around the campus doing trivial things. He spent most of his time at the accelerator, as though he had just discovered the experimental side of physics and did not tire of toying with it. Our accelerator was new and awesome, a proton-loop model with a neutron injector. It operated in the trillion-electron-volt range then; of course, the current alpha-spiral machines far exceed that, but in its day it was a colossus. The twin pylons of the high-voltage lines carrying current from the fusion plant at the edge of the Pacific seemed like titanic messengers of power, and the great dome of the accelerator building itself gleamed in mighty self-satisfaction. Jack haunted the building. He sat by the screens while undergraduates performed elementary experiments in neutrino detection and in antiparticle annihilation. Occasionally he tinkered with the control panels just to see how they worked and to find out how it felt to be master of those surging forces. But what he was doing was meaningless. It was busywork. He was deliberatly marking time.

Was it really because he needed a rest?

Or had he seen the implications of his own work at last—and been frightened?

I never asked him. In such cases I wait for a troubled younger man to come to me with his troubles. And I could not take the risk of infecting Jack's mind with my own doubts if those doubts had not already occurred to him.

At the end of his second semester of idleness he requested a formal counseling session with me. Here it comes, I thought. He's going to tell me where his work is leading, and he'll ask me if I think it's morally proper for him to continue, and then I'll be on the spot. I came to the session loaded with pills.

He said, "Leo, I'd like to resign from the University."

I was shaken. "You have a better offer?"

"Don't be absurd. I'm leaving physics."

"Leaving—physics—?"

"And getting married. Do you know Shirley Frisch? You've seen me with her. We're getting married a week from Sunday. It'll be a small wedding, but I'd like you to come, Leo."

"And then?"

"We've bought a house in Arizona. In the desert near Tucson. We'll be moving there."

"What will you do, Jack?"

"Meditate. Write, a little. There are some philosophical questions I want to consider."

"Money?" I asked. "Your University salary—"

"I've got a small inheritance that somebody invested wisely a long time ago. Shirley's also got a private income. It's nothing much, but it'll let us get by. We're dropping out of society. I felt I couldn't hide it from you any more."

I spread my hands on my desk and contemplated my knuckles for a long moment. I felt as though webs had begun to sprout between my fingers. Eventually I said, "What about your thesis, Jack?"

"Discontinued."

"You were so close to finishing it."

"I'm at a total dead end. I can't go on." His eyes met mine and remained fixed. Was he telling me that he didn't *dare* go on? Was his withdrawal at this point a matter of scientific defeat or of moral doubt? I wanted to ask. I waited for him to tell me. He said nothing. His smile was rigid and unconvincing. Finally he said, "Leo, I don't think I'd ever do anything worthwhile in physics."

"That isn't true. You—"

"I don't think I even *want* to do anything worthwhile in physics."

"Oh."

"Will you forgive me? Will you still be my friend? *Our* friend?"

I came to the wedding. It turned out I was one of four guests. The bride was a girl I knew only vaguely; she was about twenty-two, a pretty blonde, a graduate student in sociology. God knows how Jack had ever met her, with his nose pushed into his notebooks all the time, but they seemed very much in love. She was tall, almost to Jack's shoulder, with a great cascade of golden hair like finespun wire, and honey-tanned skin, and big dark eyes, and a supple, athletic body. Beyond a doubt she was beautiful, and in her short white wedding gown she looked as radiant as any bride has ever looked. The ceremony was brief and nonsectarian. Afterwards we all went to dinner, and toward sundown the bride and groom quietly disappeared. I felt a curious emptiness that night as I went home. I rummaged among old papers for lack of anything else to do, and came upon some early drafts of Jack's thesis; I stood staring at the scrawled notations for a long while, comprehending nothing.

A month later they invited me to be their guest for a week in Arizona.

I thought it was a *pro forma* invitation and politely declined, thinking I was expected to decline. Jack phoned and insisted I come. His face was as earnest as ever, but the little greenish screen clearly showed that the tension and haggardness had been ironed from it. I accepted. Their house, I found, was perfectly isolated, with miles of tawny desert on all sides. It was a fortress of comfort in all that bleakness. Jack and Shirley were both deeply tanned, magnificently happy, and wonderfully attuned to each other. They led me on a long walk into the desert my first day, laughing as jackrabbits or desert rats or long green lizards scuttered past us. They stooped to show me small gnarled plants close to the barren soil, and took me to a towering saguaro cactus whose massive corrugated green arms cast the only shade in view.

Their home became a refuge for me. It was understood that I was free to come at any time on a day's notice, whenever I felt the need to escape. Although they extended invitations from time to time, they insisted that I avail myself of the privilege of inviting myself. I did. Sometimes six or ten months went by without my making the journey to Arizona; sometimes I came for five or six weekends in a row. There was never any regular pattern. My need to visit them depended wholly upon my inner weather. *Their* weather never changed, within or without; their days were forever sunny. I never saw them quarrel or even mildly disagree. Not until the day that Vornan-19 careened into their life was there any gulf visible between them.

Gradually our relationship deepened into something subtle and intimate. I suppose I was essentially an uncle figure to them, since I was in my mid-forties, Jack was not yet thirty, and Shirley hardly into her twenties; yet the tie was deeper than that. One would have to call it love. There was nothing overtly sexual in it, though I would gladly have slept with Shirley if we had met some other way; certainly I found her physically attractive, and the attraction increased as time and the sun burnished from her some of the charming immaturity that made me at first think of her as a girl and not as a woman. But though my relationship to Jack and Shirley was a triangular one, with emotional vectors leading in many paths, it never threatened to break down into a seamy experiment in adultery. I admired Shirley, but I did not—I think—envy

Jack his physical possession of her. At night, when I heard the sounds of pleasure sometimes coming from their bedroom, my only reaction was one of delight in their happiness, even while I tossed in my own solitary bed. One time I brought a woman companion of my own to their place, with their approval; but it was a disaster. The chemistry of the weekend was all wrong. It was necessary for me to come alone, and oddly I did not feel condemned to celibacy even though my sharing of Shirley's love with Jack fell short of physical union.

We grew so close that nearly all barriers fell. On the hot days—which meant most of the time—Jack was accustomed to going about in the nude. Why not? There was no one in the neighborhood to object, and he scarcely needed to feel inhibited in the presence of his wife and his closest friend. I envied him his freedom, but I did not imitate it, because it did not seem proper to expose myself in front of Shirley. Instead I wore shorts. It was a delicate matter, and they chose a characteristically delicate way to resolve it. One August day when the temperature was well above one hundred degrees and the sun seemed to take up a quarter of the sky, Jack and I were working outside the house, tending the little garden of desert plants they cherished so warmly. When Shirley emerged to bring us some beers, I saw that she had neglected to don the two strips of fabric that were her usual garments. She was quite casual about it: setting the tray down, offering me a beer, then handing one to Jack, and both of them totally relaxed all the while. The impact of her body on me was sudden but brief. Her ordinary daily costume had been so scant that the contours of her breasts and buttocks were no mysteries to me, and so it was purely a technicality, this crossing of the line between being covered and being revealed. My first impulse was to look away, as if I were an unexpected intruder coming upon her by surprise; but I sensed that this was precisely the inference she wished to destroy, and so I made a determined effort to equal her sangfroid. I suppose it sounds comic and preposterous, but I let my eyes travel deliberately down her bareness, as though some fine statuette had been presented to me for my admiration and I was showing my gratitude by examining it in detail. My eyes lingered on the only parts of her that were new to me: the pinkish mounds of her nipples, the golden triangle of her loins. Her body, ripe and full and lustrous, gleamed as though oiled in the bright midday sun, and she was evenly tanned throughout. When I had completed my solemn, foolish inspection, I downed half my beer, arose, and gravely peeled away my shorts.

After that we ceased to observe any taboo of nudity, which made life very much more convenient in what was, after all, quite a small house. It began to seem wholly natural to me—and, I assume, to them—that modesty was irrelevant in our relationship. Once when a party of tourists took the wrong fork in the road and came down the desert track to the house, we were so unaware of our nakedness that we made no attempt to hide ourselves, and only slowly did we realize why the people in the car seemed so shocked, so eager to swing about and retreat.

One barrier remained forever unbreached. I did not speak to Jack about his work in physics, or about his reasons for abandoning it.

Sometimes he talked shop with me, inquiring after my time-reversal project, asking a hazy question or two, leading me into a discourse on whatever knot currently impeded my progress. But I suspect he did this as a therapeutic act, knowing that I had come to them because I was in an impasse, and hoping that he could bring me past the sticking-point. He did not seem to be aware of current work. Nowhere in the house did I see the familiar green spools of *Physical Review* or *Physical Review Letters*. It was as if he had performed an amputation. I tried to imagine what my life would be if I withdrew wholly from physics, and failed even to picture it. That was what Jack had done, and I did not know why, and I did not dare to ask. If the revelation ever came, it would have to come unsolicited from him.

He and Shirley lived a quiet, self-contained life in their desert paradise. They read a good deal, had an extensive musical library, and had outfitted themselves with equipment for making and playing back sonic sculptures. Shirley was the sculptor. Some of her work was quite fine. Jack wrote poetry which I failed to comprehend, contributed occasional essays on desert life to the national magazines, and claimed to be working on some large philosophical tome, the manuscript of which I never saw. Basically I think they were idle people, though not in any negative sense; they had dropped out of the competition and were sufficient unto themselves, producing little, consuming little, and thoroughly happy. By choice they had no children. They left their desert no more than twice a year, for quick trips to New York or San Francisco or London, pulling back hurriedly into their chosen environment. They had four or five other friends who visited them periodically, but I never met any of them, nor did it seem as though any of the others were as close to them as I. Most of the time Jack and Shirley were alone together, and I gather that they found one another completely rewarding. They baffled me. Outwardly they might seem simple, two children of nature romping nude in the desert warmth, untouched by the harshness of the world they had rejected; but the underlying complexity of their renunciation of the world was more than I could fathom. Though I loved them and felt that they were part of me and I of them, yet it was a delusion: they were alien beings, in the final analysis, detached from the world because they did not belong to it. It would have been better for them if they had managed to sustain their isolation.

That Christmas week when Vornan-19 descended upon the world, I had gone to their place in deepest need. My work had become hollow to me. It was the despair of fatigue; for fifteen years I had lived on the brink of success, for brinks border not only abysses but also precipices, and I had been scaling a precipice. As I climbed, the summit receded, until I felt that there was no summit at all, merely the illusion of one, and that in any event what I had been doing was not worth the dedication I had given it. These moments of total doubt come upon me frequently, and I know them to be irrational. I suppose that everyone must give way periodically to the fear that he has wasted his life, except, perhaps, for those who *have* wasted their lives and who mercifully lack the capacity to know it. What of the advertising man who breaks his soul to fill the sky with a glowing, pinwheeling cloud of propaganda? What of the middle-echelon executive who pours his life into the shuttling of tense memoranda? What of the designer of automobile hulls, the stockbroker, the college president? Do they ever have a crisis of values?

My crisis of values was upon me again. I was stymied in my work and I turned to Jack and Shirley. Shortly before Christmas I closed my office, had mail deliveries suspended, and invited myself to Arizona for an indefinite stay. My work schedule is not keyed to the semesters and holidays of the University; I work when I please, withdraw when I must.

It takes three hours to drive to Tucson from Irvine. I locked my car into the first transportation pod heading over the mountains and let myself be whirled eastward along the glittering track, programmed for a short-run trip. The clicking mind in the Sierra Nevada did the rest, omnisciently detaching me from the Phoenix-bound route at the right time, shunting me onto the Tucson track, decelerating me from my three-hundred-mile-per-hour velocity, and delivering me safely to the depot where the manual controls of my car were reactivated. The December weather on the Coast had been rainy and cool, but here the sun blazed cheerfully and the temperature was well into the eighties. I paused in Tucson to charge my car's batteries, having robbed Southern California Edison of a few dollars of revenue by forgetting to do it before I set out. Then I drove into the desert. I followed the old Interstate 89 for the first stretch, turning off onto a county road after fifteen minutes, and leaving even that modest artery shortly for the mere capillary leading to their pocket of uninhabited desert. Most of this region belongs to the Papago Indians, which is why it has avoided the plague of development enveloping Tucson, and just how Shirley and Jack acquired title to their little tract of land I am not at all sure. But they were alone, incredible as that may seem on the eve of the twenty-first century. There still are such places in the United States where one can withdraw as they had done. The final five-mile stretch I traveled was a pebbled dirt track that could be called a road only by semantic jugglery. Time dropped away; I might have been following the route of one of my own electrons, backward into the world's dawn. This was emptiness, and it had the power to draw forth torment from a cluttered soul like a heat pump soothing the dance of the molecules.

I arrived in late afternoon. Behind me lay rutted gulleys and parched earth. To my left rose purple mountains dipped in cloud. They sloped off toward the Mexican border, leading my eye straight around to the flat, coarsely pebbled desert on which the Bryant house was the only modern intrusion. A dry wash through which water had not flowed in centuries rimmed their property, I parked my car beside it and walked toward the house.

They lived in a twenty-year-old building made of redwood and glass, two stories high in the living quarters, with a sundeck to the rear. Beneath the house was its life-system: a Fermi reactor that powered the air-conditioning, the water circulators, the lighting, and the heating. Once a month the man from Tucson Electric drove out to service the unit, as required by law wherever a utility has declined to run power lines and has supplied an isolated generating unit instead. The fifty-yard storage unit below the house held a month's supply of food, too, and the water purifier was independent of city lines. Civilization could disappear entirely, and Shirley and Jack might remain unaware of it for weeks.

Shirley was on the sundeck, busy with one of her sonic sculptures, spinning a feathery thing of intricate lines and glowing textures, whose soft birdlike twitter had immense carrying power as it crossed the desert to me. She finished what she was doing before she rose and ran toward me, arms outstretched, breasts jouncing. As I caught her and embraced her, I felt some of my weariness ebb away.

"Where's Jack?" I asked.

"He's writing. He'll come out in a little while. Here, let me get you moved in. You look *terrible*, darling!"

"So they've been telling me."

"We'll fix that."

She snatched my suitcase and hurried into the house. The saucy twitching of her bare rump reassured and refreshed me, and I grinned at the two firm cheeks as they vanished from sight. I was among friends. I had come home. At the moment, I felt that I might stay among them for months.

I went to my room. Shirley had everything ready for me: fresh linens, a few spools beside the reader, a nightglow on the table, a pad and stylus and recorder if I wanted to set down my ideas. Jack appeared. He pressed a flask of beer into my hand and I thumbed it open. We winked in mutual delight.

That evening Shirley conjured a magical dinner, and afterwards, as warmth fled from the desert on this winter evening, we sprawled in their living room to talk. They said nothing whatever of my work, bless them both. Instead we discussed the Apocalyptists, for they had come to be fascinated by the cult of doom that now was infesting so many minds.

"I've been studying them closely," said Jack. "Do you follow it at all?"

"Not really."

"It happens every thousand years, it seems. As the millennium comes to its close, a conviction spreads that the world is about to end. It was very bad toward 999. At first only peasants believed it, but then some very sophisticated churchmen began to catch the fever, and that did it. There were orgies of prayer and also the other sorts of orgies."

"And when A.D. 1000 came?" I asked. "The world survived, and what happened to the cult?"

Shirley laughed. "It was quite disillusioning for them. But people don't learn."

"How do the Apocalyptists think the world is going to perish?"

"By fire," said Jack.

"The scourge of God?"

"They expect a war. They believe that the world leaders have already ordained it and that hellfires will be loosed on the first day of the new century."

"We haven't had a war of any size in fifty-odd years," I said. "The last time an atomic weapon was used in anger was 1945. Isn't it safe to assume that we've developed techniques for sidestepping the apocalypse by now?"

"Law of accumulating catastrophe," Jack said. "Static builds toward a discharge. Look at all the little wars: Korea, Vietnam, the Near East, South Africa, Indonesia—"

"Mongolia and Paraguay," Shirley offered.

"Yes. On the average, one minor war every seven or eight years. Each one creating sequences of reflexive response that help to motivate the next, because everybody's eager to put into practice the lessons of the last war. Building up a mounting intensity that's bound to explode into the Final War. Which is due to begin and end on January 1, 2000."

"Do you believe this?" I asked.

"Myself? Not really," Jack said. "I'm simply stating the theory. I don't detect any signs of imminent holocaust in the world, though I admit that all I know is what comes over the screen. Nevertheless, the Apocalyptists catch the imagination. Shirley, run those tapes of the Chicago riot, will you?"

She slipped a capsule into the slot. The entire rear wall of the room blossomed with color as the playback of the telecast began. I saw the towers of Lake Shore Drive and Michigan Boulevard; I saw bizarre figures spilling out over the highway, onto the beach, cavorting beside the icy lake. Most of them were painted in gaudy stripes like mummers on the loose. Most were partly naked, and this was not the innocent natural nudity of Jack and Shirley on a hot day, but something ugly and raw and deliberately obscene, a wanton flaunting of jiggling breasts and paint-daubed buttocks. This was a display calculated to shock: Hieronymus Bosch grotesques set loose, waggling their nakedness in the face of a world regarded as doomed. I had not paid attention to the movement before. I was startled to see a girl hardly adolescent rush before the camera, whirl, flip up her skirt, crouch and urinate in the face of another reveler who had fallen in stupor. I watched the open fornication, the grotesque tangles of bodies, the complex couplings that were more accurately triplings and quadruplings. An immensely fat old woman waddled across the beach, cheering the younger rioters on. A mountain of furniture went up in flames. Policemen, bewildered, sprayed foam on the mob but did not enter it.

"Mere anarchy is loosed upon the world," I muttered. "How long has this been going on?"

"Since July, Leo," said Shirley quietly. "You didn't know?"

"I've been very busy."

Jack said, "There's a distinct crescendo. At first it was a movement of crackpots in the Midwest—around '93, '94—a thousand members or so, convinced that they'd better pray hard because Doomsday was less than a decade away. They got the proselytizing bug and started to preach doom, only this time the message came across. And the movement got out of hand. For the last six months the idea has been building that it's foolish to waste time in anything but fun, because there's not much time left."

I shuddered. "Universal madness?"

"Quite so. On every continent the profound conviction that the bombs fall a year from January 1. Eat, drink, and be merry. It's spreading. I hate to think of what the hysteria will be like a year from now in the supposed final week of the world. We three may be the only survivors, Leo."

I stared at the screen for a few moments more, appalled.

"Shut that thing off," I said at length.

Shirley chuckled. "How could you not have heard of this, Leo?"

"I've been out of touch with everything." The screen darkened. The painted demons of Chicago still leaped obscenely through my brain. The world is going mad, I thought, and I have not noticed it. Shirley and Jack saw how rocked I was by this revelation of the Apocalyptist apocalypse, and they deftly shifted the subject, talking of the ancient Indian ruins they had discovered in the desert a few miles away. Long before midnight I showed my weariness and they saw me to bed.

Shirley returned to my room a few minutes later, she had undressed, and her bare body glowed like a holiday candle in the doorway.

"Can I get you anything, Leo?"

"I'm fine," I told her.

"Merry Christmas, darling. Or have you forgotten that too? Tomorrow's Christmas Day."

"Merry Christmas, Shirley."

I blew her a kiss, and she turned out my light. While I slept, Vornan-19 entered our world six thousand miles away, and nothing would be quite the same for any of us, ever again.

Three

I awoke late on Christmas morning. Jack and Shirley had clearly been up for hours. There was a bitter taste in my mouth and I did not want company, not even theirs; as was my privilege, I went into the kitchen and silently programmed my breakfast. They sensed my mood and stayed away. Orange juice and toast came from the output panel of the autochef. I devoured them, punched for black coffee, then dumped the dishes in the cleaner, started the cycle, and went out. I walked by myself for three hours. When I returned I felt purged. It was too cool a day for sunbathing or gardening; Shirley showed off some of her sculptures, Jack read me a little of his poetry, and I spoke hesitantly about the obstacle to my work. That evening we dined magnificently on roast turkey and chilled Chablis.

The days that followed were soothing ones. My nerves uncoiled. Sometimes I walked alone in the desert; sometimes they came with me. They took me to their Indian ruin. Jack knelt to show me the potsherds in the sand: triangular wedges of white pottery marked by black bars and dots. He indicated the sunken contours of a pitdwelling; he showed me the fragmentary foundations of a building wall made of rough stone mortared with mud.

"Is this Papago stuff?" I asked.

"I doubt it. I'm still checking, but I'm sure it's too good for the Papagos. My guess is that it's a colony of ancestral Hopis, say a thousand years back, coming downstate out of Kayenta. Shirley's supposed to bring me some tapes on archaeology next time she goes into Tucson. The data library doesn't have any of the really advanced texts."

"You could request them," I said. "It wouldn't be hard for the Tucson library to transfer facsims to the dataphone people and shoot them right out to you. If Tucson doesn't have the right books, they can scoop them fom L.A. The whole idea of this data network is that you can get what you need at home, right away, when—"

"I know," Jack said gently. "But I didn't want to start too much of a fuss. The next thing you know, I might have a team of archaeologists out here. We'll get our books the old-fashioned way, by going to the library."

"How long have you known about this site?"

"A year," he said. "There's no hurry."

I envied him his freedom from all normal pressures. How had these two done it, finding a life like this for themselves in the desert? For one jealous moment I wished it were possible for me to do the same. But I could hardly stay permanently with them, though they might not object, and the idea of living by myself in some other corner of the desert was not appealing. No. My place was at the University. So long as I had the privilege of escaping to the Bryants when the need arrived, I could seek solace in my work. And at that thought I felt a surge of joy; after only two days here, I was beginning to think hopefully of my work again!

Time flowed easily by. We celebrated the advent of 1999 with a little party at which I got mildly drunk. My tensions eased. A burst of summer warmth hit the desert during the first week in January, and we stretched naked in the sun, mindlessly happy. A winter-flowering cactus in their garden produced a cascade of yellow blooms, and bees appeared from somewhere. I let a great furry bumble-bee with thighs swollen with pollen alight on my arm, and twitching only slightly, made no effort to shoo him. After a moment he flew to Shirley and explored the warm valley between her breasts; then he vanished. We laughed. Who could fear such a fat bumblebee?

Almost ten years had gone by, now, since Jack had resigned from the University and taken Shirley into the desert. The turning of the year brought the usual reflections on the passage of time, and we had to admit that we had changed very little. It seemed as if a kind of stasis had settled over us all in the late 1980's. Though I was past 50, I had the appearance and health of a much younger man, and my hair was still black, my face unlined. For that I gave thanks, but I had paid a steep price for my preservation: I was no further along in my work this first week of 1999 than I had been the first week of 1989, I still sought ways of confirming my theory that the flow of time is two-directional and that at least on the subatomic level it can be reversed. For a full decade I had moved in roundabout ways, getting nowhere, while my fame grew willy-nilly and my name was often mentioned for the Nobel. Take it as Garfield's Law that when a theoretical physicist becomes a public figure, something has gone awry with his career. To journalists I was a glamorous wizard who would someday give the world a time machine; to myself I was a futile failure trapped in a maze of detours.

The ten years had flecked the edges of Jack's temples with gray, but otherwise time's metamorphosis had been a positive one for him. He was more muscular, a brawny man who had utterly shed that indoor pallor; his body rippled with strength and he moved with an easy grace that belied his vanished awkwardness. Exposure to the sun had darkened his skin for good. He seemed confident, potent, assured, where once he had been wary and tenative.

Shirley had gained most of all. The changes in her were slight but all to the good. I remembered her as lean, coltish, too ready to giggle, too slender in the thigh for the fullness of her breasts. The years had adjusted those minor flaws. Her golden-tan body was magnificent in its proportions now, and that made her seem all the less naked when she was nude, for she was like some Aphrodite of Phidias walking about under the Arizona sun. Ten pounds heavier than in the California days, yes, but every ounce of it placed perfectly. She was flawless, and, like Jack, she had that deep reservoir of strength, that total self-assurance, which guided her every move and every word. Her beauty was still ripening. In two or three more years she would be blinding to behold. I did not wish to think about her as she one day would be, withered and shrunken. It was hard to imagine that these two—and especially she—were condemned to the same harsh sentence under which we all must live.

To be with them was joy. I felt whole enough, in the second week of my visit, to discuss the problems of my work with Jack in some detail. He listened sympathetically, following with an effort, and seemed not to understand much. Was it true? Could a mind as fine as his have lost contact so thoroughly with physics? At any rate he listened to me, and it did me good. I was groping in darkness; I felt as though I was more distant from my goal now than I had been five or eight years before. I needed a listener, and I found him in Jack.

The difficulty lay in the annihilation of antimatter. More an electron back in time and its charge changes; it becomes a positron and immediately seeks its antiparticle. To find is to perish. A billionth of a second and the tiny explosion comes, and a photon is released. We could sustain our time-reversal thrust only by sending our particle back into a matter-free universe.

Even if we could find enough power to hurl larger particles—protons and neutrons and even alphas—backward in time, we would still enter the same trap. Whatever we sent to the past would be annihilated so swiftly that it would be the merest microevent on our tracking scanner. The newstapes to the contrary, there was no chance at all of true time travel; a man sent back in time would be a superbomb, assuming that a living thing could survive the transition into antimatter in the first place. Since this part of our theory seemed incontestable, we had been exploring the notion of a matter-free universe, seeking some pocket of nothingness into which we could thrust our backward-going traveler, containing it while we monitored it. But here we were beyond our depth.

Jack said, "You want to open up a synthetic universe?"

"Essentially."

"Can you do it?"

"In theory we can. On paper. We set up a strain pattern that breaches the wall of the continuum. Then we thrust our backward-moving electron through the breach."

"But how can you monitor it?"

"We can't," I said. "That's where we're stuck."

"Of course," Jack murmured. "Once you introduce anything but the electron into the universe, it's no longer matter-free, and you get the annihilation that you don't want. But then you've got no way of observing your own experiment."

"Call it Garfield's Uncertainty Principle," I said faintly.

"The act of observing the experiment queers it instantaneously. Do you see why we're hung up?"

"Have you made any efforts at opening this adjoining universe of yours?"

"Not yet. We don't want to go to the expense until we're sure we can do something with it. For that matter, we've got a little further checking to do before we dare try it. You don't go about ripping space-time open until you've run a mock-up of every possible consequence."

He came over to me and punched me lightly in the shoulder. "Leo, Leo, Leo, don't you ever wish you had decided to become a barber instead?"

"No. But there are times I wish physics were a little easier."

"Then you might as well have been a barber."

We laughed. Together we walked to the sundeck, where Shirley lay reading. It was a bright, crisp January afternoon, the sky a metallic blue, great slabs of clouds poised on the tips of the mountains, the sun big and warm. I felt very much at ease. In my two weeks here I had succeeded in externalizing my work problem, so that it seemed almost to belong to someone else. If I could get far enough outside it, I might find some daring new way to slice through the obstacles once I went back to Irvine.

The trouble was that I no longer thought in daring new ways. I thought in clever combinations of the old ways, and that was not good enough. I needed an outsider to examine my dilemma and show me with a quick intuitive flash which way the solution might be reached. I needed Jack. But Jack had retired from physics. He had chosen to disconnect his superb mind.

On the sundeck Shirley rolled over, sat up, grinned at us. Her body glistened with beads of perspiration. "What brings you two outdoors?"

"Despair," I said. "The walls were closing in."

"Sit down and warm up, then." She tapped a button that cut off the radio outlet. I had not even noticed that the radio was on until the sound died away. Shirley said, "I've just been listening to the latest on the man from the future."

"Who's that?" I asked.

"Vornan-19. He's coming to the United States!"

"I don't think I know anything about—"

Jack shot a tense glance at Shirley, the first time I had ever seen him reprove her. Instantly my interest was engaged. Was this something they were keeping from me?

"It's just nonsense," Jack said. "Shirley shouldn't have bothered you with it."

"Will you tell me what you're talking about?"

Shirley said, "He's the living answer to the Apocalyptists. He claims to have come back from the year 2999, as a sort of tourist, you know. He showed up in Rome, stark naked on the Spanish Stairs, and when they tried to arrest him, he knocked a policeman out with a touch of his fingertips. Since then he's been causing all sorts of confusion."

"A stupid hoax," Jack said. "Obviously some moron is tired of pretending that the world is coming to an end next January, and decided to pretend that he was a visitor from a thousand years from now. And people are believing him. It's the times we live in. When hysteria's a way of life, you follow every lunatic who comes along."

"Suppose he *is* a time traveler, though!" Shirley said.

"If he is, I'd like to meet him," I put in. "He might be able to answer a few questions I've got about time-reversal phenomena." I chuckled. Then I stopped chuckling. It wasn't funny at all, I stiffened and said, "You're right, Jack. He's nothing but a charlatan. Why are we wasting all this time talking about him?"

"Because there's a possibility he's real, Leo." Shirley got to her feet and shook out the long golden hair rippling to her shoulders. "The interviews make him out to be very strange. He talks about the future as though he's been there. Oh, maybe he's only clever, but he's entertaining. He's a man I'd like to meet."

"When did he appear?"

"Christmas Day," said Shirley.

"While I was here? And you didn't mention it?"

She shrugged. "We assumed you were following the newscasts and didn't find it an interesting topic."

"I haven't been near the screen since I came."

"Then you ought to do some catching up," she said.

Jack looked displeased. It was unusual to see this rift between them, and he had looked notably cross when Shirley had expressed a wish to meet the time traveler. Odd, I thought. With his interest in the Apocalyptists, why should he discriminate against the latest manifestation of irrationality?

My own feeling about the man from the future was a

neutral one. The business of time travel amused me, of course; I had broken my soul to prove its practical impossibility, and I was hardly likely to accept cheerfully the claim that it had been accomplished. No doubt that was why Jack had tried to shield me from this item of news, believing that I needed no distorted parodies of my own work to remind me of the problems I had fled from just before Christmas. But I was getting free of my depression; time-reversal no longer triggered bleakness in me. I was in the mood to find out more about this fraud. The man seemed to have charmed Shirley via television, and anything that charmed Shirley was of interest to me.

One of the networks ran a documentary on Vornan-19 that evening, preempting an hour of prime time usually taken up by one of the kaleidoscope shows. That in itself revealed the depth and extent of public interest in the story. The documentary was aimed at Robinson Crusoes like myself who had neglected to follow the developments thus far, and so I was able to bring myself up to date all at once.

We floated on pneumochairs before the wall screen and outlasted the commercials. Finally a resonant voice said, "What you are about to see is in part a computer simulation." The camera revealed the Piazza di Spagna on Christmas morning, with a sprinkling of figures posed on the Stairs and in the piazza as though the computer simulating them had been programmed by Tiepolo. Into this neatly reconstructed frieze of casual bystanders came the simulated image of Vornan-19 descending on a shining arc from the heavens. The computers do this sort of thing so well today. It does not really matter that a camera's eye fails to record some sudden major event, for it can always be hauled from time's abyss by a cunning re-creation. I wonder what future historians will make of these simulations . . . if the world survives past the first of next month, of course.

The descending figure was nude, but the simulators ducked the problem of the conflicting testimony of the nuns and the others by showing us only a rear view. There was no prudishness about that, I'm sure; the television coverage of the Apocalyptist revelry that Shirley and Jack had shown me had been quite explicitly revealing of the flesh, and apparently it is now a standard ploy of the networks to work anatomy into the newscasts whenever such displays fall under the protection of the Supreme Court decision on legitimate journalistic observation. I have no objection to this coverage of uncoverage; the nudity taboos are long overdue for discard, and I suppose that anything encouraging a well-informed citizenry is desirable, even pandering in the newscasts. But there is always cowardice an inch behind the façade of integrity. Vornan-19's loins went unsimulated because three nuns had sworn he had been covered by a misty nimbus, and it was easier to sidestep the issue than to risk offending the devout by contradicting the testimony of the holy sisters.

I watched Vornan-19 inspecting the piazza. I saw him mount the Spanish Stairs. I smiled as the excited policeman rushed up, proffered his cloak, and was knocked to the ground by an unseen thunderbolt.

The colloquy with Horst Klein followed. This was done most cleverly, for Klein himself was used, conversing with a dubbed simulation of the time traveler. The young German reconstructed his own conversation with Vornan, while the computer played back what Klein recalled the visitor to have said.

The scene shifted. Now we were indoors, in a high room with congruent polygons inscribed on the walls and ceiling, and with the smooth, even glow of thermoluminescence illuminating the faces of a dozen men. Vornan-19 was in custody, voluntarily, for no one could touch him without being smitten by that electric-eel voltage of his. He was being interrogated. The men about him were skeptical, hostile, amused, angered in turn. This, too, was a simulation; no one had bothered to make a record at the time.

Speaking in English, Vornan-19 repeated what he had told Horst Klein. The interrogators challenged him on various points. Aloof, tolerant of their hostility, Vornan parried their thrusts. Who was he? A visitor. Where was he from? The year 2999. How had he come here? By time transport. Why was he here? To view the medieval world at first hand.

Jack snickered. "I like that. We're medievals to him!"

"It's a convincing touch," said Shirley.

"The simulators dreamed it up," I pointed out. "So far we haven't heard an authentic word."

But shortly we did. Bridging the events of the past ten days in a few words, the program's narrator described how Vornan-19 had moved into the most imposing suite of an elegant hotel on the Via Veneto, how he was holding court there for all interested comers, how he had obtained a wardrobe of fine contemporary clothes by requesting one of Rome's costliest tailors to attend to his needs. The whole problem of credibility had seemingly been bypassed. What astonished me was the ease with which Rome appeared to accept his story at face value. Did they really believe he came from the future? Or was the Roman attitude a huge joke, a self-indulgent romp?

The screen showed us shots of Apocalyptist pickets outside his hotel, and suddenly I understood why the hoax was succeeding. Vornan-19 did have something to offer a troubled world. Accept him, and one accepted the future. The Apocalyptists were attempting to deny the future. I watched them: the grotesque masks, the painted bodies, the wanton capers, the signs held high, crying, REJOICE! THE END IS NEAR! In fury they shook their fists at the hotel and cast sacks of living light at the building, so that trickles of gleaming red and blue pigment streamed down the weathered masonry. The man from the future was the nemesis of their cult. An epoch racked by fears of imminent extinction turned to him easily, naturally, and hopefully. In an apocalyptic age all wonders are welcome.

"Last night in Rome," said the narrator, "Vornan-19 held his first live press conference. Thirty reporters representing the major global news services questioned him."

Abruptly the screen dissolved into a swirl of colors, out of which came the replay of the news conference. Not a simulation this time. Vornan himself, live, appeared before my eyes for the first time.

I was shaken.

I can use no other word. In view of my later involvement with him, let me make it quite clear that at this time I regarded him as nothing but an ingenious fraud. I felt contempt for his pretensions and despised those who, for whatever motives, were choosing to play his silly game. Nevertheless my first sight of the purported visitor had a wholly unexpected impact. He peered outward from the screen, relaxed and poised, and the effect of his presence was something more than merely three-dimensional.

He was a slim man of less than middle height, with narrow sloping shoulders, a slender feminine neck, and a finely modeled head held proudly erect. The planes of his face were pronounced: sharp cheek-bones, angular temples, a strong chin, a prominent nose. His skull was slightly too large for his frame; it was high-vaulted, longer than it was broad, and the bone structure in back would have been of interest to a phrenologist, for his skull was curiously prolonged and ridged. Its unusual features, though, fell within the range of what one might expect to find on the streets of any large city.

His hair was close-cropped and gray. His eyes, too, were gray. He might have been of any age from thirty to sixty. His skin was unlined. He wore a pale blue tunic that had the simplicity of high style, and at his throat was a neatly gathered foulard, in cerise, providing the only touch of color about him. He looked cool, graceful, alert, intelligent, charming, and somewhat disdainful. I was reminded forcefully of a sleek bluepoint Siamese cat I had once known. He had the ambivalent sexuality of a superb tom, for there is something sinuously feminine even about most male cats, and Vornan projected that same quality, that well-groomed look of pantherish grace. I don't mean to say that he was epicene in the sense of being sexless, but rather that he was androgynous, omnisexual, capable of finding and giving pleasure with anyone or anything. I stress the point that this was my instant impression, and not something that I am projecting backward out of what I later discovered about Vornan-19.

Character is defined mainly by the eyes and the mouth. Vornan's power centered there. His lips were thin, his mouth somewhat too wide, his teeth flawless, his smile dazzling. He flashed the smile like a beacon, radiating an immense warmth and concern, and just as swiftly cut it off, so that the mouth became a nullity and the center of attention shifted to the chilly, penetrating eyes. Those were the two most conspicuous sides of Vornan's personality: the instant capacity to demand and seize love, represented by the irresistible blaze of the smile; and the quick withdrawal to calculating aloofness, represented by the moonstone gleam of the eyes. Charlatan or not, he was plainly an extraordinary man, and despite my scorn for such charades as this, I felt impelled to watch him in action. The simulated version shown a few moments before, under interrogation by the bureaucrats, had had the same features, but the power was missing. The first instant's view of the live Vornan carried an immediate magnetism absent from the computerized zombie.

The camera lingered on him for perhaps thirty seconds, long enough to register his curious ability to command attention. Then it panned around the room, showing the newsmen.

Remote as I am from the heroes of the screen, I recognized at least half a dozen of them, and the fact that Vornan had been thought worthy of the time of the world's star reporters was important in itself, testimony to the effect he had already had on the world while Jack and Shirley and I lazed in the desert. The camera continued around, revealing all the gimmicks of our gadgety era: the power core of the recording instruments, the dull snout of the computer input, the boom from which the sound equipment dangled, the grid of depth-sensors that kept the three dimensions of the telecast from wandering, and the small cesium laser that provided the spotlighting. Usually all these devices are carefully kept out of sight, but for this production they had been obtrusively thrust forward—props, one might say, to demonstrate that we medievals knew a thing or two.

The press conference began with a voice saying in clipped London tones, "Mr. Vornan, would you kindly describe your assertions concerning your presence here?"

"Certainly. I have come across time to gain insight into the life processes of early technological man. My starting point was the year you reckon as 2999. I propose to tour the centers of your civilization and carry back with me a full account for the delight and instruction of my contemporaries."

He spoke smoothly and with no descernible hesitation. His English was scrubbed free of accent; it was the sort of English I have heard computers speaking, a speech cobbled together from chaste isolated phonemes and thus missing any regional taint. The robotic quality of his timbre and enunciation clearly conveyed the notion that this man was speaking a language he had learned *in vacuo*, from some sort of teaching machine; but of course a twentieth-century Finn or Basque or Uzbek who had learned English via tape would have sounded much the same way. Vornan's voice itself was flexible and well modulated, pleasant to hear.

A questioner said, "How come you speak English?"

"It seemed the most useful medieval language for me to learn."

"Isn't it spoke in your time?"

"Only in a greatly altered form."

"Tell us a little about the world of the future."

Vornan smiled—the charm again—and said patiently. "What would you like to know?"

"The population."

"I'm not sure. Several billions, at least."

"Have you reached the stars yet?"

"Oh, yes, of course."

"How long do people live in 2999?"

"Until they die," said Vornan amiably. "That is, until they choose to die."

"What if they don't so choose?"

"I suppose they'd keep on living. I'm really not sure."

"What are the leading nations of 2999?"

"We have no nations. We have the Centrality, and then there are the decentralized settlements. That is all."

"What's the Centrality?"

"A voluntary association of citizens in a single area. A city, in a sense, but something more than a city."

"Where is it?"

Vornan-19 frowned delicately. "On one of the major continents. I forget your names for the continents."

Jack looked up at me. "Shall I turn it off? He's obviously a phony. He can't even fake the details convincingly!"

"No, leave it," Shirley said. She seemed entranced. Jack tensed again, and I quickly said, "Yes, let's watch a little more. It's amusing."

". . . only one city, then?"

"Yes," Vornan replied. "Composed of those who value communal life. There's no economic need for us to cluster together, you know. We're each quite self-sufficient. What fascinates me is the need you folk have to keep your hands in each other's pockets. This business of money, for example. Without it, a man starves, a man goes naked. Am I right? You lack independent means of production. Am I right in believing that energy conversion is not yet an accomplished fact?"

A harsh American voice said, "Depends what you mean by energy conversion. Mankind's had ways of getting energy since the first fires were kindled."

Looking perturbed, Vornan said, "I mean *efficient* energy conversion. The full use of the power stored within a single— ah, a single atom. You lack this?"

I glanced sideways at Jack. He was gripping the float of his pneumochair in sudden anguish, and his features were distorted with tension. I looked away again as though I had intruded on something terribly private, and I realized that a decade-old question had been answered at least in part.

Vornan was no longer discussing energy conversion when I was able to return my attention to the screen.

". . . a tour of the world. I wish to sample the full range of experience available in this era. And I will begin in the United States of America."

"Why?"

"One likes to see the processes of decadence in motion. When one visits a crumbling culture, one does best to explore its most powerful component first. My impression is that the chaos that will come upon you will radiate outward from the United States, and therefore I wish to search for the symptoms there first." He said this with a kind of bland impersonality, as though it should be quite self-evident that our society was collapsing and that no offense could possibly be given by remarking on something so obvious. Then he flashed the smile just long enough to stun his audience into ignoring the underlying darkness of his words.

The press conference trickled to an anticlimactic end. Random questions about Vornan's world and about the method by which he had come to our time were met with such vague generalities that he seemed clearly to be mocking his questioners. Occasionally he implied that he might provide further details on some point another time; mostly he declared that he simply did not know. He was particularly evasive on all efforts to get from him a sharp description of world events in our immediate future. I gathered that he had no high regard for our attainments and was a trifle surprised to discover that we had electricity and atomic energy and space travel at our early stage in the stream of history. He made no attempt to hide his disdain, but the odd thing was that his cockiness failed to be infuriating. And when the editor of a Canadian facsimsheet said, "Just how much of all this do you really expect us to believe?" he replied quite pleasantly. "Why, feel free to believe none of it. I'm sure it makes no difference to me."

When the program was over, Shirley turned to me and said, "Now you've seen the fabulous man from tomorrow, Leo. What do you think of him?"

"I'm amused."

"Convinced?"

"Don't be silly. This is nothing but a very clever publicity dodge that's working out magnificently for somebody. But give the devil credit: he's got charm."

"He does indeed," Shirley said. She looked toward her husband. "Jack, darling, would you mind very much if I arrange to sleep with him when he comes to the States? I'm sure they've invented a few new wrinkles in sex in the next thousand years, and maybe he could teach me something."

"Very funny," Jack said.

His face was black with rage. Shirley recoiled as she saw it. It startled me that he would overreact in this way to her innocently wanton suggestion. Surely their marriage was secure enough so that she could play at infidelity without angering him. And then it struck me that he was not reacting at all to her talk of sleeping with Vornan, that he was still locked in his earlier anguish. That talk of total energy conversion—of a decentralized world in which each man was an economically self-sufficient unit—

"Do you mind?" he said, and left the room.

Shirley and I exchanged troubled glances. She bit her lip, tugged at her hair, and said softly, "I'm sorry, Leo. I know what's eating him, but I can't explain."

"I think I can guess." .

"Yes, you probably would be the one who could."

She opened the circuit that opaqued the side window. I saw Jack on the sundeck, gripping the rail, hulking forward and staring into the darkened desert. Lightning forked across the summits of the mountains in the west, and then came the instant fury of a winter rainstorm. Sheets of water cascaded across the glass paneling. Jack remained there, a statue more than a man, and let the storm unleash its force upon him. Beneath my feet I felt the purr of the house's life-system as the storage pumps sucked the rainwater into the cisterns for later use. Shirley came up beside me and put her hand on my arm. "I'm afraid," she whispered. "Leo, I'm afraid."

Four

"Come out into the desert with me," Jack said. "I'd like to talk to you, old man."

Two days had passed since the telecast of Vornan-19's press

conference. We had not turned the wallscreen on again, and the tension had ebbed from the house. I was planning to return to Irvine the following day. My work was calling me, and I felt also that I should leave Shirley and Jack in privacy while they dealt with whatever gulfs were opening in their lives. Jack had said little during the two days; he appeared to be making a conscious effort to conceal the pain he had felt that night. I was surprised and pleased by his invitation.

"Will Shirley go?" I asked.

"She doesn't need to. Just the two of us."

We left her sunbathing in the noon light, her eyes closed, her supple body upturned, her loveliness bare to the sun's caress. Jack and I walked more than a mile from the house, taking a path we rarely used. The sand was still dimpled from the heavy rainfall, and the scrubby plants were erupting in violent greenery.

Jack halted at a place where three high mica-encrusted monoliths formed a kind of natural Stonehenge, and crouched down before one of the boulders to tug at a clump of sage growing by its base. When he had succeeded in pulling the hapless plant free, he cast it aside and said, "Leo, did you ever wonder why I left the University?"

"You know I did."

"What was the story I gave you?"

"That you were at a dead end in your work," I said. "That you were bored with it, that you had lost faith in yourself and in physics, that you simply wanted to get away to your love-nest with Shirley and stay there and write and meditate."

He nodded. "It was a lie."

"I know."

"Well, partly a lie. I did want to come away here and live apart from the world, Leo. But the bit about being at a dead end: it wasn't true at all. My problem was quite the opposite. I was *not* at a dead end. God knows I wanted to be. But I saw my way clearly to the culmination of my thesis. The answers were in sight, Leo. All the answers."

Something twitched in my left cheek. "And you could stop, knowing that it was all in your grasp?"

"Yes." He scuffed at the base of the boulder, knelt, scooped sand, sifted it through his fingers. He did not look at me. At length he said, "Was it an act of moral grandeur, I wonder, or just an act of cowardice? What do you think, Leo?"

"You tell me."

"Do you know where my work was heading?"

"I think I knew it before you," I said. "But I wasn't going to point it out. I had to let you make all the decisions. You never once indicated that you saw any of the larger implications at all, Jack. As far as I could tell, you thought you were dealing with the atomic binding forces in a vacuum of theory."

"I was. For the first year and a half."

"And then?"

"I met Shirley, remember? She didn't know much about physics. Sociology, history, those were her fields. I described my work to her. She didn't understand, so I put it in simpler terms, and then still simpler terms. It was good discipline for me, verbalizing what had really been just a bunch of equations. And finally I said that what I was doing was finding out what holds atoms together internally. And she said, 'Does that mean we'd be able to take them apart without blowing things up?' 'Yes,' I said. 'Why, we could take any atom at all and liberate enough energy to run a house on it, I suppose.' Shirley gave me a queer look and said, 'That would be the end of our whole economic structure, wouldn't it?'"

"It had never occured to you before?"

"Never, Leo. Never. I was that skinny kid from M.I.T., yes? I didn't worry about applied technology. Shirley turned me upside down. I started calculating, then got on the phone to the library and had the computer run off some engineering texts for me, and Shirley gave me a little lecture on elementary economics. Then I saw, yes, by damn, somebody could take my equations and figure out a way of liberating unlimited energy. It was $E = MC^2$ all over again. I panicked. I couldn't assume the responsibility for overturning the world. My first impulse was to go to you and ask what you thought I should do."

"Why didn't you?"

He shrugged. "It was the cheap way out. Loading the burden onto you. Anyway, I realized that you probably saw the problem already, and that you would have said something about it to me unless you felt I ought to work out the moral part by myself. So I asked for that sabbatical, and spent my time fooling around at the accelerator while I thought things over. I looked up Oppenheimer and Fermi and the rest of the boys who built the atomic bomb, and asked myself what I would have done in their place. They worked in wartime, to help humanity against a really filthy enemy, and even *they* had their doubts. I wasn't doing anything that would save humanity from clear and present danger. I was simply whipping up a gratuitous bit of research that would smash the world's money structure. I saw myself as an enemy of mankind."

"With real energy conversion," I said quietly, "there'd be no more hunger, no more greed, no more monopolies—"

"There'd also be a fifty-year upheaval while the new order of things was taking shape. And the name of Jack Bryant would be accursed. Leo, I couldn't do it. I wasn't able to take the responsibility. At the end of that third year, I packed myself in. I walked away fom my own work and came out here. I committed a crime against knowledge to avoid committing a worse crime."

"And you feel guilty about it?"

"Of course I do. I feel that my whole life for the past decade has been a penance for running away. Have you ever wondered about the book I've been writing, Leo?"

"Many times."

"It's kind of autobiographical essay: an *apologia pro vita sua*. In it I explain what I was working on at the University, how I came to realize its true nature, why I halted work, and what my attitude toward my own withdrawal has been. The book's an examination of the moral responsibilities of science, you could say. By way of an appendix, I include the complete text of my thesis."

"As it was the day you stopped work?"

"No," Jack said. "The *complete* text. I told you the answers were in sight when I quit. I finished my work five years ago. It's all there in the manuscript. With a billion dollars and a decently equipped laboratory any reasonably alert corporation could translate my equations into a fully functioning power system the size of a walnut that would run forever on an input of sand."

Just then it seemed to me as if the Earth wobbled a little on its axis. I said after a long moment. "Why did you wait this long to bring the subject up?"

"That stupid newscast the other night gave me the push. The so-called man from 2999, with his idiot talk of a decentralized civilization in which every man is self-sufficient because he's got full energy conversion. It was like having a vision of the future—a future that I helped to shape."

"Surely you don't believe—"

"I don't know, Leo. It's a load of nonsense to imagine a man dropping in on us from a thousand years ahead. I was as convinced as you were that the man was all phony... until he started describing the decentralization thing."

"The idea of complete liberation of atomic energy has been around for a long time, Jack. This fellow's clever enough to grab it up and use it. It doesn't necessarily mean that he really is from the future and that your equations have actually gone into use. Forgive me, Jack, but I think you're over-estimating your own uniqueness. You've taken an idea out of the floating pool of futuristic dreams and turned it into reality, yes, but no one except you and Shirley know that, and you mustn't let his random shot fool you into thinking—"

"But suppose it *is* true, Leo?"

"If you're really worried about it, why don't you burn your manuscript?" I suggested.

He looked as shocked as if I had proposed self-mutilation.

"I couldn't do that."

"You'd protect mankind against the upheaval that you seem to feel advance guilt for causing."

"The manuscript's safe enough, Leo."

"Where?"

"Downstairs. I've built a vault for it and rigged up a deadfall in the house reactor. If anyone tries to enter the vault improperly, the safeties come out of the reactor and the house blows sky high. I don't need to destroy what I've written. It'll never fall into the wrong hands."

"Yet you assume it *has* fallen into the wrong hands, some-where in the next thousand years; so that by the time Vornan-19 is born, the world is already living on your power system. Right?"

"I don't know, Leo. The whole thing is crazy. I think I'm going crazy myself."

"Let's say for argument's sake that Vornan-19 is genuine and that such a power system is in use in A.D. 2999. Yes? Okay, but we don't know that it's the system you devised. Suppose you burn your manuscript. The act of doing that would change the future so that the economy described by Vornan-19 would never have come into existence. He himself might wink out of existence the moment your book went into the incinerator. And that way you'd know that the future was saved from the terrible fate you had created for it."

"No, Leo. Even if I burned the manuscript, *I'd* still be here. I could recreate my equations from memory. The menace is in my brain. Burning the book would prove nothing."

"There are memory-washing drugs—"

He shuddered. "I couldn't trust those."

I looked at him in horror. With a sensation like that of falling through a trapdoor, I made contact with Jack's paranoia for the first time; and the healthy, tanned extrovert of these desert years vanished forever. To think that he had come to this! Tied in knots over the possibility that a shrewd but implausible fraud represented a veritable ambassador from a distant future shaped by Jack's own suppressed creation!

"Is there anything I can do to help you?" I said softly.

"There is, Leo. One thing."

"Anything."

"Find some way to meet Vornan-19 yourself. You're an important scientific figure. You can pull the right strings. Sit down and talk with him. Find out if he's really a faker."

"Of course he is."

"Find it out, Leo."

"And if he's really what he says he is?"

Jack's eyes blazed with unsettling intensity. "Question him about his own era, then. Get him to tell you more about this atomic energy thing. Get him to tell you when it was invented—by whom. Maybe it didn't come up until five hundred years from now—an independent rediscovery, nothing to do with my work. Wring the truth out of him, Leo. I have to know."

What could I say?

Could I tell him, Jack, you've gone skully? Could I beg him to enter therapy? Could I offer a quick amateur diagnosis of paranoia? Yes, and lose forever my dearest friend. But to become a partner in psychosis by solemnly quizzing Vornan-19 this way was distasteful to me. Assuming I could ever get access to him, assuming there was some way of obtaining an individual audience, I had no wish to stain myself by treating the mountebank even for a moment as though his pretensions should be taken seriously.

I could lie to Jack. I could invent a reassuring conversation with the man.

But that was treachery. Jack's dark, tormented eyes begged for honest aid. I'll humor him, I thought.

"I'll do what I can," I promised.

His hand clasped mine. We walked quietly back to the house.

* * *

The next morning, as I packed, Shirley came into my room. She wore a clinging, pearly iridescent wrap that miraculously enhanced the contours of her body. I who had grown callously accustomed to her nakedness was reminded anew that she was beautiful, and that my unclelike love for her incorporated a nugget of repressed though irrepressible lust.

She said, "How much did he tell you out there yesterday?"

"Everything."

"About the manuscript? About what he's afraid of?"

"Yes."

"Can you help him, Leo?"

"I don't know. He wants me to get hold of the man from 2999 and check everything out with him. That may not be so easy. And it probably won't do much good even if I can."

"He's very disturbed, Leo. I'm worried about him. You know, he looks so healthy on the outside, and yet this thing has been burning through him year after year. He's lost all perspective."

"Have you thought of getting professional help for him?"

"I don't dare," she whispered. "It's the one thing not even I can suggest. This is the great moral crisis of his life, and I've got to take it that way. I can't suggest that it's a sickness. At least not yet. Perhaps if you came back here able to convince him that this man's a hoax, that would help Jack start letting go of his obsession. Will you do it?"

"Whatever I can, Shirley."

Suddenly she was in my arms. Her face was thrust into the hollow between my cheek and my shoulder; the globes of her breasts, discernible through the thin wrap, crushed themselves against my chest, and her fingertips dug into my back. She was trembling and sobbing. I held her close, until I began to tremble for another reason, and gently I broke the contact between us. An hour later I was bumping over the dirt road, heading for Tucson and the transportation pod that was waiting to bring me back to California.

I reached Irvine at nightfall. A thumb to the doorplate and my house opened for me. Sealed for three weeks, climate-proofed, it had a musty, tomblike odor. The familiar litter of papers and spools everywhere was reassuring. I went in just as a light rain began to fall. Wandering from room to room, I felt that sense of an ending that I used to know on the day after the last day of summer; I was alone again, the holiday was over, the Arizona brightness had given way to the misty dark of California winter. I could not expect to find Shirley scampering spritelike about the house, nor Jack uncoiling some characteristically involuted idea for my consideration. The homecoming sadness was even sharper this time, for I had lost the strong, sturdy Jack I had depended on for so many years, and in his place there had appeared a troubled stranger full of irrational doubts. Even golden Shirley stood revealed as no goddess but a worried wife. I had gone to them with a sickness in my own soul and had come home healed of that, but it had been a costly visit.

I cut out the opaquers and peered outside at the Pacific's surging surf, at the reddish strip of beach, at the white swirls of fog invading the twisted pines that grew where sand yielded to soil. The staleness in the house gave way as that piney salt air was sucked through the vents. I slipped a music cube into the scanner, and the thousands of tiny speakers embedded in the walls spun a skein of Bach for me. I allowed myself a few ounces of cognac. For a while I sat quietly sipping, letting the music cocoon me, and gradually I felt a kind of peace come over me. My hopeless work awaited me in the morning. My friends were in anguish. The world was convulsed by an apocalyptic cult and now was beset by a self-appointed emissary from the epochs ahead. Yet there had always been false prophets loose in the land, men had always struggled with problems so heavy they strained their souls, and the good had always been plagued with shattering doubts and turmoils. Nothing was new. I need feel no pity for myself. Live each day for itself, I thought, meet the challenges as they arise, brood not, do your best, and hope for a glorious resurrection. Fine. Let the morrow come.

After a while I remembered to reactivate my telephone. It was a mistake.

My staff knows that I am incommunicado when I am in Arizona. All incoming calls are shunted to my secretary's line, and she deals with them as she sees fit, never consulting me. But if anything of major importance comes up, she rings it into the storage cell of my home telephone so that I'll find out about it right away when I return. The instant I brought my phone to life, the storage cell disgorged its burden; the chime sounded and automatically I nudged the output switch. My secretary's long, bony face appeared on the screen.

"I'm calling on January fifth, Dr. Garfield. There have been several calls for you today from a Sanford Kralick of the White House staff. Mr. Kralick wants to speak to you urgently and insisted a number of times that he be put through to Arizona. He pushed me quite hard, too. When I finally got it across to him that you couldn't be disturbed, he asked me to have you call him at the White House as soon as possible, any hour of the day or night. He said it was on a matter vital to national security. The number is—"

That was all. I had never heard of Mr. Sanford Kralick, but of course Presidential aides come and go. This was perhaps the fourth time the White House had called me in the past eight years, since I had inadvertently become part of the available supply of learned pundits. A profile of me in one of the weekly journals for the feeble-minded had labeled me as a man to be watched, an adventurer on the frontiers of thought, a dominant force in American physics, and since then I had been manipulated to the status of a star scientist. I was occasionally asked to lend my name to this or that official statement on the National Purpose or on the Ethical Structure of Humanity; I was called to Washington to guide beefy Congressmen through the intricacies of particle theory when appropriations for new accelerators were under discussion; I was dragooned as part of the backdrop when some bold explorer of space was being awarded the Goddard Prize. The foolishness even spread to my own profession, which should have known better; occasionally I keynoted an annual meeting of the. A.A.A.S., or tried to explain to a delegation of oceanographers or archaeologists what was taking place out on my particular frontier of thought. I admit hesitantly that I came to welcome this nonsense, not for the notoriety it provided, but simply because it supplied me with a virtuous-sounding excuse for escaping from my own increasingly less rewarding work. Remember Garfield's Law: star scientists usually are men in a private creative bind. Having ceased to produce meaningful results, they go on the public-appearance circuit and solace themselves with the reverence of the ignorant.

Never once, though, had one of these Washington summonses been couched in such urgent terms. "Vital to national security," Kralick had said. Really? Or was he one of those Washingtonians for whom hyperbole is the native tongue?

My curiosity was piqued. It was dinnertime in the capital

just now. Call at any hour, Kralick had said. I hoped I would interrupt him just as he sat down to supreme de volaille at some absurd restaurant overlooking the Potomac. Hastily I punched out the White House number. The Presidential seal appeared on my screen and a ghostly computerized voice asked me my business.

"I'd like to talk to Sanford Kralick," I said.

"One moment, please."

It took more than one moment. It took about three minutes while the computer hunted up a relay number for Kralick, who was out of his office, called it, and had him brought to the phone. In time my screen showed me a somber-looking young man, surprisingly ugly, with a tapering wedge of a face and bulging orbital ridges that would have been the pride of some Neanderthal. I was relieved; I had expected one of those collapsible plastic yes-men so numerous in Washington. Whatever else Kralick might be, he at least had been stamped from the usual mold. His ugliness was in his favor.

"Dr. Garfield," he said at once. "I've been hoping you'd call! Did you have a good vacation?"

"Excellent."

"Your secretary deserves a medal for loyalty, professor. I practically threatened to call out the National Guard if she wouldn't put me through to you. She refused anyway."

"I've warned my staff that I'll vivisect anyone who lets my privacy be broken, Mr. Kralick. What can I do for you?"

"Can you come to Washington tomorrow? All expenses paid."

"What is it this time? A conference on our chances of surviving into the twenty-first century?"

Kralick grinned curtly. "Not a conference, Dr. Garfield. We need your services in a very special way. We'd like to co-opt a few months of your time and put you to work on a job that no one else in the world can handle."

"A few *months*? I don't think I can—"

"It's essential, sir. I'm not just making governmental noises now. This is big."

"May I have a detail or two?"

"Not over the phone, I'm afraid."

"You want me to fly to Washington on no day's notice to talk about something you can't tell me about?"

"Yes. If you prefer, I'll come to California to discuss it. But that would mean even more delay, and we've already forfeited so much time that—"

My hand hovered over the cutoff knob, and I made sure Kralick knew it. "Unless I get at least a clue, Mr. Kralick, I'm afraid I'll have to terminate this discussion."

He didn't look intimidated. "One clue, then."

"Yes?"

"You're aware of the so-called man from the future who arrived a few weeks ago?"

"More or less."

"What we have in mind involves him. We need you to question him on certain topics. I—"

For the second time in three days I felt that sensation of dropping through a trapdoor. I thought of Jack begging me to talk to Vornan-19; and now here was the government commanding me to do the same. The world had gone mad.

I cut Kralick off by blurting, "All right. I'll come to Washington tomorrow."

Five

The telephone screen deceives. Kralick in the screen had looked engagingly lithe and agile; Kralick in the flesh turned out to be six feet seven or so, and that look of intellectuality that made his ugly face interesting was wholly engulfed by the impression of massiveness he projected. He met me at the airport; it was ten in the morning, Washington time, when I arrived, after having taken a plane that left Los Angeles International at 10:10 A.M. Los Angeles time. Who says time-reversal is hard to accomplish?

As we sped along the autotrack to the White House, he insistently stressed the importance of my mission and his gratitude for my cooperation. He offered no details of what he wanted from me. We took the downtown shunt of the track and rolled smoothly through the White House's private bypass gate. Somewhere in the bowels of the earth I was duly scanned and declared acceptable, and we ascended into the venerable building. I wondered if the President himself would do the briefing. As it turned out, I never caught sight of the man. I was shown into the Situation Room, which bristled preposterously with communications gear. In a crystal capsule on the main table was a Venusian zoological specimen, a purplish plasmoid that tirelessly sent forth its amoebalike projections in a passable imitation of life. An inscription on the base of the capsule said that it had been found on the second expedition. I was surprised: I had not thought we had discovered so many that we could afford to leave them lying around like paperweights in the dens of the bureaucracy.

A brisk little man with cropped gray hair and a flamboyant suit entered the room, almost at a trot. His shoulders were padded like a fullback's and a row of glittering chromed spines jutted from his jacket like vertebrae gone berserk. Obviously this was a man who believed very much in being up to date.

"Marcus Kettridge," he said. "Special Assistant to the President. Glad you're with us, Dr. Garfield."

Kralick said, "What about the visitor?"

"He's been in Copenhagen. The relay came in half an hour ago. Would you like to see it before the briefing?"

"It might be an idea."

Kettridge opened his hand; a tape capsule lay on his palm, and he inserted it. A screen I had not noticed before came to life. I saw Vornan-19 strolling through the baroque fancifulness of the Tivoli Gardens, domed against the weather and showing not a trace of the Danish winter. Patterns of flashing lights stained the sky. He moved like a dancer, controlling every muscle for maximum impetus. By his side walked a blonde giantess, perhaps nineteen years old, with a corona of dazzling hair and a dreamy look on her face. She wore crotch-high shorts and a skimpy bandeau across immense breasts; she might as well have been naked. Yards of flesh showed. Vornan put his arm around her and idly touched the tip of a finger to each of the deep dimples above her monumental buttocks.

Kettridge said, "The girl's a Dane named Ulla Something that he collected yesterday at the Copenhagen Zoo. They spent the night together. He's been doing that everywhere, you know—like an emperor, summoning girls into his bed by royal command."

"Not only girls," rumbled Kralick.

"True. True. In London there was that young hairdresser."

I watched Vornan-19's progress through Tivoli. A curious throng attended him; and in his immediate presence were a dozen brawny Danish police officers with neural whips, a few people who seemed to be government officials, and half a dozen individuals who obviously were reporters. I said, "How do you keep the journalists at bay?"

"It's a pool," Kettridge snapped. "Six reporters represent all the media. They change every day. It was Vornan's idea; he said he liked publicity but he hated to have a mob around him."

The visitor had come to a pavilion where Danish youngsters were dancing. The honkings and skreeings of the band unfortunately were reproduced in perfect clarity, and the boys and girls moved in jerky discontinuity, arms and legs flailing. It was one of those places where the floor is a series of interlocking revolving slidewalks, so that as you stand in place, going through the gyrations of the dance, you are swept on an orbit through the entire hall, confronting partner after partner. Vornan stood watching this in seeming wonder for a while. He smiled that wonderful smile of his and signaled to his bovine consort. They stepped out onto the dance floor. I saw one of the officials put coins in the slot; clearly Vornan did not deign to handle money himself, and it was necessary for someone to follow after him, paying the bills.

Vornan and the Danish girl took places facing one another and caught the rhythm of the dance. There was nothing difficult about it: blatant pelvic thrusts combined with a pattern of stomping and clutching, just like all the other dances of the past forty years. The girl stood with feet flat, knees flexed, legs far apart, head tipped back; the giant cones of her breasts rose toward the faceted mirrors of the ceiling. Vornan, clearly enjoying himself, adopted the knees-in, elbows-out posture of the boys about him and started to move. He picked up the knack of it easily, after only a brief preliminary moment of uncertainty, and off he went, whirled through the hall by the mechanism beneath the floor, facing now this girl, now that, and performing the explicit erotic movements expected of him.

Nearly all the girls knew who he was, it appeared. Their gasps and expressions of awe made that apparent. The fact that a global celebrity was moving in the throng created a certain amount of confusion, throwing the girls off their pace; one simply stopped moving and stared in rapture at Vornan for the whole period of ninety seconds or so that he was her partner. But there was no serious trouble for the first seven or eight turns. Then Vornan was dancing with a plumply pretty dark-haired girl of about sixteen who became totally catatonic with terror. She froze and twisted jerkily and managed to step backward beyond the electronic guard signal at the rear of her moving strip. A buzzer sounded to warn her, but she was beyond any such guidance, and a moment later she had one foot on each of two strips heading in opposite directions. She went down, her short skirt flipping upward to reveal pudgy pink thighs, and in her fright she grabbed at the legs of the boy nearest her.

He toppled too, and in another moment I had a graphic demonstration of the domino effect, because dancers were losing their balance all over the room. Nearly everyone was on more than one strip at once and was clutching at someone else for support. A wave of collapse rippled across the great hall. And there was Vornan-19, still upright, watching the catastrophe in high good humor. His Junoesque paramour was also on her feet, 180 degrees away from him; but then a groping hand caught her ankle, and she went down like a felled oak, careening into two or three other dancers as she dropped. The scene was straight from the pit: writhing figures everywhere, arms and legs in the air, no one able to rise. The machinery of the dance pavilion finally crunched to a halt. The untangling took long minutes. Many girls were crying. Some had skinned knees or abraded rumps; one had somehow contrived to lose her skirt in the melee and was crouched in a fetal huddle. Where was Vornan? Vornan was already at the rim of the hall, safely extricating himself the instant the floor stopped moving. The blond goddess was beside him.

"He's got an immense talent for disruption," said Kettridge.

Kralick, laughing said, "This isn't as bad as the business yesterday at the smorgasbord place in Stockholm, when he punched the wrong button and got the whole table revolving."

The screen darkened. An unsmiling Kettridge turned to me. "This man will be the guest of the United States three days from now, Dr. Garfield. We don't know how long he's staying. We intend to monitor his movements closely and try to head off some of the confusion that he's been known to cause. What we have in mind, Professor, is appointing a committee of five or six leading scholars as—well, guides for the visitor. Actually they'll also be overseers, watchdogs, and . . . spies."

"Does the United States officially believe that he's a visitor from 2999?"

"Officially, yes," said Kettridge. "That is, we're going to treat him as if he's kosher."

"But—" I spluttered.

Kralick put in, "Privately, Dr. Garfield, we think he's a hoaxer. At least I do, and I believe Mr. Kettridge does. He's an extremely sharp-witted and enterprising phony. However, for purposes of public opinion, we choose to accept Vornan-19 at face value until there's some reason to think otherwise."

"For God's sake, *why*?"

"You know of the Apocalyptist movement, Dr. Garfield?" asked Kralick.

"Well, yes. I can't say I'm an expert, but—"

"So far, Vornan-19 hasn't done anything much more harmful than mesmerizing a roomful of Danish schoolgirls into falling on their butts. The Apocalyptists do real damage. They riot, they loot, they destroy. They're the force of chaos in our society. We're attempting to contain them before they rip everything apart."

"And by embracing this self-appointed ambassador from the future," I said, "you explode the chief selling point of the Apocalyptists, which is that the world is supposed to come to an end next January 1."

"Exactly."

"Very good," I said. "I had already suspected it. Now you confirm it as official policy. But is it proper to meet mass insanity with deliberate dishonesty?"

Kettridge said ponderously, "Dr. Garfield, the job of government is to maintain the stability of the governed society. When possible, we like to adhere to the Ten Commandments in so doing. But we reserve the right to meet a threat to the social structure in any feasible way, up to and including the mass annihilation of hostile forces, which I think you will regard as a more serious action than a little fibbing, and which this government has resorted to on more than one occasion. In short, if we can ward off the Apocalyptist lunacy by giving Vornan-19 a seal of approval, it's worth a bit of moral compromise."

"Besides," said Kralick, "we don't actually *know* he's a fraud. If he isn't, we're not committing any act of bad faith."

"The possibility must be very soothing to your souls," I said.

I regretted my flippancy at once. Kralick looked hurt, and I didn't blame him. *He* hadn't set this policy. One by one, the frightened governments of the world had decided to short-circuit the Apocalyptists by proclaiming Vornan to be the real thing, and the United States was merely falling in line. The decision had been taken on high; Kralick and Kettridge were merely implementing it, and I had no call to impugn their morality. As Kralick had said, it might just turn out that hailing Vornan this way would be not only useful but even correct.

Kettridge fussed with the spines of his ornate costume and did not look at me as he said, "We can understand, Dr. Garfield, that in the academic world people tend to view moral issues in the abstract, but nevertheless—"

"All right," I said wearily, "I suppose I was wrong. I had to put myself on record, that's all. Let's go past that point, Vornan-19 is coming to the United States, and we're going to roll out the red carpet for him. Fine. Now—what do you want from me?"

"Two things," said Kralick. "First: you're widely regarded, sir, as the world's ranking authority on time-reversal physics. We'd like you to provide us with your opinion as to whether it's theoretically possible for a man to travel backward in time as Vornan-19 claims to have done, and how, in your appraisal, it might have been accomplished."

"Well," I said, "I have to be skeptical, because so far we've succeeded only in sending individual electrons backward in time. This converts them into positrons—the antiparticle of the electron, identical in mass but opposite in charge—and the effect is one of virtually instant annihilation. I see no practical way to sidestep the conversion of matter into anti-matter during time-reversal, which means that to account for the purported time trip of Vornan-19, we must first explain how so much mass can be converted, and then why it is that although presumably composed of antimatter he does not touch off the annihilation effect when—"

Kralick politely cleared his throat. I stopped talking. Kralick said, "I'm sorry that I didn't make myself quite clear. We don't want an immediate reply from you. We'd like a position paper, Dr. Garfield, which you can file in the next forty-eight hours or thereabouts. We'll provide any necessary secretarial assistance. The President is quite anxious to read what you have to say."

"All right. The other thing you wanted?"

"We'd like you to serve on the committee that will guide Vornan-19 when he gets here."

"Me? Why?"

"You're a nationally known scientific figure associated in the public's mind with time travel," said Kettridge. "Isn't that reason enough?"

"Who else is going to be on this committee?"

"I'm not at liberty to reveal names, even to you," Kralick told me. "But I give you my word that they're all figures whose stature in the scientific or scholarly world is equal to your own."

"Meaning," I said, "that not one of them has said yes yet, and you're hoping to bulldoze them all."

Kralick looked hurt again. "Sorry," I said.

Kettridge, unsmiling, declared, "It was our belief that by putting you in close contact with the visitor, you would find some means of extracting information from him about the time-travel process he employed. We believed that this would be of considerable interest to you as a scientist, as well as of major value to the nation."

"Yes," I said. "True. I'd like to pump him on the subject."

"And then," said Kralick, "why should you be hostile to the assignment? We've chosen a leading historian to find out the pattern of events in our future, a psychologist who will attempt to check on the genuineness of Vornan's story, an anthropologist who'll look for cultural developments, and so on. The committee will simultaneously be examining the legitimacy of Vornan's credentials and trying to get from him anything that may be of value to us, assuming that he's what he says he is. I can't imagine any work that could be of greater significance to the nation and to humanity at this time."

I closed my eyes a moment. I felt properly chastened. Kralick was sincere in his earnest way, and so was Kettridge in his fast-talking though heavy-handed style. They needed me, honestly. And was it not true that I had reasons of my own for wanting to peer behind Vornan's mask? Jack had begged me to do it, never dreaming that it would be so easy for me to manage.

Why was I balking, then?

I saw why. It had to do with my own work and the minute possibility that Vornan-19 was a genuine traveler in time. The man who is trying to invent the wheel is not really eager to learn the details of a five-hundred-mile-per-hour turbine car. Here was I piddling around for half a lifetime with my reversed electrons, and here was Vornan-19, telling tales of vaulting across the centuries; in the depths of my soul I preferred not to think about him at all. However, Kralick and Kettridge were right: I was the man for this committee.

I told them I would serve.

They expressed their gratitude profusely, and then seemed to lose interest in me, as though they didn't plan to waste any emotion on someone who was already signed up. Kettridge disappeared, and Kralick gave me an office somewhere in the underground annex of the White House. Little blobs of living light floated in a tank on the ceiling. He told me that I had full access to the executive mansion's secretarial services, and showed me where the computer outputs and inputs were. I could make any phone calls I wanted, he said, and use any assistance I required in order to prepare my position paper on time travel for the President.

"We've arranged accommodations for you," Kralick told me. "You're in a suite right across the park."

"I thought I might go back to California this evening to wind up my affairs."

"That wouldn't be satisfactory. We have only seventy-two hours, you know, before Vornan-19 arrives in New York. We need to spend that time as efficiently as possible."

"But I had only just returned from vacation!" I protested. "I was in and out again. I need to leave instructions for my staff—to make arrangements for the laboratory—"

"That can all be done by phone, can't it, Dr. Garfield? Don't worry about the phone expense. We'd rather have you spend two or three hours on the line to California than lose all the time of having you make another round trip in the short time remaining."

He smiled. I smiled.

"All right?" he asked.

"All right," I said.

It was very clear. My options had expired the moment I

had agreed to serve on the committee. I was now part of the
Vornan Project, with no independent scope for action. I
would have only as much freedom as the Government could
spare, until this thing was over. The odd part was that I didn't
resent it, I who had always been the first to sign any petition
attacking infringement of liberties, I who had never regarded
myself as an organization man but rather as a free-lance
scholar loosely affiliated with the University. Without a murmur I let myself be pressed into service. I suppose it was all a
subliminal way of dodging the unpleasantness that awaited
me when I finally did get back into my laboratory to struggle
with my unanswered questions.

The office they had given me was cozy. The floor was
bouncy sponge glass, the walls were silvered and reflective,
and the ceiling was aglow with color. It was still early enough
to call California and find someone in the laboratory. I
notified the University proctor, first, that I'd been called into
Government service. He didn't mind. Then I spoke to my
secretary and said I'd have to extend my absence indefinitely.
I made arrangements for staff work and for monitoring my
pupils' research projects. I discussed the question of mail
delivery and maintenance of my house with the local data
utility, and over the screen came a detailed authorization
form. I was supposed to check off the things I wished the
utility to do for me and the things I did not. It was a long list:

Mow lawn
Survey sealing and climateproofing
Relay mail and messages
Gardening
Monitor storm damage
Notify sales organizations
Pay bills

And so on. I checked off nearly everything and billed the
service to the United States Government. I had learned
something from Vornan-19 already: I didn't plan to pay a bill
of my own until I was released from this job.

When I had tidied up my personal affairs, I put through a
call to Arizona. Shirley answered. She looked taut and edgy,
but she seemed to loosen a little when she saw my face on
her screen. I said, "I'm in Washington."

"What for, Leo?"

I told her. She thought I was joking at first, but I assured her that I was telling the truth.

"Wait," she said. "I'll get Jack."

She walked away from the phone. The perspective changed as she retreated, and instead of the usual head-and-shoulders view the screen showed me the tiny image of all of Shirley, a three-quarters view. She stood in the doorway, back to camera, leaning against the doorframe so that one ripe globe of a breast showed under her arm. I knew that government flunkies were monitoring my call, and it infuriated me that they should be getting this free view of Shirley's loveliness. I moved to cut off the vision, but it was too late; Shirley was gone and Jack was on screen.

"What's this?" he asked. "Shirley said—"

"I'm going to be talking to Vornan-19 in a few days."

"You shouldn't have bothered, Leo. I've been thinking about that conversation we had. I feel damned foolish about it. I said a lot of, well, unstable things, and I never dreamed that you'd drop everything and go running off to Washington to—"

"It didn't exactly happen that way, Jack. I got drafted to come out here. Vital to national security, that sort of thing. But I just wanted to tell you that as long as I'm here, I'll try to help you in what you discussed."

"I'm grateful, Leo."

"That's all. Try to relax. Maybe you and Shirley need to get away from the desert for a while."

"Maybe later on," he said. "Let's see how things work out."

I winked at him and broke the contact. He wasn't fooling me at all with his feigned cheeriness. Whatever had been boiling and bubbling inside him a few days ago was still there, even though he was trying to apologize it away as foolishness. He needed help.

One more job, now. I opened up the input and started to dictate my position paper on time-reversal. I didn't know how much copy they wanted, but I figured that it didn't really matter. I began to talk. A bright dot of green light danced along the ground-glass screen of the computer's output, typing out my words as I spoke them. Working entirely from memory and not bothering to summon from the data tanks the texts of my own publications, I reeled off a quick, nontechnical précis of my thoughts on time-reversal. The gist of it was that while time-reversal on the subatomic level had already been achieved, it did not in terms of any physical theory I understood seem possible for a human being to travel backward in time and arrive at his destination alive, regardless of the power source used to transport him. I bolstered this with a few thoughts on accumulative temporal momentum, the extension of mass into an inverted continuum, and the annihilation of antimatter. And I wound it up concluding in almost those words that Vornan-19 was plainly a fake.

Then I spent a few moments contemplating my glowing words in the vibrant but temporary green gleam on the screen. I brooded on the fact that the President of the United States, by executive decision, had chosen to look upon Vornan-19's claims as convincing ones. I pondered the efficacy of telling the President to his face that he was party to a fraud. I debated whether to forfeit my own integrity for the sake of keeping the top man's conscience from twinging, and then I said to hell with it and told the computer to print what I had dictated and transfer it to the Presidential data files.

A minute later my personal copy bounced out of the output slot, typed, justified on both margins, and neatly stitched. I folded it, put it in my pocket, and called Kralick.

"I'm finished," I said. "I'd like to get out of here, now."

He came for me. It was very late afternoon, which is to say it was a bit past midday on the time system my metabolism was accustomed to, and I was hungry. I asked Kralick about lunch. He looked a little puzzled until he realized the time-zone problem. "It's almost dinnertime for me," he said. "Look, why don't we go across the street and have a drink together, and then I'll show you to your suite in the hotel. Then I can arrange some dinner for you, if that's all right. An early dinner instead of a late lunch."

"Good enough," I told him.

Like Virgil in reverse, he guided me upward out of the maze beneath the White House, and we emerged in the open air at twilight. The city had had a light snowfall while I had been underground, I saw. Melting coils were humming in the sidewalks, and robot sweepers drifted dreamily through the streets, sucking up the slush with their long, greedy hoses. A few flakes were still falling. In the shining towers of Washington the lights glittered like jewels against the blue-black afternoon sky. Kralick and I left the White House grounds by a side gate and cut across Pennsylvania Avenue in a knight's move that brought us into a small, dim cocktail lounge. He folded his long legs under the table with difficulty.

It was one of the automatic places that had been so popular a few years back: a control console at each table, a computerized mixologist in the back room, and an elaborate array of spigots. Kralick asked me what I'd have, and I said filtered rum. He punched it into the console and ordered Scotch and soda for himself. The credit plate lit up; he pushed his card into the slot. An instant later the drinks gurgled from the spigots.

"Drink high," he said.

"The same."

I let the rum slip down my gullet. It went down easily, landing on no solid food to speak of, and began to infiltrate my nervous system. Shamelessly I asked for a refill while Kralick was still unwinding himself on his first. He tossed me a thoughtful look, as if telling himself that nothing in my dossier had indicated I was an alcoholic. But he got me the drink.

"Vornan has gone on to Hamburg," Kralick said abruptly. "He's studying night life along the Reepersbahn."

"I thought that was closed down years ago."

"They run it as a tourist attraction, complete with imitation sailors who come ashore and get into brawls. God knows how he ever heard of it, but you can bet there'll be a fine brawl there tonight." He glanced at his watch. "It's probably going on now. Six hours ahead of us. Tomorrow he's in Brussels. Then Barcelona for a bullfight. And then New York."

"God help us."

"God," said Kralick, "is bringing the world to an end in eleven months and—what is it?—sixteen days?" He laughed thickly. "Not soon enough. Not soon enough. If He'd do the job tomorrow, we wouldn't have to put up with Vornan-19."

"Don't tell me you're a crypto-Apocalyptist!"

"I'm a cryptoboozer," he said. "I started on this stuff at lunchtime and my head's spinning, Garfield. Do you know, I was a lawyer once? Young, bright, ambitious, a decent practice. Why did I want to go into the Government?"

"You ought to punch for an antistim," I said guardedly.

"You know, you're right."

He ordered himself a pill, and then, as an afterthought, ordered a third rum for me. My earlobes felt a little thick. Three drinks in ten minutes? Well, I could always have an antistim too. The pill arrived and Kralick swallowed it; he grimaced as his metabolism went through the speedup that would burn the backlog of alcohol out of it. For a long moment he sat there shivering. Then he pulled himself together.

"Sorry. It hit me all at once."

"Feel better?"

"Much," he said. "Did I say anything classified?"

"I doubt it. Except you were wishing the world would end tomorrow."

"Strictly a mood. Nothing religious about it. Do you mind if I call you Leo?"

"I'd prefer it."

"Good. Leo, look, I'm sober now, and what I'm saying is the straight orbit. I've handed you a lousy job, and I'm sorry about it. If there's anything I can do to make your life more comfortable while you're playing nursemaid to this futuristic quack, just ask me. It's not my money I'll be spending. I know you like your comforts, and you'll have them."

"I appreciate that—ah, Sanford."

"Sandy."

"Sandy."

"For instance, tonight. You came in on short notice, and I don't suppose you've had a chance to contact any friends. Would you like a companion for dinner. . . and afterward?"

That was thoughtful of him. Ministering to the needs of the aging bachelor scientist. "Thanks," I said, "but I think I'll manage by myself tonight. Get caught up with my thoughts, get coordinated to your time-zone—"

"It won't be any trouble."

I shrugged the matter aside. We nibbled small algae crackers and listened to the distant hiss of the speakers in the bar's sound system. Kralick did most of the talking. He mentioned the names of a few of my fellow members of the Vornan committee, among them F. Richard Heyman, the historian, and Helen McIlwain, the anthropologist, and Morton Fields of Chicago, the psychologist. I nodded sagely. I approved.

"We checked everything carefully," said Kralick. "I mean, we didn't want to put two people on the committee who had had a feud or something of that sort. So we searched the entire data files to trace the relationships. Believe me, it was a job. We had to reject two good candidates because they'd been involved in, well, rather irregular incidents with one of the other members of the committee, and that was a disappointment."

"You keep files on fornication among the learned?"

"We try to keep files on everything, Leo. You'd be surprised. But anyway we put a committee together, finally, finding replacements for those who wouldn't serve, and replacements for those who turned up incompatible with the others on the data check, and arranging and rearranging—"

"Wouldn't it have been simpler to write Vornan off as a hoax and forget about him?"

Kralick said, "There was an Apocalyptist rally in Santa Barbara last night. Did you hear about it?"

"No."

"A hundred thousand people gathered on the beach. In the course of getting there they did two million dollars worth of property damage, estimated. After the usual orgies they began to march into the sea like lemurs."

"Lemmings."

"Lemmings." Kralick's thick fingers hovered over the bar console a moment, then withdrew. "Picture a hundred thousand chanting Apocalyptists from all over California marching stark naked into the Pacific on a January day. We're still getting the figures on the drownings. Over a hundred, at least, and God knows how much pneumonia, and ten girls were trampled to death. They do things like that in Asia, Leo. Not here. Not here. You see what we're up against? Vornan will smash this movement. He'll tell us how it is in 2999, and people will stop believing that The End Is Nigh. The Apocalyptists will collapse. Another rum?"

"I think I ought to get to my hotel."

"Right." He uncoiled himself and we went out of the bar. As he walked around the edges of Lafayette Park, Kralick said, "I think I ought to warn you that the information media know you're in town and will start to bombard you with interview requests and whatnot. We'll screen you as well as we can, but they'll probably get through to you. The answer to all questions is—"

"No comment."

"Precisely. You're a star, Leo."

Snow was falling again, somewhat some actively than the melting coils were programmed to handle. Thin crusts of white were forming here and there on the pavement, and it was deeper in the shrubbery. Pools of newly melted water glistened. The snow twinkled like starlight as it drifted down. The stars themselves were hidden; we might have been alone in the universe. I felt a great loneliness. In Arizona now the sun was shining.

As we entered the grand old hotel where I was staying, I turned to Kralick and said, "I think I'll accept that offer of a dinner companion after all."

Six

I sensed the real power of the United States Government for the first time when the girl came to my suite about seven that evening. She was a tall blonde with hair like spun gold. Her eyes were brown, not blue, her lips were full, her posture was superb. In short, she looked astonishingly like Shirley Bryant.

Which meant that they had been keeping tabs on me for a long time, observing and recording the sort of women I usually chose, and producing one of exactly the right qualifications on a moment's notice. Did that mean that they thought Shirley was my mistress? Or that they had drawn an abstract profile of all my women, and had come up with a Shirley-like girl because I had (unconsciously!) been picking Shirley-surrogates all along?

This girl's name was Martha. I said, "You don't look like a Martha at all. Marthas are short and dark and terribly intense, with long chins. They smell of cigarettes all the time."

"Actually," Martha said, "I'm a Sidney. But the government didn't think you'd go for a girl named Sidney."

Sidney, or Martha, was an ace, a star. She was too good to be true, and I suspected that she had been created golemlike in a government laboratory to serve my needs. I asked her if that was so, and she said yes. "Later on," she said, "I'll show you where I plug in."

"How often do you need a recharge?"

"Two or three times a night, sometimes. It depends."

She was in her early twenties, and she reminded me forcibly of the co-eds around the campus. Perhaps she was a

robot, perhaps she was a call girl; but she acted like neither—
more like a lively, intelligent, mature human being who just
happened to be willing to make herself available for duties
like this. I didn't dare ask her if she did things of this sort all
the time.

Because of the snow, we ate in the hotel dining room. It
was an old-fashioned place with chandeliers and heavy drap-
eries, head waiters in evening clothes and an engraved menu
a yard long. I was glad to see it; the novelty of using menu
cubes had worn off by now, and it was graceful to read our
choices from a printed card while a live human being took
down our wishes with a pad and pencil, just as in bygone
times.

The Government was paying. We ate well. Fresh caviar,
oyster cocktails, turtle soup, Chateaubriand for two, very
rare. The oysters were the delicate little Olympias from
Puget Sound. They have much to commend them, but I miss
the true oysters of my youth. I last ate them in 1976 at the
Bicentennial Fair—when they were five dollars a dozen,
because of the pollution. I can forgive mankind for destroying
the dodo, but not for blotting out bluepoints.

Much satiated, we went back upstairs. The perfection of
the evening was marred only by a nasty scene in the lobby
when I was set upon by a few of the media boys looking for a
story.

"Professor Garfield—"

"—is it true that—"

"—words on your theory of—"

"—Vornan-19—"

"No comment." "No comment." "No comment." "No
comment."

Martha and I escaped into the elevator. I slapped a privacy
seal on my door—old-fashioned as this hotel is, it has
modern conveniences—and we were safe. She looked at me
coquettishly, but her coyness didn't last long. She was long
and smooth, a symphony in pink and gold, and she wasn't any
robot, although I found where she plugged in. In her arms I
was able to forget about men from 2999, drowning Apocalyptists, and the dust gathering on my laboratory desk. If there
is a heaven for Presidential aides, let Sandy Kralick ascend to
it when his time comes.

In the morning we breakfasted in the room, took a shower
together like newlyweds, and stood looking out the window

at the last traces of the night's snow. She dressed; her black plastic mesh sheath seemed out of place in the morning's pale light, but she was still lovely to behold. I knew I would never see her again.

As she left, she said, "Someday you must tell me about time-reversal, Leo."

"I don't know a thing about it. So long, Sidney."

"Martha."

"You'll always be Sidney to me."

I resealed the door and checked with the hotel switchboard when she was gone. As I expected, there had been dozens of calls, and all had been turned away. The switchboard wanted to know if I'd take a call from Mr. Kralick. I said I would.

I thanked him for Sidney. He was only a bit puzzled. Then he said, "Can you come to the first committee meeting at two, in the White House? A get-together session."

"Of course. What's the news from Hamburg?"

"Bad. Vornan caused a riot. He went into one of the tough bars and made a speech. The essence of it was that the most lasting historic achievement of the German people was the Third Reich. It seems that's all he knows about Germany, or something, and he started praising Hitler and getting him mixed up with Charlemagne, and the authorities yanked him out of there just in time. Half a block of nightclubs burned down before the foam tanks arrived." Kralick grinned ingenuously. "Maybe I shouldn't be telling you this. It still isn't too late for you to pull out."

I sighed and said, "Oh, don't worry, Sandy. I'm on the team for keeps now. It's the least I can do for you . . . after Sidney."

"See you at two. We'll pick you up and take you across via tunnel because I don't want you devoured by the media madmen. Stay put until I'm at your door."

"Right," I said. I put down the phone, turned, and saw what looked like a puddle of green slime gliding across my threshold and into the room.

It wasn't slime. It was a fluid audio pickup full of monomolecular ears. I was being bugged from the corridor. Quickly I went to the door and ground my heel into the puddle. A thin voice said, "Don't do that, Dr. Garfield. I'd like to talk to you. I'm from Amalgamated Network of—"

"Go away."

I finished grinding my heel. I wiped up the rest of the

mess with a towel. Then I leaned close to the floor and said to any remaining ears sticking to the woodwork, "The answer is still No Comment. Go away."

I got rid of him, finally. I adjusted the privacy seal so that it wouldn't be possible even to slide a single molecule's thickness of anything under the door, and waited out the morning. Shortly before two Sandy Kralick came for me and smuggled me into the underground tunnel leading to the White House. Washington is a maze of subterranean connections. I'm told you can get from anywhere to anywhere if you know the routes and have the right access-words handy when the scanners challenge you. The tunnels go down layer after layer. I hear there's an automated brothel six layers deep below the Capitol, for Congressional use only; and the Smithsonian is supposed to be carrying on experiments in mutagenesis somewhere below the Mall, spawning biological monstrosities that never see the light of day. Like everything else you hear about the capital, I suppose these stories are apocryphal; I suppose that the truth, if it were ever known, would be fifty times as ghastly as the fables. This is a diabolical city.

Kralick led me to a room with walls of anodized bronze somewhere beneath the West Wing of the White House. Four people were in it already. I recognized three of them. The upper levels of the scientific establishment are populated by a tiny clique, inbred, self-perpetuating. We all know one another, through interdisciplinary meetings of one kind or another. I recognized Lloyd Kolff, Morton Fields, and Aster Mikkelsen. The fourth person rose stiffly and said, "I don't believe we've met, Dr. Garfield. F. Richard Heyman."

"Yes, of course. *Spengler, Freud, and Marx*, isn't it? I remember it very fondly." I took his hand. It was moist at the fingertips, and I suppose moist at the palms too, but he shook hands in that peculiarly untrusting Central European manner by which the suspicious one seizes the fingers of the other in a remote way, instead of placing palm next to palm. We exchanged noises about how pleased we were to make the other's acquaintance.

Give me full marks for insincerity. I did not think much of F. Richard Heyman's book, which struck me as both ponderous and superficial at once, a rare feat; I did not care for the occasional reviews he wrote for the general magazines, which inevitably turned out to be neat eviscerations of his colleagues; I did not like the way he shook hands; I did not even like his name. What was I supposed to call an "F. Richard" when we had to use names? "F?" "Dick?" What about "my dear Heyman?" He was a short stocky man with a cannonball head, fringe of course red hair along the back half of his skull, and a thick reddish beard curling down over his cheeks and throat to hide what I'm sure was a chin as round as the top of his head. A thin-lipped sharklike mouth was barely visible within the foliage. His eyes were watery and unpleasant.

The other members of the committee I had no hostilities toward. I knew them vaguely, was aware of their high standings in their individual professions, and had never come to any disagreement with them in the scientific forums where we encountered one another. Morton Fields of the University of Chicago was a psychologist, affiliated with the new so-called cosmic school, which I interpreted to be a kind of secular Buddhism. They sought to unravel the mysteries of the soul by placing it in rapport with the universe as a totality, which has a pretentious sound to it. In person Fields looked like a corporation executive on the way up, say, a comptroller: lean athletic frame, high cheekbones, sandy hair, tight downturned mouth, prominent chin, pale questioning eyes. I could imagine him feeding data into a computer four days a week and spending his weekends slamming a golf ball mercilessly about the fairways. Yet he was not as pedantic as he looked.

Lloyd Kolff, I knew, was the doyen of philologists: a massive thick-bodied man, well along in his sixties, with a seamed, florid face and the long arms of a gorilla. His base of operations was Columbia, and he was a favorite among graduate students because of his robust earthiness; he knew more Sanskrit obscenities than any man of the last thirty centuries, and used them all vividly and frequently. Kolff's sideline was erotic verse, all centuries, all languages. He supposedly wooed his wife—also a philologist—by murmuring scorching endearments in Middle Persian. He would be an asset to our group, a valuable counterbalance to the stuffed shirt that I suspected F. Richard Heyman to be.

Aster Mikkelsen was a biochemist from Michigan State, part of the group involved in the life-synthesis project. I had met her at last year's A.A.A.S. conference in Seattle. Though her name has a Scandinavian ring to it, she was not one of those Nordic Junos of whom I am so scandalously fond, however. Dark-haired, sharp-boned, slender, she gave an appearance of fragility and timidity. She was hardly more than five feet tall; I doubt that she weighed a hundred pounds. I suppose she was about forty, though she looked younger. Her eyes held a wary sparkle; her features were elegant. Her clothes were defiantly chaste, modeling her boyish figure as if to advertise the fact that she had nothing to offer the voluptuary. Through my mind there speared the incongruous image of Lloyd Kolff and Aster Mikkelsen in bed together, the beefy folds of his heavy, hairy body thrust up against her slim frail form, her lean thighs and tapering calves straining in agony to contain his butting form, her ankles dug deep into his copious flesh. The mismatch of physiques was so monstrous that I had to close my eyes and look away. When I dared to open them, Kolff and Aster were standing side by side as before, the ziggurat of flesh beside the dainty nymph, and both were peering at me in alarm.

"Are you all right?" Aster asked. Her voice was high and piping, a reedy girlish sound. "I thought you were going to faint!"

"I'm a bit tired," I bluffed. I could not explain why that sudden image had come to me, nor why it left me so dazed. To cover my confusion I turned to Kralick and asked him how many other members our committee would have. One, he said: Helen McIlwain, the famed anthropologist, who was due at any moment. As though on cue, the door slid open and the divine Helen herself strode into the room.

Who has not heard of Helen McIlwain? What more can be said about her? The apostle of cultural relativism, the lady anthropologist who is no lady, the dogged student of puberty rites and fertility cults who has not hesitated to offer herself as tribeswoman and blood sister? She who pursued the quest for knowledge into the sewers of Ouagadougu to partake of skewered dog, she who wrote the basic text on the techniques of masturbation, she who had learned at first hand how virgins are initiated in the frozen wastes of Sikkim? It seemed to me that Helen had always been with us, going from one outrageous exploit to another, publishing books that in another era would have had her burned at the stake, solemnly informing the television audience of matters that might shock hardened scholars. Our paths had crossed many times, although not lately. I was surprised to see how youthful she looked; she had to be at least fifty.

She was dressed—well—flamboyantly. A plastic bar encircled her shoulders, and from it descended a black fiber cunningly designed to look like human hair. Perhaps it *was* human hair. It formed a thick cascade reaching to mid-thigh, a fetishist's delight, long and silken and dense. There was something fierce and primordial about this tent of hair in which Helen was encased; all that was missing was the bone through the nose and the ceremonial scarifications on the cheeks. Beneath the mass of hair she was nude, I think. As she moved across the room, one caught sight of glints of pinkness peeping through the hairy curtain. I had the momentary illusion that I was seeing the tip of a rosy nipple, the curve of a smooth buttock. Yet so cohesive was the sensual sweep of the long, sleek, satin-smooth strands of hair that it cloaked her body almost entirely, granting us only those fleeting views which Helen intended us to have. Her graceful, slender arms were bare. Her neck, swanlike, rose triumphantly out of the hirsuteness, and her own hair, auburn and glossy, did not suffer by comparison with her garment. The effect was spectacular, phenomenal, awesome, and absurd. I glanced at Aster Mikkelsen as Helen made her grand entrance, and saw Aster's lips flicker briefly in amusement.

"I'm sorry I was late," Helen boomed in that magnificent contralto of hers. "I've been at the Smithsonian. They've been showing me a *magnificent* set of ivory circumcision knives from Dahomey!"

"And letting you practice with them?" Lloyd Kolff asked.

"We didn't get that far. But after this silly meeting, Lloyd, darling, if you'd like to come back there with me, I'd be delighted to demonstrate my technique. On you."

"It is sixty-three years too late for that," Kolff rumbled, "as you should know. I'm surprised your memory is so short, Helen."

"Oh, yes, darling! Absolutely right! A thousand apologies. I quite forgot!" And she rushed over to Kolff, hairy garment aflutter, to kiss him on his broad cheek. Sanford Kralick bit his lip. Obviously that was something his computer had missed. F. Richard Heyman looked uncomfortable, Fields smiled, and Aster seemed bored. I began to see that we were in for a lively time.

Kralick cleared his throat. "Now that we're all here, if I could have your attention a moment..."

He proceeded to brief us on our job. He used screens, data

cubes, sonic synthesizers, and a battery of other up-to-the-minute devices by way of conveying to us the urgency and necessity of our mission. Basically, we were supposed to help make Vornan-19's visit to 1999 more rewarding and enjoyable; but also we were under instructions to keep a close watch on the visitor, tone down his more outrageous behavior if possible, and determine secretly to our own satisfaction whether he was genuine or a clever fraud.

It turned out that our own group was split on that last point. Helen McIlwain believed firmly, even mystically, that Vornan-19 *had* come from 2999. Morton Fields was of the same opinion, although he wasn't so vociferous about it. It seemed to him that there was something symbolically appropriate about having a messiah-figure come out of the future to aid us in our time of travail; and since Vornan fit the criteria, Fields was willing to accept him. On the other side, Lloyd Kolff thought the idea to taking Vornan seriously was too funny for words, while F. Richard Heyman seemed to grow purple in the face at the mere thought of embracing any notion so irrational. I likewise was unable to buy Vornan's claims. Aster Mikkelsen was neutral, or perhaps agnostic is the better word. Aster had true scientific objectivity: she wasn't going to commit herself on the time traveler until she'd had a chance to see him herself.

Some of this genteel academic bickering took place under Kralick's nose. The rest occurred at dinner that night. Just the six of us at the table in the White House, with noiseless servants gliding in and out to ply us with delicacies at the taxpayer's expense. We did a lot of drinking. Certain polarities began to expose themselves in our ill-assorted little band. Kolff and Helen clearly had slept together before and meant to do so again; they were both so uninhibited about their lustiness that it plainly upset Heyman, who seemed to have a bad case of constipation from his cranial vault clear to his insteps. Morton Fields apparently had some sexual interest in Helen too, and the more he drank the more he tried to express it, but Helen wasn't having any; she was too involved with that fat old Sanskrit-spouting Falstaff, Kolff. So Fields turned his attention to Aster Mikkelsen, who, however, seemed as sexless as the table, and deflected his heavy-handed advances with the cool precision of a woman long accustomed to such tasks. My own mood was a detached one, an old vice: I sat there, the disembodied observer, watching my distin-

guished colleagues at play. This was a group carefully selected
to eliminate personality conflicts and other flaws, I thought.
Poor Sandy Kralick believed he had assembled six flawless
savants who would serve the nation with zealous dedication.
We hadn't been convened for eight hours yet, and already the
lines of cleavage were showing up. What would happen to us
when we were thrust into the presence of the slick, unpredictable Vornan-19? I feared much.

The banquet ended close to midnight. A row of empty
wine bottles crisscrossed the table. Government flunkies
appeared and announced that they would conduct us to the
tunnels.

It turned out that Kralick had distributed us in hotels all
around town. Fields made a boozy little scene about seeing
Aster to her place, and she sidestepped him somehow. Helen
and Kolff went off together, arm in arm; as they got into the
elevator I saw his hand slide deep under the shroud of hair
that enveloped her. I walked back to my hotel. I did not turn
on the screen to find out what Vornan-19 had been up to this
evening in Europe. I suspected, quite justly, that I'd get
enough of his antics as the weeks unrolled, and that I could
do without tonight's news.

I slept poorly. Helen McIlwain haunted my dreams. I had
never before dreamed that I was being circumcised by a
redheaded witch garbed in a cloak of human hair. I trust I
don't have that dream again...ever.

Seven

At noon the next day the six of us—and Kralick—boarded the
intercity tube for New York, nonstop. An hour later we
arrived, just in time for an Apocalyptist demonstration at the
tube terminal. They had heard that Vornan-19 was due to
land in New York shortly, and they were doing a little
preliminary cutting up.

We ascended into the vast terminal hall and found it a sea
of sweaty, shaggy figures. Banners of living light drifted in the
air, proclaiming gibberish slogans or just ordinary obscenities.

Terminal police were desperately trying to keep order. Over everything came the dull boom of an Apocalyptist chant, ragged and incoherent, a cry of anarchy in which I could make out only the words "doom . . . flame . . . doom . . ."

Helen McIlwain was enthralled. Apocalyptists were at least as interesting to her as tribal witch doctors, and she tried to rush out to the terminal floor to soak up the experience at close range. Kralick asked her to come back, but it was too late; she rushed toward the mob. A bearded prophet of doom clutched at her and ripped the network of small plastic disks that was her garment this morning. The disks popped in every direction, baring a swath of Helen eight inches wide down the front from throat to waist. One bare breast jutted into view, surprisingly firm for a woman her age, surprisingly well developed for a woman of her lean, lanky build. Helen looked glassy-eyed with excitement; she clutched at her new swain, trying to extract the essence of Apocalyptism from him as he shook and clawed and pummeled her. Three burly guards went out there at Kralick's insistence to rescue her. Helen greeted the first one with a kick in the groin that sent him reeling away; he vanished under a tide of surging fanatics and we did not see him reappear. The other two brandished neural whips and used them to disperse the Apocalyptists. Howls of outrage went up; there were sharp shrill cries of pain, riding over the undercurrent of "doom . . . flame . . . doom . . ." A troop of half-naked girls, hands to hips, paraded past us like a chorus line, cutting off my view; when I could see into the mob again, I realized that the guards had cut an island around Helen and were bringing her out. She seemed transfigured by the experience. "Marvelous," she kept saying, "marvelous, marvelous, such orgasmic frenzy!" The walls echoed with "doom . . . flame . . . doom . . ."

Kralick offered Helen his jacket, and she waved it away, not caring about the bare flesh or perhaps caring very much to keep it in view. Somehow they got us out of there. As we hustled through the door, I heard one terrible cry of pain rising above everything else, the sound that I imagine a man would make as he was being drawn before quartering. I never found out who screamed that way, or why.

". . . doom . . ." I heard, and we were outside.

Cars waited. We were taken to a hotel in mid-Manhattan. On the 125th floor we had a good view of the downtown renewal area. Helen and Kolff shamelessly took a double room; the rest of us received singles. Kralick supplied each of us with a thick sheaf of tapes dealing with suggested methods of handling Vornan. I filed mine without playing anything. Looking down into the distant street, I saw figures moving in a frantic stream on the pedestrian level, patterns forming and breaking, occasionally a collision, gesticulating arms, the movements of angry ants. Now and then a flying wedge of rowdies came roaring down the middle of the street. Apocalyptists, I assumed. How long had this been going on? I had been out of touch with the world; I had not realized that at any given moment in any given city one was vulnerable to the impact of chaos. I turned away from my window.

Morton Fields came into the room. He accepted my offer of a drink, and I punched the programming studs on my room service board. We sat quietly sipping filtered rums. I hoped he wouldn't babble at me in psychology jargon. But he wasn't the babbling kind: direct, incisive, sane, that was his style.

"Like a dream, isn't it?" he asked.

"This man from the future thing?"

"This whole cultural environment. The *fin de siècle* mood."

"It's been a long century, Fields. Maybe the world is happy to see it out. Maybe all this anarchy around us is a way of celebration, eh?"

"You could have a point," he conceded. "Vornan-19's a sort of Fortinbras, come to set the time back into joint."

"You think so?"

"It's a possibility."

"He hasn't acted very helpful so far," I said. "He seems to stir up trouble wherever he goes."

"Unintentionally. He's not attuned to us savages yet, and he keeps tripping over tribal taboos. Give him some time to get to know us and he'll begin to work wonders."

"Why do you say that?"

Fields solemnly tugged his left ear. "He has charismatic powers, Garfield. *Numen*. The divine power. You can see it in that smile of his, can't you?"

"Yes. Yes. But what makes you think he'll use that charisma rationally? Why not have some fun, stir up the mobs? Is he here as a savior or just as a tourist?"

"We'll find that out ourselves, in a few days. Mind if I punch another drink?"

"Punch three," I said airily. "I don't pay the bills."

Fields regarded me earnestly. His pale eyes seemed to be having trouble focusing, as though he were wearing a pair of corneal compressors and didn't know how to use them yet. After a long silence he said, "Do you know anyone who's ever been to bed with Aster Mikkelsen?"

"Not really. Should I?"

"I was just wondering. She might be a Lesbian."

"I doubt it," I said, "somehow. Does it matter?"

Fields laughed thinly. "I tried to seduce her last night."

"So I noticed."

"I was quite drunk."

"I noticed that too."

Fields said, "Aster told me an odd thing while I was trying to get her into bed. She said she didn't go to bed with men. She put it in a kind of flat declarative uninflected way, as though it ought to be perfectly obvious to anyone but a damned idiot. I was just wondering if there was something about her I ought to know and didn't."

"You might ask Sandy Kralick," I suggested. "He's got a dossier on all of us."

"I wouldn't do that. I mean—it's a little unworthy of me—"

"To want to sleep with Aster?"

"No, to go around to that bureaucrat trying to pick up tips. I'd rather keep the matter between us."

"Between us professors?" I amplified.

"In a sense," Fields grinned, an effort that must have cost him something. "Look, old fellow, I didn't mean to push my concerns onto you. I just thought—if you know anything about—about her—"

"Her proclivities?"

"Her proclivities."

"Nothing at all. She's a brilliant biochemist," I said. "She seems rather reserved as a person. That's all I can tell you."

Fields finally went away after a while. I heard Lloyd Kolff's lusty laughter roaring through the hallways. I felt like a prisoner. What if I phoned Kralick and asked him to send me Martha/Sidney at once? I stripped and got under the shower, letting the molecules do their buzzing dance, peeling away the grime of my journey from Washington. Then I read for a while. Kolff had given me his latest book, an anthology of metaphysical love lyrics he had translated from the Phoenician texts found at Byblos. I had always thought of Phoenicians as crisp Levantine businessmen, with no time for poetry, erotic or otherwise; but this was startling stuff, raw, fiery. I had not dreamed there were so many ways of describing the female genitalia. The pages were festooned with long streamers of adjectives: a catalog of lust, an inventory of stock-in-trade. A little of it went a very long way. I wondered if he had given a copy to Aster Mikkelsen.

I must have dozed. About five in the afternoon I was awakened by a few sheets sliding out of the data slot in the wall. Kralick was sending around Vornan-19's itinerary. Standard stuff: the New York Stock Exchange, the Grand Canyon, a couple of factories, an Indian reservation or two, and—pencilled in as tentative—Luna City. I wondered if we were expected to accompany him to the Moon if he went there. Probably.

At dinner that evening Helen and Aster went into a long huddle about something. I found myself stranded next to Heyman, and was treated to a discourse on Spenglerian interpretations of the Apocalyptist movement. Lloyd Kolff told scabrous tales in several languages to Fields, who listened dolefully and drank a good deal once again. Kralick joined us for dessert to say that Vornan-19 was boarding a rocket for New York the following morning and would be among us by noon, local time. He wished us luck.

We did not go to the airport to meet Vornan. Kralick expected trouble there, and he was right; we stayed at the hotel, watching the scene of the arrival on our screens. Two rival groups had gathered at the airport to greet Vornan. There was a mass of Apocalyptists, but that was not surprising; these days there seemed to be a mass of Apocalyptists everywhere. What was a little more unsettling was the presence of a group of a thousand demonstrators whom, for lack of a better word, the announcer called Vornan's "disciples." They had come to worship. The camera played lovingly over their faces. They were not bedizened lunatics like the Apocalyptists; no, they were very middle class, most of them, very tense, under tight control, not Dionysian revelers at all. I saw the pinched faces, the clamped lips, the sober mien—and I was frightened. The Apocalyptists represented the froth of society, the drifters, the rootless. These who had come to bow the knee to Vornan were the dwellers in small suburban apartments, the depositors in savings institutions, the goers to sleep at early hours, the backbone of American life. I remarked on this to Helen McIlwain.

"Of course," she said. "It's the counterrevolution, the coming reaction to Apocalyptist excess. These people see the man from the future as the apostle of order restored." Fields had said much the same thing.

I thought of falling bodies and pink thighs in a Tivoli dance hall. "They're likely to be disappointed," I said, "if they think that Vornan's going to help them. From what I've seen, he's strictly on the side of entropy."

"He may change when he sees what power he can wield over them."

Of all the many frightening things I saw and heard those first days, Helen McIlwain's calm words were, as I look back, the most terrifying of all.

Of course, the government had had long experience in importing celebrities. Vornan's arrival was announced for one runway, and then he came in on another, at the far end of the airport, while a dummy rocket sent up for the purpose from Mexico City glided in for a landing where the man from 2999 was supposed to come down. The police contained the mob fairly well, considering. But as the two groups rushed forth onto the field, they coalesced, the Apocalyptists mingled with the disciples of Vornan, and then, abruptly, it was impossible to know which group was which. The camera zeroed in on one throbbing mass of humanity and retreated just as quickly upon the discovery that a rape was in progress beneath all the confusion. Thousands of figures swarmed about the rocket, whose dull blue sides gleamed temptingly in the feeble January sunlight; meanwhile Vornan was quetly being extracted from the true rocket a mile away. Via helicopter and transportation pod he came to us, while tanks of foam were emptied on the strugglers surrounding the blue rocket. Kralick phoned ahead to let us know that they were bringing Vornan to the hotel suite that was serving as our New York headquarters.

I felt a moment of sudden blinding panic as Vornan-19 approached the room.

How can I convey the intensity of that feeling in words? Can I say that for an instant the moorings of the universe seemed to loosen, so that the Earth was drifting free in the void? Can I say that I felt myself wandering in a world without reason, without structure, without coherence? I mean this quite seriously: it was a moment of utter fear. My various ironic, wry, mocking, detached poses deserted me; and I was left without the armor of cynicism, naked in a withering gale, facing the prospect that I was about to meet a wanderer out of time.

The fear I felt was the fear that abstraction was turning to reality. One can talk a great deal about time-reversal, one can even shove a few electrons a brief distance into the past, and yet it all remains essentially abstract. I have not seen an electron, nor can I tell you where one finds the past. Now, abruptly, the fabric of the cosmos had been ripped apart and a chilly wind blew upon me out of the future; though I tried to recapture my old skepticism, I found it was impossible. God help me, I believed that Vornan was authentic. His charisma preceded him into the room, converting me in advance. What price hard headedness? I was jelly before he appeared. Helen McIlwain stood enraptured. Fields fidgeted; Kolff and Heyman looked troubled; even Aster's icy shield was penetrated. Whatever I was feeling, they were feeling it too.

Vornan-19 entered.

I had seen him on the screens so often in the past two weeks that I felt I knew him; but when he came among us, I found myself in the presence of a being so alien that he was unknowable. And traces of that feeling lingered during the months that followed, so that Vornan was always something apart.

He was even shorter than I had expected him to be, no more than an inch or two taller than Aster Mikkelsen. In a room of big men he looked overwhelmed, with towering Kralick at one side and mountainous Kolff at the other. Yet he was in perfect command. He drew his eyes over all of us in one smooth gesture and said, "This is most kind of you, to take this trouble for me. I am flattered."

God help me. I *believed*.

We are each of us the summaries of the events of our time, the great and the small. Our patterns of thought, our clusters of prejudices, these things are determined for us by the distillate of happenings that we inhale with our every breath. I have been shaped by the small wars of my lifetime, by the detonations of atomic weapons in my childhood, by the trauma of the Kennedy assassination, by the extinction of the Atlantic oyster, by the words my first woman spoke to me in her moment of ecstasy, by the triumph of the computer, by the tingle of Arizona sunlight on my bare skin, and much else. When I deal with other human beings, I know that I have a kinship with them, that they have been shaped by some of the events that fashioned my soul, that we have at least certain points of common reference.

What had shaped Vornan?

None of the things that had shaped me. I found grounds for awe in that. The matrix from which he came was wholly different from mine. A world that spoke other languages, that had had ten centuries of further history, that had undergone unimaginable alterations of culture and motive—that was the world from which he came. Through my mind flashed an imagined view of Vornan's world, an idealized world of green fields and gleaming towers, of controlled weather and vacations in the stars, of incomprehensible concepts and inconceivable advances; and I knew that whatever I imagined would fall short of the reality, that I had no points of reference to share with him at all.

I told myself that I was being a fool to give way to such fear.

I told myself that this man was of my own time, a clever manipulator of his fellow mortals.

I fought to recover my defensive skepticism. I failed.

We introduced ourselves to Vornan. He stood in the middle of the room, faintly supercilious, listening as we recited our scientific specialties to him. The philologist, the biochemist, the anthropologist, the historian, and the psychologist announced themselves in turn. I said, "I'm a physicist specializing in time-reversal phenomena," and waited.

Vornan-19 replied, "How remarkable. You've discovered time-reversal so early in civilization! We must talk about this some time soon, Sir Garfield."

Heyman stepped forward and barked, "What do you mean, 'so early in civilization'? If you think we're a pack of sweaty savages, you—"

"Franz," Kolff muttered, catching Heyman's arm, and I found out what the *F.* in "F. Richard Heyman" stood for. Heyman subsided stonily. Kralick scowled at him. One did not welcome a guest, however suspect a guest, by snarling defiance.

Kralick said, "We've arranged for a tour of the financial district for tomorrow morning. The rest of this day, I thought, could be spent at liberty, just relaxing. Does that sound all—"

Vornan was paying no attention. He had moved in a curious gliding way across the room and was eye-to-eye with Aster Mikkelsen. Quite softly he said, "I regret that my body is soiled from long hours of traveling. I wish to cleanse myself. Would you do me the honor of bathing with me?"

We gaped. We were all braced for Vornan's habit of making outrageous requests, but we hadn't expected him to try anything so soon, and not with Aster. Morton Fields went rigid and swung around like a man of flint, clearly groping for a way to rescue Aster from her predicament. But Aster needed no rescuing. She accepted Vornan's invitation to share a bathroom with him gracefully and with no sign of hesitation. Helen grinned. Kolff winked. Fields spluttered. Vornan made a little bow—flexing his knees as well as his spine, as though he did not really know how bows were accomplished—and ushered Aster briskly from the room. It had happened so fast that we were totally stunned.

Fields managed to say finally, "We can't let him do that!"

"Aster didn't object," Helen pointed out. "It was her decision."

Heyman pounded his hand into his fist. "I resign!" he boomed. "This is an absurdity! I withdraw entirely!"

Kolff and Kralick turned to him at once. "Franz, keep your temper," Kolff roared, and Kralick said simultaneously, "Dr. Heyman, I beg of you—"

"Suppose he had asked *me* to take a bath with him?" Heyman demanded. "Are we to grant him every whim? I refuse to be a party to this idiocy!"

Kralick said, "No one's asking you to yield to obviously excessive requests, Dr. Heyman. Miss Mikkelsen was under no pressure to agree. She did it for the sake of harmony, for—well, for scientific reasons. I'm proud of her. Nevertheless, she didn't *have* to say yes, and I don't want you to feel that you—"

Helen McIlwain cut in serenely, "I'm sorry you chose to resign this quickly, Franz, love. Wouldn't you have wanted to discuss the shape of the next thousand years with him? You'll never get a chance, now. I doubt that Mr. Kralick can let you interview him as you wish if you don't cooperate, and of course there are so many other historians who'd be happy to take your place, aren't there?"

Her ploy was devilishly effective. The thought of letting some despised rival get first crack at Vornan left Heyman devastated; and soon he was muttering that he hadn't really resigned, he had only *threatened* to resign. Kralick let him wiggle on that hook for a while before agreeing to forget the whole unhappy incident, and in the end Heyman promised none too gracefully to take a more temperate attitude toward the assignment.

Fields, during all this, kept looking toward the door through which Aster and Vornan had vanished. At length he said edgily, "Don't you think you ought to find out what they're doing?"

"Taking a bath, I imagine," said Kralick.

"You've very calm about it!" Fields said. "But what if you've sent her off with a homicidal maniac? I detect certain signs in that man's posture and facial expression that lead me to believe he's not to be trusted."

Kralick lifted a thick eyebrow. "Really, Dr. Fields? Would you care to dictate a report on that?"

"Not just yet," he said sullenly. "But I think Miss Mikkelsen ought to be protected. It's too early for us to begin assuming that this future-man is motivated in any way by the mores and taboos of our society, and—"

"That's right," said Helen. "It may be his custom to sacrifice a dark-haired virgin every Thursday morning. The important thing for us to remember is that he doesn't think like us, not in any of the big ways nor in the small ones."

It was impossible to tell from her deadpan tone whether she meant it, although I suspected she didn't. As for Fields' distress, that was simple enough to explain: having been frustrated in his own designs on Aster, he was upset to find Vornan spiriting her away so readily. He was so upset, in fact, that he triggered an exasperated Kralick into revealing something that he had plainly not intended to tell us.

"My staff is monitoring Vornan at all times," Kralick snapped at the psychologist. "We've got a complete audio, video, and tactile pickup on him, and I don't believe he knows it, and I'll thank you not to *let* him know it. Miss Mikkelsen is in no danger whatever."

Fields was taken aback. I think we all were.

"Do you mean your men are *watching* them—right now?"

"Look," said Kralick in obvious annoyance. He snatched up the house phone and dialed a transfer number. Instantly the room's wallscreen lit up with a relay of what his pickup devices were seeing. We were given a view in full color and three dimensions of Aster Mikkelsen and Vornan-19.

They were stark naked. Vornan's back was to camera; Aster's was not. She had a lean, supple, narrow-hipped body and the breasts of a twelve-year-old.

They were under a molecular shower together. She was scrubbing his back.

They appeared to be having a fine time.

Eight

That evening Kralick had arranged to have Vornan-19 attend a party in his honor at the Hudson River mansion of Wesley Bruton, the utilities tycoon. Bruton's place had been completed only two or three years back; it was the work of Albert Ngumbwe, the brilliant young architect who is now designing the Pan-African capital city in the Ituri Forest. It was so much of a showplace that even I had heard of it in my California isolation: the outstanding representative of contemporary design, it was said. My curiosity was piqued. I spent most of the afternoon going over a practically opaque book by one of the architectural critics, setting the Bruton house in its context—my homework, so to say. The helicopter fleet would depart at 6:30 from the heliport atop our hotel, and we'd travel under the tightest of security arrangements. The problem of logistics was going to be a severe one in this tour; I could see, and we would have to be infiltrated from place to place like contraband. Several hundred reporters and other media pests attempted to follow Vornan everywhere, even though it was agreed that coverage would be restricted to the daily pool of six journalists. A cloud of angry Apocalyptists trailed Vornan's movements, shouting their disbelief in him. And now there was the additional headache of a gathering force of disciples, a countermob of the sleek and respectable not-quite-middle-class burghers who saw in him the apostle of law and order, and who trampled on law and order in their hectic desire to worship him. With all those to contend with, we had to move swiftly.

Toward six we began to collect in our main suite. I found Kolff and Helen there when I arrived. Kolff was dressed in high style, and he was awesome to behold: a shimmering tunic enfolded his monumental bulk, sparkling in a whole spectrum of colors, while a gigantic cummerbund in midnight blue called attention to his jutting middle. He had slicked his straggly white hair across his dome of a skull. On his vast breast were mounted a row of academic medals conferred by many governments I recognized only one, which I also have been awarded: France's Legion des Curies. Kolff flourished a full dozen of the silly things.

Helen seemed almost restrained by comparison. She wore a sleek flowing gown made of some coy polymer that was now transparent, now opaque; viewed at the proper angle, she seemed nude, but the view lasted only an instant before the long chains of slippery molecules changed their orientation and concealed her flesh. It was cunning, attractive, and even tasteful in its way. Around her throat she wore a curious amulet, blatantly phallic, so much so that it negated itself and ultimately seemed innocent. Her makeup consisted of a green lipglow and dark halos around her eyes.

Fields entered shortly, wearing an ordinary business suit, and then came Heyman, dressed in a tight evening outfit at least twenty years out of style. Both of them looked uneasy. Not long afterward Aster stepped into the room, clad in a simple thigh-length robe, and adorned by a row of small tourmalines across her forehead. Her arrival stirred tension in the room.

I jerked about guiltily, hardly able to meet her eyes. Like all the rest, I had spied on her; even though it had not been my idea to switch on that espionage pickup and peer at her in the shower. I had looked with all the others, I had put my eye to the knothole and stolen a peek. Her tiny breasts and flat, boyish buttocks were no secret to me now. Fields went rigid once again, clenching his fists; Heyman flushed and scuffed at the sponge-glass floor. But Helen, who did not believe in such concepts as guilt or shame or modesty, gave Aster a warm, untroubled greeting, and Kolff, who had transgressed so often in a long life that he had no room left for a minor bit of remorse over some unintentional voyeurism, boomed happily, "Did you enjoy your clean-getting?"

Aster said quietly, "It was amusing."

She offered no details, I could see Fields bursting to know

if she had been to bed with Vornan-19. It seemed a moot
point to me; our guest had already demonstrated a remarkable and indiscriminate sexual voracity, but on the other hand
Aster appeared well able to guard her chastity even from a
man she had bathed with. She looked cheerful and relaxed
and not at all as though she had suffered any fundamental
violation of her personality in the last three hours. I rather
hoped she *had* slept with him; it might have been a healthy
experience for her, cool and isolated woman that she was.

Kralick arrived a few minutes later, Vornan-19 in tow. He
led us all to the roof heliport, where the copters were
waiting. There were four of them: one for the six members of
the news pool, one for the six of us and Vornan, one for a
batch of White House people, and one for our security guard.
Ours was the third to take off. With a quiet whir of turbines it
launched itself into the night sky and sped northward. We
could not see the other copters at any time during the flight.
Vornan-19 peered with interest through his window at the
glowing city beneath.

"What is the population of this city, please?" he asked.

"Including the surrounding metropolitan area, about thirty
million people," said Heyman.

"All of them human?"

The question baffled us. After a moment Fields said, "If
you mean, do any of them come from other worlds, no. We
don't have any beings from other worlds on Earth. We've
never discovered any intelligent life forms in this solar system, and we don't have any of our star probes back yet."

"No," said Vornan, "I am not talking about otherworlders. I
speak of natives to Earth. How many of your thirty million
here are full-blood human, and how many are servitors?"

"Servitors? Robots, you mean?" Helen asked.

"In the sense of synthetic life-forms, no," said Vornan
patiently. "I refer to those who do not have full human status
because they are genetically other than human. You have no
servitors yet? I have trouble finding the right words to ask.
You do not build life out of lesser life? There are no—no—"
He faltered. "I cannot say. There are no words."

We exchanged troubled glances. This was practically the
first conversation any of us had had with Vornan-19, and
already we were wallowing in communication dilemmas.
Once again I felt that chill of fear, that awareness that I was in
the presence of something strange. Every skeptical rationalist

atom in my being told me that this Vornan was nothing but a gifted con-man, and yet when he spoke in this random way of an Earth populated by humans and less-than-humans, there was powerful conviction in his groping attempts to explain what he meant. He dropped the subject. We flew onward. Below us the Hudson wound sluggishly to the sea. In a while the metropolitan zone ebbed and we could make out the dark areas of the public forests, and then we were descending toward the private landing strip of Wesley Bruton's hundred-acre estate, eighty miles north of the city. Bruton owned the largest tract of undeveloped privately held land east of the Mississippi, they said. I believed it.

The house was radiant. We saw it from a distance of a quarter of a mile as we left the helicopters; it breasted a rise overlooking the river, shining with an external green light that sent streams of brightness toward the stars. A covered glidewalk carried us up the grade, through a winter garden of sculptured ice, tinted fantasies done by a master hand. Coming closer, we could make out Ngumbwe's structural design: a series of concentric translucent shells comprising a peaked pavilion taller than any of the surrounding trees. Eight or nine overlapping arches formed the roof, revolving slowly so that the shape of the house continually changed. A hundred feet above the highest arch hung a great beacon of living light, a vast yellow globe that turned and writhed and swirled on its tenuous pedestal. We could hear music, high-pitched, vibrant, coming from festoons of tiny speakers draped along the icy limbs of gaunt, monumental trees. The glidewalk guided us toward the house; a door yawned like a mouth, gaping sideways to engulf us. I caught a glimpse of myself mirrored in the glassy surface of the door, looking solemn, a bit plump, ill at ease.

Within the house chaos reigned. Ngumbwe clearly was in league with the powers of darkness; no angle was comprehensible, no line met another. From the vestibule where we stood dozens of rooms were visible, branching in every direction, and yet it was impossible to discern any pattern, for the rooms themselves were in motion, constantly rearranging not only their individual shapes but their relation to one another. Walls formed, dissolved, and were reincarnated elsewhere. Floors rose to become ceilings while new rooms were spawned beneath them. I had a sense of colossal machinery grinding and clanking in the bowels of the earth to achieve

these effects, but all was done smoothly and noiselessly. In
the vestibule itself the structure was relatively stable, but the
oval alcove had pink, clammy walls of skinlike material which
swooped down at a sharp declivity, rising again just beyond
where we stood, and twisting in midair so that the seamless
surface was that of a Möbius strip. One could walk that wall,
pass the turnover point, and leave the room for another, yet
there were no apparent exits. I had to laugh. A madman had
designed this house, another madman lived in it; but one had
to take a certain perverse pride in all this misplaced ingenuity.

"Remarkable!" Lloyd Kolff boomed. "Incredible! What do
you think of it, eh?" he asked Vornan.

Vornan smiled palely. "Quite amusing. Does the therapy
work well?"

"Therapy?"

"This is a house for curing of the disturbed? A bedlam, is
that the word?"

"This is the home of one of the world's wealthiest men,"
Heyman said stiffly, "designed by the talented young architect Albert Ngumbwe. It's considered a landmark of artistic
accomplishment."

"Charming," said Vornan-19 devastatingly.

The vestibule rotated and we moved along the clammy
surface until abruptly we were in another room. The party
was in full swing. At least a hundred people were clustered in
a diamond-shaped hall of immense size and unfathomable
dimensions; the din they made was fearful, although by some
clever prank of acoustical engineering we had not heard a
thing until we had passed the critical zone of the Möbius
strip. Now we were among the horde of elegant guests who
clearly had been celebrating the night's event long before the
arrival of the guest of honor. They danced, they sang, they
drank, they puffed clouds of multi-hued smoke. Spotlights
played upon them. I recognized dozens of faces in one
dazzled sweep across the room: actors, financiers, political
figures, playboys, spacemen. Bruton had cast a wide net
through society, capturing only the distinguished, the lively,
the remarkable. It surprised me that I could put names to so
many of the faces, and I realized that it was a measure of
Bruton's success that he could gather under one multiplicity of
roofs so many individuals that a cloistered professorial sort
like myself could recognize.

A torrent of sparkling red wine flowed from a vent high on

one wall and ran in a thick, bubbly river diagonally across the floor like water in a pig trough. A dark-haired girl clad only in silver hoops stood under it, giggling as it drenched her. I groped for her name and Helen said, "Deona Sawtelle. The computer heiress." Two handsome young men in mirror-surface tuxedos tugged at her arms, trying to pull her free, and she eluded them to frolic in the flowing wine. In a moment they joined her. Nearby a superb dark-skinned woman with jeweled nostrils screamed happily in the grip of a titanic metal figure that was rhythmically clutching her to its chest. A man with a shaven and polished skull lay stretched full length on the floor while three girls scarcely out of their teens sat stride him and, I think, tried to undo his trousers. Four scholarly gentlemen with dyed beards sang raucously in a language unknown to me, and Lloyd Kolff strode across to greet them with whoops of mysteriously expressed pleasure. A woman with golden skin wept quietly at the base of a monstrous whirling construction of ebony, jade, and brass. Through the smoky air soared mechanical creatures with clanking metal wings and peacock tails, shrieking stridently and casting glittering droppings upon the guests. A pair of apes chained with loops of interlocked ivory gaily copulated near the intersection of two acute angles of the wall. This was Nineveh; this was Babylon. I stood dazzled, repelled by the excess of it all and yet delighted, as one is delighted by cosmic audacity of any kind. Was this a typical Wesley Bruton party? Or had it all been staged for the benefit of Vornan-19? I could not imagine people behaving like this under normal circumstances. They all seemed quite natural, though; it would take only some layers of dirt and a change of scene, and this could be an Apocalyptist riot, not a gathering of the elite. I caught sight of Kralick—appalled. He stood to one side of the vanished entrance, huge and bleak-faced, his ugly features no longer looking charming as dismay filtered through his flesh. He had not intended to bring Vornan into such a place.

Where was our visitor, anyway? In the first shock of our plunge into the madhouse we had lost sight of him. Vornan had been right: this was bedlam. And there he was in the midst of it. I saw him now, alongside the river of wine. The girl in the silver hoops, the computer heiress, rose on her knees, body stained deep crimson, and ran her hand lightly down her side. The hoops opened to the gentle command

and dropped away. She offered one to Vornan, who accepted it gravely, and hurled the rest into the air. The mechanical birds snapped them up in midflight and began to devour them. The computer heiress, wholly bare now, clapped her hands in delight. One of the young men in the mirror tuxedos produced a flask from his pocket and sprayed the girl's breasts and loins, leaving a thin plastic coating. She thanked him with a curtsy, and turning again to Vornan-19, scooped up wine with her hands and offered him a drink. He sipped. The whole left half of the room went into a convulsion, the floor rising twenty feet to reveal an entirely new group of revelers emerging from a cellar somewhere. Kralick, Fields, and Aster were among those of our group who vanished from view in this rotation of the main floor. I decided I should keep close to Vornan, since no other member of our committee was assuming the responsibility. Kolff was in paroxysms of laughter with his four bearded savants; Helen stood as if in a daze, trying to record every aspect of the scene; Heyman went swirling away in the arms of a voluptuous brunette with talons affixed to her fingers. I shouldered my way across the floor. A waxen young man seized my hand and kissed it. A tottering dowager sent a swirl of vomit within six inches of my shoes, and a buzzing golden-hued metallic beetle a foot in diameter emerged from the floor to clean the mess, emitting satisfied clicks; I saw the gears meshing beneath its wings when it scuttled away. A moment later I was beside Vornan.

His lips were smeared with wine, but his smile was still magnificent. As he caught sight of me, he disengaged himself from the Sawtelle girl, who was trying to pull him into the rivulet of wine, and said to me, "This is excellent, Sir Garfield. I am having a splendid evening." His forehead furrowed. "Sir Garfield is the wrong form of address, I remember. You are Leo. It is a splendid evening, Leo. This house—it is comedy itself!"

All around us the bacchanal raged more furiously. Blobs of living light drifted at eye level; I saw one distinguished guest capture one and eat it. A fist-fight had begun between the two escorts of a bloated-looking woman who was, I realized in awe and distaste, a beauty queen of my youth. Near us two girls rolled on the floor in a vehement wrestling match, ripping away handfuls of each other's clothing. A ring of onlookers formed and clapped rhythmically as the zones of bare flesh were revealed; suddenly pink buttocks flashed and the quarrel turned into an uninhibited sapphic embrace. Vornan seemed fascinated by the flexed legs of the girl beneath, by the thrusting pelvis of her conqueror, by the moist sucking sounds of their joined lips. He inclined his head to get a better view. Yet at the same moment a figure approached us and Vornan said to me, "Do you know this man?" I had the unsettling impression that Vornan had been looking in two directions at once, taking in a different quadrant of the room with each of his eyes. Was it so?

The newcomer was a short, chunky man no taller than Vornan-19, but at least twice as wide. His immensely powerful frame was the support for a massive dolichocephalic head that rose, without virtue of a neck, from his enormous shoulders. He had no hair, not even eyebrows or lashes, which made him look far more naked than the various nude and seminude caperers reeling about in our vicinity. Ignoring me, he pushed a vast paw at Vornan-19 and said, "So you're the man from the future? Pleased to know you. I'm Wesley Bruton."

"Our host. Good evening." Vornan gave him a variant of the smile, less dazzling, more urbane, and almost at once the smile flicked away and the eyes came into play: keen, cool, penetrating. Nodding gently in my direction he said, "You know Leo Garfield, of course?"

"Only by reputation," Bruton roared. His hand was still outstretched. Vornan had not taken it. The look of expectancy in Bruton's eyes slowly curdled into bewildered disappointment and barely suppressed fury. Feeling I had to do something, I seized the hand myself, and as he mangled me I shouted, "So good of you to invite us, Mr. Bruton. It's a miraculous house." I added in a lower voice, "He doesn't understand all of our customs. I don't think he shakes hands."

The utilities magnate looked mollified. He released me and said, "What do *you* think of the place, Vornan?"

"Delightful. Lovely in its delicacy. I admire the taste of your architect, his restraint, his classicism."

I couldn't be sure whether that was meant as sincere praise or as derision. Bruton appeared to take the compliments at face value. He seized Vornan by one wrist, clamped his other hand about me, and said, "I'd like to show you some of the behind-the-scenes stuff, fellows. This ought to interest you, Professor. And I know Vornan here will go for it. Come on!"

I feared that Vornan would make use of that shock tech-

nique he had demonstrated on the Spanish Stairs and send
Bruton flying a dozen yards for having dared to lay hands on
him. But no, our guest let himself be manhandled. Bruton
bulled his way through the swirling chaos of the party, towing
us in his wake. We reached a dais in the center of the room.
An invisible orchestra sounded a terrifying chord and burst
forth with a symphony I had never heard before, bringing
loops of sound spurting from every corner of the room. A girl
in the garb of an Egyptian princess was dancing atop the dais.
Bruton clamped one hand on each of her bare thighs and
lifted her out of the way as though she were a chair. We
mounted the dais beside him; he signaled and we sank
abruptly through the floor.

"We're two hundred feet down," Bruton announced. "This
is the master control room. Look!"

He waved his arms grandly. All about us were screens
relaying images of the party. The action unfolded kaleido-
scopically in a dozen rooms at once. I saw poor Kralick
wobbling unsteadily while some femme fatale climbed on his
shoulders. Morton Fields was coiled in a compromising position about a portly woman with a broad, flat nose; Helen
McIlwain was dictating notes into the amulet at her throat, a
task that required her to give a good imitation of the fellative
act, while Lloyd Kolff was enjoying the act itself not far away,
laughing cavernously as a wide-eyed girl crouched before
him. I could not find Heyman at all. Aster Mikkelsen stood in
the midst of a room with moist, palpitating walls, looking
serene as the frenzy raged about her. Tables laden with food
moved seemingly of their own will through each room; I
watched the guests seizing tidbits, stuffing themselves, hurling
tender morsels at one another. There was a room in which
spigots of (I presume) wine or liquor dangled from the ceiling
for anyone to grasp and squeeze and draw comfort from;
there was a room that was in total darkness, but not unoccu-
pied; there was a room in which the guests took turns
donning the headband of some sensory-disruptive device.

"Watch this!" Bruton cried.

Vornan and I watched, he with mild interest, I in distress,
as Bruton yanked switches, closed contacts, tapped out computer orders in maniacal glee. Lights flickered on and off in
the upper rooms; floors and ceilings changed places; small
artificial creatures flew insanely among the shrieking, laughing guests. Shattering sounds too terrifying to be called music

resounded through the building. I thought the Earth itself would erupt in protest, and molten lava engulf us all.

"Five thousand kilowatts an hour," Bruton proclaimed.

He splayed his hands against a counterbalanced silvery globe a foot in diameter and nudged it forward on a jeweled track. Instantly one wall of the control room folded out of sight, revealing the giant shaft of a magneto-hydrodynamic generator descending into yet another sub-basement. Monitor needles did a madman's dance; dials flashed green and red and purple at us. Perspiration rolled down Wesley Bruton's face as he recited, almost hysterically, the engineering specifications of the power plant on which his palace was founded. He sang us a wild song of kilowatts. He set his grip on thick cables and massaged them in frank obscenity. He beckoned us down to see the core of his generator, and we followed, led ever deeper into the pit by this gnomish tycoon. Wesley Bruton, I remembered vaguely, had put together the holding company that distributed electricity across half the continent, and it was as though all the generating capacity of that incomprehensible monopoly were concentrated here, beneath our feet, harnessed for the sole purpose of maintaining and sustaining the architectural masterpiece of Albert Ngumbwe. The air was fiercely hot at this level. Sweat rolled down my cheeks. Bruton ripped open his jacket to bare a hairless chest banded by thick cords of muscle. Vornan-19 alone remained untroubled by the heat; he danced along beside Bruton, saying little, observing much, quite uninfected by the feverish mood of his host.

We reached the bottom. Bruton fondled the swelling flank of his generator as though it were a woman's haunch. Suddenly it must have dawned on him that Vornan-19 was less than ecstatic over this parade of wonders. He whirled and demanded. "Do you have anything like this where you come from? Is there a house that can match my house?"

"I doubt it," said Vornan gently.

"How do people live up there? Big houses? Small?"

"We tend toward simplicity."

"So you've never seen a place like mine! Nothing to equal it in the next thousand years!" Bruton paused. "But—doesn't my house still exist in your time?"

"I am not aware of that."

"Ngumbwe promised me it would last a thousand years! Five thousand! No one would tear a place like this down!

Listen, Vornan, stop and think. It must be there somewhere. A monument of the past—a museum of ancient history—"

"Perhaps it is," said Vornan indifferently. "You see, this area lies outside the Centrality. I have no firm information on what may be found there. However, I believe the primitive barbarity of this structure might have been offensive to those who lived in the Time of Sweeping, when many things changed. Much perished then through intolerance."

"Primitive—barbarity—" Bruton muttered. He looked apoplectic. I wished I had Kralick on hand to get me out of this.

Vornan went on planting barbs in the billionaire's unexpectedly thin hide. "It would have been charming to retain a place like this," he said. "To stage festivals in it, curious ceremonies in honor of the return of spring." Vornan smiled. "We might even have winters again, if only so we could experience the return of spring. And then we would dance and frolic in your house, Sir Bruton. But I think it is lost. I think it has gone, hundreds of years ago. I am not sure. I am not sure."

"Are you making fun of me?" Bruton bellowed. "Laughing at my house? Am I just a savage to you? Do—"

I cut in quickly. "As an expert on electricity, Mr. Bruton, perhaps you'd like to know something about power sources in Vornan-19's era. At one of his interviews a few weeks ago he said a few things about self-contained power sources involving total energy-conversion, and possibly he'd elaborate, now, if you'd care to question him."

Bruton forgot at once that he was angry. He used his arm to wipe away the sweat that was trickling into his browless eyes and grunted, "What's this? Tell me about this!"

Vornan put the backs of his hands together in a gesture that was as communicative as it was alien. "I regret that I know so little about technical matters."

"Tell me something, though!"

"Yes," I said, thinking of Jack Bryant in his agony and wondering if this was my moment to learn what I had to learn. "This system of self-sufficient power, Vornan. When did it come into use?"

"Oh . . . very long ago. In my day, that is."

"*How* long ago?"

"Three hundred years?" he asked himself. "Five hundred? Eight hundred? It is so difficult to calculate these things. It was long ago . . . very long ago."

"What was it?" Bruton demanded. "How big was each generating unit?"

"Quite small," said Vornan evasively. He put his hand lightly against Bruton's bare arm. "Shall we go upstairs? I am missing your so-interesting party."

"You mean it eliminated the need for power transmission altogether?" Bruton could not let go. "Everybody generated his own? Just as I'm doing down here?"

We mounted a catwalk, spidery and intricate, that swung us to an upper level. Bruton continued to pepper Vornan with questions as we threaded our route back to the master control room. I tried to interject queries that would pin down the point in time at which this great changeover had come about, hoping to be able to ease Jack's soul by telling him it had happened far in our future. Vornan danced gaily about our questions, saying little of substance. His lighthearted refusal to meet any request for information squarely aroused my suspicions once more. How could I help but swing on a pendulum, now gravely grilling Vornan about the events of future history, now cursing myself for a gullible fool as I realized he was a fraud? In the control room Vornan chose a simple method to relieve himself of the burden of our inquisitiveness. He strode to one of the elaborate panels, gave Bruton a smile of the highest voltage, and said, "This is deliciously amusing, this room of yours. I admire it greatly." He pulled three switches and depressed four buttons; then he turned a wheel ninety degrees and yanked a lengthy lever.

Bruton howled. The room went dark. Sparks flew like demons. From far above came the cacophonous wail of disembodied musical instruments and the sounds of crashing and colliding. Below us, two movable catwalks clanged together, an eerie screech rose from the generator. One screen came to life again, showing us by its pale glow the main ballroom with the guests dumped into a disheveled heap. Red warning lights began to flash. The entire house was awry, rooms orbiting rooms. Bruton was madly clawing at the controls, pressing this and twisting that, but each further adjustment he made seemed only to compound the disruption. Would the generator blow?, I wondered. Would everything come crashing down on us? I listened to a stream of curses that would have put Kolff into ecstasy. Machinery still gnashed both above and below us. The screen presented me with an out-of-focus view of Helen McIlwain riding piggyback

on the shoulders of a distressed Sandy Kralick. There were
the sounds of alarums and excursions. I had to move on.
Where was Vornan-19? I had lost sight of him in the dark.
Fitfully I edged forward, looking for the exit from the control
room. I spied a door; it was in paroxysms, moving along its
socket in arythmic quivering jerks. Crouching, I counted five
complete cycles and then, hoping I had the timing at least
approximately correct, leaped through just in time to avoid
being crushed.

"Vornan!" I yelled.

A greenish mist drifted through the atmosphere of the
room I entered now. The ceiling tilted at unlikely angles.
Bruton's guests lay slumped on the floor, some unconscious, a
few injured, at least one couple locked in a passionate embrace. I thought I caught sight of Vornan in a room vaguely
visible to my left, but I made the mistake of leaning against a
wall, and a panel responded to my pressure and pivoted,
thrusting me into a different room. I had to squat here; the
ceiling was perhaps five feet high. Scuttling across it, I
pushed open a folding screen and found myself in the main
ballroom. The waterfall of wine had become a fountain,
spurting its bubbly fluid toward the dazzling ceiling. Guests
milled vacantly, grabbing at one another for comfort and
reassurance. Underfoot buzzed the mechanical insects that
cleared away debris; half a dozen of them had caught one of
Bruton's metal birds and were rending it with tiny beaks.
None of our group could be seen. A high whining sound now
came from the fabric of the house.

I prepared myself for death, thinking it properly absurd
that I should perish in the home of one lunatic at the whim of
another while I was engaged on this lunatic mission. But still
I fought my way onward through the smoke and noise,
through the tangled, screaming figures of the elegant guests,
through the sliding walls and collapsing floors. Once more it
seemed to me I saw Vornan moving ahead of me. With
maniacal persistence I went after him, feeling that it was
somehow my duty to find him and lead him out of the
building before it demolished itself in one final expression
of petulance. But I came to a barrier beyond which I could
not pass. Invisible yet impermeable, it held me fast. "Vornan!"
I shouted, for now I saw him plainly. He was chatting with
a tall, attractive woman of middle years who seemed wholly
undisturbed by what had happened. "Vornan! It's me, Leo

Garfield!" But he could hear nothing. He gave the woman his arm, and they strolled away, sauntering in an irregular course through the chaos. I hammered with my fists against the invisible wall.

"That's no way to get out," said a husky feminine voice. "You couldn't smash that in a million years."

I turned. A vision in silver had appeared behind me: a slender girl, no older than nineteen, whose entire form gleamed in whiteness. Her hair had a silken glitter; her eyes were silver mirrors; her lips were silvered; her body was encased in a silver gown. I looked again and realized it was no gown, but merely a layer of paint; I detected nipples, a navel, twin muscle-ridges up the flat belly. From throat to toes she wore the silver spray, and by the ghostly light she seemed radiant, unreal, unattainable. I had not seen her before at the party.

"What happened?" she asked.

"Bruton took us on a tour of the control room. Vornan pressed some buttons when we weren't watching him. I think the house is going to explode."

She touched her silvery hand to her silvery lips. "No, it won't go up. But we'd better get out anyway. If it's going through random changes, it might squeeze everybody flat before things settle down. Come with me."

"You know how to get out?"

"Of course," she said. "Just follow along! There's an exit pouch three rooms from here . . . unless it's moved."

Mine not to reason why. She darted through a hatch that yawned suddenly, and mesmerized by the view of her dainty silvered rump, I followed. She led me along until I gasped with fatigue. We leaped over thresholds that undulated like serpents; we burrowed through heaps of giddy inebriates; we soared past impediments that came and went in mindless palpitations. I had never seen anything so beautiful as this burnished statue come to life, this girl of silver, nude and sleek and swift, moving purposefully through the dislocations of the house. She halted by a quivering strip of wall and said, "In here."

"Where?"

"There." The wall yawned wide. She thrust me inside and got in after me; then with a quick pirouette she moved around me, pressed on something, and we were outside the house.

The blast of January wind struck us like a whirling sword.

I had forgotten about the weather; we had been wholly shielded from it throughout the evening. Suddenly we were exposed to it, I in my light evening clothes, the girl in nudity covered only by a molecule-thick layer of silver paint. She stumbled and went down in a snowbank, rolling over as though aflame; I tugged her to her feet. Where could we go? Behind us the house churned and throbbed like a cephalopod gone berserk. Until this moment the girl had seemed to know what to do, but the frigid air numbed and stunned her, and now she trembled in paralysis, frightened and pathetic.

"The parking lot," I said.

We raced for it. It lay at least a quarter of a mile away, and we did not travel on any covered glidewalk now; we ran over frozen ground made hazardous by mounds of snow and rivers of ice. I was so stoked by excitement that I hardly noticed the cold, but it punished the girl brutally. She fell several times before we reached the lot. There it was at last. The vehicles of the rich and mighty were neatly arranged under a protective shield. Somehow we erupted through; Bruton's parking attendants had gone out of control in the general failure of power, and they made no attempt to stop us. They circled in buzzing bewilderment, flashing their lights on and off. I dragged the girl to the nearest limousine, pulled open its door, thrust her inside and dropped down beside her.

Within it was warm and womblike. She lay gasping, shivering, congealed. "Hold me!" she cried, "I'm freezing! For God's sake, hold me!"

My arms wrapped tight around her. Her slim form nestled against mine. In a moment her panic was gone; she was warm again, and as self-possessed as she had been when she led us from the house. I felt her hands against me. Willingly I surrendered to her silvered lure. My lips went to hers and came away tasting of metal; her cool thighs encircled me; I felt as though I were making love to some artfully crafted engine, but the silver paint was no more than skin deep, and the sensation vanished as I reached warm flesh beneath it. In our passionate struggles her silver hair revealed itself as a wig, it slipped away, displaying an unsilvered skull, bald as porcelain, below. I knew her now: she must be Bruton's daughter. His gene for hairlessness bred true. She sighed and drew me down into oblivion.

Nine

Kralick said, "We lost control of events. We have to keep a tighter grip on things next time. Which one of you was with Vornan when he got hold of the controls?"

"I was," I said. "There was absolutely no way of preventing what took place. He moved quickly. Neither Bruton nor I suspected that he might do any such thing."

"You can't ever let yourself get off guard with him," Kralick said in anguish. "You have to assume at any given moment that he's capable of doing the most outrageous thing imaginable. Haven't I tried to get that point across to you before?"

"We are basically rational people," said Heyman. "We do not find it easy to adjust to the presence of an irrational person."

A day had passed since the debacle at Wesley Bruton's wondrous villa. Miraculously, there had been no fatalities; Kralick had signaled for Government troops, who had pulled all the guests from the throbbing, swaying house in time. Vornan-19 had turned up standing outside the house, watching calmly as it went through its antics. The damage to the house, I heard Kralick mutter, had been several hundred thousand dollars. The Government would pay. I did not envy Kralick his job of calming Wesley Bruton down. But at least the utilities magnate could not say that he had suffered unjustly. His own urge to lionize the man from the future had brought this trouble upon him. Bruton surely had seen the reels of Vornan's trip through the capitals of Europe, and was aware that unpredictable things took place around and about Vornan. Yet Bruton had insisted on giving the party, and had insisted too on taking Vornan to the control room of his mansion. I could not feel very sorry for him. As for the guests who had been interrupted in their revelry by the cataclysm, they deserved little pity either. They had come to stare at the time traveler and to make fools of themselves. They had done both, and what harm was it if Vornan had chosen to make fools of them in return?

Kralick was right to be displeased with us, though. It was our responsibility to keep such things from happening. We had not discharged that responsibility very well on our first outing with the man from the future.

A little grimly, we prepared to continue the tour.

Today we were visiting the New York Stock Exchange. I have no idea how that came to be on Vornan's itinerary. Certainly he did not request it; I suspect that some bureaucrat in the capital decided arbitrarily that it would be a worthy propaganda move to let the futuristic sightseer have a look at the bastion of the capitalistic system. For my part I felt a little like a visitor from some alien environment myself, since I had never been near the Stock Exchange nor had any dealings with it. This is not the snobbery of the academic man, please understand. If I had time and inclination, I would gladly have joined the fun of speculating in Consolidated System Mining and United Ultronics and the other current favorites. But my salary is a good one and I have a small private income besides, ample for my needs; since life is too short to allow us to sample every experience, I have lived within my income and devoted my energy to my work, rather than to the market. In a kind of eager ignorance, then, I readied myself for our visit. I felt like a grade-school boy on an outing.

Kralick had been called back to Washington for conferences. Our governmental shepherd for the day was a taciturn young man named Holliday, who looked anything but happy at having drawn this assignment. At eleven that morning we headed downtown, traveling en masse: Vornan, the seven of us, an assortment of official hangers-on, the six members of today's media pool, and our guards. By prearrangement the Stock Exchange gallery would be closed to other visitors while we were there. Traveling with Vornan was complex enough without having to share a visitors' balcony.

Our motorcade of glossy limousines halted grandly before the immense building. Vornan looked politely bored as we were ushered inside by Exchange officials. He had said next to nothing all day; in fact, we had heard little from him since the grim homeward ride from the Bruton fiasco. I feared his silence. What mischief was he storing up? Right now he seemed wholly disconnected; neither the shrewd, calculating eyes nor the all-conquering smile were at work. Blank-faced, withdrawn, he seemed no more than a slight, ordinary man as we filed toward the visitors' gallery.

The scene was stupendous. Beyond doubt this was the home of the moneychangers.

We looked down into a room at least a thousand feet on each side, perhaps a hundred fifty feet from floor to ceiling. In the middle of everything was the great masculine shaft of the central financial computer: a glossy column twenty yards in diameter, rising from the floor and disappearing through the ceiling. Every brokerage house in the world had its direct input to that machine. Within its polished depths existed who knew how many clicking and chattering relays, how many memory cores of fantastic smallness, how many phone links, how many data tanks? With one swift bolt of a laser cannon it would be possible to sever the communications network that held together the financial structure of civilization. I looked warily at Vornan-19, wondering what deviltry he had in mind. But he seemed calm, aloof, only faintly interested in the floor of the Exchange.

About the central rod of the computer shaft were situated smaller cagelike structures, some thirty or forty of them, each with its cluster of excited, gesticulating brokers. The open space between these booths was littered with papers. Messenger boys scurried frantically about, kicking the discarded papers into clouds. Overhead, draped from one wall to the other, ran the gigantic yellow ribbon of the stock ticker, reeling off in magnified form the information that the main computer was transmitting everywhere. It seemed odd to me that a computerized stock exchange would have all this bustle and clutter on its floor, and that there would be so much paper lying about, as though the year were 1949 instead of 1999. But I did not take into account the force of tradition among these brokers. Men of money are conservative, not necessarily in ideology but certainly in habit. They want everything to remain as it has always been.

Half a dozen Stock Exchange executives came out to greet us—crisp, gray-haired men, attired in neat old-fashioned business suits. They were unfathomably rich, I suppose; and why, given such riches, they chose to spend the days of their lives in this building I could not and cannot understand. But they were friendly. I suspect they would give the same warm, open-handed greeting to a touring delegation from the social-

ist countries that have not yet adopted modified capitalism—
say, a pack of touring zealots from Mongolia. They thrust
themselves upon us, and they seemed almost as delighted to
have a gaggle of touring professors on their balcony as they
did to have a man claiming to come from the far future.

The President of the Stock Exchange, Samuel Norton,
made us a brief, courtly speech. He was a tall, well-groomed
man of middle years, easy of manner, obviously quite pleased
with his place in the universe. He told us of the history of his
organization, gave us some weighty statistics, boasted a bit
about the current Stock Exchange headquarters, which had
been built in the 1980's, and closed by saying, "Our guide
will now show you the workings of our operation in detail.
When she's finished, I'll be happy to answer any general
questions you may have—particularly those concerning the
underlying philosophy of our system, which I know must be
of great interest to you."

The guide was an attractive girl in her twenties with short,
shiny red hair and a gray uniform artfully designed to mask
her feminine characteristics. She beckoned us forward to the
edge of the balcony and said, "Below us you see the trading
floor of the New York Stock Exchange. At the present time,
four thousand one hundred twenty-five common and preferred stocks are traded on the Exchange. Dealings in bonds
are handled elsewhere. In the center of the floor you see the
shaft of our main computer. It extends thirteen stories into
the basement and rises eight stories above us. Of the hundred
floors in this building, fifty-one are used wholly or in part for
the operations of this computer, including the levels for
programming, decoding, maintenance, and record storage.
Every transaction that takes place on the floor of the Exchange
or on any of the subsidiary exchanges in other cities and
countries is noted with the speed of light within this computer. At present there are eleven main subsidiary exchanges:
San Francisco, Chicago, London, Zurich, Milan, Moscow,
Tokyo, Hong Kong, Rio de Janeiro, Addis Ababa, and—ah—
Sydney. Since these span all time zones, it is possible to carry
out securities transactions twenty-four hours a day. The New
York Exchange, however, is open only from ten in the morning
to half past three, the traditional hours, and all 'off-the-floor'
transactions are recorded and analyzed for the pre-opening
session the following morning. Our daily volume on the main
trading floor is about three hundred fifty million shares, and

roughly twice that many shares are traded each day on the subsidiary exchanges. Only a generation ago such figures would have been regarded as fantastic.

"Now, how does a securities transaction take place?

"Let us say that you, Mr. Vornan, wish to purchase one hundred shares of XYZ Space Transit Corporation. You have seen in yesterday's tapes that the market price is currently about forty dollars a share, so you know that you must invest approximately four thousand dollars. Your first step is to contact your broker, which of course can be done by a touch of your finger to your telephone. You place your order with him, and he immediately relays it to the trading floor. The particular data bank in which XYZ Space Transit transactions are recorded takes his call and notes your order. The computer conducts an auction, just as has been done in listed securities on the Exchange since 1792. The offers to sell XYZ Space Transit are matched against the offers to buy. At the speed of light it is determined that one hundred shares are available for sale at forty, and that a buyer exists. The transaction is closed and your broker notifies you. A small commission is his only charge to you; in addition there is a small fee for the computer services of the Exchange. A portion of this goes to the retirement fund of the so-called specialists who formerly handled the matching of buy and sell orders on the trading floor.

"Since everything is handled by computer, you may wonder what is taking place elsewhere on the trading floor. What you see represents a delightful Stock Exchange tradition: although not strictly necessary any longer, we maintain a staff of brokers who buy and sell securities for their own accounts, exactly as in the old days. They are following the precomputer process. Let me trace the course of a single transaction for you. . . ."

In clean, precise tones she showed us what all the mad scurrying on the floor was about. I was startled to realize that it was done purely as a charade; the transactions were unreal and at the end of each day all accounts were canceled. The computer actually handled everything. The noise, the discarded papers, the intricate gesticulations—these were reconstructions of the archaic past, performed by men whose lives had lost their purpose. It was fascinating and depressing; a ritual of money, a running-down of the capitalistic clock. Old brokers who would not retire took part in this daily amusement,

I gathered, while alongside them the monstrous shaft of the computer, which had unmanned them a decade previously, gleamed as the erect symbol of their impotence.

Our guide droned on and on, telling us of the stock ticker and the Dow-Jones averages, deciphering the cryptic symbols that drifted dreamily by on the screen, talking of bulls and bears, of short sellers, of margin requirements, of many another strange and wonderful thing. As the climax of her act she switched on a computer output and allowed us to have a squint at the boiling madhouse within the master brain, where transactions took place at improbable speeds and billions of dollars changed hands within moments.

I was awed by the awesomeness of it all. I who had never played the market felt the urge to phone my broker, if I could find one, and get plugged into the great data banks. Sell a hundred GFX! Buy two hundred CCC! Off a point! Up two! This was the core of life; this was the essence of being. The mad rhythm of it caught me completely. I longed to rush toward the computer shaft, spread my arms wide, embrace its gleaming vertical bulk. I envisioned its lines reaching out through the world, even unto the reformed socialist brethren in Moscow, threading a communion of dollars from city to city, and extending perhaps to the Moon, to our coming bases on the planets, to the stars themselves . . . capitalism triumphant!

The guide faded away. President Norton of the Stock Exchange stepped forward again, beaming pleasantly, and said, "Now, if I can help you with any further problems—"

"Yes," said Vornan mildly. "What is the purpose, please, of a stock exchange?"

The executive reddened and showed signs of shock. After all this detailed explication . . . to have the esteemed guest ask what the whole thing was about? We looked embarrassed ourselves. None of us had thought that Vornan had come here ignorant of the basic uses of this enterprise. How had he let himself be taken to the Exchange without knowing what it was he was going to see? Why had he not asked before this? I realized once again that if he were genuine, Vornan must view us as amusing apes whose plans and schemes were funny to watch for their own sake; he was not so much interested in visiting a thing called a stock exchange as he was in the fact that our Government earnestly desired him to visit that thing.

"Well," said the Stock Exchange man, "am I to understand, Mr. Vornan, that in the time that you—that you come from there is no such thing as a securities exchange?"

"Not that I know of."

"Perhaps under some other name?"

"I can think of no equivalent."

Consternation. "But how do you manage to transfer units of corporate ownership, then?"

Blankness. A shy, possibly mocking smile from Vornan-19.

"You *do* have corporate ownership?"

"Pardon," Vornan said. "I have studied your language carefully before making my journey, but there are many gaps in my knowledge. Perhaps if you could explain some of your basic terms—"

The executive's easy dignity began to flee. Norton's cheeks were mottled, his eyes were flickering like those of a beast trapped in a cage. I had seen something of the same look on Wesley Bruton's face when he had learned from Vornan that his magnificent villa, built to endure through the ages like the Parthenon and the Taj Mahal, had vanished and been forgotten by 2999, and would have been retained only as a curiosity, a manifestation of baroque foolishness, if it had survived. The Stock Exchange man could not comprehend Vornan's incomprehension, and it unnerved him.

Norton said, "A corporation is a—well, a company. That is, a group of individuals banded together to do something for profit. To manufacture a product, to perform a service, to—"

"A profit," said Vornan idly. "What is a profit?"

Norton bit his lip and dabbed at his sweaty forehead. After some hesitation he said, "A profit is a return of income above costs. A surplus value, as they say. The corporation's basic goal is to make a profit that can be divided among its owners. Thus it must be efficiently productive, so that the fixed costs of operation are overcome and the unit cost of manufacturing is lower than the market price of the product offered. Now, the reason why people set up corporations instead of simple partnerships is—"

"I do not follow," said Vornan. "Simpler terms, please. The object of this corporation is profit, to be divided among owners, yes? But what is an owner?"

"I was just coming to that. In legal terms—"

"And what use is this profit that the owners should want it?"

I sensed that a deliberate baiting was going on. I looked in worry at Kolff, at Helen, at Heyman. But they seemed hardly to be perturbed. Holliday, our Government man, was frowning a bit, but perhaps he thought Vornan-19's questions more innocent than they seemed to me.

The nostrils of the Stock Exchange man flickered ominously. His temper seemed to be held under tight restraint. One of the media men, alive to Norton's discomfiture, moved close to flash a camera in his face. He glowered at it.

"Am I to understand," Norton asked slowly, "that in your era the concept of the corporation is unknown? That the profit motive is extinct? That money itself has vanished from use?"

"I would have to say yes," Vornan replied pleasantly. "At least, as I comprehend those terms, we have nothing equivalent to them."

"This has happened *in America*?" Norton asked in incredulity.

"We do not precisely have an America," said Vornan. "I come from the Centrality. The terms are not congruous, and in fact I find it hard to compare even approximately—"

"America's gone? How could that be? When did it happen?"

"Oh, during the Time of Sweeping, I suppose. Many things changed then. It was long ago. I do not remember an America."

F. Richard Heyman saw an opportunity to scrape a little history out of the maddeningly oblique Vornan. He swung around and said, "About the Time of Sweeping that you've occasionally mentioned. I'd like to know—"

He was interrupted by a geyser of indignation from Samuel Norton.

"America gone? Capitalism extinct? It just couldn't happen! I tell you—"

One of the executive's aides moved hurriedly to his side and urgently murmured something. The great man nodded. He accepted a violet-hued capsule from the other and touched its ultrasonic snout to his wrist. There was a quick whirr, an intake of what I suppose was some kind of tranquilizing drug. Norton breathed deeply and made a visible effort to collect himself.

More temperately, the Stock Exchange leader said to Vornan, "I don't mind telling you that I find all this hard to believe. A world without America in it? A world that doesn't use money? Tell me this, will you, please: *Has the whole world gone Communist where you come from?*"

There ensued what they call a pregnant silence, during which cameras and recorders were busy catching tense, incredulous, angry, or disturbed facial expressions. I sensed impending disaster. At length Vornan said, "It is another term I do not understand. I apologize for my extreme ignorance. I fear that my world is much unlike yours. However"—at this point he produced his glittering smile, drawing the sting from his words—"it is your world, and not mine, that I have come here to discuss. Please do tell me the use of this Stock Exchange of yours."

But Norton could not shake his obsession with the contours of Vornan-19's world. "In a moment. If you'll tell *me*, first, how you make purchases of goods—a hint or two of your economic system—"

"We each have all that any person would require. Our needs are met. And now, this idea of corporation ownership—"

Norton turned away in despair. Vistas of an unimaginable future stretched before us: a world without economics, a world in which no desire went unfulfilled. Was it possible? Or was it all the oversimplified shrugging-away of details that a mountebank did not care to simulate for us? One or the other, I was beguiled. But Norton was derailed. He gestured numbly to one of the other Stock Exchange men, who came forward brightly to say, "Let's start right at the beginning. We've got this company that makes things. It's owned by a little group of people. Now, in legal terms there's a concept known as liability, meaning that the owners of a company are responsible for anything their company might do that's improper or illegal. To shift liability, they create an imaginary entity called a corporation, which bears the responsibility for any action that might be brought against them in their business capacity. Now, since each member of the owning group has a share in the ownership of this corporation, we can issue *stock*, that is, certificates representing proportional shares of beneficial interest in the . . ."

And so on and on. A basic course in economics.

Vornan beamed. He let the whole thing run its route, right to the point where the man was explaining that when an owner wished to sell his share in the company, he found it expedient to work through a central auction system that would put his stock up for the highest bidder, when Vornan quietly and devastatingly admitted that he still couldn't quite grasp the concepts of ownership, corporations, and profit, let alone the transfer of stock interests. I'm sure he said it just to annoy and goad. He was playing the part now of the man from Utopia, eliciting long explanations of our society and then playfully giving the structure itself a shove by registering ignorance of its underlying assumptions, implying that the underlying assumptions were transient and insignificant. There was a distressed huddle among the offended but stonily reserved Stock Exchange officials. It had never occurred to them that anyone might take this mock-innocent attitude. Even a child knew what money was and what corporations did, even if the concept of limited liability remained elusive.

I felt no great impulse to get mixed up in the awkwardness. My eyes roved idly here and there. Looking toward the great yellow blowup of the stock ticker, I saw:

STOCK EXCHANGE PLAYS HOST TO MAN FROM 2999

And then:

VORNAN-19 ON VISITORS GALLERY NOW

The tape began then to tell of stock transactions and of fluctuating averages. But the damage was done. Action on the trading floor came to a halt. The counterfeit buying and selling stopped, and a thousand faces were upturned to the balcony. Great shouts arose, incoherent, unintelligible. The brokers were waving and cheering. They flowed together, swirling around the trading posts, pointing, waving, crying out mysterious booming noises. What did they want? The Dow-Jones industrial averages for January, 2999? The laying-on of hands? A glimpse of the man from the future? Vornan was at the rim of the balcony, now, smiling, holding up his hands as though delivering a benediction upon capitalism. The last rites, perhaps . . . extreme unction for the financial dinosaurs.

Norton said, "They're acting strangely. I don't like this."

Holliday reacted to the note of alarm in his voice. "Let's get Vornan out of here," he murmured to a guard standing just by my elbow. "There's the look of a riot starting."

Tickertape floated through the air. The churning brokers seized long streamers of it, danced around with it, sent it coiling upward toward the balcony. I heard a few shouts against the background of noise: they wanted Vornan to come down among them. Vornan continued to acknowledge their homage.

The ticker declared:

VOLUME AT NOON: 197,452,000
DJIA: 1627.51, UP 14.32

An exodus from the trading floor had begun. The brokers were coming upstairs to find Vornan! Our group dissolved in confusion. I was growing accustomed now to making quick exits; Aster Mikkelsen stood beside me, so I seized her by the hand and whispered hoarsely. "Come on, before the trouble starts! Vornan's done it again!"

"But he hasn't done anything!"

I tugged at her. A door appeared, and we slipped quickly through it. I looked back and saw Vornan following me, surrounded by his security guards. We passed down a long glittering corridor that coiled tubelike around the entire building. Behind us came shouts, muffled and inchoate. I saw a door marked NO ADMITTANCE and opened it. I was on another balcony, this one overlooking what could only have been the gut of the master computer. Snaky strands of data leaped convulsively from tank to tank. Girls in short smocks rushed back and forth, thrusting their hands into enigmatic openings. What looked like an intestine stretched across the ceiling. Aster laughed. I pulled her after me and we went out again, into the corridor. A robotruck came buzzing up toward us. We sidestepped it. What did the tape say now? FLOOR BROKERS RUN AMOK?

"Here," Aster said. "Another door!"

We found ourselves at the lip of a dropshaft and stepped blithely into it. Down, down, down . . .

. . . and out. Into the warm arcade of Wall Street. Sirens wailed behind us, I paused, gasping, taking my bearings, and saw that Vornan was still behind me, with Holliday and the media crew right in back of him.

"Into the cars!" Holliday ordered.

We made our escape successfully. Later in the day we learned that the Dow-Jones averages had suffered a decline of 8.51 points during our visit to the Exchange, and that two elderly brokers had perished from derangement of their cardiac pacemakers during the excitement. As we sped out of New York City that night, Vornan said idly to Heyman, "You must explain capitalism to me again some time. It seems quite thrilling, in its fashion."

Ten

We had a simpler time of things at the automated brothel in Chicago. Kralick was a little leery of letting Vornan visit the place, but Vornan requested it himself, and such a request could hardly be denied without risking explosive consequences. At any rate, since such places are legal and even fashionable, there was no reason for refusing, short of lingering puritanism.

Vornan was no puritan himself. That much was clear. He had lost little time commandeering the sexual services of Helen McIlwain, as Helen bragged to us on the third night of our stewardship. There was at least a fair chance that he had had Aster too, though of course neither he nor Aster was saying anything about it. Having demonstrated an insatiable curiosity for our sexual mores, Vornan could not be kept away from the computerized bordello; and, he slyly told Kralick, it would be part of his continuing education in the mysteries of the capitalistic system. Since Kralick had not been with us at the New York Stock Exchange, he failed to see the joke.

I was delegated to be Vornan's guide. Kralick seemed embarrassed to ask it of me. But it was unthinkable to let him go anywhere without a watchdog, and Kralick had come to know me well enough to realize that I had no objections to accompanying him to the place. Neither, for that matter, had Kolff, but he was too boisterous himself for such a task, and Fields and Heyman were unfit for it on grounds of excessive morality. Vornan and I set out together through the erotic maze early on a dark afternoon, hours after we had podded into Chicago from New York.

The building was at once sumptuous and chaste: an ebony tower on the Near North Side, at least thirty stories, windowless, the façade decorated with abstract inlays. There was no indication of the building's purpose on its door. With great misgivings I ushered Vornan through the climate field, wondering what kind of chaos he would contrive to create inside.

I had never been to one of these places myself. Permit me the mild boast of saying that it had never been necessary for me to purchase sexual companionship; there had always been an ample supply available to me for no other *quid pro quo* than my own services. I wholeheartedly approved of the enabling law that had permitted their establishment, though. Why should sex not be a commodity as easily purchased as food and drink? Is it not as essential to human well-being, or nearly so? And is there not considerable revenue to be captured by licensing a public utility of eroticism, carefully regulated and heavily taxed? In the long run it was the national revenue need that had triumphed over our traditional puritanism; I wonder if the brothels would ever have come into being but for the temporary exhaustion of other tax avenues.

I did not try to explain the subtleties of all this to Vornan-19. He seemed baffled enough by the mere concept of money, let alone the idea of exchanging money for sex, or of taxing such transactions for the benefit of society as a whole. As we entered, he said pleasantly, "Why do your citizens require such places?"

"To satisfy their sexual needs."

"And they give money for this satisfaction, Leo? Money which they have obtained by performing other services?"

"Yes."

"Why not perform the services directly in return for sexual satisfaction?"

I explained briefly the role of money as a medium of exchange, and its advantages over barter. Vornan smiled. He said, "It is an interesting system. I will discuss it at great length when I get home. But why must money be paid in exchange for sexual pleasure? That seems unfair. The girls one hires here get money, and they get sexual pleasure too, so they are being paid twice."

"They don't get sexual pleasure," I said. "Just money."

"But they engage in the sexual act. And so they receive a benefit from the men who come here."

"No, Vornan. They just let themselves be used. There's no transaction of pleasure. They make themselves available to anyone, you see, and somehow that cancels out any physical pleasure in what they do."

"But surely pleasure comes when one body is joined to another, regardless of motive!"

"That isn't so. Not among us. You have to understand—"

I stopped. His expression was one of disbelief. Worse, of shock. At that moment Vornan seemed more authentically a man of another time than ever before. He was genuinely jarred by this revelation of our sexual ethos; his façade of mild amusement dropped away, and I saw the real Vornan-19, stunned and repelled by our barbarity. Lost in confusion, I could not begin to extricate myself by tracing the evolution of our way of life. Instead I suggested blurredly that we begin our tour of the building.

Vornan agreed. We moved forward across a vast internal plaza of yielding purple tile. Before us stretched a shining blank wall broken only by reception cubicles. I had been briefed on what was expected of us. Vornan entered one cubicle; I took a seat in the cubicle to the left of his.

A small output screen lit up the moment I crossed the threshold. It said, *Please reply to all questions in a clear, loud voice*. A pause. *If you have read and understood this instruction, indicate your understanding with the word* yes.

"Yes," I said. Suddenly I wondered if Vornan were capable of comprehending written instructions. He spoke English fluently, but he did not necessarily have any knowledge of the written language. I thought of going to his aid; but the brothel computer was saying something to me, and I kept my eyes on the screen.

It was quizzing me about my sexual preferences.

Female?

"Yes."

Under thirty?

"Yes." After some thought.

Preferred color of hair?

I hesitated. "Red," I said, just for the sake of variety.

Preferred physical type: Choose one by pressing button beneath the screen.

The screen showed me three feminine contours: fashionably thin and boyish, middle-of-the-road girl-next-door curvaceousness, and hypermammiferous steroid-enhanced ultra-voluptuousness. My hand wandered across the buttons. It was a temptation to go for the fleshiest, but reminding myself that I was seeking variety, I opted for the boyish figure, which in outline reminded me of Aster Mikkelsen's.

Now the computer began to grill me about the sort of lovemaking I wished to enjoy. It informed me crisply that there were extra charges for specific enumerated deviant acts. It listed the additional fee for each, and I noted in a certain chilly fascination that sodomy was five times as expensive as fellatio, and that supervised sadism was considerably costlier than masochism. But I passed up the whips and boots, and also chose to do without the use of the nongenital orifices. Let other men take their pleasure in navel or ear, I thought. I am a conservative in such matters.

The next sequence to pass across the screen was choice of positions, since I had opted for regulation congress. Something like a scene out of the *Kama Sutra* came in view: twenty-odd male and female stick figures, coupling in extravagantly imaginative ways. I have seen the temples of Konarak and Khajurao, those monuments to bygone Hindu exuberance and fertility, covered over with virile men and full-breasted women, Krishna and Radha in all the combinations and permutations man and woman have ever devised. The cluttered screen had something of the same feverish intensity, although I admit the streamlined stick figures lacked the *volupté*, the three-dimensional fleshiness of those shining stone images under the Indian sun. I brooded over the extensive choice and selected one that struck my fancy.

Lastly came the most delicate matter of all: the computer wished to know my name and ID number.

Some say that that regulation was tacked on by vindictive legislative prudes, fighting a desperate rearguard battle to scuttle the entire program of legalized prostitution. The reasoning was that no one would use the place in the knowledge that his identity was being recorded on the master computer's memory film, perhaps to be spewed forth later as part of a potentially destructive dossier. The officials in charge of the enterprise, doing their best to cope with this troublesome requirement, announced vociferously that all data would remain forever confidential; yet I suppose there are some who fear to enter the house of automated assignations simply because they must register their presence. Well, what had I to fear? My academic tenure is interruptible only for reasons of moral turpitude, and there can be nothing turpid about making use of a government-operated facility such as this. I gave my name and identifying number. Briefly I wondered how Vornan, who lacked an identifying number, would make out; evidently the computer had been forewarned of his presence, though, for he was passed through to the next stage of our processing without difficulty.

A slot opened in the base of the computer output. It contained a privacy mask, I was told, which I was to slip over my head. I withdrew the mask, distended it, and pulled it into place. The thermoplastic compound fit itself to my features as though it were a second skin, and I wondered how anything so snug could be concealing; but I caught sight of myself in the momentarily blank face of the screen, and the reflection was not that of any face I would have recognized. Mysteriously, the mask had rendered me anonymous.

The screen now told me to step forward as the door opened. I obeyed. The front of my cubicle lifted; I passed through to a helical ramp leading to some upper level of the huge building. I caught sight of other men ascending on ramps to my left and right; like spirits going to salvation they rose, borne upward by silent glidewalks, their faces hidden, their bodies tensed. From above streamed the cool radiance of a gigantic light tank, bathing us all in brilliance. A figure waved to me from an adjoining ramp. Unmistakably it was Vornan; masked though he was, I detected him by the slimness of his figure, the jauntiness of his stance, and by a certain aura of strangeness that seemed to enfold him even with his features hidden. He soared past me and disappeared, swallowed up by the pearly radiance above. A moment later I was in that zone of radiance too, and swiftly and easily I passed through another portal that admitted me to a cubicle not much larger than the one in which the computer had interviewed me.

Another screen occupied the left-hand wall. To the far side was a washstand and a molecular cleanser; the center of the cubicle was occupied by a chaste double bed, freshly made. The entire environment was grotesquely antiseptic. If this is legalized prostitution, I thought, I prefer streetwalkers... if there are any. I stood beside the bed, eyeing the screen. I was alone in the room. Had the mighty machine faltered? Where was my paramour?

But they were not finished scrutinizing me. The screen

glowed and words streamed across it: *Please remove your clothing for medical examination.*

Obediently, I stripped and placed my garments in a hopper that debouched from the wall in response to some silent signal. The hopper closed again; I suspected that my clothes would be fumigated and purified while they were in there, and I was correct. I stood naked but for my mask, Everyman reduced to his final prop, as scanners and sensors played a subtle greenish light over my body, searching for the chancres of venereal disease, most likely. The examination lasted some sixty seconds. Then the screen invited me to extend my arm, and I did so, whereupon a needle descended and speedily removed a small sample of my blood. Unseen monitors searched that fragment of mortality for the tokens of corruption, and evidently found nothing that threatened the health of the personnel of this establishment, for in another moment the screen flashed some sort of light pattern that signified I had passed my tests. The wall near the washstand opened and a girl came through.

"Hello," she said. "I'm Esther, and I'm *so* glad to know you. I'm sure we're going to be great friends."

She was wearing a gauzy smock through which I could see the outlines of her slender body. Her hair was red, her eyes were green, her face bore the look of intelligence, and she smiled with a fervor that was not altogether mechanical, I thought. In my innocence I had imagined that all prostitutes were coarse, sagging creatures with gaping pores and sullen, embittered faces, but Esther did not fit my preconceived image. I had seen girls much like her on the campus at Irvine; it was quite possible that I had seen Esther herself there. I would not ask her that time-hoared question: What's a nice girl like you doing in a place like this? But I wondered. I wondered.

Esther eyed my body appraisingly, perhaps not so much to judge my masculinity as perhaps to hunt out any medical shortcomings that the sensor system might have overlooked. Yet she managed to transform her glance into something more than a merely clinical one; it was provocative as well. I felt curiously exposed, probably because I am not accustomed to meeting young ladies for the first time under such circumstances. After her quick survey Esther crossed the room and touched her hand to a control at the base of the screen. "We don't want them peeping at us, do we?" she asked brightly, and the screen darkened. I hazarded a private guess that this was part of the regular routine, by way of convincing the customer that the great staring eye of the computer would not spy on his amours; and I guessed also that despite the conspicuous gesture of turning off the screen, the room was still being monitored and would continue to be under surveillance while I was in it. Surely the designers of this place would not leave the girls wholly at the mercies of any customer with whom they might be sharing a cubicle. I felt queasy about going to bed with someone knowing that my performance was being observed and very likely taped and coded and filed, but I overcame my hesitation, telling myself that I was here purely on a lark. This bordello was clearly no place for an educated man. It invited too much suspicion. But no doubt it suited the needs of those who had such needs.

As the glow of the screen darkened, Esther said, "Shall I turn the room light off?"

"It doesn't matter to me."

"I'll turn it down, then." She did something to the knob and the room dimmed. In a quick lithe gesture she slipped off her smock. Her body was smooth and pale, with narrow hips and small, girlish breasts whose translucent skin revealed a network of fine blue veins. She reminded me very much of Aster Mikkelsen as Aster had looked at that spy pickup the week before. Aster . . . Esther . . . for one moment of dreamy confusion I confounded the two and wondered why a world-famous biochemist would be doubling as a tart. Smiling amiably, Esther stretched out on the bed, lying on her side with her knees drawn up; it was a friendly, conversational posture, nothing blatant about it. I was grateful for that. I had expected a girl in such a place to lie back, part her legs, and say, "Come on, buddy, get aboard," and I was relieved that Esther did no such thing. It occurred to me that in my interview below, the computer had sized up my personality, marked me as a member of the inhibited academic class, and had passed along to Esther, preparing herself for work, a memorandum to the effect that I was to be treated in a dignified manner.

I sat down alongside her.

"Would you like to talk awhile?" she asked. "We have plenty of time."

"All right. You know, I've never been here before."

"I do know."

"How?"

"The computer told me. The computer tells us everything."

"*Everything?* My name?"

"Oh, no, not your name! I mean, all the *personal* things."

I said, "So what do you know about me, Esther?"

"You'll see in a little while." Her eyes sparkled mischievously. Then she said, "Did you see the man from the future when you came in?"

"The one called Vornan-19?"

"Yes. He's supposed to be here today. Just about this time. We got a special notice over the master line. They say he's awfully handsome. I've seen him on the screen. I wish I'd get a chance to meet him."

"How do you know you aren't with him right now?"

She laughed. "Oh, no! I know I'm not!"

"But I'm masked. I could be—"

"You aren't. You're just teasing me. If I was getting him, they would have notified me."

"Maybe not. Maybe he prefers secrecy."

"Well, maybe so, but anyway I know you're not the man from the future. Mask or no mask, you aren't fooling me."

I let my hand roam along the smoothness of her thigh. "What do you think of him, Esther? Do you believe he's really from the year 2999?"

"Don't you think so?"

"I'm asking you what you think."

She shrugged. Taking my hand, she drew it slowly up over her taut belly until it was cupping the small cool mound of her left breast, as though she hoped to deflect my troublesome questions by leading me into the act of passion. Pouting a little, she said, "Well, they all say he's real. The President and everyone. And they say he's got special powers. That he can give you a kind of electric shock if he wants." Esther giggled suddenly. "I wonder if—if he can shock a girl while he's—you know, while he's with her."

"Quite likely. If he's really what he says he is."

"Why don't you believe in him?"

I said, "It all seems phony to me. That a man should drop out of the sky—literally—and claim to come from a thousand years in the future. Where's the proof? How am I supposed to know he's telling the truth?"

"Well," Esther said, "there's that look in his eyes. And his smile. There's something strange about him, everyone says.

He talks strange too, not with an accent, exactly, but yet his voice comes out peculiar. I believe in him, yes. I'd like to make love with him. I'd do it for free."

"Perhaps you'll have the chance," I said.

She grinned. But she was growing restless, as though this conversation exceeded the boundaries of the usual sort of small talk she was in the habit of making with dilatory clients. I pondered the impact that Vornan-19 had had even on this crib-girl, and I wondered what Vornan might be doing elsewhere in this building at this very moment. I hoped someone in Kralick's outfit was monitoring him. Ostensibly I was in here to keep an eye on him, but, as they must have known, there was no way for me to make contact with Vornan once we were past the lobby, and I feared an outbreak of our guest's by-now-familiar capacity for creating chaos. It was beyond my control, though. I slid my hands across Esther's accessible sleekness. She lay there, lost in dreams of embracing the man from the future, while her body undulated in the passionate rhythms she knew so well. The computer had prepared her adequately for her task; as our bodies joined, she slid into the position I had chosen, and she discharged her duties with energy and a reasonable counterfeit of desire.

Afterward we rolled apart. She looked satisfactorily satisfied; part of the act, I assumed. She indicated the washstand and snapped on the molecular cleanser so that I could be purified of the stains of lust. We still had time left, and she said, "Just for the record: wouldn't *you* like to meet Vornan-19? Just to convince yourself that he's the real thing?"

I debated. Then I said gravely, "Why, yes, I think I would. But I suppose I never shall."

"It's exciting to think that he's right here in this building, isn't it? Why, he might be right next door! He might be coming here next . . . if he wants another round." She crossed the room to me and slipped her arms about me. Large, glossy eyes fastened on my own. "I shouldn't be talking about him so much. I don't know how I started. We aren't supposed to mention other men when—when—listen, did I make you happy?"

"Very much, Esther. I wish I could show—"

"Tipping isn't allowed," she said hastily as I fumbled for my credit plate. "But on the way out the computer may ask you for a report on me. They pick one out of ten customers for a sampling. I hope you'll have a good word for me."

"You know I will."

She leaned up and kissed me lightly, passionlessly, on the lips. "I like you," she said. "Honestly. That isn't just a standard line. If you ever come back here, I hope you'll ask for me."

"If I ever do, I certainly will," I said, meaning it. "That's a solemn promise."

She helped me dress. Then she vanished through her door, disappearing into the depths of the building to perform some rite of purification before taking on her next assignment. The screen came to life again, notifying me that my credit account would be billed at the standard rate, and requesting me to leave by the rear door of my cubicle. I stepped out onto the glidewalk and found myself drawn through a region of misty perfumed loveliness, a vaulted gallery whose high ceiling was festooned with strips of shimmertape; so magical was this realm that I scarcely noticed anything until I discovered that I was descending once more, gliding into a vestibule as large as the one through which I had entered, but at the opposite side of the building.

Vornan? Where was Vornan?

I emerged into the feeble light of a winter afternoon, feeling faintly foolish. The visit had been educational and recreational for me, but it had hardly served the purpose of keeping watch over our unpredictable charge. I paused on the wide plaza, wondering if I should go back inside and search out Vornan. Was it possible to ask the computer for information on a customer? While I hesitated, a voice from behind said, "Leo?"

It was Kralick, sitting in a gray-green limousine from whose hood projected the blunt snouts of a communications rig's antennae. I walked toward the car.

"Vornan's still inside," I said. "I don't know what—"

"It's all right. Get in."

I slipped through the door that the Government man held open for me. To my discomfort I found Aster Mikkelsen in the rear of the car, her head bent low over some sort of data sheets. She smiled briefly at me and went back to what she was analyzing. It troubled me to step directly from the brothel into the company of the pure Aster.

Kralick said, "I've got a full pickup running on our friend. It might interest you to know that he's on his fourth woman now, and shows no sign of running out of pep. Would you like to look?"

"No, thanks." I told him as he started to activate the screen. "That's not my kick. Is he making any trouble in there?"

"Not in his usual fashion. He's just using up a lot of girls. Going down the roster, trying out positions, capering like a goat." Muscles clenched suddenly in Kralick's cheeks. He swung about to face me and said, "Leo, you've been with this guy for nearly two weeks, now. What's your opinion? Real or fake?"

"I honestly don't know, Sandy. There are times when I'm convinced that he's absolutely authentic. Then I stop and pinch myself and say that nobody can come back in time, that it's a scientific impossibility, and that in any case Vornan's just a charlatan."

"A scientist," said Kralick heavily, "ought to begin with the evidence and construct a hypothesis around it, leading to a conclusion, right? Not start with a hypothesis and judge the evidence in terms of it."

"True," I conceded. "But what do you regard as evidence? I have experimental knowledge of time-reversal phenomena, and I know that you can't send a particle of matter back half a second without reversing its charge. I have to judge Vornan against that."

"All right. And the man of A.D. 999 also knew that it was impossible to fly to Mars. We can't venture to say what's possible a thousand years on and what isn't. And it happens that we've acquired some new evidence today."

"Which is?"

Kralick said, "Vornan consented to undergo the standard medical examination in there. The computer got a blood sample from him and a lot of other stuff, and relayed it all to us out here, and Aster's been going over it. She says he's got blood of a type she's never seen before, and that it's full of weird antibodies unknown to modern science—and that there are fifty other physical anomalies in Vornan's medical check-out. The computer also picked up traces of unusual electrical activity in his nervous system, the gimmick that he uses to shock people he doesn't like. He's built like an electric eel. I don't think he comes from this century at all, Leo. And I can't tell you how much it costs me to say a thing like that."

From the back seat Aster said in her lovely flutelike voice,

"It seems strange that we should be doing fundamental research by sending him into a whorehouse, doesn't it, Leo? But these findings are very odd. Would you like to see the tapes?"

"I wouldn't be able to interpret them, thanks."

Kralick swiveled around. "Vornan's finished with Number Four. He's requesting a fifth."

"Can you do me a favor? There's a girl in there named Esther, a slim pretty little redhead. I'd like you to arrange things with your friend the computer, Sandy. See to it that Esther is his next sweetheart."

Kralick arranged it. Vornan had requested a tall, curvy brunette for his next romance, but the computer slipped Esther in on him instead, and he accepted the substitution, I suppose, as a forgivable defect in our medieval computer technology. I asked to watch the video pickup, and Kralick switched it on. There was Esther, wide-eyed, timid, her professional poise ragged as she found herself in the presence of the man of her dreams. Vornan spoke to her elegantly, soothing her, calming her. She removed her smock and they moved toward the bed, and I had Kralick cut off the video.

Vornan was with her a long while. His insatiable virility seemed to underline his alien origin. I sat brooding, looking into nowhere, trying to let myself accept the data Kralick had collected today. My mind refused to make the jump. I could not believe, even now, that Vornan-19 was genuine, despite the chill I had felt in Vornan's presence and all the rest.

"He's had enough," Kralick said finally. "He's coming out. Aster, clean up all the equipment, fast."

While Aster concealed the monitoring pickups, Kralick sprinted from the car, got Vornan, and led him swiftly across the plaza. In the brutal winter weather there were no disciples about to throw themselves before him, nor any rampaging Apocalyptists, so for once we were able to make a clean, quick exit.

Vornan was beaming. "Your sexual customs are fascinating," he said, as we drove away. "Fascinating! So wonderfully primitive! So full of vigor and mystery!" He clapped his hands in delight. I felt the odd chill again creeping through my limbs, and it had nothing to do with the weather outside the car. I hope Esther is happy now, I thought. She'll have something to tell her grandchildren. It was the least I could have done for her.

Eleven

We dined that evening at a very special restaurant in Chicago, a place whose distinction is that it serves meats almost impossible to obtain elsewhere: buffalo steak, filet of bear, moose, elk, such birds as pheasant, partridge, grouse. Vornan had heard about it somehow and wanted to sample its mysterious delights. It was the first time we had gone to a public restaurant with him, a point that troubled us; already an ominous tendency was developing for uncontrollable crowds to gather about him everywhere, and we feared what might happen in a restaurant. Kralick had asked the restaurant management to serve its specialties at our hotel, and the restaurant was willing—for a price. But Vornan would have none of that. He wished to dine out, and dine out we did.

Our escort of Government people took precautions. They were learning fast how to cope with Vornan's unpredictable ways. It turned out that the restaurant had both a side entrance and a private dining room upstairs, so we were able to sweep our guest into the place and past the regular diners without problems. Vornan seemed displeased to find himself in an isolated room, but we pretended that in our society it was the acme of luxury to eat away from the vulgar throng, and Vornan took the story for what it was worth.

Some of us did not know the nature of the restaurant. Heyman thumbed the menu cube, peered at it for a long moment, and delivered a thick Teutonic hiss. He was sizzling in wrath over the bill of fare. "Buffalo!" he cried. "Moose! These are rare animals! We are to eat valuable scientific specimens? Mr. Kralick, I protest! This is an outrage!"

Kralick had suffered much on this jaunt, and Heyman's testiness had been nearly as much of a bother to him as Vornan's flamboyance. He said, "I beg your pardon, Professor Heyman. Everything on the menu is approved by the Department of the Interior. You know, even the herds of rare animals need to be thinned occasionally, for the good of the species. And—"

"They could be sent to other conservation preserves," Heyman rumbled, "not slaughtered for their meat! My God, what will history say of us? We who live in the last century when wild animals are found on the earth, killing and eating the priceless few survivors of a time when—"

"You want the verdict of history?" Kolff asked. "There sits history, Heyman! Ask its opinion!" He waved a beefy hand at Vornan-19, in whose authenticity he was not a believer, and guffawed until the table shook.

Serenely Vornan said, "I find it quite delightful that you should be eating these animals. I await my chance to share in the pleasure of doing so."

"But it isn't right!" Heyman spluttered. "These creatures—do any of them exist in your time? Or are they all gone—all eaten?"

"I am not certain. The names are unfamiliar. This buffalo, for example: What is it?"

"A large bovine mammal covered with shaggy brown fur," said Aster Mikkelsen. "Related to the cow. Formerly found in herds of many thousands on the western prairies."

"Extinct," said Vornan. "We have some cows, but no relatives of cows. And moose?"

"A large-horned animal of the northern forests. That's a moose head mounted on the wall, the one with the huge antlers and the long, drooping snout," said Aster.

"Absolutely extinct. Bear? Grouse? Partridge?"

Aster described each. Vornan replied gleefully that no such animals were known to exist in his era. Heyman's face turned a mottled purple. I had not known he harbored conservationist leanings. He delivered a choppy sermon on the extinction of wildlife as a symbol of a decadent civilization, pointing out that it is not barbarians who eliminate species but rather the fastidious and cultured, who seek the amusements of the hunt and of the table, or who thrust the outposts of civilization into the nesting grounds of strange and obscure creatures. He spoke with passion and even some wisdom; it was the first time I had heard the obstreperous historian say anything of the faintest value to an intelligent person. Vornan watched him with keen interest as he spoke. Gradually a look of pleasure spread across our visitor's face, and I thought I knew why: Heyman was arguing that extinction of species comes with the spread of civilization, and Vornan, who privately regarded us as little more than savages, doubtless thought that line of reasoning extremely funny.

When Heyman finished, we were eyeing one another and our menu cubes in shamefaced fashion, but Vornan broke the spell. "Surely," he said, "you will not deny me the pleasure of cooperating in the great extinction that makes my own time so barren of wildlife? After all, the animals we are about to eat tonight are already dead, are they not? Let me take back to my era the sensation of having dined on buffalo and grouse and moose, please."

Of course there was no question of dining somewhere else that night. We would eat here feeling guilty or we would eat here without guilt. As Kralick had observed, the restaurant used only licensed meat obtained through Government channels, and so was not directly causing the disappearance of any endangered species. The meat it served came from rare animals, and the prices showed it, but it was idle to blame a place like this for the hardships of twentieth-century wildlife. Still, Heyman had a point: the animals *were* going. I had seen somewhere a prediction that in another century there would be no wild animals at all except those in protected preserves. If we could credit Vornan as a genuine ambassador from posterity, that prediction had come to pass.

We ordered. Heyman chose roast chicken; the rest of us dipped into the rarities. Vornan requested and succeeded in getting a kind of smorgasbord of house specialties: a miniature filet of buffalo, a strip of moose steak, breast of pheasant, and one or two of the other unusual items.

Kolff said, "What animals *do* you have in your—ah—epoch?"

"Dogs. Cats. Cows. Mice." Vornan hesitated. "And several others."

"Nothing but domestic creatures?" asked Heyman, aghast.

"No," said Vornan, and propelled a juicy slab of meat to his mouth. He smiled pleasantly. "Delicious! What a loss we have suffered!"

"You see?" Heyman cried. "If only people had—"

"Of course," said Vornan sweetly, "we have many interesting foods of our own. I must admit there's a pleasure in putting a bit of meat from a living creature into one's mouth, but it's a pleasure that only the very few might enjoy. Most of us are rather fastidious. It takes a strong stomach to be a time traveler."

"Because we are filthy, depraved, hideous barbarians?" Heyman asked loudly, "Is that your opinion of us?"

Not at all discomfited, Vornan replied, "Your way of life is quite different from my own. Obviously. Why else would I have taken the trouble to come here?"

"Yet one way of life is not inherently superior or inferior to the other," Helen McIlwain put in, looking up fiercely from a huge slab of what I recall as elk steak. "Life may be more comfortable in one era than in another, it may be healthier, it may be more tranquil, but we may not use the terms of *superior* or *inferior*. From the viewpoint of cultural relativism—"

"Do you know," said Vornan, "that in my time such a thing as a restaurant is unknown? To eat food in public, among strangers—we find it inelegant. In the Centrality, you know, one comes in contact with strangers quite often. This is not true in the outlying regions. One is never hostile to a stranger, but one would not eat in his presence, unless one is planning to establish sexual intimacy. Customarily we reserve eating for intimate companions alone." He chuckled. "It's quite wicked of me to want to visit a restaurant. I regard you all as intimate companions, you must realize—" His hand swept the whole table, as though he would be willing to go to bed even with Lloyd Kolff if Kolff were available. "But I hope that you will grant me the pleasure of dining in public one of these days. Perhaps you were trying to spare my sensibilities by arranging for us to eat in this private room. But I ask you to let me indulge my shamelessness a bit the next time."

"Wonderful," Helen McIlwain said, mainly to herself. "A taboo on public eating! Vornan, if you'd only give us more insight into your own era. We're so eager to know anything you tell us!"

"Yes," Heyman said. "This period known as the Time of Sweeping, for instance—"

"—some information on biological research in—"

"—problems of mental therapy. The major psychoses, for example, are of great concern to—"

"—a chance to confer with you on linguistic evolution in—"

"—time-reversal phenomena. And also some information on the energy systems that—" It was my own voice, weaving through the thickened texture of our table talk. Naturally Vornan replied to none of us, since we were all babbling at once. When we realized what we were doing, we fell into embarrassed silence, awkwardly letting bits of words tumble over the brink of our discomfort to shatter in the abyss of self-consciousness. For an instant, there, our frustrations had broken through. In our days and nights of merry-go-round with Vornan-19, he had been infuriatingly elliptical about his own alleged era, dropping a hint here, a clue there, never delivering anything approaching a formal discourse on the shape of that future society from which he claimed to be an emissary. Each of us overflowed with unanswered questions.

They were not answered that night. That night we dined on the delicacies of a waning era, breast of phoenix and *entrecôte* of unicorn, and listened closely as Vornan, more conversationally inclined than usual, dropped occasional nuggets about the feeding habits of the thirtieth century. We were grateful for what we could learn. Even Heyman grew so involved in the situation that he ceased to bewail the fate of the rarities that had graced our plates.

When the time came to leave the restaurant, we found ourselves in an unhappily familiar kind of crisis. Word had circulated that the celebrated man from the future was here, and a crowd had gathered. Kralick had to order guards armed with neural whips to clear a path through the restaurant, and for a while it looked as though the whips might have to be used. At least a hundred diners left their tables and shuffled toward us as we came down from the private room. They were eager to see, to touch, to experience Vornan-19 at close range. I eyed their faces in dismay and alarm. Some had the scowls of skeptics, some the glassy remoteness of the idle curiosity-seeker; but on many was that eerie look of reverence that we had seen so often in the past week. It was more than mere awe. It was an acknowledgment of an inner messianic hunger. These people wanted to drop on their knees before Vornan. They knew nothing of him but what they had seen on their screens, and yet they were drawn to him and looked toward him to fill some void in their own lives. What was he offering? Charm, good looks, a magnetic smile, an attractive voice? Yes, and alienness, for in word and deed he was stamped with strangeness. I could almost feel that pull myself. I had been too close to Vornan to worship him; I had seen his colossal esurience, his imperial self-indulgence, his gargantuan appetite for sensual pleasure of all sorts, and once one has seen a messiah coveting food and impaling legions of willing women, it is hard to feel truly reverent toward him. Nevertheless, I sensed his power. It had begun to transform my own evaluation of him. I had started as a skeptic, hostile and almost belligerent about it; that mood had softened, until I had virtually ceased to add the inevitable qualifier, *"if* he is genuine," to everything I thought about Vornan-19. It was not merely the evidence of the blood sample that swayed me, but every aspect of Vornan's conduct. I found it now harder to believe he might be a fraud than that he had actually come to us out of time, and this of course left me in an untenable position vis-à-vis my own scientific specialty. I was forced to embrace a conclusion that I still regarded as physically impossible: doublethink in the Orwellian sense. That I could be trapped like this was a tribute to Vornan's power; and I believed I understood something of what these people desired as they pressed close, straining to lay hands on the visitor as he passed before them.

Somehow we got out of the restaurant without any unpleasant incident. The weather was so frigid that there were only a few stragglers in the street. We sped past them and into the waiting cars. Blank-faced chauffeurs convoyed us to our hotel. Here, as in New York, we had a string of connected rooms in the most secluded part of the building. Vornan excused himself at once when we came to our floor. He had been sleeping with Helen McIlwain for the past few nights, but it seemed that our trip to the brothel had left him temporarily without interest in women, not too surprisingly. He disappeared into his room. The guards sealed it at once. Kralick, looking drained and pale, went off to file his nightly report to Washington. The rest of us assembled in one of the suites to unwind a bit before going to bed.

The committee of six had been together long enough now for a variety of patterns to manifest themselves. We were still divided on the question of Vornan's authenticity, but not as sharply as before. Kolff, an original skeptic, was still positive of Vornan's phoniness, though he admired Vornan's technique as a confidence man. Heyman, who had also come out against Vornan at the outset, was not so sure now; it clearly went against his nature to say so, but he was wavering in Vornan's direction, mainly on the basis of a few tantalizing hints Vornan had dropped on the course of future history. Helen McIlwain continued to accept Vornan as authentic. Morton Fields, on the other hand, was growing disgruntled and backing away from his original positive appraisal. I think he was jealous of Vornan's sexual prowess and was trying to get revenge by disavowing his legitimacy.

The original neutral, Aster, had chosen to wait until more evidence was in. Evidence had come in. Aster now was wholly of the opinion that Vornan came from further along the human evolutionary track, and she had biochemical proof that satisfied her of that. As I have noted, I too had been swayed toward Vornan, though purely on emotional grounds;

scientifically he remained an impossibility for me. Thus we
now had two True Believers, two vacillating ex-skeptics inclined to take Vornan's story at face value, one former believer moving to the opposite pole, and one remaining diehard
apostate. Certainly the movement had been to Vornan's benefit. He was winning us.

So far as the emotional crosscurrents within our group
went, they were strong and violent. We agreed on just one
thing: that we were all heartily sick of F. Richard Heyman.
The very sight of the historian's coarse reddish beard had
become odious to me. We were weary of his pontificating, his
dogmatism, and his habit of treating the rest of us as not-too-
bright undergraduates. Morton Fields, too, was outlasting his
welcome in our midst. Behind his ascetic façade he had
revealed himself as a mere lecher, which I did not really
mind, and as a conspicuously unsuccessful one, which I found
objectionable. He had lusted after Helen and had been
turned away; he had lusted after Aster and had failed utterly.
Since Helen practiced a kind of professional nymphomania,
operating under the assumption that a lady anthropologist
had a duty to study *all* of mankind at the closest possible
range, her rejection of Fields was the most cutting kind of
rebuff. Before our tour was a week old, Helen had bedded
down with all of us at least once, except for Sandy Kralick,
who was too much in awe of her to think of her in sexual
terms, and for poor Fields. Small wonder that his soul was
souring. I suppose Helen had some private scholarly disagreement with him, dating back prior to the Vornan assignment, that motivated her unsubtle psychological castration of
him. Fields' next move had been toward Aster; but Aster was
as unworldly as an angel, and blithely fended him off without
seeming even to comprehend what he wanted from her.
(Even though Aster had taken that shower with Vornan, none
of us could believe that anything carnal had taken place
between them. Aster's crystalline innocence seemed proof
even against Vornan's irresistible masculine charm, we felt.)
Thus Fields had the sexual problems of a pimply adolescent, and as you might imagine, those problems erupted in
many ways during ordinary social discussions. He expressed
his frustrations by erecting opaque façades of terminology
behind which he glowered and raged and spat. This drew the
disapproval of Lloyd Kolff, who in his Falstaffian heartiness
could see Fields only as something to be deplored; when

Fields got annoying enough, Kolff tended to slap him down with a jovial growl that only made matters worse. With Kolff I had no quarrel; he swilled his way pleasantly from night to night and made a cheerfully ursine companion on what might otherwise have been a more dreary assignment. I was grateful, too, for Helen McIlwain's company, and not only in bed. Monomaniac though she might be on the subject of cultural relativism, she was lively, well-informed, and enormously entertaining; she could always be depended on to puncture some immense procedural debate with a few choice words on the amputation of the clitoris among North African tribeswomen or on ceremonial scarification in New Guinea puberty rites. As for Aster the unfathomable, Aster the impenetrable, Aster the inscrutable, I could not honestly say that I liked her, but I found her an agreeable quasi-feminine enigma. It troubled me that I had seen her bareness via that spy pickup; enigmas should remain total enigmas, and now that I had looked upon Aster bare, I felt that her mystery had in part been breached. She seemed deliciously chaste, a Diana of biochemistry, magically sustained at the age of sixteen forever. In our frequent debates over ways and means of dealing with Vornan, Aster seldom spoke, but what she did have to say was invariably reasonable and just.

Our traveling circus moved along, forging westward from Chicago as January ebbed. Vornan was as indefatigable a sightseer as he was a lover. We took him to factories, power plants, museums, highway interchanges, weather-control stations, transportation monitor posts, fancy restaurants, and a good deal more, some of it at official request, some of it at Vornan's insistence. He managed to stir up a good deal of trouble for us nearly everywhere. Perhaps by way of establishing that he was beyond "medieval" morality, he abused the hospitality of his hosts in a variety of delicately outrageous ways: seducing victims of all available sexes, flagrantly insulting sacred cows, and indicating unmistakably that he regarded the gadgety, formidably scientific world in which we lived as quaintly primitive. I found his thumb-to-nose insolence cheerfully refreshing; he fascinated as well as repelled. But others, both in and out of our group, did not think so. Nevertheless, the very outrageousness of his behavior seemed to guarantee the authenticity of his claim, and there were surprisingly few protests at his antics. He was immune, the guest of the world, the wanderer out of time; and the world, though baffled and uncertain, received him cordially.

We did our best to head off calamities. We learned how to shield Vornan from pompous, easily vulnerable individuals who would surely call forth some mischief from him. We had seen him stare in playful awe at the immense bosom of a matronly patron of the arts who was guiding us through the splendid museum in Cleveland; he regarded the deep valley between the two upthrust white peaks with such keen concentration that we should have anticipated trouble, but we failed to intervene when Vornan abruptly reached out a finger, gaily plunged it into that cosmic cleavage, and produced the mildest of his puzzling repertoire of electric shocks. After that we kept busty middle-aged women in low-cut dresses away from him. We learned to shunt him away from other such targets for the puncturing of vanity, and if we had one success for each dozen failures, that was sufficient.

Where we did not do so well was in extracting information from him about the epoch from which he said he came or about anything that had taken place between then and now. He let us have a morsel occasionally, such as his vague reference to an undescribed political upheaval that he referred to as the Time of Sweeping. He mentioned visitors from other stars, and talked a bit about the political structure of the ambiguous national entity he called the Centrality, but in essence he told us nothing. There was no substance to his words; he gave us only sketchy outlines.

Each of us had ample opportunity to question him. He submitted in obvious boredom to our interrogations, but slid away from any real grilling. I spoke to him for several hours one afternoon in St. Louis, trying to pump him on the subjects of most immediate interest to me. I drew blanks.

"Won't you tell me a little about how you reached our time, Vornan? The actual transport mechanism?"

"You want to know about my time machine?"

"Yes. Yes. Your time machine."

"It's not really a machine, Leo. That is, you mustn't think of it as having levers and dials and such."

"Will you describe it for me?"

He shrugged. "That isn't easy. It's—well, more of an abstraction than anything else. I didn't see much of it. You step into a room, and a field begins to operate, and—" His voice trailed off. "I'm sorry. I'm not a scientist. I just saw the room, really."

"Others operated the machine?"

"Yes, yes, of course. I was only the passenger."

"And the force that moves you through time—"

"Honestly, love, I can't imagine what it's like."

"Neither can I, Vornan. That's the whole trouble. Everything I know about physics shrieks out that you can't send a living man back through time."

"But I'm here, Leo. I'm the proof."

"Assuming that you ever traveled through time."

He looked crestfallen. His hand caught mine; his fingers were cool and oddly smooth. "Leo," he said, wounded, "are you expressing suspicion?"

"I'm simply trying to find out how your time machine works."

"I'd tell you if I knew. Believe me, Leo. I have nothing but the warmest feelings for you personally, and for all the earnest, struggling, sincere individuals I've found here in your time. But I just don't know. Look, if you got into your car and drove back into the year 800, and someone asked you to explain how that car works, would you be able to do it?"

"I'd be able to explain some fundamental principles. I couldn't build an automobile myself, Vornan, but I know what makes it move. You aren't even telling me that."

"It's infinitely more complex."

"Perhaps I could *see* the machine."

"Oh, no," said Vornan lightly. "It's a thousand years up the line. It tossed me here, and it will bring me back when I choose to leave, but the machine itself, which I tell you is not exactly a machine, stays up there."

"How," I asked, "will you give the signal to be taken back?"

He pretended not to have heard. Instead he began questioning me about my university responsibilities; his trick was standard, to meet an awkward question with his own line of interrogation. I could not wring a drop of information from him. I left the session with my basic skepticism reborn. He could not tell me about the mechanics of travel in time because he had not traveled in time. Q.E.D.: phony. He was just as evasive on the subject of energy conversion. He would not tell me when it had come into use, how it worked, who was credited with its invention.

The others, though, occasionally had better luck with

Vornan. Most notably Lloyd Kolff, who, probably because he had voiced doubts of Vornan's genuineness to Vornan himself, was treated to a remarkable disquisition. Kolff had not troubled much to interrogate Vornan in the early weeks of our tour, possibly because he regarded Vornan as a synthetic artifact, possibly because he was too lazy to bother. The old philologist had revealed an awesomely broad streak of indolence; he was quite clearly coasting on professional laurels earned twenty or thirty years before, and now preferred to spend his time wenching and feasting and accepting the sincere homage of younger men in his discipline. I had discovered that old Lloyd had not published a meaningful paper since 1980. It began to seem as if he regarded our current assignment as a mere joyride, a relaxing way to pass a winter that might otherwise have to be endured in the grayness of Morningside Heights. But in Denver one snowbound February night Kolff finally decided to tackle Vornan from the linguistic angle. I don't know why.

They were closeted a long time. Through the thin walls of the hotel we could hear Kolff's booming voice chanting rhythmically in a language none of us understood: reciting Sanskrit erotic verse for Vornan, maybe. Then he translated, and we could catch an occasional salacious word, even a wanton line or two about the pleasures of love. We lost interest after a while; we had heard Kolff's recitals before. When I bothered to eavesdrop again, I caught Vornan's light laughter cutting like a silver scalpel through Kolff's earthy boomings, and then I dimly detected Vornan speaking in an unknown tongue. Matters seemed serious in there. Kolff halted him, asked a question, recited something of his own, and Vornan spoke again. At that point Kralick came into our room to give us copies of the morning's itinerary—we were taking Vornan to a gold mine, no less—and we ceased to pay attention to Kolff's interrogation.

An hour later Kolff came into the room where the rest of us sat. He looked flushed and shaken. He tugged heavily at a meaty earlobe, clutched the rolls of flesh on the back of his neck, cracked his knuckles with a sound like that of ricocheting bullets. "Damn," he muttered. "By everlasting eternal damn!" Striding across the room, he stood for a while at the window, peering out at snowcapped skyscrapers, and then he said, "Is there what to drink?"

"Rum, Bourbon, Scotch," Helen said. "Help yourself."

Kolff barreled over to the table where the half-empty bottles stood, picked up the Bourbon, and poured himself a slug that would paralyze a hippo. He downed it straight, in three or four greedy gulps, and let the glass drop to the spongy floor. He stood with feet firmly planted, worrying his earlobe. I heard him cursing in what might have been Middle English.

At length Aster said, "Did you learn anything from him?"

"Yah. Very much." Kolff sank into an armchair and switched the vibrator on. "I learned from him that he is no phony!"

Heyman gasped. Helen looked astonished, and I had never seen her poise shaken before. Fields blurted, "What the hell do you mean, Lloyd?"

"He talked to me . . . in his own language," Kolff said thickly. "For half an hour. I have taped it all. I'll give it to the computer tomorrow for analysis. But I can tell it was not faked. Only a genius of linguistics could have invented a language like that, and he would not have done it so well." Kolff smacked his forehead. "My God! My God! A man out of time! How can it be?"

"You understood him?" Heyman asked.

"Give me more to drink," said Kolff. He accepted the Bourbon bottle from Aster and put it to his lips. He scratched his hairy belly. He passed his hand before his eyes as though trying to sweep away cobwebs. Eventually he said, "No, I did not understand him. I detected only patterns. He speaks the child of English . . . but it is an English as far from our time as the language of the Anglo-Saxon Chronicle. It is full of Asian roots. Bits of Mandarin, bits of Bengali, bits of Japanese. There is Arabic in it, I am sure. And Malay. It is a chop suey of language." Kolff belched. "You know, our English, it is already a big stew. It has Danish, Norman French, Saxon, a mess of things, two streams, a Latin and a Teutonic. So we have duplicate words, we have *preface* and *foreword*, we have *perceive* and *know*, *power* and *might*. Both streams, though, they flow from the same source, the old Indo-European *mutter*-tongue. Already in Vornan's time they have changed that. They have taken in words from other ancestral groups. Stirred everything all around. Such a language! You can say anything in a language like that. Anything! But the roots only are there. The words are polished like pebbles in a stream, all roughness smoothed away, the inflections gone. He makes ten sounds and he conveys twenty sentences. The grammar—it would take me fifty years more to *find* the grammar. And five hundred to understand it. The withering away of grammar—a bouillabaisse of sounds, a pot-au-feu of language—incredible, incredible! There has been another vowel shift, far more radical than the last one. He speaks...like poetry. Dream poetry no one can understand. I caught bits, only pieces..." Kolff fell silent. He massaged the huge bowl of his belly. I had never seen him serious before. It was a profoundly moving moment.

Fields shattered it. "Lloyd, how can you be sure you aren't imagining all this? A language you can't understand, how can you interpret it? If you can't detect a grammar, how do you know it isn't just gibberish he was drooling?"

"You are a fool," Kolff replied easily. "You should take your head and have the poison pumped out of it. But then your skull would collapse."

Fields sputtered. Heyman stood up and walked back and forth in quick penguinlike strides; he seemed to be going through a new internal crisis. I felt great uneasiness myself. If Kolff had been converted, what hope remained that Vornan might not be what he claimed to be? The evidence was mounting. Perhaps all this was a boozy figment of Kolff's decaying brain. Perhaps Aster had misread the data of Vornan's medical examination. Perhaps. Perhaps. God help me, I did not *want* to believe Vornan was real, for where would that leave my own scientific accomplishments, and it pained me to know that I was violating that fuzzy abstraction, the code of science, by setting up an *a priori* structure for my own emotional convenience. Like it or not, that structure was toppling. Maybe. How long, I wondered, would I try to prop it up? When would I accept, as Aster had accepted, as Kolff had now accepted? When Vornan made a trip in time before my eyes?

Helen said sweetly, "Why don't you play us the tape, Lloyd?"

"Yes. Yes. The tape." He produced a small recording cube, and fumbling a bit, managed to press it into the pickup slot of a playback unit. He thumbed for sonic and suddenly there flowed through the room a stream of soft, eroded sounds. I strained to hear. Vornan spoke liltingly, playfully, artfully, varying pitch and timbre, so that his speech was close to song, and now and then a tantalizing fragment of a comprehensible word seemed to whirl past my ears. But I understood nothing. Kolff made steeples of his thick fingers, nodded and smiled, waved his shoe at some particularly critical moment, murmured now and then, "Yes? You see? You *see*?" but I saw not, neither did I hear; it was pure sound, now pearly, now azure, now deep turquoise, all of it mysterious, none of it intelligible. The cube whirled to its finish, and when it was over we sat silently, as if the melody of Vornan's words still lingered, and I knew that nothing had been proven, not to me, though Lloyd might choose to accept these sounds as the child of English. Solemnly Kolff rose and pocketed the cube. He turned to Helen McIlwain, whose features were transfigured as though she had attended some incredibly sacred rite. "Come," he said, and touched her bony wrist. "It is the time for sleeping, and not a night for sleeping alone. Come." They went out together. I still heard Vornan's voice, gravely declaiming some lengthy passage in a language centuries unborn, or possibly rattling off a skein of nonsense, and I felt lulled to dreaminess by the sound of the future or the sound of ingenious fraud.

Twelve

Our caravan moved westward from snowy Denver to a sunny welcome in California, but I did not remain with the others. A great restlessness had come over me, an impatience to get away from Vornan and Heyman and Kolff and the rest at least for a little while. I had been on this tour for over a month, now, and it was telling on me. So I asked Kralick for permission to take a brief leave of absence; he granted it and I headed south into Arizona, to the desert home of Jack and Shirley Bryant, with the understanding that I would rejoin the group a week later in Los Angeles.

It had been early January when I had last seen Jack and Shirley; now it was mid-February, so hardly any time had really passed. Yet inwardly a great deal of time must have elapsed, for them and for me. I saw changes in them. Jack looked drawn and frayed, as though he had been sleeping poorly lately; his motions were nervous and jerky, and I was

reminded of the old Jack, the pallid eastern boy who had
come to my laboratory so many years ago. He had retrogressed.
The calm of the desert had fled from him. Shirley too seemed
to be under some kind of strain. The sheen of her golden hair
was dulled, and her postures now were rigid ones; I saw
trusses of taut muscles form again and again in her throat.
Her response to tension was an overcompensating gaiety. She
laughed too often and too loudly; her voice rose unnaturally
in pitch, becoming shrill, harsh, and vibrant. She seemed
much older; if she had looked twenty-five in December
instead of her proper thirty-odd, now she seemed at the
brink of her forties. All this I noticed in the first few minutes
of my arrival, when such alterations are the most conspicuous. But I said nothing of what I saw, and just as well, for the
first words were Jack's:

"You look tired, Leo. This business must have taken a lot
out of you."

And Shirley:

"Yes, poor Leo. All that silly traveling around. You need a
good rest. Can't you contrive to stay here longer than a
week?"

"Am I that much of a wreck?" I asked. "Is it so obvious?"

"A little Arizona sunshine will work wonders," Shirley said,
and laughed in that dreadful new way of hers.

That first day we did little but soak up Arizona sunshine.
We lay, the three of us, on their sundeck, and after these
weeks of soggy eastern winter it was pure delight to feel the
warmth on my bare skin. Tactful as always, neither of them
brought up the subject of my recent activities that day; we
sunned and dozed, chatted a little, and in the evening feasted
on grilled steak and a fine bottle of Chambertin '88. As the
chill of night swept down on the desert, we sprawled on the
thick rug to listen to Mozart's dancing melodies, and all that I
had done and seen in the last weeks sloughed away and
became unreal to me.

In the morning I woke early, for my inner clock was
confused by the crossing of time zones, and walked for a
while in the desert. Jack was up when I returned. He sat at
the edge of the dry wash, carving something from a bit of
gnarled, greasy-looking wood. As I drew near, he blurted,
"Leo, did you find out anything about—"

"No."

"—energy conversion."

I shook my head. "I've tried, Jack. But there's no way to learn anything from Vornan that he doesn't want to tell you. And he won't give hard data on anything. He's devilish about answering questions."

"I'm in knots, Leo. The possibility that something I've devised will wreck society—"

"Drop it, will you? You've penetrated a frontier, Jack. Publish your work and accept your Nobel, and to hell with any misuse that posterity hands out. You've done pure research. Why crucify yourself over possible applications?"

"The men who developed the bomb must have said the same things," Jack murmured.

"Have any bombs been dropping lately? Meanwhile your house runs on a pocket reactor. You might be lighting wood fires if those old boys hadn't found out about nuclear fission."

"But their souls—their *souls*—"

I lost patience. "We revere their damned souls! They were scientists; they did their best, and they got somewhere. And changed the world, sure, but they had to. There was a war then, you know? Civilization was endangered. They invented something that caused a lot of trouble, yeah, but it did a lot of good, too. You haven't even invented anything. Equations. Basic principles. And here you sit pitying yourself because you think you've betrayed mankind! All you've done has been to use your *brain*, Jack, and if that's a betrayal of mankind in your philosophy, then you'd better—"

"All right, Leo," he said quietly. "I plead guilty to a charge of self-pity and voluntarily solicited martyrdom. Sentence me to death and then let's change the subject. What's your considered opinion of this man Vornan? Real? Fake? You've seen him at close range."

"I don't know."

"Good old Leo," he said savagely. "Always incisive! Always ready with the firm answer!"

"It isn't that simple, Jack. Have you been watching Vornan on the screens?"

"Yes."

"Then you know he's complex. A tricky bastard, the trickiest I've ever seen."

"But don't you have some intuitive feel, Leo, some immediate response, a yes or a no, true or false?"

"I have," I said.

"Keeping it a secret?"

I moistened my lips and scuffed at the sandy ground. "What I intuit is that Vornan-19 is what he says he is."

"A man from 2999?"

"A traveler out of the future," I said.

Behind me, Shirley laughed in a sharp crescendo. "That's wonderful, Leo! You've finally learned how to embrace the irrational!"

She had come up behind us, nude, a goddess of the morning, heart-stoppingly beautiful, her hair like a flag in the breeze. But her eyes were too brilliant, shining with that new fixed glitter.

"The irrational is a thorny mistress," I said. "I'm not happy to share my bed with her."

"Why do you think he's real?" Jack pressed.

I told him about the blood sample and about Lloyd Kolff's experience with Vornan's spoken language. I added some purely intuitive impressions I had gathered. Shirley seemed delighted, Jack pensive. He said finally, "You don't know a thing about the scientific background of his supposed means of time transport?"

"Zero. He isn't saying."

"Small wonder. He wouldn't want 2999 invaded by a bunch of hairy barbarians who've whipped up a time machine out of his description."

"Maybe that's it—a security matter," I said.

Jack closed his eyes. He rocked back and forth on his haunches. "If he's real, then the energy thing is real, and the possibility still exists that—"

"Cut it, Jack," I said fiercely. "Snap out!"

With an effort he interrupted his lamentations. Shirley tugged him to his feet. I said, "What's for breakfast?"

"What about brook trout, straight out of the freeze?"

"Good enough." I slapped her amiably on her firm rump to send her scampering into the house. Jack and I strolled after her. He was calmer now.

"I'd like to sit down myself and talk with this Vornan," Jack said. "Ten minutes, maybe. Could you arrange that?"

"I doubt it. Very few private interviews are being granted. The Government's keeping him on a tight rein—or trying to. And I'm afraid if you aren't a bishop or a holding-company president or a famous poet, you won't stand a chance. But it doesn't matter, Jack. He won't tell you what you want to know. I'm sure of it."

"Still, I'd like to try to get it out of him. Keep it in mind."

I promised that I would, but I saw little chance of it. We managed to get into less problematical topics at breakfast, Afterward, Jack disappeared to finish something he was writing, and Shirley and I went to the sundeck. She was worried about Jack, she said; he was so totally obsessed with what the future might think of him. She did not know how to get him unwound. "It's nothing new, you understand. It's been going on ever since I've known him, since he was with you at the University. But since Vornan showed up, it's become fifty times as bad. He genuinely thinks now that his manuscript is going to reshuffle all of future history. He said last week that he wished the Apocalyptists were right: He wants the world to be blown up next January. He's sick, Leo."

"I see. But it's a sickness that he won't try to cure."

In a low voice, leaning close to me so that I could have put my lips to hers, she said, "Were you holding anything back from him? Tell me the truth. What did Vornan say about energy?"

"Nothing. I swear."

"And do you really believe he's—"

"Most of the time. I'm not convinced. You know, I've got scientific reservations."

"Aside from them?"

"I believe," I said.

We were silent. I let my eyes roam down the ridge of her spine to the blossoming of her hips. Beads of perspiration glittered on her upturned tawny buttocks. Her toes were outstretched and pressed close in a little gesture of tension.

She said, "Jack wants to meet Vornan."

"I know."

"So do I. Let me confess it, Leo. I'm hungry for him."

"Most women are."

"I've never been unfaithful to Jack. But I would be, with Vornan. I'd tell Jack first, of course. But I'm drawn to him. Just seeing him on television, I want to touch him, to have him against me, in me. Am I shocking you, Leo?"

"Don't be silly."

"The comforting thing is that I know I'll never get the chance. There must be a million women ahead of me in line. Have you noticed, Leo, the hysteria that's building up over this man? It's almost a cult. It's killing off Apocalyptism practically overnight. Last fall everyone thought the world was about to end, and now everyone thinks we're going to fill up with tourists from the future. I watch the faces of the people on the screens, the ones who follow Vornan around, cheering, kneeling. He's like a messiah. Does any of this sound sensible to you?"

"All of it does. I'm not blind, Shirley. I've seen it up close."

"It frightens me."

"Me also."

"And when you say you think he's real—you, hard-headed old Leo Garfield—that's even more scary." Shirley gave me the shrill giggle again. "Living out here on the edge of nowhere, I sometimes think the whole world's crazy except Jack and me."

"And lately you've had your doubts about Jack."

"Well, yes." Her hand covered mine. "Why should people be responding to Vornan like this?"

"Because there's never been anyone like him before."

"He's not the first charismatic figure to come along."

"He's the first one peddling this particular tale," I said. "And the first in the era of modern communications. The whole world can see him in three dimensions and natural color all the time. He gets to them. His eyes—his smile—the man's got a power, Shirley. You feel it through the screen. I feel it close up."

"What will happen, eventually?"

"Eventually he'll go back to 2999," I said lightly, "and write a best-seller about his primitive ancestors."

Shirley laughed hollowly and we let the conversation trickle to nothingness. Her words troubled me. Not that I was surprised to find she was drawn to Vornan, for she was far from alone in that; what upset me was her willingness to admit it to me. I resented becoming the confidant of her passions. A woman admits her illicit desires to a harem eunuch, perhaps, or to another woman, but not to a man whom she realizes has suppressed designs of his own on her. Surely she knew that but for my respect for their marriage, I would have reached out for her long ago and would have been received willingly. So why tell me such things, knowing that they must hurt me? Did she think I would use my supposed influence to lure Vornan into her bed? That out of love for her I would play the panderer?

We lazed away the day. Toward late afternoon Jack came to me and said, "Maybe you aren't interested, but Vornan's on the screen. He's being interviewed in San Diego by a panel of theologians and philosophers and stuff. Do you want to watch?"

Not really, I thought. I had come here to escape from Vornan, and somehow no moment passed without mention of him. But I failed to answer, and Shirley said yes. Jack activated the screen nearest us, and there was Vornan, big as life, radiating charm in three dimensions. The camera gave us a view of the panel: five distinguished experts in eschatology, some of whom I recognized. I spied the long nose and drooping brows of Milton Clayhorn, one of the pundits of our San Diego campus, the man who, they say, has been devoting his career to getting Christ out of Christianity. I saw the blunt features and time-freckled skin of Dr. Naomi Gersten, behind whose hooded eyes lurked six thousand years of Semitic anguish. The other three seemed familiar; I suspected they had been neatly chosen to represent each creed. We had come in late in the discussion, but as it turned out, just in time for the detonation of Vornan's megaton bomb.

"—no organized religious movement in your era whatever?" Clayhorn was saying. "A withering away of the church, so to speak?"

Vornan nodded curtly.

"But the religious idea itself," Clayhorn vociferated. "That can't be gone! There are certain eternal verities! Man must establish a relationship delineating the boundaries of the universe and the boundaries of his own soul. He—"

"Perhaps," Dr. Gersten said to Vornan in her small cracked voice, "you could tell us if you understand at all what we mean by religion, eh?"

"Certainly. A statement of human dependence on a more powerful external force," said Vornan, looking pleased with himself.

A furry-voiced moderator said, "I think that's an excellent formulation, don't you, Monsignor?"

I recognized now the long-chinned man in the turned-about collar: Meehan, a television priest, a figure of fair charisma himself, who spent a moment summoning resonance and said, "Yes, that's excellently put, in its fashion. It's refreshing to know that our guest comprehends the concept of religion, even if"—the Monsignor showed a momentary crack in his façade—"as he says, our present-day religions have ceased to play a meaningful role in the life of his times. I venture to say that perhaps Mr. Vornan is underestimating the strength of religion in his day, and possibly is, as so many individuals do today, projecting his personal lack of belief onto society as a whole. Might I have a comment on that?"

Vornan smiled. Something ominous sparkled in his eyes. I felt the clutch of fear. Using the eyes and the lips at once! He was cranking up the catapult for a blow that would smash the enemy walls. The panel members saw it too. Clayhorn cringed. Dr. Gersten seemed to vanish like a wary tortoise into the folds of her own neck. The famed Monsignor braced himself as if for the blade of the guillotine.

Vornan said mildly, "Shall I tell you what we have learned of man's relationship to the universe? We have discovered, you see, the manner by which life came into being on the earth, and our knowledge of the Creation has had its effect on our religious beliefs. I am not an archaeologist, please understand, and I can give no details beyond what I say here. But this is what we now know: Once, in the distant past, our planet was wholly lifeless. There was a sea covering nearly everything, with rocks here and there, and both sea and land were lacking even in the merest microbe. Then our planet was visited by explorers from another star. They did not land. They merely orbited our world and saw that it was without life, and thus of no interest to them. They paused only long enough to jettison certain garbage that had accumulated aboard their ship, and then journeyed elsewhere, while the garbage they had dumped descended through the atmosphere of the earth and found its way into the sea, introducing certain factors that created a chemical disturbance which set in motion the beginning of the process that resulted in the phenomenon known as"—the panel was in turmoil; the camera swung in mercilessly to reveal the grimaces, the scowls, the wild eyes, the stony jaws, the gaping lips—"life on earth."

Thirteen

At the end of my week of reprieve I kissed Shirley good-bye, told Jack to go easy on himself, and sped off to Tucson to be podded to Los Angeles. I arrived there only hours after the rest of the team had come up the coast from San Diego. The impact of that interview with Vornan still reverberated through the land. Perhaps never before in human history had a major theological dogma been enunciated over television on a global hookup; certainly this one spread through the world even as the contamination of the primordial garbage had infected the sterile seas. Quietly, amiably, with great delicacy and restraint, Vornan had undermined the religious faith of four billion human beings. One had to admire his skill, surely.

Jack and Shirley and I had watched the unfolding of the reaction in cool fascination. Vornan had presented his belief as received fact, the result of careful investigation and of corroborative detail obtained from beings who had visited the world of his time. As usual, he offered no substructure of data, merely the bald, elliptical statement. But anyone who had swallowed the news that a man had come to us from 2999 would not have much difficulty swallowing that man's story of the Creation; all it took was flexible jaws. WORLD STARTED FROM GARBAGE, said the tapes the next day, and swiftly the concept moved into the public domain.

The Apocalyptists, who had been quiescent for a few weeks, came back to life. They led vigorous protest rallies through the cities of the world. The screen showed us their fixed faces, their gleaming eyes, their defiant banners. I learned something I had not suspected previously about this mushroom cult: it was a patchwork of disparate components, made up of the alienated, the rootless, the youthfully rebellious, and—amazingly—the devout. In the midst of the orgies of the Apocalyptists, among all the scatological rites and exhibitionist fervor, were the shabby, slab-jawed Fundamentalists, the quintessence of American Gothic, deeply persuaded that the world would indeed shortly come to its finish. We saw these people now for the first time dominant in the Apocalyptist riots. They did not commit bestialities themselves, but they paraded among the fornicators, benevolently accepting the shamelessness as a sign of the approaching end. To these people Vornan was Antichrist and his creation-from-garbage dogma was thunderous blasphemy.

To others it was The Word. The inchoate band of Vornan-worshipers that had been taking form in every city now had not only a prophet but a creed. We are trash and the descendants of trash, and we must put aside all mystical self-exaltation and accept reality, these people said. There is no God, and Vornan is His prophet! When I came to Los Angeles I found both these conflicting groups in full panoply, and Vornan under heavy guard. Only with great difficulty did I manage to get back to our group. They had to fly me in by helicopter, putting me down on the roof of a hotel in downtown Los Angeles, while far below me the Apocalyptists capered and the worshipers of Vornan sought to abase themselves before their idol. Kralick led me to the edge of the roof and had me look down at the swirling, writhing mass in the streets.

"How long has this been going on?" I asked.

"Since nine this morning. We arrived at eleven. We could call in troops, but for the moment we'll just sit tight. The mob stretches from here to Pasadena, they say."

"That's impossible! We—"

"Look out there."

It was true. A ribbon of brightness wound through the streets, coiling past the sparkling towers of the city's reconstructed nucleus, weaving toward the distant stack of freeways and vanishing somewhere to the east. I could hear cries, shouts, gurgles. I did not want to look any longer. It was a siege.

Vornan was greatly amused at the forces he had unleashed. I found him holding court in the customary suite on the hotel's eighty-fifth floor; about him were Kolff, Heyman, Helen, and Aster, a few media people, and a great deal of equipment. Fields was not there. I learned later that he was sulking, having made another pass at Aster the night before in San Diego. Vornan was speaking about California weather, I think, when I came in. He rose at once and glided to me, seizing my elbows and locking his eyes to mine.

"Leo, old man! How we've missed you!"

I was taken off stride by his chummy approach. But I managed to say, "I've been following your progress by screen, Vornan."

"You heard the San Diego interview?" Helen asked.

I nodded. Vornan seemed very pleased with himself. He waved vaguely toward the window and said, "There's a big mob out there. What do you think they want?"

"They're waiting for your next revelation," I told him.

"The gospel according to St. Vornan," Heyman muttered darkly.

From Kolff, later, I got confusing news. He had run

Vornan's speech samples through the departmental computer at Columbia, with uncertain results. The computer was baffled by the structure of the language, and had sorted everything out into phonemes without coming to conclusions. Its analysis indicated the possibility that Kolff was right in thinking of the words as an evolved language, and also the possibility that Vornan had simply been mouthing noises at random, occasionally hitting on some combination of sounds that seemed to represent a futuristic version of a contemporary word. Kolff looked despondent. In his first flush of enthusiasm he had released his evaluation of Vornan's talk to the media, and that had helped to fan the global hysteria; but now he was not at all sure that he had made the correct interpretation. "If I am wrong," he said, "I have destroyed myself, Leo. I have lent all my prestige to nonsense, and if that is so, I have no more prestige." He was shaking. He seemed to have lost twenty pounds in the few days since I had last seen him; pockets of loose skin dangled on his face.

"Why not run a recheck?" I asked. "Get Vornan to repeat what he taped for you before. Then feed both tapes to the computer and check the correlation function. If he was improvising gibberish the last time, he won't be able to duplicate it."

"My friend, that was my first thought."

"And?"

"He will not speak to me in his language again. He has lost interest in my researches. He refuses to utter a syllable."

"That sounds suspicious to me."

"Yes," said Kolff sadly. "Of course it is suspicious. I tell him that by doing this simple thing, he can destroy forever all doubts about his origin, and he says no. I tell him that by refusing, he is inviting us to regard him as an impostor, and he says he does not care. Is he bluffing? Is he a liar? Or does he genuinely not care? Leo, I am destroyed."

"You heard a linguistic pattern, didn't you, Lloyd?"

"Certainly I did. But it may have been only an illusion—a coincidental striking of sound values." He shook his head like a wounded walrus, muttered something in Persian or Pushtu, and went shuffling away, bowed, sagging. And I realized that Vornan had diabolically canceled out one of the major arguments for accepting him as genuine. Deliberately. Wantonly. He was toying with us . . . with all of us.

Dinner was served to us at the hotel that night. There was

no question of our going outside, not with thousands of people in the streets about us. One of the networks screened a documentary on Vornan's progress through the land, and we watched it. Vornan watched with us, although in the past he had not shown much interest in what the media had to say about him. In a way I wished he had not seen it. The documentary concentrated on the impact he had had on mass emotions, and showed things I had not suspected: Adolescent girls in Illinois writhing in drug-induced ecstasy before a tridim photo of our visitor. Africans lighting immense ceremonial bonfires in whose greasy blue smoke the image of Vornan was said to take form. A woman in Indiana who had collected tapes of every telecast dealing with the man from the future, and who was selling replicas of them mounted in special reliquaries. We saw a massive westward movement under way; hordes of curiosity-seekers were spilling across the continent, hoping to catch up with Vornan as he moved about. The camera's eye descended into the swirling mobs we had been seeing so often, showing us the fixed faces of fanatics. These people wanted revelation from Vornan; they wanted prophecies; they wanted divine guidance. Excitement flickered like heat-lightning wherever he went. If Kolff ever let that cube of Vornan's speech get into public circulation, it would provoke a new manifestation of glossolalia, I realized—a wild outburst of speaking in tongues as holy babbling became the way to salvation once more. I was frightened. In the slower moments of the documentary I stole glances at Vornan and saw him nodding in satisfaction, eminently pleased with the stir he was causing. He seemed to revel in the power that publicity and curiosity had placed in his hands. Anything he might choose to say would be received with high interest, discussed and discussed again, and swiftly would harden into an article of faith accepted by millions. It has been given only to a very few men in history to have such power, and none of Vornan's charismatic predecessors had had his access to communications channels.

It terrified me. Up to now he had seemed wholly unconcerned by the world's response to him, as aloof as he had been the day he strolled naked up the Spanish Stairs while a Roman policeman shouted at him to halt. Now, though, a feedback was appearing. He watched his own documentaries. Was he enjoying the confusion he engendered? Was he consciously planning new upheavals? Vornan acting in lighthearted innocence created chaos enough; Vornan motivated by deliberate malice could smash civilization. I had been scornful of him at first, and then amused by him. Now I was afraid of him.

Our gathering broke up early. I saw Fields speaking urgently to Aster; she shook her head, shrugged, and walked away from him, leaving him scowling. Vornan went up to him and touched him lightly on the shoulder. I have no idea what Vornan said to him, but Fields' expression was even darker afterward. He went out, trying to slam a slamproof door. Kolff and Helen left together. I lingered awhile for no particular reason. My room was next to Aster's, and we walked down the hall together. We stood awhile talking in front of her door. I had the odd impression that she was going to invite me in to spend the night; she seemed more animated than usual, eyelashes fluttering, delicate nostrils flaring. "Do you know how much longer we'll be on this tour?" she asked me. I told her that I didn't know. She was thinking of getting back to her laboratory, she said, but then she confessed wryly, "I'd leave right now except that I'm getting interested in this despite myself. Interested in Vornan. Leo, do you notice that he's changing?"

"How?"

"Becoming more aware of what's happening around him. He was so divorced from it at first, so alien. Do you remember the time he asked me to take a shower with him?"

"I can't forget it."

"If it had been another man, I would have refused, of course. But Vornan was so blunt about it—the way a child would be. I knew he meant no harm. But now—now he seems to want to *use* people. He isn't just sightseeing any more. He's manipulating everyone. Very subtly."

I told her that I had thought all these thoughts too, during the television program a little earlier. Her eyes glowed; points of rosiness sprouted in her cheeks. She moistened her lips, and I waited for her to tell me that she and I had much in common and ought to know one another better; but all she said was, "I'm afraid, Leo. I wish he'd go back where he came from. He's going to make real trouble."

"Kralick and Company will prevent that."

"I wonder." She flashed a nervous smile. "Well, good night, Leo. Sleep well."

She was gone. I stared for a long moment at her closed

door, and the stolen image of her slim body drifted up out of my memory bank. Aster had not had much physical appeal for me up till now; she hardly seemed a woman at all. Suddenly I understood what Morton Fields saw in her. I desired her fiercely. Was this, too, some of Vornan's mischief? I smiled. I was blaming him for everything now. My hand rested on the plate of Aster's door, and I debated asking her to admit me, but I entered my own room instead. I sealed the door, undressed, prepared myself for sleep. Sleep did not come. I went to the window to stare at the mobs, but the mobs had dissipated. It was past midnight. A slice of moon dangled over the sprawling city. I drew out a blank notepad and began to sketch some theorems that had drifted into my mind during dinner: a way of accounting for a double reversal of charge during time travel. Problem: assuming that time-reversal is possible, create a mathematical justification for conversion from matter to anti-matter to matter again before the completion of a journey. I worked quickly and for a while even convincingly. I came to the verge of picking up the phone and getting a data hookup with my computer so I could run some verifying mockups of the system. Then I saw the flaw near the beginning of my work, the stupid algebraic error, the failure to keep my signs straight. I crumpled the sheets and threw them away in disgust.

I heard a tapping at my door. A voice: "Leo? Leo, are you awake?"

I nudged the scanner beside my bed and got a dim image of my visitor. Vornan! Instantly I sprang up and unsealed the door. He was dressed in a thin green tunic as though to go out. His presence astonished me, for I knew that Kralick sealed him in his room each night, and at least in theory there was no way for Vornan to break that seal, which was supposed to protect him but which also imprisoned him. Yet he was here.

"Come in," I said. "Is anything wrong?"

"Not at all. Were you sleeping?"

"Working. Trying to calculate how your blasted time machine works, in fact."

He laughed lightly. "Poor Leo. You'll wear out your brain with all that thinking."

"If you really felt sorry for me, you'd give me a hint or two about it."

"I would if I could," he said. "But it's impossible. I'll explain why downstairs."

"Downstairs?"

"Yes. We're going out for a little walk. You'll accompany me, won't you, Leo?"

I gaped. "There's a riot going on outside. We'll be killed by the hysterical mob!"

"I think the mob has gone away," said Vornan. "Besides, I have *these*." He extended his hand. In his palm lay two limp plastic masks of the sort we had worn at the Chicago brothel. "No one will recognize us. We'll stroll the streets of this wonderful city in disguise. I want to go out, Leo. I'm tired of official promenades. I feel like exploring again."

I wondered what to do. Call Kralick and have Vornan locked into his room again? That was the sensible response. Masks or not, it was rash to leave the hotel without a guard. But it would be a betrayal to turn Vornan in like that. Obviously he trusted me more than any of the others; perhaps there was even something he wished to tell me in confidence, beyond the range of Kralick's spy-pickups. I would have to take the risks in the hope of winning from him some nugget of valuable information.

"All right. I'll go with you."

"Quickly, then. If someone monitors your room—"

"What about *your* room?"

He laughed smugly. "My room has been adjusted. Those who pry will think I am still in it. But if I am seen in here as well—get dressed, Leo."

I threw on some clothing and we left the room. I sealed it from the outside. In the hall lay three of Kralick's men, sound asleep; the green globe of an anesthetic balloon drifted in the air, and as its temperature-sensitive scanning plate picked up my thermals it homed in on me. Vornan lazily reached up for it, caught its trailing strand of plastic tape, and tugged it down to turn it off. He grinned conspiratorially at me. Then, like a boy running away from home, he darted across the hall, motioning to me to follow him. At a nudge a service door in the corridor opened, revealing a tumbletube for linens. Vornan beckoned me to enter.

"We'll land in the laundry room!" I protested.

"Don't be foolish, Leo. We'll get off before the last stop."

Mine not to reason why. I entered the tumbletube with him and down we caromed, flushed like debris to the depths

of the building. A catchnet erupted across the tube unexpectedly
and we bounced into it. I thought it was some kind of trap,
but Vornan said simply, "It's a safety device to keep hotel
employees from falling into the linen conveyor. I've been
talking to the chambermaids, you see. Come on!" He stepped
out of the net, which I suppose had been activated by
mass-detectors along the sides of the tube, and we perched
on a ledge of the chute while he opened a door. For a man
who scarcely understood what a stock exchange was, he had a
remarkably complete knowledge of the inner workings of this
hotel. The catchnet withdrew into the tube wall the moment
I was out of it; an instant later some soiled linens zoomed past
us from above and vanished into the maw of the laundry pit
somewhere far below. Vornan beckoned again. We went
scrambling down a narrow passageway lit from above by strips
of cold light, and emerged finally in one of the hallways of the
hotel. By a prosaic staircase we took ourselves to a sublobby
and out unnoticed into the street.

All was quiet. We could see where the rioters had been.
Stenciled slogans gleamed up from the sidewalk and glistened
on the sides of buildings: THE END IS NEAR, PREPARE TO MEET
YOUR MAKER, stuff like that, the classic billboard ruminations.
Bits of clothing were scattered everywhere. Mounds of foam
told me that the riot had not been dispersed without effort.
Here and there a few sleepers lay, stunned or drunk or
simply resting; they must have crept out of the shadows after
the police had cleared the area.

We donned our masks and moved silently through the
mildness of the Los Angeles night. Here in the early hours of
morning little was taking place in the downtown district; the
towers all about us were hotels and office buildings, and the
nightlife went elsewhere. We strolled at random. Occasionally an advert balloon dawdled through the sky a few hundred
feet above us, flashing its gaudy incitements. Two blocks from
our hotel we paused to examine the window of a shop selling
spy devices. Vornan seemed wholly absorbed. The shop was
closed, of course, and yet as we lingered on a sensor plate
embedded in the pavement a mellifluous voice told us the
store hours and invited us to return in daytime. Two doors
down we came to a sportsman's shop specializing in fishing
equipment. Our presence tripped another sidewalk trigger
that yielded a sales talk aimed at deep-sea fishermen. "You've
come to the right place," a mechanical voice proclaimed. "We

carry a full line. Hydrophotometers, plankton samplers, mud penetrometers, light-scattering meters, tide recorders, hydrostatic actuators, radar buoys, clinometers, sludge detectors, liquid-level indicators—"

We moved on.

Vornan said, "I love your cities. The buildings are so tall—the merchants are so aggressive. We have no merchants, Leo."

"What do you do if you need a sludge detector or a plankton sampler?"

"They are available," he said simply. "I rarely need such things."

"Why have you told us so little about your time, Vornan?"

"Because I have come here to learn, not to teach."

"But you're not rushed for time. You could reciprocate. We're morbidly curious about the shape of things to come. And you've said so little. I have only the vaguest picture of your world."

"Tell me how it seems to you."

"Fewer people than we have today," I said. "Very sleek, very orderly. Gadgets kept in the background, yet anything at all available when needed. No wars. No nations. A simple, pleasant, happy world. It's hard for me to believe in it."

"You've described it well."

"But how did it come to get that way, Vornan? That's what we want to know! Look at the world you've been visiting. A hundred suspicious nations. Superbombs. Tension. Hunger and frustration. Millions of hysterical people hunting for a receptacle for their faith. What happened? How did the world settle down?"

"A thousand years is a long time, Leo. Much can happen."

"What *did* happen, though? Where did the present nations go? Tell me about the crises, the wars, the upheavals."

We halted under a lamppost. Instantly its photosensors detected us and stepped up the output of light. Vornan said, "Suppose you tell me, Leo, about the organization, rise, and decline of the Holy Roman Empire."

"Where'd you hear about the Holy Roman Empire?"

"From Professor Heyman. Tell me what you know about the Empire, Leo."

"Why—next to nothing, I guess. It was some kind of European confederation seven or eight hundred years ago. And—and—"

"Exactly. You know nothing about it at all."

"I'm not claiming to be a practicing historian, Vornan."

"Neither am I," he said quietly. "Why do you think I should know anything more about the Time of Sweeping than you do about the Holy Roman Empire? It's ancient history to me. I never studied it. I had no interest in learning about it."

"But if you were planning to come back on a time trip, Vornan, you should have made it your business to study history the way you studied English."

"I needed English in order to communicate. I had no need of history. I am not here as a scholar, Leo. Only as a tourist."

"And you know nothing of the science of your era either, I suppose?"

"Nothing at all," he said cheerfully.

"What *do* you know? What do you do in 2999?"

"Nothing. Nothing."

"You have no profession?"

"I travel. I observe. I please myself."

"A member of the idle rich?"

"Yes, except we have no idle rich. I guess you'd call me idle, Leo. Idle and ignorant."

"And is everyone in 2999 idle and ignorant? Are work and scholarship and effort obsolete?"

"Oh, no, no, no," Vornan said. "We have many diligent souls. My somatic brother Lunn-31 is a collector of light impulses, a ranking authority. My good friend Mortel-91 is a connoisseur of gestures. Pol-13, whose beauty you would appreciate, dances in the psychodrome. We have our artists, our poets, our learned ones. The celebrated Ekki-89 has labored fifty years on his revivification of the Years of Flame. Sator-11 has assembled a complete set of crystal images of the Seekers, all of his own making. I am proud of them."

"And you, Vornan?"

"I am nothing. I do nothing. I am quite an ordinary man, Leo." There was a note in his voice I had not heard before, a throb that I took for sincerity. "I came here out of boredom, out of the lust for diversion. Others are possessed by their commitment to the endeavors of the spirit. I am an empty vessel, Leo. I can tell you no science, no history. My perceptions of beauty are rudimentary. I am ignorant. I am idle. I search the worlds for my pleasures, but they are shallow pleasures." Through the mask came the filtered gleam of his wondrous smile. "I am being quite honest with you, Leo. I hope this explains my failure to answer the questions of you and your friends. I am quite unsatisfactory, a man of many shortcomings. Does my honesty distress you?"

It did more than that. It appalled me. Unless Vornan's sudden burst of humility was merely a ploy, he was labeling himself a dilettante, a wastrel, an idler—a nobody out of time, diverting himself among the sweaty primitives because his own epoch had momentarily ceased to amuse him. His evasiveness, the voids in his knowledge, all seemed comprehensible now. But it was hardly flattering to know that this was our time traveler, that we had merited nothing better than Vornan. And I found it ominous that a self-proclaimed shallow floater had the power over our world that Vornan had effortlessly gained. Where would his quest for amusement lead him? And what, if any, restraints would he care to impose on himself?

I said as we walked on, "Why have no other visitors from your era come to us?"

Vornan chuckled. "What makes you think I am the first?"

"We've never—no one has—there hasn't been—" I paused, dithering, once more the victim of Vornan's gift for opening trapdoors in the fabric of the universe.

"I am no pioneer," he said gently. "There have been many here before me."

"Keeping their identity secret?"

"Of course. It pleased me to reveal myself. More serious-minded individuals go about things surreptitiously. They do their work in silence and depart."

"How many have there been?"

"I scarcely could guess."

"Visiting all eras?"

"Why not?"

"Living among us under assumed identities?"

"Yes, yes, of course," Vornan said lightly. "Often holding public office, I believe. Poor Leo! Did you think that I was blazing a trail, a miserable fool like me?"

I swayed, more sickened by this than anything. Our world honeycombed by strangers out of time? Our nations perhaps guided by these wanderers? A hundred, a thousand, fifty thousand travelers popping in and out of history? No. No. No. No. My mind rebelled at that. Vornan was playing with me now. There could be no alternative. I told him I did not believe him. He laughed. He said, "I give you my permission not to believe me. Do you hear that sound?"

I heard a sound, yes. It was a sound like that of a waterfall, coming from the direction of Pershing Square. There are no waterfalls in Pershing Square. Vornan sprinted forward. I hurried after him, my heart pounding, my skull throbbing. I could not keep up. He halted after a block and a half to wait for me. He pointed ahead. "Quite a number of them," he said, "I find this very exciting!"

The dispersed mob had regrouped, milling about Pershing Square and now beginning to overflow. A phalanx of capering humanity rolled toward us, filling the street from edge to edge. I could not tell for a moment which mob it was, the Apocalyptists or those who sought Vornan to worship him, but then I saw the crazily painted faces, the baleful banners, the zigging metal coils held high overhead as symbols of heavenly fire, and I knew that these were the prophets of doom bearing down on us.

I said, "We've got to get out of here. Back to the hotel!"

"I want to see this."

"We'll be trampled, Vornan!"

"Not if we're careful. Stay with me, Leo. Let the tide sweep over us."

I shook my head. The vanguard of the Apocalyptist mob was only a block from us. Wielding flares and sirens, the rioters were streaming in a wild rush toward us, screams and shrieks puncturing the air. Merely as bystanders, we might suffer at the hands of the mob; if we were recognized through our masks, we were dead. I caught Vornan's wrist and tugged in anguish, trying to drag him down a side street that led to the hotel. For the first time I felt his electrical powers. A low-voltage jolt made my hand leap back. I clamped it to him again, and this time he transmitted a burst of stunning energy that sent me reeling away, muscles twitching in a dislocated dance. I dropped to my knees and crouched half dazed while Vornan gaily raced toward the Apocalyptists, his arms spread wide.

The bosom of the mob enfolded him. I saw him slip between two of the front runners and vanish into the core of the surging, shouting mass. He was gone. I struggled dizzily to my feet, knowing that I had to find him, and took three or four uncertain steps forward. An instant later the Apocalyptists were upon me.

I managed to stay on my feet long enough to throw off the effects of the shock Vornan had given me. About me moved the cultists, faces thick with red and green paint; the acrid tang of sweat was in the air, and mysteriously, I spied one

Apocalyptist to whose chest was strapped the hissing little globe of an ion-dispersal deodorant; this was strange territory for the fastidious. I was whirled around. A girl with bare jiggling breasts, whose nipples glowed with luminescence, hugged me. "The end is coming!" she shrilled. "Live while you can!" She clawed at my hands and pressed them to her breasts. I clutched warm flesh for a moment, before the current of the mob whirled her away from me; when I looked down at my palms I saw the luminescent imprints gleaming in them, like watchful eyes. Musical instruments of indeterminate ancestry honked and blared. Three high-stepping boys, arms locked, paraded before me, kicking at anyone who came close. A towering man in a goat's mask exposed his maleness jubilantly, and a heavy-thighed woman rushed toward him, offered herself, and clung tight. An arm snaked around my shoulders. I whirled and saw a gaunt, bony, grinning figure leaning toward me; a girl, I thought, from her costume and the long snarled silken hair, but then "her" blouse fell open and I saw the flat shining hairless chest with the two small dark circlets.

"Have a drink," the boy said, and thrust a squeeze-flask at me. I could not refuse. The snout of the flask went between my lips and I tasted something bitter and thin. Turning away, I spat it out, but the flavor remained like a stain on my tongue.

We were marching fifteen or twenty abreast in several directions at once, though the prevailing movement was back toward the hotel. I fought my way against the tide, hunting for Vornan. Hands clutched at me again and again. I stumbled over a couple locked in lust on the sidewalk; they were inviting destruction and did not seem to mind. It was like a carnival, but there were no floats, and the costumes were wildly individualistic.

"Vornan!" I bellowed. And the mob took it up, magnifying the cry. "Vornan . . . Vornan . . . Vornan . . . kill Vornan . . . doom . . . flame . . . doom . . . Vornan . . ." It was the dance of death. A figure loomed before me, face marked with pustulent sores, dripping lesions, gaping cavities; a woman's hand rose to caress it and the makeup smeared so that I could see the handsome unmarred face beneath the artificial horrors. Here came a young man nearly seven feet high, waving a smoky torch and yelling of the Apocalypse; there was a flat-nosed girl drenched in sweat, rending her garments; two pomaded young men tweaked her breasts, laughed, kissed one another, and catapulted on. I called out again, "Vornan!"

Then I caught sight of him. He was standing quite still, like a boulder in a flowing stream, and curiously the rampaging mob was passing on either side of him as it roared forward. Several feet of open space remained inviolate around him, as though he had carved a private pocket in the throng. He stood with arms folded, surveying the madness about him. His mask had been ripped, so that his cheek showed through it, and he was daubed with paint and glowing substances. I struggled toward him, was carried away by a sudden inner surge within the main flow, and fought my way back to him with elbows and knees, hammering a route through tons of flesh. When I was within a few feet of him I understood why the rioters were bypassing him. Vornan had created a little dike all around himself out of stacked human bodies, piling them two or three high on each side. They seemed dead, but as I watched, a girl who had been lying to Vornan's left stumbled to her feet and went reeling away. Vornan promptly reached toward the next Apocalyptist to come along, a cadaverous man whose bald skull was stained deep blue. A touch of Vornan's hand and the man collapsed, falling neatly into place to restore the rampart. Vornan had built a living wall with his electricity. I jumped over it and thrust my face close to his.

"For God's sake let's get out of here!" I yelled.

"We are in no danger, Leo. Keep calm."

"Your mask's ripped. What if you're recognized?"

"I have my defenses." He laughed. "What delight this is!"

I knew better than to try to seize him again. In his careless rapture he would stun me a second time and add me to his rampart, and I might not survive the experience. So I stood beside him, helpless. I watched a heavy foot descend on the hand of an unconscious girl who lay near me; when the foot moved on, the shattered fingers quivered convulsively, bending at the joints in a way that human hands do not normally bend. Vornan turned in a full circle, taking everything in.

He said to me, "What makes them believe the world is going to end?"

"How would I know? It's irrational. They're insane."

"Can so many people be insane at once?"

"Of course."

"And do they know the day the world ends?"

"January 1, 2000."

"Quite close. Why that day in particular?"

"It's the beginning of a new century," I said, "of a new

millennium. Somehow people expect extraordinary things to happen then."

With lunatic pedantry Vornan said, "But the new century does not begin until 2001. Heyman has explained it to me. It is not correct to say that the century starts when—"

"I know all that. But no one pays attention to it. Damn you, Vornan, let's not stand here debating calendrics! I want to get away from here!"

"Then go."

"With you."

"I'm enjoying this. Look there, Leo!"

I looked. A nearly naked girl garbed as a witch rode on the shoulders of a man with horns sprouting from his forehead. Her breasts were painted glossy black, the nipples orange. But the sight of such grotesquerie did nothing to me now. I did not even trust Vornan's improvised barricade. If things got any wilder—

Police copters appeared abruptly. Long overdue, too. They hovered between the buildings, no more than a hundred feet up, and the whirr of their rotors sent a chilling draft upon us. I watched the dull gray nozzles extrude from the white globular bellies above us; then came the first spurts of the antiriot foam. The Apocalyptists seemed to welcome it. They rushed forward, trying to get into position under the nozzles; some of them stripped off what few garments they wore and bathed in it. The foam came bubbling down, expanding as it met the air, foaming a thick viscous soapiness that filled the street and made movement almost impossible. Moving now in angular jerks like machines running down, the demonstrators lurched to and fro, fighting their way through the layers of foam. Its taste was oddly sweet. I saw a girl get a jolt of it in the face and stumble, blinded, mouth and nostrils engulfed in the stuff. She fell to the pavement and disappeared totally, for by now at least three feet of foam rose from the ground, cool, sticky, cutting all of us off at our thighs. Vornan knelt and drew the girl back into view, although she would not suffocate where she was. He cleared the foam tenderly from her face and ran his hands over her moist, slippery flesh. When he gripped her breasts, her eyes opened and he said quietly to her, "I am Vornan-19." His lips went to hers. When he released her, she scrambled away on her knees, burrowing through the foam. To my horror I saw that Vornan was without his mask.

We could scarcely move at all, now. Police robots were in the street, great shining domes of metal that buzzed easily through the foam, seizing the trapped demonstrators and hustling them into groups of ten or twelve. Sanitation mechs were already out to suck up the excess foam. Vornan and I stood near the outer border of the scene; slowly we sloshed through the foam and reached an open street. No one seemed to notice us. I said to Vornan, "Will you listen to reason now? Here's our chance to get back to the hotel without any more trouble."

"We have had little trouble so far."

"There'll be big trouble if Kralick finds out what you've been up to. He'll restrict your freedom, Vornan. He'll keep an army of guards outside your door and put a triple seal on it."

"Wait," he said. "I want something. Then we can go."

He darted back into the mob. By now the foam had hardened to a doughy consistency, and those in it were wallowing precariously. In a moment Vornan returned. He was dragging a girl of about seventeen who seemed dazed and terrified. Her costume was of transparent plastic, but flecks of foam were clinging to it, conveying a probably unwanted modesty. "Now we can go to the hotel," he said to me. And to the girl he whispered, "I am Vornan-19. The world does not end in January. Before dawn I will prove it to you."

Fourteen

We did not have to sneak back into the hotel. A cordon of searchers had spread out for blocks around it; within moments after we had escaped from the foam, Vornan tripped an identity-signal and some of Kralick's men picked us up. Kralick was in the hotel lobby, monitoring the detector screens and looking half berserk with anxiety. When Vornan strode up to him, still tugging the quivering Apocalyptist girl, I thought Kralick would have a fit. Blandly Vornan apologized for any trouble he might have caused, and asked to be conducted to his room. The girl accompanied him. I had an uncomfortable session with Kralick when they were out of sight.

"How did he get out?" he demanded.

"I don't know. He gimmicked the seal on his room, I suppose." I tried to persuade Kralick that I had meant to give an alarm when Vornan left the hotel, but had been prevented by circumstances beyond my control. I doubt that I convinced him, but at least I got across to him the fact that I had done my best to keep Vornan from becoming involved with the Apocalyptists, and that the entire exploit had been none of my doing.

There was a noticeable tightening of security in the weeks that followed. In effect, Vornan-19 became the prisoner and not merely the guest of the United States Government. Vornan had been more or less an honored prisoner all along, for Kralick had suspected it was unwise to let him move about freely; but aside from sealing his room at night and posting guards, no attempt had been made to exert physical restraint on him. Somehow he had coped with the seal and drugged his guards, but Kralick prevented a repetition by using better seals, self-tripping alarms, and more guards.

It worked, in the sense that Vornan did not go on any further unauthorized expeditions. But I think that that was more a matter of Vornan's own choice than of Kralick's added precautions. After his experience with the Apocalyptists, Vornan seemed to subside considerably; he became a more orthodox tourist, looking at this and that but holding back his more demoniacal comments. I feared this subdued version of our guest the way I would fear a quiescent volcano. But in fact he committed no new outrageous transgressions of propriety, stepped on no toes, was in many ways the model of tact. I wondered what he was storing up for us.

And so the weeks of the tour dragged on. We looked at Disneyland with Vornan, and although the place had been visibly refurbished, it plainly bored him. He was not interested in seeing synthetic reconstructions of other times and other places; he wanted to experience the United States of 1999 at first hand. At Disneyland he paid more attention to the other customers than to the amusements themselves. We swept him through the park unheralded, moving in a small close-knit group, and for once he attracted little attention. It was as if anyone who saw Vornan at Disneyland assumed that what he saw was part of the park, a clever plastic imitation of the man out of time, and passed by with no more than a nod and a smile.

We took him to Irvine and showed him the trillion-volt accelerator. That was my idea: I wanted a chance to get back to the campus for a few days, to visit my office and my house and be sure that all was still well. Letting Vornan near the accelerator was something of a calculated risk, I thought, remembering the havoc he had produced at Wesley Bruton's villa; but we saw to it that Vornan never came within reach of any of the control equipment. He stood beside me, gravely watching the screens, as I smashed atoms for him. He seemed interested, but it was the superficial interest a child might have shown: he liked the pretty patterns.

For a moment I forgot everything except the joy of manipulating the huge machine. I stood at the operating panel, with billions of dollars of equipment stretching above and before me, pulling switches and levers with the same glee Wesley Bruton had displayed while making his house work wonders. I pulverized atoms of iron and sent neutrons spraying madly about. I sent a stream of protons along the track and cut in the neutron injector so that the screen was spattered with the bright bursts of demolition lines. I conjured up quarks and antiquarks. I went through my entire repertoire, and Vornan nodded innocently, smiling, pointing. He could have deflated me as he had done the Stock Exchange man, simply by asking what the point of all this cumbersome apparatus might be, but he did not. I am not sure if his restraint was a matter of courtesy toward me—for I flattered myself that Vornan was closer to me than to any of the others who traveled with him—or if it was simply that for the moment his vein of impishness was played out, and he was content to stand and watch respectfully.

We took him next to the fusion plant on the coast. Again, this was my doing, though Kralick agreed it might be useful. I still had hopes, however flickering, of squeezing from Vornan some data on the energy sources of his era. Jack Bryant's too-sensitive conscience spurred me on. But the attempt was a failure. The manager of the plant explained to Vornan how we had captured the fury of the sun itself, setting up a proton-proton reaction within a magnetic pinch, and tapping power from the transmutation of hydrogen to helium. Vornan was permitted to enter the relay room where the plasma was regulated by sensors operating above the visible spectrum. What we were seeing was not the raging plasma itself—direct viewing of that was impossible—but a simulation, a recreation, a curve following peak for peak every fluctuation of the soup of stripped-down nuclei within the pinch tank. It had been years since I had visited the plant myself, and I was awed. Vornan kept his own counsel. We waited for disparaging remarks; none came. He did not bother to compare our medieval scientific accomplishments with the technology of his own age. This new Vornan lacked bite.

Next we doubled back through New Mexico, where Pueblo Indians dwell in a living museum of anthropology. This was Helen McIlwain's big moment. She led us through the dusty mud village trailing anthropological data. Here in early spring the regular tourist season had not yet begun, and so we had the pueblo to ourselves; Kralick had arranged with the local authorities to close the reservation to outsiders for the day, so that no Vornan-seekers would come up from Albuquerque or down from Santa Fe to make trouble. The Indians themselves came shuffling out of their flat-roofed adobes to stare, but I doubt that many of them knew who Vornan was, and I doubt that any of them cared. They were pudgy people, round-faced, flat-nosed, not at all the hawk-featured Indians of legend. I felt sorry for them. They were Federal employees, in a sense, paid to stay here and live in squalor. Although they were permitted television and automobiles and electricity, they may not build houses in the modern styles, and must continue to grind corn meal, perform their ceremonial dances, and turn out pottery for sale to visitors. Thus we guard our past.

Helen introduced us to the leaders of the village: the governor, the chief, and the heads of two of the so-called secret societies. They seemed like sharp, sophisticated men, who could just as easily be running automobile agencies in Albuquerque. We were taken around, into a few of the houses, even down into the kiva, the town religious center, formerly sacrosanct. Some children did a ragged dance for us. In a shop at the edge of the plaza we were shown the pottery and turquoise-and-silver jewelry that the women of the village produced. One case held older pottery, made in the first half of the twentieth century, handsome stuff with a smooth finish and elegant semi-abstract patterns of birds and deer; but these pieces were priced at hundreds of dollars apiece, and from the look on the face of the salesgirl I gathered that they were not really for sale at all; they were tribal treasures, souvenirs of happier times. The real stock-in-trade consisted of cheap, flimsy little jugs. Helen said with scorn, "You see how they put the paint on *after* the pot's been fired, now? It's deplorable. Any child can do it. The University of New Mexico is trying to revive the old ways, but the people here argue that the tourists like the fake stuff better. It's brighter, livelier—and cheaper." Vornan drew a sour glare from Helen when he expressed his opinion that the so-called touristware was more attractive than the earlier pottery. I think he said it only to tease her, but I am not sure; Vornan's esthetic standards were always unfathomable, and probably to him the debased current work seemed as authentic a product of the remote past as the really fine pottery in the display case.

We had only one minor Vornan incident at the pueblo. The girl running the showroom was a slim adolescent beauty with long soft shining black hair and fine features that looked more Chinese than Indian; we were all quite taken by her, and Vornan seemed eager to add her to his collection of conquests. I don't know what would have happened if he had asked the girl to stage a command performance in his bed that night. Luckily, he never got that far. He was eyeing the girl in obvious lust as she moved about the showroom; I saw it, and so did Helen. When we left the building, Vornan turned as if to go back in and announce his desire. Helen blocked his way, looking more like a witch than ever, her eyes blazing against her flaming mop of red hair.

"*No*," she said fiercely. "You *can't*!"

That was all. And Vornan obeyed. He smiled and bowed to Helen and walked away. I hadn't expected him to do that.

The new meek Vornan was a revelation to us all, but the public at large preferred the revelations of the Vornan it had come to know in January and February. Against all likelihood, interest in Vornan's deeds and words grew more passionate with each passing week; what might have been a nine-days' wonder was on its way toward becoming the sensation of the age. Some clever huckster assembled a quick, flimsy book about Vornan and called it *The New Revelation*. It contained transcripts of all of Vornan-19's press conferences and media appearances since his arrival at Christmastime, with some choppy commentary tying everything together. The book appeared in the middle of March, and some measure of its significance can be gathered from the fact that it came out not only in tape, cube, and facsim editions, but also in a printed text—a book, that is, in the old sense. A California publisher produced it as a slim paperbound volume with a bright red jacket and the title in incandescent ebony letters; an edition of a million copies sold out within a week. Very shortly, pirated editions were emerging from underground presses everywhere, despite the frantic attempts of the copyright owner to protect his property. Uncountable millions of *The New Revelation* flooded the land. I bought one myself, as a keepsake. I saw Vornan reading a copy. Both the genuine edition and the various ersatz ones had the same black-on-red color scheme, so that at a glance they were indistinguishable, and in the early weeks of spring those paper-bound books covered the nation like a strange red snowfall.

The new creed had its prophet, and now it had its gospel too. I find it hard to see what sort of spiritual comfort could be derived from *The New Revelation*, and so I suppose the book was more of a talisman than a scripture; one did not take counsel from it, one merely carried it about, drawing sustenance from the feel of the shiny covers against the hands. Whenever we traveled with Vornan and a crowd assembled, copies of the book were held aloft like flashcards at a college football game, creating a solid red backdrop speckled with the dark letters of the title.

There were translations. The Germans, the Poles, the Swedes, the Portuguese, the French, the Russians, all had their own versions of *The New Revelation*. Someone on Kralick's staff was collecting the things and forwarding them to us wherever we went. Kralick usually turned them over to Kolff, who showed a weird bitter interest in each new edition. The book made its way into Asia, and reached us in Japanese, in several of the languages of India, in Mandarin, and in Korean. Appropriately, a Hebrew edition appeared, the right language for any holy book. Kolff liked to arrange the little red books in rows, shifting the patterns about. He spoke dreamily of making a translation of his own, into Sanskrit or perhaps Old Persian; I am not sure if he was serious.

Since the episode of his interview with Vornan, Kolff had been slipping into some kind of senile decay. He had been badly shocked by the computer's views on Vornan's speech sample; the ambiguity of that report had punctured his own buoyant conviction that he had heard the voice of the future, and now, chastened and humiliated, he had fallen back from his first enthusiastic verdict. He was not at all sure that Vornan was genuine or that he had really heard the ghosts of words in the liquid flow of Vornan's prattle. Kolff had lost faith in his own judgment, his own expertise, and we could see him crumbling now. This great Falstaff of a man was at least partly a humbug, as we had discovered during our tour; though his gifts were great and his learning was vast, he knew that his lofty reputation had been undeserved for decades, and abruptly he stood exposed as an uncertain maunderer. In pity for him I asked Vornan to grant Kolff a second interview and to repeat whatever it was he had recited the first time. Vornan would not do it.

"It is useless," he said, and refused to be prodded.

Kolff subdued seemed hardly to be Kolff at all. He ate little, said less, and by the beginning of April had lost so much weight that he seemed unrecognizable. His clothes and his skin itself hung slack on his shrunken frame. He moved along with us from place to place, but he was shambling blindly, hardly aware of what was happening about him. Kralick, concerned, wanted to relieve Kolff of his assignment and send him home. He discussed the matter with the rest of us, but Helen's opinion was decisive. "It'll kill him," she said. "He'll think he's being fired for incompetence."

"He's a sick man," said Kralick. "All this traveling—"

"It's a useful function."

"But he isn't being useful any more," Kralick pointed out. "He hasn't contributed anything in weeks. He just sits there playing with those copies of the book. Helen, I can't take the responsibility. He belongs in a hospital."

"He belongs with us."

"Even if it kills him?"

"Even if it kills him," Helen said vigorously. "Better to die in harness than to creep away thinking you're an old fool."

Kralick let her win the round, but we were fearful, for we could see the inward rot spreading through old Lloyd day by day. Each morning I expected to be told that he had slipped away in his sleep; but each morning he was there, gaunt, gray-skinned, his nose now jutting like a pyramid in his diminished face. We journeyed to Michigan so that Vornan could see Aster's life-synthesis project; and as we walked the aisles of that eerie laboratory, Kolff clumped along behind us, a delegate from the walking dead witnessing the spawning of artificial life.

Aster said, "This was one of our earliest successes, if you can call it a success. We never could figure out what phylum to put it in, but there's no doubt that it's alive and that it breeds true, so in that sense the experiment was successful."

We peered into a huge tank in which a variety of underwater plants grew. Between the green fronds swam slender azure creatures, six to eight inches long; they were eyeless, propelled themselves by ripplings of a dorsal fin that ran their entire length, and were crowned by gaping mouths rimmed with agile translucent tentacles. At least a hundred of them were in the tank. A few appeared to be budding; smaller representatives of their kind protruded from their sides.

"We intended to manufacture coelenterates," Aster explained. "Basically, that's what we have here: a giant free-swimming anemone. But coelenterates don't have fins, and this one does, and knows how to use it. We didn't engineer that fin. It developed spontaneously. There's the phantom of a segmented body structure, too, which is an attribute belonging to a higher phylum. Metabolically, the thing is capable of adapting to its environment far more satisfactorily than most invertebrates; it lives in fresh or salt water, gets along in a temperature spectrum of about a hundred degrees, and handles any sort of food. So we've got a super-coelenterate. We'd like to test it in natural conditions, perhaps dump a few in a pond nearby, but frankly we're afraid to let the thing loose." Aster smiled self-consciously. "We've also been trying vertebrate synthesis lately, with rather less to show for it. Here . . ."

She indicated a tank in which a small brown creature lay limply on the bottom, moving in an occasional random twitch. It had two boneless-looking arms and a single leg; the missing leg did not seem ever to have been there. A whiplike tail drifted feebly about. To me it looked like a sad salamander. Aster seemed quite proud of it, though, for it had a well-developed skeletal structure, a decent nervous system, a surprisingly good set of eyes, and a full complement of internal organs. It did not, however, reproduce itself. They were still working on that. In the meantime, each of these synthetic vertebrates had to be built up cell by cell from the basic genetic material, which very much limited the scope of the experiment. But this was awesome enough.

Aster was in her element, now, and she led us on tirelessly, down one avenue of the long, brightly lit room and up the next, past giant frosted flasks and looming, sinister centrifuges, along alcoves occupied by fractionating columns, into annexes where mechanical agitators chuttered busily in reaction vats containing somber iridescent amber fluids. We peered through long fiber telescopes to spy on sealed rooms in which light, temperature, radiation, and pressure were meticulously controlled. We saw blowups of electron photomicrographs and garnet holograms that showed us the internal structures of mysterious cellular groups. Aster sprinkled her running commentary liberally with words laden with symbolic significance, a lab jargon that had its own mystic rhythm; we heard of photometric titrators, platinum crucibles, hydraulic plethysmographs, rotary microtomes, densitometers, electrophoresis cells, collodion bags, infrared microscopes, flowmeters, piston burettes, cardiotachometers: an incomprehensible and wonderful vocabulary. Painstakingly Aster revealed how the protein chains of life were put together and made to replicate themselves; she spelled everything out simply and beautifully, and there were the wriggling mock-coelenterates and the flabby pseudo-salamanders to tell us of achievement. It was altogether marvelous.

As she drew us along, Aster fished for what concerned her most: Vornan's comments. She knew that some sort of not-quite-human life existed in Vornan's time, for he had spoken in ambiguous terms at one of our early meetings of "servitors," which did not have full human status because they were genetically unhuman, life-forms built out of "lesser life." From what he had said, these servitors did not seem to be synthetic creations, but rather some kind of composites constructed of humbler germ plasm drawn from living things: dog-people, cat-people, gnu-people. Naturally Aster wished to know more, and she had just as naturally learned not a shred more from Vornan-19. Now she probed again, getting nowhere. Vornan remained distantly polite. He asked a few questions: How soon, he wanted to know, would Aster be able to synthesize imitation humans? Aster looked hazy. "Five, ten, fifteen years," she said.

"If the world lasts that long," said Vornan slyly.

We all laughed, more an explosion of tensions than any real show of amusement. Even Aster, who had never displayed anything like a sense of humor, flashed a thin, mechanical smile. She turned away and indicated a tank mounted in a pressure capsule.

"This is our latest project," she said. "I'm not quite sure how it stands now, since as you all know I've been away from the laboratory since January. You see here an effort to synthesize a mammalian embryo. We have several embryos in various stages of development. If you'll come closer . . ."

I looked and saw a number of fishlike things coiled within small membrane-bounded cells. My stomach tightened in nervous response to the sight of these big-headed little creatures, born from a mess of amino acids, ripening toward who knew what kind of maturity. Even Vornan looked impressed.

Lloyd Kolff grunted something in a language I did not understand: three or four words, thick, harsh, guttural. His voice carried an undertone of anguish. I looked toward him and saw him standing rigid, one arm brought up at an acute angle across his chest, the other pointing straight out from his side. He seemed to be performing some extremely complex ballet step and had become frozen in mid-pirouette. His face was deep blue, the color of Ming porcelain; his red-rimmed eyes were wide and frightful. He stood that way a long moment. Then he made a little chittering noise in the back of his throat and pitched forward onto the stone top of a laboratory table. He clutched convulsively; flasks and burners went sliding and crashing to the floor. His thick hands seized the rim of a small tank and pulled it over, spilling a dozen sleek little synthetic coelenterates. They flapped and quivered at our feet. Lloyd sagged slowly, losing his grip on the table and toppling in several stages, landing flat on his back. His eyes were still open. He uttered one sentence, with marvelously distinct diction: Lloyd Kolff's valedictory to the world. It was in some ancient language, perhaps. None of us could identify it afterward or repeat even a syllable. Then he died.

"Life support!" Aster yelled. "Hurry!"

Two laboratory assistants came scuttling up almost at once with a life-support rig. Kralick, meanwhile, had dropped beside Kolff and was trying mouth-to-mouth resuscitation. Aster got him away, and crouching efficiently beside Kolff's bulky, motionless form, ripped open his clothing to reveal the deep chest matted with gray hair. She gestured and one of her assistants handed her a pair of electrodes. She put them in place and gave Kolff's heart a jolt. The other assistant was already uncapping a hypodermic and pushing it against Kolff's arm. We heard the whirr of the ultrasonic snout while it rose through the frequencies to the functional level. Kolff's big body shivered as the hormones and the electricity hit it simultaneously; his right hand rose a few inches, fist clenched, and dropped back again. "Galvanic response," Aster muttered. "Nothing more."

But she didn't give up. The life-support rig had a full complement of emergency devices, and she put them all into use. A chest compressor carried on artificial respiration; she injected refrigerants into his bloodstream to prevent brain decay; the electrodes rhythmically assaulted the valves of his heart. Kolff was nearly concealed by the assortment of first-aid equipment covering him.

Vornan knelt and peered intently into Kolff's staring eyes. He observed the slackness of the features. He put a tentative hand forth to touch Kolff's mottled cheek. He noted the mechanisms that pumped and squeezed and throbbed on top of the fallen man. Then he rose and said quietly to me, "What are they trying to do to him, please?"

"Bring him back to life."

"This is death, then?"

"Death, yes."

"What happened to him?"

"His heart stopped working, Vornan. Do you know what the heart is?"

"Yes, yes."

"Kolff's heart was tired. It stopped. Aster's trying to start it again. She won't succeed."

"Does this happen often, this thing of death?"

"Once at least in everybody's lifetime," I said bitterly. A doctor had been summoned now. He pulled more apparatus from the life-support rig and began making an incision in Kolff's chest. I said to Vornan. "How does death come in your time?"

"Never suddenly. Never like this. I know very little about it."

He seemed more fascinated with the presence of death even than he had been with the creation of life in this same room. The doctor toiled; but Kolff did not respond, and the rest of us stood in a ring like statues. Only Aster moved, picking up the creatures that Kolff in his last convulsion had spilled. Some of them too were dead, a few from exposure to air, the others from being crushed by heedless feet. But some survived. She put them back in a tank.

At length the doctor rose, shaking his head.
I looked at Kralick. He was weeping.

Fifteen

Kolff was buried in New York with high academic honors. Out of respect we halted our tour for a few days. Vornan attended the funeral; he was vastly curious about our customs of interment. His presence at the ceremony nearly caused a crisis, for the gowned academics pressed close to get a glimpse of him, and at one point I thought the coffin itself would be overturned in the confusion. Three books went into Kolff's grave with him. Two were works of his own; the third was the Hebrew translation of *The New Revelation*. I was enraged by that, but Kralick told me it had been Kolff's own idea. Three or four days before the end he had given Helen McIlwain a sealed tape that turned out to contain burial instructions.

After the period of mourning we headed west again to continue Vornan's tour. It was surprising how fast the death of Kolff ceased to matter to us; we were five now instead of six, but the shock of his collapse dwindled and shortly we were back to routine. As the season warmed, though, certain quiet changes in mood became apparent. Distribution of *The New Revelation* seemed complete, since virtually everyone in the country had a copy, and the crowds that attended Vornan's movements were larger every day. Subsidiary prophets were springing up, interpreters of Vornan's message to humanity. The focus for much of this activity was in California, as usual, and Kralick took good care to keep Vornan out of that state. He was perturbed by this gathering cult, as was I, as were all of us. Vornan alone seemed to enjoy the presence of his flock. Even he sometimes seemed a bit apprehensive, as when he landed at an airport to find a sea of red-covered volumes gleaming in the sunlight. At least it was my impression that the really huge mobs made him ill at ease; but most of the time he seemed to revel in the attention he gained. One California newspaper had suggested quite seriously that Vornan be nominated to run for the Senate in the next election. I found Kralick gagging over the facsim of that one when it came in. "If Vornan ever sees this," he said, "we could be in a mess."

There was to be no Senator Vornan, luckily. In a calmer moment we persuaded ourselves that he could not meet the residence requirements; and, too, we doubted that the courts would accept a member of the Centrality as a citizen of the United States, unless Vornan had some way of demonstrating the Centrality to be the legally constituted successor-in-fact to the sovereignty of the United States.

The schedule called for Vornan to be taken to the Moon at the end of May to see the recently developed resort there. I begged off from this; I had no real wish to visit the pleasure palaces of Copernicus, and it seemed to me that I could use the extra time to get my personal affairs in order at Irvine as the semester ended. Kralick wanted me to go, especially since I had already had one leave of absence; but he had no practical way of compelling me, and in the end he let me have another leave. A committee of four could manage Vornan as well as a committee of five, he decided.

But it was a committee of three by the time they actually did depart for the lunar base.

Fields resigned on the eve of the departure. Kralick should have seen it coming, since Fields had been grumbling and muttering for weeks, and was in obvious rebellion against the entire assignment. As a psychologist, Fields had been studying Vornan's responses to the environment as we moved about, and had come up with two or three contradictory and mutually exclusive evaluations. Depending on his own emotional weather, Fields concluded that Vornan was or was not an impostor, and filed reports covering almost every possibility. My private evaluation of Fields' evaluations was that they were worthless. His cosmic interpretations of Vornan's actions were in themselves empty and vapid, but I could have forgiven that if only Fields had managed to sustain the same opinion for more than two consecutive weeks.

His resignation from the committee, though, did not come on ideological grounds. It was provoked by nothing more profound than petty jealousy. And I must admit, little as I liked Fields, that I sympathized with him in this instance.

The trouble arose over Aster. Fields was still pursuing her in a kind of hopeless romantic quest which was as repugnant to the rest of us as it was depressing for him. She did not want him; that was quite clear, even to Fields. But proximity does strange things to a man's ego, and Fields kept trying. He bribed hotel clerks to put his room next to Aster's and searched for ways to slip into her bedroom at night. Aster was annoyed, though not as much as if she'd been a real flesh-and-blood woman; in many ways she was as artificial as her own coelenterates, and she minimized the Byronic heavings and pantings of her too-ardent swain.

As Helen McIlwain told me, Fields grew more and more visibly worked up over this treatment. Finally one night when everyone was gathered together, he asked Aster point-blank to spend the night with him. She said no. Fields then delivered himself of some blistering commentary on the defects in Aster's libido. Loudly and angrily he accused her of frigidity, perversity, malevolence, and several other varieties of bitchiness. In a way, everything he said about Aster was probably true, with one limiting factor: she was an *unintentional* bitch. I don't think she had been trying to tease or provoke him at all. She had simply failed to understand what sort of response was expected of her.

This time, though, she remembered that she was a woman, and disemboweled Fields in a notably feminine way. In front of Fields, in front of everyone, she invited Vornan to share her bed with her that night. She made it quite clear that she was offering herwelf to Vornan without reservations. I wish I had seen that. As Helen put it, Aster looked female for the first time: eyes aglow, lips drawn back, face flushed, claws unsheathed. Naturally Vornan obliged her. Away they went together, Aster as radiant as a bride on her wedding night. For all I know, she thought of it that way.

Fields could take no more. I hardly blame him. Aster had cut him up in a fairly ultimate way, and it was too much to expect him to stick around for more of the same. He told Kralick he was quitting. Kralick naturally appealed to Fields to stay on, calling it his patriotic duty, his obligation to science, and so forth—a set of abstractions which I know are as hollow to Kralick as to the rest of us. It was a ritualized speech, and Fields ignored it. That night he packed up and cleared out, thus sparing himself, according to Helen, the sight of Aster and Vornan coming forth from the nuptial chambers the next morning in a fine full gleam of recollected delights.

I was back in Irvine while all this went on. Like any ordinary citizen I followed Vornan's career by screen, when I remembered to tune in. My few months with him now seemed even less real than when they were happening; I had to make an effort to convince myself that I had not dreamed the whole thing. But it was no dream. Vornan was up there on the Moon, being shepherded about by Kralick, Helen, Heyman, and Aster. Kolff was dead. Fields had gone back to Chicago. He called me from there in the middle of June; he was writing a book on his experiences with Vornan, he said, and wanted to check a few details with me. He said nothing about his motives for resigning.

I forgot about Fields and his book within the hour. I tried to forget about Vornan-19, too. I returned to my much-neglected work, but I found it flat, weary, stale, and unprofitable. Wandering aimlessly around the laboratory, shuffling through the tapes of old experiments, occasionally tapping out something new on the computer, yawning my way through conferences with the graduate students. I suppose I cut a pathetic figure: King Lear among the elementary particles, too old, too dull-witted, too frazzled to grasp my own questions. I sensed the younger men patronizing me that month. I felt eighty years old. Yet none of them had any suggestions for breaking through the barrier that contained our research. They were stymied too; the difference was that they were confident something would turn up if we only kept on searching, while I seemed to have lost interest not only in the search but in the goal.

Naturally they were very curious about my views on the authenticity of Vornan-19. Had I learned anything about his method of moving through time? Did I think he really *had* moved in time? What theoretical implications could be found in the fact of his visit?

I had no answers. The questions themselves became tedious. And so I wandered through a month of idleness, stalling, faking. Possibly I should have left the University again and visited Shirley and Jack. But my last visit there had been a disturbing one, revealing unexpected gulfs and craters in their marriage, and I was afraid to go back for fear I would discover that my one remaining place of refuge was lost to me. Nor could I keep running away from my work, depressing and moribund though it was. I stayed in California. I visited my laboratory every day or two. I checked through the papers of my students. I avoided the cascades of media people who wanted to question me about Vornan-19. I slept a good deal, sometimes twelve and thirteen hours at a stretch, hoping to sleep my way through this period of doldrums entirely. I read novels and plays and poetry in an obsessive way, going on binges. You can guess my mood from the statement that I worked myself through the Prophetic Books of Blake in five consecutive nights, without skipping a word. Those inspired ravings clog my mind even now, half a year later. I read all of Proust, too, and much of Dostoyevsky, and a dozen anthologies of the nightmares that passed for plays in the Jacobean era. It was all apocalyptic art for an apocalyptic era, but much of it faded as fast as it moved across my glazed retina, leaving only a residue: Charlus, Svidrigailov, the Duchess of Malfi, Vindice, Swann's Odette. The foggy dreams of Blake remain: Enitharmon and Urizen, Los, Orc, majestic Golgonooza:

> But blood & wounds & dismal cries &
> clarions of war.
> And hearts laid open to the light by the
> broad grizly sword,
> And bowels hidden in hammered steel
> ripp'd forth upon the ground.
> Call forth thy smiles of soft deceit, call
> forth thy cloudy tears!
> We hear thy sights in trumpets shrill
> when Morn shall blood renew.

During this fevered time of solitude and inner confusion I paid little attention to the pair of conflicting mass movements that troubled the world, the one coming in, the other going out. The Apocalyptists were not extinct by any means, and their marches and riots and orgies still continued, although in a kind of dogged stubbornness not too different from the galvanic twitches of Lloyd Kolff's dead arm. Their time was over. Not too many of the world's uncommitted people now cared to believe that Armageddon was due to arrive on January 1, 2000—not with Vornan roaming about as living evidence to the contrary. Those who took part in the Apocalyptist uprisings now, I gathered, were those for whom orgy and destruction had become a way of life; there was nothing theological in their posturings and cavortings any longer. Within this group of rowdies there was a hard core of the devout, looking forward hungrily to imminent Doomsday, but these fanatics were losing ground daily. In July, with less than six months left before the designated day of holocaust, it appeared to impartial observers that the Apocalyptist creed would succumb to inertia long before mankind's supposed final weeks arrived. Now we know that that is not so, for as I speak these words, only eight days remain before the hour of truth appears; and the Apocalyptists are still very much with us. It is Christmas eve, 1999, tonight—the anniversary of Vornan's manifestation in Rome, I now realize.

If in July the Apocalyptists seemed to be fading, that other cult, the nameless one of Vornan-worship, was certainly gathering momentum. It had no thesis and no purpose; the aim of its adherents seemed only to be to get close to the figure of Vornan and scream their excited approbation of him. *The New Revelation* was its only scripture: a disjointed, incoherent patchwork of interviews and press conferences, studded here and there with tantalizing nuggets Vornan had dropped. I could construct just two tenets of Vornanism: that life on earth is an accident caused by the carelessness of interstellar visitors, and that the world will not be destroyed next January 1. I suppose religions have been founded on slimmer bases than these, but I can think of no examples. Yet the Vornanites continued to gather around the charismatic, enigmatic figure of their prophet. Surprisingly, many followed him to the Moon, creating crowds there that had not been seen since the opening of the commercial resort in Copernicus some years back. The rest assembled around giant screens erected in open plazas by canny corporations, and watched en masse the relays from Luna. And I in turn occasionally turned in on pickups from those mass meetings.

What troubled me most about this movement was its formlessness. It was awaiting the shaper's hand. If Vornan chose to, he could give direction and impetus to his cult, merely by delivering a few ex cathedra pronouncements. He could call for holy wars, for political upheavals, for dancing in the streets, for abstinence from stimulants, for over-indulgence in stimulants—and millions would obey. He had not cared to make use of his power thus far. Perhaps it was only gradually dawning on him that the power was available to him. I had seen Vornan turn a private party into a shambles with a few casual movements of his hand; what could he not do once he grasped the levers that control the world?

The strength of his cult was appalling, and so was the speed at which it grew. His absence on the Moon seemed not to matter at all. Even from a distance he exerted a pull, as powerful and as mindless as the tug of the Moon itself on our seas. He was, more accurately than the cliché can convey, all things to all men; there were those who loved him for his gaudy nihilism, and others who saw him as a symbol of stability in a tottering world. I don't doubt that his basic appeal was as a deity: not Jehovah, not Wotan, not a remote, and bearded father-figure, but as a handsome, dynamic, buoyant Young God, the incarnation of springtime and light, the creative and the destructive forces bound into a single synthesis. He was Apollo. He was Baldur. He was Osiris. But also he was Loki, and the old mythmakers had not contemplated that particular combination.

His visit to Luna was extended several times. I believe it was the intention of Kralick—on behalf of the Government— to keep Vornan away from Earth as long as possible, so that the dangerous emotions engendered by his arrival in the last year of the old millennium might have a chance to subside. He had been scheduled to stay only to the end of June, but late in July he was still there. On the screens we caught glimpses of him in the gravity baths, or gravely examining the hydroponics tanks, or jet-skiing, or mingling with a select group of international celebrities at the gambling tables. And I noticed Aster beside him quite often, looking oddly regal, her slim body bedecked in startlingly revealing, astonishingly un-Aster-like costumes. Hovering in the background occasionally were Helen and Heyman, an ill-assorted pair linked by mutual detestation, and I sometimes picked out the looming figure of Sandy Kralick, dour-faced, grim, lost in contemplation of his unlikely assignment.

At the end of July I was notified that Vornan was returning and that my services would again be needed. I was instructed to go to the San Francisco spaceport to await Vornan's landing a week hence. A day later I received a copy of an unpleasant little pamphlet which I'm sure did not improve the flavor of Sandy Kralick's mood. It was a glossy-covered thing bound in red to imitate *The New Revelation;* its title was *The Newest Revelation* and its author was Morton Fields. A signed copy came to me compliments of the author. Before long, millions were in circulation, not because the booklet had any inherent interest but because it was coveted by others who collected any scrap of printed matter dealing with the advent of Vornan-19.

The Newest Revelation was Fields' ugly memoir of his

experiences on tour with Vornan. It was his way of venting his spleen against Aster, mainly. It did not name her—for fear of the libel laws, I suppose—but no one could fail to identify her, since there were only two women on the committee and Helen McIlwain was mentioned by name. The portrait of Aster that emerged was not one that corresponded to the Aster Mikkelsen I had known; Fields showed her as a treacherous, sly, deceitful, and above all else amoral minx who had prostituted herself to the members of the committee, who had driven Lloyd Kolff into his grave with her insatiable sexual appetite, and who had committed every abomination known to man with Vornan-19. Among her lesser crimes was her deliberate sadistic torment of the one virtuous and sane member of our group, who was of course Morton Fields. Fields had written:

"This vicious and wanton woman took a strange delight in sharpening her claws on me. I was her easiest victim. Because I made it clear from the start I disliked her, she set out to snare me into her bed—and when I rebuffed her, she grew more determined to add me to her collection of scalps. Her provocations grew flagrant and shameful, until in a weak moment I found myself about to yield to them. Then, of course, with great glee she denounced me as a Don Juan, callously humiliating me before the others, and . . ."

And so on. The whining tone was maintained consistently throughout. Fields ticked each of us off unsparingly. Helen McIlwain was a giddy post-adolescent, somewhat overripe; Lloyd Kolff was a superannuated dodderer making his way through gluttony, lechery, and the shrewd use of a mind that contained nothing but erotic verse; F. Richard Heyman was an arrogant stuffed shirt. (I did not find Fields' characterization of Heyman unjust.) Kralick was dismissed as a Government flunkey, trying hard to save everyone's face at once, and willing to make any compromise at all to avoid trouble. Fields was quite blunt about the Government's role in the Vornan affair. He said openly that the President had ordered complete acceptance of Vornan's claims in order to deflate the Apocalyptists; this of course was true, but no one had admitted it publicly before, certainly not anyone so highly placed in the circles around Vornan as was Fields. Luckily he buried his complaint in a long, clotted passage devoted to a paranoid flaying of the national psyche, and I suspect the point was overlooked by most readers.

I came off fairly well in Fields' assessments. He described me as aloof, superficial, falsely profound, a mock-philosopher who invariably recoiled in terror from any hard issue. I am not pleased with those indictments, but I suspect that I must plead guilty to the charges. Fields touched on my excessive venery, on my lack of real commitment to any cause, and on my easy tolerance of the defects of those about me. Yet there was no venom in his paragraph on me; to him, I seemed neither fool nor villain, but rather a neutral figure of little interest. So be it.

Fields' nasty gossip about his fellow committeemen alone would not have won his book much of a following outside academic circles, nor would I be speaking of it at such great length. The core of his essay was his "newest revelation"—his analysis of Vornan-19. Muddled, mazy, stilted, and dreary though it was, this section managed to carry enough of Vornan's charisma to gain it readership. And thus Fields' foolish little book achieved an influence out of all proportion to its real content.

He devoted only a few paragraphs to the question of Vornan's authenticity. Over the course of the past six months Fields has held a variety of contradictory views on that subject, and he managed to pile all the contradictions into a short space here. In effect he said that probably Vornan was not an impostor, but that it would serve us all right if he were, and in any case it did not matter. What counted was not the absolute truth concerning Vornan, but only his impact on 1999. In this I think Fields was correct. Fraud or not, Vornan's effect on us was undeniable, and the power of his passage through our world was genuine even if Vornan-as-time-traveler may not have been.

So Fields dispensed with that problem in a cluster of blurred ambiguities and moved on to an interpretation of Vornan's culture-role among us. It was very simple, said Fields. Vornan was a god. He was deity and prophet rolled into one, an omnipotent self-advertiser, offering himself as the personification of all the vague, unfocused yearnings of a planet whose people had had too much comfort, too much tension, too much fear. He was a god for our times, giving off electricity that may or may not have been produced by surgically implanted power-packs; a god who Zeus-like took mortals to his bed; a troublemaker of a god; a slippery, elusive, evasive, self-indulgent god, offering nothing and

accepting much. You must realize that in summarizing Fields'
thoughts I am greatly compressing them and also untangling
them, cutting away the brambles and thorns of excessive
dogmatism and leaving only the inner theory with which I
myself wholly agree. Surely Fields had caught the essence of
our response to Vornan.

Nowhere in *The Newest Revelation* did Fields claim that
Vornan-19 was *literally* divine, any more than he offered a
final opinion on the genuineness of his claim to have come
from the future. Fields did not care whether or not Vornan
was genuine, and he certainly did not think that he was in
any way a supernatural being. What he was really saying—
and I believe it wholeheartedly—was that *we ourselves had
made Vornan into a god*. We had needed a deity to preside
over us as we entered our new millennium, for the old gods
had abdicated; and Vornan had come along to fill our need.
Fields was analyzing humanity, not assessing Vornan.

But of course humanity in the mass is not capable of
absorbing such subtle distinctions. Here was a book bound in
red which said that Vornan was a god! Never mind the
hedgings and fudgings, never mind the scholarly obfuscations.
Vornan's divine status was officially proclaimed! And from "he
is a god" to "He is God" is a very short journey. *The Newest
Revelation* became a sacred scripture. Did it not say in
words, in printed words, that Vornan was divine? Could one
ignore such words?

The magical process followed expectations. The little red
pamphlet was translated into every language of mankind,
serving as it did as the holy justification of the madness of
Vornan-worship. The faithful had an additional talisman to
carry about. And Morton Fields became the St. Paul of the
new creed, the press agent of the prophet. Although he
never saw Vornan again, never took an active part in the
movement he unwittingly helped to encourage, Fields through
his foul little book has already become an invisible presence
of great significance in the movement that now sweeps the
world. I suspect that he is due to be elevated to a lofty place
in the canon of saints, once the new hagiologies have been
written.

Reading my advance copy of Fields' book at the beginning
of August, I failed to guess the impact it would have. I read it
quickly and with the sort of cold fascination one feels upon
lifting a boulder at the seashore to disclose squirming white

things beneath; and then I tossed it aside, amused and repelled, and forgot all about it until its importance became manifest. Duly I reported to San Francisco to greet Vornan when he landed from space. The usual subterfuges and precautions were in effect at the spaceport. While a roaring crowd waved *The New Revelation* aloft under a gray fogbound sky, Vornan moved through a subterranean channel to a staging area at the edge of the spaceport.

He took my hand warmly. "Leo, you should have come," he said. "It was pure delight. The triumph of your age, I'd say, that resort on the Moon. What have you been doing?"

"Reading, Vornan. Resting. Working."

"To good effect?"

"To no effect whatever."

He looked sleek, relaxed, as confident as always. Some of his radiance had transferred itself to Aster, who stood beside him in a frankly possessive way, no longer the blank, absent, crystalline Aster I remembered, but a warmly passionate woman fully awakened to her own soul at last. However he had worked this miracle, it was undoubtedly his most impressive achievement. Her transformation was remarkable. My eyes met hers and in their liquid depths I saw a secret smile. On the other hand, Helen McIlwain looked old and drained, her features slack, her hair coarse, her posture slumped. For the first time she seemed to be a woman in middle age. Later I discovered what had harrowed her: she felt defeated by Aster, for she had assumed all along that Vornan regarded her as a kind of consort, and quite clearly that role had passed to Aster. Heyman, too, seemed weakened. The Teutonic heaviness I so disliked was gone from him. He said little, offered no greeting, and appeared remote, distracted, dislocated. He reminded me of Lloyd Kolff in his final weeks. Prolonged exposure to Vornan obviously had its dangers. Even Kralick, tough and resilient, looked badly overextended. His hand was shaking as he held it toward mine, and the fingers splayed apart from one another, requiring of him a conscious effort to unite them.

On the surface, though, the reunion was a pleasant one. Nothing was said about any strains that might have developed, nor about the apostasy of the odious Fields. I rode with Vornan in a motorcade to downtown San Francisco, and cheering multitudes lined the route, occasionally blocking it, just as though someone of the highest importance had arrived.

We resumed the interrupted tour.

Vornan had by now seen about as much of the United States as was deemed a representative sample, and the itinerary called for him to go abroad. Theoretically the responsibility of our Government should have ended at that point. We had not shepherded Vornan about in the earliest days of his visit to the twentieth century, when he had been exploring (and demoralizing) the capitals of Europe; we should have handed him on to others now that he was moving westward. But responsibilities have a way of institutionalizing themselves. Sandy Kralick was stuck with the job of conveying Vornan from place to place, for he was the world's leading authority on that chore; and Aster, Helen, Heyman and myself were swept along in Vornan's orbit. I did not object. I was blatantly eager to escape from the need to confront my own work.

So we traveled. We headed into Mexico, toured the dead cities of Chichén Itzá and Uxmal, prowled Mayan pyramids at midnight, and cut over to Mexico City for a view of the hemisphere's most vibrant metropolis. Vornan took it all in quietly. His chastened mood, first in evidence in the spring, had remained with him here at the end of summer. No longer did he commit verbal outrages, no longer did he utter unpredictably scabrous comments, no longer could he be depended on to upset any plan or program in which he was involved. His actions seemed perfunctory and spasmodic now. He did not bother to infuriate us. I wondered why. Was he sick? His smile was as dazzling as ever, but there was no vitality behind it; he was all façade, now. He was going through the idle motions of a global tour and responding in a purely mechanical way to all he saw. Kralick seemed concerned. He, too, preferred Vornan the demon to Vornan the automaton, and wondered why the animation had gone out of him.

I spent a good deal of time with Vornan as we whirled westward from Mexico City to Hawaii, and on from there to Tokyo, Peking, Angkor, Melbourne, Tahiti, and Antarctica. I had not entirely given up my hope of getting hard information from him on the scientific points that were of concern to me; but although I failed in that, I learned a bit more about Vornan himself. I discovered why he was so flaccid these days.

He had lost interest in us.

We bored him. Our passions, our monuments, our foolishnesses, our cities, our foods, our conflicts, our neuroses—he had sampled everything, and the taste had palled. He was, he confessed to me, deathly weary of being hauled to and fro on the face of our world.

"Why don't you go back to your own time, then?" I asked.

"Not yet, Leo."

"But if we're so tiresome to you—"

"I think I'll stay, anyhow. I can endure the boredom a while longer. I want to see how things turn out."

"What things?"

"Things," he said.

I repeated this to Kralick, who merely shrugged. "Let's hope he sees how things turn out fast," Kralick said. "He's not the only one who's tired of traveling around."

The pace of our journey was stepped up, as though Kralick wished to sicken Vornan thoroughly of the twentieth century. Sights and textures blurred and swirled; we zigzagged out of the white wastes of the Antarctic into the tropic swelter of Ceylon, and darted through India and the Near East, went by felucca up the Nile, trekked into the heart of Africa, sped from one shining capital to the next. Wherever we went, even in the most backward countries, the reception was a frenzied one. Thousands turned out to hail the visiting deity. By now—it was nearly October—the message of *The Newest Revelation* had had time to sink in. Fields' analogies were transformed into assertions; there was no Vornanite Church in any formal sense, but quite plainly the unfocused mass hysteria was coalescing into a religious movement.

My fears that Vornan would try to take hold of this movement proved unfounded. The crowds bored him as much as laboratories and power plants now did. From enclosed balconies he hailed the roaring throngs like a Caesar, with upraised palm; but I did not fail to notice the flicker of the nostrils, the barely suppressed yawn. "What do they want from me?" he asked, almost petulantly.

"They want to love you," Helen said.

"But why? Are they so empty?"

"Terribly empty," Helen murmured.

Heyman said distantly, "If you went among them, you'd feel their love."

Vornan seemed to shiver. "It would be unwise. They would destroy me with their love."

I remembered Vornan in Los Angeles six months before, gleefully plunging into a mad mob of Apocalyptists. He had shown no dread of their desperate energies then. True, he had been masked, but the risks had still been great. The image of Vornan with a pile of stunned cultists forming a living barricade came to me. What joy he had felt in the midst of that chaos! Now he feared the love of the mobs that yearned for him. This was a new Vornan, then, a cautious one. Perhaps at last he was aware of the forces he had helped to unleash, and had grown more serious in his appraisal of danger. That freewheeling Vornan of the early days was gone.

In mid-October we were in Johannesburg, scheduled to hop the Atlantic for a tour of South America. South America was primed and ready for him. The first signs of organized Vornanism were appearing there: in Brazil and Argentina there had been prayer meetings attended by thousands; and we heard that churches were being founded, though the details were fragmentary and uninformative. Vornan showed no curiosity about this development. Instead he turned to me suddenly late one afternoon and said, "I wish to rest for a while, Leo."

"To take a nap?"

"No, to rest from traveling. The crowds, the noise, the excitement—I have had enough. I want quietness now."

"You'd better talk to Kralick."

"First I must talk to you. Some weeks ago, Leo, you spoke to me of friends of yours in a quiet place. A man and a woman, a former pupil of yours, do you know the ones I mean?"

I knew. I went rigid. In an idle moment I had told Vornan about Jack and Shirley, about the pleasure it gave me to flee to them at times of internal crisis or fatigue. In telling him, I had hoped to draw from him some parallel declaration, some detail of his own habits and relationships in that world of the future that seemed yet so unreal to me. But I had not anticipated *this*.

"Yes," I said tensely. "I know who you mean."

"Perhaps we could go there together, Leo. You and I, and these two people, without the others, without the guards, the noise, the crowds. We could quietly disappear. I must renew my energies. This trip has been a strain for me, you know. And I want to see people of this era in day-to-day life. What I have seen so far has been a show, a pageant. But just to sit quietly and talk—I would like it very much. Could you arrange it for me, Leo?"

I was taken off balance. The sudden warmth of Vornan's appeal disarmed me; and automatically I found myself calculating that we might learn much about Vornan this way, yes, that Jack, Shirley, and I, sipping cocktails in the Arizona sunlight, might pry from the visitor facts that had remained concealed during his highly public progress around the world. I was aware of what we might try to get from Vornan; and deluded by the undemanding Vornan of recent months, I failed to take into account what Vornan might try to get from us. "I'll talk to my friends," I promised. "And to Kralick. I'll see what I can do about it, Vornan."

Sixteen

Kralick was bothered at first by the disruption of the carefully balanced itinerary; South America, he said, would be very disappointed to learn that Vornan's arrival would be postponed. But the positive aspects of the scheme were apparent to him as well. He thought it might be useful to get Vornan-19 off into a different kind of environment, away from the crowds and the cameras. I think he welcomed the chance to escape from Vornan for a while himself. In the end he approved the proposal.

Then I called Jack and Shirley.

I felt hesitant about dropping Vornan on them, even though they had both begged me to arrange something like this. Jack was desperately eager to talk to Vornan about total conversion of energy, though I knew he'd learn nothing. And Shirley... Shirley had confessed to me that she was physically drawn to the man from 2999. It was for her sake that I hesitated. Then I told myself that whatever Shirley might feel toward Vornan was something for Shirley herself to resolve, and that if anything happened between Shirley and Vornan, it would be only with Jack's consent and blessing. In which case I did not have to feel responsible.

When I told them what had been proposed, they both

thought I was joking. I had to work hard to persuade them that I really could bring Vornan to them. At length they decided to believe me, and I saw them exchange offscreen glances; then Jack said, "How soon is this going to come about?"

"Tomorrow, if you're ready for it."

"Why not?" Shirley said.

I searched her face for a betrayal of her desire. But I saw nothing except simple excitement.

"Why not?" Jack agreed. "But tell me this: is the place going to be overrun by reporters and policemen? I won't put up with that."

"No," I said. "Vornan's whereabouts are going to be kept secret from the press. There won't be a media man in sight. And I suppose the access roads to your place will be guarded, just in case, but you won't be bothered with security people. I'll make sure they stay far away."

"All right," Jack said. "Bring him, then."

Kralick had the South American trip postponed, and announced that Vornan was going to an undisclosed place for a private holiday of indeterminate length. We let it leak out that he would be vacationing at a villa somewhere in the Indian Ocean. Amid great show of significance, a private plane left Johannesburg the next morning bound for the island of Mauritius. It sufficed to keep the press baffled and misled. A little later that morning Vornan and I boarded a small jet and headed across the Atlantic. We changed planes in Tampa and were in Tucson by early afternoon. A car was waiting there. I told the Government chauffeur to get lost, and drove down to Jack and Shirley's place myself. Kralick, I knew, had spread a surveillance net in a fifty-mile radius around the house, but he had agreed not to let any of his men come closer unless I requested help. We would be undisturbed. It was a flawless late-autumn afternoon, the sky sharp and flat, free of clouds, the taut blueness practically vibrating. The mountains seemed unusually distinct. As I drove, I noticed the occasional golden gleam of a Government copter high overhead. They were watching us . . . from a distance.

Shirley and Jack were in front of the house when we drove up. Jack wore a ragged shirt and faded jeans; Shirley was dressed in a skimpy halter and shorts. I had not seen them since the spring, and I had spoken to them only a few times. It struck me that the tensions I had observed in them in the spring had continued to erode them over the succeeding months. They both looked edgy, coiled, compressed, in a way that could not altogether be credited to the arrival of their celebrated guest.

"This is Vornan-19," I said. "Jack Bryant. Shirley."

"Such a pleasure," Vornan said gravely. He did not offer his hand, but bowed in an almost Japanese way, first to Jack, then to Shirley. An awkward silence followed. We stood staring at each other under the harsh sun. Shirley and Jack behaved almost as though they had never believed in Vornan's existence until this moment; they seemed to regard him as some fictional character unexpectedly conjured into life. Jack clamped his lips together so firmly that his cheeks throbbed. Shirley, never taking her eyes from Vornan, rocked back and forth on the balls of her bare feet. Vornan, self-contained and affable, studied the house, its environment, and its occupants with cool curiosity.

"Let me show you to your room," Shirley blurted.

I fetched the luggage: a suitcase apiece for Vornan and myself. My own grip was nearly empty, holding nothing more than a few changes of clothing; but I had to struggle to lift Vornan's. Naked he had come into this world, but he had accumulated a good deal on his travels: clothing, knickknacks, a random miscellany. I hauled it into the house. Shirley had given Vornan the room I usually occupied, and a storage room near the sundeck had been hastily converted into an auxiliary guest room for me. That seemed quite proper. I set his suitcase down, and left Shirley with him to instruct him in the use of the household appliances. Jack took me to my own room.

I said, "I want you to realize, Jack, that this visit can be ended at any time. If Vornan gets to be too much for you, just say the word and we'll pull out. I don't want you going to any trouble on his account."

"That's all right. I think this is going to be interesting, Leo."

"No doubt. But it might also be strenuous."

He smiled fitfully. "Will I get a chance to talk to him?"

"Of course."

"You know about what."

"Yes. Talk all you like. There won't be much else to do. But you won't get anywhere, Jack."

"I can try, at least." In a low voice he added, "He's shorter than I thought he'd be. But impressive. Very impressive. He's got a kind of natural power to dominate, doesn't he?"

"Napoleon was a short man," I reminded him. "Also Hitler."

"Does Vornan know that?"

"He doesn't seem to be much of a student of history," I said, and we both laughed.

A little while later Shirley came out of Vornan's room and encountered me in the hall. I don't think she expected to find me there, for I caught a quick glimpse of her face, and she was wholly without the mask that we wear in front of others. Her eyes, her nostrils, her lips, all revealed raw emotion, churning conflicts. I wondered if Vornan had attempted anything in the five minutes they had been together. Certainly what I saw on Shirley's face was purely sexual, a tide of desire flooding toward the surface. An instant later she realized I was looking at her, and the mask slipped swiftly into place. She smiled nervously. "He's all settled in," she said. "I like him, Leo. You know, I expected him to be cold and forbidding, some kind of robotlike thing. But he's polite and courtly, a real gentleman in his strange way."

"He's quite the charmer, yes."

Telltale points of color lingered in her cheeks. "Do you think it was a mistake for us to say he could come here?"

"Why should it be a mistake?"

She moistened her lips. "There's no telling what might happen. He's beautiful, Leo. He's irresistible."

"Are you afraid of your own desires?"

"I'm afraid of hurting Jack."

"Then don't do anything without Jack's consent," I said, feeling more than ever like an uncle. "It's that simple. Don't get carried away."

"What if I do, Leo? When I was in the room with him—I saw him *looking* at me so hungrily—"

"He looks at all beautiful women that way. But surely you know how to say no, Shirley."

"I'm not sure I'd want to say no."

I shrugged. "Should I call Kralick and say that we'd like to leave?"

"No!"

"Then you'll have to be the watchdog of your own chastity, I'm afraid. You're an adult, Shirley. You ought to be able to keep from sleeping with your house guest if you think it would be unwise. That's never been much of a problem for you before."

She recoiled, startled, at my gratuitous final words. Her face crimsoned again beneath the deep tan. She peered at me as if she had never seen me in clear focus before. I felt angry at myself for my foolishness. In one breath I had cheapened a decade-long relationship. But the taut moment passed. Shirley relaxed as though going through a series of inner exercises, and said at last in a calm voice, "You're right, Leo. It won't really be a problem."

The evening was surprisingly free from tension. Shirley produced a magnificent meal, and Vornan was lavish in his praise; it was, he said, the first dinner he had eaten in anyone's home, and he was delighted by it. Afterwards we strolled together at twilight. Jack walked beside Vornan, and I with Shirley, but we stayed close to one another. Jack pointed out a kangaroo rat that had emerged from hiding a little early and went hopping madly over the desert. We saw a few jackrabbits and some lizards. It forever astonished Vornan that wild animals should be on the loose. Later, we returned to the house for drinks, and sat pleasantly like four old friends, talking of nothing in particular. Vornan seemed to accommodate himself perfectly to the personalities of his hosts. I began to think that I had been uneasy over nothing.

The curious tranquility continued for several days more. We slept late, explored the desert, reveled in eighty-degree heat, talked, ate, peered at the stars. Vornan was restrained and almost cautious. Yet he spoke more of his own time here than was usual for him. Pointing to the stars, he tried to describe the constellations he knew, but he failed to find any, not even the Dipper. He talked of food taboos and how daring it would be for him to sit at a table with his hosts in a parallel situation in 2999. He reminisced lazily about his ten months among us, like a traveler who is close to the end of his journey and beginning to look back at remembered pleasures.

We were careful not to tune in on any news broadcasts while Vornan was around. I did not want him to know that there had been riots of disappointment in South America over the postponement of his visit, nor that a kind of Vornan-hysteria was sweeping the world, with folk everywhere looking toward the visitor for all the answers to the riddles of the universe. In his past pronouncements Vornan had smugly let it be known that he would eventually supply all the answers to everything, and this promissory note seemed to be infinitely negotiable, even though in fact Vornan had raised more questions than answers. It was good to keep him in isolation here, far from the nodes of control that he might so easily seize.

On the fourth morning we woke to brilliant sunlight. I cut out my window-opaquers and found Vornan already on the sundeck. He was nude, stretched cozily in a webfoam cradle, basking in the brightness. I tapped on the window. He looked up, saw me, smiled. I stepped outside just as he rose from the cradle. His sleek, smooth body might almost have been made of some seamless plastic substance; his skin was without blemish and he had no body hair whatever. He was neither muscular nor flabby, and seemed simultaneously frail and powerful. I know that sounds paradoxical. He was also formidably male. "It's wonderfully warm out here, Leo," he said. "Take off your clothes and join me."

I held back. I had not told Vornan of the free-and-easy nudism of my earlier visits to this house; and thus far all the proprieties had been carefully observed. But of course Vornan had no nudity taboos; and now that he had made the first move, Shirley was quick to follow. She emerged on the deck, saw Vornan bare and myself clad in nightclothes, and said smilingly, "Yes, that's quite all right. I meant to suggest that yesterday. We aren't foolish about our bodies here." And having made that declaration of liberalism, she stripped away the flimsy wrap she had been wearing and lay down to enjoy the sun. Vornan watched in what struck me as remarkably aloof curiosity as Shirley revealed her supple, magnificently endowed body. He seemed interested, but only in a theoretical way. This was not the ravenously wolfish Vornan I knew. Shirley, though, betrayed profound inner discomfort. A flush swept nearly to the base of her throat. Her movements were exaggeratedly casual. Her eyes strayed guiltily to Vornan's loins a moment, then quickly pulled away. Her nipples gave her away, rising in sudden excitement. She knew it, and hastily rolled over to lie on her belly, but not before I had noticed the effect. When Shirley and Jack and I had sunbathed together, it had been as innocent as in Eden; but the stiffening of those two nubs of erectile tissue bluntly advertised how she felt about being nude in front of a nude Vornan.

Jack appeared a while later. He took in the situation with

an amused glance: Shirley sprawled out with upturned buttocks, Vornan peeled and dozing, I pacing the sundeck in distress. "A beautiful day," he said, a little too enthusiastically. He was wearing shorts and he kept them on. "Shall I get breakfast, Shirl?"

Neither Shirley nor Vornan bothered to get dressed at all that morning. She seemed determined to achieve the same informality that had been the hallmark of my visits here; and after her first moments of confusion, she did indeed subside into a more natural acceptance of the situation. Oddly, Vornan appeared to be totally indifferent to her body. That was apparent to me long before Shirley realized it. Her little coquettishnesses, her deftly subtle movements, flexing a shapely thigh or inflating her rib cage to send her breasts rising, were wholly lost on him. Since he evidently came from a culture where nudity among near-strangers was nothing remarkable, that was not too strange—except that Vornan's attitude toward women had always been so predatory in the past months, and it was mysterious that he so conspicuously did not respond to Shirley's loveliness.

I got down to the buff too. Why not? It was comfortable, and it was the mode. But I found I could not relax. In the past I had not been aware that sunbathing with Shirley generated any obvious tension within me. Now, though, such a torrent of yearning roared through me at times that I became dizzy and had to grip the rail of the sundeck and look away.

Jack's behavior also was odd. Nakedness was wholly natural to him here, but he kept his shorts on for a full day and a half after Vornan had precipitated the rest of us into stripping. He was almost defiant about it—working in the garden, hacking at a bush in need of pruning, sweat rolling down his broad back and staining the waistband of his shorts. Shirley asked him, finally, why he was being so modest. "I don't know," he said strangely. "I hadn't noticed it." He kept the shorts on.

Vornan looked up and said, "It is not on my account, is it?" Jack laughed. He touched the snap of his shorts and wriggled out of them, chastely turning his back to us. Though he went without them thereafter, he appeared markedly unhappy about it.

Jack seemed captivated by Vornan. They talked long and earnestly over drinks; Vornan listened thoughtfully, saying something now and then, while Jack unreeled a strand of words. I paid little attention to these discussions. They talked of politics, time travel, energy conversion, and many other things, each conversation quickly becoming a monologue. I wondered why Vornan was so patient, but of course there was little else to do here. After a while I withdrew into myself and simply lay in the sun, resting. I realized that I was terribly tired. This year had been a formidable drain on me. I dozed. I basked. I sipped flasks of cooling drinks. And I let destruction enfold my dearest friends without remotely sensing the pattern of events.

I did see the vague discontent rising in Shirley. She felt ignored and rebuffed, and even I could understand why. She wanted Vornan. And Vornan, who had commandeered so many dozens of women, treated her with glacial respect. As if belatedly embracing bourgeois morality, Vornan declined to enter any of Shirley's gambits, backing away with just the right degree of tact. Had someone told him that it was improper to seduce the wife of one's host? Propriety had never troubled Vornan in the past. I could credit his miraculous display of continence now only to his streak of innate mischief. He would take a woman to bed out of impishness—as with Aster, say—but now it amused him to thwart Shirley simply because she was beautiful and bare and obviously available. It was, I thought, an outburst of the devilish old Vornan, the deliberate thumber of the nose.

Shirley grew almost desperate about it. Her clumsiness offended me, the involuntary witness. I saw her sidle up beside Vornan to press the firmness of a breast into his back as she pretended to reach for his discarded drinkflask; I saw her invite him brazenly with her eyes; I saw her stretch out in carefully wanton postures that she had always instinctively avoided in the past. None of it did any good. Perhaps if she had entered Vornan's bedroom in the dark hours and thrown herself upon him, she would have had what she wanted from him, but her pride would not let her go quite that far. And so she grew coarse and shoddy with frustration. Her ugly shrill giggle returned. She made remarks to Jack or to Vornan or to me that revealed scarcely hidden hostilities. She spilled things and dropped things. The effect of all this on me was a depressing one, for I too had shown tact with Shirley, not just over a few days but across a decade; I had resisted temptation, I had denied myself the forbidden pleasure of taking my friend's wife. She had never offered herself to me the way she now offered herself to Vornan. I did not enjoy the sight of her this way, nor did I find pleasure in the ironies of the situation.

Jack was totally unaware of his wife's torment. His fascination with Vornan left him no opportunity to observe what was taking place about him. In his desert isolation Jack had had no chance in years to make new friends, and little enough contact with his old ones. Now he took to Vornan precisely as a lonely boy would take to some odd newcomer on his block. I choose that simile deliberately; there was something adolescent or even subadolescent about Jack's surrender to Vornan. He talked endlessly, delineating himself against the background of his University career, describing the reasons for his desert withdrawal, even taking Vornan down into that workshop I had never entered, where he showed the guest the secret manuscript of his autobiography. No matter how intimate the subject, Jack spoke freely, like a child hauling out his most prized toys to display. He was buying Vornan's attention with a frantic effort. Jack appeared to regard Vornan as a chum. I who had always thought of Vornan as unutterably alien, who had come to accept him as genuine largely because he inspired such mysterious dread in me, found it bewildering to see Jack succumbing this way. Vornan seemed pleased and amused. Occasionally they disappeared into the workshop for several hours at a time. I told myself that this was all some ploy on Jack's part to wangle from Vornan the information he desired. It was clever of Jack, was it not, to construct so intense a relationship for the sake of picking Vornan's mind?

But Jack got no information from Vornan. And in my blindness I was aware of nothing.

How could I have failed to see it? That look of bemused and dreamy confusion that Jack wore much of the time now? The moments when his eyes dropped and he turned away from Shirley or from me, cheeks glowing in unknown embarrassments? Even when I saw Vornan slip his hand possessively onto Jack's bare shoulder, I remained blind.

Shirley and I spent more time together in those days than on any previous visit, for Jack and Vornan were forever off by themselves. I did not take advantage of my opportunity. We said little, but lay side by side, baking in the sun; Shirley seemed so taut and keyed up that I scarcely knew what to say to her, and so I kept silent. Arizona was gripped by an autumn heat wave. Warmth came boiling out of Mexico toward us, making us sluggish. Shirley's bare skin gleamed like fine bronze. The fatigue washed from me. Several times Shirley seemed about to speak, and the words died in her throat. A fabric of tension took form. In a subliminal way I felt trouble in the air, the way one feels a summer storm coming on. But I had no idea what was awry; I hovered in a cocoon of heat, detecting uncertain emanations of impending cataclysm, and not until the actual moment of disaster did I grasp the truth of the situation.

It happened on the twelfth day of our visit. We were only a day short of November, now, but the unseasonal warmth was staying on; at noon the sun was like a blazing eye whose fiery stare was impossible to meet, and I could not remain outdoors. I excused myself from Shirley—Jack and Vornan were nowhere about—and went to my room. As I opaqued the window, I paused to peer out at Shirley, lying torpid on the sundeck, eyes shielded, her left knee drawn up, her breasts slowly rising and falling, her skin glistening with sweat. She was the image of total relaxation, I thought, the languid beautiful woman drowsing in the heat of noon. And then I caught sight of her left hand, fiercely clenched, so tightly fisted that it trembled at the wrist and muscles throbbed the length of her arm; and I understood that her pose was a conscious counterfeit of tranquility, maintained by sheer force of will.

I darkened the room and stretched out on my bed. The cool indoor air was refreshing. Perhaps I slept. My eyes opened when I heard the sound of someone at my door. I sat up.

Shirley rushed in. She looked wild: eyes glaring in horror, lips drawn back, breasts heaving. Her face was crimson. Bright beads of sweat, I saw with curious clarity, covered her skin, and there was a shining rivulet in the valley of her bosom. "Leo—" she said in a rusty choking voice. "Oh, God, Leo!"

"What is it? What happened?"

She stumbled across the room and sagged forward, her knees against my mattress. She seemed almost in a state of shock. Her jaws worked, but no words came forth.

"Shirley!"

"Yes," she muttered. "Yes, Jack—Vornan—oh, Leo, I was right about them! I didn't want to believe it, but I was right. I saw them! I saw them!"

"What are you talking about?"

"It was time for lunch," she said, gulping for calm. "I woke up on the sundeck and went looking for them. They were in Jack's workshop, as usual. They didn't answer when I knocked, and I pushed the door open, and then I saw why they hadn't answered. They were busy. With each other. With... each ... other. Arms and legs all over each other. I saw. I stood there maybe half a minute watching it. Oh, Leo, Leo, Leo!"

Her voice rose to a piercing shriek. She flung herself forward in despair, sobbing, shattered. I caught her as she lurched into me. The heavy globes of her breasts pressed with tips of flame against my cool skin. In the eye of my mind I could see the scene she had described for me; now the obviousness of it all struck me, and I gasped at my own stupidity, at Vornan's callousness, and at Jack's innocence. I squirmed as I pictured for myself Vornan wrapped about him like some giant predatory invertebrate, and then there was no time for further thought. Shirley was in my arms, trembling and bare and sweat-sticky and weeping. I comforted her and she clung to me, looking only for an island of stability in a suddenly quaking world; and the embrace of comfort that I offered her rapidly became something quite different. I could not control myself, and she did not resist, but rather she welcomed my invasion in relief or out of revenge, and at long last my body pierced hers and we fell joined and heaving to the pillow.

Seventeen

I had Kralick get Vornan and me out of there hours later. I did not explain anything to anyone. I merely said that it was necessary for us to leave. There were no farewells. We dressed and packed, and I drove with Vornan to Tucson, where Kralick's men picked us up.

Looking back, I see how panicky my flight was. Perhaps I should have stayed with them. Perhaps I should have tried to help them rebuild themselves. But in that chaotic instant I felt I had to flee. The atmosphere of guilt was too stifling; the texture of interwoven shames was too tight. What had taken place between Vornan and Jack and what had taken place between Shirley and me were inextricably bound into the fabric of the catastrophe, as for that matter was what had not taken place between Shirley and Vornan. And I had brought the serpent among them. In the moment of crisis I had forfeited any moral advantage I might have had by yielding to my impulse and then by running away. I was the guilty one. I was responsible.

I may never see either of them again.

I know too much of their secret shame, and like one who has stumbled upon a file of yellowed correspondence belonging to some dear one, I feel that my unwanted knowledge falls now as a sword holding me apart from them. That may change. Already, nearly two months later, I see the episode in a different light. We all managed to look equally ugly and equally weak at once, all three of us, puppets spun about by Vornan's artfully constructed whim; and that shared knowledge of our frailty may draw us together. I don't know. I do know, though, that whatever Shirley and Jack had shared only with each other lies broken and trampled and beyond repair.

A montage of faces comes to me: Shirley flushed and dizzied in the grip of passion, eyes closed, mouth gaping. Shirley sickened and sullen afterward, slumping to the floor, crawling away from me like an injured insect. Jack coming up from the workshop, dazed and pale as if he had been the victim of a rape, walking carefully through a world made unreal. And Vornan looking complacent, cheerfully replete, quite satisfied with his work and even more pleased to discover what Shirley and I had done. I could not feel real anger toward him. He was still as much a beast of prey as ever, and had renounced nothing. He had rebuffed Shirley not out of some excess of conventionality but only because he was stalking a different quarry.

To Kralick I said nothing. He could tell that the Arizona interlude had been a disaster, but I gave him no details, and he pressed for none. We met in Phoenix; he had flown there from Washington when he got my message. The trip to South America, he said, had been hastily reinstated and we were due in Caracas the following Tuesday.

"Count me out," I said. "I've had enough of Vornan. I'm resigning from the committee, Sandy."

"Don't."

"I have to. It's a personal matter. I've given you close to a year, but now I've got to pick up the pieces of my own life."

"Give us one month more," he pleaded. "It's important. Have you been following the news, Leo?"

"Now and then."

"The world is in the grip of a Vornan mania. It gets worse each day. Those two weeks or so he was off in the desert only inflamed it. Do you know, a false Vornan showed up in Buenos Aires on Sunday and proclaimed a Latin American empire? In just fifteen minutes he collected a mob of fifty thousand. The damage ran into the millions, and it could have been worse if a sniper hadn't shot him."

"*Shot* him? What for?"

Kralick shook his head. "Who knows? It was pure hysteria. The crowd tore the assassin to pieces. It took two days to convince everyone that it had been a fake Vornan. And then we've heard rumors of false Vornana in Karachi, Istanbul, Peking, Oslo. It's that foul book Fields wrote. I could flay him."

"What does this have to do with me, Sandy?"

"I need to have you beside Vornan. You've spent more time with him than anyone else. You know him well, and I think he knows you and trusts you. It may not be possible for anyone else to control him."

"I have no way of controlling him," I said, thinking of Jack and Shirley. "Isn't that obvious by now?"

"But at least with you we have a chance. Leo, if Vornan ever harnesses the power that's at his command, he'll turn this world upside down. At a word from him, fifty million people would cut their own throats. You've been out of touch. You can't comprehend how this is building. Maybe you can head him off if he starts to realize his own potential."

"The way I headed him off when he wrecked Wesley Bruton's villa, eh?"

"That was early in the game. We know better now, we don't let Vornan near dangerous equipment. And what he did to Bruton's place is just a sample of what he can do to the whole world."

I laughed harshly. "In that case, why take risks? Have him killed."

"For God's sake, Leo—"

"I mean it. There are ways of arranging it. A big, clever Government bastard like you doesn't need instructions in

Machiavellianism. Get rid of Vornan while you still can, before he sets himself up as Emperor Vornan with a bodyguard of ten thousand. You take care of it and let me go back to my laboratory, Sandy."

"Be serious. How—"

"I *am* serious. If you don't want to assassinate him, try persuading him to go back where he belongs."

"We can't do that either."

"What *are* you going to do, then?"

"I told you," said Kralick patiently. "Keep him on tour until he gets sick of it. Watch him all the time. Make sure he stays happy. Feed him all the women he can handle."

"And men too," I put in.

"Little boys, if we have to. We're sitting on a megabomb, Leo, and we're trying like hell to keep it from exploding. If you want to walk out on us at this point, go ahead. But when the explosion comes, you're likely to feel it even in your ivory tower. What's the answer now?"

"I'll stick," I said bitterly.

So I rejoined the traveling circus, and so it was that I was on hand for the final events of Vornan's story. I had not expected Kralick to succeed in talking me into it. I had for at least a few hours believed I was quit of Vornan, whom I did not hate for what he had done to my friends, but whom I regarded as an ultimate peril. I had been quite serious in suggesting that Kralick have him destroyed. Now I found myself committed to accompany him once more; but now I chose to keep my distance from him even when I was with him, stifling the good fellowship that had begun to develop. Vornan knew why. I'm sure of that. He did not seem troubled by my new coolness toward him.

The crowds were immense. We had seen howling mobs before, but we had never seen mobs howling like these. At Caracas they estimated one hundred thousand turned out—all that could squeeze into the big downtown plaza—and we stared in amazement as they bellowed their delight in Spanish. Vornan appeared on a balcony to greet them; it was like a Pope delivering his blessing. They screamed for him to make a speech. We had no facilities for it, though, and Vornan merely smiled and waved. The sea of red-covered books churned madly. I did not know if they waved *The New Revelation* or *The Newest Revelation*, but it scarcely mattered.

He was interviewed that night on Venezuelan television.

The network rigged a simultaneous-translation channel, for Vornan knew no Spanish. What message, he was asked, did he have for the people of Venezuela? "The world is pure and wonderful and beautiful," Vornan replied solemnly. "Life is holy. You can shape a paradise while you yet live." I was astonished. These pieties were out of character for our mischievous friend, unless this was the sign of some new malice in the making.

The crowds were even greater in Bogotá. Shrill cries echoed through the thin air of the plateau. Vornan spoke again, and again it was a sermon of platitudes. Kralick was worried. "He's warming up for something," he said to me. "He's never talked like this before. He's making a real effort to reach them directly, instead of letting them come to him."

"Call off the tour, then," I suggested.

"We can't. We're committed."

"Forbid him to make speeches."

"How?" he asked, and there was no answer.

Vornan himself seemed fascinated by the size of the throngs that came out to see him. These were no mere knots of curiosity seekers; these were giant hordes who knew that a strange god walked the earth, and longed for a glimpse. Clearly he felt his power over them now, and was beginning to exert it. I noticed, though, that he no longer exposed himself physically to the mobs. He seemed to fear harm, and drew back, keeping to balconies and within sealed cars.

"They're crying for you to come down and walk among them," I told him as we faced a roaring multitude in Lima. "Can't you hear it, Vornan?"

"I wish I could do it," he said.

"There's nothing stopping you."

"Yes. Yes. There are so many of them. There would be a stampede."

"Put on a crowd shield," Helen McIlwain suggested.

Vornan swung around. "What is that, please?"

"Politicians wear them. A crowd shield is an electronic sphere of force that surrounds the wearer. It's designed specifically to protect public figures in mobs. If anyone gets too close, the shield delivers a mild shock. You'd be perfectly safe, Vornan."

To Kralick he said, "Is this so? Can you get me such a shield?"

"I think it can be arranged," Kralick said.

The next day, in Buenos Aires, the American Embassy delivered a shield to us. It had last been used by the President on his Latin American tour. An Embassy official demonstrated it, strapping on the electrodes, taping the power pack to his chest. "Try and come near me," he said, beckoning. "Cluster around."

We approached him. A gentle amber glow enveloped him. We pushed forward, and abruptly we began to strike an impenetrable barrier. There was nothing painful about the sensation, but in its subtle way it was thoroughly effective; we were thrown back, and it was impossible to come within three feet of the wearer. Vornan looked delighted. "Let me try it," he said. The Embassy man put it on him and instructed him in its use. Vornan laughed and said, "All of you, crowd around me, now. Shove and push. Harder! Harder!" There was no touching him. Pleased, Vornan said, "Good. Now I can go among my people."

Quietly, later, I said to Kralick, "Why did you let him have that thing?"

"He asked for it."

"You could have told him they didn't work well or something like that, Sandy. Isn't there a possibility that the shield will conk out at a critical moment?"

"Not normally," Kralick said. He picked up the shield, uncoiled it, and snapped back the panel to the rear of the power pack. "There's only one weak spot in the circuitry, and that's here, this integrated module. You can't see it, really. It's got a tendency to overload under certain circumstances and degenerate, causing a shield failure. But there's a redundancy circuit that automatically cuts in, Leo, and takes over within a couple of microseconds. Actually there's only one way a crowd shield can fail, and that's if it's deliberately sabotaged. Say, if someone jimmies the back-up circuit, and then the main module overloads. But I don't know anyone who'd do a thing like that."

"Except Vornan, perhaps."

"Well, yes. Vornan's capable of anything. But I hardly think he'll want to play around with his own shield. For all intents he'll be wholly safe wearing the shield."

"Well, then," I said, "aren't you afraid of what will happen now that he can get out among the mobs and really lay the charisma on?"

"Yes," said Kralick.

Buenos Aires was the scene of the greatest excitement over Vornan we had yet experienced. This was the city where a false Vornan had arisen, and the presence of the real one was electric to the Argentines. The broad, tree-lined Avenida 9 de Julio was packed from end to end, with only the obelisk in its center puncturing the mass of flesh. Through this chaotic, surging mob moved Vornan's cavalcade. Vornan wore his crowd shield; the rest of us were not so protected, and huddled nervously within our armored vehicles. From time to time Vornan leaped out and strode into the crowd. The shield worked—no one could get close to him—but the mere fact that he was among them sent the crowd into ecstasies. They pushed up close, coming to the absolute limit of the electronic barrier and flattening themselves against it, while Vornan beamed and smiled and bowed. I said to Kralick, "We're becoming accomplices to the madness. We should never have let this happen."

Kralick gave me a crooked grin and told me to relax. But I could not relax. That night Vornan again allowed himself to be interviewed, and what he said was bluntly utopian. The world was badly in need of reform; too much power had concentrated in too few hands; an era of universal affluence was imminent, but it would take the cooperation of the enlightened masses to bring it about. "We were born from trash," he said, "but we have the capacity to become gods. I know it can be done. In my time there is no disease, there is no poverty, there is no suffering. Death itself has been abolished. But must mankind wait a thousand years to enjoy these benefits? You must act now. *Now.*"

It seemed like a call to revolution.

As yet Vornan had put forth no specific program. He was uttering only generalized calls for a transformation of our society. But even that was far beyond the sly, oblique, flippant remarks he had customarily made in the early months of his stay. It was as if his capacity for troublemaking had been greatly enlarged; he recognized now that he could stir up infinitely more mischief by addressing himself to the mobs in the street than by poking fun at selected individuals. Kralick seemed as aware of this as I was; I did not understand why he allowed the tour to continue, why he saw to it that Vornan had access to communications channels. He seemed helpless to halt the course of events, helpless to interrupt the revolution that he himself had served to manufacture.

Of Vornan's motives we knew nothing. On the second day in Buenos Aires he again went into the throng. This time the mob was far greater than on the day before, and in a kind of obstinate insistence they surrounded Vornan, trying desperately to reach and touch him. We had to get him out of there, finally, with a scoop lowered from a copter. He was pale and shaken as he rid himself of the crowd shield. I had never seen Vornan look rattled before, but this crowd had done it. He eyed the shield skeptically and said, "Possibly there are dangers in this. How trustworthy is the shield?"

Kralick assured him that it was loaded with redundancy features that made it foolproof. Vornan looked doubtful. He turned away, trying to compose himself; it was actually refreshing to see a symptom of fear in him. I could hardly fault him for fearing that crowd, even with a shield.

We flew from Buenos Aires to Rio de Janeiro in the early hours of November 19. I tried to sleep, but Kralick came to my compartment and woke me. Behind him stood Vornan. In Kralick's hand was the coiled slimness of a crowd shield.

"Put this on," he said.

"What for?"

"So you can learn how to use it. You're going to wear it in Rio."

My lingering sleepiness vanished. "Listen, Sandy, if you think I'm going to expose myself to those crowds—"

"Please," said Vornan. "I want you beside me, Leo."

Kralick said, "Vornan's been feeling uneasy about the size of the mobs for the last few days, and he doesn't want to go down there alone anymore. He asked me if I could get you to accompany him. He wants only you."

"It's true, Leo," Vornan said. "I can't trust the others. With you beside me I'm not afraid."

He was damnably persuasive. One glance, one plea, and I was ready to walk through millions of screaming cultists with him. I told him I'd do as he wished, and he touched his hand to mine and murmured his thanks softly but movingly. Then he went away. The moment he was gone, I saw the lunacy of it; and as Kralick pushed the crowd shield toward me, I shook my head. "I can't," I said. "Get Vornan. Tell him I changed my mind."

"Come on, Leo. Nothing can happen to you."

"If I don't go out there, Vornan doesn't go either?"

"That's correct."

"Then we've solved our problem," I said. "I'll refuse to put the shield on. Vornan won't be able to mingle with the multitudes. We'll cut him off from the source of his power. Isn't that what we want?"

"No."

"No?"

"We want Vornan to be able to reach the people. They love him. They need him. We don't dare deny them their hero."

"Give them their hero, then. But not with me next to him."

"Don't start that again, Leo. You're the one he asked for. If Vornan doesn't make an appearance in Rio, it's going to screw up international relations and God knows what else. We can't risk frustrating that mob by not producing him."

"So I'm thrown to the wolves?"

"The shields are safe, Leo! Come on. Help us out one last time."

The intensity of Kralick's concern was compelling, and in the end I agreed to honor my promise to Vornan. As we rocketed eastward over the dwindling wilderness of the Amazon basin, twenty miles high, Kralick taught me how to use the crowd shield. By the time we began our arc of descent, I was an expert. Vornan was visibly pleased that I had agreed to accompany him. He spoke freely of the excitement he felt in the midst of a throng, and of the power he felt he exerted over those who clustered about him. I listened and said little. I studied him with care, recording in my mind the look of his face, the gleam of his smile, for I had the feeling that his visit to our medieval epoch might soon be drawing to its close.

The crowd at Rio exceeded anything we had seen before. Vornan was scheduled to make a public appearance on the beach; we rolled through the streets of the magnificent city, heading for the sea, and there was no beach in sight, only a sea of heads lining the shore, a jostling, shoving, incredibly dense mob that stretched from the white towers of the oceanfront buildings to the edge of the waves, and even out into the water. We were unable to penetrate that mass, and had to take to the air. By copter we traversed the length of the beach. Vornan glowed with pride. "For me," he said softly. "They come here for me. Where is my speech machine?"

Kralick had furnished him with yet another gadget: a translator, rigged to turn Vornan's words into fluent Portuguese. As we hovered over that forest of dark upraised arms,

Vornan spoke, and his words boomed out into the bright summer air. I cannot vouch for the translation, but the words he used were eloquent and moving. He spoke of the world from which he came, telling of its serenity and harmony, describing its freedom from striving and strife. Each human being, he said, was unique and valued. He contrasted that with our own bleak, harried time. A mob such as he saw beneath him, he said, was inconceivable in his day, for only a shared hunger brings a mob together, and no hunger so clawing could exist there. Why, he asked, did we choose to live this way? Why not rid ourselves of our rigidities and our prides, cast away our dogmas and our idols, hurl down the barriers that fence each human heart? Let every man love his fellow man as a brother. Let false cravings be abolished. Let the desire for power perish. Let a new age of benevolence be ushered in.

These were not new sentiments. Other prophets had offered them. But he spoke with such monstrous sincerity and fervor that he seemed to be minting each sentimental cliché anew. Was this the Vornan who had laughed in the face of the world? Was this the Vornan who had used human beings as toys and tools? This pleading, cajoling, thrilling orator? This saint? I was close to tears myself as I listened to him. And the impact on those down on the beach—those following this on a global network—who could calculate that?

Vornan's mastery was complete. His slim, deceptively boyish figure occupied the center of the world's stage. We were his. With sincerity instead of mockery now his weapon, he had conquered all.

He finished speaking. To me he said, "Now let us go down among them, Leo."

We put on our shields. I was at the edge of terror; and Vornan himself, peering over the lip of the copter's hatch into that swirling madhouse below, seemed to falter a moment and draw back from the descent. But they were waiting. They cried out for him in love-thickened voices. For once the magnetism worked the other way; Vornan was drawn forward.

"Go first," he told me. "Please."

With suicidal bravado I seized the grips and let myself be swung down a hundred feet to the beach. A clearing opened for me. I touched ground and felt shifting sand at my feet. People rushed toward me; then, seeing that I was not their prophet, they halted. Some rebounded from my shield. I felt invulnerable, and my fear ebbed as I saw how the amber glow repelled those who came too close.

Now Vornan was descending. A low roar rumbled from ten thousand throats and rushed up the scale to become an intolerable shriek. They recognized him. He stood beside me, aglow with his own power, proud of himself, swollen with joy. I knew what he was thinking: for a nobody he had done pretty well for himself. It is given to few men to become gods in their own lifetimes.

"Walk beside me," he said.

He lifted his arms and strode slowly forward, majestic, awesome. Like a lesser apostle I accompanied him. No one paid heed to me; but worshipers flung themselves at him, their faces distorted and transfigured, their eyes glassy. None could touch him. The wondrous field turned all away, so that there was not even the impact of collision. We walked ten feet, twenty, thirty. The crowd opened for us, then surged inward again, no one willing to accept the reality of the shield. Protected as I was, I felt the enormous pent-up strength of that mob. Perhaps a million Brazilians surrounded us; perhaps five million. This was Vornan's grandest moment. On, on, on he moved, nodding, smiling, reaching forth his hand, graciously accepting the homage offered.

A gigantic black man stripped to the waist loomed before him, shining with sweat, skin nearly purple. He stood for a moment outlined against the brilliant summer sky. "Vornan!" he shouted in a voice like thunder. "Vornan!" He stretched both his hands toward Vornan—

And seized his arm.

The image is engraved on my mind: that jet-black hand gripping the light-green fabric of Vornan's garment. And Vornan turning, frowning, looking at the hand, suddenly realizing that his shield had ceased to protect him.

"*Leo!*" he screamed.

There was a terrible inward rush. I heard cries of ecstasy. The crowd was going wild.

Before me dangled the grips of the copter's scoop. I seized them and was pulled aloft to safety. I looked down only after climbing aboard; I saw the formless surging of the mob on the beach, and shuddered.

There were several hundred fatalities. No trace of Vornan was ever discovered.

Eighteen

It is over, now, and yet it is just beginning. I do not know if Vornan's disappearance will steady us or destroy us. We may not know that for a while.

I have lived in Rio for six weeks, but in such isolation that I might as well have been on the Moon. When the others left, I remained. My apartment is a small one, just two rooms, not far from the beach where Vornan's final act was played. I have not left my apartment in over a month. My food is delivered through the house data-channel; I take no exercise; I have no friends in this city. I cannot even understand the language.

Since the fifth of December I have occupied myself by dictating this memoir, which shortly will be done. I do not intend to seek publication. I have set down, as accurately as recollection permits, the whole story of Vornan-19's stay among us, and of my involvement with him. I will seal the tape and have it placed in a vault, to be opened in not less than one hundred years. I have no wish to add to the flood of gospels now appearing: perhaps my testimony will be of some use a century hence, but I will not have it employed now to feed the fires that are raging in the world. I wish I could feel confident that by the time someone breaks my seal of silence, all this will have receded into oblivion. But I doubt that that will be the case.

So many ambiguities remain. Did Vornan perish in that mob or did he return to his own time? Was that black giant a courier come to fetch him? Or did Vornan transmit himself into the future at the instant his shield failed? I wonder. And why did the shield fail, anyway? Kralick had sworn that it was proof against all but deliberate sabotage. Did Kralick gimmick the shield out of fear of Vornan's growing power? And did he then use me as the cat's-paw in his conspiracy, persuading me to cooperate so that an uneasy Vornan would agree to put the flawed shield on and go into the crowd? If that is so, I am an accessory after the fact, I who pretend to abhor violence. But I am not sure that Vornan was murdered; I am not even sure that Vornan died. All I know beyond doubt is that he has gone from us.

I think he is dead. We could not risk Vornan's further presence among us. The conspirators who slew Caesar felt they were performing a public service. With Vornan gone, the question remains: can we survive his departure?

We have written the proper climax for the myth. When a young god comes among us, we slay him. Now he surely is dismembered Osiris and murdered Tammuz and lamented Baldur. Now the hour of redemption and resurrection must follow, and I fear it. Vornan alive might have undone himself in time, revealing himself to the world as foolish, vain, ignorant, and amoral, a mingling of peacock and wolf. Vornan gone is another matter. He is beyond our control now that we have martyred him. Those who needed him will wait for his successor, for someone to fill the void now created. I do not think we will lack for successors. We are coming into an age of prophets. We are coming into an era of new gods. We are coming into a century of flame. I fear that I may live to see the Time of Sweeping of which Vornan spoke.

Enough. It is nearly midnight, and tonight is the thirty-first of December. At the stroke the century will turn, for all but the purists. There is revelry in the streets. There is dancing and singing. I hear coarse shouts and the dull boom of fireworks. The sky blazes with light. If there are any Apocalyptists left, they must await the next hour in dread or in bliss, dreaming of approaching doom. It will be the year 2000 before long. The sound of that is strange to me.

It is time to leave my apartment at last. I will go out into the streets, among the crowds, and celebrate the birth of the new year. I need no shield; I am in no danger now, except only the danger in which we all must live. Now the century dies. I will go out.

BORN WITH
THE DEAD

For Brian and Margaret Aldiss,
who live too far away

One

And what the dead had no speech for, when living,
They can tell you, being dead: the communication
Of the dead is tongued with fire beyond the language of
    the living.

                               T.S. Eliot: *Little Gidding*

Supposedly his late wife Sybille was on her way to Zanzibar.
That was what they told him, and he believed it. Jorge Klein
was at that stage in his search when he would believe
anything, if belief would only lead him to Sybille. Anyway, it
wasn't so absurd that she would go to Zanzibar. Sybille had
always wanted to go there. In some unfathomable obsessive
way the place had seized the center of her consciousness long
ago. When she was alive it hadn't been possible for her to go
there, but now, loosed from all bonds, she would be drawn
toward Zanzibar like a bird to its nest, like Ulysses to Ithaca,
like a moth to a flame.

The plane, a small Air Zanzibar Havilland FP-803, took off
more than half empty from Dar es Salaam at 0915 on a mild
bright morning, gaily circled above the dense masses of
mango trees, red-flowering flamboyants, and tall coconut
palms along the aquamarine shores of the Indian Ocean, and
headed northward on the short hop across the strait to
Zanzibar. This day—Tuesday, the ninth of March, 1993—would
be an unusual one for Zanzibar: five deads were aboard the
plane, the first of their kind ever to visit that fragrant isle.
Daud Mahmoud Barwani, the health officer on duty that
morning at Zanzibar's Karume Airport, had been warned of
this by the emigration officials on the mainland. He had no
idea how he was going to handle the situation, and he was
apprehensive: these were tense times in Zanzibar. Times are
always tense in Zanzibar. Should he refuse them entry? Did

203

deads pose any threat to Zanzibar's ever-precarious political stability? What about subtler menaces? Deads might be carriers of dangerous spiritual maladies. Was there anything in the Revised Administrative Code about refusing visas on grounds of suspected contagions of the spirit? Daud Mahmoud Barwani nibbled moodily at his breakfast—a cold chapatti, a mound of cold curried potato—and waited without eagerness for the arrival of the deads.

Almost two and a half years had passed since Jorge Klein had last seen Sybille: the afternoon of Saturday, October 13, 1990, the day of her funeral. That day she lay in her casket as though merely asleep, her beauty altogether unmarred by her final ordeal: pale skin, dark lustrous hair, delicate nostrils, full lips. Iridescent gold and violet fabric enfolded her serene body; a shimmering electrostatic haze, faintly perfumed with a jasmine fragrance, protected her from decay. For five hours she floated on the dais while the rites of parting were read and the condolences were offered—offered almost furtively, as if her death were a thing too monstrous to acknowledge with a show of strong feeling; then, when only a few people remained, the inner core of their circle of friends, Klein kissed her lightly on the lips and surrendered her to the silent dark-clad men whom the Cold Town had sent. She had asked in her will to be rekindled; they took her away in a black van to work their magic on her corpse. The casket, retreating on their broad shoulders, seemed to Klein to be disappearing into a throbbing gray vortex that he was helpless to penetrate. Presumably he would never hear from her again. In those days the deads kept strictly to themselves, sequestered behind the walls of their self-imposed ghettos; it was rare ever to see one outside the Cold Towns, rare even for one of them to make oblique contact with the world of the living.

So a redefinition of their relationship was forced on him. For nine years it had been Jorge and Sybille, Sybille and Jorge, I and thou forming we, above all we, a transcendental we. He had loved her with almost painful intensity. In life they had gone everywhere together, had done everything together, shared research tasks and classroom assignments, thought interchangeable thoughts, expressed tastes that were nearly always identical, so completely had each permeated the other. She was a part of him, he of her, and until the moment of her unexpected death he had assumed it would be like that forever. They were still young, he thirty-eight, she thirty-four, decades to look forward to. Then she was gone. And now they were mere anonymities to one another, she not Sybille but only a dead, he not Jorge but only a warm. She was somewhere on the North American continent, walking about, talking, eating, reading, and yet she was gone, lost to him, and it behooved him to accept that alteration in his life, and outwardly he did accept it, but yet, though he knew he could never again have things as they once had been, he allowed himself the indulgence of a lingering wistful hope of regaining her.

Shortly the plane was in view, dark against the brightness of the sky, a suspended mote, an irritating fleck in Barwani's eye, growing larger, causing him to blink and sneeze. Barwani was not ready for it. When Ameri Kombo, the flight controller in the cubicle next door, phoned him with the routine announcement of the landing, Barwani replied, "Notify the pilot that no one is to debark until I have given clearance. I must consult the regulations. There is possibly a peril to public health." For twenty minutes he let the plane sit, all hatches sealed, on the quiet runway. Wandering goats emerged from the shrubbery and inspected it. Barwani consulted no regulations. He finished his modest meal; then he folded his arms and sought to attain the proper state of tranquility. These deads, he told himself, could do no harm. They were people like all other people, except that they had undergone extraordinary medical treatment. He must overcome his superstitious fear of them: he was no peasant, no silly clove-picker, nor was Zanzibar an abode of primitives. He would admit them, he would give them their anti-malaria tablets as though they were ordinary tourists, he would send them on their way. Very well. Now he was ready. He phoned Ameri Kombo. "There is no danger," he said. "The passengers may exit."

There were nine altogether, a sparse load. The four warms emerged first, looking somber and a little congealed, like people who had had to travel with a party of uncaged cobras. Barwani knew them all: the German consul's wife, the merchant Chowdhary's son, and two Chinese engineers, all returning from brief holidays in Dar. He waved them through the gate without formalities. Then came the deads, after an interval of half a minute: probably they had been sitting together at one end of the nearly empty plane and the others had been at the other. There were two women, three men, all of them tall and surprisingly robust-looking. He had expected them to shamble, to shuffle, to limp, to falter, but they moved with aggressive strides, as if they were in better health now than when they had been alive. When they reached the gate, Barwani stepped forward to greet them, saying softly, "Health regulations, come this way, kindly." They were breathing, undoubtedly breathing: he tasted an emanation of liquor from the big red-haired man, a mysterious and pleasant sweet flavor, perhaps anise, from the dark-haired woman. It seemed to Barwani that their skins had an odd waxy texture, an unreal glossiness, but possibly that was his imagination; white skins had always looked artificial to him. The only certain difference he could detect about the deads was in their eyes, a way they had of remaining unnervingly fixed in a single intense gaze for many seconds before shifting. Those were the eyes, Barwani thought, of people who had looked upon the Emptiness without having been swallowed into it. A turbulence of questions erupted within him: What is it like, how do you feel, what do you remember, where did you go? He left them unspoken. Politely he said, "Welcome to the isle of cloves. We ask you to observe that malaria has been wholly eradicated here through extensive precautionary measures, and to prevent recurrence of unwanted disease we require of you that you take these tablets before proceeding further." Tourists often objected to that; these people swallowed their pills without a word of protest. Again Barwani yearned to reach toward them, to achieve some sort of contact that might perhaps help him to transcend the leaden weight of being. But an aura, a shield of strangeness, surrounded these five, and though he was an amiable man who tended to fall into conversations easily with strangers, he passed them on in silence to Mponda the immigration man.

Mponda's high forehead was shiny with sweat, and he chewed at his lower lip; evidently he was as disturbed by the deads as Barwani. He fumbled forms, he stamped a visa in the wrong place, he stammered while telling the deads that he must keep their passports overnight. "I shall post them by messenger to your hotel in the morning," Mponda promised them, and sent the visitors onward to the baggage pickup area with undue haste.

* * *

Klein had only one friend with whom he dared talk about it, a colleague of his at UCLA, a sleek supple Parsee sociologist from Bombay named Framji Jijibhoi, who was as deep into the elaborate new subculture of the deads as a warm could get. "How can I accept this?" Klein demanded. "I can't accept it at all. She's out there somewhere, she's alive, she's—"

Jijibhoi cut him off with a quick flick of his fingertips. "No, dear friend," he said sadly, "not alive, not alive at all, merely rekindled. You must learn to grasp the distinction."

Klein could not learn to grasp the distinction. Klein could not learn to grasp anything having to do with Sybille's death. He could not bear to think that she had passed into another existence from which he was totally excluded. To find her, to speak with her, to participate in her experience of death and whatever lay beyond death, became his only purpose. He was inextricably bound to her, as though she were still his wife, as though Jorge-and-Sybille still existed in any way.

He waited for letters from her, but none came. After a few months he began trying to trace her, embarrassed by his own compulsiveness and by his increasingly open breaches of the etiquette of this sort of widowerhood. He traveled from one Cold Town to another—Sacramento, Boise, Ann Arbor, Louisville—but none would admit him, none would even answer his questions. Friends passed on rumors to him, that she was living among the deads of Tucson, of Roanoke, of Rochester, of San Diego, but nothing came of these tales; then Jijibhoi, who had tentacles into the world of the rekindled in many places, and who was aiding Klein in his quest even though he disapproved of its goal, brought him an authoritative-sounding report that she was at Zion Cold Town in southeastern Utah. They turned him away there too, but not entirely cruelly, for he did manage to secure plausible evidence that that was where Sybille really was.

In the summer of '92 Jijibhoi told him that Sybille had emerged from Cold Town seclusion. She had been seen, he said, in Newark, Ohio, touring the municipal golf course at Octagon State Memorial in the company of a swaggering red-haired archaeologist named Kent Zacharias, also a dead, formerly a specialist in the mound-building Hopewellian cultures of the Ohio Valley. "It is a new phase," said Jijibhoi, "not unanticipated. The deads are beginning to abandon their early philosophy of total separatism. We have started to observe them as tourists visiting our world—exploring the life-death interface, as they like to term it. It will be very interesting, dear friend." Klein flew at once to Ohio and without ever actually seeing her, tracked her from Newark to Chillicothe, from Chillicothe to Marietta, from Marietta into West Virginia, where he lost her trail somewhere between Moundsville and Wheeling. Two months later she was said to be in London, then in Cairo, then Addis Ababa. Early in '93 Klein learned, via the scholarly grapevine—an ex-Californian now at Nyerere University in Arusha—that Sybille was on safari in Tanzania and was planning to go, in a few weeks, across to Zanzibar.

Of course. For ten years she had been working on a doctoral thesis on the establishment of the Arab Sultanate in Zanzibar in the early nineteenth century—studies unavoidably interrupted by other academic chores, by love affairs, by marriage, by financial reverses, by illnesses, death, and other responsibilities—and she had never actually been able to visit the island that was so central to her. Now she was free of all entanglements. Why shouldn't she go to Zanzibar at last? Why not? Of course: she was heading for Zanzibar. And so Klein would go to Zanzibar too, to wait for her.

As the five disappeared into taxis, something occurred to Barwani. He asked Mponda for the passports and scrutinized the names. Such strange ones: Kent Zacharias, Nerita Tracy, Sybille Klein, Anthony Gracchus, Laurence Mortimer. He had never grown accustomed to the names of Europeans. Without the photographs he would be unable to tell which were the women, which the men. Zacharias, Tracy, Klein . . . ah. *Klein*. He checked a memo, two weeks old, tacked to his desk. Klein, yes. Barwani telephoned the Shirazi hotel—a project that consumed several minutes—and asked to speak with the American who had arrived ten days before, that slender man whose lips had been pressed tight in tension, whose eyes had glittered with fatigue, the one who had asked a little service of Barwani, a special favor, and had dashed him a much-needed hundred shillings as payment in advance. There was a lengthy delay, no doubt while porters searched the hotel, looking in the men's room, the bar, the lounge, the garden, and then the American was on the line. "The person about whom you inquired has just arrived, sir," Barwani told him.

TWO

> The dance begins. Worms underneath fingertips, lips beginning to pulse, heartache and throat-catch. All slightly out of step and out of key, each its own tempo and rhythm. Slowly, connections. Lip to lip, heart to heart, finding self in other, dreadfully, tentatively, burning...notes finding themselves in chords, chords in sequence, cacophony turning to polyphonous contrapuntal chorus, a diapason of celebration.
>
> R.D. Laing: *The Bird of Paradise*

Sybille stands timidly at the edge of the municipal golf course at Octagon State Memorial in Newark, Ohio, holding her sandals in her hand and surreptitiously working her toes into the lush, immaculate carpet of dense, close-cropped lime-green grass. It is a summer afternoon in 1992, very hot; the air, beautifully translucent, has that timeless midwestern shimmer, and the droplets of water from the morning sprinkling have not yet burned off the lawn. Such extraordinary grass! She hadn't often seen grass like that in California, and certainly not at Zion Cold Town in thirsty Utah. Kent Zacharias, towering beside her, shakes his head sadly. "A golf course!" he mutters. "One of the most important prehistoric sites in North America and they make a golf course out of it! Well, I suppose it could have been worse. They might have bulldozed the whole thing and turned it into a municipal parking lot. Look, there, do you see the earthworks?"

She is trembling. This is her first extended journey outside the Cold Town, her first venture into the world of the warms since her rekindling, and she is picking up threatening vibrations from all the life that burgeons about her. The park is surrounded by pleasant little houses, well kept. Children on bicycles rocket through the streets. In front of her, golfers are merrily slamming away. Little yellow golf carts clamber with lunatic energy over the rises and dips of the course. There are platoons of tourists who, like herself and Zacharias, have come to see the Indian mounds. There are dogs running free. All this seems menacing to her. Even the vegetation—the thick grass, the manicured shrubs, the heavy-leafed trees with low-hanging boughs—disturbs her. Nor is the nearness of Zacharias reassuring, for he too seems inflamed with undeadlike vitality; his face is florid, his gestures are broad and overanimated, as he points out the low flat-topped mounds, the grassy bumps and ridges making up the giant joined circle and octagon of the ancient monument. Of course, these mounds are the mainspring of his being, even now, five years post mortem. Ohio is his Zanzibar.

"—once covered four square miles. A grand ceremonial center, the Hopewellian equivalent of Chichén Itzá, of Luxor, of—" He pauses. Awareness of her distress has finally filtered through the intensity of his archaeological zeal. "How are you doing?" he asks gently.

She smiles a brave smile. Moistens her lips. Inclines her head toward the golfers, toward the tourists, toward the row of darling little houses outside the rim of the park. Shudders.

"Too cheery for you, is it?"

"Much," she says.

Cheery. Yes. A cheery little town, a magazine-cover town, a chamber-of-commerce town. Newark lies becalmed on the breast of the sea of time: but for the look of the automobiles, this could be 1980 or 1960 or perhaps 1940. Yes. Motherhood, baseball, apple pie, church every Sunday. Yes. Zacharias nods and makes one of the signs of comfort at her. "Come," he whispers. "Let's go toward the heart of the complex. We'll lose the twentieth century along the way."

With brutal imperial strides he plunges into the golf course. Long-legged Sybille must work hard to keep up with him. In a moment they are within the embankment, they have entered the sacred octagon, they have penetrated the vault of the past, and at once Sybille feels they have achieved a successful crossing of the interface between life and death. How still it is here! She senses the powerful presence of the forces of death, and those dark spirits heal her unease. The encroachments of the world of the living on these precincts of the dead become insignificant: the houses outside the park are no longer in view, the golfers are mere foolish incorporeal shadows, the bustling yellow golf carts become beetles, the wandering tourists are invisible.

She is overwhelmed by the size and symmetry of the

ancient site. What spirits sleep here? Zacharias conjures
them, waving his hands like a magician. She has heard so
much from him already about these people, these Hopewellians—
What did they call themselves? How can we ever know?
—who heaped up these ramparts of earth twenty centuries
ago. Now he brings them to life for her with gestures and low
urgent words. He whispers fiercely:

—Do you see them?

And she does see them. Mists descend. The mounds
reawaken; the mound-builders appear. Tall, slender, swarthy,
nearly naked, clad in shining copper breastplates, in necklaces of flint disks, in bangles of bone and mica and tortoise
shell, in heavy chains of bright lumpy pearls, in rings of stone
and terra cotta, in armlets of bears' teeth and panthers' teeth,
in spool-shaped metal ear-ornaments, in furry loincloths.
Here are priests in intricately woven robes and awesome
masks. Here are chieftains with crowns of copper rods,
moving in frosty dignity along the long earthen-walled avenue. The eyes of these people glow with energy. What an
enormously vital, enormously profligate culture they sustain
here! Yet Sybille is not alienated by their throbbing vigor, for
it is the vigor of the dead, the vitality of the vanished.

Look, now. Their painted faces, their unblinking gazes.
This is a funeral procession. The Indians have come to these
intricate geometrical enclosures to perform their acts of worship, and now, solemnly parading along the perimeters of the
circle and the octagon, they pass onward, toward the mortuary zone beyond. Zacharias and Sybille are left alone in the
middle of the field. He murmurs to her:

—Come. We'll follow them.

He makes it real for her. Through his cunning craft she has
access to this community of the dead. How easily she has
drifted backward across time! She learns here that she can
affix herself to the sealed past at any point; it's only the
present, open-ended and unpredictable, that is troublesome.
She and Zacharias float through the misty meadow, no sensation of feet touching ground; leaving the octagon, they travel
now down a long grassy causeway to the place of the burial
mounds, at the edge of a dark forest of wide-crowned oaks.
They enter a vast clearing. In the center the ground has been
plastered with clay, then covered lightly with sand and fine
gravel; on this base the mortuary house, a roofless four-sided
structure with walls consisting of rows of wooden palisades,

has been erected. Within this is a low clay platform topped by a rectangular tomb of log cribbing, in which two bodies can be seen: a young man, a young woman, side by side, bodies fully extended, beautiful even in death. They wear copper breastplates, copper ear ornaments, copper bracelets, necklaces of gleaming yellowish bears' teeth.

Four priests station themselves at the corners of the mortuary house. Their faces are covered by grotesque wooden masks topped by great antlers, and they carry wands two feet long, effigies of the death-cup mushroom in a wood sheathed with copper. One priest commences a harsh, percussive chant. All four lift their wands and abruptly bring them down. It is a signal; the depositing of grave-goods begins. Lines of mourners bowed under heavy sacks approach the mortuary house. They are unweeping, even joyful, faces ecstatic, eyes shining, for these people know what later cultures will forget, that death is no termination but rather a natural continuation of life. Their departed friends are to be envied. They are honored with lavish gifts, so that they may live like royalty in the next world: out of the sacks come nuggets of copper, meteoric iron, and silver, thousands of pearls, shell beads, beads of copper and iron, buttons of wood and stone, heaps of metal ear-spools, chunks and chips of obsidian, animal effigies carved from slate and bone and tortoise shell, ceremonial copper axes and knives, scrolls cut from mica, human jawbones inlaid with turquoise, dark coarse pottery, needles of bone, sheets of woven cloth, coiled serpents fashioned from dark stone, a torrent of offerings, heaped up around and even upon the two bodies.

At length the tomb is choked with gifts. Again there is a signal from the priests. They elevate their wands and the mourners, drawing back to the borders of the clearing, form a circle and begin to sing a somber, throbbing funeral hymn. Zacharias, after a moment, sings with them, wordlessly embellishing the melody with heavy melismas. His voice is a rich *basso cantante*, so unexpectedly beautiful that Sybille is moved almost to confusion by it, and looks at him in awe. Abruptly he breaks off, turns to her, touches her arm, leans down to say:

—You sing too.

Sybille nods hesitantly. She joins the song, falteringly at first, her throat constricted by self-consciousness; then she finds herself becoming part of the rite, somehow, and her tone becomes more confident. Her high clear soprano soars brilliantly above the other voices.

Now another kind of offering is made: boys cover the mortuary house with heaps of kindling—twigs, dead branches, thick boughs, all sorts of combustible debris—until it is quite hidden from sight, and the priests cry a halt. Then, from the forest, comes a woman bearing a blazing firebrand, a girl, actually, entirely naked, her sleek fair-skinned body painted with bizarre horizontal stripes of red and green on breasts and buttocks and thighs, her long glossy black hair flowing like a cape behind her as she runs. Up to the mortuary house she sprints; breathlessly she touches the firebrand to the kindling, here, here, here, performing a wild dance as she goes, and hurls the torch into the center of the pyre. Skyward leap the flames in a ferocious rush. Sybille feels seared by the blast of heat. Swiftly the house and tomb are consumed.

While the embers still glow, the bringing of earth gets under way. Except for the priests, who remain rigid at the cardinal points of the site, and the girl who wielded the torch, who lies like discarded clothing at the edge of the clearing, the whole community takes part. There is an open pit behind a screen of nearby trees; the worshipers, forming lines, go to it and scoop up soil, carrying it to the burned mortuary house in baskets, in buckskin aprons, in big moist clods held in their bare hands. Silently they dump their burdens on the ashes and go back for more.

Sybille glanced at Zacharias; he nods; they join the line. She goes down into the pit, gouges a lump of moist black clayey soil from its side, takes it to the growing mound. Back for another, back for another. The mound rises rapidly, two feet above ground level now, three, four, a swelling circular blister, its outlines governed by the unchanging positions of the four priests, its tapering contours formed by the tamping of scores of bare feet. Yes, Sybille thinks, this is a valid way of celebrating death, this is a fitting rite. Sweat runs down her body, her clothes become stained and muddy, and still she runs to the earth-quarry, runs from there to the mound, runs to the quarry, runs to the mound, runs, runs, transfigured, ecstatic.

Then the spell breaks. Sometimes goes wrong, she does not know what, and the mists clear, the sun dazzles her eyes, the priests and the mound-builders and the unfinished mound disappear. She and Zacharias are once again in the octagon, golf carts roaring past them on every side. Three children and their parents stand just a few feet from her, staring, staring, and a boy about ten years old points to Sybille and says in a voice that reverberates through half of Ohio, "Dad, what's wrong with those people? Why do they look so weird?"

Mother gasps and cries, "*Quiet*, Tommy, don't you have any manners?" Dad, looking furious, gives the boy a stinging blow across the face with the tips of his fingers, seizes him by the wrist, tugs him toward the other side of the park, the whole family following in their wake.

Sybille shivers convulsively. She turns away, clasping her hands to her betraying eyes. Zacharias embraces her. "It's all right," he says tenderly. "The boy didn't know any better. It's all right."

"Take me away from here!"

"I want to show you—"

"Some other time. Take me away. To the motel. I don't want to see anything. I don't want anybody to see me."

He takes her to the motel. For an hour she lies face down on the bed, racked by dry sobs. Several times she tells Zacharias she is unready for this tour, she wants to go back to the Cold Town, but he says nothing, simply strokes the tense muscles of her back, and after a while the mood passes. She turns to him and their eyes meet and he touches her and they make love in the fashion of the deads.

Three

Newness is renewal: *ad hoc enim venit, ut renovemur in illo;* making it new again, as on the first day; *herrlich wie am ersten Tag.* Reformation, or renaissance; rebirth. Life is Phoenix-like, always being born again out of its own death. The true nature of life is resurrection; all life is life after death, a second life, reincarnation. *Totus hic ordo revolubilis testatio est resurrectionis mortuorum.* The universal pattern of recurrence bears witness to the resurrection of the dead.

Norman O. Brown: *Love's Body*

'The rains shall be commencing shortly, gentleman and lady," the taxi driver said, speeding along the narrow highway to

Zanzibar Town. He had been chattering steadily, wholly unafraid of his passengers. He must not know what we are, Sybille decided. "Perhaps in a week or two they begin. These shall be the long rains. The short rains come in the last of November and December."

"Yes, I know," Sybille said.

"Ah, you have been to Zanzibar before?"

"In a sense," she replied. In a sense she had been to Zanzibar many times, and how calmly she was taking it, now that the true Zanzibar was beginning to superimpose itself on the template in her mind, on that dream-Zanzibar she had carried about so long! She took everything calmly now: nothing excited her, nothing aroused her. In her former life the delay at the airport would have driven her into a fury: a ten-minute flight, and then to be trapped on the runway twice as long! But she had remained tranquil throughout it all, sitting almost immobile, listening vaguely to what Zacharias was saying and occasionally replying as if sending messages from some other planet. And now Zanzibar, so placidly accepted. In the old days she had felt a sort of paradoxical amazement whenever some landmark familiar from childhood geography lessons or the movies or travel posters—the Grand Canyon, the Manhattan skyline, Taos Pueblo—turned out in reality to look exactly as she imagined it would; but now here was Zanzibar, unfolding predictably and unsurprisingly before her, and she observed it with a camera's cool eye, unmoved, unresponsive.

The soft, steamy air was heavy with a burden of perfumes, not only the expected pungent scent of cloves but also creamier fragrances which perhaps were those of hibiscus, frangipani, jacaranda, bougainvillaea, penetrating the cab's open window like probing tendrils. The imminence of the long rains was a tangible pressure, a presence, a heaviness in the atmosphere: at any moment a curtain might be drawn aside and the torrents would start. The highway was lined by two shaggy green walls of palms broken by tin-roofed shacks; behind the palms were mysterious dark groves, dense and alien. Along the edge of the road was the usual tropical array of obstacles: chickens, goats, naked children, old women with shrunken, toothless faces, all wandering around untroubled by the taxi's encroachment on their right-of-way. On through the rolling flatlands the cab sped, out onto the peninsula on which Zanzibar Town sits. The temperature seemed to be rising perceptibly minute by minute; a fist of humid heat was clamping tight over the island. "Here is the waterfront, gentleman and lady," the driver said. His voice was an intrusive hoarse purr, patronizing, disturbing. The sand was glaringly white, the water a dazzling glassy blue; a couple of dhows moved sleepily across the mouth of the harbor, their lateen sails bellying slightly as the gentle sea breeze caught them. "On this side, please—" An enormous white wooden building, four stories high, a wedding cake of long verandahs and cast-iron railings, topped by a vast cupola. Sybille, recognizing it, anticipated the driver's spiel, hearing it like a subliminal pre-echo: "Beit al-Ajaib, the House of Wonders, former government house. Here the Sultan was often make great banquets, here the famous of all Africa came homaging. No longer in use. Next door the old Sultan's Palace, now Palace of People. You wish to go in House of Wonders? Is open: we stop, I take you now."

"Another time," Sybille said faintly. "We'll be here awhile."

"You not here just a day like most?"

"No, a week or more. I've come to study the history of your island. I'll surely visit the Beit al-Ajaib. But not today."

"Not today, no. Very well: you call me, I take you any- where. I am Ibuni." He gave her a gallant toothy grin over his shoulder and swung the cab inland with a ferocious lurch, into the labyrinth of winding streets and narrow alleys that was Stonetown, the ancient Arab quarter.

All was silent here. The massive white stone buildings presented blank faces to the streets. The windows, mere slits, were shuttered. Most doors—the famous paneled doors of Stonetown, richly carved, studded with brass, cunningly inlaid, each door an ornate Islamic masterpiece—were closed and seemed to be locked. The shops looked shabby, and the small display windows were speckled with dust. Most of the signs were so faded Sybille could barely make them out:

PREMCHAND'S EMPORIUM
MONJI'S CURIOS
ABDULLAH'S BROTHERHOOD STORE
MOTILAL'S BAZAAR

The Arabs were long since gone from Zanzibar. So were most of the Indians, though they were said to be creeping back. Occasionally, as it pursued its intricate course through the maze of Stonetown, the taxi passed elongated black limousines, probably of Russian or Chinese make, chauffeur-driven, occupied by dignified self-contained dark-skinned men in white robes. Legislators, so she supposed them to be, en route to meetings of state. There were no other vehicles in sight, and no pedestrians except for a few women, robed entirely in black, hurrying on solitary errands. Stonetown had none of the vitality of the countryside; it was a place of ghosts, she thought, a fitting place for vacationing deads. She glanced at Zacharias, who nodded and smiled, a quick quirky smile that acknowledged her perception and told her that he too had had it. Communication was swift among the deads and the obvious rarely needed voicing.

The route to the hotel seemed extraordinarily involuted, and the driver halted frequently in front of shops, saying hopefully, "You want brass chests, copper pots, silver curios, gold chains from China?" Though Sybille gently declined his suggestions, he continued to point out bazaars and emporiums, offering earnest recommendations of quality and moderate price, and gradually she realized, getting her bearings in the town, that they had passed certain corners more than once. Of course: the driver must be in the pay of shopkeepers who hired him to lure tourists.

"Please take us to our hotel," Sybille said, and when he persisted in his huckstering—"Best ivory here, best lace" —she said it more firmly, but she kept her temper. Jorge would have been pleased by her transformation, she thought; he had all too often been the immediate victim of her fiery impatience. She did not know the specific cause of the change. Some metabolic side-effect of the rekindling process, maybe, or maybe her two years of communion with Guidefather at the Cold Town, or was it, perhaps, nothing more than the new knowledge that all of time was hers, that to let oneself feel hurried now was absurd?

"Your hotel is this," Ibuni said at last.

It was an old Arab mansion—high arches, innumerable balconies, musty air, electric fans turning sluggishly in the dark hallways. Sybille and Zacharias were given a sprawling suite on the third floor, overlooking a courtyard lush with palms, vermilion nandi, kapok trees, poinsettia, and agapanthus. Mortimer, Gracchus, and Nerita had long since arrived in the other cab and were in an identical suite one floor below. "I'll have a bath," Sybille told Zacharias. "Will you be in the bar?"

"Very likely. Or strolling in the garden."

He went out. Sybille quickly shed her travel-sweaty clothes. The bathroom was a Byzantine marvel, elaborate swirls of colored tile, an immense yellow tub standing high on bronze eagle-claw-and-globe legs. Lukewarm water dribbled in slowly when she turned the tap. She smiled at her reflection in the tall oval mirror. There had been a mirror somewhat like it at the rekindling house. On the morning after her awakening, five or six deads had come into her room to celebrate with her her successful transition across the interface, and they had had that big mirror with them; delicately, with great ceremoniousness, they had drawn the coverlet down to show herself to her in it, naked, slender, narrow-waisted, high-breasted, the beauty of her body unchanged, marred neither by dying or by rekindling, indeed enhanced by it, so that she had become more youthful-looking and even radiant in her passage across that terrible gulf.

—You're a very beautiful woman.

That was Pablo. She would learn his name and all the other names later.

—I feel such a flood of relief. I was afraid I'd wake up and find myself a shriveled ruin.

—That could not have happened, Pablo said.

—And never will happen, said a young woman. Nerita, she was.

—But deads do age, don't they?

—Oh, yes, we age, just as the warms do. But not *just* as.

—More slowly?

—Very much more slowly. And differently. All our biological processes operate more slowly, except the functions of the brain, which tend to be quicker than they were in life.

—Quicker?

—You'll see.

—It all sounds ideal.

—We are extremely fortunate. Life has been kind to us. Our situation is, yes, ideal. We are the new aristocracy.

—The new aristocracy—

Sybille slipped slowly into the tub, leaning back against the cool porcelain, wriggling a little, letting the tepid water slide up as far as her throat. She closed her eyes and drifted peacefully. All of Zanzibar was waiting for her. *Streets I never thought I should visit.* Let Zanzibar wait. Let Zanzibar wait. *Words I never thought to speak. When I left my body on a distant shore.* Time for everything, everything in its due time.

—You're a very beautiful woman, Pablo had told her, not meaning to flatter.

Yes. She had wanted to explain to them, that first morning, that she didn't really care all that much about the appearance of her body, that her real priorities lay elsewhere, were "higher," but there hadn't been any need to tell them that. They understood. They understood everything. Besides, she *did* care about her body. Being beautiful was less important to her than it was to those women for whom physical beauty was their only natural advantage, but her appearance mattered to her; her body pleased her and she knew it was pleasing to others, it gave her access to people, it was a means of making connections, and she had always been grateful for that. In her other existence her delight in her body had been flawed by the awareness of the inevitability of its slow steady decay, the certainty of the loss of that accidental power that beauty gave her, but now she had been granted exemption from that: she would change with time but she would not have to feel, as warms must feel, that she was gradually falling apart. Her rekindled body would not betray her by turning ugly. No.

—We are the new aristocracy—

After her bath she stood a few minutes by the open window, naked to the humid breeze. Sounds came to her: distant bells, the bright chatter of tropical birds, the voices of children singing in a language she could not identify. Zanzibar! Sultans and spices, Livingstone and Stanley, Tippu Tib the slaver, Sir Richard Burton spending a night in this very hotel room, perhaps. There was a dryness in her throat, a throbbing in her chest: a little excitement coming alive in her after all. She felt anticipation, even eagerness. All Zanzibar lay before her. Very well. Get moving, Sybille, put some clothes on, let's have lunch, a look at the town.

She took a light blouse and shorts from her suitcase. Just then Zacharias returned to the room, and she said, not looking up, "Kent, do you think it's all right for me to wear these shorts here? They're—" A glance at his face and her voice trailed off. "What's wrong?"

"I've just been talking to your husband."

"He's *here*?"

"He came up to me in the lobby. Knew my name. 'You're Zacharias,' he said, with a Bogarty little edge to his voice, like a deceived movie husband confronting the Other Man. 'Where is she? I have to see her.'"

"Oh, no, Kent."

"I asked him what he wanted with you. 'I'm her husband,' he said, and I told him, 'Maybe you were her husband once, but things have changed,' and then—"

"I can't imagine Jorge talking tough. He's such a *gentle* man, Kent! How did he look?"

"Schizoid," Zacharias said. "Glassy eyes, muscles bunching in his jaws, signs of terrific pressure all over him. He knows he's not supposed to do things like this, doesn't he?"

"Jorge knows exactly how he's supposed to behave. Oh, Kent, what a stupid mess! Where is he now?"

"Still downstairs. Nerita and Laurence are talking to him. You don't want to see him, do you?"

"Of course not."

"Write him a note to that effect and I'll take it down to him. Tell him to clear off."

Sybille shook her head. "I don't want to hurt him."

"Hurt him? He's followed you halfway around the world like a lovesick boy, he's tried to violate your privacy, he's disrupted an important trip, he's refused to abide by the conventions that govern the relationships of warms and deads, and you—"

"He loves me, Kent."

"He loved you. All right, I concede that. But the person he loved doesn't exist any more. He has to be made to realize that."

Sybille closed her eyes. "I don't want to hurt him. I don't want you to hurt him either."

"I won't hurt him. Are you going to see him?"

"No," she said. She grunted in annoyance and threw her shorts and blouse into a chair. There was a fierce pounding at her temples, a sensation of being challenged, of being threatened, that she had not felt since that awful day at the Newark mounds. She strode to the window and looked out, half expecting to see Jorge arguing with Nerita and Laurence in the courtyard. But there was no one down there except a houseboy who looked up as if her bare breasts were beacons and gave her a broad dazzling smile. Sybille turned her back to him and said dully, "Go back down. Tell him that it's impossible for me to see him. Use that word. Not that I *won't* see him, not that I *don't want to* see him, not that it isn't *right* for me to see him, just that it's impossible. And then phone the airport. I want to go back to Dar on the evening plane."

"But we've only just arrived!"

"No matter. We'll come back some other time. Jorge is very persistent; he won't accept anything but a brutal rebuff, and I can't do that to him. So we'll leave."

Klein had never seen deads at close range before. Cautiously, uneasily, he stole quick intense looks at Kent Zacharias as they sat side by side on rattan chairs among the potted palms in the lobby of the hotel. Jijibhoi had told him that it hardly showed, that you perceived it more subliminally than by any outward manifestation, and that was true; there was a certain look about the eyes, of course, the famous fixity of the deads, and there was something oddly pallid about Zacharias' skin *beneath* the florid complexion, but if Klein had not known what Zacharias was, he might not have guessed it. He tried to imagine this man, this red-haired red-faced dead archaeologist, this digger of dirt mounds, in bed with Sybille. Doing with her whatever it was that the deads did in their couplings. Even Jijibhoi wasn't sure. Something with hands, with eyes, with whispers and smiles, not at all genital—so Jijibhoi believed. *This is Sybille's lover I'm talking to. This is Sybille's lover.* How strange that it bothered him so. She had had affairs when she was living; so had he; so had everyone; it was the way of life. But he felt threatened, overwhelmed, defeated, by this walking corpse of a lover.

Klein said, "Impossible?"

"That was the word she used."

"Can't I have ten minutes with her?"

"Impossible."

"Would you let me see her for a few moments, at least? I'd just like to find out how she looks."

"Don't you find it humiliating, doing all this scratching around just for a glimpse of her?"

"Yes."

"And you still want it?"

"Yes."

Zacharias sighed. "There's nothing I can do for you. I'm sorry."

"Perhaps Sybille is tired from having done so much traveling. Do you think she might be in a more receptive mood tomorrow?"

"Maybe," Zacharias said. "Why don't you come back then?"

"You've been very kind."

"*De nada.*"

"Can I buy you a drink?"

"Thanks, no," Zacharias said. "I don't indulge any more. Not since—" He smiled.

Klein could smell whiskey on Zacharias' breath. All right, though. All right. He would go away. A driver waiting outside the hotel grounds poked his head out of his cab window and said hopefully, "Tour of the island, gentleman? See the clove plantations, see the athlete stadium?"

"I've seen them already," Klein said. He shrugged. "Take me to the beach."

He spent the afternoon watching turquoise wavelets lapping pink sand. The next morning he returned to Sybille's hotel, but they were gone, all five of them, gone on last night's flight to Dar, said the apologetic desk clerk. Klein asked if he could make a telephone call, and the clerk showed him an ancient instrument in an alcove near the bar. He phoned Barwani. "What's going on?" he demanded. "You told me they'd be staying at least a week!"

"Oh, sir, things change," Barwani said softly.

Four

What portends? What will the future bring? I do not know, I have no presentiment. When a spider hurls itself down from some fixed point, consistently with its nature, it always sees before it only an empty space wherein it can find no foothold however much it sprawls. And so it is with me: always before me an empty space; what drives me forward is a consistency which lies behind me. This life is topsy-turvy and terrible, not to be endured.

Soren Kierkegaard: *Either/Or*

* * *

Jijibhoi said, "In the entire question of death who is to say what is right, dear friend? When I was a boy in Bombay it was not unusual for our Hindu neighbors to practice the rite of suttee, that is, the burning of the widow on her husband's funeral pyre, and by what presumption may we call them barbarians? Of course"—his dark eyes flashed mischievously—"we *did* call them barbarians, though never when they might hear us. Will you have more curry?"

Klein repressed a sigh. He was getting full, and the curry was fiery stuff, of an incandescence far beyond his usual level of tolerance; but Jijibhoi's hospitality, unobtrusively insistent, had a certain hieratic quality about it that made Klein feel like a blasphemer whenever he refused anything in his home. He smiled and nodded, and Jijibhoi, rising, spooned a mound of rice into Klein's plate, buried it under curried lamb, bedecked it with chutneys and sambals. Silently, unbidden, Jijibhoi's wife went to the kitchen and returned with a cold bottle of Heinekens. She gave Klein a shy grin as she set it down before him. They worked well together, these two Parsees, his hosts.

They were an elegant couple—striking, even. Jijibhoi was a tall, erect man with a forceful aquiline nose, dark Levantine skin, jet-black hair, a formidable mustache. His hands and feet were extraordinarily small; his manner was polite and reserved; he moved with a quickness of action bordering on nervousness. Klein guessed that he was in his early forties, though he suspected his estimate could easily be off by ten years in either direction. His wife—strangely, Klein had never been told her name—was younger than her husband, nearly as tall, fair of complexion—a light-olive tone—and voluptuous of figure. She dressed invariably in flowing silken saris; Jijibhoi affected western business dress, suits and ties in style twenty years out of date. Klein had never seen either of them bareheaded: she wore a kerchief of white linen, he a brocaded skullcap that might lead people to mistake him for an Oriental Jew. They were childless and self-sufficient, forming a closed dyad, a perfect unit, two segments of the same entity, conjoined and indivisible, as Klein and Sybille once had been. Their harmonious interplay of thought and gesture made them a trifle disconcerting, even intimidating, to others. As Klein and Sybille once had been.

Klein said, "Among your people—"

"Oh, very different, very different, quite unique. You know of our funeral custom?"

"Exposure of the dead, isn't it?"

Jijibhoi's wife giggled. "A very ancient recycling scheme!"

"The Towers of Silence," Jijibhoi said. He went to the dining room's vast window and stood with his back to Klein, staring out at the dazzling lights of Los Angeles. The Jijibhois' house, all redwood and glass, perched precariously on stilts near the crest of Benedict Canyon, just below Mulholland: the view took in everything from Hollywood to Santa Monica. "There are five of them in Bombay," said Jijibhoi, "on Malabar Hill, a rocky ridge overlooking the Arabian Sea. They are centuries old, each one circular, several hundred feet in circumference, surrounded by a stone wall twenty or thirty feet high. When a Parsee dies—do you know of this?"

"Not as much as I'd like to know."

"When a Parsee dies, he is carried to the Towers on an iron bier by professional corpse-bearers; the mourners follow in procession, two by two, joined hand to hand by holding a white handkerchief between them. A beautiful scene, dear Jorge. There is a doorway in the stone wall through which the corpse-bearers pass, carrying their burden. No one else may enter the Tower. Within is a circular platform paved with large stone slabs and divided into three rows of shallow, open receptacles. The outer row is used for the bodies of males, the next for those of females, the innermost one for children. The dead one is given a resting-place; vultures rise from the lofty palms in the gardens adjoining the Towers; within an hour or two, only bones remain. Later, the bare, sun-dried skeleton is cast into a pit at the center of the Tower. Rich and poor crumble together there into dust."

"And all Parsees are—ah—buried in this way?"

"Oh, no, no, by no means," Jijibhoi said heartily. "All ancient traditions are in disrepair nowadays, do you not know? Our younger people advocate cremation or even conventional interment. Still, many of us continue to see the beauty of our way."

"—beauty?—"

Jijibhoi's wife said in a quiet voice, "To bury the dead in the ground, in a moist tropical land where diseases are highly contagious, seems not sanitary to us. And to burn a body is to waste its substance. But to give the bodies of the dead to the efficient hungry birds—quickly, cleanly, without fuss—is to us a way of celebrating the economy of nature. To have one's bones mingle in the pit with the bones of the entire community is, to us, the ultimate democracy."

"And the vultures spread no contagions themselves, feeding as they do on the bodies of—"

"Never," said Jijibhoi firmly. "Nor do they contract our ills."

"And I gather that you both intend to have your bodies returned to Bombay when you—" Aghast, Klein paused, shook his head, coughed in embarrassment, forced a weak smile. "You see what this radioactive curry of yours has done to my manners? Forgive me. Here I sit, a guest at your dinner table, quizzing you about your funeral plans!"

Jijibhoi chuckled. "Death is not frightening to us, dear friend. It is—one hardly needs say it, does one?—it is a natural event. For a time we are here, and then we go. When our time ends, yes, she and I will give ourselves to the Towers of Silence."

His wife added sharply, "Better there than the Cold Towns! Much better!"

Klein had never observed such vehemence in her before.

Jijibhoi swung back from the window and glared at her. Klein had never seen that before either. It seemed as if the fragile web of elaborate courtesy that he and these two had been spinning all evening was suddenly unraveling, and that even the bonds between Jijibhoi and his wife were undergoing strain. Agitated now, fluttery, Jijibhoi began to collect the empty dishes, and after a long awkward moment said, "She did not mean to give offense."

"Why should I be offended?"

"A person you love chose to go to the Cold Towns. You might think there was implied criticism of her in my wife's expression of distaste for—"

Klein shrugged. "She's entitled to her feelings about rekindling. I wonder, though—"

He halted, uneasy, fearing to probe too deeply.

"Yes?"

"It was irrelevant."

"Please," Jijibhoi said. "We are old friends."

"I was wondering," said Klein slowly, "if it doesn't make things hard for you, spending all your time among deads, studying them, mastering their ways, devoting your whole career to them, when your wife evidently despises the Cold

Towns and everything that goes on in them. If the theme of
your work repels her, you must not be able to share it with
her."

"Oh," Jijibhoi said, tension visibly going from him, "if it
comes to that, I have even less liking for the entire rekindling
phenomenon than she."

"You do?" This was a side of Jijibhoi that Klein had never
suspected. "It repels you? Then why did you choose to make
such an intensive survey of it?"

Jijibhoi looked genuinely amazed. "What? Are you saying
one must have personal allegiance to the subject of one's field
of scholarship?" He laughed. "You are of Jewish birth, I
think, and yet your doctoral thesis was concerned, was it not,
with the early phases of the Third Reich?"

Klein winced. "Touché!"

"I find the subculture of the deads irresistible, as a sociologist," Jijibhoi went on. "To have such a radical new aspect of
human existence erupt during one's career is an incredible
gift. There is no more fertile field for me to investigate. Yet I
have no wish, none at all, ever to deliver myself up for
rekindling. For me, my wife, it will be the Towers of Silence,
the hot sun, the obliging vultures—and finis, the end, no
more, terminus."

"I had no idea you felt this way. I suppose if I'd known
more about Parsee theology, I might have realized—"

"You misunderstand. Our objections are not theological. It
is that we share a wish, an idiosyncratic whim, not to
continue beyond the allotted time. But also I have serious
reservations about the impact of rekindling on our society. I
feel a profound distress at the presence among us of these
deads, I feel a purely private fear of these people and the
culture they are creating, I feel even an abhorrence for—"
Jijibhoi cut himself short. "Your pardon. That was perhaps too
strong a word. You see how complex my attitudes are toward
this subject, my mixture of fascination and repulsion? I exist
in constant tension between those poles. But why do I tell
you all this, which if it does not disturb you, must surely bore
you? Let us hear about your journey to Zanzibar."

"What can I say? I went, I waited a couple of weeks for her
to show up, I wasn't able to get near her at all, and I came
home. All the way to Africa and I never even had a glimpse of
her."

"What a frustration, dear Jorge!"

"She stayed in her hotel room. They wouldn't let me go upstairs to her."

"They?"

"Her entourage," Klein said. "She was traveling with four other deads, a woman and three men. Sharing her room with the archaeologist, Zacharias. He was the one who shielded her from me, and did it very cleverly, too. He acts as though he owns her. Perhaps he does. What can you tell me, Framji? Do the deads marry? Is Zacharias her new husband?"

"It is very doubtful. The terms 'wife' and 'husband' are not in use among the deads. They form relationships, yes, but pair-bonding seems to be uncommon among them, possibly altogether unknown. Instead they tend to create supportive pseudo-familial groupings of three or four or even more individuals, who—"

"Do you mean that all four of her companions in Zanzibar are her lovers?"

Jijibhoi gestured eloquently. "Who can say? If you mean in a physical sense, I doubt it, but one can never be sure. Zacharias seems to be her special companion, at any rate. Several of the others may be part of her pseudo-family also, or all, or none. I have reason to think that at certain times every dead may claim a familial relationship to all others of his kind. Who can say? We perceive the doings of these people, as they say, through a glass, darkly."

"I don't see Sybille even that well. I don't even know what she looks like now."

"She has lost none of her beauty."

"So you've told me before. But I want to see her myself. You can't really comprehend, Framji, how much I want to see her. The pain I feel, not able—"

"Would you like to see her right now?"

Klein shook in a convulsion of amazement. "What? What do you mean? Is she—"

"Hiding in the next room? No, no, nothing like that. But I do have a small surprise for you. Come into the library." Smiling expansively, Jijibhoi led the way from the dining room to the small study adjoining it, a room densely packed from floor to ceiling with books in an astonishing range of languages—not merely English, French, and German, but also Sanskrit, Hindi, Gujerati, Farsi, the tongues of Jijibhoi's polyglot upbringing among the tiny Parsee colony of Bombay, a community in which no language once cherished was ever discarded. Pushing aside a stack of dog-eared professional journals, he drew forth a glistening picture-cube, activated its inner light with a touch of his thumb, and handed it to Klein.

The sharp, dazzling holographic image showed three figures in a broad grassy plain that seemed to have no limits and was without trees, boulders, or other visual interruptions, an endlessly unrolling green carpet under a blank death-blue sky. Zacharias stood at the left, his face averted from the camera; he was looking down, tinkering with the action of an enormous rifle. At the far right stood a stocky, powerful-looking dark-haired man whose pale, harsh-featured face seemed all beard and nostrils. Klein recognized him: Anthony Gracchus, one of the deads who had accompanied Sybille to Zanzibar. Sybille stood beside him, clad in khaki slacks and a crisp white blouse. Gracchus' arm was extended; evidently he had just pointed out a target to her, and she was intently aiming a gun nearly as big as Zacharias'.

Klein shifted the cube about, studying her face from various angles, and the sight of her made his fingers grow thick and clumsy, his eyelids to quiver. Jijibhoi had spoken truly: she had lost none of her beauty. Yet she was not at all the Sybille he had known. When he had last seen her, lying in her casket, she had seemed to be a flawless marble image of herself, and she had that same surreal statuary appearance now. Her face was an expressionless mask, calm, remote, aloof; her eyes were glossy mysteries; her lips registered a faint, enigmatic, barely perceptible smile. It frightened him to behold her this way, so alien, so unfamiliar. Perhaps it was the intensity of her concentration that gave her that forbidding marmoreal look, for she seemed to be pouring her entire being into the task of taking aim. By tilting the cube more extremely, Klein was able to see what she was aiming at: a strange awkward bird moving through the grass at the lower left, a bird larger than a turkey, round as a sack, with ash-gray plumage, a whitish breast and tail, yellow-white wings, and short, comical yellow legs. Its head was immense and its black bill ended in a great snubbed hook. The creature seemed solemn, rather dignified, and faintly absurd; it showed no awareness that its doom was upon it. How odd that Sybille should be about to kill it, she who had always detested the taking of life: Sybille the huntress now, Sybille the lunar goddess, Sybille-Diana!

Shaken, Klein looked up at Jijibhoi and said, "Where was this taken? On that safari in Tanzania, I suppose."

"Yes. In February. This man is the guide, the white hunter."

"I saw him in Zanzibar. Gracchus, his name is. He was one of the deads traveling with Sybille."

"He operates a hunting preserve not far from Kilimanjaro," Jijibhoi said, "that is set aside exclusively for the use of the deads. One of the more bizarre manifestations of their sub-culture, actually. They hunt only those animals which—"

Klein said impatiently, "How did you get this picture?"

"It was taken by Nerita Tracy, who is one of your wife's companions."

"I met her in Zanzibar too. But how—"

"A friend of hers is an acquaintance of mine, one of my informants, in fact, a valuable connection in my researches. Some months ago I asked him if he could obtain something like this for me. I did not tell him, of course, that I meant it for you." Jijibhoi looked close. "You seem troubled, dear friend."

Klein nodded. He shut his eyes as though to protect them from the glaring surfaces of Sybille's photograph. Eventually he said in a flat, toneless voice, "I have to get to see her."

"Perhaps it would be better for you if you would abandon—"

"*No.*"

"Is there no way I can convince you that it is dangerous for you to pursue your fantasy of—"

"No," Klein said. "Don't even try. It's necessary for me to reach her. Necessary."

"How will you accomplish this, then?"

Klein said mechanically, "By going to Zion Cold Town."

"You have already done that. They would not admit you."

"This time they will. They don't turn away deads."

The Parsee's eyes widened. "You will surrender your own life? Is this your plan? What are you saying, Jorge?"

Klein, laughing, said, "That isn't what I meant at all."

"I am bewildered."

"I intend to infiltrate. I'll disguise myself as one of them. I'll slip into the Cold Town the way an infidel slips into Mecca." He seized Jijibhoi's wrist. "Can you help me? Coach me in their ways, teach me their jargon?"

"They'll find you out instantly."

"Maybe not. Maybe I'll get to Sybille before they do."

"This is insanity," Jijibhoi said quietly.

"Nevertheless. You have the knowledge. Will you help me?"

Gently Jijibhoi withdrew his arm from Klein's grasp. He crossed the room and busied himself with an untidy bookshelf for some moments, fussily arranging and rearranging. At length he said, "There is little I can do for you myself. My knowledge is broad but not deep, not deep enough. But if you insist on going through with this, Jorge, I can introduce you to someone who may be able to assist you. He is one of my informants, a dead, a man who has rejected the authority of the Guidefathers, a person who is *of* the deads but not *with* them. Possibly he can instruct you in what you would need to know."

"Call him," Klein said.

"I must warn you he is unpredictable, turbulent, perhaps even treacherous. Ordinary human values are without meaning to him in his present state."

"Call him."

"If only I could discourage you from—"

"Call him."

Five

Quarreling brings trouble. These days lions roar a great deal. Joy follows grief. It is not good to beat children much. You had better go away now and go home. It is impossible to work today. You should go to school every day. It is not advisable to follow this path, there is water in the way. Never mind, I shall be able to pass. We had better go back quickly. These lamps use a lot of oil. There are no mosquitoes in Nairobi. There are no lions here. There are people here, looking for eggs. Is there water in the well? No, there is none. If there are only three people, work will be impossible today.

D. V. Perrott: *Teach Yourself Swahili*

Gracchus signals furiously to the porters and bellows, "*Shika njia hii hii!*" Three turn, two keep trudging along. "*Ninyi nyote!*" he calls. "*Fanga kama hivi!*" He shakes his head, spits, flicks sweat from his forehead. He adds, speaking in a lower voice and in English, taking care that they will not hear him, "Do as I say, you malevolent black bastards, or you'll be deader than I am before sunset!"

Sybille laughs nervously. "Do you always talk to them like that?"

"I try to be easy on them. But what good does it do, what good does any of it do? Come on, let's keep up with them."

It is less than an hour after dawn, but already the sun is very hot, here in the flat dry country between Kilimanjaro and Serengeti. Gracchus is leading the party northward across the high grass, following the spoor of what he thinks is a quagga, but breaking a trail in the high grass is hard work and the porters keep veering away toward a ravine that offers the tempting shade of a thicket of thorn trees, and he constantly has to harass them in order to hold them to the route he wants. Sybille has noticed that Gracchus shouts fiercely to his blacks, as if they were no more than recalcitrant beasts, and speaks of them behind their backs with a rough contempt, but it all seems done for show, all part of his white-hunter role: she has also noticed, at times when she was not supposed to notice, that privately Gracchus is in fact gentle, tender, even loving among the porters, teasing them—she supposes—with affectionate Swahili banter and playful mock-punches. The porters are role-players too: they behave in the traditional manner of their profession, alternately deferential and patronizing to the clients, alternately posing as all-knowing repositories of the lore of the bush and as simple, guileless savages fit only for carrying burdens. But the clients they serve are not quite like the sportsmen of Hemingway's time, since they are deads, and secretly the porters are terrified of the strange beings whom they serve. Sybille has seen them muttering prayers and fondling amulets whenever they accidentally touch one of the deads, and has occasionally detected an unguarded glance conveying unalloyed fear, possibly revulsion. Gracchus is no friend of theirs, however jolly he may get with them: they appear to regard him as some sort of monstrous sorcerer and the clients as fiends made manifest.

Sweating, saying little, the hunters move in single file, first the porters with the guns and supplies, then Gracchus, Zacharias, Sybille, Nerita constantly clicking her camera, and

Mortimer. Patches of white cloud drift slowly across the immense arch of the sky. The grass is lush and thick, for the short rains were unusually heavy in December. Small animals scurry through it, visible only in quick flashes, squirrels and jackals and guinea-fowl. Now and then larger creatures can be seen: three haughty ostriches, a pair of snuffling hyenas, a band of Thomson gazelles flowing like a tawny river across the plain. Yesterday Sybille spied two wart hogs, some giraffes, and a serval, an elegant big-eared wildcat that slithered along like a miniature cheetah. None of these beasts may be hunted, but only those special ones that the operators of the preserve have introduced for the special needs of their clients; anything considered native African wildlife, which is to say anything that was living here before the deads leased this tract from the Masai, is protected by government decree. The Masai themselves are allowed to do some lion-hunting, since this is their reservation, but there are so few Masai left that they can do little harm. Yesterday, after the wart hogs and before the giraffes, Sybille saw her first Masai, five lean, handsome, long-bodied men, naked under skimpy red robes, drifting silently through the bush, pausing frequently to stand thoughtfully on one leg, propped against their spears. At close range they were less handsome—toothless, fly-specked, herniated. They offered to sell their spears and their beaded collars for a few shillings, but the safarigoers had already stocked up on Masai artifacts in Nairobi's curio shops, at astonishingly higher prices.

All through the morning they stalk the quagga, Gracchus pointing out hoofprints here, fresh dung there. It is Zacharias who has asked to shoot a quagga. "How can you tell we're not following a zebra?" he asks peevishly.

Gracchus winks. "Trust me. We'll find zebras up ahead too. But you'll get your quagga. I guarantee it."

Ngiri, the head porter, turns and grins. "*Piga quagga m'uzuri, bwana,*" he says to Zacharias, and winks also, and then—Sybille sees it plainly—his jovial confident smile fades as though he has had the courage to sustain it only for an instant, and a veil of dread covers his dark glossy face.

"What did he say?" Zacharias asks.

"That you'll shoot a fine quagga," Gracchus replies.

Quaggas. The last wild one was killed about 1870, leaving only three in the world, all females, in European zoos. The Boers had hunted them to the edge of extinction in order to feed their tender meat to Hottentot slaves and to make from their striped hides sacks for Boer grain, leather *veldschoen* for Boer feet. The quagga of the London zoo died in 1872, that in Berlin in 1875, the Amsterdam quagga in 1883, and none was seen alive again until the artificial revival of the species through breedback selection and genetic manipulation in 1990, when this hunting preserve was opened to a limited and special clientele.

It is nearly noon, now, and not a shot has been fired all morning. The animals have begun heading for cover; they will not emerge until the shadows lengthen. Time to halt, pitch camp, break out the beer and sandwiches, tell tall tales of harrowing adventures with maddened buffaloes and edgy elephants. But not quite yet. The marchers come over a low hill and see, in the long sloping hollow beyond, a flock of ostriches and several hundred grazing zebras. As the humans appear, the ostriches begin slowly and warily to move off, but the zebras, altogether unafraid, continue to graze. Ngiri points and says, *"Piga quagga, bwana."*

"Just a bunch of zebras," Zacharias says.

Gracchus shakes his head. "No. Listen. You hear the sound?"

At first no one perceives anything unusual. But then, yes, Sybille hears it: a shrill barking neigh, very strange, a sound out of lost time, the cry of some beast she has never known. It is a song of the dead. Nerita hears it too, and Mortimer, and finally Zacharias. Gracchus nods toward the far side of the hollow. There, among the zebras, are half a dozen animals that might almost be zebras, but are not—unfinished zebras, striped only on their heads and foreparts; the rest of their bodies are yellowish brown, their legs are white, their manes are dark-brown with pale stripes. Their coats sparkle like mica in the sunshine. Now and again they lift their heads, emit that weird percussive whistling snort, and bend to the grass again. Quaggas. Strays out of the past, relicts, rekindled specters. Gracchus signals and the party fans out along the peak of the hill. Ngiri hands Zacharias his colossal gun. Zacharias kneels, sights.

"No hurry," Gracchus murmurs. "We have all afternoon."

"Do I seem to be hurrying?" Zacharias asks. The zebras now block the little group of quaggas from his view, almost as if by design. He must not shoot a zebra, of course, or there will be trouble with the rangers. Minutes go by. Then the

screen of zebras abruptly parts and Zacharias squeezes his
trigger. There is a vast explosion; zebras bolt in ten directions, so that the eye is bombarded with dizzying stroboscop-
ic waves of black and white; when the convulsive confusion
passes, one of the quaggas is lying on its side, alone in the
field, having made the transition across the interface. Sybille
regards it calmly. Death once dismayed her, death of any
kind, but no longer.

"Piga m'uzuri!" the porters cry exultantly.

"Kufa," Gracchus says. "Dead. A neat shot. You have your
trophy."

Ngiri is quick with the skinning-knife. That night, camping
below Kilimanjaro's broad flank, they dine on roast quagga,
deads and porters alike. The meat is juicy, robust, faintly
tangy.

Late the following afternoon, as they pass through cooler
stream-broken country thick with tall, scrubby gray-green
vase-shaped trees, they come upon a monstrosity, a shaggy
shambling thing twelve or fifteen feet high, standing upright
on ponderous hind legs and balancing itself on an incredibly
thick, heavy tail. It leans against a tree, pulling at its top
branches with long forelimbs that are tipped with ferocious
claws like a row of sickles; it munches voraciously on leaves
and twigs. Briefly it notices them, and looks around, studying
them with small stupid yellow eyes; then it returns to its
meal.

"A rarity," Gracchus says. "I know hunters who have been
all over this park without ever running into one. Have you
ever seen anything so ugly?"

"What is it?" Sybille asks.

"Megatherium. Giant ground sloth. South American, really, but we weren't fussy about geography when we were
stocking this place. We have only four of them, and it costs
God knows how many thousands of dollars to shoot one.
Nobody's signed up for a ground sloth yet. I doubt anyone
will."

Sybille wonders where the beast might be vulnerable to a
bullet: surely not in its dim peanut-sized brain. She wonders,
too, what sort of sportsman would find pleasure in killing
such a thing. For a while they watch as the sluggish monster
tears the tree apart. Then they move on.

* * *

Gracchus shows them another prodigy at sundown: a pale dome, like some huge melon, nestling in a mound of dense grass beside a stream. "Ostrich egg?" Mortimer guesses.

"Close. Very close. It's a moa egg. World's biggest bird. From New Zealand, extinct since about the eighteenth century."

Nerita crouches and lightly taps the egg. "What an omelet we could make!"

"There's enough there to feed seventy-five of us," Gracchus says. "Two gallons of fluid, easy. But of course we mustn't meddle with it. Natural increase is very important in keeping this park stocked."

"And where's mama moa?" Sybille asks. "Should she have abandoned the egg?"

"Moas aren't very bright," Gracchus answers. "That's one good reason why they became extinct. She must have wandered off to find some dinner. And—"

"Good God," Zacharias blurts.

The moa has returned, emerging suddenly from a thicket. She stands like a feathered mountain above them, limned by the deep-blue of twilight: an ostrich, more or less, but a magnified ostrich, an ultimate ostrich, a bird a dozen feet high, with a heavy rounded body and a great thick hose of a neck and taloned legs sturdy as saplings. Surely this is Sinbad's rukh, that can fly off with elephants in its grasp! The bird peers at them, sadly contemplating the band of small beings clustered about her egg; she arches her neck as though readying for an attack, and Zacharias reaches for one of the rifles, but Gracchus checks his hand, for the moa is merely rearing back to protest. It utters a deep mournful mooing sound and does not move. "Just back slowly away," Gracchus tells them. "It won't attack. But keep away from the feet; one kick can kill you."

"I was going to apply for a license on a moa," Mortimer says.

"Killing them's a bore," Gracchus tells him. "They just stand there and let you shoot. You're better off with what you signed up for."

What Mortimer has signed up for is an aurochs, the vanished wild ox of the European forests, known to Caesar, known to Pliny, hunted by the hero Siegfried, altogether exterminated by the year 1627. The plains of East Africa are not a comfortable environment for the aurochs and the herd that has been conjured by the genetic necromancers keeps to itself in the wooded highlands, several days' journey from the haunts of quaggas and ground sloths. In this dark grove the hunters come upon troops of chattering baboons and solitary big-eared elephants and, in a place of broken sunlight and shadow, a splendid antelope, a bull bongo with a fine curving pair of horns. Gracchus leads them onward, deeper in. He seems tense: there is peril here. The porters slip through the forest like black wraiths, spreading out in arching crab-claw patterns, communicating with one another and with Gracchus by whistling. Everyone keeps weapons ready in here. Sybille half expects to see leopards draped on overhanging branches, cobras slithering through the undergrowth. But she feels no fear.

They approach a clearing.

"Aurochs," Gracchus says.

A dozen of them are cropping the shrubbery: big short-haired long-horned cattle, muscular and alert. Picking up the scent of the intruders, they lift their heavy heads, sniff, glare. Gracchus and Ngiri confer with eyebrows. Nodding, Gracchus mutters to Mortimer, "Too many of them. Wait for them to thin off." Mortimer smiles. He looks a little nervous. The aurochs has a reputation for attacking without warning. Four, five, six of the beasts slip away, and the others withdraw to the edge of the clearing, as if to plan strategy; but one big bull, sour-eyed and grim, stands his ground, glowering. Gracchus rolls on the balls of his feet. His burly body seems, to Sybille, a study in mobility, in preparedness.

"Now," he says.

In the same moment the bull aurochs charges, moving with extraordinary swiftness, head lowered, horns extended like spears. Mortimer fires. The bullet strikes with a loud whonking sound, crashing into the shoulder of the aurochs, a perfect shot, but the animal does not fall, and Mortimer shoots again, less gracefully ripping into the belly, and then Gracchus and Ngiri are firing also, not at Mortimer's aurochs but over the heads of the others, to drive them away, and the risky tactic works, for the other animals go stampeding off into the woods. The one Mortimer has shot continues toward him, staggering now, losing momentum, and falls practically at his feet, rolling over, knifing the forest floor with its hooves.

"Kufa," Ngiri says. "Piga nyati m'uzuri, bwana."

Mortimer grins. *"Piga,"* he says.

Gracchus salutes him. "More exciting than moa," he says.

"And these are mine," says Nerita three hours later, indicating a tree at the outer rim of the forest. Several hundred large pigeons nest in its boughs, so many of them that the tree seems to be sprouting birds rather than leaves. The females are plain—light-brown above, gray below—but the males are flamboyant, with rich, glossy blue plumage on their wings and backs, breasts of a wine-red chestnut color, iridescent spots of bronze and green on their necks, and weird, vivid eyes of a bright, fiery orange. Gracchus says, "Right. You've found your passenger pigeons."

"Where's the thrill in shooting pigeons out of a tree?" Mortimer asks.

Nerita gives him a withering look. "Where's the thrill in gunning down a charging bull?" She signals to Ngiri, who fires a shot into the air. The startled pigeons burst from their perches and fly in low circles. In the old days, a century and a half ago in the forests of North America, no one troubled to shoot passenger pigeons on the wing: the pigeons were food, not sport, and it was simpler to blast them as they sat, for that way a single hunter might kill thousands of birds in one day. Thus it took only fifty years to reduce the passenger pigeon population from uncountable sky-blackening billions to zero. Nerita is more sporting. This is a test of her skill, after all. She aims her shotgun, shoots, pumps, shoots, pumps. Stunned birds drop to the ground. She and her gun are a single entity, sharing one purpose. In moments it is all over. The porters retrieve the fallen birds and snap their necks. Nerita has the dozen pigeons her license allows: a pair to mount, the rest for tonight's dinner. The survivors have returned to their tree and stare placidly, unreproachfully, at the hunters.

"They breed so damned fast," Gracchus mutters. "If we aren't careful, they'll be getting out of the preserve and taking over all of Africa."

Sybille laughs. "Don't worry. We'll cope. We wiped them out once and we can do it again, if we have to."

Sybille's prey is a dodo. In Dar, when they were applying for their licenses, the others mocked her choice: a fat flightless bird, unable to run or fight, so feeble of wit that it fears nothing. She ignored them. She wants a dodo because to her it is the essence of extinction, the prototype of all that is dead and vanished. That there is no sport in shooting foolish dodos means little to Sybille. Hunting itself is meaningless for her.

Through this vast park she wanders as in a dream. She sees ground sloths, great auks, quaggas, moas, heath hens, Javan rhinos, giant armadillos, and many other rarities. The place is an abode of ghosts. The ingenuities of the genetic craftsmen are limitless; someday, perhaps, the preserve will offer trilobites, tyrannosaurs, mastodons, saber-toothed cats, baluchitheria, even—why not?—packs of Australopithecines, tribes of Neanderthals. For the amusement of the deads, whose games tend to be somber. Sybille wonders whether it can really be considered killing, this slaughter of laboratory-spawned novelties. Are these animals real or artificial? Living things, or cleverly animated constructs? Real, she decides. Living. They eat, they metabolize, they reproduce. They must seem real to themselves, and so they are real, realer, maybe, than dead human beings who walk again in their own cast-off bodies.

"Shotgun," Sybille says to the closest porter.

There is the bird, ugly, ridiculous, waddling laboriously through the tall grass. Sybille accepts a weapon and sights along its barrel. "Wait," Nerita says. "I'd like to get a picture of this." She moves slantwise around the group, taking exaggerated care not to frighten the dodo, but the dodo does not seem to be aware of any of them. Like an emissary from the realm of darkness, carrying good news of death to those creatures not yet extinct, it plods diligently across their path. "Fine," Nerita says. "Anthony, point at the dodo, will you, as if you've just noticed it? Kent, I'd like you to look down at your gun, study its bolt or something. Fine. And Sybille, just hold that pose—aiming—yes—"

Nerita takes the picture.

Calmly Sybille pulls the trigger.

"*Kazi imekwisha,*" Gracchus says. "The work is finished."

Six

Although to be driven back upon oneself is an uneasy affair at best, rather like trying to cross a border with borrowed credentials, it seems to be now the one condition necessary to the beginnings of real self-respect. Most of our platitudes notwithstanding, self-deception remains the most difficult deception. The tricks that work on others count for nothing in that very well-lit back alley where one keeps assignations with oneself: no winning smiles will do here, no prettily drawn lists of good intentions.

Joan Didion: *On Self-Respect*

"You better believe what Jeej is trying to tell you," Dolorosa said. "Ten minutes inside the Cold Town, they'll have your number. Five minutes."

Jijibhoi's man was small, rumpled-looking, forty or fifty years old, with untidy long dark hair and wide-set smoldering eyes. His skin was sallow and his face was gaunt. Such other deads as Klein had seen at close range had about them an air of unearthly serenity, but not this one: Dolorosa was tense, fidgety, a knuckle-cracker, a lip-gnawer. Yet somehow there could be no doubt he was a dead, as much a dead as Zacharias, as Gracchus, as Mortimer.

"They'll have my what?" Klein asked.

"Your number. Your number. They'll know you aren't a dead, because it can't be faked. Jesus, don't you even speak English? Jorge, that's a foreign name. I should have known. Where are you from?"

"Argentina, as a matter of fact, but I was brought to California when I was a small boy. In 1955. Look, if they catch me, they catch me. I just want to get in there and spend half an hour talking with my wife."

"Mister, you don't have any wife any more."

"With Sybille," Klein said, exasperated. "To talk with Sybille, my—my former wife."

"All right. I'll get you inside."

"What will it cost?"

"Never mind that," Dolorosa said. "I owe Jeej here a few favors. More than a few. So I'll get you the drug—"

"Drug?"

"The drug the Treasury agents use when they infiltrate the Cold Towns. It narrows the pupils, contracts the capillaries, gives you that good old zombie look. The agents always get caught and thrown out, and so will you, but at least you'll go in there feeling that you've got a convincing disguise. Little oily capsule, one every morning before breakfast."

Klein looked at Jijibhoi. "Why do Treasury agents infiltrate the Cold Towns?"

"For the same reasons they infiltrate anywhere else," Jijibhoi said. "To spy. They are trying to compile dossiers on the financial dealings of the deads, you see, and until proper life-defining legislation is approved by Congress there is no precise way of compelling a person who is deemed legally dead to divulge—"

Dolorosa said, "Next, the background. I can get you a card of residence from Albany Cold Town in New York. You died last December, okay, and they rekindled you back east because—let's see—"

"I could have been attending the annual meeting of the American Historical Association in New York," Klein suggested. "That's what I do, you understand, professor of contemporary history at UCLA. Because of the Christmas holiday my body couldn't be shipped back to California, no room on any flight, and so they took me to Albany. How does that sound?"

Dolorosa smiled. "You really enjoy making up lies, Professor, don't you? I can dig that quality in you. Okay, Albany Cold Town, and this is your first trip out of there, your drying-off trip—that's what it's called, drying-off—you come out of the Cold Town like a new butterfly just out of its cocoon, all soft and damp, and you're on your own in a strange place. Now, there's a lot of stuff you'll need to know about how to behave, little mannerisms, social graces, that kind of crap, and I'll work on that with you tomorrow and Wednesday and Friday, three sessions; that ought to be enough. Meanwhile let me give you the basics. There are only three things you really have to remember while you're inside:

"(1) Never ask a direct question.

"(2) Never lean on anybody's arm. You know what I mean?

"(3) Keep in mind that to a dead the whole universe is plastic, nothing's real, nothing matters a hell of a lot, it's all only a joke. Only a joke, friend, only a joke."

Early in April he flew to Salt Lake City, rented a car, and drove out past Moab into the high plateau rimmed by red-rock mountains where the deads had built Zion Cold Town.

This was Klein's second visit to the necropolis. The other had been in the late summer of '91, a hot, parched season when the sun filled half the sky and even the gnarled junipers looked dazed from thirst; but now it was a frosty afternoon, with faint pale light streaming out of the wintry western hills and occasional gusts of light snow whirling through the iron-blue air. Jijibhoi's route instructions pulsed from the memo screen on his dashboard. Fourteen miles from town, yes, narrow paved lane turns off highway, yes, discreet little sign announcing PRIVATE ROAD, NO ADMITTANCE, yes, a second sign a thousand yards in, ZION COLD TOWN, MEMBERS ONLY, yes, and then just beyond that the barrier of green light across the road, the scanner system, the roadblocks sliding like scythes out of the underground installations, a voice on an invisible loudspeaker saying, "If you have a permit to enter Zion Cold Town, please place it under your left-hand windshield wiper."

That other time he had had no permit, and he had gone no farther than this, though at least he had managed a little colloquy with the unseen gatekeeper out of which he had squeezed the information that Sybille was indeed living in that particular Cold Town. This time he affixed Dolorosa's forged card of residence to his windshield, and waited tensely, and in thirty seconds the roadblocks slid from sight. He drove on, along a winding road that followed the natural contours of a dense forest of scrubby conifers, and came at last to a brick wall that curved away into the trees as though it encircled the entire town. Probably it did. Klein had an overpowering sense of the Cold Town as a hermetic city, ponderous and sealed as old Egypt. There was a metal gate in the brick wall; green electronic eyes surveyed him, signaled their approval, and the wall rolled open.

He drove slowly toward the center of town, passing through a zone of what he supposed were utility buildings—storage depots, a power substation, the municipal waterworks, whatever, a bunch of grim windowless one-story cinderblock affairs—and then into the residential district, which was not much lovelier. The streets were laid out on a rectangular grid; the buildings were squat, dreary, impersonal, homogeneous. There was practically no automobile traffic, and in a dozen blocks he saw no more than ten pedestrians, who did not even glance at him. So this was the environment in which the deads chose to spend their second lives. But why such deliberate bleakness? "You will never understand us," Dolorosa had warned. Dolorosa was right. Jijibhoi had told him that Cold Towns were something less than charming, but Klein had not been prepared for this. There was a glacial quality about the place, as though it were wholly entombed in a block of clear ice: silence, sterility, a mortuary calm. Cold Town, yes, aptly named. Architecturally, the town looked like the worst of all possible cheap-and-sleazy tract developments, but the psychic texture it projected was even more depressing, more like that of one of those ghastly retirement communities, one of the innumerable Leisure Worlds or Sun Manors, those childless joyless retreats where colonies of that other kind of living dead collected to await the last trumpet. Klein shivered.

At last, another few minutes deeper into the town, a sign of activity, if not exactly of life: a shopping center, flat-topped brown stucco buildings around a U-shaped courtyard, a steady flow of shoppers moving about. All right. His first test was about to commence. He parked his car near the mouth of the U and strolled uneasily inward. He felt as if his forehead were a beacon, flashing glowing betrayals at rhythmic intervals:

FRAUD   INTRUDER   INTERLOPER   SPY

Go ahead, he thought, seize me, seize the impostor, get it over with, throw me out, string me up, crucify me. But no one seemed to pick up the signals. He was altogether ignored. Out of courtesy? Or just contempt? He stole what he hoped were covert glances at the shoppers, half expecting to run across Sybille right away. They all looked like sleepwalkers, moving in glazed silence about their errands. No smiles, no chatter: the icy aloofness of these self-contained people heightened the familiar suburban atmosphere of the shopping center into surrealist intensity, Norman Rockwell with an overlay of Dali or De Chirico. The shopping center looked like all other shopping centers: clothing stores, a bank, a record shop, snack bars, a florist, a TV-stereo outlet, a theater, a five-and-dime. One difference, though, because apparent as Klein wandered from shop to shop: the whole place was automated. There were no clerks anywhere, only the ubiquitous data screens, and no doubt a battery of hidden scanners to discourage shoplifters. (Or did the impulse toward petty theft perish with the body's first death?) The customers selected all the merchandise themselves, checked it out via data screens, touched their thumbs to charge-plates to debit their accounts. Of course. No one was going to waste his precious rekindled existence standing behind a counter to sell tennis shoes or cotton candy. Nor were the dwellers in the Cold Towns likely to dilute their isolation by hiring a labor force of imported warms. Somebody here had to do a little work, obviously—how did the merchandise get into the stores?—but, in general, Klein realized, what could not be done here by machines would not be done at all.

For ten minutes he prowled the center. Just when he was beginning to think he must be entirely invisible to these people, a short, broad-shouldered man, bald but with oddly youthful features, paused in front of him and said, "I am Pablo. I welcome you to Zion Cold Town." This unexpected puncturing of the silence so startled Klein that he had to fight to retain appropriate deadlike imperturbability. Pablo smiled warmly and touched both his hands to Klein's in friendly greeting, but his eyes were frigid, hostile, remote, a terrifying contradiction. "I've been sent to bring you to the lodging-place. Come: your car."

Other than to give directions, Pablo spoke only three times during the five-minute drive. "Here is the rekindling house," he said. A five-story building, as inviting as a hospital, with walls of dark bronze and windows black as onyx. "This is Guidefather's house," Pablo said a moment later. A modest brick building, like a rectory, at the edge of a small park. And, finally: "This is where you will stay. Enjoy your visit." Abruptly he got out of the car and walked rapidly away.

This was the house of strangers, the hotel for visiting deads, a long low cinderblock structure, functional and unglamorous, one of the least seductive buildings in this city of stark disagreeable buildings. However else it might be with the deads, they clearly had no craving for fancy architecture. A voice out of a data screen in the spartan lobby assigned him to a room: a white-walled box, square, high of ceiling. He had his own toilet, his own data screen, a narrow bed, a chest of drawers, a modest closet, a small window that gave him a view of a neighboring building just as drab as this. Nothing had been said about rental; perhaps he was a guest of the city. Nothing had been said about anything. It seemed that he had been accepted. So much for Jijibhoi's gloomy assurance that he would instantly be found out, so much for Dolorosa's insistence that they would have his number in ten minutes or less. He had been in Zion Cold Town for half an hour. Did they have his number?

"Eating isn't important among us," Dolorosa had said.

"But you do eat?"

"Of course we eat. It just isn't *important*."

It was important to Klein, though. Not *haute cuisine*, necessarily, but some sort of food, preferably three times a day. He was getting hungry now. Ring for room service? There were no servants in this city. He turned to the data screen. Dolorosa's first rule: *Never ask a direct question*. Surely that didn't apply to the data screen, only to his fellow deads. He didn't have to observe the niceties of etiquette when talking to a computer. Still, the voice behind the screen might not be that of a computer after all, so he tried to employ the oblique, elliptical conversational style that Dolorosa said the deads favored among themselves:

"Dinner?"

"Commissary."

"Where?"

"Central Four," said the screen.

Central Four? All right. He would find the way. He changed into fresh clothing and went down the long vinyl-floored hallway to the lobby. Night had come; street lamps were glowing; under cloak of darkness the city's ugliness was no longer so obtrusive, and there was even a kind of controlled beauty about the brutal regularity of its streets.

The streets were unmarked, though, and deserted. Klein walked at random for ten minutes, hoping to meet someone heading for the Central Four commissary. But when he did come upon someone, a tall and regal woman well advanced in years, he found himself incapable of approaching her. (*Never ask a direct question. Never lean on anybody's arm.*) He walked alongside her, in silence and at a distance, until she turned suddenly to enter a house. For ten minutes more he wandered alone again. This is ridiculous, he thought: dead or warm, I'm a stranger in town, I should be entitled to a little assistance. Maybe Dolorosa was just trying to complicate things. On the next corner, when Klein caught sight of a man hunched away from the wind, lighting a cigarette, he went boldly over to him. "Excuse me, but—"

The other looked up. "Klein?" he said. "Yes. Of course. Well, so you've made the crossing too!"

He was one of Sybille's Zanzibar companions, Klein realized. The quick-eyed, sharp-edged one—Mortimer. A member of her pseudo-familial grouping, whatever that might be. Klein stared sullenly at him. This had to be the moment when his imposture would be exposed, for only some six weeks had passed since he had argued with Mortimer in the gardens of Sybille's Zanzibar hotel, not nearly enough time for someone to have died and been rekindled and gone through his drying-off. But a moment passed and Mortimer said nothing. At length Klein said, "I just got here. Pablo showed me to the house of strangers and now I'm looking for the commissary."

"Central Four? I'm going there myself. How lucky for you." No sign of suspicion in Mortimer's face. Perhaps an elusive smile revealed his awareness that Klein could not be what he claimed to be. *Keep in mind that to a dead the whole universe is plastic, it's all only a joke.* "I'm waiting for Nerita," Mortimer said. "We can all eat together."

Klein said heavily, "I was rekindled in Albany Cold Town. I've just emerged."

"How nice," Mortimer said.

Nerita Tracy stepped out of a building just beyond the corner—a slim, athletic-looking woman, about forty, with short reddish-brown hair. As she swept toward them, Mortimer said, "Here's Klein, who we met in Zanzibar. Just rekindled, out of Albany."

"Sybille will be amused."

"Is she in town?" Klein blurted.

Mortimer and Nerita exchanged sly glances. Klein felt abashed. *Never ask a direct question.* Damn Dolorosa!

Nerita said, "You'll see her before long. Shall we go to dinner?"

The commissary was less austere than Klein had expected: actually quite an inviting restaurant, elaborately constructed on five or six levels divided by lustrous dark hangings into small, secluded dining areas. It had the warm, rich look of a tropical resort. But the food, which came automat-style out of revolving dispensers, was prefabricated and cheerless—another jarring contradiction. *Only a joke, friend, only a joke.* In any case he was less hungry than he had imagined at the hotel. He sat with Mortimer and Nerita, picking at his meal, while their conversation flowed past him at several times the speed

of thought. They spoke in fragments and ellipses, in peri-
phrastics and aposiopeses, in a style abundant in chiasmus,
metonymy, meiosis, oxymoron, and zeugma; their dazzling
rhetorical techniques left him baffled and uncomfortable,
which beyond much doubt was their intention. Now and
again they would dart from a thicket of indirection to skewer
him with a quick corroborative stab: Isn't that so, they would
say, and he would smile and nod, nod and smile, saying, Yes,
yes, absolutely. Did they know he was a fake, and were they
merely playing with him, or had they, somehow, impossibly,
accepted him as one of them? So subtle was their style that
he could not tell. A very new member of the society of the
rekindled, he told himself, would be nearly as much at sea
here as a warm in deadface.

Then Nerita said—no verbal games, this time—"You still
miss her terribly, don't you?"

"I do. Some things evidently never perish."

"Everything perishes," Mortimer said. "The dodo, the
aurochs, the Holy Roman Empire, the T'ang Dynasty, the
walls of Byzantium, the language of Mohenjo-daro."

"But not the Great Pyramid, the Yangtze, the coelacanth,
or the skullcap of Pithecanthropus," Klein countered. "Some
things persist and endure. And some can be regenerated.
Lost languages have been deciphered. I believe the dodo and
the aurochs are hunted in a certain African park in this very
era."

"Replicas," Mortimer said.

"Convincing replicas. Simulations as good as the original."

"Is that what you want?" Nerita asked.

"I want what's possible to have."

"A convincing replica of lost love?"

"I might be willing to settle for five minutes of conversation with her."

"You'll have it. Not tonight. See? There she is. But don't
bother her now." Nerita nodded across the gulf in the center
of the restaurant; on the far side, three levels up from where
they sat, Sybille and Kent Zacharias had appeared. They
stood for a brief while at the edge of their dining alcove,
staring blandly and emotionlessly into the restaurant's central
well. Klein felt a muscle jerking uncontrollably in his cheek,
a damning revelation of undeadlike uncoolness, and pressed
his hand over it, so that it twanged and throbbed against his
palm. She was like a goddess up there, manifesting herself in

her sanctum to her worshipers, a pale shimmering figure, more beautiful even than she had become to him through the anguished enhancements of memory, and it seemed impossible to him that that being had ever been his wife, that he had known her when her eyes were puffy and reddened from a night of study, that he had looked down at her face as they made love and had seen her lips pull back in that spasm of ecstasy that is so close to a grimace of pain, that he had known her crochety and unkind in her illness, short-tempered and impatient in health, a person of flaws and weaknesses, of odors and blemishes, in short a human being, this goddess, this unreal rekindled creature, this object of his quest, this Sybille. Serenely she turned, serenely she vanished into her cloaked alcove. "She knows you're here," Nerita told him. "You'll see her. Perhaps tomorrow." Then Mortimer said something maddeningly oblique, and Nerita replied with the same off-center mystification, and Klein once more was plunged into the river of their easy dancing wordplay, down into it, down and down and down, and as he struggled to keep from drowning, as he fought to comprehend their interchanges, he never once looked toward the place where Sybille sat, not even once, and congratulated himself on having accomplished that much at least in his masquerade.

That night, lying alone in his room at the house of strangers, he wonders what he will say to Sybille when they finally meet, and what she will say to him. Will he dare bluntly to ask her to describe to him the quality of her new existence? That is all that he wants from her, really, that knowledge, that opening of an aperture into her transfigured self; that is as much as he hopes to get from her, knowing as he does that there is scarcely a chance of regaining her, but will he dare to ask, will he dare even that? Of course his asking such things will reveal to her that he is still a warm, too dense and gross of perception to comprehend the life of a dead; but he is certain she will sense that anyway, instantly. What will he say, what will he say? He plays out an imagined script of their conversation in the theater of his mind:
  —Tell me what it's like, Sybille, to be the way you are now.
  —Like swimming under a sheet of glass.
  —I don't follow.
  —Everything is quiet where I am, Jorge. There's a peace that passeth all understanding. I used to feel sometimes that I

was caught up in a great storm, that I was being buffeted by every breeze, that my life was being consumed by agitations and frenzies, but now, now, I'm at the eye of the storm, at the place where everything is always calm. I observe rather than let myself be acted upon.

—But isn't there a loss of feeling that way? Don't you feel that you're wrapped in an insulating layer? Like swimming under glass, you say—that conveys being insulated, being cut off, being almost numb.

—I suppose you might think so. The way it is, is that one no longer is affected by the unnecessary.

—It sounds to me like a limited existence.

—Less limited than the grave, Jorge.

—I never understood why you wanted rekindling. You were such a world-devourer, Sybille, you lived with such intensity, such passion. To settle for the kind of existence you have now, to be only half-alive—

—Don't be a fool, Jorge. To be half-alive is better than to be rotting in the ground. I was so young. There was so much else still to see and do.

—But to see it and do it half-alive?

—Those were your words, not mine. I'm not alive at all. I'm neither less nor more than the person you knew. I'm another kind of being altogether. Neither less nor more, only different.

—Are all your perceptions different?

—Very much so. My perspective is broader. Little things stand revealed as little things.

—Give me an example, Sybille.

—I'd rather not. How could I make anything clear to you? Die and be with us, and you'll understand.

—You know I'm not dead?

—Oh, Jorge, how funny you are!

—How nice that I can still amuse you.

—You look so hurt, so tragic. I could almost feel sorry for you. Come: ask me anything.

—Could you leave your companions and live in the world again?

—I've never considered that.

—Could you?

—I suppose I could. But why should I? This is my world now.

—This ghetto.

—Is that how it seems to you?

—You lock yourselves into a closed society of your peers, a tight subculture. Your own jargon, your own wall of etiquette and idiosyncrasy. Designed, I think, mainly to keep the outsiders off balance, to keep them feeling like outsiders. It's a defensive thing. The hippies, the blacks, the gays, the deads—same mechanism, same process.

—The Jews, too. Don't forget the Jews.

—All right, Sybille, the Jews. With their little tribal jokes, their special holidays, their own mysterious language, yes, a good case in point.

—So I've joined a new tribe. What's wrong with that?

—Did you need to be part of a tribe?

—What did I have before? The tribe of Californians? The tribe of academics?

—The tribe of Jorge and Sybille Klein.

—Too narrow. Anyway, I've been expelled from that tribe. I needed to join another one.

—Expelled?

—By death. After that there's no going back.

—You could go back. Any time.

—Oh, no, no, no, Jorge, I can't, I can't, I'm not Sybille Klein any more, I never will be again. How can I explain it to you? There's no way. Death brings on changes. Die and see. Jorge. Die and see.

Nerita said, "She's waiting for you in the lounge."

It was a big, coldly furnished room at the far end of the other wing of the house of strangers. Sybille stood by a window through which pale, chilly morning light was streaming. Mortimer was with her, and also Kent Zacharias. The two men favored Klein with mysterious oblique smiles—courteous or derisive, he could not tell which. "Do you like our town?" Zacharias asked. "Have you been seeing the sights?" Klein chose not to reply. He acknowledged the question with a faint nod and turned to Sybille. Strangely, he felt altogether calm at this moment of attaining a years-old desire: he felt nothing at all in her presence, no panic, no yearning, no dismay, no nostalgia, nothing, nothing. As though he were truly a dead. He knew it was the tranquility of utter terror.

"We'll leave you two alone," Zacharias said. "You must have so much to tell each other." He went out, with Nerita and Mortimer. Klein's eyes met Sybille's and lingered there. She was looking at him coolly, in a kind of impersonal appraisal. That damnable smile of hers, Klein thought: dying turns them all into Mona Lisas.

She said, "Do you plan to stay here long?"

"Probably not. A few days, maybe a week." He moistened his lips. "How have you been, Sybille? How has it been going?"

"It's all been about as I expected."

What do you mean by that? Can you give me some details? Are you at all disappointed? Have there been any surprises? What has it been like for you, Sybille? Oh, Jesus—

—Never ask a direct question—

He said, "I wish you had let me visit with you in Zanzibar."

"That wasn't possible. Let's not talk about it now." She dismissed the episode with a casual wave. After a moment she said, "Would you like to hear a fascinating story I've uncovered about the early days of Omani influence in Zanzibar?"

The impersonality of the question startled him. How could she display such absolute lack of curiosity about his presence in Zion Cold Town, his claim to be a dead, his reasons for wanting to see her? How could she plunge so quickly, so coldly, into a discussion of archaic political events in Zanzibar?

"I suppose so," he said weakly.

"It's a sort of Arabian Nights story, really. It's the story of how Ahmad the Sly overthrew Abdullah ibn Muhammad Alawi."

The names were strange to him. He had indeed taken some small part in her historical researches, but it was years since he had worked with her, and everything had drifted about in his mind, leaving a jumbled residue of Ahmads and Hasans and Abdullahs. "I'm sorry," he said. "I don't recall who they were."

Unperturbed, Sybille said, "Certainly you remember that in the eighteenth and early nineteenth centuries the chief power in the Indian Ocean was the Arab state of Oman, ruled from Muscat on the Persian Gulf. Under the Busaidi dynasty, founded in 1744 by Ahmad ibn Said al-Busaidi, the Omani extended their power to East Africa. The logical capital for their African empire was the port of Mombasa, but they were unable to evict a rival dynasty reigning there, so the Busaidi looked toward nearby Zanzibar—a cosmopolitan island of mixed Arab, Indian, and African population. Zanzibar's strategic placement on the coast and its spacious and well-protected harbor made it an ideal base for the East African slave trade that the Busaidi of Oman intended to dominate."

"It comes back to me now, I think."

"Very well. The founder of the Omani Sultanate of Zanzibar was Ahmad ibn Majid the Sly, who came to the throne of Oman in 1811—do you remember?—upon the death of his uncle Abd-er-Rahman al-Busaidi."

"The names sound familiar," Klein said doubtfully.

"Seven years later," Sybille continued, "seeking to conquer Zanzibar without the use of force, Ahmad the Sly shaved his beard and mustache and visited the island disguised as a soothsayer, wearing yellow robes and a costly emerald in his turban. At that time most of Zanzibar was governed by a native ruler of mixed Arab and African blood, Abdullah ibn Muhammad Alawi, whose hereditary title was Mwenyi Mkuu. The Mwenyi Mkuu's subjects were mainly Africans, members of a tribe called the Hadimu. Sultan Ahmad, arriving in Zanzibar Town, gave a demonstration of his soothsaying skills on the waterfront and attracted so much attention that he speedily gained an audience at the court of the Mwenyi Mkuu. Ahmad predicted a glowing future for Abdullah, declaring that a powerful prince famed throughout the world would come to Zanzibar, make the Mwenyi Mkuu his high lieutenant, and confirm him and his descendants as lords of Zanzibar forever.

"'How do you know these things?' asked the Mwenyi Mkuu.

"'There is a potion I drink,' Sultan Ahmad replied, 'that enables me to see what is to come. Do you wish to taste of it?'

"'Most surely I do,' Abdullah said, and Ahmad thereupon gave him a drug that sent him into rapturous transports and showed him visions of paradise. Looking down from his place near the footstool of Allah, the Mwenyi Mkuu saw a rich and happy Zanzibar governed by his children's children's children. For hours he wandered in fantasies of almighty power.

"Ahmad then departed, and let his beard and mustache grow again, and returned to Zanzibar ten weeks later in his full regalia as Sultan of Oman, at the head of an imposing and powerful armada. He went at once to the court of the Mwenyi Mkuu and proposed, just as the soothsayer had prophesied, that Oman and Zanzibar enter into a treaty of alliance under which Oman would assume responsibility for much of Zanzibar's external relations—including the slave trade—while guaranteeing the authority of the Mwenyi Mkuu over domestic affairs. In return for his partial abdication of authority, the Mwenyi Mkuu would receive financial compensation from Oman. Remembering the vision the soothsayer had revealed to him, Abdullah at once signed the treaty, thereby legitimizing what was, in effect, the Omani conquest of Zanzibar. A great feast was held to celebrate the treaty, and, as a mark of honor, the Mwenyi Mkuu offered Sultan Ahmad a rare drug used locally, known as *borqash*, or 'the flower of truth.' Ahmad only pretended to put the pipe to his lips, for he loathed all mind-altering drugs, but Abdullah, as the flower of truth possessed him, looked at Ahmad and recognized the outlines of the soothsayer's face behind the Sultan's new beard. Realizing that he had been deceived, the Mwenyi Mkuu thrust his dagger, the tip of which was poisoned, deep into the Sultan's side and fled the banquet hall, taking up residence on the neighboring island of Pemba. Ahmad ibn Majid survived, but the poison consumed his vital organs and the remaining ten years of his life were spent in constant agony. As for the Mwenyi Mkuu, the Sultan's men hunted him down and put him to death along with ninety members of his family, and native rule in Zanzibar was therewith extinguished."

Sybille paused. "Is that not a gaudy and wonderful story?" she asked at last.

"Fascinating," Klein said. "Where did you find it?"

"Unpublished memoirs of Claude Richburn of the East India Company. Buried deep in the London archives. Strange that no historian ever came upon it before, isn't it? The standard texts simply say that Ahmad used his navy to bully Abdullah into signing the treaty, and then had the Mwenyi Mkuu assassinated at the first convenient moment."

"Very strange," Klein agreed. But he had not come here to listen to romantic tales of visionary potions and royal treacheries. He groped for some way to bring the conversation to a more personal level. Fragments of his imaginary dialogue with Sybille floated through his mind. *Everything is quiet where I am, Jorge. There's a peace that passeth all understanding. Like swimming under a sheet of glass. The way it is, is that one no longer is affected by the unnecessary. Little things stand revealed as little things. Die and be with us, and you'll understand*. Yes. Perhaps. But did she really believe any of that? He had put all the words in her mouth; everything he had imagined her to say was his own construct, worthless as a key to the true Sybille. Where would he find the key, though?

She gave him no chance. "I will be going back to Zanzibar soon," she said. "There's much I want to learn about this incident from the people in the back country—old legends about the last days of the Mwenyi Mkuu, perhaps variants on the basic story—"

"May I accompany you?"

"Don't you have your own research to resume, Jorge?" she asked, and did not wait for an answer. She walked briskly toward the door of the lounge and went out, and he was alone.

Seven

I mean what they and their hired psychiatrists call "delusional systems." Needless to say, "delusions" are always officially defined. We don't have to worry about questions of real or unreal. They only talk out of expediency. It's the *system* that matters. How the data arrange themselves inside it. Some are consistent, others fall apart.

Thomas Pynchon: *Gravity's Rainbow*

Once more the deads, this time only three of them, coming over on the morning flight from Dar. Three was better than five, Daud Mahmoud Barwani supposed, but three was still more than a sufficiency. Not that those others, two months back, had caused any trouble, staying just the one day and flitting off to the mainland again, but it made him uncomfortable to think of such creatures on the same small island as himself. With all the world to choose, why did they keep coming to Zanzibar?

"The plane is here," said the flight controller.

Thirteen passengers. The health officer let the local people through the gate first—two newspapermen and four legisla-

tors coming back from the Pan-African Conference in Capetown—
and then processed a party of four Japanese tourists, unsmiling
owlish men festooned with cameras. And then the deads: and
Barwani was surprised to discover that they were the same
ones as before, the red-haired man, the brown-haired man
without the beard, the black-haired woman. Did deads have
so much money that they could fly from America to Zanzibar
every few months? Barwani had heard a tale to the effect that
each new dead, when he rose from his coffin, was presented
with bars of gold equal to his own weight, and now he
thought he believed it. No good will come of having such
beings loose in the world, he told himself, and certainly none
from letting them into Zanzibar. Yet he had no choice.
"Welcome once again to the isle of cloves," he said unctuously,
and smiled a bureaucratic smile, and wondered, not for the
first time, what would become of Daud Mahmoud Barwani
once his days on earth had reached their end.

"—Ahmad the Sly versus Abdullah Something," Klein said.
"That's all she would talk about. The history of Zanzibar." He
was in Jijibhoi's study. The night was warm and a late-season
rain was falling, blurring the million sparkling lights of the
Los Angeles basin. "It would have been, you know, gauche to
ask her any direct questions. Gauche. I haven't felt so gauche
since I was fourteen. I was helpless among them, a foreigner,
a child."

"Do you think they saw through your disguise?" Jijibhoi
asked.

"I can't tell. They seemed to be toying with me, to be
having sport with me, but that may just have been their
general style with any newcomer. Nobody challenged me.
Nobody hinted I might be an impostor. Nobody seemed to
care very much about me or what I was doing there or how I
had happened to become a dead. Sybille and I stood face to
face, and I wanted to reach out to her, I wanted her to reach
out to me, and there was no contact, none, none at all, it was
as though we had just met at some academic cocktail party
and the only thing on her mind was the new nugget of
obscure history she had just unearthed, and so she told me all
about how Sultan Ahmad outfoxed Abdullah and Abdullah
stabbed the Sultan." Klein caught sight of a set of familiar
books on Jijibhoi's crowded shelves—Oliver and Mathew,
History of East Africa, books that had traveled everywhere

with Sybille in the years of their marriage. He pulled forth Volume I, saying, "She claimed that the standard histories give a sketchy and inaccurate description of the incident and that she's only now discovered the true story. For all I know, she was just playing a game with me, telling me a piece of established history as though it were something nobody knew till last week. Let me see—Ahmad, Ahmad, Ahmad—"

He examined the index. Five Ahmads were listed, but there was no entry for a Sultan Ahmad ibn Majid the Sly. Indeed, an Ahmad ibn Majid was cited, but he was mentioned only in a footnote and appeared to be an Arab chronicler. Klein found three Abdullahs, none of them a man of Zanzibar. "Something's wrong," he murmured.

"It does not matter, dear Jorge," Jijibhoi said mildly.

"It does. Wait a minute." He prowled the listings. Under *Zanzibar, Rulers,* he found no Ahmads, no Abdullahs; he did discover a Majid ibn Said, but when he checked the reference he found that he had reigned somewhere in the second half of the nineteenth century. Desperately Klein flipped pages, skimming, turning back, searching. Eventually he looked up and said, "It's all wrong!"

"The Oxford *History of East Africa?*"

"The details of Sybille's story. Look, she said this Ahmad the Sly gained the throne of Oman in 1811, and seized Zanzibar seven years later. But the book says that a certain Seyyid Said al-Busaidi became Sultan of Oman in 1806, and ruled for *fifty years.* He was the one, not this nonexistent Ahmad the Sly, who grabbed Zanzibar, but he did it in 1828, and the ruler he compelled to sign a treaty with him, the Mwenyi Mkuu, was named Hasan ibn Ahmad Alawi, and—" Klein shook his head. "It's an altogether different cast of characters. No stabbings, no assassinations, the dates are entirely different, the whole thing—"

Jijibhoi smiled sadly. "The deads are often mischievous."

"But why would she invent a complete fantasy and palm it off as a sensational new discovery? Sybille was the most scrupulous scholar I ever knew! She would never—"

"That was the Sybille you knew, dear friend. I keep urging you to realize that this is another person, a new person, within her body."

"A person who would lie about history?"

"A person who would tease," Jijibhoi said.

"Yes," Klein muttered. "Who would tease." *Keep in mind*

*that to a dead the whole universe is plastic, nothing's real,
nothing matters a hell of a lot.* "Who would tease a stupid,
boring, annoyingly persistent ex-husband who has shown up
in her Cold Town, wearing a transparent disguise and pretending
to be a dead. Who would invent not only an anecdote but
even its principals, as a joke, a game, a *jeu d'esprit*. Oh,
God. Oh, God, how cruel she is, how foolish I was! It was her
way of telling me she knew I was a phony dead. Quid pro
quo, fraud for fraud!"

"What will you do?"

"I don't know," Klein said.

What he did, against Jijibhoi's strong advice and his own
better judgment, was to get more pills from Dolorosa and
return to Zion Cold Town. There would be a fitful joy, like
that of probing the socket of a missing tooth, in confronting
Sybille with the evidence of her fictional Ahmad, her imaginary Abdullah. Let there be no more games between us, he
would say. Tell me what I need to know, Sybille, and then let
me go away; but tell me only truth. All the way to Utah he
rehearsed his speech, polishing and embellishing. There was
no need for it, though, since this time the gate of Zion Cold
Town would not open for him. The scanners scanned his
forged Albany card and the loudspeaker said, "Your credentials are invalid."

Which could have ended it. He might have returned to Los
Angeles and picked up the pieces of his life. All this semester
he had been on sabbatical leave, but the summer term was
coming and there was work to do. He did return to Los
Angeles, but only long enough to pack a somewhat larger
suitcase, find his passport, and drive to the airport. On a
sweet May evening a BOAC jet took him over the Pole to
London, where, barely pausing for coffee and buns at an
airport shop, he boarded another plane that carried him
southeast toward Africa. More asleep than awake, he watched
the dreamy landmarks drifting past: the Mediterranean, coming and going with surprising rapidity, and the tawny carpet
of the Libyan Desert, and the mighty Nile, reduced to a
brown thread's thickness when viewed from a height of ten
miles. Suddenly Kilimanjaro, mist-wrapped, snow-bound,
loomed like a giant double-headed blister to his right, far
below, and he thought he could make out to his left the
distant glare of the sun on the Indian Ocean. Then the big

needle-nosed plane began its abrupt swooping descent, and he found himself, soon after, stepping out into the warm humid air and dazzling sunlight of Dar es Salaam.

Too soon, too soon. He felt unready to go on to Zanzibar. A day or two of rest, perhaps: he picked a Dar hotel at random, the Agip, liking the strange sound of its name, and hired a taxi. The hotel was sleek and clean, a streamlined affair in the glossy 1960's style, much cheaper than the Kilimanjaro, where he had stayed briefly on the other trip, and located in a pleasant leafy quarter of the city, near the ocean. He strolled about for a short while, discovered that he was altogether exhausted, returned to his room for a nap that stretched on for nearly five hours, and awakening groggy, showered and dressed for dinner. The hotel's dining room was full of beefy red-faced fair-haired men, jacketless and wearing open-throated white shirts, all of whom reminded him disturbingly of Kent Zacharias; but these were warms, Britishers from their accents, engineers, he suspected, from their conversation. They were building a dam and a power plant somewhere up the coast, it seemed, or perhaps a power plant without a dam; it was hard to follow what they said. They drank a good deal of gin and spoke in hearty booming shouts. There were also a good many Japanese businessmen, of course, looking trim and restrained in dark-blue suits and narrow ties, and at the table next to Klein's were five tanned curly-haired men talking in rapid Hebrew—Israelis, surely. The only Africans in sight were waiters and bartenders. Klein ordered Mombasa oysters, steak, and a carafe of red wine, and found the food unexpectedly good, but left most of it on his plate. It was late evening in Tanzania, but for him it was ten o'clock in the morning, and his body was confused. He tumbled into bed, meditated vaguely on the probable presence of Sybille just a few air-minutes away in Zanzibar, and dropped into a sound sleep from which he awakened, what seemed like many hours later, to discover that it was still well before dawn.

He dawdled away the morning sightseeing in the old native quarter, hot and dusty, with unpaved streets and rows of tin shacks, and at midday returned to his hotel for a shower and lunch. Much the same national distribution in the restaurant— British, Japanese, Israeli—though the faces seemed different. He was on his second beer when Anthony Gracchus came in.

The white hunter, broad-shouldered, pale, densely bearded, clad in khaki shorts, khaki shirt, seemed almost to have stepped out of the picture-cube Jijibhoi had once shown him. Instinctively Klein shrank back, turning toward the window, but too late: Gracchus had seen him. All chatter came to a halt in the restaurant as the dead man strode to Klein's table, pulled out a chair unasked, and seated himself; then, as though a motion-picture projector had been halted and started again, the British engineers resumed their shouting, sounding somewhat strained now. "Small world," Gracchus said. "Crowded one, anyway. On your way to Zanzibar, are you, Klein?"

"In a day or so. Did you know I was here?"

"Of course not." Gracchus' harsh eyes twinkled slyly. "Sheer coincidence is what this is. She's there already."

"She is?"

"She and Zacharias and Mortimer. I hear you wiggled your way into Zion."

"Briefly," Klein said. "I saw Sybille. Briefly."

"Unsatisfactorily. So once again you've followed her here. Give it up, man. Give it up."

"I can't."

"*Can't!*" Gracchus scowled. "A neurotic's word, *can't*. What you mean is *won't*. A mature man can do anything he wants to that isn't a physical impossibility. Forget her. You're only annoying her, this way, interfering with her work, interfering with her—" Gracchus smiled. "With her life. She's been dead almost three years, hasn't she? Forget her. The world's full of other women. You're still young, you have money, you aren't ugly, you have professional standing—"

"Is this what you were sent here to tell me?"

"I wasn't sent here to tell you anything, friend. I'm only trying to save you from yourself. Don't go to Zanzibar. Go home and start your life again."

"When I saw her at Zion," Klein said, "she treated me with contempt. She amused herself at my expense. I want to ask her why she did that."

"Because you're a warm and she's a dead. To her you're a clown. To all of us you're a clown. It's nothing personal, Klein. There's simply a gulf in attitudes, a gulf too wide for you to cross. You went to Zion drugged up like a Treasury man, didn't you? Pale face, bulgy eyes? You didn't fool anyone. You certainly didn't fool *her*. The game she played with you was her way of telling you that. Don't you know that?"

"I know it, yes."

"What more do you want, then? More humiliation?"

Klein shook his head wearily and stared at the tablecloth. After a moment he looked up, and his eyes met those of Gracchus, and he was astounded to realize that he trusted the hunter, that for the first time in his dealings with the deads he felt he was being met with sincerity. He said in a low voice, "We were very close, Sybille and I, and then she died, and now I'm nothing to her. I haven't been able to come to terms with that. I need her, still. I want to share my life with her, even now."

"But you can't."

"I know that. And still I can't help doing what I've been doing."

"There's only one thing you *can* share with her," Gracchus said. "That's your death. She won't descend to your level: you have to climb to hers."

"Don't be absurd."

"Who's absurd, me or you? Listen to me, Klein. I think you're a fool, I think you're a weakling, but I don't dislike you, I don't hold you to blame for your own foolishness. And so I'll help you, if you'll allow me." He reached into his breast pocket and withdrew a tiny metal tube with a safety catch at one end. "Do you know what this is?" Gracchus asked. "It's a self-defense dart, the kind all the women in New York carry. A good many deads carry them, too, because we never know when the reaction will start, when the mobs will turn against us. Only we don't use anesthetic drugs in ours. Listen, we can walk into any tavern in the native quarter and have a decent brawl going in five minutes, and in the confusion I'll put one of these darts into you, and we'll have you in Dar General Hospital fifteen minutes after that, crammed into a deep-freeze unit, and for a few thousand dollars we can ship you unthawed to California, and this time Friday night you'll be undergoing rekindling in, say, San Diego Cold Town. And when you come out of it you and Sybille will be on the same side of the gulf, do you see? If you're destined to get back together with her, ever, that's the only way. That way you have a chance. This way you have none."

"It's unthinkable," Klein said.

"Unacceptable, maybe. But not unthinkable. Nothing's

unthinkable once somebody's thought it. You think it some
more. Will you promise me that? Think about it before you
get aboard that plane for Zanzibar. I'll be staying here tonight
and tomorrow, and then I'm going out to Arusha to meet
some deads coming in for the hunting, and any time before
then I'll do it for you if you say the word. Think about it. Will
you think about it? Promise me that you'll think about it."

"I'll think about it," Klein said.

"Good. Good. Thank you. Now let's have lunch and change
the subject. Do you like eating here?"

"One thing puzzles me. Why does this place have a clientele that's exclusively non-African? Does it dare to discriminate against blacks in a black republic?"

Gracchus laughed. "It's the blacks who discriminate, friend.
This is considered a second-class hotel. All the blacks are at
the Kilimanjaro or the Nyerere. Still, it's not such a bad
place. I recommend the fish dishes, if you haven't tried them,
and there's a decent white wine from Israel that—"

Eight

O Lord, methought what pain it was to drown!
What dreadful noise of water in mine ears!
What sights of ugly death within mine eyes!
Methoughts I saw a thousand fearful wracks;
A thousand men that fishes gnawed upon;
Wedges of gold, great anchors, heaps of pearl,
Inestimable stones, unvalued jewels,
All scatt'red in the bottom of the sea.
Some lay in dead men's skulls, and in the holes
Where eyes did once inhabit there were crept,
As 'twere in scorn of eyes, reflecting gems
That wooed the slimy bottom of the deep
And mocked the dead bones that lay scatt'red by.
                              Shakespeare: *Richard III*

"—Israeli wine," Mick Dongan was saying. "Well, I'll try
anything once, especially if there's some neat little irony

attached to it. I mean, there we were in Egypt, in *Egypt*, at this fabulous dinner party in the hills at Luxor, and our host is a Saudi prince, no less, in full tribal costume right down to the sunglasses, and when they bring out the roast lamb he grins devilishly and says, 'Of course we could always drink Mouton-Rothschild, but I do happen to have a small stock of select Israeli wines in my cellar, and because I think you are, like myself, a connoisseur of small incongruities, I've asked my steward to open a bottle or two of'—Klein, do you see that girl who just came in?" It is January, 1981, early afternoon, a fine drizzle in the air. Klein is lunching with six colleagues from the history department at the Hanging Gardens atop the Westwood Plaza. The hotel is a huge ziggurat on stilts; the Hanging Gardens is a rooftop restaurant, ninety stories up, in freaky neo-Babylonian décor, all winged bulls and snorting dragons of blue and yellow tile, waiters with long curly beards and scimitars at their hips—gaudy nightclub by dark, campy faculty hangout by day. Klein looks to his left. Yes, a handsome woman, mid-twenties, coolly beautiful, serious-looking, taking a seat by herself, putting a stack of books and cassettes down on the table before her. Klein does not pick up strange girls: a matter of moral policy, and also a matter of innate shyness. Dongan teases him. "Go on over, will you? She's your type, I swear. Her eyes are the right color for you, aren't they?"

Klein has been complaining, lately, that there are too many blue-eyed girls in southern California. Blue eyes are disturbing to him, somehow, even menacing. His own eyes are brown. So are hers: dark, warm, sparkling. He thinks he has seen her occasionally in the library. Perhaps they have even exchanged brief glances. "Go on," Dongan says. "Go *on*, Jorge. Go." Klein glares at him. He will not go. How can he intrude on this woman's privacy? To force himself on her—it would almost be like rape. Dongan smiles complacently; his bland grin is a merciless prod. Klein refuses to be stampeded. But then, as he hesitates, the girl smiles too, a quick shy smile, gone so soon he is not altogether sure it happened at all, but he is sure enough, and he finds himself rising, crossing the alabaster floor, hovering awkwardly over her, searching for some inspired words with which to make contact, and no words come, but still they make contact the old-fashioned way, eye to eye, and he is stunned by the intensity of what passes between them in that first implausible moment.

"Are you waiting for someone?" he mutters, shaken.

"No." The smile again, far less tentative. "Would you like to join me?"

She is a graduate student, he discovers quickly. Just got her master's, beginning now on her doctorate—the nineteenth-century East African slave trade, particular emphasis on Zanzibar. "How romantic," he says. "Zanzibar! Have you been there?"

"Never. I hope to go some day. Have you?"

"Not ever. But it always interested me, ever since I was a small boy collecting stamps. It was the last country in my album."

"Not in mine," she says. "Zululand was."

She knows him by name, it turns out. She had even been thinking of enrolling in his course on Nazism and Its Offspring. "Are you South American?" she asks.

"Born there. Raised here. My grandparents escaped to Buenos Aires in '37."

"Why Argentina? I thought that was a hotbed of Nazis."

"Was. Also full of German-speaking refugees, though. All their friends went there. But it was too unstable. My parents got out in '55, just before one of the big revolutions, and came to California. What about you?"

"British family. I was born in Seattle. My father's in the consular service. He—"

A waiter looms. They order sandwiches offhandedly. Lunch seems very unimportant now. The contact still holds. He sees Conrad's *Nostromo* in her stack of books; she is halfway through it, and he has just finished it, and the coincidence amuses them. Conradis one of her favorites, she says. One of his, too. What about Faulkner? Yes, and Mann, and Virginia Woolf, and they share even a fondness for Hermann Broch, and a dislike for Hesse. How odd. Operas? *Freischütz, Holländer, Fidelio*, yes. "We have very Teutonic tastes," she observes.

"We have very similar tastes," he adds. He finds himself holding her hand.

"Amazingly similar," she says.

Mick Dongan leers at him from the far side of the room; Klein gives him a terrible scowl. Dongan winks. "Let's get out of here," Klein says, just as she starts to say the same thing.

They talk half the night and make love until dawn. "You ought to know," he tells her solemnly over breakfast, "that I decided long ago never to get married and certainly never to have a child."

"So did I," she says. "When I was fifteen."

They were married four months later. Mick Dongan was his best man.

Gracchus said, as they left the restaurant, "You will think things over, won't you?"

"I will," Klein said. "I promised you that."

He went to his room, packed his suitcase, checked out, and took a cab to the airport, arriving in plenty of time for the afternoon flight to Zanzibar. The same melancholy little man was on duty as health officer when he landed, Barwani. "Sir, you have come back," Barwani said. "I thought you might. The other people have been here several days already."

"The other people?"

"When you were here last, sir, you kindly offered me a retainer in order that you might be informed when a certain person reached this island." Barwani's eyes gleamed. "That person, with two of her former companions, is here now."

Klein carefully placed a twenty-shilling note on the health officer's desk.

"At which hotel?"

Barwani's lips quirked. Evidently twenty shillings fell short of expectations. But Klein did not take out another banknote, and after a moment Barwani said, "As before. The Zanzibar House. And you, sir?"

"As before," Klein said. "I'll be staying at the Shirazi."

Sybille was in the garden of the hotel, going over that day's research notes, when the telephone call came from Barwani. "Don't let my papers blow away," she said to Zacharias, and went inside.

When she returned, looking bothered, Zacharias said, "Is there trouble?"

She sighed. "Jorge. He's on his way to his hotel now."

"What a bore," Mortimer murmured. "I thought Gracchus might have brought him to his senses."

"Evidently not," Sybille said. "What are we going to do?"

"What would you like to do?" Zacharias asked.

She shook her head. "We can't allow this to go on, can we?"

The evening air was humid and fragrant. The long rains had come and gone, and the island was in the grip of the new season's lunatic fertility: outside the window of Klein's hotel room some vast twining vine was putting forth monstrous trumpet-shaped yellow flowers, and all about the hotel grounds everything was in blossom, everything was in a frenzy of moist young leaves. Klein's sensibility reverberated to that feeling of universal vigorous thrusting newness; he paced the room, full of energy, trying to devise some feasible stratagem. Go immediately to see Sybille? Force his way in, if necessary, with shouts and alarums, and demand to know why she had told him that fantastic tale of imaginary sultans? No. No. He would do no more confronting, no more lamenting; now that he was here, now that he was close by her, he would seek her out calmly, he would talk quietly, he would invoke memories of their old love, he would speak of Rilke and Woolf and Broch, of afternoons in Puerto Vallarta and nights in Santa Fe, of music heard and caresses shared, he would rekindle not their marriage, for that was impossible, but merely the remembrance of the bond that once had existed, he would win from her some acknowledgment of what had been, and then he would soberly and quietly exorcise that bond, he and she together, they would work to free him by speaking softly of the change that had come over their lives, until, after three hours or four or five, he had brought himself with her help to an acceptance of the unacceptable. That was all. He would demand nothing, he would beg for nothing, except only that she assist him for one evening in ridding his soul of this useless, destructive obsession. Even a dead, even a capricious, wayward, volatile, whimsical, wanton dead, would surely see the desirability of that, and would freely give him her cooperation. Surely. And then home, and then new beginnings, too long postponed.

He made ready to go out.

There was a soft knock at the door. "Sir? Sir? You have visitors downstairs."

"Who?" Klein asked, though he knew the answer.

"A lady and two gentlemen," the bellhop replied. "The taxi

has brought them from the Zanzibar House. They wait for
you in the bar."

"Tell them I'll be down in a moment."

He went to the iced pitcher on the dresser, drank a glass of
cold water mechanically, unthinkingly, poured himself a second, drained that too. This visit was unexpected; and why
had she brought her entourage along? He had to struggle to
regain that centeredness, that sense of purpose understood,
which he thought he had attained before the knock. Eventually he left the room.

They were dressed crisply and impeccably this damp night,
Zacharias in a tawny frock coat and pale-green trousers,
Mortimer in a belted white caftan trimmed with intricate
brocade, Sybille in a simple lavender tunic. Their pale faces
were unmarred by perspiration; they seemed perfectly com-
posed, models of poise. No one sat near them in the bar. As
Klein entered, they stood to greet him, but their smiles
appeared sinister, having nothing of friendliness in them.
Klein clung tight to his intended calmness. He said quietly,
"It was kind of you to come. May I buy drinks for you?"

"We have ours already," Zacharias pointed out. "Let us be
your hosts. What will you have?"

"Pimm's Number Six," Klein said. He tried to match their
frosty smiles. "I admire your tunic, Sybille. You all look so
debonair tonight that I feel shamed."

"You never were famous for your clothes," she said.

Zacharias returned from the counter with Klein's drink. He
took it and toasted them gravely.

After a short while Klein said, "Do you think I could talk
privately with you, Sybille?"

"There's nothing we have to say to one another that can't
be said in front of Kent and Laurence."

"Nevertheless."

"I prefer not to, Jorge."

"As you wish." Klein peered straight into her eyes and saw
nothing there, nothing, and flinched. All that he had meant
to say fled his mind. Only churning fragments danced there:
Rilke, Broch, Puerto Vallarta. He gulped at his drink.

Zacharias said, "We have a problem to discuss, Klein."

"Go on."

"The problem is you. You're causing great distress to
Sybille. This is the second time, now, that you've followed
her to Zanzibar, to the literal end of the earth, Klein, and

you've made several attempts besides to enter a closed sanctuary in Utah under false pretenses, and this is interfering with Sybille's freedom, Klein, it's an impossible, intolerable interference."

"The deads are dead," Mortimer said. "We understand the depths of your feelings for your late wife, but this compulsive pursuit of her must be brought to an end."

"It will be," Klein said, staring at a point on the stucco wall midway between Zacharias and Sybille. "I want only an hour or two of private conversation with my—with Sybille, and then I promise you that there will be no further—"

"Just as you promised Anthony Gracchus," Mortimer said, "not to go to Zanzibar."

"I wanted—"

"We have our rights," said Zacharias. "We've gone through hell, literally through hell, to get where we are. You've infringed on our right to be left alone. You bother us. You bore us. You annoy us. We hate to be annoyed." He looked toward Sybille. She nodded. Zacharias' hand vanished into the breast pocket of his coat. Mortimer seized Klein's wrist with astonishing suddenness and jerked his arm forward. A minute metal tube glistened in Zacharias' huge fist. Klein had seen such a tube in the hand of Anthony Gracchus only the day before.

"No," Klein gasped. "I don't believe—*no!*"

Zacharias plunged the cold tip of the tube quickly into Klein's forearm.

"The freezer unit is coming," Mortimer said. "It'll be here in five minutes or less."

"What if it's late?" Sybille asked anxiously. "What if something irreversible happens to his brain before it gets here?"

"He's not even entirely dead yet," Zacharias reminded her. "There's time. There's ample time. I spoke to the doctor myself, a very intelligent Chinese, flawless command of English. He was most sympathetic. They'll have him frozen within a couple minutes of death. We'll book cargo passage aboard the morning plane for Dar. He'll be in the United States within twenty-four hours, I guarantee that. San Diego will be notified. Everything will be all right, Sybille!"

Jorge Klein lay slumped across the table. The bar had emptied the moment he had cried out and lurched forward: the half-dozen customers had fled, not caring to mar their holidays by sharing an evening with the presence of death, and the waiters and bartenders, big-eyed, terrified, lurked in the hallway. A heart attack, Zacharias had announced, some kind of sudden attack, maybe a stroke, where's the telephone? No one had seen the tiny tube do its work.

Sybille trembled. "If anything goes wrong—"

"I hear the sirens now," Zacharias said.

From his desk at the airport Daud Mahmoud Barwani watched the bulky refrigerated coffin being loaded by grunting porters aboard the morning plane for Dar. And then, and then, and then? They would ship the dead man to the far side of the world, to America, and breathe new life into him, and he would go once more among men. Barwani shook his head. These people! The man who was alive is now dead, and these dead ones, who knows what they are? Who knows? Best that the dead remain dead, as was intended in the time of first things. Who would have foreseen a day when the dead returned from the grave? Not I. And who can foresee what we will all become, a hundred years from now? Not I. Not I. A hundred years from now I will sleep, Barwani thought. I will sleep, and it will not matter to me at all what sort of creatures walk the earth.

Nine

We die with the dying:
See, they depart, and we go with them.
We are born with the dead:
See, they return, and bring us with them.
T.S. Eliot: Little Gidding

On the day of his awakening he saw no one except the attendants at the rekindling house, who bathed him and fed him and helped him to walk slowly around his room. They said nothing to him, nor he to them; words seemed irrelevant. He felt strange in his skin, too snugly contained, as though all his life he had worn ill-fitting clothes and now had for the first time encountered a competent tailor. The images that his eyes brought him were sharp, unnaturally clear, and faintly haloed by prismatic colors, an effect that imperceptibly vanished as the day passed. On the second day he was visited by the San Diego Guidefather, not at all the formidable patriarch he had imagined, but rather a cool, efficient executive, about fifty years old, who greeted him cordially and told him briefly of the disciplines and routines he must master before he could leave the Cold Town. "What month is this?" Klein asked, and Guidefather told him it was June, the seventeenth of June, 1993. He had slept four weeks.

Now it is the morning of the third day after his awakening, and he has guests: Sybille, Nerita, Zacharias, Mortimer, Gracchus. They file into his room and stand in an arc at the foot of his bed, radiant in the glow of light that pierces the narrow windows. Like demigods, like angels, glittering with a dazzling inward brilliance, and now he is of their company. Formally they embrace him, first Gracchus, then Nerita, then Mortimer. Zacharias advances next to his bedside, Zacharias who sent him into death, and he smiles at Klein and Klein returns the smile, and they embrace. Then it is Sybille's turn: she slips her hand between his, he draws her close, her lips brush his cheek, his touch hers, his arm encircles her shoulders.

"Hello," she whispers.

"Hello," he says.

They ask him how he feels, how quickly his strength is returning, whether he has been out of bed yet, how soon he will commence his drying-off. The style of their conversation is the oblique, elliptical style favored by the deads, but not nearly so clipped and cryptic as the way of speech they normally would use among themselves; they are favoring him, leading him inch by inch into their customs. Within five minutes he thinks he is getting the knack.

He says, using their verbal shorthand, "I must have been a great burden to you."

"You were, you were," Zacharias agrees. "But all that is done with now."

"We forgive you," Mortimer says.

"We welcome you among us," declares Sybille.

They talk about their plans for the months ahead. Sybille is nearly finished with her work on Zanzibar; she will retreat to Zion Cold Town for the summer months to write her thesis. Mortimer and Nerita are off to Mexico to tour the ancient temples and pyramids; Zacharias is going to Ohio, to his beloved mounds. In the autumn they will reassemble at Zion and plan the winter's amusement: a tour of Egypt, perhaps, or Peru, the heights of Machu Picchu. Ruins, archaeological sites, delight them; in the places where death has been busiest, their joy is most intense. They are flushed, excited, verbose—virtually chattering, now. Away we will go, to Zimbabwe, to Palenque, to Angkor, to Knossos, to Uxmal, to Nineveh, to Mohenjo-daro. And as they go on and on, talking with hands and eyes and smiles and even words, even words, torrents of words, they blur and become unreal to him, they are mere dancing puppets jerking about a badly painted stage, they are droning insects, wasps or bees or mosquitoes, with all their talk of travels and festivals, of Boghazköy and Babylon, of Megiddo and Masada, and he ceases to hear them, he tunes them out, he lies there smiling, eyes glazed, mind adrift. It perplexes him that he has so little interest in them. But then he realizes that it is a mark of his liberation. He is freed of old chains now. Will he join their set? Why should he? Perhaps he will travel with them, perhaps not, as the whim takes him. More likely not. Almost certainly not. He does not need their company. He has his own interests. He will follow Sybille about no longer. He does not need, he does not want, he will not seek. Why should he become one of them, rootless, an amoral wanderer, a ghost made flesh? Why should he embrace the values and customs of these people who had given him to death as dispassionately as they might swat an insect, only because he had bored them, because he had annoyed them? He does not hate them for what they did to him, he feels no resentment that he can identify, he merely chooses to detach himself from them. Let them float on from ruin to ruin, let them pursue death from continent to continent; he will go his own way. Now that he has crossed the interface, he finds that Sybille no longer matters to him.

—*Oh, sir, things change—*

"We'll go now," Sybille said softly.

He nods. He makes no other reply.

"We'll see you after your drying-off," Zacharias tells him, and touches him lightly with his knuckles, a farewell gesture used only by the deads.

"See you," Mortimer says.

"See you," says Gracchus.

"Soon," Nerita says.

Never, Klein says, saying it without words, but so they will understand. Never. Never. Never. I will never see any of you. I will never see you, Sybille. The syllables echo through his brain, and the word, *never, never, never,* rolls over him like the breaking surf, cleansing him, purifying him, healing him. He is free. He is alone.

"Goodbye," Sybille calls from the hallway.

"Goodbye," he says.

It was years before he saw her again. But they spent the last days of '99 together, shooting dodos under the shadow of mighty Kilimanjaro.

THOMAS
THE PROCLAIMER

One
Moonlight, Starlight, Torchlight

How long will this night last? The blackness, though moon-pierced, star-pierced, torch-pierced, is dense and tangible. They are singing and chanting in the valley. Bitter smoke from their firebrands rises to the hilltop where Thomas stands, flanked by his closest followers. Fragments of old hymns dance through the trees. "Rock of Ages, Cleft for Me." "O God, Our Help in Ages Past." "Jesus, Lover of My Soul, Let Me to Thy Bosom Fly." Thomas is the center of all attention. A kind of invisible aura surrounds his blocky, powerful figure, an unseen crackling electrical radiance. Saul Kraft, at his side, seems eclipsed and obscured, a small, fragile-looking man, overshadowed now but far from unimportant in the events of this night. "Nearer, My God, to Thee." Thomas begins to hum the tune, then to sing. His voice, though deep and magical, the true charismatic voice, tumbles randomly from key to key: the prophet has no ear for music. Kraft smiles sourly at Thomas' dismal sounds.

> *"Watchman, tell us of the night,*
> *What its signs of promise are,*
> *Traveler, o'er yon mountain's height,*
> *See that glory-beaming star!"*

Ragged shouts from below. Occasional sobs and loud coughs. What is the hour? The hour is late. Thomas runs his hands through his long, tangled hair, tugging, smoothing, pulling the strands down toward his thick shoulders. The familiar gesture, beloved by the multitudes. He wonders if he should make an appearance. They are calling his name; he hears the

rhythmic cries punching through the snarl of clashing hymns.
Tho-mas! Tho-mas! Tho-mas! Hysteria in their voices. They
want him to come forth and stretch out his arms and make
the heavens move again, just as he caused them to stop. But
Thomas resists that grand but hollow gesture. How easy it is
to play the prophet's part! He did not cause the heavens to
stop, though, and he knows that he cannot make them move
again. Not of his own will alone, at any rate.

"What time is it?" he asks.

"Quarter to ten," Kraft tells him. Adding, after an instant's
thought: "P.M."

So the twenty-four hours are nearly up. And still the sky
hangs frozen. Well, Thomas? Is this not what you asked for?
Go down on your knees, you cried, and beg him for a Sign, so
that we may know He is still with us, in this our time of need.
And render up to Him a great shout. And the people knelt
throughout all the lands. And begged. And shouted. And the
Sign was given. Why, then, this sense of foreboding? Why
these fears? Surely this night will pass. Look at Kraft. Smiling
serenely. Kraft has never known any doubts. Those cold eyes,
those thin wide lips, the fixed expression of tranquility.

"You ought to speak to them," Kraft says.

"I have nothing to say."

"A few words of comfort for them."

"Let's see what happens, first. What can I tell them now?"

"Empty of words, Thomas? You, who have had so much to
proclaim?"

Thomas shrugs. There are times when Kraft infuriates him:
the little man needling him, goading, scheming, never letting
up, always pushing this Crusade toward some appointed goal
grasped by Kraft alone. The intensity of Kraft's faith exhausts
Thomas. Annoyed, the prophet turns away from him. Thomas
sees scattered fires leaping on the horizon. Prayer meetings?
Or are they riots? Peering at those distant blazes, Thomas
jabs idly at the tuner of the radio before him.

"... rounding out the unprecedented span of twenty-four
hours of continuous daylight in much of the Eastern Hemisphere, an endless daybreak over the Near East and an
endless noon over Siberia, eastern China, the Philippines,
and Indonesia. Meanwhile western Europe and the Americas
remain locked in endless night..."

"... then spake Joshua to the Lord in the day when the
Lord delivered up the Amorites before the children of Israel,

and he said in the sight of Israel, Sun, stand thou still upon Gibeon; and thou, Moon, in the valley of Ajalon. And the sun stood still, and the moon stayed, until the people had avenged themselves upon their enemies. Is this not written in the book of Jasher? So the sun stood still in the midst of heaven, and hasted not to go down about a whole day . . ."

" . . . an astonishing culmination, apparently, to the campaign led by Thomas Davidson of Reno, Nevada, known popularly as Thomas the Proclaimer. The shaggy-bearded, long-haired, self-designated Apostle of Peace brought his Crusade of Faith to a climax yesterday with the world-wide program of simultaneous prayer that appears to have been the cause of . . ."

> *"Watchman, does its beauteous ray*
> *Aught of joy or hope foretell?*
> *Traveler, yes; it brings the day,*
> *Promised day of Israel."*

Kraft says sharply, "Do you hear what they're singing, Thomas? You've got to speak to them. You got them into this; now they want you to tell them you'll get them out of it."

"Not yet, Saul."

"You mustn't let your moment slip by. Show them that God still speaks through you!"

"When God is ready to speak again," Thomas says frostily, "I'll let His words come forth. Not before." He glares at Kraft and punches for another change of station.

" . . . continued meetings in Washington, but no communiqué as yet. Meanwhile, at the United Nations . . ."

" . . . Behold, He cometh with clouds; and every eye shall see Him, and they also which pierced Him: and all kindreds of the Earth shall wail because of Him. Even so, Amen . . ."

" . . . outbreaks of looting in Caracas, Mexico City, Oakland, and Vancouver. But in the daylight half of the world, violence and other disruption has been slight, though an unconfirmed report from Moscow . . ."

" . . . and when, brethren, when did the sun cease in its course? At six in the morning, brethren, six in the morning, Jerusalem time! And on what day, brethren? Why, the sixth of June, the sixth day of the sixth month! *Six—six—six!* And what does Holy Writ tell us, my dearly beloved ones, in the thirteenth chapter of Revelations? That a beast shall rise up out of the sea, having seven heads and ten horns, and upon his horns ten crowns, and upon his heads the name of blasphemy. And the Holy Book tells us the number of the beast, beloved, and the number is six hundred three score and six, wherein we see again the significant digits, *six—six— six!* Who then can deny that these are the last days, and that the Apocalypse must be upon us? Thus in this time of woe and fire as we sit upon this stilled planet awaiting His judgment, we must . . ."

". . . latest observatory report confirms that no appreciable momentum effects could be detected as the Earth shifted to its present period of rotation. Scientists agree that the world's abrupt slowing on its axis should have produced a global catastrophe leading, perhaps, to the destruction of all life. However, nothing but minor tidal disturbances have been recorded so far. Two hours ago, we interviewed Presidential Science Adviser Raymond Bartell, who made this statement:

"'Calculations now show that the Earth's period of rotation and its period of revolution have suddenly become equal; that is, the day and the year now have the same length. This locks the Earth into its present position relative to the sun, so that the side of the Earth now enjoying daylight will continue indefinitely to do so, while the other side will remain permanently in night. Other effects of the slowdown that might have been expected include the flooding of coastal areas, the collapse of most buildings, and a series of earthquakes and volcanic eruptions, but none of these things seem to have happened. For the moment we have no rational explanation of all this, and I must admit it's a great temptation to say that Thomas the Proclaimer must have managed to get his miracle, because there isn't any other apparent way of . . .'"

". . . I am Alpha and Omega, the beginning and the ending, saith the Lord, which is, and which was, and which is to come, the Almighty . . ."

With a fierce fingerthrust Thomas silences all the radio's clamoring voices. Alpha and Omega! Apocalyptist garbage! The drivel of hysterical preachers pouring from a thousand transmitters, poisoning the air! Thomas despises all these criers of doom. None of them knows anything. No one understands. His throat fills with a turbulence of angry incoherent words, almost choking him. A coppery taste of denunciations. Kraft again urges him to speak. Thomas glowers. Why doesn't Kraft do the speaking himself, for once? He's a truer believer than I am. He's the real prophet. But of course the idea is ridiculous. Kraft has no eloquence, no fire. Only ideas and visions. He'd bore everybody to splinters. Thomas succumbs. He beckons with his fingertips. "The microphone," he mutters. "Let me have the microphone."

Among his entourage there is fluttery excitement. "He wants the mike!" they murmur. "Give him the mike!" Much activity on the part of the technicians.

Kraft presses a plaque of cold metal into the Proclaimer's hand. Grins, winks. "Make their hearts soar," Kraft whispers. "Send them on a trip!" Everyone waits. In the valley the torches bob and weave; have they begun dancing down there? Overhead the pocked moon holds its corner of the sky in frosty grasp. The stars are chained to their places. Thomas draws a deep breath and lets the air travel inward, upward, surging to the recesses of his skull. He waits for the good lightheadedness to come upon him, the buoyancy that liberates his tongue. He thinks he is ready to speak. He hears the desperate chanting: *Tho-mas! Tho-mas! Tho-mas!* It is more than half a day since his last public statement. He is tense and hollow; he has fasted throughout this Day of the Sign, and of course he has not slept. No one has slept.

"Friends," he begins. "Friends, this is Thomas."

The amplifiers hurl his voice outward. A thousand loudspeakers drifting in the air pick up his words and they bounce across the valley, returning as jagged echoes. He hears cries, eerie shrieks; his own name ascends to him in blurry distortions. *Too-mis! Too-mis! Too-mis!*

"Nearly a full day has passed," he says, "since the Lord gave us the Sign for which we asked. For us it has been a long day of darkness, and for others it has been a day of strange light, and for all of us there has been fear. But this I say to you now: BE . . . NOT . . . AFRAID. For the Lord is good and we are the Lord's."

Now he pauses. Not only for effect; his throat is raging. He signals furiously and Kraft, scowling, hands him a flask. Thomas takes a deep gulp of the good red wine, cool, strong. Ah. He glances at the screen beside him; the video pickup relayed from the valley. What lunacy down there! Wild-eyed, sweaty madmen, half-naked and worse, jumping up and down! Crying out his name, invoking him as though he were divine. *Too-mis! Too-mis!*

"There are those who tell you now," Thomas goes on, "that the end of days is at hand, that judgment is come. They talk of apocalypses and the wrath of God. And what do I say to that? I say: BE ... NOT ... AFRAID. The Lord God is a God of mercy. We asked Him for a Sign, and a Sign was given. Should we not therefore rejoice? Now we may be certain of His presence and His guidance. Ignore the doom-sayers. Put away your fears. We live now in God's love!"

Thomas halts again. For the first time in his memory he has no sense of being in command of his audience. Is he reaching them at all? Is he touching the right chords? Or has he begun already to lose them? Maybe it was a mistake to let Kraft nag him into speaking so soon. He thought he was ready; maybe not. Now he sees Kraft staring at him, aghast, pantomiming the gestures of speech, silently telling him, *Get with it, you've got to keep talking now!* Thomas' self-assurance momentarily wavers, and terror floods his soul, for he knows that if he falters at this point he may well be destroyed by the forces he has set loose. Teetering at the brink of an abyss, he searches frantically for his customary confidence. Where is that steely column of words that ordinarily rises unbidden from the depths of him? Another gulp of wine, fast. Good. Kraft, nervously rubbing hands together, essays a smile of encouragement. Thomas tugs at his hair. He pushes back his shoulders, thrusts out his chest. Be not afraid! He feels control returning after the frightening lapse. They are his, all those who listen. They have always been his. What are they shouting in the valley now? No longer his name, but some new cry. He strains to hear. Two words. What are they? *De-dum! De-dum! De-dum!* What? *De-dum! De-dum! De-dum, too-mis, de-dum!* What? What? "The sun," Kraft says. The sun? Yes. They want the sun. "The sun! The sun! The sun!"

"The sun," Thomas says. "Yes. This day the sun stands still, as our Sign from Him. BE NOT AFRAID! A long dawn over Jerusalem has He decreed, and a long night for us, but not so very long, and soon sped." Thomas feels the power surging at last. Kraft nods to him, and Thomas nods back and spits a stream of wine at Kraft's feet. He is aware of that consciousness of risk in which the joy of prophecy lies: I will bring forth what I see, and trust to God to make it real. That feeling of risk accepted, of triumph over doubt. Calmly he says, "The Day of the Sign will end in a few minutes. Once more the world will turn, and moon and stars will move across the sky. So put down your torches, and go to your homes, and offer up joyful prayers of thanksgiving to Him, for this night will pass, and dawn will come at the appointed hour."

How do you know, Thomas? Why are you so sure?

He hands the microphone to Saul Kraft and calls for more wine. Around him are tense faces, rigid eyes, clamped jaws. Thomas smiles. He goes among them, slapping backs, punching shoulders, laughing, embracing, winking ribaldly, poking his fingers playfully into their ribs. Be of good cheer, ye who follow my way! Share ye not my faith in Him? He asks Kraft how he came across. Fine, Kraft says, except for that uneasy moment in the middle. Thomas slaps Kraft's back hard enough to loosen teeth. Good old Saul. My inspiration, my counselor, my beacon. Thomas pushes his flask toward Kraft's face. Kraft shakes his head. He is fastidious about drinking, about decorum in general, as fastidious as Thomas is disreputable. You disapprove of me, don't you, Saul? But you need my charisma. You need my energy and my big loud voice. Too bad, Saul, that prophets aren't as neat and housebroken as you'd like them to be. "Ten o'clock," someone says. "It's now been going on for twenty-four hours."

A woman says, "The moon! Look! Didn't the moon just start to move again?"

From Kraft: "You wouldn't be able to see it with the naked eye. Not possibly. No way."

"Ask Thomas! Ask him!"

One of the technicians cries, "I can feel it! The Earth is turning!"

"Look, the stars!"

"Thomas! Thomas!"

They rush to him. Thomas, benign, serene, stretching forth his huge hands to reassure them, tells them that he has felt it too. Yes. There is motion in the universe again. Perhaps the turnings of the heavenly bodies are too subtle to be detected in a single glance, perhaps an hour or more will be needed for verification, and yet he knows, he is sure, he is absolutely sure. The Lord has withdrawn His Sign. The

Earth turns. "Let us sleep now," Thomas says joyfully, "and greet the dawn in happiness."

Two
The Dance of the Apocalyptists

In late afternoon every day a band of Apocalyptists gathers by the stinking shore of Lake Erie to dance the sunset in. Their faces are painted with grotesque nightmare stripes; their expressions are wild; they fling themselves about in jerky, lurching steps, awkward and convulsive, the classic death-dance. Two immense golden loudspeakers, mounted like idols atop metal spikes rammed into the soggy soil, bellow abstract rhythms at them from either side. The leader of the group stands thigh-deep in the fouled waters, chanting, beckoning, directing them with short blurted cries: "People . . . holy people . . . chosen people . . . blessed people . . . persecuted people . . . Dance! . . . Dance! . . . The end . . . is near . . ." And they dance. Fingers shooting electrically into the air, elbows ramming empty space, knees rising high, they scramble toward the lake, withdraw, advance, withdraw, advance, three steps forward and two steps back, a will-you-won't-you-will-you-won't-you approach to salvation.

They have been doing this seven times a week since the beginning of the year, this fateful, terminal year, but only in the week since the Day of the Sign have they drawn much of an audience. At the outset, in frozen January, no one would bother to come to watch a dozen madmen capering on the windswept ice. Then the cult began getting sporadic television coverage, and that brought a few curiosity seekers. On the milder nights of April perhaps thirty dancers and twenty onlookers could be found at the lake. But now it is June, apocalyptic June, when the Lord in all His majesty has revealed Himself, and the nightly dances are an event that brings thousands out of Cleveland's suburbs. Police lines hold the mob at a safe distance from the performers. A closed-circuit video loop relays the action to those on the outskirts of the crowd, too far away for a direct view. Network copters hover, cameras ready in case something unusual happens—the death of a dancer, the bursting loose of the mob, mass conversions, another miracle, anything. The air is cool to-night. The sun, delicately blurred and purpled by the smoky haze that perpetually thickens this region's sky, drops toward the breast of the lake. The dancers move in frenzied patterns, those in the front rank approaching the water, dipping their toes, retreating. Their leader, slapping the lake, throwing up fountaining spumes, continues to exhort them in a high, strained voice.

"People . . . holy people . . . chosen people . . ."

"Hallelujah! Hallelujah!"

"Come and be sealed! Blessed people . . . persecuted people . . . Come! Be! Sealed! Unto! The! Lord!"

"Hallelujah!"

The spectators shift uneasily. Some nudge and snigger. Some, staring fixedly, lock their arms and glower. Some move their lips in silent prayer or silent curses. Some look tempted to lurch forward and join the dance. Some will. Each night, there are a few who go forward. Each night, also, there are some who attempt to burst the police lines and attack the dancers. In June alone seven spectators have suffered heart seizures at the nightly festival: five fatalities.

"Servants of God!" cries the man in the water.

"Hallelujah!" reply the dancers.

"The year is speeding! The time is coming!"

"Hallelujah!"

"The trumpet shall sound! And we shall be saved!"

"Yes! Yes! Yes! Yes!"

Oh, the fervor of the dance! The wildness of the faces! The painted stripes swirl and run as sweat invades the thick greasy pigments. One could strew hot coals on the shore, now, and the dancers would advance all the same, oblivious, blissful. The choreography of their faith absorbs them wholly at this moment and they admit of no distractions. There is so little time left, after all, and such a great output of holy exertion is required of them before the end! June is almost half-spent. The year itself is almost half-spent. January

approaches: the dawning of the new millennium, the day of
the final trump, the moment of apocalypse. January 1, 2000:
six and a half months away. And already He has given the
Sign that the end of days is at hand. They dance. Through
ecstatic movement comes salvation.

"Fear God, and give glory to Him; for the hour of His
Judgment is come!"

"Hallelujah! Amen!"

"And worship Him that made heaven, and earth, and the
sea, and the fountains of waters!"

"Hallelujah! Amen!"

They dance. The music grows more intense: prickly blurts
of harsh tone flickering through the air. Spectators begin to
clap hands and sway. Here comes the first convert of the
night, now, a woman, middle-aged, plump, beseeching her
way through the police cordon. An electronic device checks
her for concealed weapons and explosive devices; she is found
to be harmless; she passes the line and runs, stumbling, to
join the dance.

"For the great day of His wrath is come; and who shall be
able to stand?"

"Amen!"

"Servants of God! Be sealed unto Him, and be saved!"

"Sealed . . . sealed . . . We shall be sealed . . . We shall be
saved . . ."

"And I saw four angels standing on the four corners of the
Earth, holding the four winds of the Earth, that the wind
should not blow on the Earth, nor on the sea, nor on any
tree," roars the man in the water. "And I saw another angel
ascending from the east, having the seal of the living God:
and he cried with a loud voice to the four angels, to whom it
was given to hurt the Earth and the sea, saying, Hurt not the
Earth, neither the sea, nor the trees, till we have sealed the
servants of our God in their foreheads."

"Sealed! Hallelujah! Amen!"

"And I heard the number of them which were sealed: and
there were sealed an hundred and forty and four thousand of
all the tribes of the children of Israel."

"Sealed! Sealed!"

"Come to me and be sealed! Dance and be sealed!"

The sun drops into the lake. The purple stain of sunset
spreads across the horizon. The dancers shriek ecstatically
and rush toward the water. They splash one another; they

offer frantic baptisms in the murky lake; they drink, they spew forth what they have drunk, they drink again. Surrounding their leader. Seeking his blessing. An angry thick mutter from the onlookers. They are disgusted by this hectic show of faith. A menagerie, they say. A circus sideshow. These freaks. These godly freaks. Whom we have come to watch, so that we may despise them.

And if they are right? And if the world *does* end next January 1, and we go to hellfire, while *they* are saved? Impossible. Preposterous. Absurd. But yet, who's to say? Only last week the Earth stood still a whole day. We live under His hand now. We always have, but now we have no liberty to doubt it. We can no longer deny that He's up there, watching us, listening to us, thinking about us. And if the end is really coming, as the crazy dancers think, what should I do to prepare for it? Should I join the dance? God help one. God help us all. Now the darkness falls. Look at the lunatics wallowing in the lake.

"Hallelujah! Amen!"

Three
The Sleep of Reason
Produces Monsters

When I was about seven years old, which is to say somewhere in the late 1960's, I was playing out in front of the house on a Sunday morning, perhaps stalking some ladybirds for my insect collection, when three freckle-faced Irish kids who lived on the next block came wandering by. They were on their way home from church. The youngest one was my age, and the other two must have been eight or nine. To me they were Big Boys: ragged, strong, swaggering, alien. My father was a college professor and theirs was probably a bus conductor or a coal miner, and so they were as strange to me as a trio of tourists from Patagonia would have been. They stopped and watched me for a minute, and then the biggest one called me out into the street, and he asked me how it was that they never saw me in church on Sundays.

The simplest and most tactful thing for me to tell them would have been that I didn't happen to be Roman Catholic. That was true. I think that all they wanted to find out was what church I *did* go to, since I obviously didn't go to theirs. Was I Jewish, Moslem, Presbyterian, Baptist, what? But I was a smug little snot then, and instead of handling the situation diplomatically, I cheerfully told them that I didn't go to church because I didn't believe in God.

They looked at me as though I had just blown my nose on the American flag.

"Say that again?" the biggest one demanded.

"I don't believe in God," I said. "Religion's just a big fake. My father says so, and I think he's right."

They frowned and backed off a few paces and conferred in low, earnest voices, with many glances in my direction. Evidently I was their first atheist. I assumed we would now have a debate on the existence of the Deity: they would explain to me the motives that led them to use up so many valuable hours on their knees inside the Church of Our Lady of the Sorrows, and then I would try to show them how silly it was to worry so much about an invisible old man in the sky. But a theological disputation wasn't their style. They came out of their huddle and strolled toward me, and I suddenly detected menace in their eyes, and just as the two smaller ones lunged at me I slipped past them and started to run. They had longer legs, but I was more agile; besides, I was on my home block and knew the turf better. I sprinted halfway down the street, darted into an alley, slipped through the open place in the back of the Allertons' garage, doubled back up the street via the rear lane, and made it safely into our house by way of the kitchen door. For the next couple of days I stayed close to home after school and kept a wary watch, but the pious Irish lads never came around again to punish the blasphemer. After that I learned to be more careful about expressing my opinions on religious matters.

But I never became a believer. I had a natural predisposition toward skepticism. *If you can't measure it, it isn't there.* That included not only Old Whiskers and His Only Begotten Son, but all the other mystic baggage that people liked to carry around in those tense credulous years: the flying saucers, Zen Buddhism, the Atlantis cult, Hare Krishna, macrobiotics, telepathy and other species of extrasensory perception, theosophy, entropy-worship, astrology, and such. I was willing to accept neutrinos, quasars, the theory of continental drift, and the various species of quarks, because I respected the evidence for their existence; I couldn't buy the other stuff, the irrational stuff, the assorted opiates of the masses. When the Moon is in the seventh house, etc., etc.—sorry, no. I clung to the path of reason as I made my uneasy journey toward maturity, and hardheaded little Billy Gifford, smarty-pants bug collector, remained unchurched as he ripened into Professor William F. Gifford, Ph.D., of the Department of Physics, Harvard. I wasn't *hostile* to organized religion, I just ignored it, as I might ignore a newspaper account of a jai-alai tournament in Afghanistan.

I envied the faithful their faith, oh, yes. When the dark times got darker, how sweet it must have been to be able to rush to Our Lady of the Sorrows for comfort! *They* could pray, *they* had the illusion that a divine plan governed this best of all possible worlds, while I was left in bleak, stormy limbo, dismally aware that the universe makes no sense and that the only universal truth there is, is that Entropy Eventually Wins.

There were times when I wanted genuinely to be able to pray, when I was weary of operating solely on my own existential capital, when I wanted to grovel and cry out, *Okay, Lord, I give up, You take it from here.* I had favors to ask of Him. God, let my little girl's fever go down. Let my plane not crash. Let them not shoot *this* President too. Let the races learn how to live in peace before the blacks get around to burning down my street. Let the peace-loving enlightened students not bomb the computer center this semester. Let the next kindergarten drug scandal not erupt in my boy's school. Let the lion lie down with the lamb. As we zoomed along on the Chaos Express, I was sometimes tempted toward godliness the way the godly are tempted toward sin. But my love of divine reason left me no way to opt for the irrational. Call it stiffneckedness, call it rampant egomania: no matter how bad things got, Bill Gifford wasn't going to submit to the tyranny of a hobgoblin. Even a benevolent one. Even if I had favors to ask of Him. So much to ask; so little faith. Intellectual honesty *über alles*, Gifford! While every year things were a little worse than the last.

When I was growing up, in the 1970's, it was fashionable

for educated and serious-minded people to get together and tell each other that western civilization was collapsing. The Germans had a word for it, *Schadenfreude,* the pleasure one gets from talking about catastrophes. And the 1970's were shadowed by catastrophes, real or expected: the pollution escalation, the population explosion, Vietnam and all the little Vietnams, the supersonic transport, black separatism, white backlash, student unrest, extremist women's lib, the neofascism of the New Left, the neonihilism of the New Right, a hundred other varieties of dynamic irrationality going full blast, yes, ample fuel for the *Schadenfreude* syndrome. Yes, my parents and their civilized friends said solemnly, sadly, gleefully, it's all blowing up, it's all going smash, it's all whooshing down the drain. Through the fumes of the Saturday-night pot came the inevitable portentous quotes from Yeats: *Things fall apart; the center cannot hold; mere anarchy is loosed upon the world.* Well, what shall we do about it? Perhaps it's really beyond our control now. Brethren, shall we pray? Lift up your voices unto Him! But I can't. I'd feel like a damned fool. Forgive me, God, but I must deny You! *The best lack all conviction, while the worst are full of passionate intensity.*

And of course everything got much more awful than the doomsayers of the 1970's really expected. Even those who most dearly relished enumerating the calamities to come still thought, beneath their grim joy, that somehow reason ulti-mately would triumph. The most gloomy Jeremiah entertained secret hopes that the noble ecological resolutions would eventually be translated into meaningful environmental ac-tion, that the crazy birth spiral would be checked in time, that the strident rhetoric of the innumerable protest groups would be tempered and modulated as time brought them the beginning of a fulfillment of their revolutionary goals—but no. Came the 1980's, the decade of my young manhood, and all the hysteria jumped to the next-highest energy level. That was when we began having the Gas Mask Days. The pro-grammed electrical shutdowns. The elegantly orchestrated international chaos of the Third World People's Prosperity Group. The airport riots. The black rains. The Computer Purge. The Brazilian Pacification Program. The Claude Harkins Book List with its accompanying library-burnings. The Eco-logical Police Action. The Genetic Purity League and its even more frightening black counterpart. The Children's Crusade for Sanity. The Nine Weeks' War. The Night of the Lasers. The center had long ago ceased to hold; now we were strapped to a runaway wheel. Amidst the furies I studied, married, brought forth young, built a career, fought off daily terror, and like everyone else, waited for the inevitable final calamity.

Who could doubt that it would come? Not you, not I. And not the strange wild-eyed folk who emerged among us like dark growths pushing out of rotting logs, the Apocalyptists, who raised *Schadenfreude* to the sacramental level and organized an ecstatic religion of doom. The end of the world, they told us, was scheduled for January 1, A.D. 2000, and upon that date, 144,000 elite souls, who had "sealed" themselves unto God by devotion and good works, would be saved; the rest of us poor sinners would be hauled before the Judge. I could see their point. Although I rejected their talk of the Second Coming, having long ago rejected the First, and although I shared neither their confidence in the exact date of the apocalypse nor their notions of how the survivors would be chosen, I agreed with them that the end was close at hand. The fact that for a quarter of a century we had been milking giddy cocktail-party chatter out of the impending collapse of western civilization didn't of itself guarantee that western civilization wasn't going to collapse; *some* of the things people like to say at cocktail parties can hit the target. As a physicist with a decent understanding of the entropic process, I found all the signs of advanced societal decay easy to identify: for a century we had been increasing the complexity of society's functions so that an ever-higher level of organization was required in order to make things run, and for much of that time we had simultaneously been trending toward total universal democracy, toward a world consisting of several billion self-governing republics with a maximum of three citizens each. Any closed system which experiences simultaneous sharp increases in mechanical complexity and in entropic diffusion is going to go to pieces long before the maximum distribution of energy is reached. The pattern of consents and contracts on which civilization is based is destroyed; every social interaction, from parking your car to settling an international boundary dispute, becomes a problem that can be handled only by means of force, since all "civilized" techniques of reconciling disagreement have been suspended as irrelevant; when the delivery of mail is a matter of private negotiation between the citizen and his postman, what hope is there for the rule of reason? Somewhere, somehow, we had passed a point of no return—in 1984, 1972, maybe even that ghastly day in November of 1963—and nothing now could save us from plunging over the brink.

Nothing?

Out of Nevada came Thomas, shaggy Thomas, Thomas the Proclaimer, rising above the slot machines and the roulette wheels to cry, If ye have faith, ye shall be saved! An anti-Apocalyptist prophet, no less, whose message was that civilization still might be preserved, that it was not yet too late. The voice of hope, the enemy of entropy, the new Apostle of Peace. Though to people like me he looked just as wild-eyed and hairy and dangerous and terrifyingly psychotic as the worshipers of the holocaust, for he, like the Apocalyptists, dealt in forces operating outside the realm of sanity. By rights he should have come out of the backwoods of Arkansas or the crazier corners of California, but he didn't, he was a desert rat, a Nevadan, a sand-eating latter-day John the Baptist. A true prophet for our times, too, seedy, disreputable, a wine-swiller, a cynic. Capable of beginning a global telecast sermon with a belch. An ex-soldier who had happily napalmed whole provinces during the Brazilian Pacification Program. A part-time dealer in bootlegged hallucinogens. An expert at pocket-picking and computer-jamming. He had gone into the evangelism business because he thought he could make an easy buck that way, peddling the Gospels and appropriating the collection box, but a funny thing had happened to him, he claimed: he had seen the Lord, he had discovered the error of his ways, he had become inflamed with righteousness. Hiding not his grimy past, he now offered himself as a walking personification of redemption: *Look ye, if I can be saved from sin, there's hope for everyone!* The media picked him up. That magnificent voice of his, that great mop of hair, those eyes, that hypnotic self-confidence—perfect. He walked from California to Florida to proclaim the coming millennium. And gathered followers, thousands, millions, all those who weren't yet ready to let Armageddon begin, and he made them pray and pray and pray, he held revival meetings that were beamed to Karachi and Katmandu and Addis Ababa and Shanghai, he preached no particular theology and no particular scripture, but only a smooth ecumenical theism that practically anybody could swallow, whether he be

Confucianist or Moslem or Hindu. Listen, Thomas said, there *is* a God, some kind of all-powerful being out there whose divine plan guides the universe, and He watches over us, and don't you believe otherwise! And He is good and will not let us come to harm if we hew to His path. And He has tested us with all these troubles, in order to measure the depth of our faith in Him. So let's show Him, brethren! Let's all pray together and send up a great shout unto Him! For He would certainly give a Sign, and the unbelievers would at last be converted, and the epoch of purity would commence. People said, Why not give it a try? We've got a lot to gain and nothing to lose. A vulgar version of the old Pascal wager: if He's really there, He may help us, and if He's not, we've only wasted a little time. So the hour of beseeching was set.

In faculty circles we had a good deal of fun with the whole idea, we brittle worldly rational types, but sometimes there was a nervous edge to our jokes and a forced heartiness to our laughter, as if some of us suspected that Pascal might have been offering pretty good odds, or that Thomas might just have hit on something. Naturally I was among the skeptics, though as usual I kept my doubts to myself. (The lesson learned so long ago, the narrow escape from the Irish lads.) I hadn't really paid much attention to Thomas and his message, any more than I did to football scores or children's video programs: not my sphere, not my concern. But as the day of prayer drew near, the old temptation beset me. *Give in at last, Gifford. Bow your head and offer homage. Even if He's the myth you've always known He is, do it. Do it!* I argued with myself. I told myself not to be an idiot, not to yield to the age-old claims of superstition. I reminded myself of the holy wars, the Inquisition, the lascivious Renaissance popes, all the crimes of the pious. *So what, Gifford? Can't you be an ordinary humble God-fearing human being for once in your life? Down on your knees beside your brethren? Read your Pascal. Suppose He exists and is listening, and suppose your refusal is the one that tips the scales against mankind? We're not asking so very much.* Still I fought the sly inner voice. To believe is absurd, I cried. I must not let despair stampede me into the renunciation of reason, even in this apocalyptic moment. Thomas is a cunning ruffian and his followers are hysterical grubby fools. *And you're an arrogant elitist, Gifford. Who may live long enough to repent his arrogance*. It was psychological warfare, Gifford vs. Gifford, reason vs. faith.

In the end reason lost. I was jittery, off balance, demoralized. The most astonishing people were coming out in support of Thomas the Proclaimer, and I felt increasingly isolated, a man of ice, heart of stone, the village atheist scowling at Christmas wreaths. Up until the final moment I wasn't sure what I was going to do, but then the hour struck and I found myself in my study, alone, door locked, safely apart from wife and children—who had already, all of them, somewhat defiantly announced their intentions of participating—and there I was on my knees, feeling foolish, feeling preposterous, my cheeks blazing, my lips moving, saying the words. *Saying the words*. Around the world the billions of believers prayed, and I also. I too prayed, embarrassed by my weakness, and the pain of my shame was a stone in my throat.

And the Lord heard us, and He gave a Sign. And for a day and a night (less 1×12–4 sidereal day) the Earth moved not around the sun, neither did it rotate. And the laws of momentum were confounded, as was I. Then Earth again took up its appointed course, as though nothing out of the ordinary had occurred. Imagine my chagrin. I wish I knew where to find those Irish boys. I have some apologies to make.

Four

Thomas Preaches in the Marketplace

I hear what you're saying. You tell me I'm a prophet. You tell me I'm a saint. Some of you even tell me I'm the Son of God come again. You tell me I made the sun stand still over Jerusalem. Well, no, I didn't do that, the Lord Almighty did that, the Lord of Hosts. Through His divine Will, in response to your prayers. And I'm only the vehicle through which your prayers were channeled. I'm not any kind of saint, folks. I'm not the Son of God reborn, or any of the other crazy things you've been saying I am. I'm only Thomas.

Who am I?

I'm just a voice. A spokesman. A tool through which His will was made manifest. I'm not giving you the old humility act, friends, I'm trying to make you see the truth about me.

Who am I?

I'll tell you who I was, though you know it already. I was a bandit, I was a man of evil, I was a defiler of the law. A killer, a liar, a drunkard, a cheat! I did what I damned pleased. I was a law unto myself. If I ever got caught, you bet I wouldn't have whined for mercy. I'd have spit in the judge's face and taken my punishment with my eyes open. Only I never got caught, because my luck was running good and because this is a time when a really bad man can flourish, when the wicked are raised high and the virtuous are ground into the mud. Outside the law, that was me! Thomas the criminal! Thomas the brigand, thumbing his nose! Doing bad was my religion, all the time—when I was down there in Brazil with those flamethrowers, or when I was freelancing your pockets in our cities, or when I was ringing up funny numbers on the big computers. I belonged to Satan if ever a man did, that's the truth, and then what happened? The Lord came along to Satan and said to him, Satan, give me Thomas, I have need of him. And Satan handed me over to Him, because Satan is God's servant too.

And the Lord took me and shook me and knocked me around and said, Thomas, you're nothing but trash!

And I said, I know that, Lord, but who was it who made me that way?

And the Lord laughed and said, You've got guts, Thomas; talking back to me like that. I like a man with guts. But you're wrong, fellow. I made you with the potential to be a saint or a sinner, and you chose to be a sinner, yes, your own free will! You think I'd bother to create people to be wicked? I'm not interested in creating puppets, Thomas, I set out to make me a race of *human beings*. I gave you your options and you opted for evil, eh, Thomas? Isn't that the truth?

And I said, Well, Lord, maybe it is; I don't know.

And the Lord God grew annoyed with me and took me again and shook me again and knocked me around some more, and when I picked myself up I had a puffed lip and a bloody nose, and He asked me how I would do things if I

could live my life over again from the start. And I looked
Him right in the eye and said, Well, Lord, I'd say that being
evil paid off pretty well for me. I lived a right nice life and I
had all my happies and I never spent a day behind bars, oh,
no. So tell me, Lord, since I got away with everything the
first time, why shouldn't I opt to be a sinner again?

And he said, Because you've done that already, and now it's
time for you to do something else.

I said, What's that, Lord?

He said, I want you to do something important for me,
Thomas. There's a world out there full of people who've lost
all faith, people without hope, people who've made up their
minds it's no use trying any more, the world's going to end. I
want to reach those people somehow, Thomas, and tell them
that they're wrong. And show them that they can shape their
own destiny, that if they have faith in themselves and in me
they can build a good world.

I said, That's easy, Lord. Why don't You just appear in the
sky and say that to them, like You just did to me?

He laughed again and said, Oh, no, Thomas, that's much
too easy. I told you, I don't run a puppet show. They've got to
want to lift themselves up out of despair. They've got to take
the first step by themselves. You follow me, Thomas?

Yes, Lord, but where do I come in?

And He said, You go to them, Thomas, and you tell them
all about your wasted, useless, defiant life, and then tell them
how the Lord gave you a chance to do something worthwhile
for a change, and how you rose up above your evil self and
accepted the opportunity. And then tell them to gather and
pray and restore their faith, and ask for a Sign from on high.
Thomas, if they listen to you, if they pray and it's sincere
prayer, I promise you I *will* give them a Sign, I *will* reveal
myself to them, and all doubt will drop like scales from their
eyes. Will you do that thing for me, Thomas?

Friends, I listened to the Lord, and I discovered myself
shaking and quivering and bursting into sweat, and in a
moment, in the twinkling of an eye, I wasn't the old filthy
Thomas any more, I was somebody new and clean, I was a
man with a high purpose, a man with a belief in something
bigger and better than his own greedy desires. And I went
down among you, changed as I was, and I told my tale, and
all of you know the rest of the story, how we came freely
together and offered up our hearts to Him, and how He

vouchsafed us a miracle these two and a half weeks past, and gave us a Sign that He still watches over us.

But what do I see now, in these latter days after the giving of the Sign? What do I see?

Where is that new world of faith? Where is that new dream of hope? Where is mankind shoulder to shoulder, praising Him and working together to reach the light?

What do I see? I see this rotting planet turning black inside and splitting open at the core. I see the cancer of doubt. I see the virus of confusion. I see His Sign misinterpreted on every hand, and its beauty trampled on and destroyed.

I still see painted fools dancing and beating on drums and screaming that the world is going to be destroyed at the end of this year of nineteen hundred and ninety-nine. What madness is this? Has God not spoken? Has he not told us joyful news? God is with us! God is good! Why do these Apocalyptists not yet accept the truth of His Sign?

Even worse! Each day new madnesses take form! What are these cults sprouting up among us? Who are these people who demand of God that He return and spell out His intentions, as though the Sign wasn't enough for them? And who are these cowardly blasphemers who say we must lie down in fear and weep piteous tears, because we have invoked not God but Satan, and destruction is our lot? Who are these men of empty souls who bleat and mumble and snivel in our midst? And look at your lofty churchmen, in their priestly robes and glittering tiaras, trying to explain away the Sign as some accident of nature! What talk is this from God's own ministers? And behold the formerly godless ones, screeching like frightened monkeys now that their godlessness has been ripped from them! What do I see? I see madness and terror on all sides, where I should see only joy abounding!

I beg you, friends, have care, take counsel with your souls. I beg you, think clearly now if you ever have thought at all. Choose a wise path, friends, or you will throw away all the glory of the Day of the Sign and lay waste to our great achievement. Give no comfort to the forces of darkness. Keep away from these peddlers of lunatic creeds. Strive to recapture the wonder of that moment when all mankind spoke with a single voice. I beg you—how can you have doubt of Him now?—I beg you—faith—the triumph of faith—let us not allow—let us—not allow—not—allow—

(Jesus, my throat! All this shouting, it's like swallowing fire.
Give me that bottle, will you? Come on, give it here! The
wine. The wine. Now. Ah. Oh, that's better! Much better,
oh, yes. No, wait, give it back—good, good—stop looking at
me like that, Saul. Ah. *Ah*.)

And so I beseech you today, brothers and sisters in the
Lord—brothers and sisters (what was I saying, Saul? what did
I start to say?)—I call upon you to rededicate yourselves—to
pledge yourselves to—to (is that it? I can't remember)—to a
new Crusade of Faith, that's what we need, a purging of all
our doubts and all our hesitations and all our (oh, Jesus, Saul,
I'm lost, I don't remember where the hell I'm supposed to
be. Let the music start playing. Quick. That's it. Good and
louder. Louder.) Folks, let's all sing! Raise your voices joyously
unto Him!

I shall praise the Lord my God,
Fountain of all power . . .

That's the way! Sing! Everybody sing!

Five

Ceremonies
of Innocence

Throughout the world the quest for an appropriate response
to the event of June 6 continues. No satisfactory interpretation of that day's happenings has yet been established, though
many have been proposed. Meanwhile passions run high;
tempers easily give way; a surprising degree of violence has
entered the situation. Clearly the temporary slowing of the
earth's axial rotation must have imposed exceptional emotional stress on the entire global population, creating severe
strains that have persisted and even intensified in the succeeding
weeks. Instances of seemingly motiveless crimes, particularly
arson and vandalism, have greatly increased. Government

authorities in Brazil, India, the United Arab Republic, and
Italy have suggested that clandestine revolutionary or coun-
terrevolutionary groups are behind much of this activity,
taking advantage of the widespread mood of uncertainty to
stir discontent. No evidence of this has thus far been made
public. Much hostility has been directed toward the organized religions, a phenomenon for which there is as yet no
generally accepted explanation, although several sociologists
have asserted that this pattern of violent anticlerical behavior
is a reaction to the failure of most established religious bodies
as of this time to provide official interpretations of the so-
called miracle of June 6. Reports of the destruction by mob
action of houses of worship of various faiths, with accompanying injuries or fatalities suffered by ecclesiastical personnel,
have come from Mexico, Denmark, Burma, Puerto Rico,
Portugal, Hungary, Ethiopia, the Philippines, and, in the
United States, Alabama, Colorado, and New York. Statements
are promised shortly by leaders of most major faiths. Meanwhile a tendency has developed in certain ecclesiastical quarters toward supporting a mechanistic or rationalistic causation
for the June 6 event; thus on Tuesday the Archbishop of York,
stressing that he was speaking as a private citizen and not as a
prelate of the Church of England, declared that we should
not rule out entirely the possibility of a manipulation of the
Earth's movements by superior beings native to another
planet, intent on spreading confusion preparatory to conquest. Modern theologians, the Archbishop said, see no
inherent impossibility in the doctrine of a separate act of
creation that brought forth an intelligent species on some
extraterrestrial or extragalactic planet, nor is it inconceivable,
he went on, that it might be the Lord's ultimate purpose to
cause a purging of sinful mankind at the hands of that other
species. Thus the slowing of the Earth's rotation may have
been an attempt by these enemies from space to capitalize on
the emotions generated by the recent campaign of the so-
called prophet Thomas the Proclaimer. A spokesman for the
Coptic Patriarch of Alexandria, commenting favorably two
days later on the Archbishop's theory, added that in the
private view of the Patriarch it seems less implausible that
such an alien species should exist than that a divine miracle of
the June 6 sort could be invoked by popular demand. A
number of other religious leaders, similarly speaking unofficially,
have cautioned against too rapid acceptance of the divine

origin of the June 6 event, without as yet going so far as to embrace the Archbishop of York's suggestion. On Friday Dr. Nathan F. Scharf, President of the Central Conference of American Rabbis, urgently appealed to American and Israeli scientists to produce a computer-generated mathematical schema capable of demonstrating how a unique but natural conjunction of astronomical forces might have resulted in the June 6 event. The only reply to this appeal thus far has come from Ssu-ma Hsiang-ju, Minister of Science of the People's Republic of China, who has revealed that a task force of several hundred Chinese astronomers is already at work on such a project. But his Soviet counterpart, Academician N. V. Posilippov, has on the contrary called for a revision of Marxist-Leninist astronomical theory to take into account what he terms "the possibility of intervention by as yet undefined forces, perhaps of supernatural aspect, in the motions of the heavenly bodies." We may conclude, therefore, that the situation remains in flux. Observers agree that the chief beneficiaries of the June 6 event at this point have been the various recently founded apocalyptic sects, who now regard the so-called Day of the Sign as an indication of the imminent destruction of life on Earth. Undoubtedly much of the current violence and the other irrational behavior can be traced to the increased activity of such groups. A related manifestation is the dramatic expansion in recent weeks of older millenarian sects, notably the Pentecostal churches. The Protestant world in general has experienced a rebirth of the Pentecostal-inspired phenomenon known as glossolalia, or "speaking in tongues," a technique for penetrating to revelatory or prophetic levels by means of unreined ecstatic outbursts *illalum gha ghollim ve illalum ghollim ghaznim kroo! Aiha! Kroo illalum nildaz sitamon ghaznim* of seemingly random syllables in no language known to the speaker; the value of this practice has *mehigioo camaleelee honistar zam* been a matter of controversy in religious circles for many centuries.

Six

The Woman Who
Is Sore at Heart
Reproaches Thomas

I knew he was in our country and I had to get to see him because he was the one who made all this trouble for me. So I went to his headquarters, the place where the broadcasts were being made that week, and I saw him standing in the middle of a group of his followers. A very handsome man, really, somewhat too dirty and wild-looking for my tastes, but you give him a shave and a haircut and he'd be quite attractive in my estimation. Big and strong he is, and when you see him you want to throw yourself into his arms, though of course I was in no frame of mind to do any such thing just then and in any case I'm not that sort of woman. I went right toward him. There was a tremendous crowd in the street, but I'm not discouraged easily, my husband likes to call me his "little bulldog" sometimes, and I just bulled my way through that mob, a little kicking and some elbowing and I think I bit someone's arm once and I got through. There was Thomas and next to him that skinny little man who's always with him, that Saul Kraft, who I guess is his press agent or something. As I got close, three of his bodyguards looked at me and then at each other, probably saying oh-oh, here comes another crank dame, and they started to surround me and move me away, and Thomas wasn't even looking at me, and I began to yell, saying I had to talk to Thomas, I had something important to say. And then this Saul Kraft told them to let go of me and bring me forward. They checked me out for concealed weapons and then Thomas asked me what I wanted.

I felt nervous before him. Such a famous man. But I planted my feet flat on the ground and stuck my jaw up the way Dad taught me, and I said, "You did all this. You've wrecked me, Thomas. You've got me so I don't know if I'm standing on my head or right side up."

He gave me a funny sideways smile. "I did?"

"Look," I said, "I'll tell you how it was. I went to Mass every week, my whole family, Church of the Redeemer on Wilson's Avenue. We put money in the plate, we did everything the fathers told us to do, we tried to live good Christian lives, right? Not that we really thought much about God. Whether He was actually up there listening to me saying my paternoster. I figured He was too busy to worry much about me, and I couldn't be too concerned about him, because He surpasses my understanding, you follow? Instead I prayed to the fathers. To me Father McDermott was like God Himself, in a way, not meaning any disrespect. What I'm trying to say is that the average ordinary person, they don't have a very close relationship with God, you follow? With the church, yes, with the fathers, but not with God. Okay. Now you come along and say the world is in a mess, so let's pray to God to show Himself like in the olden times. I ask Father McDermott about it and he says it's all right, it's permitted even though it isn't an idea that came from Rome, on such-and-such day we'll have this world moment of prayer. So I pray, and the sun stands still. June 6, you made the sun stand still."

"Not me. *Him.*" Thomas was smiling again. And looking at me like he could read everything in my soul.

I said, "You know what I mean. It's a miracle, anyway. The biggest miracle since, I don't know, since the Resurrection. The next day we need help, guidance, right? My husband and I, we go to church. *The church is closed.* Locked tight. We go around back and try to find the fathers. Nobody there but a housekeeper and she's scared. Won't open up. Why is the church shut? They're afraid of rioters, she says. Where's Father McDermott? He's gone to the Archdiocese for a conference. So have all the other fathers. Go away, she says. Nobody's here. You follow me, Thomas? Biggest miracle since the Resurrection, *and they close the church the next day.*"

Thomas said, "They got nervous, I guess."

"Nervous? Sure they were nervous. That's my whole point. Where were the fathers when we needed them? Conferring at the Archdiocese. The Cardinal was holding a special meeting about the crisis. *The crisis,* Thomas! God Himself works a miracle, and to the church it's a crisis! What am I supposed to do? Where does it leave me? I need the church, the church has always been telling me that, and all of a sudden the church locks its doors and says to me, Go figure it out by yourself, lady, we won't have a bulletin for a couple of days. The church was scared!

I think they were afraid the Lord was going to come in and say we don't need priests any more, we don't need churches, all this organized-religion stuff hasn't worked out so well anyway, so let's forget it and move right into the Millennium."

"Anything big and strange always upsets the people in power," Thomas said, shrugging. "But the church opened again, didn't it?"

"Sure, four days later. Business as usual, except we aren't supposed to ask any questions about June 6 yet. Because they don't have The Word from Rome yet, the interpretation, the official policy." I had to laugh. "Three weeks, almost, since it happened, and the College of Cardinals is still in special consistory, trying to decide what position the church ought to take. Isn't that crazy, Thomas? If the Pope can't recognize a miracle when he sees one, what good is the whole church?"

"All right," Thomas said, "but why blame me?"

"Because you took my church away from me. I can't trust those people any more. I don't know what to believe. We've got God right here beside us, and the church isn't giving any leadership. What do we do now? How do we handle this thing?"

"Have faith, my child," he said, "and pray for salvation, and remain steadfast in your righteousness." He said a lot of other stuff like that too, rattling it off like he was a computer programmed to deliver blessings. I could tell he wasn't sincere. He wasn't trying to answer me, just to calm me down and get rid of me.

"No," I said, breaking in on him. "That stuff isn't good enough. *Have faith. Pray a lot.* I've been doing that all my life. Okay, we prayed and we got God to show Himself. What now? What's your program, Thomas? Tell me that. What do you want us to do? You took our church away—what will you give us to replace it?"

I could tell he didn't have any answers.

His face turned red and he tugged on the ends of his hair and looked at Saul Kraft in a sour way, almost like he was saying I-told-you-so with his eyes. Then he looked back at me and I saw either sorrow or fear in his face, I don't know which, and I realized right then that this Thomas is just a human being like you and me, a scared human being, who doesn't really understand what's happening and doesn't know how to go on from this point. He tried to fake it. He told me again to pray, never underestimate the power of prayer, et cetera, et cetera, but his heart wasn't in his words. He was stuck. *What's your program, Thomas?* He doesn't have any. He hasn't thought things through past the point of getting the Sign from God. He can't help us now. There's your Thomas

for you, the Proclaimer, the prophet. He's scared. We're all
scared, and he's just one of us, no different, no wiser. And last
night the Apocalyptists burned the shopping center. You know, if
you had asked me six months ago how I'd feel if God gave us a
Sign that He was really watching over us, I'd have told you that I
thought it would be the most wonderful thing that had ever
happened since Jesus in the manger. But now it's happened. And
I'm not so sure how wonderful it is. I walk around feeling that
the ground might open up under my feet any time. I don't know
what's going to happen to us all. God has come, and it ought to
be beautiful, and instead it's just scary. I never imagined it would
be this way. Oh, God. God I feel so lost. God I feel so empty.

Seven
An Insight of
Discerners

Speaking before an audience was nothing new for me, of course.
Not after all the years I've spent in classrooms, patiently instructing
each season's hairy new crop of young in the mysteries of tachyon
theory, anterior-charge particles, and time-reversal equations.
Nor was this audience a particularly alien or frightening one: it
was made up mainly of faculty people from Harvard and M.I.T.,
some graduate students, and a sprinkling of lawyers, psycholo-
gists, and other professional folk from Cambridge and the outskirts. All of us part of the community of scholarship, so to speak.
The sort of audience that might come together to protest the
latest incident of ecological rape or of preventive national liberation. But one aspect of my role this evening was unsettling to
me. This was in the truest sense a religious gathering; that is, we
were meeting to discuss the nature of God and to arrive at some
comprehension of our proper relationship to Him. And I was the
main speaker, me, old Bill Gifford, who for nearly four decades
had regarded the Deity as an antiquated irrelevance. I was this
flock's pastor. How strange that felt.

"But I believe that many of you are in the same predicament," I told them. "Men and women to whom the religious impulse has been something essentially foreign. Whose lives were complete and fulfilled although prayer and ritual were wholly absent from them. Who regarded the concept of a supreme being as meaningless and who looked upon the churchgoing habits of those around them as nothing more than lower-class superstitiousness on the one hand and middle-class pietism on the other. And then came the great surprise of June 6—forcing us to reconsider doctrines we had scorned, forcing us to reexamine our basic philosophical constructs, forcing us to seek an acceptable explanation of a phenomenon that we had always deemed impossible and implausible. All of you, like myself, suddenly found yourselves treading very deep metaphysical waters."

The nucleus of this group had come together on an ad hoc basis the week after It happened, and since then had been meeting two or three times a week. At first there was no formal organizational structure, no organizational name, no policy; it was merely a gathering of intelligent and sophisticated New Englanders who felt unable to cope individually with the altered nature of reality and who needed mutual reassurance and reinforcement. That was why I started going, anyway. But within ten days we were groping toward a more positive purpose: no longer simply to learn how to *accept* what had befallen humanity, but to find some way of turning it to a useful purpose. I had begun articulating some ideas along those lines in private conversation, and abruptly I was asked by several of the leaders of the group to make my thoughts public at the next meeting.

"An astonishing event has occurred," I went on. "A good many ingenious theories have been proposed to account for it—as, for example, that the Earth was brought to a halt through the workings of an extrasensory telekinetic force generated by the simultaneous concentration of the entire world population. We have also heard the astrological explanations—that the planets or the stars were lined up in a certain once-in-a-universe's-lifetime way to bring about such a result. And there have been the arguments, some of them coming from quite surprising places, in favor of the notion that the June 6 event was the doing of malevolent creatures from outer space. The telekinesis hypothesis has a certain superficial plausibility, marred only by the fact that experimenters in the past have never been able to detect even an iota of telekinetic ability in any human being or combination

of human beings. Perhaps a simultaneous world-wide effort
might generate forces not to be found in any unit smaller than
the total human population, but such reasoning requires an
undesirable multiplication of hypotheses. I believe that most
of you here agree with me that the other explanations of the
June 6 event beg one critical question: Why did the slowing
of the Earth occur so promptly, in seemingly direct response
to Thomas the Proclaimer's campaign of global prayer? Can
we believe that a unique alignment of astrological forces just
happened to occur the day after that hour of prayer? Can we
believe that the extragalactic fiends just happened to meddle
with the Earth's rotation on that particular day? The element
of coincidence necessary to sustain these and other arguments is fatal to them, I think.

"What are we left with, then? Only with the explanation
that the Lord Almighty, heeding mankind's entreaties, performed
a miracle so that we should be confirmed in our faith in Him.

"So I conclude. So do many of you. But does it necessarily
follow that mankind's sorry religious history, with all its holy
wars, its absurd dogmas, its childish rituals, its fastings and
flagellations, is thereby justified? Because you and you and
you and I were bowled over on June 6, blasted out of our
skepticism by an event that has no rational explanation,
should we therefore rush to the churches and synagogues and
mosques and enroll immediately in the orthodoxy of our
choice? I think not. I submit that our attitudes of skepticism
and rationalism were properly held, although our aim was
misplaced. In scorning the showy, trivial trappings of organized faith, in walking past the churches where our neighbors
devoutly knelt, we erred by turning away also from the
matter that underlay their faith: the existence of a supreme
being whose divine plan guides the universe. The spinning of
prayer wheels and the mumbling of credos seemed so inane
to us that, in our revulsion for such things, we were led to
deny all notions of a higher order, of a teleological universe,
and we embraced the concept of a wholly random cosmos.
And then the Earth stood still for a day and a night.

"How did it happen? We admit it was God's doing, you and
I, amazed though we are to find ourselves saying so. We have
been hammered into a posture of belief by that inexplicable
event. But what do we mean by 'God'? Who is He? An old
man with long white whiskers? Where is He to be found?
Somewhere between the orbits of Mars and Jupiter? Is He a

supernatural being, or merely an extraterrestrial one? Does
he too acknowledge a superior authority? And so on, an
infinity of new questions. We have no valid knowledge of His
nature, though now we have certain knowledge of His existence.

"Very well. A tremendous opportunity now exists for us the
discerning few, for us who are in the habit of intellectual
activity. All about us we see a world in frenzy. The Apocalyptists swoon with joy over the approaching catastrophe, the
glossolaliacs chatter in maniac glee, the heads of entrenched
churchly hierarchies are aghast at the possibility that the
Millennium may really be at hand; everything is in flux,
everything is new and strange. New cults spring up. Old
creeds dissolve. And this is our moment. Let us step in and
replace credulity and superstition with reason. An end to
cults; an end to theology; an end to blind faith. Let it be our
goal to relate the events of that awesome day to some
principle of reason, and develop a useful, dynamic, *rational*
movement of rebirth and revival—not a religion per se but
rather a cluster of belief, based on the concept that a divine
plan exists, that we live under the authority of a supreme or
at least superior being, and that we must strive to come to
some kind of rational relationship with this being.

"We've already had the moral strength to admit that our
old intuitive skepticism was an error. Now let us provide an
attractive alternate for those of us who still find ritualistic
orthodoxy unpalatable, but who fear a total collapse into
apocalyptic disarray if no steps are taken to strengthen mankind's spiritual insight. Let us create, if we can, a purely
secular movement, a nonreligious religion, which offers the
hope of establishing a meaningful dialogue between Us and
Him. Let us make plans. Let us find powerful symbols with
which we may sway the undecided and the confused. Let us
march forth as crusaders in a dramatic effort to rescue humanity from unreason and desperation."

And so forth. I think it was a pretty eloquent speech,
especially coming from someone who isn't in the habit of
delivering orations. A transcript of it got into the local paper
the next day and was reprinted all over. My "us the discerning few" line drew a lot of attention, and spawned an instant
label for our previously unnamed movement. We became
known as the Discerners. Once we had a name, our status
was different. We weren't simply a group of concerned citizens any longer. Now we constituted a cult—a skeptical,

rational, antisuperstitious cult, true, but nevertheless a cult, a sect, the newest facet of the world's furiously proliferating latter-day craziness.

Eight
An Expectation of Awaiters

I know it hasn't been fashionable to believe in God these last twenty thirty forty years people haven't been keeping His path much but I always did even when I was a little boy I believed truly and I loved Him and I wanted to go to church all the time even in the middle of the week I'd say to Mother let's go to church I genuinely enjoyed kneeling and praying and feeling him near me but she'd say no Davey you've got to wait till Sunday for that it's only Wednesday now. So as they say I'm no stranger to His ways and of course when they called for that day of prayer I prayed with all my heart that he might give us a Sign but even so I'm no fool I mean I don't accept everything on a silver platter I ask questions I have doubts I test things and probe a little I'm not one of your ordinary country bumpkins that takes everything on faith. In a way I suppose I could be said to belong to the discerning few although I don't want any of you to get the idea I'm a Discerner oh no I have no sympathy whatever with that atheistic bunch. Anyway we all prayed and the Sign came and my first reaction was joy I don't mind telling you I wept for joy when the sun stood still feeling that all the faith of a lifetime had been confirmed and the godless had better shiver in their boots but then a day or so later I began to think about it and I asked myself how do we know that the Sign really came from God? How can we be sure that the being we have invoked is really on our side I asked myself and of course I had no good answer to that. For all I knew we

had conjured up Satan the Accursed and what we imagined
was a miracle was really a trick out of the depths of hell
designed to lead us all to perdition. Here are these Discerners
telling us that they repent their atheism because they know
now that God is real and God is with us but how naïve they
are they aren't even allowing for the possibility that the Sign
is a snare and a delusion I tell you we can't be sure the thing
is we absolutely *can't be sure*. The Sign might have been
from God or from the Devil and we don't know we won't
know until we receive a second Sign which I await which I
believe will be coming quite soon. And what will that second
Sign tell us? I maintain that that has not yet been decided on
high it may be a Sign announcing our utter damnation or it
may be a Sign welcoming us to the Earthly Paradise and we
must await it humbly and prayerfully my friends we must
pray and purify ourselves and prepare for the worst as well as
for the best. I like to think that in a short while God Himself
will present Himself to us not in any indirect way like
stopping the sun but rather in a direct manifestation
either as God the Father or as God the Son and we will all
be saved but this will come about *only if we remain
righteous*. If we succumb to error and evil we will bring it
to pass that the Devil's advent will descend on us for as
Thomas has said himself our destiny is in our hands as well
as in His and I believe the first Sign was only the start of a
process that will be decided for good or for evil in the days
just ahead. Therefore I Davey Strafford call upon you my
friends to keep the way of the faith for we must not waver
in our hope that He Who Comes will be lovingly inclined
toward us and I say that this is our time of supreme test
and if we fail it we may discover that it is Satan who shows
up to claim our souls. I say once more we cannot interpret
the first Sign we can only have faith that it is truly from
God and we must pray that this is so while we await the
ultimate verdict of heaven therefore we have obtained the
rental of a vacant grocery store on Coshocton Avenue
which we have renamed the First Church of the Awaiters
of Redemption and we will pray round the clock there are
seventeen of us now and we will pray in three-hour shifts
five of us at a time in rotation the numbers increasing as
our expected rapid growth takes place I trust you will
come to us and swell our voices for we must pray we've
got to there's no other hope now just pray a lot in order

that He Who Comes may be benevolent and I ask you to keep praying and have a trusting heart in this our time of waiting.

Nine

A Crying of Proclaimers

Kraft enters the room as Thomas puts down the telephone. "Who were you talking to?" Kraft asks.

"Gifford the Discerner, calling from Boston."

"Why are you answering the phone yourself?"

"There was no one else here."

"There were three apostles in the outer office who could have handled the call, Thomas."

Thomas shrugs. "They would have had to refer it to me eventually. So I answered. What's wrong with that?"

"You've got to maintain distance between yourself and ordinary daily routines. You've got to stay up there on your pedestal and not go around answering telephones."

"I'll try, Saul," says Thomas heavily.

"What did Gifford want?"

"He'd like to merge his group and ours."

Kraft's eyes flash. "To merge? *To merge?* What are we, some sort of manufacturing company? We're a movement. A spiritual force. To talk mergers is nonsense."

"He means that we should start working together, Saul. He says we should join forces because we're both on the side of sanity."

'Exactly what is that supposed to mean?"

"That we're both anti-Apocalyptist. That we're both working to preserve society instead of to bury it."

"An oversimplification," Kraft says. "We deal in faith and he deals in equations. We believe in a Divine Being and he believes in the sanctity of reason. Where's the meeting point?"

"The Cincinnati and Chicago fires are our meeting point, Saul. The Apocalyptists are going crazy. And now these Awaiters too, these spokesmen for Satan—no. We have to act. If I put myself at Gifford's disposal—"

"At his *disposal?*"

"He wants a statement from me backing the spirit if not the substance of the Discerner philosophy. He thinks it'll serve to calm things a little."

"He wants to co-opt you for his own purposes."

"For the purposes of mankind, Saul."

Kraft laughs harshly. "How naîve you can be, Thomas! Where's your sense? You can't make an alliance with atheists. You can't let them turn you into a ventriloquist's dummy who—"

"They believe in God just as much as—"

"You have power, Thomas. It's in your voice, it's in your eyes. They have none. They're just a bunch of professors. They want to borrow your power and make use of it to serve their own ends. They don't want you, Thomas, they want your charisma. I forbid this alliance."

Thomas is trembling. He towers over Kraft, but his entire body quivers and Kraft remains steady. Thomas says, "I'm so tired, Saul."

"Tired?"

"The uproar. The rioting. The fires. I'm carrying too big a burden. Gifford can help me. With planning, with ideas. That's a clever bunch, those people."

"I can give you all the help you need."

"No, Saul! What have you been telling me all along? That prayer is sufficient unto every occasion! Faith! Faith! Faith! Faith moves mountains! Well? You were right, yes, you channeled your faith through me and I spoke to the people and we got ourselves a miracle, but what now? What have we really accomplished? Everything's falling apart, and we need strong souls to build and rebuild, and you aren't offering anything new. You—"

"The Lord will provide for—"

"Will He? Will He, Saul? How many thousands dead already, since June 6? How much property damage? Government paralyzed. Transportation breaking down. New cults. New prophets. Here's Gifford saying, Let's join hands, Thomas, let's try to work together, and you tell me—"

"I forbid this," Kraft says.

"It's all agreed. Gifford's going to take the first plane west, and—"

"I'll call him. He mustn't come. If he does I won't let him see you. I'll notify the apostles to bar him."

"No, Saul."

"We don't need him. We'll be ruined if we let him near you."

"Why?"

"Because he's godless and our movement's strength proceeds from the Lord!" Kraft shouts. "Thomas, what's happened to you? Where's your fire? Where's your zeal? Where's my old swaggering Thomas who talked back to God? Belch, Thomas, Spit on the floor, scratch your belly, curse a little. I'll get you some wine. It shocks me to see you sniveling like this. Telling me how tired you are, how scared."

"I don't feel like swaggering much these days, Saul."

"Damn you, swagger anyway! The whole world is watching you! Here, listen—I'll rough out a new speech for you that you'll deliver on full hookup tomorrow night. We'll outflank Gifford and his bunch. We'll co-opt *him*. What you'll do, Thomas, is call for a new act of faith, some kind of mass demonstration, something symbolic and powerful, something to turn people away from despair and destruction. We'll follow the Discerner line *plus* our own element of faith. You'll denounce all the false new cults and urge everyone to—to— let me think—to make a pilgrimage of some kind?—a coming together—a mass baptism, that's it, a march to the sea, everybody bathing in God's own sea, washing away doubt and sin. Right? A rededication to faith." Kraft's face is red. His forehead gleams. Thomas scowls at him. Kraft goes on, "Stop pulling those long faces. You'll do it and it'll work. It'll pull people back from the abyss of Apocalypticism. Positive goals, that's our approach. Thomas the Proclaimer cries out that we must work together under God. Yes? Yes. We'll get this thing under control in ten days, I promise you. Now go have yourself a drink. Relax. I've got to call Gifford, and then I'll start blocking in your new appeal. Go on. And stop looking so glum. Thomas! We hold a mighty power in our hands. We're wielding the sword of the Lord. You want to turn all that over to Gifford's crowd? Go. Go. Get some rest, Thomas."

Ten

A Prostration of Propitiators

ALL PARISH CHAIRMEN PLEASE COPY AND DISTRIBUTE. The Reverend August Hammacher to his dearly beloved brothers and sisters in Christ, members of the Authentic Church of the Doctrine of Propitiation, this message from Central Shrine: greetings and blessings. Be you hereby advised that we have notified Elder Davey Strafford of the First Church of the Awaiters of Redemption that as of this date we no longer consider ourselves in communion with his church, on grounds of irremediable doctrinal differences. It is now forbidden for members of the Authentic Church to participate in the Awaiter rite or to have any sacramental contact with the instrumentalities of the Awaiter creed, although we shall continue to remember the Awaiters in our prayers and to strive for their salvation as if they were our own people.

The schism between ourselves and the Awaiters, which has been in the making for more than a week, arises from a fundamental disagreement over the nature of the Sign. It is of course our belief, greatly strengthened by the violent events of recent days, that the Author of the Sign was Satan and that the Sign foretells a coming realignment in heaven, the probable beneficiaries of which are to be the Diabolical Forces. In expectation of the imminent establishment of the Dark Powers on Earth, we therefore direct our most humble homage to Satan the Second Incarnation of Christ, hoping that when He comes among us He will take cognizance of our obeisance and spare us from the ultimate holocaust.

Now the Awaiters hold what is essentially an agnostic position, saying that we cannot know whether the Sign pro-

309

ceeds from God or from Satan, and that pending further
revelation we must continue to pray as before to the Father
and the Son, so that perhaps through our devotions we may
stave off the advent of Satan entirely. There is one point of
superficial kinship between their ideas and ours, which is an
unwillingness to share the confidence of Thomas the Proclaimer
on the one hand, and the Discerners on the other, that the
Sign is God's work. But it may be seen that a basic conflict of
doctrine exists between ourselves and the Awaiters, for they
refuse to comprehend our teachings concerning the potential
benevolence of Satan, and cling to an attitude that may be
deemed dangerously offensive by Him. Unwilling to commit
themselves finally to one side or the other, they hope to steer
a cautious middle course, not realizing that when the Dark
One comes He will chastise all those who failed to accept the
proper meaning of the revelation of June 6. We have hoped
to sway the Awaiters to our position, but their attitude has
grown increasingly abusive as we have exposed their doctrinal
inconsistencies, and now we have no option but to pronounce
excommunication upon them. For what does Revelation say?
"I know thy works, that thou art neither cold nor hot: I would
thou wert cold or hot. So then because thou art lukewarm,
and neither cold nor hot, I will spue thee out of my mouth."
We cannot risk being tainted by these lukewarm Awaiters
who will not bow the knee to the Dark One, though they
admit the possibility (but not the inevitability) of His Advent.

However, dearly loved friends in Christ, I am happy to
reveal that we have this day established preliminary communion with the United Diabolist Apocalyptic Pentecostal Church
of the United States, the headquarters of which is in Los
Angeles, California. I need not here recapitulate the deep
doctrinal chasms separating us from the Apocalyptist sects in
general; but although we abhor certain teachings even of this
Diabolist faction, we recognize large areas of common belief
linking us, and hope to wean the United Diabolist Apocalyp-
tics entirely from their errors in the course of time. This is by
no means to be interpreted as presently authorizing commu-
nicants of the Authentic Church of the Doctrine of Propitiation to take part in Apocalyptist activities, even those which
are nondestructive, but I do wish to advise you of the
possibility of a deeper relationship with at least one Apocalyptist group even as we sever our union with the Awaiters.
Our love goes out to all of you, from all of us at Central

Shrine. We prostrate ourselves humbly before the Dark One whose triumph is ordained. In the name of the Father, the Son, the Holy Ghost, and He Who Comes. Amen.

Eleven
The March to the Sea

It was the most frightening thing ever. Like an army invading us. Like a plague of locusts. They came like the locusts came upon the land of Egypt when Moses stretched out his hand. Exodus 10:15 tells it: *For they covered the face of the whole earth, so that the land was darkened; and they did eat every herb of the land, and all the fruit of the trees which the hail had left: and there remained not any green thing in the trees, or in the herbs of the field, through all the land of Egypt.* Like a nightmare. Lucy and me were the Egyptians and all of Thomas' people, they were the locusts.

Lucy wanted to be in the middle of it all along. To her, Thomas was like a holy prophet of God from the moment he first started to preach, although I tried to tell her back then that he was a charlatan and a dangerous lunatic with a criminal record. Look at his face, I said, look at those eyes! A lot of good it did me. She kept a scrapbook of him like he was a movie star and she was a fifteen-year-old girl instead of a woman of seventy-four. Pictures of him, texts of all his speeches. She got angry at me when I called him crazy or unscrupulous: we had our worst quarrel in maybe thirty years when she wanted to send him $500 to help pay for his television expenses and I absolutely refused. Naturally after the Day of the Sign she came to look upon him as being right up there in the same exalted category as Moses and Elijah and John the Baptist, one of the true anointed voices of the Lord, and I guess I was starting to think of him that way too, despite myself. Though I didn't like him or trust him I sensed he had a special power. When everybody was praying for the Sign I prayed too, not so much because I thought it would come about but just to avoid trouble with Lucy, but I did put my heart into the prayer, and when the Earth stopped turning a shiver ran all through me and I got such a jolt of amazement that I thought I might be having a stroke. So I apologized to Lucy for all I had said about Thomas. I still suspected he was a madman and a charlatan, but I couldn't deny that he had something of the saint and prophet about him too. I suppose it's possible for a man to be a saint and a charlatan both. Anything's possible. I understand that one of these new religions is saying that Satan is actually an incarnation of Jesus, or the fourth member of the Trinity, or something like that. Honestly.

Well then all the riotings and burnings began when the hot weather came and the world seemed to be going crazy with things worse not better after God had given His Sign, and Thomas called for this Day of Rededication, everybody to go down to the sea and wash off his sins, a real old-time total-immersion revival meeting where we'd all get together and denounce the new cults and get things back on the right track again.

And Lucy came to me all aglow and said, Let's go, let's be part of it. I think there were supposed to be ten gathering-places all around the United States, New York and Houston and San Diego and Seattle and Chicago and I don't remember which else, but Thomas himself was going to attend the main one at Atlantic City, which is just a little ways down the coast from us, and the proceedings would be beamed by live telecast to all the other meetings being held here and overseas. She hadn't ever seen Thomas in person. I told her it was crazy for people our age to get mixed up in a mob of the size Thomas always attracts. We'd be crushed, we'd be trampled, we'd die sure as anything. Look, I said, we live right here by the seashore anyway, the ocean is fifty steps from our front porch; so why ask for trouble? We'll stay here and watch the praying on television, and then when everybody goes down into the sea to be purified we can go right here on our own beach and we'll be part of things in a way without taking the risks. I could see that Lucy was disappointed about not seeing Thomas in person but after all she's a sensible woman and I'm going to be eighty next November and there had already been some pretty wild scenes at each of Thomas' public appearances.

The big day dawned and I turned on the television and

then of course we got the news that Atlantic City had banned Thomas' meeting at the last minute on the grounds of public safety. A big oil tanker had broken up off shore the night before and an oil slick was heading toward the beach, the mayor said. If there was a mass meeting on the beach that day it would interfere with the city's pollution-prevention procedures, and also the oil would endanger the health of anybody who went into the water, so the whole Atlantic City waterfront was being cordoned off, extra police brought in from out of town, laser lines set up, and so forth. Actually the oil slick wasn't anywhere near Atlantic City and was drifting the other way, and when the mayor talked about public safety he really meant the safety of his city, not wanting a couple of million people ripping up the boardwalk and breaking windows. So there was Atlantic City sealed off and Thomas had this immense horde of people already collected, coming from Philadelphia and Trenton and Wilmington and even Baltimore, a crowd so big it couldn't be counted, five, six, maybe ten million people. They showed it from a helicopter view and everybody was standing shoulder to shoulder for about twenty miles in this direction and fifty miles in that direction, that's how it seemed, anyway, and about the only open place was where Thomas was, a clearing around fifty yards across with his apostles forming a tight ring protecting him.

Where was this mob going to go, since it couldn't get into Atlantic City? Why, Thomas said, everybody would just march up the Jersey coast and spread out along the shore from Long Beach Island to Sandy Hook. When I heard that I wanted to jump into the car and start heading for maybe Montana, but it was too late: the marchers were already on their way, all the mainland highways were choked with them. I went up on the sundeck with our binoculars and I could see the first of them coming across the causeway, walking seventy or eighty abreast, and a sea of faces behind them going inland on and on back toward Manahawkin and beyond. Well it was like the Mongol hordes of Genghis Khan. One swarm went south toward Beach Haven and the other came up through Surf City and Loveladies and Harvey Cedars in our direction. Thousands and thousands and thousands of them. Our island is long and skinny like any coastal sandspit, and it's pretty well built up both on the beach side and on the bay side, no open space except the narrow streets, and there wasn't *room* for all those people. But they kept on coming, and as I watched through the binoculars I thought I was getting dizzy because I imagined some of the houses on the beach side were moving too, and then I realized that the houses *were* moving, some of the flimsier ones, they were being pushed right off their foundations by the press of humanity. Toppling and being ground underfoot, entire houses, can you imagine? I told Lucy to pray, but she was already doing it, and I got my shotgun ready because I felt I had to try at least to protect us, but I said to her that this was probably going to be our last day alive and I kissed her and we told each other how good it had been, all of it, fifty-three years together. And then the mob came spilling through our part of the island. Rushing down to the beach. A berserk crazy multitude.

And Thomas was there, right close to our place. Bigger than I thought he'd be, and his hair and beard were all tangled up, and his face was red and peeling some from sunburn—he was that close, I could see the sunburn—and he was still in the middle of his ring of apostles, and he was shouting through a bullhorn, but no matter how much amplification they gave him from the copter-borne speakers overhead it was impossible to understand anything he was saying. Saul Kraft was next to him. He looked pale and frightened. People were rushing into the water, some of them fully clothed and some stark naked, until the whole shoreline was packed right out to where the breakers begin. As more and more people piled into the water the ones in front were pushed beyond their depth, and I think this was when the drownings started. I know I saw a number of people waving and kicking and yelling for help and getting swept out to sea. Thomas remained on shore, shouting through the bullhorn. He must have realized it was all out of control, but there was nothing he could do. Until this point the thrust of the mob was all forward, toward the sea, but now there was a change in the flow: some of those in the water tried to force their way back up onto land, and smashed head on into those going the other way. I thought they were coming up out of the water to avoid being drowned, but then I saw the black smears on their clothing and I thought, *the oil slick!* and yes, there it was, not down by Atlantic City but up here by us, right off the beach and moving shoreward. People in the water were getting bogged down in it, getting it all over their hair and faces, but they couldn't reach the shore because of the rush still heading in the opposite direction. This was when the tramplings started as the ones coming out of the water, coughing and choking and blinded with oil, fell under the feet of those still trying to get into the sea.

I looked at Thomas again and he was like a maniac. His face was wild and he had thrown the bullhorn away and he was just screaming, with angry cords standing out on his neck and forehead. Saul Kraft went up to him and said something and Thomas turned like the wrath of God, turned and rose up and brought his hands down like two clubs on Saul Kraft's head, and you know Kraft is a small man and he went down like he was dead, with blood all over his face. Two or three apostles picked him up and carried him into one of the beachfront houses. Just then somebody managed to slip through the cordon of apostles and went running toward Thomas. He was a short, plump man wearing the robes of one of the new religions, an Awaiter or Propitiator or I don't know what, and he had a laser-hatchet in his hand. He shouted something at Thomas and lifted the hatchet. But Thomas moved toward him and stood so tall that the assassin almost seemed to shrink, and the man was so afraid that he couldn't do a thing. Thomas reached out and plucked the hatchet from his hand and threw it aside. Then he caught the man and started hitting him, tremendous close-range punches, slam slam slam, all but knocking the man's head off his shoulders. Thomas didn't look human while he was doing that. He was some kind of machine of destruction. He was bellowing and roaring and running foam from his mouth, and he was into this terrible deadly rhythm of punching, slam slam slam. Finally he stopped and took the man by both hands and flung him across the beach, like you'd fling a rag doll. The man flew maybe twenty feet and landed and didn't move. I'm certain Thomas beat him to death. There's your holy prophet for you, your saint of God. Suddenly Thomas's whole appearance changed: he became terribly calm, almost frozen, standing there with his arms dangling and his shoulders hunched up and his chest heaving from all that hitting. And he began to cry. His face broke up like winter ice on a spring pond and I saw the tears. I'll never forget that: Thomas the Proclaimer all alone in the middle of that madhouse on the beach, sobbing like a new widow.

I didn't see anything after that. There was a crash of glass from downstairs and I grabbed my gun and went down to see, and I found maybe fifteen people piled up on the livingroom

floor who had been pushed right through the picture window
by the crowd outside. The window had cut them all up and
some were terribly maimed and there was blood on everything, and more and more and more people kept flying
through the place where the window had been, and I heard
Lucy screaming and my gun went off and I don't know what
happened after that. Next I remember it was the middle of
the night and I was sitting in our completely wrecked house
and I saw a helicopter land on the beach, and a tactical squad
began collecting bodies. There were hundreds of dead just on
our strip of beach. Drowned, trampled, choked by oil, heart
attacks, everything. The corpses are gone now but the island
is a ruin. We're asking the government for disaster aid. I don't
know: is a religious meeting a proper disaster? It was for us.
That was your Day of Rededication, all right: a disaster.
Prayer and purification to bring us all together under the
banner of the Lord. May I be struck dead for saying this if I
don't mean it with all my heart: I wish the Lord and all his
prophets would disappear and leave us alone. We've had
enough religion for one season.

Twelve
The Voice from
the Heavens

Saul Kraft, hidden behind nine thousand dollars' worth of
security devices, an array of scanners and sensors and shunt-
gates and trip-vaults, wonders why everything is going so
badly. Perhaps his choice of Thomas as the vehicle was an
error. Thomas, he has come to realize, is too complicated, too
unpredictable—a dual soul, demon and angel inextricably
merged. Nevertheless the Crusade had begun promisingly
enough. Working through Thomas, he had coaxed God Almighty into responding to the prayers of mankind, hadn't he?
How much better than that do you need to do?
But now. This nightmarish carnival atmosphere every-

where. These cults, these other prophets. A thousand interpretations of an event whose meaning should have been crystal-clear. The bonfires. Madness crackling like lightning across the sky. Maybe the fault was in Thomas. The Proclaimer had been deficient in true grace all along. Possibly any mass movement centered on a prophet who had Thomas' faults of character was inherently doomed to slip into chaos.

Or maybe the fault was mine, O Lord.

Kraft has been in seclusion for many days, perhaps for several weeks; he is no longer sure when he began this retreat. He will see no one, not even Thomas, who is eager to make amends. Kraft's injuries have healed and he holds no grievance against Thomas for striking him: the fiasco of the Day of Rededication had driven all of them a little insane there on the beach, and Thomas' outburst of violence was understandable if not justifiable. It may even have been of divine inspiration, God inflicting punishment on Kraft through the vehicle of Thomas for his sins. The sin of pride, mainly. To turn Gifford away, to organize the Day of Rededication for such cynical motives—

Kraft fears for his soul, and for the soul of Thomas.

He dares not see Thomas now, not until he has regained his own spiritual equilibrium; Thomas is too turbulent, too tempestuous, emits such powerful emanations of self-will; Kraft must first recapture his moral strength. He fasts much of the time. He tries to surrender himself fully in prayer. But prayer will not come: he feels cut off from the Almighty, separated from Him as he has never been before. By bungling this holy Crusade he must have earned the Lord's displeasure. A gulf, a chasm, parts them; Kraft is earthbound and helpless. He abandons his efforts to pray. He prowls his suite restlessly, listening for intruders, constantly running security checks. He switches on his closed-circuit video inputs, expecting to see fires in the streets, but all is calm out there. He listens to news bulletins on the radio: chaos, turmoil, everywhere. Thomas is said to be dead; Thomas is reported on the same day to be in Istanbul, Karachi, Johannesburg, San Francisco; the Propitiators have announced that on the twenty-fourth of November, according to their calculations, Satan will appear on Earth to enter into his sovereignty; the Pope, at last breaking his silence, has declared that he has no idea what power might have been responsible for the startling happenings of June 6, but thinks it would be rash to attribute the

event to God's direct intervention without some further
evidence. So the Pope has become an Awaiter too. Kraft
smiles. Marvelous! Kraft wonders if the Archbishop of Can-
terbury is attending Propitiator services. Or the Dalai Lama
consorting with the Apocalyptists. Anything can happen now.
Gog and Magog are let loose upon the world. Kraft no longer
is surprised by anything. He feels no astonishment even
when he turns the radio on late one afternoon and finds that
God Himself seems to be making a broadcast.

God's voice is rich and majestic. It reminds Kraft somewhat of the voice of Thomas, but God's tone is less fervid,
less evangelical; He speaks in an easy but serious-minded
way, like a senator campaigning for election to his fifth term
of office. There is a barely perceptible easternness to God's
accent: He could be a senator from Pennsylvania, maybe, or
Ohio. He has gone on the air, He explains, in the hope of
restoring order to a troubled world. He wishes to reassure
everyone: no apocalypse is planned, and those who anticipate.
the imminent destruction of the world are most unwise. Nor
should you pay heed to those who claim that the recent Sign
was the work of Satan. It certainly was not, God says, not at
all, and propitiation of the Evil One is uncalled for. By all
means let's give the Devil his due, but nothing beyond that.
All I intended when I stopped the Earth's rotation, God
declares, was to let you know that I'm here, looking after
your interests. I wanted you to be aware that in the event of
really bad trouble down there I'll see to it—

Kraft, lips clamped tautly, changes stations. The resonant
baritone voice pursues him.

—that peace is maintained and the forces of justice are
strengthened in—

Kraft turns on his television set. The screen shows nothing
but the channel insignia. Across the top of the screen gleams
a bright-green title:

ALLEGED VOICE OF GOD

and across the bottom, in frantic scarlet, is a second caption:

BY LIVE PICKUP FROM THE MOON

The Deity, meanwhile, has moved smoothly on to new
themes. All the problems of the world, He observes, can be

attributed to the rise and spread of atheistic socialism. The false prophet Karl Marx, aided by the Antichrist Lenin and the subsidiary demons Stalin and Mao, have set loose in the world a plague of godlessness that has tainted the entire twentieth century and, here at the dawn of the twenty-first, must at last be eradicated. For a long time the zealous godly folk of the world resisted the pernicious Bolshevik doctrines, God continues, His voice still lucid and reasonable; but in the past twenty years an accommodation with the powers of darkness has come into effect, and this has allowed spreading corruption to infect even such splendidly righteous lands as Japan, Brazil, the German Federal Republic, and God's own beloved United States of America. The foul philosophy of coexistence has led to a step-by-step entrapment of the forces of good, and as a result—

Kraft finds all of this quite odd. Is God speaking to every nation in English, or is He speaking Japanese to the Japanese, Hebrew to the Israelis, Croatian to the Croats, Bulgarian to the Bulgars? And when did God become so staunch a defender of the capitalist ethic? Kraft recalls something about driving moneychangers out of the temple, long ago. But now the voice of God appears to be demanding a holy war against communism. Kraft hears Him calling on the legions of the sanctified to attack the Marxist foe wherever the red flag flies. Sack embassies and consulates, burn the houses of ardent left-wingers, destroy libraries and other sources of dangerous propaganda, the Lord advises. He says everything in a level, civilized tone.

Abruptly, in midsentence, the voice of the Almighty vanishes from the airwaves. A short time later an announcer, unable to conceal his chagrin, declares that the broadcast was a hoax contrived by bored technicians in a satellite relay station. Investigations have begun to determine how so many radio and television stations let themselves be persuaded to transmit it as a public-interest item. But for many godless Marxists the revelation comes too late. The requested sackings and lootings have occurred in dozens of cities. Hundreds of diplomats, guards, and clerical workers have been slain by maddened mobs bent on doing the Lord's work. Property losses are immense. An international crisis is developing, and there are scattered reports of retribution against American citizens in several eastern European countries. We live in

strange times, Kraft tells himself. He prays. For himself. For
Thomas. For all mankind. Lord have mercy. Amen. Amen.
Amen.

Thirteen
The Burial of Faith

The line of march begins at the city line and runs westward out of town into the suburban maze. The marchers,
at least a thousand of them, stride vigorously forward even
though a dank, oppressive heat enfolds them. On they go,
past the park dense with the dark-green leaves of late
summer, past the highway cloverleaf, past the row of
burned motels and filling stations, past the bombed reservoir, past the cemeteries, heading for the municipal
dumping-grounds.

Gifford, leading the long sober procession, wears ordinary classroom clothes: a pair of worn khaki trousers, a
loose-fitting gray shirt, and old leather sandals. Originally
there had been some talk of having the most important
Discerners come garbed in their academic robes, but
Gifford had vetoed that on the grounds that it wasn't in
keeping with the spirit of the ceremony. Today all of the
old superstitions and pomposities were to be laid to rest;
why then bedeck the chief iconoclasts in hieratic costume
as though they were priests, as though this new creed
were going to be just as full of mummery as the outmoded
religions it hoped to supplant?

Because the marchers are so simply dressed, the contrast is
all the more striking between the plain garments they wear
and the elaborate, rich-textured ecclesiastical paraphernalia
they carry. No one is empty-handed; each has some vest-
ment, some sacred artifact, some work of scripture. Draped
over Gifford's left arm is a large white linen alb, ornately
embroidered, with a dangling silken cincture. The man behind him carries a deacon's dalmatic; the third marcher has a
handsome chasuble; the fourth, a splendid cope. The rest of

the priestly gear is close behind: amice, stole, maniple, vimpa. A frosty-eyed woman well along in years waves a crozier aloft; the man beside her wears a mitre at a mockingly rakish angle. Here are cassocks, surplices, hoods, tippets, cottas, rochets, mozettas, mantellettas, chimeres, and much more: virtually everything, in fact, save the papal tiara itself. Here are chalices, crucifixes, thuribles, fonts; three men struggle beneath a marvelously carved fragment of a pulpit; a little band of marchers displays Greek Orthodox outfits, the rhason and the sticharion, the epitrachelion and the epimanikia, the sakkos, the epigonation, the zone, the omophorion; they brandish ikons and enkolpia, dikerotrikera and dikanikion. Austere Presbyterian gowns may be seen, and rabbinical yarmulkes and tallithim and tfilin. Farther back in the procession one may observe more exotic holy objects, prayer wheels and tonkas, sudras and kustis, idols of fifty sorts, things sacred to Confucianists, Shintoists, Parsees, Buddhists both Mahayana and Hinayana, Jains, Sikhs, animists of no formal rite, and others. The marchers have shofars, mezuzahs, candelabra, communion trays, even collection plates; no portable element of faith has been ignored. And of course the holy books of the world are well represented: an infinity of Old and New Testaments, the Koran, the Bhagavad-Gita, the Upanishads, the Tao Te Ching, the Vedas, the Vedanta Sutra, the Talmud, the Book of the Dead, and more. Gifford has been queasy about destroying books, for that is an act with ugly undertones; but these are extreme times, and extreme measures are required. Therefore he has given his consent even for that.

Much of the material the marchers carry was freely contributed, mostly by disgruntled members of congregations, some of it given by disaffected clergymen themselves. The other objects come mostly from churches or museums plundered during the civil disturbances. But the Discerners have done no plundering of their own; they have merely accepted donations and picked up some artifacts that rioters had scattered in the streets. On this point Gifford was most strict: acquisitions of material by force was prohibited. Thus the robes and emblems of the newly founded creeds are seen but sparsely today, since Awaiters and Propitiators and their like would hardly have been inclined to contribute to Gifford's festival of destruction.

They have reached the municipal dump now. It is a vast flat wasteland, surprisingly aseptic-looking: there are large areas of meadow, and the unreclaimed regions of the dump have been neatly graded and mulched, in readiness for the scheduled autumn planting of grass. The marchers put down their burdens and the chief Discerners come forward to take spades and shovels from a truck that has accompanied them. Gifford looks up; helicopters hover and television cameras bristle in the sky. This event will have extensive coverage. He turns to face the others and intones, "Let this ceremony mark the end of all ceremonies. Let this rite usher in a time without rites. Let reason rule forevermore."

Gifford lifts the first shovelful of soil himself. Now the rest of the diggers set to work, preparing a trench three feet deep, ten to twelve feet wide. The topsoil comes off easily, revealing strata of cans, broken toys, discarded television sets, automobile tires, and garden rakes. A mound of debris begins to grow as the digging team does its task; soon a shallow opening gapes. Though it is now late afternoon, the heat has not diminished, and those who dig stream with sweat. They rest frequently, panting, leaning on their tools. Meanwhile those who are not digging stand quietly, not putting down that which they carry.

Twilight is near before Gifford decides that the trench is adequate. Again he looks up at the cameras, again he turns to face his followers.

He says, "On this day we bury a hundred thousand years of superstition. We lay to rest the old idols, the old fantasies, the old errors, the old lies. The time of faith is over and done with; the era of certainty opens. No longer do we need theologians to speculate on the proper way of worshiping the Lord; no longer do we need priests to mediate between ourselves and Him; no longer do we need man-made scriptures that pretend to interpret His nature. We have all of us felt His hand upon our world, and the time has come to approach Him with clear eyes, with an alert, open mind. Hence we give to the earth these relics of bygone epochs, and we call upon discerning men and women everywhere to join us in this ceremony of renunciation."

He signals. One by one the Discerners advance to the edge of the pit. One by one they cast their burdens in: albs, chasubles, copes, mitres, Korans, Upanishads, yarmulkes, crucifixes. No one hurries; the Burial of Faith is serious business. As it proceeds, a drum roll of dull distant thunder reverberates along the horizon. A storm on the way? Just heat lightning, perhaps, Gifford decides. The ceremony continues. In with the maniple. In with the shofar. In with the cassock. Thunder again: louder, more distinct. The sky darkens. Gifford attempts to hasten the tempo of the ceremony, beckoning the Discerners forward to drop their booty. A blade of lightning slices the heavens and this time the answering thunderclap comes almost instantaneously, *ka-thock*. A few drops of rain. The forecast had been in error. A nuisance, but no real harm. Another flash of lightning. A tremendous crash. That one must have struck only a few hundred yards away. There is some nervous laughter. "We've annoyed Zeus," someone says. "He's throwing thunderbolts." Gifford is not amused; he enjoys ironies, but not now, not now. And he realizes that he has become just credulous enough, since the sixth of June, to be at least marginally worried that the Almighty might indeed be about to punish this sacrilegious band of Discerners. A flash again. *Ka-thock!* The clouds now split asunder and torrents of rain abruptly descend. In moments, shirts are pasted to skins, the floor of the pit turns to mud, rivulets begin to stream across the dump.

And then, as though they had scheduled the storm for their own purposes, a mob of fierce-faced people in gaudy robes burst into view. They wield clubs, pitchforks, rake handles, cleavers, and other improvised weapons; they scream incoherent, unintelligible slogans; and they rush into the midst of the Discerners, laying about them vigorously. "Death to the godless blasphemers!" is what they are shrieking, and similar phrases. Who are they, Gifford wonders? Awaiters. Propitiators. Diabolists. Apocalyptists. Perhaps a coalition of all cultists. The television helicopters descend to get a better view of the melee, and hang just out of reach, twenty or thirty feet above the struggle. Their powerful floodlights provide apocalyptic illumination. Gifford finds hands at his throat: a crazed woman, howling, grotesque. He pushes her away and she tumbles into the pit, landing on a stack of mud-crusted Bibles. A frantic stampede has begun; his people are rushing in all directions, followed by the vengeful servants of the Lord, who wield their weapons with vindictive glee. Gifford sees his friends fall, wounded, badly hurt, perhaps slain. Where are the police? Why are they giving no protection? "Kill all the blasphemers!" a maniac voice shrills near him.

He whirls, ready to defend himself. A pitchfork. He feels a strange cold clarity of thought and moves swiftly in, feinting, seizing the handle of the pitchfork, wresting it from his adversary. The rain redoubles its force; a sheet of water comes between Gifford and the other, and when he can see again, he is alone at the edge of the pit. He hurls the pitchfork into the pit and instantly wishes he had kept it, for three of the robed ones are coming toward him. He breaks into a cautious trot, tries to move past them, puts on a sudden spurt of speed, and slips in the mud. He lands in a puddle; the taste of mud is in his mouth; he is breathless, terrified, unable to rise. They fling themselves upon him. "Wait," he says. "This is madness!" One of them has a club. "No," Gifford mutters. "No. No. No. No."

Fourteen
The Seventh Seal

1. And when he had opened the seventh seal, there was silence in heaven about the space of half an hour.

2. And I saw the seven angels which stood before God; and to them were given seven trumpets.

3. And another angel came and stood at the altar, having a golden censer; and there was given unto him much incense, that he should offer it with the prayers of all saints upon the golden altar which was before the throne.

4. And the smoke of the incense, which came with the prayers of the saints, ascended up before God out of the angel's hand.

5. And the angel took the censer, and filled it with fire of the altar, and cast it into the earth: and there were voices, and thunderings, and lightnings, and an earthquake.

6. And the seven angels which had the seven trumpets prepared themselves to sound.

7. The first angel sounded, and there followed hail and fire mingled with blood, and they were cast upon the earth: and the third part of trees was burnt up, and all green grass was burnt up.

8. *And the second angel sounded, and as it were a great mountain burning with fire was cast into the sea: and the third part of the sea became blood;*

9. *And the third part of the creatures which were in the sea, and had life, died; and the third part of the ships were destroyed.*

10. *And the third angel sounded, and there fell a great star from heaven, burning as it were a lamp, and it fell upon the third part of the rivers, and upon the fountains of waters;*

11. *And the name of the star is called Wormwood: and the third part of the waters became wormwood; and many men died of the waters, because they were made bitter.*

12. *And the fourth angel sounded, and the third part of the sun was smitten, and the third part of the moon, and the third part of the stars; so as the third part of them was darkened, and the day shone not for a third part of it, and the night likewise.*

13. *And I beheld, and heard an angel flying through the midst of heaven, saying with a loud voice, Woe, woe, woe, to the inhabiters of the earth by reason of the other voices of the trumpet of the three angels, which are yet to sound!*

Fifteen
The Flight of
the Prophet

All, all over. Thomas weeps. The cities burn. The very lakes are afire. So many thousands dead. The Apocalyptists dance, for though the year is not yet sped the end seems plainly in view. The Church of Rome has pronounced anathema on Thomas, denying his miracle: he is the Antichrist, the Pope has said. Signs and portents are seen everywhere. This is the season of two-headed calves and dogs with cats' faces. New prophets have arisen. God may shortly return, or He may not; revelations differ. Many people now pray for an end to all such visitations and miracles. The Awaiters no longer Await, but now ask that we be spared from His next coming; even the Diabolists and the Propitiators cry, Come not, Lucifer. Those who begged a Sign from God in June would be content now only with God's renewed and prolonged absence. Let Him neglect us; let Him dismiss us from His mind. It is a time of torches and hymns. Rumors of barbaric warfare come from distant continents. They say the neutron bomb has been used in Bolivia. Thomas' last few followers have asked him to speak with God once more, in the hope that things can still be set to rights, but Thomas refuses. The lines of communication to the Deity are closed. He dares not reopen them: see, see how many plagues and evils he has let loose as it is! He renounces his prophethood. Others may dabble in charismatic mysticism if they so please. Others may kneel before the burning bush or sweat in the glare of the pillar of fire. Not Thomas. Thomas' vocation is gone. All over. All, all, all over.

He hopes to slip into anonymity. H shaves his beard and docks his hair; he obtains a new wardrobe, bland and undistinguished; he alters the color of his eyes; he practices walking in a slouch to lessen his great height. Perhaps he has not lost his pocket-picking skills. He will go silently into the cities, head down, fingers on the ready, and thus he will make his way. It will be a quieter life.

Disguised, alone, Thomas goes forth. He wanders unmolested from place to place, sleeping in odd corners, eating in dim rooms. He is in Chicago for the Long Sabbath, and he is in Milwaukee for the Night of Blood, and he is in St. Louis for the Invocation of Flame. These events leave him unaffected. He moves on. The year is ebbing. The leaves have fallen. If the Apocalyptists tell us true, mankind has but a few weeks left. God's wrath, or Satan's, will blaze over the land as the year 2000 sweeps in on December's heels. Thomas scarcely minds. Let him go unnoticed and he will not mind if the universe tumbles about him.

"What do you think?" he is asked on a street corner in Los Angeles. "Will God come back on New Year's Day?"

A few idle loungers, killing time. Thomas slouches among them. They do not recognize him, he is sure. But they want an answer. "Well? What do you say?"

Thomas makes his voice furry and thick, and mumbles,

"No, not a chance. He's never going to mess with us again. He gave us a miracle and look what we made out of it."

"That so? You really think so?"

Thomas nods. "God's turned His back on us. He said, Here, I give you proof of My existence, now pull yourselves together and get somewhere. And instead we fell apart all the faster. So that's it. We've had it. The end is coming."

"Hey, you might be right!" Grins. Winks.

This conversation makes Thomas uncomfortable. He starts to edge away, elbows out, head bobbing clumsily, shoulders hunched. His new walk, his camouflage.

"Wait," one of them says. "Stick around. Let's talk a little."

Thomas hesitates.

"You know, I think you're right, fellow. We made a royal mess. I tell you something else: we never should have started all that stuff. Asking for a Sign. Stopping the Earth. Would have been a lot better off if that Thomas had stuck to picking pockets, let me tell you."

"I agree three hundred percent," Thomas says, flashing a quick smile, on-off. "If you'll excuse me—"

Again he starts to shuffle away. Ten paces. An office building's door opens. A short, slender man steps out. *Oh, God! Saul!* Thomas covers his face with his hand and turns away. Too late. No use. Kraft recognizes him through all the alterations. His eyes gleam. "Thomas!" he gasps.

"No. You're mistaken. My name is—"

"Where have you been?" Kraft demands. "Everyone's searching for you, Thomas. Oh, it was wicked of you to run away, to shirk your responsibilities. You dumped everything into our hands, didn't you? But you were the only one with the strength to lead people. You were the only one who—"

"Keep your voice down," Thomas says hoarsely. No use pretending. "For the love of God, Saul, stop yelling at me! Stop saying my name! Do you want everyone to know that I'm—"

"That's exactly what I want," Kraft says. By now a fair crowd has gathered, ten people, a dozen. Kraft points. "Don't you know him? That's Thomas the Proclaimer! He's shaved and cut his hair, but can't you see his face all the same? There's your prophet! There's the thief who talked with God!"

"No, Saul!"

"Thomas?" someone says. And they all begin to mutter it.

"Thomas? Thomas? Thomas?" They nod heads, point, rub chins, nod heads again. "Thomas? Thomas?"

Surrounding him. Staring. Touching him. He tries to push them away. Too many of them, and no apostles, now. Kraft is at the edge of the crowd, smiling, the little Judas! "Keep back," Thomas says. "You've got the wrong man. I'm not Thomas. I'd like to get my hands on him myself. I—I—" *Judas! Judas!* "Saul!" he screams. And then they swarm over him.

GOING

One

In the early spring of 2095, with his one hundred thirty-sixth birthday coming on, Henry Staunt decided quite abruptly that the moment had arrived for him to Go. He would notify the Office of Fulfillment, get himself a congenial Guide, take a suite in one of the better Houses of Leavetaking. With the most pleasant season of the year about to unfurl, the timing would be ideal; he could make his farewells and renunciations during these cool green months and get decently out of the way before summer's blazing eye was open.

This was the first time that he had ever seriously considered Going, and he felt some surprise that the notion had stolen upon him so suddenly. Why, he wondered, was he willing to end it this morning, when he clearly had not been last week, last month, last year? What invisible watershed had he unknowingly crossed, what imperceptible valley of decision? Perhaps this was only a vagrant morning mood; perhaps by noon he would find himself eager to live another hundred years, after all. Eh? No, not likely. He was aware of the resolution, hard and firm, embedded, encapsulated, shining like a glittering pellet at the core of his soul. *Arrange for your Going, Henry.* Nothing equivocal about that. A tone of certainty. Of finality. Still, he thought, we must not hurry into this. First let me understand my own motives in coming to this decision. The unexamined death is not worth requesting.

He had heard that it was useful, when thoughts of Going first came into one's mind, to consult that book of Hallam's—the handbook of dying, the anatomy of world-renunciation. Very well. Staunt touched a bright enameled control stud and the screen opposite the window flowered into color. "Sir?" the library machine asked him.

Staunt said, "Hallam's book. The one about dying."

"The Turning of the Wheel: Departure as Consolation, sir?"

"Yes."

Instantly its title page was on the screen. Staunt picked up the scanning rod and pressed it here and there and there, randomly, bringing this page and that into view. He admired the clarity of the image. The type was bold and elegant, the margins were wide; not for several moments did he begin paying attention to the text.

. . . essential that the decision, when it is made, be made for the proper reasons. Although sooner or later we must all turn the wheel, abandoning the world to those who await a place in it, nevertheless no one should leave in resentment, thinking that he has been driven too soon from the worldly sphere. It is the task of the civilized man to bring himself, in the fullness of time, to an acceptance of the knowledge that his life has been completed; Going should not be undertaken by anyone who is not wholly ready, and attaining that state of readiness should be our lifelong goal. Too often we delude ourselves into thinking we are truly ready, when actually we have not reached readiness at all, and choose Going out of unworthy or shallow motives. How tragic it is to arrive at the actual moment of Leavetaking and to realize that one has deceived oneself, that one's motivations are false, that one is, in fact, not in the least ready to Go!

There are many improper reasons for choosing to Go, but they all may be classified as expressions of the desire to escape. One who is experiencing emotional frustration, or difficulty with his work, or a deterioration of health, or intense fatigue, or disappointment of some kind, may, in a moment of dark whim, apply to a House of Leavetaking; but his real intention is a trivial one, that is, to punish the cruel world by escaping from it. One should never look upon Going as a way of getting even. I must point out again that Going is something more than mere suicide. Going is not a petulant, irrational, vindictive deed. It is a positive act, an act of willing renunciation, a deeply moral act; one does not enter into it lightly, solely to escape. One does not say: I loathe you, foul world, therefore I take my leave, and good riddance. One says: I love you, fair world, but I have experienced your joys to the fullest, and now remove myself so that others may know the same joys.

When one first considers Going, therefore, one must strive to discover if one has attained true readiness—that is, the genuine willingness to put aside the world for the sake of others—or if one is simply seeking to satisfy the ego through the gesture of suicide—

There was much more in that vein. He would read it some other time. He turned the screen off.

So. To find the motive for wanting to Go. Walking slowly through the cool, spacious rooms of his old suburban house, Staunt searched for his reasons. His health? Perfect. He was tall, slender, still strong, with his own teeth, and a full head of thick, close-cropped white hair. He hadn't had major surgery since the pancreas transplant nearly seventy years before. Each year he had his arteries retuned, his eyesight adjusted, and his metabolism enhanced, but at his age those were routine things; basically he was a very healthy man. With the right sort of medical care, and everyone nowadays had the right sort of medical care, his body would go on functioning smoothly for decades more.

When then? Emotional problems? Hardly. He had his friends; he had his family; his life had never been more serene than it was now. His work? Well, he rarely worked any longer: some sketches, some outlines for future compositions, but he knew he would never get around to finishing them. No matter. He had only happy thoughts about his work. Worries over the state of the world? No, the world was in fine shape. Rarely finer.

Boredom, perhaps. Perhaps. He had grown weary of his tranquil life, weary of being content, weary of his beautiful surroundings, weary of going through the motions of life. That could be it. He went to the thick clear window of the living room and peered out at the view that had given him so much delight for so many years. The lawn, still pale from winter, sloped evenly and serenely toward the brook, where stubby skunk cabbages clustered. The dogwoods held the first hints of color; the crocuses were not quite finished; the heavy buds of the daffodils would be bursting by Saturday. All was well outside. Lovely. As it always was, this time of year. Yet he was unmoved. It did not sadden him to think that he would probably not see another spring. There's the heart of it, Staunt thought: I must be ripe for Going, because I don't care to stay. It's that simple. I've done all I care to do, I've seen all I care to see; now I might just as well move along. The wheel has to turn. Others are waiting to fill my place. It is a far, far better thing I do, et cetera, et cetera.

"Get me the Office of Fulfillment," he told his telephone. A gentle female face appeared on the small screen.

Staunt smiled. "My name's Henry Staunt, and I think I'm ready to Go. Would you send a Guide over as soon as you can?"

Two

An hour later, as Staunt stood by the studio window listening to one of his favorites among his own compositions, the string quartet of 2038, a green-blue copter descended and came fluttering to a halt on his lawn, resting on a cushion of air a short distance above the tips of the grass. It bore on its hull the symbol of the Office of Fulfillment—a wheel and a set of enmeshed gears. The hatch of the copter lifted and, to Staunt's surprise, Martin Bollinger got out. Bollinger was a neighbor, a friend of long standing, possibly the closest friend Staunt had these days; he often came over for visits; lately there had been some talk of Staunt's setting a group of Bollinger's poems to music; but what was Bollinger doing riding around in a Fulfillment Office copter?

Jauntily Bollinger approached the house. He was short, compact, buoyant, with sparkling brown eyes and soft, wavy hair. Staunt supposed he must be seventy or so, eighty at most. Still a young man. Prime of life. It made Staunt feel youthful just to have Bollinger around, and yet he knew that to Bollinger, Bollinger was no youngster. Staunt hadn't felt like a boy when *he* was eighty, either. But living to one hundred thirty-six changes your perspective about what's old.

From outside Bollinger said, "Can I come in, Henry?"

"Let him in," Staunt murmured. One of the sensors in the studio wall picked up the command and relayed it to the front door, which opened. "Tell him I'm in the studio," Staunt said, and the house guided Bollinger in. With a flick of two fingers Staunt cut down the volume of the music.

Bollinger, as he entered, nodded, and said pleasantly, "I've always loved that quartet."

Staunt embraced him. "So have I. How good to see you, Martin."

"I'm sorry it's been so long. Two weeks, isn't it?"

"I'm glad you've come. Although—to be really honest—I'm not going to be free this afternoon, Martin. I'm expecting someone else."

"Oh?"

"In fact, someone from the very organization whose vehicle you seem to have borrowed. How do you happen to come here in one of their copters, anyway?"

"Why not?" Bollinger asked.

"I can't understand why you should. It makes no sense."

"When I come on official business, I use an official copter, Henry."

"Official business?"

"You asked for a Guide."

Staunt was shaken. "*You?*"

"When they told me who had called, I insisted I be given the assignment, or I'd resign instantly. So I came. So here I am."

"I never realized you were with Fulfillment, Martin!"

"You never asked."

Staunt managed a baffled smile. "How long ago did you go into it?"

"Eight, ten years. A while ago."

"And why?"

"A sense of public duty. We all have to help out if the wheel's going to keep turning smoothly. Eh, Henry? Eh?" Bollinger came closer to Staunt, looked up at him, staring straight into his eyes, and flashed an unexpectedly brilliant, somehow overpowering grin. Then he said in a crisp, aggressive tone, "What's all this about wanting to Go, Henry?"

"The idea came to me this morning. I was strolling around the house when suddenly I realized there was no further point in my staying here. I'm done: why not admit it? Turn the wheel. Clear a space."

"You're still relatively young."

Staunt laughed harshly. "Coming up on one hundred and thirty-six."

"I know men of one hundred sixty and one hundred seventy who haven't even dreamed of Going."

"That's their problem. I'm ready."

"Are you ill, Henry?"

"Never felt better."

"Are you in any kind of trouble, then?"

"None whatever. My life is unutterably tranquil. I have only the purest of motives in applying for Leavetaking."

Bollinger seemed agitated. He paced the studio, picked up and set down one of Staunt's Polynesian carvings, clasped his hands to his elbows, and said finally, "We have to talk about this first, Henry. We have to talk about this!"

"I don't understand. Isn't it a Guide's function to speed me serenely on the way to oblivion? You sound as if you're trying to talk me out of Going!"

"It's the Guide's function," Bollinger said, "to serve the best interests of the Departing One, whatever those interests may be. The Guide may attempt to persuade the Departing One to delay his Going, or not to Go at all, if in his judgment that's the proper course to take."

Staunt shook his head. "There's a whole bustling world full of healthy young people out there who want to have more children, and who can't have them unless useless antiquities like myself get out of the way. I volunteer to make some space available. Are you telling me that you'd *oppose* my Going, Martin, if—"

"Maintaining the level of population at a consistent quantity is only one aspect of our work," Bollinger said. "We're also concerned with maintaining quality. We don't want useful older citizens taking themselves out of the world merely to make room for a newcomer whose capabilities we can't predict. If a man still has something important to give society—"

"I have nothing important left to give."

"If he does," Bollinger went on smoothly, "we will try to discourage him from Going until he's given it. In your case I think Going may be somewhat premature, and so I've wangled the assignment to be your Guide so that I can help you explore the consequences of what you propose to do, and perhaps—"

"What do you think I still can offer the world, Martin?"

"Your music."

"Haven't I written enough?"

"We can't be certain of that. You may have a masterpiece or

two lurking in you." Bollinger began to pace again. "Henry, have you read Hallam's *Turning of the Wheel*?"

"I've glanced at it. This morning, in fact."

"Did you look at the section in which he explains why our society is unique in western civilization?"

"It may have slipped my mind."

Bollinger said, "Henry, ours is the first that accepts the concept of suicide as a virtuous act. In the past, you know, suicide was considered filthy and evil and cowardly; religions condemned it as an attack against the will of God, and even people who weren't religious tended to try to cover it up when a friend or a relative killed himself. Well, we're into a different concept. Since our medical skills are now so highly developed that almost no one ever dies naturally, even enlightened birth-limitation measures can't keep the world from filling up with people. So long as anyone is born at all, and no one dies, there's a constant and dangerous build-up of population, so that—"

"Yes, yes, but—"

"Let me finish. To cope with our population problem, we eventually decided to regard the voluntary ending of one's life as a noble sacrifice, and so forth. Hence the whole mystique of Going. Even so, we haven't entirely lost our old moral outlook on suicide. We still don't want valuable people to Go, because we feel *they have no right* to throw away their gifts, to deprive us of what they have to give. And so one of the functions of the Office of Fulfillment is to lead the old and useless toward the exit in a civilized and gentle way, but another of our functions is to keep the old and useful from Going too soon. Therefore—"

"I understand," Staunt said softly. "I agree with the philosophy. I merely deny that I'm useful any more."

"That's open to question."

"Can it be, Martin, that you're letting personal factors interfere with your judgment?"

"What do you mean? That I'd keep you from Going because I prize your friendship so dearly?"

"I mean my promise to set your poems to music."

Bollinger reddened faintly. "That's absurd. Do you believe that my ego is so bound up in those poems that I'd meddle with your Going, simply so that you'd live to—No. I like to think that my judgment is objective."

"You could be wrong. You might disqualify yourself from being my Guide. Simply on the chance that—"

"No. I'm your guide."

"Are we going to fight, then, over whether I'll be allowed to Go?"

"Of course not, Henry. We just want you to understand the significance of the step you've asked to take."

"The significance is that I'll die. Is that such a complicated thing to understand?"

Bollinger looked disturbed by Staunt's blunt choice of words. One tried not to connect Going and dying. One was supposed to resort to the euphemisms.

He said, "Henry, I just want to follow orderly procedure."

"Which is?"

"We'll get you into a House of Leavetaking. Then we'll ask you to examine your soul and see if you're as truly ready to Go as you think you are. That's all. The final decision about when you Go will remain in your hands. If you insisted, you could Go this evening; we wouldn't stop you. Couldn't. But of course such haste would be unseemly."

"As you say."

"The House of Leavetaking I recommend for you," Bollinger said, "is known as Omega Prime. It's in Arizona—beautiful desert country rimmed with mountains—and the staff is superb. I could show you brochures on several others, but—"

"I'll trust your judgment."

"Fine. May I use the phone?"

It took less than a minute for Bollinger to book the reservation. For the first time, Staunt felt a sense of inexorability about the course of events. He was on his way out. There would be no turning back now. He would never have the audacity to cancel his Going once he had taken up residence at Omega Prime. But why, he wondered, was he showing even these faint tremors of hesitation? Had Bollinger already begun to undermine his resolution?

"There," Bollinger said. "They'll have your suite ready in an hour. Would you like to leave tonight?"

"Why not?"

"Under our procedures," Bollinger said, "your family will be notified as soon as you've arrived there. I'll do it myself. A custodian will be appointed for your house; it'll be sealed and under guard pending transfer of your property to your heirs. At the House of Leavetaking you'll have all the legal advice you'll require, assistance in making a distribution of assets, et cetera, et cetera. There'll be no loose ends left dangling. It'll all go quite smoothly."

"Splendid."

"And that completes the official part of my visit. You can stop thinking of me as your Guide for a while. Naturally, I'll be with you a good deal of the time at the House of Leavetaking, handling any queries you may have, doing whatever I can to make things easier for you. For the moment, though, I'm here simply as your friend, not as your Guide. Would you care to talk? Not about Going, I mean. About music, politics, the weather, anything you like."

Staunt said, "Somehow I don't feel very talkative."

"Shall I leave you alone?"

"I think that would be best. I'm starting to think of myself as a Departing One, Martin. I'd like a few hours to get a accustomed to the idea."

Bollinger bowed awkwardly. "It must be a difficult moment for you. I don't want to intrude. I'll come back just before dinnertime, all right?"

"Fine," Staunt said.

Three

Afterward, feeling adrift, Staunt wandered aimlessly through his house, wondering how soon it would be before he changed his mind. He put no credence in Bollinger's flattering, hopeful hypothesis that he might yet have important works of art to give the world; Staunt knew better. If he had ever owed a debt of creativity to mankind, that debt had long since been paid in full, and civilization need not fear it would be losing anything significant by his Going. Even so, he might find it difficult, after all, to remove himself from all he loved. Would the sight of his familiar possessions shake his decision? Here were the memorabilia of a long, comfortable life: the African masks, the Pueblo pots, the Mozart manuscript, the little Elizabethan harpsichord, the lunar boulder, the Sung bowl, the Canopic jars, the Persian miniatures, the dueling pistols,

the Greek coins, all the elegant things that had collected him
in his years of traveling. Once it had seemed unbearable to
him that he might ever be parted from these precious objects. They had taken on life for him, so that when a clumsy
cleaning machine knocked a Cypriote statuette to the floor
and smashed it, he had wept not for the monetary loss, but
for the pain he imagined the little clay creature was suffering,
for the humiliation it must feel at being ruined. He imagined
it hurling bitter reproaches at him: *I survived four thousand
years so that I might become yours, and you let me get
broken!* As a child might pretend that her dolls were alive,
and talk to them, and apologize to them for fancied slights. It
was, he had known all along, a foolish, sentimental, even
contemptible attitude, this attachment he had to his inani-
mate belongings, this solemn fond concern for their "comfort"
and "feelings," this way of speaking of them as "he" or "she"
instead of "it," of worrying about whether some prized piece
was receiving a place of display that was properly satisfying to
its ego. He acknowledged the half-submerged notion that he
had created a family, a special entity, by assembling this
hodgepodge of artifacts from a hundred cultures and a hundred eras.

Now, though, he deliberately confronted himself with ugly
reality: when he had Gone, his "family" would be scattered,
his beloved things sold or given away, some of them surely
lost or broken in transit, some ending up on the dusty shelves
of ignorant people, none of them ever again to know the
warmth of ownership he had lavished on them. And he did
not care. Except in the most remote, abstract way, he simply
did not care. Today the life was gone out of them, and they
were merely masks and pots and bits of bone and pieces of
paper—objects, interesting and valuable and attractive, but
lacking all feeling. Objects. They needed no coddling. He
was under no obligation to them to worry about their welfare.
Somehow, without his noticing it, his possessions had ceased
to be his pets, and he felt no pain at the thought of parting
from them. I must indeed be ready to Go, he told himself.

Here in the little alcove off the studio, was his *real* family.
A stack of portrait cubes: his wife, his son, his daughter, his
children's children, his children's children's children, each of
them recorded in a gleaming plastic box, a couple of inches
high. There were so many of them—dozens! He had had only
the socially approved two children, and so had his own

children, and none of his grandchildren or great-grandchildren had had more than three, and yet look at the clutter of cubes! The multitude of them was the most vivid possible argument in favor of the idea of Going. One simply had to make room, or everyone would be overwhelmed by the tide of oncoming young ones. Of course in a world where practically no one ever died except voluntarily, and that only at a great old age, families did tend to accumulate amazingly as the generations came along. Even a small family, and these days there was no other kind, was bound to become immense over the course of eighty or ninety years through the compounding progressions of controlled but persistent fertility. All additions, no subtractions. Or very few. And so the numbers mounted. Look at all the cubes!

The cubes were clever things: computer-actuated personality simulations. Everyone got himself cubed at least once, and those who were particularly hungry for the odd sort of immortality that cubing conferred, had new cubes made every few years. The process itself was a simple electronic transfer; it took about an hour to make a cube. The scanning machines recorded your voice and patterns of speech, your motion habits, your facial gestures, your whole set of standard reactions and responses. A battery of concise, cunningly perceptive personality tests yielded a character profile. This, too, went into the cube. They ended by having your soul in a box. Plug the cube into a receptor slot, and you came to life on a screen, smiling as you would smile, moving as you would move, sounding as you would sound, saying things you were likely to say. Of course, the thing on the screen was unreal, a mechanical mock-up, a counterfeit approximation of the person who had been cubed; but it was programmed to respond to conversation and to initiate its own conversational gambits without the stimulus of prior inputs, to absorb new data and change its outlook in the light of what it heard; in short, it behaved not like a frozen portrait but like a convincing imitation of the living person from whom it had been drawn.

Staunt studied the collection of cubes. He had five of his son, spanning Paul's life from early middle age to early old age; Paul faithfully sent his father a new cube at the beginning of each decade. Three cubes of his daughter. A number of the grandchildren. The proud parents sent him cubes of the young ones when they were ten or twelve years old, and grandchildren themselves, when they were adults, sent ...ng more mature versions of themselves. By now he had four or five cubes of some of them. Each year there were new cubes: an updating of someone's old one, or some great-great-grandchild getting immortalized for the first time, and everything landing on the patriarch's shelf. Staunt rather liked the custom.

He had only one cube of his wife. They had developed the process about fifty years ago, and Edith had been dead since '47, forty-eight years back. Staunt and his wife had been among the first to be cubed; just as well, for her time had been short, though they hadn't known it. Even now, not all deaths were voluntary. Edith had died in a copter crash, and Staunt, close to ninety, had not remarried. Having the cube of her had been a great comfort to him in the years just after her death. He rarely played it now, mainly because of its technical imperfections; since the process was so new when her cube had been made, the simulation was only approximate, and her movements were jerky and awkward, not much like those of the graceful Edith he had known. He had no idea how long it had been since he had last played her. Impulsively, he slipped her cube into the slot.

The screen brightened, and there was Edith. Supple, alert, aglow. Long creamy-white hair, a purple wrap, her favorite gold pin clasped to her shoulder. She had been in her late seventies when the cube was made; she looked hardly more than fifty. Their marriage had lasted half a century. Staunt had only recently realized that the span of his life without her was now nearly as long as the span of his life with her.

"You're looking well, Henry," she said as soon as her image appeared.

"Not bad for an old relic. It's 2095, Edith. I'll be one hundred thirty-six."

"You haven't switched me on in a while, then. Not for five years, in fact."

"No. But it isn't that I haven't thought of you, Edith. It's just that I've tended to drift away from everything I once loved. I've become a sleepwalker, in a way. Wandering through the days, filling in my time."

"Have you been well?"

"Well enough," Staunt said. "Healthy. Astonishingly healthy. I can't complain."

"Are you composing?"

"Very little, these days. Nothing, really. I've made some sketches for intended work, but that's all."

"I'm sorry. I was hoping you'd have something to play for me."

"No," he said. "Nothing."

Over the years, he had faithfully played each of his new compositions to Edith's cube, just as he had kept her up to date on the doings of their family and friends, on world events, on cultural fads. He had not wanted her cube to remain fixed forever in 2046. To have her constantly learning, growing, changing, helped to sustain his illusion that the Edith on the screen was the real Edith. He had even told her the details of her own death.

"How are the children?" she asked.

"Fine. I see them often. Paul's in fine shape, a tough old man just like his father. He's ninety-one, Edith. Does it puzzle you to be the mother of a son who's older than you are?"

She laughed. "Why should I think of it that way? If he's ninety-one, I'm one hundred twenty-five."

"Of course. Of course." If she wanted it like that.

"And Crystal's eighty-seven. Yes, that *is* a little strange. I can't help thinking of her as a young woman. Why, her children must be old themselves, and they were just babies!"

"Donna is sixty-one. David is fifty-eight. Henry is forty-seven."

"Henry?" Edith said, her face going blank. After a moment's confusion she recovered. "Oh, yes. The third child, the little accident. Your namesake. I forgot him for a moment." Henry had been born soon after Edith's death; Staunt had told her cube about him, but imprinting of post-cubing events never took as well as the original programming; she had lost the datum for a moment. As if to cover her embarrassment, Edith began asking him about all the other grandchildren, the great-grandchildren, the whole horde that had accumulated after her lifetime. She called forth names, assigned the right children to the right parents, scampered up and down the entire Staunt family tree, showing off to please him.

But he forced an abrupt switch of subject. "I want to tell you, Edith, that I've decided it's time for me to Go."

Again the blank look. "Go? Go where?"

"You know what I mean. *Going.*"

"No, I don't. Really, I don't."

"To a House of Leavetaking."

"I still don't follow."

He struggled against being impatient with her. "I've explained the idioms to you. Long ago. They've been in use at least thirty or forty years. It's voluntary termination of life, Edith. I've discussed it with you. Everyone comes to it sooner or later."

"You've decided to die?"

"To Go, yes, to die, to Go."

"Why?"

"Because of the boredom. The loneliness. I've outlived most of my early friends. I've outlived my own talent. I've outlived *myself*, Edith. A hundred thirty-six years. And I could go on another fifty. But why bother? To live just for the sake of living?"

"Poor Henry. You always had such a wonderful capacity for being interested in things. The day wasn't long enough for you, with your collections, and your books, and your music, and traveling around the world, and your friends—"

"I've read everything I want to read. I've seen the whole world. I'm tired of collecting things."

"Perhaps I was the lucky one, then. A decent number of years, a happy life, and then out. Quickly."

"No. I've enjoyed living on like this, Edith. I kept my health, I didn't go senile—it's been good, all of it. Except for not having you with me. But I've stopped enjoying things. Quite suddenly I've realized that there's no point in staying any longer. The wheel has to turn. The old have to clear themselves away. Somewhere there are people waiting to have a child, waiting for a vacancy in the world, and it's up to me to create that vacancy."

"Have you told Paul and Crystal?"

"Not yet. I made the decision just today. But I'll notify them—or it'll be done for me. They'll have most of my property. I'll give my cube of you to Paul. Everything's handled very efficiently for a Departing One."

"How soon will you—Go?"

Staunt shrugged. "I don't know yet. A month, two months—there's no rush about it."

"You sound as though you don't really want to do it."

He shook his head. "I want to, Edith. But in a civilized way. Taking my leave properly. I've lived a long time; I can't let go in a single day. But I won't stay here much longer."

"I'll miss you, Henry."

He pondered the intricacies of that. The cube missing the living man. Chuckling, he said, "Paul will play my cube to you, and yours to me. We'll talk to each other through the machinery. We'll always be there for each other."

The image of Edith reached a hand toward him. He cursed the clumsiness of the simulation. Gently he touched his fingertips to the screen, making a kind of contact with her across the decades, across the barriers separating them. He blew a kiss to her. Then, quickly, before sentimentality overcame him, he pulled her cube from the slot and set it beside those of his son and daughter. In haste, nearly stumbling, he went on into his studio.

The big room held the tangible residue of his long career. Over here, the music itself, in recorded performance: disks and cassettes for the early works, sparkling playback cubes for the later ones. Here were the manuscripts, uniformly bound in red half-morocco, one of his little vanities. Here were the scrapbooks of reviews and the programs of concerts. Here were the trophies. Here were the volumes of his critical writings. Staunt had been a busy man. He looked at the titles stamped on the bindings of the manuscripts: the symphonies, the string quartets, the concerti, the miscellaneous chamber works, the songs, the sonatas, the cantatas, the operas. So much. So much. He had tried his hand at virtually every form. His music was polite, agreeable, conservative, even a bit academic, yet he made no apologies for it: he had followed his own inner voices wherever they led, and if he had not been led to rebellion and fulminations, so be it. He had given pleasure through his work. He had added to the world's small stock of beauty. It was a respectable life's accomplishment. If he had had more passion, more turbulence, more dynamism, perhaps, he would have shaken the world as Beethoven had, as Wagner. Well, the great gesture had never been his to brandish; yet he had done his best, and in his way he had achieved enough. Some men heal the sick, some men soothe the souls of the troubled, some men invent wondrous machines—and some make songs and symphonies, because they must, and because it is all they can do to enrich the world into which they had been thrust. Even now, with his life's flame burning low, with everything suddenly seeming pointless and hollow to him, Staunt felt no sense of having wasted his time filling this room with what it held. Never in the past hundred years had a week gone by without a performance of one of his compositions somewhere. That was sufficient justification for having written, for having lived.

He turned on the synthesizer and rested his fingers lightly on the keys, and of their own will they played the opening theme of his *Venus* symphony of 1989, his first mature work. How far away all that seemed now—the glittering autumn of triumphs as he conducted it himself in a dozen capitals, the critics agog, everyone from the disgruntled Brahms-fanciers to the pundits of the avant-garde rushing to embrace him as the savior of serious music. Of course, there had been a reaction to that hysterical overpraise later, when the modernists decided that no one so popular could possibly be good and the conservatives began to find him too modern, but such things were only to be expected. He had gone his own way. Eventually others had recognized his genius—a limited and qualified genius, a small and tranquil genius, but genius nevertheless. As the world emerged from the storms of the twentieth century's bitter second half, as the new society of peace and harmony took shape on the debris of the old, Staunt created the music a quieter era needed, and became its lyric voice.

Here. He pushed a cube into a playback slot. The sweet outcry of his wind quintet. Here: *The Trials of Job*, his first opera. Here: *Three Orbits for Strings and Stasis Generator.* Here: *Polyphonies for Five Worlds*. He got them all going at once, bringing wild skeins of sound out of the room's assortment of speakers, and stood in the middle, trembling a little, accepting the sonic barrage and untangling everything in his mind.

After perhaps four minutes he cut off the sound. He did not need to play the music; it was all within his head, whenever he wanted it. Lightly he caressed the smooth, glossy black backs of his scrapbooks, with all the documentation of his successes and his occasional failures neatly mounted. He ran his fingers along the rows of bound manuscripts. So much. So very much. Such a long productive live. He had no complaints.

He told his telephone to get him the Office of Fulfillment again.

"My Guide is Martin Bollinger," he said. "Would you let him know that I'd like to be transferred to the House of Leavetaking as soon as possible?"

Four

Bollinger, sitting beside him in the copter, leaned across him and pointed down.

"That's it," he said. "Omega Prime, right below."

The House of Leavetaking seemed to be a string of gauzy white tentlike pavilions, arranged in a U-shape around a courtyard garden. The late afternoon sun tinged the pavilions with gold and red. Bare fangs of purplish mountains rose on the north and east; on the other side of Omega Prime the flat brown Arizona desert, pocked with cacti and palo verde, stretched toward the dark horizon.

The copter landed silently. When the hatch opened, Staunt felt the blast of heat. "We don't modulate the outdoor climate here," Bollinger explained. "Most Departing Ones seem to prefer it that way. Contact with the natural environment."

"I don't mind," Staunt said. "I've always loved the desert."

A welcoming party had gathered by the time he emerged from the copter. Three members of Omega Prime's staff, in smocks monogrammed with the Fulfillment insignia. Four withered oldsters, evidently awaiting their own imminent Going. A transport robot, with its wheelchair seat already in position. Staunt, picking his way carefully over the rough, pebble-strewn surface of the landing field, was embarrassed by the attention. He said in a low voice to Bollinger, "Tell them I don't need the chair. I can still walk. I'm no invalid."

They clustered around him, introducing themselves: Dr. James, Miss Elliot, Mr. Falkenbridge. Those were the staff people. The four Departing Ones croaked their names at him too, but Staunt was so astonished by their appearance that he forgot to pay attention. The shriveled faces, the palsied clawlike hands, the parchment skin—did he look like that, too? It was years since he had seen anyone his own age. He had the impression that he had come through his fourteen decades well preserved, but perhaps that was only an illusion born of vanity, perhaps he really was as much of a ruin as

347

these four. Unless they were much older than he, one hundred seventy-five, one hundred eighty years old, right at the limits of what was now the human span of mortality. Staunt stared at them in wonder, awed and dismayed by their gummy grins.

Falkenbridge, a husky red-haired young man, apparently some sort of orderly, was trying to ease him into the wheelchair. Irritably Staunt shook him off, saying, "No. No. I'll manage. Martin, tell him I don't need it."

Bollinger whispered something to Falkenbridge. The young man shrugged and sent the transport robot away. Now they all began walking toward the House of Leavetaking, Falkenbridge on Staunt's right, Miss Elliot on his left, both of them staying close to him in case he should topple.

He found himself under unexpectedly severe strain. Possibly refusing the wheelchair had been foolish bravado. The fierce dry heat, the fatigue of his ninety-minute rocket journey across the continent, the coarse texture of the ground, all conspired to make his legs wobbly. Twice he came close to falling. The first time Miss Elliot gently caught his elbow and steadied him; the second, he managed to recover himself, after a short half-stumble that sent pain shooting through his left ankle.

Suddenly, all at once, he was feeling his age. In a single day he had begun to dodder, as though his decision to enter a House of Leavetaking had stripped him of all his late-staying vigor. No. No. He rejected the idea. He was merely tired, as a man his age had every right to be; with a little rest he'd be himself again. He walked faster, despite the effort it cost him. Sweat trickled down his cheeks. There was a stitch in his side. His entire left leg ached.

At last they reached the entrance to Omega Prime.

He saw now that what had seemed to be gauzy tents, viewed from above, were in fact sturdy and substantial plastic domes, linked by an intricate network of covered passageways. The courtyard around which they were grouped, contained elaborate plantings of desert flora: giant stiff-armed cacti, looping white-whiskered succulents, odd and angular thorny things. The plants had been grouped with remarkable grace and subtleness around an assortment of strange boulders and sleek stone slabs; the effect was one of extraordinary beauty. Staunt stood a moment contemplating it. Bollinger said gently, "Why not go to your suite first? The garden will still be here this evening."

He had an entire dome to himself. Interior walls divided it into a bedroom, a sitting room, and a kind of utility room; everything was airy and tastefully simple, and the temperature was twenty-five degrees cooler than outside. A window faced the garden.

The staff people and the quartet of Departing Ones vanished, leaving Staunt alone with his Guide. Bollinger said, "Each of the residents has a suite like this. You can eat here, if you like, although there's a community dining room under the courtyard. There are recreational facilities there too—a library, a theater, a game room—but you can spend all of your time perfectly happily right where you are."

Staunt lowered himself gingerly into a webfoam hammock. As his weight registered, tiny mechanical hands began to massage his back. Bollinger smiled.

"This is your data terminal," he said, handing Staunt a copper-colored rod about eight inches long. "It's a standard access unit. You can get any book in the library—and there are thousands of them—screened on request, and you can play whatever music you'd like, and it's also a telephone input. Ask it to connect you with anyone at all. Go on. Ask."

"My son Paul," Staunt said.

"Ask it," said Bollinger.

Staunt activated the terminal and gave it Paul's name and access number. Instantly a screen came to life just beside the hammock. Staunt's son appeared in its silvery depths. The screen could almost have been a mirror, a strange sort of time-softening mirror that was capable of taking the face of a very old man and reflecting it as that of a man who was merely old. Staunt beheld someone who was a younger version of himself, though far from young: cool gray eyes, thin lips, lean bony face, a dense mane of white hair.

Paul's face was deeply lined but still vigorous. At the age of ninety-one he had not yet retired from the firm of architects he headed. So long as a man's health was good and his mind was sound and he still found his career rewarding, there was no reason to retire; when mind or body failed or career lost its savor, that was the time to withdraw and make oneself ready to Go.

Staunt said, "I'm calling you from Omega Prime."

"What's that, Henry?"

"You've never heard of it? A House of Leavetaking in Arizona. It looks like a lovely place. Martin Bollinger brought me here this evening."

Paul looked startled. "Are you thinking of Going, Henry?"

"I am."

"You never told me you had any such thing in mind!"

"I'm telling you now."

"Are you in poor health?"

"I feel fine," Staunt said. "Everyone asks me that, and I say the same thing. My health is excellent."

"Then why—"

"Do I have to justify it? I've lived long enough. My life is over."

"But you've been so alert, so *involved*—"

"It's my decision to make. It's ungracious of you to quarrel with me over it."

"I'm not quarreling," Paul said. "I'm trying to adapt to it. You know, you've been part of my life for nine decades. I don't give a damn what the social conventions are: I can't simply smile and nod and say how sweet when my father announces he's going to die."

"To Go."

"To Go," Paul muttered. "Whatever. Have you told Crystal?"

"You're the first member of the family to know. Except for your mother, that is."

"My mother?"

"The cube," said Staunt.

"Oh. Yes. The cube." A thin, edgy laugh. "All right. I'll tell the others. I suppose I'll have to learn how to be head of the family, finally. You're not going to be doing this immediately, are you?"

"Naturally not. Where do you get such ideas? I'll have a proper Leavetaking. Graceful. Serene. A few weeks, a month or two—the usual thing."

"And we can visit you?"

"I'll expect you to," Staunt said. "That's part of the ritual."

"What about—pardon me—what about the legal aspects? Disposition of property, things like that?"

"It'll all be managed in the customary way. The Office of Fulfillment is supposed to help me. Don't worry: you'll get everything that's coming to you."

"That isn't a kind way to phrase it, Henry."

"I don't have to be kind any more. I don't even have to make sense. I'm just a crazy old man getting ready to go."

"Henry—Father—"

"All right. I'm sorry. Somehow this conversation hasn't worked right at all. Shall we start it over?"

"I'd like to," Paul said.

Staunt realized he was quivering. The muscles of his face were drawn taut. He made a deliberate attempt to relax, and after a moment, said quietly, "It's a perfectly normal, desirable step to take. I'm old and tired and lonely and bored. I'm no use to myself or to anybody else, and there's really no sense troubling my doctors to keep me functioning any longer. So I'm going to Go. I'd rather Go now, when I'm still reasonably healthy and clear-witted, instead of trying to hang on another few decades until I've slid into senility. I've moved to Omega Prince, and you'll all come to visit me before my Leavetaking, and it'll be a peaceful and beautiful Going, I hope. That's all. There's nothing to weep about. In forty or fifty years you'll understand all this a lot better."

"I understand it now," Paul said. "You caught me by surprise when you called, but I understand. Of course. Of course. We don't want to lose you, but that's only our selfishness talking. You've lived a full life, and, well, the wheel has to turn."

How smoothly he does it, Staunt thought. How easily he slips into the jargon. How readily he agrees with me, after his first reflexive moment of shock. *Yes, Henry, certainly, Henry, it's wise of you to Go, Henry, you've lived long enough.* Staunt wondered which was the fraud: Paul's initial resistance to the idea of his Going, or his philosophical acquiescence. And what difference did it make? Why, Staunt asked himself, should I be offended if my son thinks it's right for me to Go when I was offended two minutes earlier by his trying to talk me out of it?

He was beginning to be unsure of his own ground. Perhaps he *did* want to be talked out of it.

I must read Hallam shortly, he told himself.

He said to Paul, "I have a great deal to do this evening. I'll call you tomorrow. Or you call me."

The screen went blank.

Bollinger said, "He took it rather well, I thought. The children don't always accept the idea that a parent is Going. They accept the theory of Leavetaking, but they always assume that it's someone else's old folks who'll Go."

"They want their own parents to live forever, even if the parents don't feel like staying around any longer?"

"That's it."

"What if someone *does* feel like staying forever?" Staunt asked.

Bollinger shrugged. "We never try to force the issue. We

hint a little, as subtly as we know how, if someone is one hundred forty or one hundred fifty or so, and really a wreck, but clinging to life anyway. For that matter, if he's eighty or ninety, even, and just going through the motions of living, held together by his doctors alone, we'll try to encourage Going. We have gentle ways of working through doctors or friends or relatives, trying to overcome the fear of dying in the ones who linger, trying to get across the idea that it's not only best for society for them to move on, it's best for themselves. If they don't take the hint, there's nothing we can do. Involuntary euthanasia just isn't part of our system."

"How old," Staunt asked, "are the oldest living people now?"

"I think the oldest ones known are something like one hundred seventy-five or one hundred eighty. Which means they were born in the early part of the twentieth century, around the time of the First World War. Anyone born before that simply spent too much of his life in the era of medieval medicine to hope for a really long span. But if you were born, say, in 1920, you were still only fifty-five or sixty when the era of organ transplants and computerized health services and laser surgery was beginning, and if you were lucky enough to be in good shape in the 1970's, the 1980's, why, you could be kept going just about indefinitely thereafter. Into the era of tissue regeneration and all the rest. A few from the early twentieth century did hang on into the era of total medicine, and some of them are still with us. Politely declining to Go."

"How much longer can they last?"

"Hard to say," Bollinger replied. "We just don't know what the practical limits of the human life-span are. Our experience with total medicine doesn't go back far enough. I've heard it said that two hundred or two hundred ten is the top figure, but in another twenty or thirty years we may have some people who've reached that figure, and we'll find that we can keep them going beyond it. Maybe there *is* no top limit, now that we can do the things we do to rebuild a decaying body. But how hideously antisocial it is of them to hang around for century after century just to test our medical skills!"

"But if they're making valuable contributions to society through all those hundreds of years—"

"*If,*" Bollinger said. "But the fact is that ninety, ninety-five percent of all people never make any contributions to society, even when they're young. They just occupy space, do jobs that could really be done better by machines, sire children who aren't any more gifted than they are—and hang on, living and living and living. We don't want to lose anyone who's valuable, Henry; I've been through that with you already. But most people aren't valuable to begin with, and get less valuable as they go along, and there's no reason in the universe why they should live past one hundred or one hundred ten, let alone to two hundred or three hundred or whatever."

"That's a harsh philosophy. Cynical, even."

"I know. But read Hallam. The wheel's got to turn. We've reached an average life-span that would have seemed wild fantasy as late as the time when you were a child, Henry, but that doesn't mean we have to strive to make everyone immortal. Not unless people are willing to give up having children, and they aren't. It's a finite planet. If there's inflow, there has to be outflow, and I like to think that those flowing out are the ones who have the least to offer to the rest of us. The decrepit, the feeble, the slow-witted, the mean-souled. Thank God, most old folks agree. For every one who absolutely won't give up his grip on life, there are fifty who are glad to go once they've hit one hundred or so. And as the remainder get even older, they change their minds about staying, just as you've done lately. Not many want to go on past one hundred fifty. The few who do, well, we'll look on them as experiments in geriatrics, and let them be."

"How old are those four who met my copter?" Staunt asked.

"I couldn't tell you. One hundred twenty, one hundred thirty, something like that. Most of those who arrange for Leavetaking now are people born between 1960 and 1980."

"Of my generation, then."

"I suppose, yes."

"Do I look as bad as they do? They're a bunch of walking mummies, Martin. I'd have guessed they were fifty years older than I am."

"I doubt that very much."

"But I'm not like them, am I? I've got my teeth. My hair. My real eyes. I look old, but not ancient. Or am I fooling myself, Martin? Am I really a dried-up nightmare too? Is it just that I've grown accustomed to the way I look, I haven't noticed the changes, decade after decade as I get older and older?"

"There's a mirror," Bollinger said. "Answer your own questions."

Staunt stared at himself. Lines and wrinkles, yes: a contour map of time, the valleys and ravines of a long life. Blotches on the skin. The glittering eyes deeply recessed; the cheeks fleshless, revealing the sharp outlines of the skull beneath. An old face, tremendously old. But yet not like *their* faces. He was no mummy yet. He imagined that a man of the twentieth century would guess him to be no more than eighty or eighty-five, just as a man of the twentieth century would guess Paul to be in his late sixties and Martin Bollinger in his late fifties. Those others, those four, showed their true ages. It must take all the magic at their doctors' command to keep them together. And now, weary of cheating death, they've come here to Go and be over with the farce. Whereas I am still strong, whereas I could continue easily, if only I wanted to continue.

"Well?" Bollinger asked.

"I'm in pretty good shape," Staunt said. "I'm quitting while I'm ahead. It's the right way to do it." He picked up the data terminal again. "I wonder if they have any of my music in storage here," he said, and opened the access node and made a request; and the room flooded with the first chords of his Twelfth Symphony. He was pleased. He closed his eyes and listened. When the movement ended, he looked around the room, and found that Bollinger had gone.

Five

Dr. James came to see him a little while later, as night was enfolding the desert. Staunt was standing by the window, watching the brilliant stars appear, when the room annunciator told him of his visitor.

The doctor was a youngish man—forty, fifty, Staunt was no longer good at guessing ages—with a long fragile-looking nose and a gentle, faintly unctuous, I-want-you-to-have-a-lovely-Going sort of manner. His first words to Staunt were, "I've been looking through your medical file. I really must congratulate you on the excellent state of your health."

"There's something about music that keeps people in good shape," Staunt said.

"Are you a conductor?"

"A composer. But I've conducted my own works quite often. Waving the baton—it's obviously good exercise."

"I don't know much about music, I'm afraid. Some afternoon you must program some of your favorite pieces for me." The doctor grinned shyly. "The simpler ones. Music for an unsophisticated medic, if you've written any." He was silent a moment. Then he said, "You really do have an excellent medical history. Your doctor's computer transferred your whole file to us this afternoon when your reservation was made. Naturally, while you're with us we want you to remain in perfect health and comfort. You'll receive the same kind of care here that you were getting at home—the muscle therapies, the ion-balance treatments, the circulatory clearances, and so forth. Including any special supportive therapy that may become necessary. Not that I anticipate someone like you to need a great deal of that."

"I could last another fifty years, eh?"

Dr. James looked abashed. His plump cheeks glowed. "That choice is entirely up to you, Mr. Staunt."

"Don't worry. I'm not about to change my mind."

"No one here will hurry you," the doctor said. "We've had people remain at Omega Prime for three, even four years. Each man's Leavetaking is the most important event in his life, after all; he's entitled to go about it at his own pace, to disengage himself from the world as gradually as he wants. You do understand that there is no cost to you for any part of your residence here. The government underwrites the whole business."

"I think Martin Bollinger explained that to me."

"Good. Let me discuss with you, then, some of your Leavetaking options. Many Departing Ones prefer to begin their withdrawal from the world by making a grand tour—a kind of farewell to all the great sights, the Pyramids, the Taj Mahal, Notre Dame, the Sahara, Antarctica, whatever. We can make any such travel arrangements you'd like. We have several organized tours, on which you'd travel with five or six or ten other Departing Ones and several Guides—a one-month tour of the most famous places, a two-month tour, or a three-month tour. These are packaged in advance, but we can make changes in itinerary by unanimous consent of the Departing Ones. Or, if you prefer, you could travel alone, that is, just you and your Guide, to any part of the world that—"

Staunt looked at him in astonishment. Was this man a doctor or a travel agent?

And did he want to take any such tour? It was vaguely tempting. At government expense to see the temples of Chichén Itzá by moonlight, to float over the Andes and descend into Machu Picchu, to smell the scent of cloves on Zanzibar, to look up at a sequoia's distant blue-green crown, to see the hippos jostling in the Nile, to roam the crumbling dusty streets of Babylon, to drift above the baroque intricacies of the Great Barrier Reef, to see the red sandstone spires of Utah, to tramp along the Great Wall of China, to make his farewells to lakes and deserts and mountains and valleys, to cities and wastelands, to penguins, to polar bears—

But he had seen all those places. Why go back? Why bother to make a breathless pilgrimage, dragging his flimsy bones from place to place? Once was enough. He had his memories.

"No," he said. "If I had any desire to travel anywhere, I wouldn't have thought of Going in the first place. If you follow me. The flavor's gone out of everything, do you see? I don't have the motivation for hauling myself around. Not even to make sentimental gestures of farewell."

"As you wish, Mr. Staunt. Most Departing Ones do take advantage of the travel option. But you'll find no coercion here. If you feel no urge to travel, why, stay right where you are."

"Thank you. What are some of the other Leavetaking options?"

"It's customary for the Departing Ones to seek experiences they may have missed during their lifetimes, or to repeat ones that they found particularly rewarding. If there's some special type of food that you enjoy—"

"I was never a gourmet."

"Or works of music you want to hear again, masterpieces you'd like to live with one last time—"

"There are some," Staunt said. "Not many. Most of them bore me now. When Mozart and Bach and Beethoven begin to bore a man, he knows it's time to Go. Do you know, even Staunt has begun to seem less interesting to me lately?"

Dr. James did not smile.

He said, "In any event, you'll find that we're programmed for every imaginable work of music, and if there are any you know of that we don't have and ought to have, I hope you'll tell us. It's the same with books. Your screen can give you any work in any language—just put in the requisition. A number of Departing Ones use this opportunity at last to read *War and Peace*, or *Ulysses*, or *The Tale of Genji*, say."

"Or *The Encyclopaedia Britannica*," Staunt said, "from 'Aardvark' to 'Zwingli.' "

"You think you're joking. We had a Departing One here five years ago who set out to do just that."

"How far did he get?" Staunt wanted to know. "'Antimony'? 'Betelgeuse'?"

" 'Magnetism,' I think. He was quite dedicated to the job."

"Perhaps I'll do some reading, too, doctor. Not the *Britannica*. But Hallam, at least. Maybe Montaigne, and maybe Hobbes, and maybe Ben Jonson. For about sixty years I've been meaning to read my way through Ben Jonson. I suppose this is my last chance."

"Another option," Dr. James said, "is a memory jolt."

"Which is?"

"Chemical stimulation of the mnemonic centers. It stirs up the memories, awakens things you may not have thought about for eighty or ninety years, sends images and textures and odors and colors of past experiences through your mind in a remarkably vivid way. In a sense, it's a trip through your entire past. I don't know any Departing One who's done it and not come out of it in a kind of ecstasy, a radiant glow of joy."

Staunt frowned. "I'd guess that it could be a painful experience. Disturbing. Depressing."

"Not at all. Never. It's emotion recollected in tranquility: the experiences may have been painful originally, but the replay of them never is. The jolt allows you to come to terms with all that you've been and done. I've known people to ask to Go within an hour of coming out of the jolt, and not because they were depressed; they simply want to take their leave on a high note."

"I'll think about it," Staunt said.

"Other than the things I've mentioned, your period of

Leavetaking is completely unstructured. You write the script.
Your family will come to see you, and your friends; I think
you'll get to know some of the other Departing Ones here;
there'll be Leavetaking parties as one by one they opt to Go,
and then there'll be Farewell ceremonies for them, and
they'll Go; and eventually, a month, six months, as you
choose, you'll request your own Leavetaking party and Farewell ceremony, and finally you'll Go. You know, Mr. Staunt, I
feel a tremendous sense of exhilaration here every day,
working with these wonderful Departing Ones, helping to
make their last weeks beautiful, watching the serenity with
which they Go. My own time of Going is still ninety or a
hundred years away, I suppose, and yet in a way I look
forward to it now; I feel a certain impatience, knowing that
the happiest hours of my life will come at the very end of it.
To Go when still healthy, to step voluntarily out of the world
in an atmosphere of peace and fulfillment, to know that you
cap a long and successful life by the noblest of all deeds,
letting the wheel turn, giving younger people an opportunity
to occupy your place—how marvelous it all is!"

"I wish," Staunt said, "that I could orchestrate your aria.
Shimmering tremolos in the strings—the plaintive wail of the
oboes—harps, six harps, making celestial noises—and then a
great crescendo of trombones and French horns and bas-
soons, a sort of Valhalla music welling up—"

Looking baffled, Dr. James said, "I told you, I don't really
know much about music."

"I'm sorry. I shouldn't mock, not at my age. I'm sure it *is*
beautiful and marvelous. I'm very happy to be here."

"A pleasure to have you," said Dr. James.

Six

Staunt did not feel up to having dinner in the community
dining room; he had had a long journey, crossing several time
zones, and his appetite was awry. He ordered a light meal,
juice and soup and fruit, and it arrived almost instantaneously
via a subterranean conveyor system. He ate sparingly. Before

I Go, he promised himself, I will have steak au poivre again, and escargots, and a curry of lamb, and all the other things I never cared much for while I was young enough to digest them. James offers me a chance; why not take it? I will become a preposthumous gourmet. Even if it kills me. Better to Go like that than by drinking whatever tasteless potion it is they give you at the end.

After dinner he asked where Bollinger was.

"Mr. Bollinger has gone home," Staunt was told. "But he'll be back the day after tomorrow. He'll spend three days a week with you while you're here."

Staunt supposed it was unreasonable of him to expect his Guide to devote all his time to him. But Bollinger might at least have stayed around for the first night. Unless the idea was to have the Departing One make his own adaptation to life in the House of Leavetaking.

He toyed with his data terminal, testing its resources. For a while he amused himself by pulling obscure music from the machine: medieval organa, Hummel sonatas, eighteenth-century German opera, odd electronic things from the middle of the twentieth century. But it was impossible to win that game; apparently, if the music had ever been recorded, the computer had access to it. Staunt turned next to books, asking for Hobbes and Hallam, Montaigne and Jonson—not screenings but actual print-out copies of his own, and within minutes after he placed the requisitions, the fresh crisp sheaves of pages began arriving on the same conveyor that had brought his dinner. He put the books aside without looking through them. Perhaps some telephone calls, he thought: my daughter, maybe, or a friend or two. But everyone he knew seemed to live in the East or in Europe, and it was some miserable early hour of the morning there. Staunt gave up the idea of talking to anyone. He dropped into a dull leaden mood. Why had he come to these three little plastic rooms in the desert, giving up his fine well-tended house, his treasures of art, his dogwoods, his books? Surrendering everything for this sterile halfway station on the road to death? I could call Dr. James, I suppose, and tell him I'd like to Go right now. Save the staff some trouble, save the taxpayers some money, save my family the bother of going through the Farewell rituals. How is Going managed, anyway? He believed it was a drug. Something sweet and pleasant, and then the body goes to sleep. A tranquil death, like Socrates', just a chill climbing quickly through the legs toward the heart. Tonight. Tonight. To Go tonight.

No.

I must play the game properly. I must do my Going with style.

He turned to the terminal and said, "I'd like someone to show me down to the recreation center."

Miss Elliot, the nurse, appeared, as though she had been stored waiting in a box just outside his suite. So far as Staunt still had the capacity to tell, she was a handsome girl, golden-haired and buxom, with fine clear skin and large glossy blue eyes, but there was something remote and impersonal and mechanical about her; she could almost have been a robot. "The recreation center? Certainly, Mr. Staunt." She offered her arm. He gestured as if to refuse it, but then, remembering his earlier struggle to walk, took it anyway, and leaned heavily on her as they went out. Thus I accept my mortality. Thus I speed my final decline.

A dropshaft took them into an immense, brightly lit area somewhere far underground. There was a moving slidewalk here; Miss Elliot guided him onto it and they trundled along a few hundred yards, to a step-off turntable that fed him smoothly into the recreation center.

It was a good-sized room, divided chapel-fashion at its far end into smaller rooms. Staunt saw screens, data terminals, playback units, and other access equipment, all of it duplicating what every Departing One had in his own suite. But of course they came here out of loneliness; it might be more comforting to do one's reading or listening in public, he thought. There also were games of various kinds suitable for the very old, nothing that required any great degree of stamina or coordination: stochastic chess, polyrhythmers, double-orbit, things like that. We slide into childhood on our way to the grave.

There were about fifty Departing Ones in the center, he guessed. Most of them looked as old as the four who had met his copter earlier in the day; a few, frighteningly, seemed even older. Some looked much younger, no more than seventy or eighty. Staunt thought at first they might be Guides, but he saw on their faces a certain placid slackness that seemed common to all these Departing Ones, a look of dim mindless content, of resignation, of death-in-life. Evidently, one did not have to be heavily stricken in years to feel the readiness to Go.

"Shall I introduce you to some of the other Departing Ones?" Miss Elliot asked.

"Please. Yes."

She took him around. This is Henry Staunt, she said again and again. The famous composer. And she told him their names. He recognized none of them. David Golding, Michael Green, Ella Freeman, Seymour Church, Katherine Parks. Names. Withered faces. Miss Elliot supplied no identifying tags for any of them, as she had done for him; no "Ella Freeman, the famous actress," no "David Golding, the famous astronaut," no "Seymour Church, the famous financier." They had not been actresses or astronauts or financiers. God alone knew what they had been; Miss Elliot wasn't saying, and Staunt found himself without the energy to ask. Accountants, stockbrokers, housewives, teachers, programmers. Anything. Nothing. Just people. Ordinary people. Survivors from previous geological epochs. So old, so old, so old. In hardly any of them could Staunt detect the glimmer of life, and he saw for the first time how fortunate he had been to reach this great old age of his intact. The walking dead. Seymour Church, the famous zombie. Katherine Parks, the famous somnambulist. None of them seemed ever to have heard of him. Staunt was not surprised at that; even a famous composer learns early in life that he will be famous only among a minority of his countrymen. But still, those blank looks, those unfocused eyes. Pleased to meet you, Mr. Stout. How d'ye do, Mr. Stint. Hello. Hello. Hello.

"Have you met some interesting people?" Miss Elliot said, passing close to Staunt half an hour later.

"I'm more tired than I thought," Staunt said. "Perhaps you should take me back to my suite."

Already the names of the other Departing Ones were slipping from his mind. He had had brief, fragmentary conversations with six or seven of them, but they could not keep their minds on what they were saying, and neither, he discovered, could he. A terrible fatigue that he had never known before was settling over him. Senility must be contagious, he decided. Thirty minutes among the Departing Ones and I am as they are. I must get away.

Miss Elliot guided him to his room. Mr. Falkenbridge, the orderly, appeared unbidden, helped him undress, and put him to bed. Staunt lay awake a long time in the unfamiliar bed, his tense mind ticking relentlessly. A time-zone problem, he thought. He was tempted to ask for a sedative, but as he searched for the strength to sit up and ring for Miss Elliot, sleep suddenly captured him and drew him down into a pit of darkness.

Seven

In the next few days he managed to get to know some of the others. It was a task he imposed on himself. Throughout his life Staunt had negotiated, sometimes with difficulty, the narrow boundary between reserve and snobbery, trying to keep to himself without seeming to reject the company of others, and he was particularly eager not to withdraw into self-sufficiency at this time of all times. So he sought out his fellow Departing Ones and did what he could to scale the barriers separating them from him.

It was late in life to be making new friends, though. He found it hard to communicate much about himself to them, or to draw from them anything of consequence beyond the bare facts of their lives. As he suspected, they were a dull lot, people who had never achieved anything in particular except longevity. Staunt did not hold that against them: he saw no reason why everyone had to bubble with creativity, and he had deeply loved many whose only gifts had been gifts of friendship. But these people, coming now to the end of their days, were hollowed by time's erosions, and there was so little left of them that even ordinary human warmth had been worn away. They answered his questions perfunctorily and rarely responded with questions of their own. "A composer? How nice. I used to listen to music sometimes." He succeeded in discovering that Seymour Church had been living in the House of Leavetaking for eight months at his son's insistence but did not want to Go; that Ella Freeman had had (or believed she had had) a love affair, more than a century ago, with a man who later became President; that David Golding had been married six times and was inordinately proud of it;

that each of these Departing Ones clung to some such trifling biographical datum that gave him a morsel of individual identity. But Staunt was unable to penetrate beyond that one identifying datum; either nothing else was in them, or they could not or would not reveal themselves to him. A dull lot, but Staunt was no longer in a position to choose his companions for their merits.

During his first week in Arizona most of the members of his family came to see him, beginning with Paul and young Henry, Crystal's son. They stayed with him for two days. David, Crystal's other son, arrived a little later, along with his wife, their children, and one of their grandchildren; then Paul's two daughters showed up, and an assortment of youngsters. Everyone, even the young ones, wore sickly-sweet expressions of bliss. They were determined to look upon Staunt's Going as a beautiful event. In their conversations with him they never spoke of Going at all, only of family gossip, music, springtime, flowers, reminiscences. Staunt played their game. He had no more wish for emotional turmoil than they did; he wanted to back amiably out of their lives, smiling and bowing. He was careful, therefore, not to imply in anything he said that he was shortly going to end his life. He pretended that he had merely come to this place in the desert for a brief vacation.

The only one who did not visit him, aside from a few great-grandchildren, was his daughter Crystal. When he tried to phone her, he got no reply. His callers avoided any mention of her. Was she ill, Staunt wondered? Dead, even? "What are you trying to hide from me?" he asked his son finally. "Where's Crystal?"

"Crystal's fine," Paul said.

"That's not what I asked. Why hasn't she come here?"

"Actually she hasn't been entirely well."

"As I suspected. She's seriously ill, and you think the shock of hearing about it will harm me."

Paul shook his head. "It isn't like that at all."

"What's wrong with her?" Visions of cancer, heart surgery, brain tumors. "Has she had some kind of transplant? Is she in a hospital?"

"It isn't a physical problem. Crystal's simply suffering from fatigue. She's gone to Luna Dome for a rest."

"I spoke to her last month," Staunt said. "She looked all right then. I want the truth, Paul."

"The truth."

"The truth, yes."

Paul's eyes closed wearily for a moment, and in that moment Staunt saw his son for what he was, an old man, though not so old a man as he. After a pause Paul said in a flat, toneless voice, "The trouble is that Crystal hasn't accepted your Going very well. I called her about it, right after you told me, and she became hysterical. She thinks you're being hoodwinked, that your Guide is part of a conspiracy to do away with you, that your decision is at least ten or fifteen years premature. And she can't speak calmly about it, so we felt it was best to get her away where she wasn't likely to speak to you, to keep her from disturbing you. There. That's the story. I wasn't going to tell you."

"Silly of you to hide it."

"We didn't want to spoil your Going with a lot of carrying on."

"My Going won't spoil that easily. I'd like to talk to her, Paul. She may benefit from whatever help I can give her. If I can make her see Going for what it really is—if I can convince her that her outlook is unhealthy—Paul, set up a call to Luna Dome for me, will you? The Fulfillment people will pay. Crystal needs me. I have to make her understand."

"If you insist," Paul said.

Somehow, though, technical problems prevented the placing of the call that day, and the next, and the one after that. And then Paul left the House of Leavetaking. When Staunt phoned him at home to find out where on the moon Crystal actually was, he became evasive and said that she had recently transferred from one sanatorium to another. It would be a few more days, Paul said, before the call could be placed. Seeing his son's agitation, Staunt ceased pressing the issue. They did not want him to talk to Crystal. Crystal's hysterics would ruin his Going, they felt. They would not give him the chance to soothe her. So be it. He could not fight them. This must be a difficult time for the whole family; if they wished to think that Crystal would upset him so terribly, he would let the matter drop, for a while. Perhaps he could speak to her later. There would be time before his Going. Perhaps. Perhaps.

Eight

Every Monday, Wednesday, and Friday, Martin Bollinger came to him, usually in midafternoon, an hour or so after lunch. Generally Staunt received his Guide in his suite, although sometimes, on the cooler days, they strolled together through the garden. Their meetings invariably fell into three well-defined segments. First, Bollinger would display lively interest in Staunt's current activities. What books are you reading? Have you been listening to music? Are there any interesting Departing Ones for you to talk with? Is the staff taking good care of you? Do your relatives visit you often enough? Has the urge to compose anything come over you? Is there anyone you'd especially like to see? Are you thinking of traveling at all? And so on and so on, the same questions surfacing frequently.

When the questions were over, Bollinger would glide into the second phase, a conversation with a quiet autumnal tone, a recollection of vanished days. Sometimes he spoke as though Staunt had already Gone; he talked of Staunt's compositions in the same way he might refer to those of some early master. The symphonies, Bollinger would say: what a testament, what a mighty cumulative structure, nothing like them since Mahler, surely. The quartets, obviously akin to Beethoven's, yet thoroughly contemporary, true expressions of their composer and his times. And Staunt would nod, solemnly accepting Bollinger's verdicts in curious, dreamy objectivity. They would talk of mutual friends in the same way, viewing them as closed books, as cubes rather than as living, evolving persons. Staunt saw that Bollinger was helping to place distance between him and the life he had lived. Already, he felt remote from that life. After several weeks in the House of Leavetaking, he was coming to look upon himself more as someone who had very carefully studied Henry Staunt's biography than as the actual living Staunt, the inhabitant of Staunt's body.

The third phase of each meeting saw Bollinger turn quite frankly to matters directly related to Staunt's Going. Constantly he pressed Staunt to examine his motives, and he avoided the false gentleness with which everyone else seemed to treat him. The Guide was pursuing truth. Do you truly wish to Go, Henry? If so, have you started to give thought to the date of your Leavetaking? Will you stay in the world another five weeks? Three months? Six? No, no one's rushing you. Stay a year, if you want. I merely wonder if you've looked realistically, yet, at what it means to Go. Whether you comprehend your purpose in asking for it. Get behind the euphemism, Henry. Going is dying. The termination of all. For you, the end of the universe. Is this what you want, Henry? Is it? Is it? Is it? I'm not trying to make it harder for you. I'm trying to make it more pure. A truly spiritual Going, the rarest kind. But only if you're ready. Are you aware that you can withdraw from the whole undertaking at any point? It isn't cowardly to turn away from Going. See Hallam: Going isn't suicide, it's a sweet renunciation, properly reserved only for those who fully understand their motives. Anyone can kill himself in a fit of gloom. A proper going requires spiritual strength. Some people enroll in a House of Leavetaking two, even three times before they can take that last step. Yes, they go through the entire ritual of Farewell, almost to the end— and then they say they want to go home, and we send them home. We never push. We are not interested in sending victims out of the world. Only volunteers whose eyes are open. Have you been reading Hallam, Henry? Our philosopher of death. Look into yourself before you leap. Ask yourself, Is this what I want?

"What I want is to Go," Staunt would reply. But he could not tell Bollinger how long it would actually be before he would find himself ready to take his leave.

There seemed to be some pattern in this thrice-weekly pas de deux of conversation with his Guide. Bollinger appeared to be maneuvering him patiently and circuitously toward some sort of apocalyptic burst of joyful insight, a radiant moment of comprehension in which he would be able to say, feeling worthy of Hallam as he did, "Now I shall Go." But the maneuvers did not seem successful. Often, Staunt came away from Bollinger confused and depressed, less certain than ever of his desire to Go.

By the fourth week, most of his time was being given over

to reading. Music had largely palled for him. His family, having made the obligatory first round of visits, had stopped coming; they would not return to the House of Leavetaking until word reached them that he was in the final phase of his Going and ready for his Farewell ceremony. He had said all he cared to say to his friends. The recreation center bored him and the company of the other Departing Ones chilled him. Therefore he read. At the outset, he went about it dutifully, mechanically, taking it up solely as a chore for the improvement of his mind in its final hours. Like an old pharoah trying to repair his looks before he must be delivered into the hands of the mummifiers, Staunt meant to polish his soul with philosophy while he still had the chance. It was in that spirit that he plodded through Hobbes, whose political ideas had set him ablaze when he was nineteen, and who merely seemed crabbed and sour now. *It may seem strange to some man, that has not well weighed these things; that nature should thus dissociate, and render men apt to invade, and destroy one another: and he may therefore, not trusting to this inference, made from the passions, desire perhaps to have the same confirmed by experience. Let him therefore consider with himself, when taking a journey, he arms himself, and seeks to go well accompanied; when going to sleep, he locks his doors; when even in his house he locks his chests; and this when he knows there be laws, and public officers, armed, to revenge all injuries shall be done him; what opinion he has of his fellow-subjects, when he rides armed; of his fellow citizens, when he locks his doors; and of his children, and servants, when he locks his chests. Does he not there as much accuse mankind by his actions, as I do by my words?* Growing up in a tense, bleak world of peace that was really war, Staunt had found it easy to accept Hobbes' dark teachings. Now he was not so sure that the natural condition of mankind was a state of conflict, every man at war with every other man. Something had changed in the world, it seemed. Or in Staunt. He put Hobbes away in displeasure.

He was almost afraid to turn to Montaigne, fearing that that other great guide of his youth might also have soured over the long decades. But no. Instantly the old charm claimed him. *I cannot accept the way in which we fix the span of our lives. I have observed that the sages hold it to be much shorter than is commonly supposed.* "What!" said the younger Cato to those who would prevent him from killing *himself, "am I now of an age to be reproached with yielding up my life too soon?" And yet he was but forty-eight years of age. He thought that age very ripe and well advanced, considering how few men reach it.* Yes. Yes. And: *Wherever your life ends, it is all there. The profit of life is not in its length but in the use we put it to: many a man has lived long, who has lived little; see to it as long as you are here. It lies in your will, not in the number of years, to make the best of life. Did you think never to arrive at a place you were incessantly making for? Yet there is no road but has an end. And if society is any comfort to you, is not the world going the selfsame way as you?* Yes. Perfect. Staunt read deep into the night, and sent for a bottle of Château d'Yquem from the House of Leavetaking's well-stocked cellars, and solemnly toasted old Montaigne in his own sleek wine, and read on until morning. *There is no road but has an end.*

When he was done with Montaigne, he turned to Ben Jonson, first the familiar works, *Volpone* and *The Silent Woman* and *The Case is Altered*, then the black, explosive plays of later years, *Bartholomew Fair* and *the New Inn* and *The Devil Is An Ass*. Staunt had always felt a strong affinity for the Elizabethans, and particularly for Jonson, that crackling, hissing, scintillating man, whose stormy, sprawling plays blazed with a nightmarish intensity that Shakespeare, the greater poet, seemed to lack. As he had always vowed he would, Staunt submerged himself in Jonson, until the sound and rhythm of Jonson's verse echoed and reechoed like thunder in his overloaded brain, and the texture of Jonson's mind seemed inlaid on his own. *The Magnetic Lady, Cynthia's Revels, Catiline his Conspiracy*—no play was too obscure, too hermetic, for Staunt in his gluttony. And one afternoon during this period he found himself doing an unexpected thing. From his data terminal he requested a printout of the final pages of *The New Inn*'s first act, with an inch of blank space between each line. At the top of the sheet he wrote carefully, *The New Inn, an Opera by Henry Staunt, from the play of Ben Jonson*. Then, turning to Lovel's long speech, "O thereon hangs a history, mine host," Staunt began to pencil musical notations beneath the words, idly at first, then with sudden earnest fervor as the proper contours of the vocal line suggested themselves to him. Within minutes he had turned the entire speech into an aria and had even scribbled some preliminary marginal notes to himself about orchestration.

The style of the music was strange to him, a spare, lean, angular sort of melodiousness, thorny and complex, with a curiously archaic flavor. It was the sort of music Alban Berg might have written during an extended visit to the early seventeenth century. It did not sound much like Staunt's own kind of thing. My late style, he thought. Probably the aria was impossible to sing. No matter: this was how the muse had called it forth. It was the first sustained composing Staunt had done in years. He stared at the completed aria in wonder, astonished that music could still flow from him like that, welling up without conscious command from the gushing spring within.

For an instant he was tempted to feed what he had written into a synthesizer and get back a rough orchestration. To hear the sound of it, with the baritone riding tensely over the swooping strings, might carry him on to set down the next page of the score, and the next, and the next. He resisted. The world already had enough operas that no one listened to. Shaking his head, smiling sadly, he dated the page, initialed it in his customary way, jotted down an opus number—by guesswork, for he was far from his ledgers—and, folding the sheet, put it away among his papers. Yet the music went on unfolding in his mind.

Nine

In his ninth week at the House of Fulfillment, finding himself stranded in stagnant waters, Staunt sought Dr. James and applied for the memory-jolt treatment. It seemed to be the only option left, short of Going, and he rarely contemplated Going these days. He was done with Jonson, and the impulse to request other books had not come to him; he peeked occasionally at his single page of *The New Inn*, but did not resume work on it; he was guarded and aloof in his conversations with Bollinger and with his occasional visitors; he realized that he was sliding imperceptibly into a deathlike passivity, without actually coming closer to his exit. He would not return to his former life, and he could not yet surrender and Go. Possibly the memory jolt would nudge him off dead center.

"It'll take six hours to prepare you," Dr. James said, his long nose twitching with enthusiasm for Staunt's project. "The brain has to be cleared of all fatigue products, and the autonomic nervous system needs a tuning. When would you like to begin?"

"Now," Staunt said.

They cleansed and tuned him, and took him back to his suite and put him to bed, and hooked him into his metabolic monitor. "If you get overexcited," Dr. James explained, "the monitor will automatically adjust the intensity of your emotional flow downward." Staunt was willing to take his chances with the intensity of his emotional flow, but the medic was insistent. The monitor stayed on. "It isn't psychic pain we're worried about," Dr. James said. "There's never any of that. But sometimes—an excess of remembered love, do you know?—a burst of happiness—it could be too much, we've found." Staunt nodded. He would not argue the point. The doctor produced a hypodermic and pressed its ultrasonic snout against Staunt's arm. Briefly Staunt wondered whether this was all a trick, whether the drug would really send him to his Going rather than for a trip along his time-track, but he pushed the irrational notion aside, and the snout made its brief droning sound and the mysterious dark fluid leaped into his veins.

Ten

He hears the final crashing chords of *The Trials of Job*, and the curtain, a sheet of dense purple light, springs up from the floor of the stage. Applause. Curtain calls for the singers. The conductor on stage, now, bowing, smiling. The chorus master, even. Cascades of cheers. All about him swirl the glittering mobile chandeliers of the Haifa Opera House. Someone is shouting incomprehensible jubilant words in his ear: the language is Hebrew, Staunt realizes. He says, Yes, yes, thank you so very much. They want him to stand and acknowledge the applause. Edith sits beside him, flushed with excitement, her eyes sparkling. His mind supplies the date: September 9, 1999. "Let them see you," Edith whispers through the tumult. A hand claps his shoulder. Wild eyes blazing into his own: Mannheim, the critic. "The opera of the century!" he cries. Staunt forces himself to rise. They are screaming his name. *Staunt! Staunt! Staunt!* The audience is his. Two thousand berserk Israelis, his to command. What shall he say to them? *Sieg! Heil! Sieg! Heil!* He chokes on his own appalling unvoiced joke. In the end he can do nothing but wave and grin and topple back into his seat. Edith rubs his arm lovingly. His glowing bride. His night of triumph. To write an opera at all these days is a mighty task; to enjoy a premiere like this is heavenly. Now the audience wants an encore. The conductor at his station. The curtain fades. Job alone on stage: his final scene, the proud bass voice crying, "Behold, I am vile," and the voice of the Lord replying to him out of a thousand loudspeakers, filling all the world with sound: "Deck thyself now with majesty and excellency." Staunt weeps at his own music. If I live a hundred years, I will never forget this night, he tells himself.

Eleven

"The copter went down so suddenly, Mr. Staunt. They had it on the stabilizer beam all through the storm, but you know it isn't always possible—"

"And my wife? And my wife?"

"We're so sorry, Mr. Staunt."

Twelve

He sits at the keyboard fretting over the theory and harmony. His legs are not yet long enough to reach the piano's pedals: a

nuisance, but temporary. He closes his eyes and strikes the
keyboard. This is the key of C major, the easy one. The tonic
chord. The dominant. Why did they wait so long to tell him
about these things? He builds chord after chord. *I will now
moderate into the key of D minor. Modulate. I do this and
this and this.* He is nine years old. All this long hot Sunday
afternoon he has explored this wondrous other language of
sounds. While his family sits frozen by the television set.
"Henry? Henry, they're going to be coming out of the
module any minute!" He shrugs. What does the moonwalk
matter to him? The moon is dead and far away. And this is the
world of D minor. He has his own exploring to do today.
"Henry, he's out! He came down the ladder!" Fine. Tonic.
Dominant. And the diminished seventh. The words are strange.
But how easy it is to go deeper and deeper into the maze of
sound.

Thirteen

"The faculty and students take great pleasure, Mr. Staunt, to
present you on the occasion of your one-hundredth birthday
with this memorial of a composer who shared your divine
productivity if not your blessed longevity: the original manuscript of Mozart's 'Divertimento in B,' Köchel number—"

Fourteen

"A boy, yes. We're calling him Paul, after Edith's father. And
what an odd feeling it is to tell myself I have a son. You know,
I'm forty-five years old. More than half my life gone, I
suppose. And now a son."

Fifteen

The sun is huge in the sky, and the beach is ablaze with shimmering heat-furies, and beyond the crescent of pink sand the green Caribbean rests against its bed like water in a quiet tub. These are the hours when he remains under cover, in some shady hammock, reading, perhaps making notes for an essay or his next composition. But there is the girl again, crouched by the shore, gently poking at the creatures of the tidal pool, the shy anemones and the little sea-slugs and the busy hermit crabs. So he must expose his vulnerable skin, for tomorrow he will fly back to New York, and this may be his last chance to introduce himself to her. He has watched her through this whole week of vacation. Not a girl, exactly. Surely at least twenty-five years old. Very much her own person: self-contained, coolly precise, alert, elegant. Tempting. He has rarely felt so drawn toward anyone. Preserving his bachelorhood has been no chore for him; he glides as easily from woman to woman as he does from city to city. But there is something about the eyes of this Edith, something about her smile, that pulls him. He knows he is being foolish. All this is pure fantasy: he has no idea what she is like, where her interests lie. That look of intelligence and sympathy may be all his own invention; the girl inside the face may in truth be drab and empty, some programmer on holiday, her soul a dull haze of daydreams about glamorous holovision stars. Yet he must approach. The sun pounds his sensitive skin. She looks up, smiling, from the tidal pool. A purple sea-slug crawls lightly across her palm. He kneels beside her. She offers him the sea-slug, and he lets it crawl on his hand, and they laugh, and she points out limpets and periwinkles and barnacles for him, until there is a kind of contact between them through the creatures of this salty pond, and at last he says, feeling clumsy about it, "We haven't even introduced ourselves. I'm Henry Staunt."

"I know," Edith says. "The composer."
And it all becomes so much easier.

Sixteen

"—and the gold medal for the outstanding work in extended symphonic form by a student under sixteen years of age goes, as I'm sure everyone has already realized, to Henry Staunt, who—"

Seventeen

"And my wife? And my wife?"
"We're so sorry, Mr. Staunt."

Eighteen

"As long as we're getting into that end of the evening, Henry, I'll allow myself the privilege of delivering a little analysis, too. Do you know what the real trouble with you is? With your music, with your soul, with everything? You don't suffer. You've never been touched by pain, or, if you have, it doesn't sink in. Look, you're forty years old, and you've never known anything but success, and your music is played everywhere, an incredible achievement for a living composer, and you could pass for thirty. Or even twenty-seven. Time doesn't claw you. I don't recommend suffering, mind you, but I do say it tempers an artist's soul; it adds a richness of texture that—forgive me—you lack, Henry. You know, you could live to be a very old man, considering the way you don't seem to age, and someday, when you're ninety-seven or one hundred five or something like that, you may realize that you've never really intersected reality, that you've kept yourself insulated, and that in a sense you haven't really lived at all or created anything at all or—forgive me, Henry. I take it all back, even if you are still smiling. Not even a friend should say things like that. Not even a friend."

Nineteen

"The Pulitzer Prize for Music for the year 2002—"

Twenty

"I Edith do take thee Henry to be my lawful wedded husband—"

Twenty-One

"It isn't as if she was a bride, Henry. God knows it's terrible to lose her that way, but she was yours for fifty years, Henry, *fifty years*, the kind of marriage most people hardly dare to dream of having, and if she's gone, well, be content that you had the fifty, at least."

"I wish we had crashed together, though."

"Don't be childish. You're—what?—eighty-five, eighty-seven

years old? You've got fifteen or twenty healthy and productive years ahead of you. More, if you're lucky. People live to fantastic ages nowadays. You might see one hundred ten or one hundred fifteen."

"Without Edith, what good is that?"

Twenty-Two

"Put your hands in the middle of the keyboard. Spread the fingers out as wide as you can. Wider. Wider. That's the boy! Now, Henry, this is what we call middle C—"

Twenty-Three

In haste, stumbling, he goes on into his studio. The big room holds the tangible residue of his long career. Over here, the music itself, in recorded performance: disks and cassettes for the early works, sparkling playback cubes for the later ones. Here are the manuscripts, uniformly bound in red half-morocco, one of his little vanities. Here are the scrapbooks of reviews and the programs of concerts. Here are the trophies. Here are the volumes of his critical writings. Staunt has been a busy man. He looks at the titles stamped on the bindings of the manuscripts: the symphonies, the string quartets, the concerti, the miscellaneous chamber works, the songs, the sonatas, the cantatas, the operas. So much. So much. Staunt feels no sense of having wasted his time, though, filling this room with what it holds. Never in the past hundred years has a week gone by without a performance of one of his compositions somewhere. That is sufficient justification for having written, for having lived. And yet, one hundred thirty-six years is such a long time.

He pushes cubes into playback slots, getting three of his

works going at once, bringing wild skeins of sound out of the room's assortment of speakers, and stands in the middle, trembling a little, accepting the sonic barrage. After perhaps four minutes he cuts off the sound and orders his telephone to ring up the Office of Fulfillment.

"My Guide is Martin Bollinger," he says. "Would you let him know that I'd like to be transferred to the House of Leavetaking as soon as possible?"

Twenty-Four

Dr. James had told him, long before, that Departing Ones invariably came out of memory jolts in a state of ecstasy, and that frequently they were in such raptures that they insisted on Going immediately, before the high could ebb. Emerging from the drug, Staunt searched in vain for the ecstasy. Where? He was wholly calm. For some hours past, or maybe just a few minutes—he had no idea how long the memory jolt had lasted—he had tasted morsels of his past, scraps of conversation, bits of scenery, random textures of contact, a stew of incidents, nonchronological, unsorted. His music and his wife. His wife and his music. A pretty thin gruel for one hundred thirty-six years of life. Where were the storms? Where were the tempests? A single great tragedy, yes, and otherwise everything tranquil. Too orderly a life, too sane, too empty, and now, permitted to review it, he found himself with nothing to grasp but applause, which slipped through his fingers, and his love of Edith, and even that had lost its magic. Where was that excess of remembered love that Dr. James had said could be dangerous? Perhaps they had monitored him too closely, tuning down the intensity of his spirit. Or perhaps it was his spirit that was at fault. Old and dry, pale and lean.

Unlike the others he had heard about, he did not request immediate Going after his voyage. Without that terminal ecstasy, why Go? He felt not exactly depressed but certainly lowered; his tour of his yesterdays had thrust him into a sort of stasis, a paralysis of the will, that left him hung up as before, enmeshed by the strands of his own quiet past.

But if Staunt remained unready to Go, not so with others. "You are invited to the Farewell ceremony of David Golding," Miss Elliot told him the day after his memory jolt.

Golding was the man who had had six wives—outliving some, divorcing some, being divorced by some. His heroic husbandry was no longer apparent: now he was small and gnarled and fleshless, and because he was nearly blind, his pinched ungenerous face was disfigured by the jutting cones of two optical transducers. They said he was one hundred twenty-five years old, but to Staunt he looked at least two hundred. For the Farewell ceremony, though, the technicians of the House of Leavetaking had transformed the little old man into something sublime. His face gleamed with make-up that obliterated the crevices of decades; he held himself buoyantly upright, no doubt inflated into a semblance of his ancient virility by some drug; he was clad in a radiant, shimmering gown. Scores of relatives and friends surrounded him in the Chambers of Farewell, a brightly decorated underground suite opposite the recreation center. Staunt, as he entered, was dismayed by the size of the crowd. So many, so young, so noisy.

Ella Freeman sidled up to him and touched her shriveled hand to Staunt's arm. "Look there: two of his wives. He hadn't seen one in sixty years. And his sons. All of them, his sons. Two or three by each wife!"

The ceremony, conducted by the relatively young man who was Golding's Guide, was elegiac in tone, brief, sweet. Standing under the emblem of the Office of Fulfillment, the wheel and the gears, the Guide spoke briefly of the philosophy of making room for others, of the beauty of a willing departure. Then he praised the Departing One in vague, general terms; one of his sons delivered a more specific eulogy; lastly, Seymour Church, chosen to represent Golding's companions at the House of Leavetaking, croaked out a short, almost incoherent speech of farewell. To this the Departing One, who seemed transfigured with joy and already at least halfway into the next world, made reply in a few faint syllables, blurrily expressing gratitude for his long and happy life. Golding barely appeared to comprehend what was going on; he sat beaming in a kind of throne, dreamy, distant. Staunt wondered if he had been drugged into a stupor.

When the speeches were done, refreshments were served. Then, accompanied only by his closest kin, fifteen or twenty people, Golding was ushered into the innermost room of the Chambers of Farewell. The door slid shut behind him, and in his absence the Leavetaking party proceeded merrily.

There were four such events in the next five weeks. At two of them—the Goings of Michael Green and Katherine Parks— Staunt was asked to give the speech of farewell. It was a task that he performed gracefully, serenely, and, he thought, with a good deal of eloquence. He spoke for ten minutes about Michael Green, for close to fifteen about Katherine Parks, talking not so much about the Departing Ones, whom he had scarcely come to know well, but about the entire philosophy of Going, the beauty and wonder of the act of world-renunciation. It was not customary for the giver of the speech of farewell to manage such sustained feats, and his audience listened in total fascination; if the occasion had permitted it, Staunt suspected, they would have applauded.

So he had a new vocation, and several Departing Ones whom he did not know at all accelerated their own Goings so that they would not fail to have Staunt speak at the rites. It was summer now, and Arizona was caught in glistening tides of heat. Staunt never went outdoors any longer; he spent much of his time mingling in the recreation center, doing research, so to speak, for future oratory. He rarely read these days. He never listened to music. He had settled into a pleasing, quiet routine. This was his fourth month at the House of Leavetaking. Except for Seymour Church, who still refused to be nudged into Going, Staunt was now the senior Departing One in point of length of residence. And at the end of July, Church at last took his leave. Staunt, of course, spoke, touching on the Departing One's slow journey toward Going, and it was difficult for him to avoid self-conscious references to his own similar reluctance. Why do I tarry here? Staunt wondered. Why do I not say the word?

Every few weeks his son Paul visited him. Staunt found their meetings difficult. Paul, showing signs of strain and anxiety, always seemed on the verge of blurting out, "Why don't you Go, already?" And Staunt would have no answer, for he did not know the answer. He had read Hallam four times. Philosophically and psychologically he was prepared to Go. Yet he remained.

Twenty-Five

In mid-August Martin Bollinger entered his suite, held out a sheet of paper, and said, "What's this, Henry?"

Staunt glanced at it. It was a photocopy of the aria from *The New Inn*. "Where did you find that?" he asked.

"One of the staff people came across it while tidying your room."

"I thought we were entitled to privacy."

"This isn't an inquisition, Henry. I'm just curious. Have you started to compose again?"

"That scrap is all I wrote. It was months ago."

"It's fascinating music," Bollinger said.

"Is it, now? I thought it was rather harsh and forced, myself."

"No. No. Not at all. You always talked about a Ben Jonson opera, didn't you? And now you've begun it."

"I was enlivening a dull day," said Staunt. "Mere scribbling."

"Henry, would you like to get out of this place?"

"Are we back to *that*?"

"Obviously you still have music in you. Perhaps a great opera."

"Which you mean to squeeze out of me, eh? Don't talk nonsense. There's nothing left in me, Martin. I'm here to Go."

"You haven't Gone, though."

"You've noticed that," Staunt said.

"It was made clear to you at the beginning that you wouldn't be rushed. But I've begun to suspect, Henry, that you aren't interested in Going at all, that you're marking time here, perhaps incubating this opera, perhaps coming to terms with something indigestible in your soul. Whatever. You don't *have* to Go. We'll send you home. Finish *The New Inn*. Think the thoughts you want to think. Reapply for Going next year or the year after."

"You want that opera out of me, don't you?"

"I want you to be happy," said Bollinger. "I want your Going to be *right*. The bit of music here is just a clue to your inner state."

"There won't be any opera, Martin. And I don't plan to leave Omega Prime alive. To have put my family through this ordeal, and then to come home, to tell them it's all been just a holiday lark out here—no. No."

"As you wish," Bollinger said. He smiled and turned away leaving an unspoken question hanging like a sword between them: *If you want to Go, Henry, why don't you Go?*

Twenty-Six

Staunt realized that he had taken on the status of a permanent Departing One, a kind of curator emeritus of the House of Fulfillment. Here he was, enjoying this life of ease and dignity, accepting the soft-voiced attentions of those who meant to slide him gently from the world, playing his role of patriarch among the shattered hulks that were the other Departing Ones here. Each week new ones came; he greeted them solemnly, helped them blend with those already in residence, and, in time, presided over their Goings. And he stayed on. Why? Why? Surely not out of fear of dying. Why, then, was he making a career out of his Going?

So that he might have the prestige of being a hero of his time, possibly—an exponent of noble renunciation, a practitioner of joyful departure. Making much glib talk of turning the wheel and creating a place for those to come— a twenty-first-century Sydney Carton, standing by the guillotine and praising the far, far better thing that he will do, only he finds himself enjoying the part so much that he forgets to kneel and present his neck to the blade.

Or maybe he is only interrupting the boredom of a too-bland life with a feigned fling at dying. The glamour of becoming a Departing One injecting interesting complexities

into a static existence. But diversion and not death his real
object. Yes? If that's it, Henry, go home and write your opera;
the holiday should have ended by now.

He came close to summoning Bollinger and asking to be
sent home. But he fought the impulse down. To leave
Omega Prime now would be the true cowardice. He owed
the world a death. He had occupied this body long enough.
His place was needed; soon he would Go. Soon. Soon.
Soon.

Twenty-Seven

At the beginning of September there were four days in a row
of rain, an almost unknown occurrence in that part of Arizona. Miss Elliot said that the Hopi, doing their annual snake
dances on their mesas far to the north, had overdone things
this year and sent rain clouds all through the state. Staunt, to
the horror of the staff, went out each day to stand in the
rain, letting the cool drops soak his thin gown, watching
the water sink swiftly into the parched red soil. "You'll catch
your death of cold," Mr. Falkenbridge told him sternly.
Staunt laughed.

He requested another wide-spaced print-out of *The New
Inn* and tried to set the opening scene. Nothing came. He
could not find the right vocal line, nor could he recapture the
strange color of the earlier aria. The tones and textures of
Ben Jonson were gone from his head. He gave the project up
without regret.

There were three Farewell ceremonies in eight days. Staunt
attended them all, and spoke at two of them.

Arbitrarily, he chose September 19 as the day of his own
Going. But he told no one about his decision, and September
19 came and went with Staunt unchanged.

At the end of the month he told Martin Bollinger, "I'm a
fraud. I haven't gotten an inch closer to Going in all the time
I've been here. I never wanted to Go at all. I still want to
live, to see and do things, to experience things. I came here
out of desperation, because I was stale, I was bored, I needed

novelty. To toy with death, to live a little scenario of dying—
that was all I was after. Excitement. An event in an eventless
life: Henry Staunt Prepares to Die. I've been using all you
people as players in a cynical charade."

Bollinger said quietly, "Shall I arrange for you to go home,
then, Henry?"

"No. No. Get me Dr. James. And notify my family that my
Farewell ceremony will be held a week from today. It's time
for me to Go."

"But if you still want to live—"

"What better time to Go?" Staunt asked.

Twenty-Eight

They were all here, close around him. Paul had come, and
Crystal, too, back from the moon and looking feeble, and all
the grandchildren and the great-grandchildren, and the friends,
the conductors and the younger composers and some critics,
more than a hundred people in all coming to see him off.
Staunt, undrugged but already beginning to ascend, had
moved coolly among them, thanking them for attending his
Leavetaking party, welcoming them to his Farewell ceremony. He was amazed at how calm he was. Seated now in the
throne of honor, he listened to the final orations and endured
without objection a scrambled medley of his most famous
compositions, obviously assembled hastily by someone inexpert in such matters. Martin Bollinger, giving the main
eulogy, quoted heavily from Hallam: "Too often we delude
ourselves into thinking we are truly ready, when actually we
have not reached readiness at all, and choose Going out of
unworthy or shallow motives. How tragic it is to arrive at the
actual moment of Leavetaking and to realize that one has
deceived oneself, that one's motivations are false, that one is,
in fact, not in the least ready to Go!"

How true, Staunt told himself. And yet how false. For here
I am ready to Go and yet not in the least ready, and in my
unreadiness lies my readiness.

Bollinger finished what he had to say, and one of the

Departing Ones, a man named Bradford who had come to
Omega Prime in August, began to fumble through the usual
final speech. He stammered and coughed and lost the thread
of his words, for he was one hundred forty years old and due
for Going himself next week, but somehow he made it to the
end, Staunt, paying little attention, beamed at his son and his
daughter, his horde of descendants, his admirers, his doctors.
He understood now why Departing Ones generally seemed
detached from their own Farewell ceremonies: the dreary
drone of the speeches launched them early into the shores of
paradise.

And then they were serving the refreshments, and now
they were about to wheel him into the innermost room. And
Staunt said, "May I speak also?"

They looked at him, appalled, frightened, obviously fearing
he would wreck the harmony of the occasion with this
unconventional, ill-timed intrusion. But they could not refuse. He had delivered so many eulogies for others—now he
would speak for himself.

Softly Staunt said, making them strain their ears to hear it,
"I accept the concept of the turning wheel, and I gladly yield
my place to those who are to come. But let me tell you that
this is not an ordinary Going. You know, when I came here I
thought I was weary of the world and ready to Go, but yet I
stayed, I held back from the brink, I delayed, I pretended.
I even—Martin knows this—began another opera. I was told
I could go home, and I refused. Hallam forgive me, but I
refused. For his way is not the only way of Going. Because
life still seems sweet, I give it up today. And so I take my
final pleasure: that of relinquishing the only thing left to me
worth keeping."

They were whispering. They were staring.

I have said all the wrong things, he thought. I have spoiled
the day for them. But whose Going is it? Why should I care
about them?

Martin Bollinger, bending low, murmured, "It's still not too
late, Henry. We can stop everything right now."

"The final temptation," Staunt said. "And I withstand it.
Bring down the curtain. I'm ready to Go."

They wheeled him to the innermost chamber. When they
offered him the cup, he seized it, winked at Martin Bollinger,
and drained it in a single gulp.

DYING
INSIDE

For B and T and C and me—
we sweated it out

One

So, then, I have to go downtown to the University and forage for dollars again. It doesn't take much cash to keep me going—$200 a month will do nicely—but I'm running low, and I don't dare try to borrow from my sister again. The students will shortly be needing their first term papers of the semester; that's always a steady business. The weary, eroding brain of David Selig is once more for hire. I should be able to pick up $75 worth of work on this lovely golden October morning. The air is crisp and clear. A high-pressure system covers New York City, banishing humidity and haze. In such weather my fading powers still flourish. Let us go then, you and I, when the morning is spread out against the sky. To the Broadway-IRT subway. Have your tokens ready, please.

You and I. To whom do I refer? I'm heading downtown alone, after all. *You and I*.

Why, of course I refer to myself and to that creature which lives within me, skulking in its spongy lair and spying on unsuspecting mortals. That sneaky monster within me, that ailing monster, dying even more swiftly than I. Yeats once wrote a dialogue of self and soul; why then shouldn't Selig, who is divided against himself in a way poor goofy Yeats could never have understood, speak of his unique and perishable gift as though it were some encapsulated intruder lodged in his skull? Why not? Let us go then, you and I. Down the hall. Push the button. Into the elevator. There is a stink of garlic in it. These peasants, these swarming Puerto Ricans, they leave their emphatic smells everywhere. My neighbors. I love them. Down. Down.

It is 10:43 A.M., Eastern Daylight Savings Time. The current temperature reading in Central Park is 57°. The humidity stands at 28% and the barometer is 30.30 and falling, with the wind northeast at 11 miles per hour. The forecast is for fair skies and sunny weather today, tonight, and tomorrow, with the highs in the low to middle 60's. The chance of precipitation is zero today and 10% tomorrow. Air quality level is rated good. David Selig is 41 and counting. Slightly above medium height, he has the lean figure of a bachelor accustomed to his own meager cooking, and his customary facial expression is a mild, puzzled frown. He blinks a lot. In his faded blue denim jacket, heavy-duty boots, and 1969-vintage striped bells he presents a superficially youthful appearance, at least from the neck down; but in fact he looks like some sort of refugee from an illicit research laboratory where the balding, furrowed heads of anguished middle-aged men are grafted to the reluctant bodies of adolescent boys. How did this happen to him? At what point did his face and scalp begin to grow old? The dangling cables of the elevator hurl shrieks of mocking laughter at him as he descends from his two-room refuge on the twelfth floor. He wonders if those rusty cables might be even older than he is. He is of the 1935 vintage. This housing project, he suspects, might date from 1933 or 1934. The Hon. Fiorello H. LaGuardia, Mayor. Though perhaps it's younger— just immediately pre-war, say. (Do you remember 1940, Duvid? That was the year we took you to the World's Fair. This is the trylon, that's the perisphere.) Anyway the buildings are getting old. What isn't?

The elevator halts grindingly at the 7th floor. Even before the scarred door opens I detect a quick mental flutter of female Hispanic vitality dancing through the girders. Of course, the odds are overwhelming that the summoner of the elevator is a young Puerto Rican wife—the house is full of them, the husbands are away at work at this time of day—but all the same I'm pretty certain that I'm reading her psychic emanations and not just playing the hunches. Sure enough. She is short, swarthy, maybe about 23 years old, and very pregnant. I can pick up the double neural output clearly: the quicksilver darting of her shallow, sensual mind and the furry, blurry thumpings of the fetus, about six months old, sealed within her hard bulging body. She is flat-faced and broad-hipped, with little glossy eyes and a thin, pinched mouth. A second child, a dirty girl of about two, clutches her mother's thumb. The babe giggles up at me and the woman favors me with a brief, suspicious smile as they enter the elevator.

They stand with their backs toward me. Dense silence.

Buenos dias, señora. Nice day, isn't it, ma'am? What a lovely little child. But I remain mute. I don't know her; she looks just like all the others who live in this project, and even her cerebral output is standard stuff, unindividuated, indistinguishable: vague thoughts of plantains and rice, this week's lottery results, and tonight's television highlights. She is a dull bitch but she is human and I love her. What's her name? Maybe it's Mrs. Altagracia Morales. Mrs. Amantina Figueroa. Mrs. Filomena Mercado. I love their names. Pure poetry. I grew up with plump clumping girls named Sondra Wiener, Beverly Schwartz, Sheila Weisbard. Ma'am, can you possibly be Mrs. Inocencia Fernandez? Mrs. Clodómira Espinosa? Mrs. Bonifacia Colon? Perhaps Mrs. Esperanza Dominguez. Esperanza. Esperanza. I love you, Esperanza. Esperanza springs eternal in the human breast. (I was there last Christmas for the bullfights. Esperanza Springs, New Mexico; I stayed at the Holiday Inn. No, I'm kidding.) Ground floor. Nimbly I step forward to hold the door open. The lovely stolid pregnant chiquita doesn't smile at me as she exits.

To the subway now, hippity-hop, one long block away. This far uptown the tracks are still elevated. I sprint up the cracking, peeling staircase and arrive at the station level hardly winded at all. The results of clean living, I guess. Simple diet, no smoking, not much drinking, no acid or mesc, no speed. The station, at this hour, is practically deserted. But in a moment I hear the wailing of onrushing wheels, metal on metal, and simultaneously I pick up the blasting impact of a sudden phalanx of minds all rushing toward me at once out of the north, packed aboard the five or six cars of the oncoming train. The compressed souls of those passengers form a single inchoate mass, pressing insistently against me. They quiver like trembling jellylike bites of plankton squeezed brutally together in some oceanographer's net, creating one complex organism in which the separate identities of all are lost. As the train glides into the station I am able to pick up isolated blurts and squeaks of discrete selfhood: a fierce jab of desire, a squawk of hatred, a pang of regret, a sudden purposeful inner mumbling, rising from the confusing totality the way odd little scraps and stabs of melody rise from the murky orchestral smear of a Mahler symphony. The power is deceptively strong in me today. I'm picking up plenty. This is the strongest it's been in weeks.

Surely the low humidity is a factor. But I'm not deceived into thinking that the decline in my ability has been checked. When I first began to lose my hair, there was a happy period when the process of erosion seemed to halt and reverse itself, when new patches of fine dark floss began to sprout on my denuded forehead. But after an initial freshet of hope I took a more realistic view: this was no miraculous reforestation but only a twitch of the hormones, a temporary cessation of decay, not to be relied upon. And in time my hairline resumed its retreat. So too in this instance. When one knows that something is dying inside one, one learns not to put much trust in the random vitalities of the fleeting moment. Today the power is strong yet tomorrow I may hear nothing but distant tantalizing murmurs.

I find a seat in the corner of the second car, open my book, and wait out the ride downtown. I am reading Beckett again, *Malone Dies;* it plays nicely to my prevailing mood, which as you have noticed is one of self-pity. *My time is limited. It is thence that one fine day, when all nature smiles and shines, the rack lets loose its black unforgettable cohorts and sweeps away the blue for ever. My situation is truly delicate. What fine things, what momentous things, I am going to miss through fear, fear of falling back into the old error, fear of not finishing in time, fear of revelling, for the last time, in a last outpouring of misery, impotence and hate. The forms are many in which the unchanging seeks relief from its formlessness.* Ah yes, the good Samuel, always ready with a word or two of bleak comfort.

Somewhere about 180th Street I look up and see a girl sitting diagonally opposite me and apparently studying me. She is in her very early twenties, attractive in a sallow way, with long legs, decent breasts, a bush of auburn hair. She has a book too—the paperback of *Ulysses*, I recognize the cover— but it lies neglected on her lap. Is she interested in me? I am not reading her mind; when I entered the train I automatically stopped my inputs down to the minimum, a trick I learned when I was a child. If I don't insulate myself against scattershot crowd-noises on trains or in other enclosed public places I can't concentrate at all. Without attempting to detect her signals, I speculate on what she's thinking about me, playing a game I often play. *How intelligent he looks . . . . He must have suffered a good deal, his face is so much older than his body . . . tenderness in his eyes . . . so sad they look . . . a poet,*

a scholar.... I bet he's very passionate ... pouring all his
pent-up love into the physical act, into screwing.... What's
he reading? Beckett? Yes, a poet, a novelist he must be ... maybe
somebody famous.... I mustn't be too agressive, though.
He'll be turned off by pushiness. A shy smile, that'll catch
him.... One thing leads to another.... I'll invite him up for
lunch.... Then, to check on the accuracy of my intuitive
perceptions, I tune in on her mind. At first there is no signal.
My damnable waning powers betraying me again! But then it
comes—static, first, as I get the low-level muzzy ruminations
of all the passengers around me, and then the clear sweet
tone of her soul. She is thinking about a karate class she will
attend later this morning on 96th Street. She is in love with
her instructor, a brawny pockmarked Japanese. She will see
him tonight. Dimly through her mind swims the memory of
the taste of sake and the image of his powerful naked body
rearing above her. There is nothing in her mind about me. I
am simply part of the scenery, like the map of the subway
system on the wall above my head. Selig, your egocentricity
kills you every time. I note that she does indeed wear a shy
smile now, but it is not for me, and when she sees me staring
at her the smile vanishes abruptly. I return my attention to
my book.

The train treats me to a long sweaty unscheduled halt in
the tunnel between stations north of 137th Street; eventually
it gets going again and deposits me at 116th Street, Columbia
University. I climbed toward the sunlight. I first climbed
these stairs a full quarter of a century ago, October '51, a
terrified high-school senior with acne and a crew-cut, coming
out of Brooklyn for my college entrance interview. Under the
bright lights in University Hall. The interviewer terribly
poised, mature—why, he must have been 24, 25 years old.
They let me into their college, anyway. And then this was my
subway station every day, beginning in September '52 and
continuing until I finally got away from home and moved up
close to the campus. In those days there was an old cast-iron
kiosk at street level marking the entrance to the depths; it
was positioned between two lanes of traffic, and students,
their absent minds full of Kierkegaard and Sophocles and
Fitzgerald, were forever stepping in front of cars and getting
killed. Now the kiosk is gone and the subway entrances are
placed more rationally, on the sidewalks.

I walk along 116th Street. To my right, the broad green-

sward of South Field; to my left, the shallow steps rising to
Low Library. I remember South Field when it was an athletic
field in the middle of the campus: brown dirt, basepaths,
fence. My freshman year I played softball there. We'd go to
the lockers in University Hall to change, and then, wearing
sneakers, polo shirts, dingy gray shorts, feeling naked amidst
the other students in business suits or ROTC uniforms, we'd
sprint down the endless steps to South Field for an hour of
outdoor activity. I was good at softball. Not much muscle, but
quick reflexes and a good eye, and I had the advantage of
knowing what was on the pitcher's mind. He'd stand there
thinking, *This guy's too skinny to hit, I'll give him a high fast
one*, and I'd be ready for it and bust it out into left field,
circling the bases before anyone knew what was happening.
Or the other side would try some clumsy bit of strategy like
hit-and-run, and I'd move effortlessly over to gather up the
grounder and start the double play. Of course it was only
softball and my classmates were mostly pudgy dubs who
couldn't even run, let alone read minds, but I enjoyed the
unfamiliar sensation of being an outstanding athlete and
indulged in fantasies of playing shortstop for the Dodgers.
The *Brooklyn* Dodgers, remember? In my sophomore year
they ripped up South Field and turned it into a fine grassy
showplace divided by a paved promenade, in honor of the
University's 200th birthday. Which happened in 1954. Christ,
so very long ago. I grow old ... I grow old ... I shall wear the
bottoms of my trousers rolled. The mermaids singing, each to
each. I do not think that they will sing to me.

I go up the steps and take a seat about fifteen feet to the
left of the bronze statue of Alma Mater. This is my office in
fair weather or foul. The students know where to look for me,
and when I'm there the word quickly spreads. There are five
or six other people who provide the service I provide—
impecunious graduate students, mostly, down on their luck—
but I'm the quickest and most reliable, and I have an
enthusiastic following. Today, though, business gets off to a
slow start. I sit for twenty minutes, fidgeting, peering into
Beckett, staring at Alma Mater. Some years ago a radical
bomber blew a hole in her side, but there's no sign of the
damage now. I remember being shocked at the news, and
then shocked at being shocked—why should I give a damn
about a dumb statue symbolic of a dumb school? That was
about 1969, I guess. Back in the Neolithic.

"Mr. Selig?"

Big brawny jock looming above me. Colossal shoulders, chubby innocent face. He's deeply embarrassed. He's taking Comp Lit 18 and needs a paper fast, on the novels of Kafka, which he hasn't read. (This is the football season; he's the starting halfback and he's very very busy.) I tell him the terms and he hastily agrees. While he stands there I covertly take a reading of him, getting the measure of his intelligence, his probable vocabulary, his style. He's smarter than he appears. Most of them are. They could write their own papers well enough if they only had the time. I make notes, setting down my quick impressions of him, and he goes away happy. After that, trade is brisk: he sends a fraternity brother, the brother sends a friend, the friend sends one of *his* fraternity brothers, a different fraternity, and the daisy-chain lengthens until by early afternoon I find I've taken on all the work I can handle. I know my capacity. So all is well. I'll eat regularly for two or three weeks, without having to tap my sister's grudging generosity. Judith will be pleased not to hear form me. Home, now, to begin my ghostly tasks. I'm good— glib, earnest, profound in a convincingly sophomoric way— and I can vary my styles. I know my way around literature, psychology, anthropology, philosophy, all the soft subjects. Thank God I kept my own term papers; even after twenty-odd years they can still be mined. I charge $3.50 a typed page, sometimes more if my probing reveals that the client has money. A minimum grade of B+ guaranteed or there's no fee. I've never had to make a refund.

Two

When he was seven and a half years old and causing a great deal of trouble for his third-grade teacher, they sent little David to the school psychiatrist, Dr. Hittner, for an examination. The school was an expensive private one on a quiet leafy street in the Park Slope section of Brooklyn; its orientation was socialist-progressive, with a smarmy pedagogical under-pinning of warmed-over Marxism and Freudianism and John

Deweyism, and the psychiatrist, a specialist in the disturbances of middle-class children, paid a call every Wednesday afternoon to peer into the soul of the current problem child. Now it was David's turn. His parents gave their consent, of course. They were deeply concerned about his behavior. Everyone agreed that he was a brilliant child: he was extraordinarily precocious, with a reading-comprehension score on the twelve-year-old level, and adults found him almost frighteningly bright. But he was uncontrollable in class, raucous, disrespectful; the schoolwork, hopelessly elementary for him, bored him to desperation; his only friends were the class misfits, whom he persecuted cruelly; most of the children hated him and the teachers feared his unpredictability. One day he had up-ended a hallway fire extinguisher simply to see if it would spray foam as promised. It did. He brought garter snakes to school and let them loose in the auditorium. He mimed classmates and even teachers with vicious accuracy. "Dr. Hittner would just like to have a little chat with you," his mother told him. "He's heard you're a very special boy and he'd like to get to know you better." David resisted, kicking up a great fuss over the psychiatrist's name. "Hitler? Hitler? I don't want to talk to Hitler!" It was the fall of 1942 and the childish pun was an inevitable one, but he clung to it with irritating stubbornness. "Dr. Hitler wants to see me. Dr. Hitler wants to get to know me." And his mother said. "No, Duvid, it's *Hittner, Hittner,* with an *n*." He went anyway. He strutted into the psychiatrist's office, and when Dr. Hittner smiled benignly and said, "Hello, there, David," David shot forth a stiff arm and snapped: *"Heil!"*

Dr. Hittner chuckled. "You've got the wrong man," he said. "I'm *Hittner,* with an *n*." Perhaps he had heard such jokes before. He was a huge man with a long horsey face, a wide fleshy mouth, a high curving forehead. Watery blue eyes twinkled behind rimless glasses. His skin was soft and pink and he had a good tangy smell, and he was trying hard to seem friendly and amused and big-brotherly, but David couldn't help picking up the impression that Dr. Hittner's brotherliness was just an act. It was something he felt with most adults: they smiled a lot, but inside themselves they were thinking things like, *What a scary brat, what a creepy little kid.* Even his mother and father sometimes thought things like that. He didn't understand why adults said one thing with their faces and another with their minds, but he was accustomed to it. It was something he had come to expect and accept.

"Let's play some games, shall we?" Dr. Hittner said.

Out of the vest pocket of his tweed suit he produced a little plastic globe on a metal chain. He showed it to David; then he pulled on the chain and the globe came apart into eight or nine pieces of different colors. "Watch closely, now, while I put it back together," said Dr. Hittner. His thick fingers expertly reassembled the globe. Then he pulled it apart again and shoved it across the desk toward David. "Your turn. Can you put it back together too?"

David remembered that the doctor had started by taking the E-shaped white piece and fitting the D-shaped blue piece into one of its grooves. Then had come the yellow piece, but David didn't recall what to do with it; he sat there a moment, puzzled, until Dr. Hittner obligingly flashed him a mental image of the proper manipulation. David did it and the rest was easy. A couple of times he got stuck, but he was always able to pull the answer out of the doctor's mind. Why does he think he's testing me, David wondered, if he keeps giving me so many hints? What's he proving? When the globe was intact David handed it back. "Would you like to keep it?" Dr. Hittner asked.

"I don't need it," David said. But he pocketed it anyway.

They played a few more games. There was one with little cards about the size of playing cards, with drawings of animals and birds and trees and houses on them; David was supposed to arrange them so that they told a story, and then tell the doctor what the story was. He scattered them at random on the desk and made up a story as he went along. "The duck goes into the forest, you see, and he meets a wolf, so he turns into a frog and jumps over the wolf right into the elephant's mouth, only he escapes out of the elephant's tushie and falls into a lake, and when he comes out he sees the pretty princess here, who says come home and I'll give you gingerbread, but he can read her mind and he sees that she's really a wicked witch, who—" Another game involved slips of paper that had big blue ink-blots on them. "Do any of these shapes remind you of real things?" the doctor asked. "Yes," David said, "this is an elephant, see, his tail is here and here all crumpled up, and this is his tushie, and this is where he makes pee-pee." He had already discovered that Dr. Hittner

became very interested when he talked about tushies or
pee-pee, so he gave the doctor plenty to be interested about,
finding such things in every ink-blot picture. This seemed a
very silly game to David, but apparently it was important to
Dr. Hittner, who scribbled notes on everything David was
saying. David studied Dr. Hittner's mind while the psychiatrist wrote things down. Most of the words he picked up were
incomprehensible, but he did recognize a few, the grown-up
terms for the parts of the body that David's mother had
taught him: *penis, vulva, buttocks, rectum,* things like
that. Obviously Dr. Hittner liked those words a great
deal, so David began to use them. "This is a picture of an
eagle that's picking up a little sheep and flying away with
it. This is the eagle's penis, down here, and over here is
the sheep's rectum. And in the next one there's a man and
a woman, and they're both naked, and the man is trying to
put his penis inside the woman's vulva only it won't fit,
and—" David watched the fountain pen flying over the
paper. He grinned at Dr. Hittner and turned to the next
ink-blot.

Next they played word games. The doctor spoke a word
and asked David to say the first word that came into his head.
David found it more amusing to say the first word that came
into Dr. Hittner's head. It took only a fraction of a second to
pick it up, and Dr. Hittner didn't seem to notice what was
going on. The game went like this:

"Father."
"Penis."
"Mother."
"Bed."
"Baby."
"Dead."
"Water."
"Belly."
"Tunnel."
"Shovel."
"Coffin."
"Mother."

Were those the right words to say? Who was the winner in
this game? Why did Dr. Hittner seem so upset?

Finally they stopped playing games and simply talked.
"You're a very bright little boy," Dr. Hittner said. "I don't
have to worry about spoiling you by telling you that, because

you know it already. What do you want to be when you grow up?"

"Nothing."

"*Nothing?*"

"I just want to play and read a lot of books and swim."

"But how will you earn a living?"

"I'll get money from people when I need it."

"If you find out how, I hope you'll tell me the secret," the doctor said. "Are you happy here in school?"

"No."

"Why not?"

"The teachers are too strict. The work is too dumb. The children don't like me."

"Do you ever wonder why they don't like you?"

"Because I'm smarter than they are," David said. "Because I—" Ooops. Almost said it. *Because I can see what they're thinking.* Mustn't ever tell anyone that. Dr. Hittner was waiting for him to finish the sentence. "Because I make a lot of trouble in class."

"And why do you do that, David?"

"I don't know. It gives me something to do, I guess."

"Maybe if you didn't make so much trouble, people would like you more. Don't you want people to like you?"

"I don't care. I don't need it."

"Everybody needs friends, David."

"I've got friends."

"Mrs. Fleischer says you don't have very many, and that you hit them a lot and make them unhappy. Why do you hit your friends?"

"Because I don't like them. Because they're dumb."

"Then they aren't really friends, if that's how you feel about them."

Shrugging, David said, "I can get along without them. I have fun just being by myself."

"Are you happy at home?"

"I guess so."

"You love your mommy and daddy?"

A pause. A feeling of great tension coming out of the doctor's mind. This is an important question. Give the right answer, David. Give him the answer he wants.

"Yes," David said.

"Do you ever wish you had a baby brother or sister?"

No hesitation now. "No."

"Really, no? You like being all alone?"

David nodded. "The afternoons are the best time. When I'm home from school and there's nobody around. Am I going to have a baby brother or sister?"

Chuckles from the doctor. "I'm sure I don't know. That would be up to your mommy and daddy, wouldn't it?"

"You won't tell them to get one for me, will you? I mean, you might say to them that it would be good for me to have one, and then they'd go and get one, but I really don't want—" I'm in trouble, David realized suddenly.

"What makes you think I'd tell your parents it would be good for you to have a baby brother or sister?" the doctor asked quietly, not smiling now at all.

"I don't know. It was just an idea." Which I found inside your head, doctor. And now I want to get out of here. I don't want to talk to you any more. "Hey, your name isn't really Hittner, is it? With an *n*? I bet I know your real name. *Heil!*"

Three

I never could send my thoughts into anybody else's head. Even when the power was strongest in me, I couldn't transmit. I could only receive. Maybe there are people around who do have that power, who can transmit thoughts even to those who don't have any special receiving gift, but I wasn't ever one of them. So right there I was condemned to be society's ugliest toad, the eavesdropper, the voyeur. Old English proverb: *He who peeps through a hole may see what will vex him.* Yes. In those years when I was particularly eager to communicate with people, I'd work up fearful sweats trying to plant my thoughts in them. I'd sit in a classroom staring at the back of some girl's head, and I'd think hard at her: *Hello, Annie, this is David Selig calling, do you read me? Do you read me? I love you, Annie. Over. Over and out.* But Annie never read me, and the currents of her mind would roll on like a placid river, undisturbed by the existence of David Selig.

No way, then, for me to speak to other minds, only to spy on them. The way the power manifests itself in me has always been highly variable. I never had much conscious control over it, other than being able to stop down the intensity of input and to do a certain amount of fine tuning; basically I had to take whatever came drifting in. Most often I would pick up a person's surface thoughts, his subvocalizations of the things he's just about to say. These would come to me in a clear conversational manner, exactly as though he *had* said them, except the tone of voice was different, it was plainly not a tone produced by the vocal apparatus. I don't remember any period even in my childhood when I confused spoken communication with mental communication. This ability to read surface thoughts has been fairly consistent throughout: I still can anticipate verbal statements more often than not, especially when I'm with someone who has the habit of rehearsing what he intends to say.

I could also and to some extent still can anticipate immediate intentions, such as the decision to throw a short right jab to the jaw. My way of knowing such things varies. I might pick up a coherent inner verbal statement—*I'm now going to throw a short right jab to his jaw*—or, if the power happens to be working on deeper levels that day, I may simply pick up a series of non-verbal instructions to the muscles, which add up in a fraction of a second to the process of bringing the right arm up for a short jab to the jaw. Call it body language on the telepathic wavelength.

Another thing I've been able to do, though never consistently, is tune in to the deepest layers of the mind—where the soul lives, if you will. Where the consciousness lies bathed in a murky soup of indistinct unconscious phenomena. Here lurk hopes, fears, perceptions, purposes, passions, memories, philosophical positions, moral policies, hungers, sorrows, the whole ragbag accumulation of events and attitudes that defines the private self. Ordinarily some of this bleeds through to me even when the most superficial mental contact is established: I can't help getting a certain amount of information about the coloration of the soul. But occasionally—hardly ever, now—I fasten my hooks into the real stuff, the whole person. There's ecstasy in that. There's an electrifying sense of contact. Coupled, of course, with a stabbing, numbing sense of guilt, because of the totality of my voyeurism: how much more of a peeping tom can a person be? Incidentally, the soul speaks a universal language. When I look into the mind of Mrs. Esperanza Dominguez, say, and I get a gabble of Spanish out of it, I don't really know what she's thinking, because I don't understand very much Spanish. But if I were to get into the depths of her soul I'd have complete comprehension of anything I picked up. The mind may think in Spanish or Basque or Hungarian or Finnish, but the soul thinks in a languageless language accessible to any prying sneaking freak who comes along to peer at its mysteries.

No matter. It's all going from me now.

Four

Paul F. Bruno
Comp Lit 18, Prof. Schmitz
October 15, 1976

The Novels of Kafka

In the nightmare world of *The Trial* and *The Castle*, only one thing is certain: that the central figure, significantly known by the initial K, is doomed to frustration. All else is dreamlike and unsure; courtrooms spring up in tenements, mysterious warders devour one's breakfast, a man thought to be Sordini is actually Sortini. The central fact is certain, though: K will fail in his attempt to attain grace.

The two novels have the same theme and approximately the same basic structure. In both, K seeks for grace and is led to the final realization that it is to be withheld from him. (*The Castle* is unfinished, but its conclusion seems plain.) Kafka brings his heroes into involvement with their situations in opposite ways: in *The Trial*, Joseph K. is passive until he is jolted into the action of the book by the unexpected arrival of the two warders; in *The Castle*, K is first shown as an active character making efforts on his own behalf to reach the mysterious Castle. To be sure, though, he has originally been summoned by the Castle; the action did not originate in himself, and thus he began as as passive a character as Joseph K. The distinction is that *The*

Trial opens at a point earlier in the time-stream of the action—at the earliest possible point, in fact. *The Castle* follows more closely the ancient rule of beginning in *medias res*, with K already summoned and trying to reach the Castle.

Both books get off to rapid starts. Joseph K. is arrested in the very first sentence of *The Trial*, and his counterpart K arrives at what he thinks is going to be the last stop before the Castle on the first page of that novel. From there, both K's struggle futilely toward their goals (in *The Castle*, simply to get to the top of the hill; in *The Trial*, first to understand the nature of his guilt, and then, despairing of this, to achieve acquittal without understanding). Both actually get farther from their goals with each succeeding action. *The Trial* reaches its peak in the wonderful Cathedral scene, quite likely the most terrifying single sequence in any of Kafka's work, in which K is given to realize that he is guilty and can never be acquitted; the chapter that follows, describing K's execution, is little more than an anticlimactic appendage. *The Castle*, less complete than *The Trial*, lacks the counterpart of the Cathedral scene (perhaps Kafka was unable to devise one?) and thus is artistically less satisfying than the shorter, more intense, more tightly constructed *Trial*.

Despite their surface artlessness, both novels appear to be built on the fundamental threepart structure of the tragic rhythm, labeled by the critic Kenneth Burke as "purpose, passion, perception." *The Trial* follows this scheme with greater success than does the incomplete *Castle;* the purpose, to achieve acquittal, is demonstrated through as harrowing a passion as any fictional hero has undergone. Finally, when Joseph K. has been reduced from his original defiant, self-confident attitude to a fearful, timid state of mind, and he is obviously ready to capitulate to the forces of the Court, the time is at hand for the final moment of perception.

The agent used to bring him to the scene of the climax is a classically Kafkaesque figure—the mysterious "Italian colleague who was on his first visit to the town and had influential connexions that made him important to the Bank." The theme that runs through all of Kafka's work, the impossibility of human communication, is repeated here: though Joseph has spent half the night studying

Italian in preparation for the visit, and is half asleep in
consequence, the stranger speaks an unknown southern
dialect which Joseph cannot understand. Then—a crown-
ing comic touch—the stranger shifts to French, but his
French is just as difficult to follow, and his bushy mustache
foils Joseph's attempts at lip-reading.

Once he reaches the Cathedral, which he has been
asked to show to the Italian (who, as we are not surprised
to find, never keeps the date), the tension mounts. Joseph
wanders through the building, which is empty, dark, cold,
lit only by candles flickering far in the distance, while night
inexplicably begins fast to fall outside. Then the priest calls
to him, and relates the allegory of the Doorkeeper. It is
only when the story is ended that we realize we did not at
all understand it; far from being the simple tale it had
originally seemed to be, it reveals itself as complex and
difficult. Joseph and the priest discuss the story at great
length, in the manner of a pair of rabbinical scholars
disputing a point in the Talmud. Slowly its implications
sink in, and we and Joseph see that the light streaming
from the door to the Law will not be visible for him until it
is too late.

Structurally the novel is over right here. Joseph has
received the final perception that acquittal is impossible;
his guilt is established, and he is not yet to receive grace.
His quest is ended. The final element of the tragic rhythm,
the perception that ends the passion, has been reached.

We know that Kafka planned further chapters showing
the progress of Joseph's trial through various later stages,
ending in his execution. Kafka's biographer Max Brod says
the book could have been prolonged infinitely. This is true,
of course, it is inherent in the nature of Joseph K.'s guilt
that he could never get to the highest Court, just as the
other K could wander for all time without ever reaching
the Castle. But structurally the novel ends in the Cathedral; the rest of what Kafka intended would not have added
anything essential to Joseph's self-knowledge. The Cathedral scene shows us what we have known since page one:
that there is no acquittal. The action concludes with that
perception.

The Castle, a much longer and more loosely constructed
book, lacks the power of *The Trial*. It rambles. The passion
of K is much less clearly defined, and K is a less consistent

character, not as interesting psychologically as he is in *The Trial*. Whereas in the earlier book he takes active charge of his case as soon as he realizes his danger, in *The Castle* he quickly becomes the victim of the bureaucracy. The transit of character in *The Trial* is from early passivity to activity back to passive resignation after the epiphany in the Cathedral. In *The Castle* K undergoes no such clearcut changes; he is an active character as the novel opens, but soon is lost in the nightmare maze of the village below the Castle, and sinks deeper and deeper into degradation. Joseph K. is almost an heroic character, while K of *The Castle* is merely a pathetic one.

The two books represent varying attempts at telling the same story, that of the existentially disengaged man who is suddenly involved in a situation from which there is no escape, and who, after making attempts to achieve the grace that will release him from his predicament, succumbs. As they exist today, *The Trial* is unquestionably the greater artistic success, firmly constructed and at all times under the author's technical control. *The Castle*, or rather the fragment of it we have, is potentially the greater novel, however. Everything that was in *The Trial* would have been in *The Castle*, and a great deal more. But, one feels, Kafka abandoned work on *The Castle* because he saw he lacked the resources to carry it through. He could not handle the world of the Castle, with its sweeping background of Brueghelesque country life, with the same assurance as he did the urban world of *The Trial*. And there is a lack of urgency in *The Castle;* we are never too concerned over K's doom because it is inevitable; Joseph K., though, is fighting more tangible forces, and until the end we have the illusion that victory is possible for him. *The Castle*, also, is too ponderous. Like a Mahler symphony, it collapses of its own weight. One wonders if Kafka had in mind some structure enabling him to end *The Castle*. Perhaps he never intended to close the novel at all, but meant to have K wander in ever-widening circles, never arriving at the tragic perception that he can never reach the Castle. Perhaps this is the reason for the comparative formlessness of the later work: Kafka's discovery that the true tragedy of K, his archetypical hero-as-victim figure, lies not in his final perception of the impossibility of attaining grace, but in the fact that he will never reach even as much as that

final perception. Here we have the tragic rhythm, a structure found throughout literature, truncated to depict more
pointedly the contemporary human condition—a condition
so abhorrent to Kafka. Joseph K., who actually reaches a
form of grace, thereby attains true tragic stature; K, who
simply sinks lower and lower, might symbolize for Kafka
the con-temporary individual, so crushed by the general
tragedy of the times that he is incapable of any tragedy on
an individual level. K is a pathetic figure, Joseph K. a
tragic one. Joseph K. is a more interesting character, but
perhaps it was K whom Kafka understood more deeply.
And for K's story no ending is possible, perhaps, save the
pointless one of death.

That's not so bad. Six double-spaced typed pages. At $3.50
per, it earns me a cool $21 for less than two hours' work, and
it'll earn the brawny halfback, Mr. Paul F. Bruno, a sure B+
from Prof. Schmitz. I'm confident of that because the very
same paper, differing only in a few minor stylistic flourishes,
got me a B from the very demanding Prof. Dupee in May,
1955. Standards are lower today, after two decades of academic
inflation. Bruno may even rack up an A – for the Kafka job.
It's got just the right quality of earnest intelligence, with the
proper undergraduate mixture of sophisticated insight and
naive dogmatism, and Dupee found the writing "clear and
forceful" in '55, according to his note in the margin. All right,
now. Time out for a little chow mein, with maybe a side order
of eggroll. Then I'll tackle *Odysseus as a Symbol of Society* or
perhaps *Aeschylus and the Aristotelian Tragedy*. I can't work
from my own old term papers for those, but they shouldn't be
too tough to do. Old typewriter, old humbugger, stand me
now and ever in good stead.

Five

Aldous Huxley thought that evolution has designed our brains
to serve as filters, screening out a lot of stuff that's of no real
value to us in our daily struggle for bread. Visions, mystical

experiences, psi phenomena such as telepathic messages from other brains—all sorts of things along these lines would forever be flooding into us were it not for the action of what Huxley called, in a little book entitled *Heaven and Hell*, "the cerebral reducing valve." Thank God for the cerebral reducing valve! If we hadn't evolved it, we'd be distracted all the time by scenes of incredible beauty, by spiritual insights of overwhelming grandeur, and by searing, utterly honest mind-to-mind contact with our fellow human beings. Luckily, the workings of the valve protect us—most of us—from such things, and we are free to go about our daily lives, buying cheap and selling dear.

Of course, some of us seem to be born with defective valves. I mean the artists like Besch or El Greco, whose eyes did not see the world as it appears to thee and me; I mean the visionary philosophers, the ecstatics and the nirvana-attainers; I mean the miserable freakish flukes who can read the thoughts of others. Mutants, all of us. Genetic sports.

However, Huxley believed that the efficiency of the cerebral reducing valve could be impaired by various artificial means, thus giving ordinary mortals access to the extrasensory data customarily seen only by the chosen few. The psychedelic drugs, he thought, have this effect. Mescaline, he suggested, interferes with the enzyme system that regulates cerebral function, and by so doing "lowers the efficiency of the brain as an instrument for focusing mind on the problems of life on the surface of our planet. This . . . seems to permit the entry into consciousness of certain classes of mental events, which are normally excluded, because they possess no survival value. Similar intrusions of biologically useless, but aesthetically and sometimes spiritually valuable, material may occur as the result of illness or fatigue; or they may be induced by fasting, or a period of confinement in a place of darkness and complete silence."

Speaking for himself, David Selig can say very little about the psychedelic drugs. He had only one experience with them, and it wasn't a happy one. That was in the summer of 1968, when he was living with Toni.

Though Huxley thought highly of the psychedelics, he didn't see them as the only gateway to visionary experience. Fasting and physical mortification could get you there also. He wrote of mystics who "regularly used upon themselves the whip of knotted leather or even of iron wire. These beatings were the equivalent of fairly extensive surgery without anaesthetics, and their effects on the body chemistry of the penitent were considerable. Large quantities of histamine and adrenalin were released while the whip was actually being plied; and when the resulting wounds began to fester (as wounds practically always did before the age of soap), various toxic substances, produced by the decomposition of protein, found their way into the bloodstream. But histamine produces shock, and shock affects the mind no less profoundly than the body. Moreover, large quantities of adrenalin may cause hallucinations, and some of the products of its decomposition are known to induce symptoms resembling those of schizophrenia. As for toxins from wounds—these upset the enzyme systems regulating the brain, and lower its efficiency as an instrument for getting on in a world where the biologically fittest survive. This may explain why the Curé d'Ars used to say that, in the days when he was free to flagellate himself without mercy, God would refuse him nothing. In other words, when remorse, self-loathing, and the fear of hell release adrenalin, when self-inflicted surgery releases adrenalin and histamine, and when infected wounds release decomposed protein into the blood, the efficiency of the cerebral reducing valve is lowered and unfamiliar aspects of Mind-at-Large (including psi phenomena, visions, and, if he is philosophically and ethically prepared for it, mystical experiences) will flow into the ascetic's consciousness.

Remorse, self-loathing, and the fear of hell. Fasting and prayer. Whips and chains. Festering wounds. Everybody to his own trip, I suppose, and welcome to it. As the power fades in me, as the sacred gift dies, I toy with the idea of trying to revive it by artificial means. Acid, mescaline, psilocybin? I don't think I'd care to go there again. Mortification of the flesh? That seems obsolete to me, like marching off to the Crusades or wearing spats: something that simply isn't appropriate for 1976. I doubt that I could get very deep into flagellation, anyway. What does that leave? Fasting and prayer? I could fast, I suppose. Prayer? To whom? To what? I'd feel like a fool. Dear God, give me my power again. Dear Moses, please help me. Crap on that. Jews don't pray for favors, because they know nobody will answer. What's left, then? Remorse, self-loathing, and the fear of hell? I have those three already, and they do me no good. We must try some other way of goading the power back to life. Invent something new. Flagellation of the mind, perhaps? Yes. I'll try that. I'll get out the metaphorical cudgels and let myself have it. Flagellation of the aching, weakening, throbbing, dissolving mind. The treacherous, hateful mind.

Six

But why does David Selig want his power to come back? Why not let it fade? It's always been a curse to him, hasn't it? It's cut him off from his fellow men and doomed him to a loveless life. Leave well enough alone, Duvid. Let it fade. Let it fade. On the other hand, without the power, what are you? Without that one faltering unpredictable unsatisfactory means of contact with them, how will you be able to touch them at all? Your power joins you to mankind, for better or for worse, in the only joining you have: you can't bear to surrender it. Admit it. You love it and you despise it, this gift of yours. You dread losing it despite all it's done to you. You'll fight to cling to the last shreds of it, even though you know the struggle's hopeless. Fight on, then. Read Huxley again. Try acid, if you dare. Try flagellation. Try fasting, at least. All right, fasting. I'll skip the chow mein. I'll skip the eggroll. Let's slide a fresh sheet into the typewriter and think about Odysseus as a symbol of society.

Seven

Hark to the silvery jangle of the telephone. The hour is late. Who calls? Is it Aldous Huxley from beyond the grave, urging me to have courage? Dr. Hittner, with some important questions about making pee-pee? Toni, to tell me she's in the neighborhood with a thousand mikes of dynamite acid and is it okay to come up? Sure. Sure. I stare at the telephone, clueless. My power even at its height was never equal to the task of penetrating the consciousness of the American Telephone & Telegraph Company. Sighing, I pick up the receiver on the fifth ring and hear the sweet contralto voice of my sister Judith.

"Am I interrupting something?" Typical Judith opening.

"A quiet night at home. I'm ghosting a term paper on *The Odyssey*. Got any bright ideas for me, Jude?"

"You haven't called in two weeks."

"I was broke. After that scene the last time I didn't want to bring up the subject of money, and lately it's been the only subject I can think of talking about, so I didn't call."

"Shit," she says, "I wasn't angry at you."

"You sounded mad as hell."

"I didn't mean any of that stuff. Why did you think I was serious? Just because I was yelling? Do you really believe that I regard you as—as—what did I call you?"

"A shiftless sponger, I think."

"A shiftless sponger. Shit. I was tense that night, Duv; I had personal problems, and my period was coming on besides. I lost control. I was just shouting the first dumb crap that came into my head, but why did you believe I meant it? You of all people shouldn't have thought I was serious. Since when do you take what people say with their mouths at face value?"

"You were saying it with your head too, Jude."

"I was?" Her voice is suddenly small and contrite. "Are you sure?"

"It came through loud and clear."

"Oh, Jesus, Duv, have a heart! In the heat of the moment I could have been thinking anything. But underneath the anger—*underneath*, Ðuv—you must have seen that I didn't mean it. That I love you, that I don't want to drive you away from me. You're all I've got, Duv, you and the baby."

Her love is unpalatable to me, and her sentimentalism is even less to my taste. I say, "I don't read much of what's underneath any more, Jude. Not much comes through these days. Anyway, look, it isn't worth hassling over. I *am* a shiftless sponger, and I *have* borrowed more from you than you can afford to give. The black sheep big brother feels enough guilt as it is. I'm damned if I'm ever going to ask for money from you again."

"Guilt? You talk about guilt, when I—"

"No," I warn her, "don't you go on a guilt trip now, Jude. Not now." Her remorse for her past coldness toward me has a flavor even more stinking than her newfound love. "I don't feel up to assigning the ratio of blames and guilts tonight."

"All right. All right. Are you okay now for money, though?"

"I told you, I'm ghosting term papers. I'm getting by."

"Do you want to come over here for dinner tomorrow night?"

"I think I'd better work instead. I've got a lot of papers to write, Jude. It's the busy season."

"It would be just the two of us. And the kid, of course, but I'll put him to sleep early. Just you and me. We could talk. We've got so much to talk about. Why don't you come over, Duv? You don't need to work all day and all night. I'll cook up something you like. I'll do the spaghetti and hot sauce. Anything. You name it." She is pleading with me, this icy sister who gave me nothing but hatred for twenty-five years. Come over and I'll be a mama for you, Duv. Come let me be loving, brother.

"Maybe the night after next. I'll call you."

"No chance for tomorrow?"

"I don't think so," I say. There is silence. She doesn't want to beg me. Into the sudden screeching silence I say, "What have you been doing with yourself, Judith? Seeing anyone interesting?"

"Not seeing anyone at all." A flinty edge to her voice. She is two and half years into her divorce; she sleeps around a good deal; juices are souring in her soul. She is 31 years old. "I'm between men right now. Maybe I'm off men altogether. I don't care if I never do any screwing again ever."

I throttle a somber laugh. "What happened to that travel agent you were seeing? Mickey?"

"Marty. That was just a gimmick. He got me all over Europe for 10% of the fare. Otherwise I couldn't have afforded to go. I was using him."

"So?"

"I felt shitty about it. Last month I broke off. I wasn't in love with him. I don't think I even liked him."

"But you played around with him long enough to get a trip to Europe, first."

"It didn't cost *him* anything, Duv. I had to go to bed with him; all he had to do was fill out a form. What are you saying, anyway? That I'm a whore?"

"Jude—"

"Okay, I'm a whore. At least I'm trying to go straight for a while. Lots of fresh orange juice and plenty of serious reading. I'm reading Proust now, would you believe that? I just finished *Swann's Way* and tomorrow—"

"I've still got some work to do tonight, Jude."

"I'm sorry. I didn't mean to intrude. Will you come for dinner this week?"

"I'll think about it. I'll let you know."

"Why do you hate me so much, Duv?"

"I don't hate you. And we were about to get off the phone, I think."

"Don't forget to call," she says. Clutching at straws.

Eight

Toni. I should tell you about Toni now.

I lived with Toni for seven weeks, one summer eight years ago. That's as long as I've ever lived with anybody, except my parents and my sister, whom I got away from as soon as I decently could, and myself, whom I can't get away from at all. Toni was one of the two great loves of my life, the other being Kitty. I'll tell you about Kitty some other time.

Can I reconstruct Toni? Let's try it in a few swift strokes. She was 24 that year. A tall coltish girl, five feet six, five feet seven. Slender. Agile and awkward, both at once. Long legs, long arms, thin wrists, thin ankles. Glossy black hair, very straight, cascading to her shoulders. Warm, quick brown eyes, alert and quizzical. A witty, shrewd girl, not really well educated but extraordinarily wise. The face by no means conventionally pretty—too much mouth, too much nose, the cheekbones too high—but yet producing a sexy and highly attractive effect, sufficient to make a lot of heads turn when she enters a room. Full, heavy breasts. I dig busty women: I often need a soft place to rest my tired head. So often so tired. My mother was built 32-A, no cozy pillows there. She couldn't have nursed me if she'd wanted to, which she didn't. (Will I ever forgive her for letting me escape from the womb? Ah, now, Selig, show some filial piety, for God's sake!)

I never looked into Toni's mind except twice, once on the day I met her and once a couple of weeks after that, plus a third time on the day we broke up. The third time was a sheer disastrous accident. The second was more or less an accident too, not quite. Only the first was a deliberate probe. After I realized I loved her I took care never to spy on her head. *He who peeps through a hole may see what will vex him.* A lesson I learned very young. Besides, I didn't want Toni to suspect anything about my power. My curse. I was afraid it might frighten her away.

That summer I was working as an $85-a-week researcher, latest in my infinite series of odd jobs, for a well-known professional writer who was doing an immense book on the political machinations involved in the founding of the State of Israel. Eight hours a day I went through old newspaper files for him in the bowels of the Col ia library. Toni was a junior editor for the publishing house that was bringing out his book. I met her one afternoon in late spring at his posh apartment on East End Avenue. I went over there to deliver a bundle of notes on Harry Truman's 1948 campaign speeches and she happened to be there, discussing some cuts to be made in the early chapters. Her beauty stung me. I hadn't been with a woman in months. I automatically assumed she was the writer's mistress—screwing editors, I'm told, is standard practice on certain high levels of the literary profession—but my old peeping-tom instincts quickly gave me the true scoop. I tossed a fast probe at him and found that his mind was a cesspool of frustrated longings for her. He ached for her and she had no yen for him at all, evidently. Next I poked into *her* mind. I sank in, deep, finding myself in warm, rich loam. Quickly got oriented. Stray fragments of autobiography bombarded me, incoherent, non-linear: a divorce, some good sex and some bad sex, college days, a trip to the Caribbean, all swimming around in the usual chaotic way. I got past that fast and checked out what I was after. No, she wasn't sleeping with the writer. Physically he registered absolute zero for her. (Odd. To me he seemed attractive, a romantic and appealing figure, so far as a drearily heterosexual soul like me is able to judge such things.) She didn't even like his writing, I learned. Then, still rummaging around, I learned something else, much more surprising: *I* seemed to be turning her on. Forth from her came the explicit line: *I wonder if he's free tonight*. She looked upon the aging researcher, a venerable 33 and already going thin on top, and did not find him repellent. I was so shaken by that—her dark-eyed glamour, her leggy sexiness, aimed at *me*—that I got the hell out of her head, fast. "Here's the Truman stuff," I said to my employer. "There's more coming in from the Truman Library in Missouri." We talked a few minutes about the next assignment he had for me, and then I made as though to leave. A quick guarded look at her.

"Wait," she said. "We can ride down together. I'm just about done here."

The man of letters shot me a poisonous envious glance. Oh, God, fired again. But he bade us both civil goodbyes. In the elevator going down we stood apart. Toni in this corner, I in that one, with a quivering wall of tension and yearning separating and uniting us. I had to struggle to keep from reading her; I was afraid, terrified, not of getting the wrong answer but of getting the right one. In the street we stood apart also, dithering a moment. Finally I said I was getting a cab to take me to the Upper West Side—me, a cab, on $85 a week!—and could I drop her off anywhere? She said she lived on 105th and West End. Close enough. When the cab stopped outside her place she invited me up for a drink. Three rooms, indifferently furnished: mostly books, records, scatter-rugs, posters. She went to pour some wine for us and I caught her and pulled her around and kissed her. She trembled against me, or was I the one who was trembling?

Over a bowl of hot-and-sour soup at the Great Shanghai, a little later that evening, she said she'd be moving in a couple of days. The apartment belonged to her current roommate—male—with whom she'd split up just three days before. She had no place to stay. "I've got only one lousy room," I said, "but it has a double bed." Shy grins, hers, mine. So she moved in. I didn't think she was in love with me, not at all, but I wasn't going to ask. If what she felt for me wasn't love, it was good enough, the best I could hope for; and in the privacy of my own head I could feel love for her. She had needed a port in a storm. I had happened to offer one. If that

was all I meant to her now, so be it. So be it. There was time
for things to ripen.

We slept very little, our first two weeks. Not that we were
screwing all the time, though there was a lot of that; but we
talked. We were new to each other, which is the best time of
any relationship, when there are whole pasts to share, when
everything pours out and there's no need to search for things
to say. (Not quite everything poured out. The only thing I
concealed from her was the central fact of my life, the fact
that had shaped my every aspect.) She talked of her marriage—
young, at 20, and brief, and empty—and of how she had lived
in the three years since its ending—a succession of men, a
dip into occultism and Reichian therapy, a newfound dedication to her editing career. Giddy weeks.

* * *

Then, our third week. My second peep into her mind. A
sweltering June night, with a full moon sending cold illumination through the slatted blinds into our room. She was
sitting astride me—her favorite position—and her body, very
pale, wore a white glow in the eerie darkness. Her long lean
form rearing far above me. Her face half hidden in her own
dangling unruly hair. Her eyes closed. Her lips slack. Her
breasts, viewed from below, seeming even bigger than they
really were. Cleopatra by moonlight. She was rocking and
jouncing her way to a private ecstasy, and her beauty and the
strangeness of her so overwhelmed me that I could not resist
watching her at the moment of climax, watching on all levels,
and so I opened the barrier that I had so scrupulously
erected, and, just as she was coming, my mind touched a
curious finger to her soul and received the full uprushing
volcanic intensity of her pleasure. I found no thought of me
in her mind. Only sheer animal frenzy, bursting from every
nerve. I've seen that in other women, before and after Toni,
as they come: they are islands, alone in the void of space,
aware only of their bodies and perhaps of that intrusive rigid
rod against which they thrust. When pleasure takes them it is
a curiously impersonal phenomenon, no matter how titanic
its impact. So it was then with Toni. I didn't object; I knew
what to expect and I didn't feel cheated or rejected. In fact
my joining of souls with her at that awesome moment served
to trigger my own coming and to treble its intensity. I lost

contact with her then. The upheavals of orgasm shatter the fragile telepathic link. Afterwards I felt a little sleazy at having spied, but not overly guilty about it. How magical a thing it was, after all, to have been with her in that moment. To be aware of her joy not just as mindless spasms of her loins but as jolts of brilliant light flaring across the dark terrain of her soul. An instant of beauty and wonder, an illumination never to be forgotten. But never to be repeated, either. I resolved, once more, to keep our relationship clean and honest. To take no unfair advantage of her. To stay out of her head forever after.

* * *

Despite which, I found myself some weeks later entering Toni's consciousness a third time. By accident. By damnable abominable accident. Oy, that third time!

That bummer—that disaster—

That catastrophe—

Nine

In the early spring of 1945, when he was ten years old, his loving mother and father got him a little sister. That was exactly how they phrased it: his mother, smiling her warmest phony smile, hugging him, telling him in her best this-is-how-we-talk-to-bright-children tone, "Dad and I have a wonderful surprise for you, David. We're going to get a little sister for you."

It was no surprise, of course. They had been discussing it among themselves for months, maybe for years, always making the fallacious assumption that their son, clever as he was, didn't understand what they were talking about. Thinking that he was unable to associate one fragment of conversation with another, that he was incapable of putting the proper antecedents to their deliberately vague pronouns, their torrent of "it" and "him." And, naturally, he had been reading their minds. In those days the power was sharp and clear; lying in his bedroom, surrounded by his dog-eared books and his stamp albums, he could effortlessly tune in on everything that went on behind the closed door of theirs, fifty feet away. It was like an endless radio broadcast without commercials. He could listen to WJZ, WHN, WEAF, WOR, all the stations on the dial, but the one he listened to most was WPMS, Paul-and-Martha-Selig. They had no secrets from him. He had no shame about spying. Preternaturally adult, privy to all their privities, he meditated daily on the raw torrid stuff of married life: the financial anxieties, the moments of sweet undifferentiated lovingness, the moments of guiltily suppressed hatred for the wearisome eternal spouse, the copulatory joys and anguishes, the comings together and the fallings apart, the mysteries of failed orgasms and wilted erections, the intense and terrifyingly singleminded concentration on the growth and proper development of The Child. Their minds poured forth a steady stream of rich yeasty foam and he lapped it all up. Reading their souls was his game, his toy, his religion, his revenge. They never suspected he was doing it. That was one point on which he constantly sought reassurance, anxiously prying for it, and constantly he was reassured: they didn't dream his gift existed. They merely thought he was abnormally intelligent, and never questioned the means by which he learned so much about so many improbable things. Perhaps if they had realized the truth, they would have choked him in his crib. But they had no inkling. He went on comfortably spying, year after year, his perceptions deepening as he came to comprehend more and more of the material his parents unwittingly offered.

He knew that Dr. Hittner—baffled, wholly out of his depth with the strange Selig child—believed it would be better for everyone if David had a sibling. That was the word he used, *sibling*, and David had to fish the meaning out of Hittner's head as though out of a dictionary. Sibling: a brother or a sister. Oh, the treacherous horse-faced bastard! The one thing young David had asked Hittner not to suggest, and naturally he had suggested it. But what else could he have expected? The desirability of siblings had been in Hittner's mind all along, lying there like a grenade. David, picking his mother's mind one night, had found the text of a letter from Hittner. *The only child is an emotionally deprived child. Without the rough-and-tumble interplay with siblings he has no way of learning the best techniques of relating to his peers, and he develops a dangerously burdensome relation with his parents, for whom he becomes a companion instead of a dependent.*

Hittner's universal panacea: lots of siblings. As though there are no neurotics in big families.

David was aware of his parents' frantic attempts at filling Hittner's prescription. No time to waste; the boy grows older all the time, siblingless, lacking each day the means of learning the best techniques of relating to his peers. And so, night after night, the poor aging bodies of Paul and Martha Selig grapple with the problem. They force themselves sweatily onward to self-defeating prodigies of lustfulness, and each month the bad news comes in a rush of blood: there will be no sibling this time. But at last the seed takes root. They said nothing about that to him, ashamed, perhaps, to admit to an eight-year-old that such things as sexual intercourse occurred in their lives. But he knew. He knew why his mother's belly was beginning to bulge and why they still hesitated to explain it to him. He knew, too, that his mother's mysterious "appendicitis" attack of July, 1944, was actually a miscarriage. He knew why they both wore tragic faces for months afterward. He knew that Martha's doctor had told her that autumn that it really wasn't wise for her to be having babies at the age of 35, that if they were going to insist on a second child the best course was to adopt one. He knew his father's traumatic response to that suggestion: *What, bring into the household a bastard that some shiksa threw away?* Poor old Paul lay tossing awake every night for weeks, not even confessing to his wife why he was so upset, but unknowingly spilling the whole thing to his nosy son. The insecurities, the irrational hostilities. *Why do I have to raise a stranger's brat, just because this psychiatrist says it'll do David some good? What kind of garbage will I be taking into the house? How can I love this child that isn't mine? How can I tell it that it's a Jew when—who knows?—it may have been made by some Irish mick, some Italian bootblack, some carpenter?* All this the all-perceiving David perceives. Finally the elder Selig voices his misgivings, carefully edited, to his wife, saying, Maybe Hittner's wrong, maybe this is just a phase David's going through and another child isn't the right answer at all. Telling her to consider the expense, the changes they'd have to make in their way of life—they're not young, they've grown settled in their ways, a child at this time of their lives, the getting up at four in the morning the crying, the diapers. And David silently cheering his father on, because who needs this intruder, this sibling, this enemy of the peace? But

Martha tearfully fights back, quoting Hittner's letter, reading key passages out of her extensive library on child psychology, offering damning statistics on the incidence of neurosis, maladjustment, bed-wetting, and homosexuality among only children. The old man yields by Christmas. *Okay, okay, we'll adopt, but let's not take just anything, hear? It's got to be Jewish.* Wintry weeks of touring the adoption agencies, pretending all the while to David that these trips to Manhattan are mere innocuous shopping excursions. He wasn't fooled. How could anyone fool this omniscient child? He had only to look behind their foreheads to know that they were shopping for a sibling. His one comfort was the hope that they would fail to find one. This was still wartime: if you couldn't buy a new car, maybe you couldn't get siblings either. For many weeks that appeared to be the case. Not many babies were available, and those that were seemed to have some grave defect: insufficiently Jewish, or too fragile-looking, or two cranky, or of the wrong sex. Some boys were available but Paul and Martha had decided to get David a little sister. Already that limited things considerably, since people tended not to give girls up for adoption as readily as they did boys, but one snowy night in March David detected an ominous note of satisfaction in the mind of his mother, newly returned from yet another shopping trip, and, looking more closely, he realized that the quest was over. She had found a lovely little girl, four months old. The mother, aged 19, was not only certifiably Jewish but even a college girl, described by the agency as "extremely intelligent." Not so intelligent, evidently, as to avoid being fertilized by a handsome, young air force captain, also Jewish, while he was home on leave in February, 1944. Though he felt remorse over his carelessness he was unwilling to marry the victim of his lusts, and was now on active duty in the Pacific, where so far as the girl's parents were concerned, he should only be shot down ten times over. They had forced her to give the child out for adoption. David wondered why Martha hadn't brought the baby home with her that very afternoon, but soon he discovered that several weeks of legal formalities lay ahead, and April was well along before his mother finally announced, "Dad and I have a wonderful surprise for you, Duvid."

They named her Judith Hannah Selig, after her adoptive father's recently deceased mother. David hated her instantly. He had been afraid they were going to move her into his bedroom, but no, they set up her crib in their own room; nevertheless, her crying filled the whole apartment night after night, unending raucous wails. It was incredible how much noise she could emit. Paul and Martha spent practically all their time feeding her or playing with her or changing her diapers, and David didn't mind that very much, for it kept them busy and took some of the pressure off him. But he loathed having Judith around. He saw nothing cute about her pudgy limbs and curly hair and dimpled cheeks. Watching her while she was being changed, he found some academic interest in observing her little pink suit, so alien to his experience; but once he had seen it his curiosity was assuaged. *So they have a slit instead of a thing. Okay, but so what?* In general she was an irritating distraction. He couldn't read properly because of the noise she made, and reading was his one pleasure. The apartment was always full of relatives or friends, paying ceremonial vists to the new baby, and their stupid conventional minds flooded the place with blunt thoughts that impinged like mallets on David's vulnerable consciousness. Now and then he tried to read the baby's mind, but there was nothing in it except vague blurry formless globs of cloudy sensation; he had had more rewarding insights reading the minds of dogs and cats. She didn't appear to have any thoughts. All he could pick up were feelings of hunger, of drowsiness, and of dim orgasmic release as she wet her diaper. About ten days after she arrived, he decided to try to kill her telepathically. While his parents were busy elsewhere he went to their room, peered into his sister's bassinet, and concentrated as hard as he could on draining her unformed mind out of her skull. If only he could manage somehow to suck the spark of intellect from her, to draw her consciousness into himself, to transform her into an empty mindless shell, she would surely die. He sought to sink his hooks into her soul. He stared into her eyes and opened his power wide, taking her entire feeble output and pulling for more. *Come . . . . come . . . . your mind is sliding toward me . . . . I'm getting it, I'm getting all of it . . . . zam! I have your whole mind!* Unmoved by his conjurations, she continued to gurgle and wave her arms about. He stared more intensely, redoubling the vigor of his concentration. Her smile wavered and vanished. Her brows puckered into a frown. Did she know he was attacking her, or was she merely bothered by the faces he was making? *Come . . . . come . . . . your mind is sliding toward me . . . .*

For a moment he thought he might actually succeed. But then she shot him a look of frosty malevolence, incredibly fierce, truly terrifying coming from an infant, and he backed away, frightened, fearing some sudden counterattack. An instant later she was gurgling again. She had defeated him. He went on hating her, but he never again tried to harm her. She, by the time she was old enough to know what the concept of hatred meant, was well aware of how her brother felt about her. And she hated back. She proved to be a far more efficient hater than he was. Oh, was she ever an expert at hating.

Ten

The subject of this composition is My Very First Acid Trip.

My first and my last, eight years ago. Actually it wasn't my trip at all, but Toni's. D-lysergic acid diethlyamide has never passed through my digestive tract, if truth be told. What I did was hitchhike on Toni's trip. In a sense I'm still a hitchhiker on that trip, that very bad trip. Let me tell you.

This happened in the summer of '68. That summer was a bad trip all in itself. Do you remember '68 at all? That was the year we all woke up to the fact that the whole business was coming apart. I mean American society. That pervasive feeling of decay and imminent collapse, so familiar to us all—it really dates from '68, I think. When the world around us became a metaphor for the process of violent entropic increase that had been going on inside our souls—inside my soul, at any rate—for some time.

That summer Lyndon Baines MacBird was in the White House, just barely, serving out his time after his abdication in March. Bobby Kennedy had finally met the bullet with his name on it, and so had Martin Luther King. Neither killing was any surprise; the only surprise was that they had been so long in coming. The blacks were burning down the cities— back then, it was their *own* neighborhoods they burned, remember? Ordinary everyday people were starting to wear freaky clothes to work, bells and body shirts and mini-

miniskirts, and hair was getting longer even for those over 25.
It was the year of sideburns and Buffalo Bill mustachios.
Gene McCarthy, a Senator from—where? Minnesota? Wis-
consin?—was quoting poetry at news conferences as part of
his attempt to gain the Democratic presidential nomination,
but it was a sure bet that the Democrats would give it to
Hubert Horatio Humphrey when they got together for their
convention in Chicago. (And wasn't that convention a lovely
festival of American patriotism?) Over in the other camp
Rockefeller was running hard to catch up with Tricky Dick,
but everybody knew where that was going to get him. Babies
were dying of malnutrition in a place called Biafra, which you
don't remember, and the Russians were moving troops into
Czechoslovakia in yet another demonstration of socialist brotherhood. In a place called Vietnam, which you probably wish
you didn't remember either, we were dumping napalm on
everything in sight for the sake of promoting peace and
democracy, and a lieutenant named William Calley had recently
coordinated the liquidation of 100-odd sinister and dangerous
old men, women, and children at the town of Mylai, only we
didn't know anything about that yet. The books everybody
was reading were *Couples, Myra Breckinridge, The Confessions of Nat Turner,* and *The Monkey Game.* I forget that
year's movies. *Easy Rider* hadn't happened yet and *The
Graduate* was the year before. Maybe it was the year of
Rosemary's Baby. Yes, that sounds right: 1968 was the devil's
year for sure. It was also the year when a lot of middle-class
middle-aged people started using, self-consciously, terms like
"pot" and "grass" when they meant "marijuana." Some of
them were smoking it as well as talking it. (Me. Finally
turning on at the age of 33.) Let's see, what else? President
Johnson nominated Abe Fortas to replace Earl Warren as
Chief Justice of the Supreme Court. Where are you now,
Chief Justice Fortas, when we need you? The Paris peace
talks, believe it or not, had just begun that summer. In later
years it came to seem that the talks had been going on since
the beginning of time, as eternal and everlasting as the Grand
Canyon and the Republican Party, but no, they were invented
in 1968. Denny McLain was on his way toward winning 31
games that season. I guess McLain was the only human being
who found 1968 a worthwhile experience. His team lost the
World Series, though. (No. What am I saying? The Tigers
won, 4 games to 3. But Mickey Lolich was the star, not

McLain.) That was the sort of year it was. Oh, Christ, I've forgotten one significant chunk of history. In the spring of '68 we had the riots at Columbia, with radical students occupying the campus ("*Kirk Must Go!*") and classes being suspended ("*Shut It Down!*") and final exams called off and nightly confrontations with the police, in the course of which a good many undergraduate skulls were laid open and much high-quality blood leaked into the gutters. How funny it is that I pushed that event out of my mind, when of all things I've listed here it was the only one I actually experienced at first hand. Standing at Broadway and 116th Street watching platoons of cold-eyed fuzz go racing toward Butler Library. ("Fuzz" is what we called policemen before we started calling them "pigs," which happened a little later that same year.) Holding my hand aloft in the forked V-for-Peace gesture and screaming idiotic slogans with the best of them. Cowering in the lobby of Furnald Hall as the blue-clad nighstick brigade went on its rampage. Debating tactics with a ragged-bearded SDS gauleiter who finally spat in my face and called me a stinking liberal fink. Watching sweet Barnard girls ripping open their blouses and waving their bare breasts at horny, exasperated cops, while simultaneously shrieking ferocious Anglo-Saxonisms that the Barnard girls of my own remote era hadn't ever heard. Watching a group of young shaggy Columbia men ritualistically pissing on a pile of research documents that had been liberated from the filing cabinet of some hapless instructor going for his doctorate. It was then that I knew there could be no hope for mankind, when even the best of us were capable of going berserk in the cause of love and peace and human equality. On those dark nights I looked into many minds and found only hysteria and madness, and once, in despair, realizing I was living in a world where two factions of lunatics were battling for control of the asylum, I went off to vomit in Riverside Park after a particularly bloody riot and was caught unawares (me, caught unawares!) by a lithe 14-year-old black mugger who smilingly relieved me of $22.

I was living near Columbia in '68, in a seedy residence hotel on 114th Street, where I had one medium-big room plus kitchen and bathroom privileges, cockroaches at no extra charge. It was the very same place where I had lived as an undergraduate in my junior and senior years, 1955–56. The building had been going downhill even then and was an abominable hellhole when I came back to it twelve years later—the courtyard was littered with broken hypodermic needles the way another building's courtyard might be littered with cigarette butts—but I have an odd way, maybe masochistic, of not letting go of bits of my past however ugly they may be, and when I needed place to live I picked that one. Besides, it was cheap—$14.50 a week—and I had to be close to the University because of the work I was doing, researching that Israel book. Are you still following me? I was telling you about my first acid trip, which was really Toni's trip.

We had shared our shabby room nearly seven weeks—a bit of May, all of June, some of July—through thick and thin, heat waves and rainstorms, misunderstandings and reconciliations, and it had been a happy time, perhaps the happiest of my life. I loved her and I think she loved me. I haven't had much love in my life. That isn't intended as a grab for your pity, just as a simple statement of fact, objective and cool. The nature of my condition diminishes my capacity to love and be loved. A man in my circumstances, wide open to everyone's innermost thoughts, really isn't going to experience a great deal of love. He is poor at giving love because he doesn't much trust his fellow human beings: he knows too many of their dirty little secrets, and that kills his feelings for them. Unable to give, he cannot get. His soul, hardened by isolation and ungivingness, becomes inaccessible, and so it is not easy for others to love him. The loop closes upon itself and he is trapped within. Nevertheless I loved Toni, having taken special care not to see too deeply into her, and I didn't doubt my love was returned. What defines love, anyway? We preferred each other's company to the company of anyone else. We excited one another in every imaginable way. We never bored each other. Our bodies mirrored our souls' closeness: I never failed of erection, she never lacked for lubrication, our couplings carried us both to ecstasy. I'd call these things the parameters of love.

On the Friday of our seventh week Toni came home from her office with two small squares of white blotting paper in her purse. In the center on each square was a faint blue-green stain. I studied them a moment or two, without comprehending.

"Acid," she said finally.

"Acid?"

"You know. LSD. Teddy gave them to me."

Teddy was her boss, the editor-in-chief. LSD, yes. I knew. I had read Huxley on mescaline in 1957. I was fascinated and tempted. For years I had flirted with the psychedelic experience, even once attempting to volunteer for an LSD research program at the Columbia Medical Center. I was too late signing up, though; and then, as the drug became a fad, came all the horror stories of suicides, psychoses, bad trips. Knowing my vulnerabilities, I decided it was the part of wisdom to leave acid to others. Though still I was curious about it. And now these squares of blotting paper sitting in the palm of Toni's hand.

"It's supposed to be dynamite stuff," she said. "Absolutely pure, laboratory quality. Teddy's already tripped on a tab from this batch and he says it's very smooth, very clean, no speed in it or any crap like that. I thought we could spend tomorrow tripping, and sleep it off on Sunday."

"Both of us?"

"Why not?"

"Do you think it's safe for both of us to be out of our minds at the same time?"

She gave me a peculiar look. "Do you think acid drives you out of your mind?"

"I don't know. I've heard a lot of scary stories."

"You've never tripped?"

"No," I said. "Have you?"

"Well, no. But I've watched friends of mine while they were tripping." I felt a pang at this reminder of the life she had led before I met her. "They don't go out of their minds, David. There's a kind of wild high for an hour or so when things sometimes get jumbled up, but basically somebody who's tripping sits there as lucid and as calm as—well, Aldous Huxley. Can you imagine Huxley out of his mind? Gibbering and drooling and smashing furniture?"

"What about the fellow who killed his mother-in-law while he was on acid, though? And the girl who jumped out of a window?"

Toni shrugged. "They were unstable," she said loftily. "Perhaps murder or suicide was where they were really at, and the acid just gave them the push they needed to go and do it. But that doesn't mean you would, or me. Or maybe the doses were too strong, or the stuff was cut with some other drug. Who knows? Those are one-in-a-million cases. I have friends who've tripped fifty, sixty times, and they've never had any trouble." She sounded impatient with me. There was a patronizing, lecturing tone in her voice. Her esteem for me seemed clearly diminished by these old-maid hesitations of mine; we were on the threshold of a real rift. "What's the matter, David? Are you afraid to trip?"

"I think it's unwise for both of us to trip at once, that's all. When we aren't sure where the stuff is going to take us.

"Tripping together is the most loving thing two people can do," she said.

"But it's a risky thing. We just don't know. Look, you can get more acid if you want it, can't you?"

"I suppose so."

"Okay, then. Let's do this thing in an orderly way, one step at a time. There's no hurry. You trip tomorrow and I'll watch. I'll trip on Sunday and you'll watch. If we both like what the acid does to our heads, we can trip together next time. All right, Toni? All right?"

It wasn't all right. I saw her begin to speak, begin to frame some argument, some objection; but also I saw her catch herself, back up, rethink her position, and decide not to make an issue of it. Although I at no time entered her mind, her facial expressions made her sequence of thoughts wholly evident to me. "All right," she said softly. "It isn't worth a hassle."

Saturday morning she skipped breakfast—she'd been told to trip on an empty stomach—and, after I had eaten, we sat for a time in the kitchen with one of the squares of blotting paper lying innocently on the table between us. We pretended it wasn't there. Toni seemed a little clutched; I didn't know whether she was bothered about my insisting that she trip without me or just troubled, here at the brink of it, by the whole idea of tripping. There wasn't much conversation. She filled an ashtray with a great dismal mound of half-smoked cigarettes. From time to time she grinned nervously. From time to time I took her hand and smiled encouragingly. During this touching scene various of the tenants with whom we shared the kitchen on this floor of the hotel drifted in and out. First Eloise, the sleek black hooker. Then Miss Theotokis, the grim-faced nurse who worked at St. Luke's. Mr. Wong, the mysterious little roly-poly Chinese who always walked around in his underwear. Aitken, the scholarly fag from Toledo, and his cadaverous mainlining roommate, Donaldson.

A couple of them nodded to us but no one actually said anything, not even "Good morning." In this place it was proper to behave as though your neighbors were invisible. The fine old New York tradition. About half past ten in the morning Toni said, "Get me some orange juice, will you?" I poured a glass from the container in the refrigerator that was labeled with my name. Giving me a wink and a broad toothy smile, all false bravado, she wadded up the blotting paper and pushed it into her mouth, bolting it and gulping the orange juice as a chaser.

"How long will it take to hit?" I asked.

"About an hour and a half," she said.

In fact it was more like fifty minutes. We were back in our own room, the door locked, faint scratchy sounds of Bach coming from the portable phonograph. I was trying to read, and so was Toni; the pages weren't turning very fast. She looked up suddenly and said, "I'm starting to feel a little funny."

"Funny how?"

"Dizzy. A slight touch of nausea. There's a prickling at the back of my neck."

"Can I get you anything? Glass of water? Juice?"

"Nothing, thanks. I'm fine. Really I am." A smile, timid but genuine. She seemed a little apprehensive but not at all frightened. Eager for the voyage. I put down my book and watched her vigilantly, feeling protective, almost wishing that I'd have some occasion to be of service to her. I didn't want her to have a bad trip but I wanted her to need me.

She gave me bulletins on the progress of the acid through her nervous system. I took notes until she indicated that the scratching of pencil against paper was distracting her. Visual effects were beginning. The walls looked a trifle concave to her, and the flaws in the plaster were taking on extraordinary texture and complexity. The color of everything was unnaturally bright. The shafts of sunlight coming through the dirty window were prismatic, shattering and spewing pieces of the spectrum over the floor. The music—I had a stack of her favorite records on the changer—had acquired a curious new intensity; she was having difficulty following melodic lines, and it seemed to her that the turntable kept stopping and starting, but the sound itself, as sound, had some indescribable quality of density and tangibility that fascinated her.

There was a whistling sound in her ears, too, as of air rushing past her cheeks. She spoke of a pervading sense of strangeness— "I'm on some other planet," she said twice. She looked flushed, excited, happy. Remembering the terrible tales I had heard of acid-induced descents into hell, harrowing accounts of grueling bummers lovingly recounted for the delight of the millions by the diligent anonymous journalists of *Time* and *Life*, I nearly wept in relief at this evidence that my Toni would come through her journey unscathed. I had feared the worst. But she was making out all right. Her eyes were closed, her face was serene and exultant, her breathing was deep and relaxed. Lost in transcendental realms of mystery was my Toni. She was barely speaking to me now, breaking her silences only every few minutes to murmur something indistinct and oblique. Half an hour had passed since she first had reported strange sensations. As she drifted deeper into her trip, my love for her grew deeper also. Her ability to cope with acid was proof of the basic toughness of her personality, and that delighted me. I admire capable women. Already I was planning my own trip for the next day—selecting the musical accompaniment, trying to imagine the sort of interesting distortions of reality I'd experience, looking forward to comparing notes with Toni afterward. I was regretting the cowardice that had deprived me of the pleasure of tripping with Toni this day.

But what is this, now? What's happening to my head? Why this sudden feeling of suffocation? The pounding in my chest? The dryness in my throat? The walls are flexing; the air seems close and heavy; my right arm is suddenly a foot longer than the left one. These are effects Toni had noticed and described a little while ago. Why do I feel them now? I tremble. Muscles leap about of their own accord in my thighs. Is this what they call a contact high? Merely being so close to Toni while she trips—did she breathe particles of LSD at me, have I inadvertently turned on through some contagion of the atmosphere?

"My dear Selig," says my armchair smugly, "how can you be so foolish? Obviously you're picking these phenomena right out of her mind!"

Obviously? Is it so obvious? I consider the possibility. Am I reading Toni without knowing it? Apparently I am. In the past some effort of concentration, however slight, has always been necessary in order for me to manage a fine-focus peep into another head. But it seems that the acid must intensify her outputs and bring them to me unsolicited. What other explanation can there be? She is broadcasting her trip; and somehow I have tuned to her wavelength, despite all my noble resolutions about respecting her privacy. And now the acid's strangenesses, spreading across the gap between us, infect me as well.

Shall I get out of her mind?

The acid effects distract me. I look at Toni and she seems transformed. A small dark mole on her lower cheek, near the corner of her mouth, flashes a vortex of blazing color: red, blue, violet, green. Her lips are too full, her mouth too wide. All those teeth. Row upon row upon row, like a shark. Why have I never noticed that predatory mouth before? She frightens me. Her neck elongates; her body compresses; her breasts move about like restless cats beneath her familiar red sweater, which itself has taken on an ominous, threatening purplish tinge. To escape her I glance toward the window. A pattern of cracks that I have never been aware of before runs through the soiled panes. In a moment, surely, the shattered window will implode and shower us with fiery fragments of glass. The building across the street is unnaturally squat today. There is menace in its altered form. The ceiling is coming toward me, too. I hear muffled drumbeats overhead—the footsteps of my upstairs neighbor, I tell myself—and I imagine cannibals preparing their dinner. Is this what tripping is like? Is this what the young of our nation have been doing to themselves, voluntarily, even eagerly, for the sake of amusement?

I should turn this off, before it freaks me altogether. I want out.

Well, easily done. I have my ways of stopping down the inputs, of blocking the flow. Only they don't work this time. I am helpless before the power of the acid. I try to shut myself away from these unfamiliar and unsettling sensations, and they march onward into me all the same. I am wide open to everything emanating from Toni. I am caught up in it. I go deeper and deeper. This is a trip. This is a bad trip. This is a very bad trip. How odd: Toni was having a good trip, wasn't she? So it seemed to one outside observer. Then why do I, accidentally hitchhiking on her trip, find myself having a bad one?

Whatever is in Toni's mind floods into mine. Receiving

another's soul is no new experience for me, but this is a transfer such as I have never had before, for the information, modulated by the drug, comes to me in ghastly distortions. I am an unwilling spectator in Toni's soul, and what I see is a feast of demons. Can such darkness really live within her? I saw nothing like this those other two times: has the acid released some level of nightmare not accessible to me before? Her past is on parade. Gaudy images, bathed in a lurid light. Lovers. Copulations. Abominations. A torrent of menstrual blood, or is that scarlet river something more sinister? Here is a clot of pain: what is that, cruelty to others, cruelty to self? And look how she gives herself to that army of monstrous men! They advance mechanically, a thundering legion. Their rigid cocks blaze with a terrible red light. One by one they plunge into her, and I see the light streaming from her loins as they plow her. Their faces are masks. I know none of them. Why am I not on line too? Where am I? Where am I? Ah, there: off to one side, insignificant, irrelevant. Is that thing me? Is that how she really sees me? A hairy vampire bat, a crouching huddled bloodsucker? Or is that merely David Selig's own image of David Selig, bouncing between us like the reflections in a barber shop's parallel mirrors? God help me, am I laying my own bad trip on her, then reading it back from her and blaming her for harboring nightmares not of her own making?

How can I break this link?

I stumble to my feet. Staggering, splay-footed, nauseated. The room whirls. Where is the door? The doorknob retreats from me. I lunge for it.

"David?" Her voice reverberates unendingly. "David David David David David David—"

"Some fresh air," I mutter. "Just stepping outside a minute—"

It does no good. The nightmare images pursue me through the door. I lean against the sweating wall, clinging to a flickering sconce. The Chinaman drifts by me as though a ghost. Far away I hear the telephone ringing. The refrigerator door slams, and slams again, and slams again, and the Chinaman goes by me a second time from the same direction, and the doorknob retreats from me, as the universe folds back upon itself, locking me into a looped moment. Entropy decreases. The green wall sweats green blood. A voice like thistles says, "Selig? Is something wrong?" It's Donaldson, the junkie. His face is a skull's face. His hand on my shoulder is all bones. "Are you sick?" he asks. I shake my head. He leans toward me until his empty eyesockets are inches from my face, and studies me a long moment. He says, "You're *tripping*, man! Isn't that right? Listen, if you're freaking out, come on down the hall, we've got some stuff that might help you."

"No. No problem."

I go lurching into my room. The door, suddenly flexible, will not close; I push it with both hands, holding it in place until the latch clicks. Toni is sitting where I left her. She looks baffled. Her face is a monstrous thing, pure Picasso; I turn away from her, dismayed.

"David?"

Her voice is cracked and harsh, and seems to be pitched in two octaves at once, with a filling of scratchy wool between the top tone and the bottom. I wave my hands frantically, trying to get her to stop talking, but she goes on, expressing concern for me, wanting to know what's happening, why I've been running in and out of the room. Every sound she makes is torment for me. Nor do the images cease to flow from her mind to mine. That shaggy toothy bat, wearing my face, still glowers in a corner of her skull. Toni, I thought you loved me. Toni, I thought I made you happy. I drop to my knees and explore the dirt-encrusted carpet, a million years old, a faded thinning threadbare piece of the Pleistocene. She comes to me, bending down solicitously, she who is tripping looking after the welfare of her untripping companion, who mysteriously is tripping also. "I don't understand," she whispers. "You're crying, David. Your face is all blotchy. Did I say something wrong? Please don't carry on, David. I was having such a good trip, and now—I just don't understand—"

The bat. The bat. Spreading its rubbery wings. Baring its yellow fangs.

Biting. Sucking. Drinking.

I choke a few words out: "I'm—tripping—too—"

My face pushed against the carpet. The smell of dust in my dry nostrils. Trilobites crawling through my brain. A bat crawling through hers. Shrill laughter in the hallway. The telephone. The refrigerator door: slam, slam, slam! The cannibals dancing upstairs. The ceiling pressing against my back. My hungry mind looting Toni's soul. He who peeps through a may see what will vex him. Toni says, "You took the r acid? When?"

"I didn't."

"Then how can you be tripping?"

I make no reply. I crouch, I huddle, I sweat, I moan. This is the descent into hell. Huxley warned me. I didn't want Toni's trip. I didn't ask to see any of this. My defenses are destroyed now. She overwhelms me. She engulfs me.

Toni says, "Are you reading my mind, David?"

"Yes." The miserable ultimate confession. "I'm reading your mind."

"What did you say?"

"I said I'm reading your mind. I can see every thought. Every experience. I see myself the way you see me. Oh, Christ, Toni, Toni, Toni, it's so awful!"

She tugs at me and tries to pull me up to look at her. Finally I rise. Her face is horribly pale; her eyes are rigid. She asks for clarifications. What's this about reading minds? Did I really say it, or is it something her acid-blurred mind invented? I really said it, I tell her. You asked me if I was reading your mind and I said yes, I was.

"I never asked any such thing," she says.

"I heard you ask it."

"But I didn't—" Trembling, now. Both of us. Her voice is bleak. "You're trying to bum-trip me, aren't you, David? I don't understand. Why would you want to hurt me? Why are you messing me up? It was a good trip. *It was a good trip.*"

"Not for me," I say.

"You weren't tripping."

"But I was."

She gives me a look of total imcomprehension and pulls away from me and throws herself on the bed, sobbing. Out of her mind, cutting through the grotesqueries of the acid images, comes a blast of raw emotion: fear, resentment, pain, anger. She thinks I've deliberately tried to injure her. Nothing I can say now will repair things. Nothing can ever repair things. She despises me. I am a vampire to her, a bloodsucker, a leech; she knows my gift for what it is. We have crossed some fatal threshold and she will never again think of me without anguish and shame. Nor I her. I rush from the room, down the hall to the room shared by Donaldson and Aitken. "Bad trip," I mutter. "Sorry to trouble you, but—"

* * *

I stayed with them the rest of the afternoon. They gave me a tranquilizer and brought me gently through the downslope of the trip. The psychedelic images still came to me out of Toni for half an hour or so, as though an inexorable umbilical chain linked us across all the length of the hallway; but then to my relief the sense of contact began to slip and fade, and suddenly, with a kind of audible click at the moment of severance, it was gone altogether. The flamboyant phantoms ceased to vex my soul. Color and dimension and texture returned to their proper states. And at last I was free from that merciless reflected self-image. Once I was fully alone in my own skull again I felt like weeping to celebrate my deliverance, but no tears would come, and I sat passively, sipping a Bromo-Seltzer. Time trickled away. Donaldson and Aitken and I talked in a peaceful, civilized, burned-out way about Bach, medieval art, Richard M. Nixon, pot, and a great many other things. I hardly knew these two, yet they were willing to surrender their time to ease a stranger's pain. Eventually I felt better. Shortly before six o'clock, thanking them gravely, I went back to my room. Toni was not there. The place seemed oddly altered. Books were gone from the shelves, prints from the walls; the closet door stood open and half the things in it were missing. In my befuddled, fatigued state it took me a moment or two to grasp what had happened. At first I imagined burglary, abduction, but then I saw the truth. She had moved out.

Eleven

Today there is a hint of encroaching winter in the air: it takes tentative nips at the cheeks. October is dying too quickly. The sky is mottled and unhealthy-looking, cluttered by sad, heavy, low-hanging clouds. Yesterday it rained, skinning yellow leaves from the trees, and now they lie pasted to the pavement of College Walk, their tips fluttering raggedly in the harsh breeze. There are puddles everywhere. As I settled down beside Alma Mater's massive green form I primly spread newspaper sheets, selected portions of today's issue of

The Columbia Daily Spectator, over the cold damp stone steps. Twenty-odd years ago, when I was a foolishly ambitious sophomore dreaming of a career in journalism—how sly, a reporter who reads minds!—*Spec* seemed central to my life; now it serves only for keeping my rump dry.

Here I sit. Office hours. On my knees rests a thick manila folder, held closed by a ballsy big rubber band. Within, neatly typed, each with its own coppery paperclip, are five term papers, the products of my busy week. *The Novels of Kafka. Shaw as Tragedian. The Concept of Synthetic A Priori Statements. Odysseus as a Symbol of Society. Aeschylus and the Aristotelian Tragedy.* The old academic bullshit, confirmed in its hopeless fecality by the cheerful willingness of these bright young men to let an old grad turn the stuff out for them. This is the day appointed for delivering the goods and, perhaps, picking up some new assignments. Five minutes to eleven. My clients will be arriving soon. Meanwhile I scan the passing parade. Students hurrying by, clutching mounds of books. Hair rippling in the wind, breasts bobbling. They all look frighteningly young to me, even the bearded ones. Especially the bearded ones. Do you realize that each year there are more and more young people in the world? Their tribe ever increases as the old farts drop off the nether end of the curve and I shuttle graveward. Even the professors look young to me these days. There are people with doctorates who are fifteen years younger than I am. Isn't that a killer? Imagine a kid born in 1950 who has a doctorate already. In 1950 I was shaving three times a week, and masturbating every Wednesday and Saturday; I was a hearty pubescent *bulyak* five feet nine inches tall, with ambitions and griefs and knowledge, with an identity. In 1950 today's newly fledged Ph.D.'s were toothless infants just squirting from the womb, their faces puckered, their skins sticky with amniotic juices. How can those infants have doctorates so soon? Those infants have lapped me as I plod along the track.

I find my own company wearisome when I descend into self-pity. To divert myself I try to touch the minds of passersby and learn what I can learn. Playing my old game, my only game. Selig the voyeur, the soul-vampire, ripping off the intimacies of innocent strangers to cheer his chilly heart. But no: my head is full of cotton today. Only muffled murmurs come to me, indistinct, content-free. No discrete words, no flashes of identity, no visions of soul's essence. This is one of the bad days. All inputs converge into unintelligibility; each bit of information is identical to all others. It is the triumph of entropy. I am reminded of Forster's Mrs. Moore, listening tensely for revelation in the echoing Marabar caves, and hearing only the same monotonous noise, the same meaningless all-dissolving sound: *Boum.* The sum and essence of mankind's earnest strivings: *Boum.* The minds flashing past me on College Walk now give me only: *Boum.* Perhaps it is all I deserve. Love, fear, faith, churlishness, hunger, self-satisfaction, every species of interior monolog, all come to me with identical content. *Boum.* I must work to correct this. It is not too late to wage war against entropy. Gradually, sweating, struggling, scrabbling for solid purchase, I widen the aperture, coaxing my perceptions to function. Yes. Yes. Come back to life. Get it up, you miserable spy! Give me my fix! Within me the power stirs. The inner murk clears a bit; stray scraps of isolated but coherent thought find their way into me. *Neurotic but not altogether psycho yet. Going to see the department head and tell him to shove it up. Tickets for the opera, but I have to. Fucking is fun, fucking is very important, but there's more. Like standing on a very high diving board about to take a plunge.* This scratchy chaotic chatter tells me nothing except that the power is not yet dead, and I take comfort enough in that. I visualize the power as a sort of worm wrapped around my cerebrum, a poor tired worm, wrinkled and shrunken, its once-glossy skin now ulcerous with shabby, flaking patches. That is a relatively recent image, but even in happier days I always thought of the gift as something apart from myself, something intrusive. An inhabitant. It and me, me and it. I used to discuss such things with Myquist. (Has he entered these exhalations yet? Perhaps not. A person I once knew, a certain Tom Myquist, a former friend of mine. Who carried a somewhat similar intruder within his skull.) Myquist didn't like my outlook. "That's schizoid, man, setting up a duality like that. Your power is you. You are your power. Why try to alienate yourself from your own brain?" Probably Nyquist was right, but it's much too late. It and me is how it will be, till death do us part.

Here is my client, the bulky halfback, Paul F. Bruno. His face is swollen and purple, and he is unsmiling, as though Saturday's heroics have cost him some teeth. I flip the rubber

band down, extract *The Novels of Kafka*, and offer the paper
to him. "Six pages," I say. He has given me a ten-dollar
advance. "You owe me another eleven bucks. Do you want to
read it first?"

"How good is it?"

"You won't be sorry."

"I'll take your word for it." He manages a painful, close-
mouthed grin. Pulling forth his thick wallet, he crosses my
palm with greenbacks. I slip quickly into his mind, just for
the hell of it now that my power is working again, a fast
psychic rip-off, and pick up the surface levels: loose teeth at
the football game, a sweet compensatory blow-job at the frat
house Saturday night, vague plans for getting laid after next
Saturday's game, etc., etc. Concerning the present transaction I detect guilt, embarrassment, even some annoyance
with me for having helped him. Oh, well: the gratitude of the
goy. I pocket his money. He favors me with a curt nod and
tucks *The Novels of Kafka* under his immense forearm.
Hastily, in shame, he goes hustling down the steps and off in
the direction of Hamilton Hall. I watch his broad retreating
back. A sudden gust of malevolent wind, rising off the
Hudson, comes knifing eastward and cuts me bone-deep.

Bruno has paused at the sundial, where a slender black
student close to seven feet tall has intercepted him. A
basketball player, obviously. The black wears a blue varsity
jacket, green sneakers, and tight tubular yellow slacks. His
legs alone seem five feet long. He and Bruno talk for a
moment. Bruno points toward me. The black nods. I am
about to gain a new client, I realize. Bruno vanishes and the
black trots springlegged across the walk, up the steps. He is
very dark, almost purple-skinned, yet his features have a
Caucasian sharpness, fierce cheekbones, proud aquiline nose,
thin frosty lips. He is formidably handsome, some kind of
walking statuary, some sort of idol. Perhaps his genes are not
negroid at all: an Ethiopan, maybe, some tribesman of the
Nile bulrushes? Yet he wears his midnight mass of kinky hair
in a vast aggressive Afro halo a foot in diameter or more,
fastidiously trimmed. I would not have been surprised by
scarified cheeks, a bone through the nostrils. As he nears me,
my mind, barely slit-wide, picks up peripheral generalized
emanations of his personality. Everything is predictable, even
stereotyped: I expect him to be touchy, cocky, defensive,
hostile, and what comes to me is a bouillabaisse of ferocious

racial pride, overwhelming physical self-satisfaction, explosive mistrust of others—especially whites. All right. Familiar patterns.

His elongated shadow falls suddenly upon me as the sun momentarily pierces the clouds. He sways bouncily on the balls of his feet. "Your name Selig?" he asks. I nod. "Yahya Lumumba," he says.

"Pardon me?"

"*Yahya Lumumba.*" His eyes, glossy white against glossy purple, blaze with fury. From the impatience of his tone I realize that he is telling me his name, or at least the name he prefers to use. His tone indicates also that he assumes it's a name everyone on this campus will recognize. Well, what would I know of college basketball stars? He could throw the ball through the hoop fifty times a game and I'd still not have heard of him. He says, "I hear you do term papers, man."

"That's right."

"You got a good recommend from my pal Bruno there. How much you charge?"

"$3.50 a page. Typed, double-spaced."

He considers it. He shows many teeth and says, "What kind of fucking rip-off is that?"

"It's how I earn my living, Mr. Lumumba." I hate myself for that toadying, cowardly *mister*. "That's about $20 for an average-length paper. A decent job takes a fair amount of time, right?"

"Yeah. Yeah." An elaborate shrug. "Okay, I'm not hassling you, man. I got need for your work. You know anything about Europydes?"

"Euripides?"

"That's what I said." He's baiting me, coming on with exaggerated black mannerisms, talking watermelon-nigger at me with his *Europydes*. "That Greek cat who wrote plays."

"I know who you mean. What sort of paper do you need, Mr. Lumumba?"

He pulls a scrap of a notebook sheet from a breast pocket and makes a great show of consulting it. "The prof he wants us to compare the 'Electra' theme in Europydes, Sophocles, and Eesk—Aysk—"

"Aeschylus?"

"Him, yeah. Five to ten pages. It due by November 10. Can you swing it?"

"I think so," I say, reaching for my pen. "It shouldn't be

any trouble at all," especially since there resides in my files a
paper of my own, vintage 1952, covering this very same hoary
old humanities theme. "I'll need some information about you
for the heading. Exact spelling of your name, the name of
your professor, the course number—" He starts to tell me
these things. As I jot them down, I simultaneously open the
aperture of my mind for my customary scan of the client's
interior, to give me some idea of the proper tone to use in the
paper. Will I be able to do a convincing job of faking the kind
of essay Yahya Lumumba is like to turn in? It will be a taxing
technical challenge if I have to write in black hipster jargon,
coming on all cool and jazzy and snotty, every line laughing in
the ofay prof's fat face. I imagine I could do it: but does
Lumumba want me to? Will he think I'm mocking *him* if I
adopt the jiveass style and seem to be putting him on as he
might put on the prof? I must know these things. So I slip my
snaky tendrils past his woolly scalp into the hidden gray jelly.
Hell, big black man. Entering, I pick up a somewhat more
immediate and vivid version of the generalized persona he
constantly projects: the hyped-up black pride, the mistrust of
the paleface stranger, the chuckling enjoyment of his own
lean long-legged muscular frame. But these are mere residual
attitudes, the standard furniture of his mind. I have not yet
reached the level of this-minute thought. I have not penetrated
to the essential Yahya Lumumba, the unique individual whose
style I must assume. I push deeper. As I sink in, I sense a
distinct warming of the psychic temperature, an outflow of
heat, comparable perhaps to what a miner might experience
five miles down, tunneling toward the magmatic fires at the
earth's core. This man Lumumba is constantly boiling within,
I realize. The glow from his tumultuous soul warns me to be
careful, but I have not yet gained the information I seek, and
so I go onward, until abruptly the molten frenzy of his stream
of consciousness hits me with terrible force. *Fucking Jew
bigbrain shithead Christ how I hate the little bald mother
conning me three-fifty a page I ought to jew him down I
ought to bust his teeth the exploiter the oppressor he wouldn't
charge a Jew that much I bet special price for niggers sure
well I ought to jew him down that's a good one jew him down
I ought to bust his teeth pick him up throw him into the trash
what if I wrote the fucking paper myself show him but I can't
shit I can't that's the whole fucking trouble mom I can't
Europydes Sophocles Eeskilus who knows shit about them I*

*got other stuff on my mind the Rutgers game one-on-one
down the court gimme the ball you dumb prick that's it and
it's up and in for Lumumba! and wait folks he was fouled in
the act of shooting now he goes to the line big confident easy
six feet ten inches tall holder of every Columbia scoring
record bounces the ball once twice up, swish! Lumumba on
his way to another big evening tonight folks Europydes
Sophocles Eeskilus why the fuck do I have to know anything
about them write anything about them what good is it to a
black man those old dead Greek fuckers how are they relevant to the black experience relevant relevant relevant not to
me just to the Jews shit what do any of them know four
hundred years of slavery we got other stuff on our minds
what do any of them know especially this shithead mother
here I got to pay him twenty bucks to do something I'm not
good enough to do for myself who says I have to what good is
any of it why why why why*

A roaring furnace. The heat is overwhelming. I've been in
contact with intense minds before, far more intense even
than this one, but that was when I was younger, stronger,
more resilient. I can't handle this volcanic blast. The force of
his contempt for me is magnified factorially by the force of
the self-contempt that needing my services makes him feel.
He is a pillar of hatred. And my poor enfeebled power can't
take it. Some sort of automatic safety device cuts in to protect
me from an overload; the mental receptors shut themselves
down. This is a new experience for me, a strange one, this
load-shedding phenomenon. It is as though limbs are dropping off, ears, balls, anything disposable, leaving nothing but
a smooth torso. The inputs fall away, the mind of Yahya
Lumumba retreats and is inaccessible to me, and I find
myself involuntarily reversing the process of penetration until
I can feel only his most superficial emanations, then not even
those, only a gray furry exudation marking the mere presence
of him alongside me. All is indistinct. All is muffled. *Boum.*
We are back to that again. There is a ringing in my ears: it is
an artifact of the sudden silence, a silence loud as thunder. A
new stage on my downward path. Never have I lost my grip
and slipped from a mind like this. I look up, dazed, shattered.
Yahya Lumumba's thin lips are tightly compressed; he stares
down at me in distaste, having no inkling of what has occurred. I say faintly, "I'd like ten dollars now in advance. The
rest you pay when I deliver the paper." He tells me coldly

that he has no money to give me today. His next check from the scholarship fund isn't due until the beginning of the coming month. I'll just have to do the job on faith, he says. Take it or leave it, man. "Can you manage five?" I ask. "As a binder. Faith isn't enough. I have expenses." He glares. He draws himself to his full height; he seems nine or ten feet tall. Without a word he takes a five-dollar bill from his wallet, crumples it, scornfully tosses it into my lap. "I'll see you here the morning of November 9," I call after him, as he stalks away. Europydes, Sophocles, Eeskilus. I sit stunned, shivering, listening to the bellowing silence. *Boum. Boum. Boum.*

Twelve

In his more flamboyantly Dostoevskian moments, David Selig liked to think of his power as a curse, a savage penalty for some unimaginable sin. The mark of Cain, perhaps. Certainly his special ability had caused a lot of trouble for him, but in his saner moments he knew that calling it a curse was sheer self-indulgent melodramatic bullshit. The power was a divine gift. The power brought ecstasy. Without the power he was nothing, a schmendrick; with it he was a god. Is that a curse? Is that so terrible? Something funny happens when gamete meets gamete, and destiny cries, Here, Selig-baby: be a god! This you would spurn? Sophocles, age 88 or so, was heard to express his great relief at having outlived the pressures of the physical passions. I am freed at last from a tyrannical master, said the wise and happy Sophocles. Can we then assume that Sophocles, had Zeus given him a chance retroactively to alter the entire course of his days, would have opted for lifelong impotence? Don't kid yourself, Duvid: no matter how badly the telepathy stuff fucked you up, and it fucked you up pretty badly, you wouldn't have done without it for a minute. Because the power brought ecstasy.

The power brought ecstasy. That's the whole megillah in a single crisp phrase. Mortals are born into a vale of tears and they get their kicks wherever they can. Some, seeking pleasure, are compelled to turn to sex, drugs, booze, television, movies, pinochle, the stock market, the racetrack, the roulette wheel, whips and chains, collecting first editions, Caribbean cruises, Chinese snuff bottles, Anglo-Saxon poetry, rubber garments, professional football games, whatever. Not him, not the accursed David Selig. All he had to do was sit quietly with his apparatus wide open and drink in the thoughtwaves drifting on the telepathic breeze. With the greatest of ease he lived a hundred vicarious lives. He heaped his treasurehouse with the plunder of a thousand souls. Ecstasy. Of course, the ecstatic part was all quite some time ago.

The best years were those between the ages of fourteen and twenty-five. Younger, and he was still too naive, too unformed, to wring much appreciation from the data he took in. Older, and his growing bitterness, his sour sense of isolation, damped his capacity for joy. Fourteen to twenty-five, though. The golden years. Ah!

It was so very much more vivid then. Life was like a waking dream. There were no walls in his world; he could go anywhere and see anything. The intense flavor of existence. Steeped in the rich juices of perception. Not until Selig was past forty did he realize how much he had lost, over the years, in the way of fine focus and depth of field. The power had not begun detectibly to dim until he was well along in his thirties, but it obviously must have been fading by easy stages all through his manhood, dwindling so gradually that he remained unaware of the cumulative loss. The change had been absolute, qualitative rather than quantitative. Even on a good day, now, the inputs did not begin to approach the intensity of those he remembered from his adolescence. In those remote years the power had brought him not only bits of subcranial conversation and scattered snatches of soul, as now, but also a gaudy universe of colors, textures, scents, densities: the world through an infinity of other sensory intakes, the world captured and played out for his delight on the glassy radiant spherical screen within his mind.

* * *

For instance. He lies propped against an itchy August haystack in a hot Brueghelesque landscape, shortly past noon. This is 1950 and he hangs becalmed midway between his fifteenth birthday and his sixteenth. Some sound effects,

Maestro: Beethoven's Sixth, bubbling up gently, sweet flutes and playful piccolos. The sun dangles in a cloudless sky. A gentle wind stirs the willows bordering the cornfield. The young corn trembles. The brook burbles. A starling circles overhead. He hears crickets. He hears the drone of a mosquito, and watches calmly as it zeroes in on his bare, hairless, sweat-shiny chest. His feet are bare too; he wears only tight, faded blue jeans. City boy, digging the country.

The farm is in the Catskills, twelve miles north of Ellenville. It is owned by the Schieles, a tribe of tawny Teutons, who produce eggs and an assortment of vegetable crops and who supplement their earnings every summer by renting out their guest house to some family of urban Yids looking for rural solace. This year the tenants are Sam and Annette Stein of Brooklyn, New York, and their daughter Barbara. The Steins have invited their close friends, Paul and Martha Selig, to spend a week on the farm with their son David and their daughter Judith. (Sam Stein and Paul Selig are hatching a scheme, destined ultimately to empty their bank accounts and destroy the friendship between the two families, to enter into a partnership and act as jobbers for replacement parts for television sets. Paul Selig is forever attempting unwise business ventures.) Today is the third day of the visit, and this afternoon, mysteriously, David finds himself utterly alone. His father has gone on an all-day hike with Sam Stein: in the serenity of the nearby hills they will plot the details of their commercial coup. Their wives have driven off, taking five-year-old Judith with them, to explore the antique shops of Ellenville. No one remains on the premises except the tight-lipped Schieles, going somberly about their unending chores, and sixteen-year-old Barbara Stein, who has been David's classmate from the third grade on through high school. Willy-nilly, David and Barbara are thrown together for the day. The Steins and the Seligs evidently have some unvoiced hope that romance will blossom between their offspring. This is naïve of them. Barbara, a lush and reasonably beautiful dark-haired girl, sleek-skinned and long-legged, sophisticated and smooth of manner, is six months older than David chronologically, and three or four years ahead of him in social development. She does not actually dislike him, but she regards him as strange, disturbing, alien, and repellent. She has no knowledge of his special gift—no one does; he's seen to that—but she's had seven years to observe him at close range, and she knows there's something fishy about him. She is a conventional girl, plainly destined to marry early (a doctor, a lawyer, an insurance broker) and have lots of babies, and the chances of romance flowering between her and anyone as dark-souled and odd as David Selig are slight. David knows this very well and he is not at all surprised, or even dismayed, when Barbara slips away in mid-morning. "If anyone asks," she says, "tell them I went for a stroll in the woods." She carries a paperback poetry anthology. David is not deceived by it. He knows she goes off to screw 19-year-old Hans Schiele at every chance she gets.

So he is left to his own resources. No matter. He has ways of entertaining himself. He wanders the farm for a while, peering at the hen-coop and the combine, and then settles down in a quiet corner of the fields. Time for mind-movies. Lazily he casts his net. The power rises and goes forth, looking for emanations. What shall I read, what shall I read? Ah. A sense of contact. His questing mind has snared another mind, a buzzing one, small, dim, intense. It is a bee's mind, in fact: David is not limited only to contact with humans. Of course there are no verbal outputs from the bee, nor any conceptual ones. If the bee thinks at all, David is incapable of detecting those thoughts. But he does get into the bee's head. He experiences a strong sense of what it is like to be tiny and compact and winged and fuzzy. How *dry* the universe of a bee is: bloodless, desiccated, arid. He soars. He swoops. He evades a passing bird, as monstrous as a winged elephant. He burrows deep into a steamy, pollen-laden blossom. He goes aloft again. He sees the world through the bee's faceted eyes. Everything breaks into a thousand fragments, as though seen through a cracked glass; the essential color of everything is gray, but odd hues lurk at the corners of things, peripheral blues and scarlets that do not correspond in any way to the colors he knows. The effect, he might have said twenty years later, is an extremely trippy one. But the mind of a bee is a limited one. David bores easily. He abandons the insect abruptly and, zooming his perceptions barnward, clicks into the soul of a hen. She is laying an egg! Rhythmic internal contractions, pleasurable and painful, like the voiding of a mighty turd. Frenzied squawks. The smarmy hen-coop odor, sharp and biting. A sense of too much straw all about. The world looks dark and dull to this bird. *Heave. Heave*. Oooh! Orgasmic excitement! The egg slides through

the hatch and lands safely. The hen subsides, fulfilled, exhausted.
David departs from her in this moment of rapture. He
plunges deep into the adjoining woods, finds a human mind,
enters it. How much richer and more intense it is to make
communion with his own species. His identity blurs into that
of his communicant who is Barbara Stein, who is getting laid
by Hans Schiele. She is naked and lying on a carpet of last
year's fallen leaves. Her legs are spread and her eyes are
closed. Her skin is damp with sweat. Hans' fingers dig into
the soft flesh of her shoulders and his cheek, rough with
blond stubble, abrades her cheek. His weight presses down
on her chest, flattening her breasts and emptying her lungs.
With steady thrusts and unvarying tempo he penetrates her,
and as his long stiff member slowly and patiently rams into
her again and again, throbbing sensation spreads in eddying
rippled outward from her loins, growing less intense with
distance. Through her mind David observes the impact of the
hard penis against the tender, slippery internal membranes.
He picks up her clamorous heartbeat. He notices her hammering her heels against the calves of Hans' legs. He is aware
of the slickness of her own fluids on her buttocks and thighs.
And now he senses the first dizzying spasms of orgasm. David
struggles to remain with her, but he knows he won't succeed;
clinging to the consciousness of someone who's coming is like
trying to ride a wild horse. Her pelvis bucks and heaves, her
fingernails desperately rake her lover's back, her head twists
to one side, she gulps for air, and, as she erupts with
pleasure, she catapults David from her unsaddled mind. He
travels only a short way, into the stolid soul of Hans Schiele,
who unknowingly grants the virgin voyeur a few instants of
knowledge of what it is like to be stoking the furnace of
Barbara Stein, thrust and thrust and thrust and thrust, her
inner muscles clamping fiercely against the swollen prod, and
then, almost immediately, comes the tickle of Hans' onrushing
climax. Hungry for information, David holds on with all his
strength, hoping to keep contact right through the tumult of
fulfillment, but no, he is flipped free, he tumbles uncontrollably,
the world goes swinging past him in giddy streaks of color,
until—click!—he finds a new sanctuary. All is calm here. He
glides through a dark cold environment. He has no weight;
his body is long and slender and agile; his mind is nearly a
void, but through it run faint chilly flickering perceptions of a
low order. He has entered the consciousness of a fish, per-

haps a brook trout. Downstream he moves in the swiftly rushing creek, taking delight in the smoothness of his motions and the delicious texture of the pure icy water flowing past his fins. He can see very little and smell even less; information comes to him in the form of minute impacts on his scales, tiny deflections and interferences. Easily he responds to each incoming news item, now twisting to avoid a fang of rock, now fluttering his fins to seize some speedy subcurrent. The process is fascinating, but the trout itself is a dull companion, and David, having extracted the troutness of the experience in two or three minutes, leaps gladly to a more complex mind the moment he approaches one. It is the mind of gnarled old Georg Schiele, Hans' father, who is at work in a remote corner of the cornfield. David has never entered the elder Schiele's mind before. The old man is a grim and forbidding character, well past sixty, who says little and stalks dourly through his day-long round of chores with his heavy-jowled face perpetually locked in a frosty scowl. David occasionally wonders whether he once might have been a concentration-camp attendant, though he knows the Schieles came to America in 1935. The farmer gives off so unpleasant a psychic aura that David has steered clear of him, but so bored is he with the trout that he slips into Schiele now, slides down through dense layers of unintelligible Deutsch ruminations, and strikes bottom in the basement of the farmer's soul, the place where his essence lives. Astonishment: old Schiele is a mystic, an ecstatic! No dourness here. No dark Lutheran vindictiveness. This is pure Buddhism: Schiele stands in the rich soil of his fields, leaning on his hoe, feet firmly planted, communing with the universe. God floods his soul. He touches the unity of all things. Sky, trees, earth, sun, plants, brook, insects, birds—everything is one, part of a seamless whole, and Schiele resonates in perfect harmony with it. How can this be? How can such a bleak, inaccessible man entertain such raptures in his depths? Feel his joy! Sensations drench him! Birdsong, sunlight, the scent of flowers and clods of upturned earth, the rustling of the sharp-bladed green cornstalks, the trickle of sweat down the reddened deep-channeled neck, the curve of the planet, the fleecy premature outline of the full moon—a thousand delights enfold this man. David shares his pleasure. He kneels in his mind, reverent, awed. The world is a mighty hymn. Schiele breaks from his stasis, raises his hoe, brings it down; heavy muscles go taut and metal digs into earth, and everything is as it should be, all conforms to the divine plan. Is this how Schiele goes through his days? Is such happiness possible? David is surprised to find tears bulging in his eyes. This simple man, this narrow man, lives in daily grace. Suddenly sullen, bitterly envious, David rips his mind free, whirls, projects it towards the woods, drops down into Barbara Stein again. She lies back, sweat-sticky, exhausted. Through her nostrils David receives the stink of semen already going sour. She rubs her hands over her skin, plucking stray bits of leaf and grass from herself. Idly she touches her softening nipples. Her mind is slow, dull, almost as empty as the trout's, just now: sex seems to have drained her of personality. David shifts to Hans and finds him no better. Lying by Barbara's side, still breathing hard after his exertions, he is torpid and depressed. His wad is shot and all desire is gone from him; peering sleepily at the girl he has just possessed, he is conscious mainly of body odors and the untidiness of her hair. Through the upper levels of his mind wanders a wistful thought, in English punctuated by clumsy German, of a girl from an adjoining farm who will do something to him with her mouth that Barbara refuses to do. Hans will be seeing her on Saturday night. Poor Barbara, David thinks, and wonders what she would say if she knew what Hans is thinking. Idly he tries to bridge their two minds, entering both in the mischievous hope that thoughts may flow from one to the other, but he miscalculates his span and finds himself returning to old Schiele, deep in his ecstasy, while holding contact with Hans as well. Father and son, old and young, priest and profaner. David sustains the twin contact a moment. He shivers. He is filled with a thundering sense of the wholeness of life.

* * *

It was like that all the time, in those years: an endless trip, a gaudy voyage. But powers decay. Time leaches the colors from the best of visions. The world becomes grayer. Entropy beats us down. Everything fades. Everything goes. Everything dies.

Thirteen

Judith's dark, rambling apartment fills with pungent smells. I hear her in the kitchen, bustling, dumping spices into the pot: hot chili, oregano, tarragon, cloves, garlic, powdered mustard, sesame oil, curry powder, God knows what else. Fire burn and cauldron bubble. Her famous fiery spaghetti sauce is in the making, a compound product of mysterious antecedents, part Mexican in inspiration, part Szechuan, part Madras, part pure Judith. My unhappy sister is not really much of a domestic type, but the few dishes she can cook she does extraordinarily well, and her spaghetti is celebrated on three continents; I'm convinced there are men who go to bed with her just to have dining-in privileges here.

I have arrived unexpectedly early, half an hour before the appointed time, catching Judith unprepared, not even dressed, so I am on my own while she readies dinner. "Fix yourself a drink," she calls to me. I go to the sideboard and pour a shot of dark rum, then into the kitchen for ice cubes. Judith, flustered, wearing housecoat and headband, flies madly about, breathlessly selecting spices. She does everything at top speed. "Be with you in another ten minutes," she gasps, reaching for the pepper mill. "Is the kid making a lot of trouble for you?"

My nephew, she means. His name is Paul, in honor of our father which art in heaven, but she never calls him that, only "the baby," "the kid." Four years old. Child of divorce, destined to be as taut-strung as his mother. "He's not bothering me at all," I assure her, and go back to the livingroom.

The apartment is one of those old, immense West Side jobs, roomy and high-ceilinged, which carries with it some sort of aura of intellectual distinction simply because so many critics, poets, playwrights, and choreographers have lived in similar apartments in this very neighborhood. Giant livingroom with many windows looking out over West End Avenue; formal dining room; big kitchen; master bedroom; child's room; maid's room; two bathrooms. All for Judith and her

cub. The rent is cosmic, but Judith can manage it. She gets
well over a thousand a month from her ex, and earns a
modest but decent living of her own as an editor and translator; aside from that she has a small income from a portfolio of
stocks, shrewdly chosen for her a few years ago by a lover
from Wall Street, which she purchased with her inherited
share of our parents' surprisingly robust savings. (My share
went to clean up accumulated debts; the whole thing melted
like June snow.) The place is furnished half in 1960 Greenwich
Village and half in 1970 Urban Elegance—black pole-lamps,
gray string chairs, red brick bookcases, cheap prints, and
wax-encrusted Chianti bottles on the one hand; leather cou-
ches, Hopi pottery, psychedelic silkscreens, glass-topped
coffee-tables, and giant potted cacti on the other. Bach harpsichord sonatas tinkle from the thousand-dollar speaker
system. The floor, ebony-dark and mirror-bright, gleams between the lush, thick area rugs. A pile of broken-backed
paperbacks clutters one wall. Opposite it stand two rough
unopened wooden crates, wine newly arrived from her vint-
ner. A good life my sister leads here. Good and miserable.

The kid eyes me untrustingly. He sits twenty feet away, by
the window, fiddling with some intricate plastic toy but keeping
close watch on me. A dark child, slender and tense like his
mother, aloof, cool. No love is lost between us: I've been inside
his head and I know what he thinks of me. To him I'm one of
the many men in his mother's life, a real uncle being not very
different from the innumerable uncle-surrogates forever sleeping over; I suppose he thinks I'm just one of her lovers who
shows up more often than most. An understandable error. But
while he resents the others merely because they compete with
him for her affection, he looks coldly upon me because he
thinks I've caused his mother pain; he dislikes me for her sake.
How shrewdly he's discerned the decades-old network of hostilities and tensions that shapes and defines my relationship
with Judith! So I'm an enemy. He'd gut me if he could.

I sip my drink, listen to Bach, smile insincerely at the kid,
and inhale the aroma of spaghetti sauce. My power is practically quiescent; I try not to use it much here, and in any case
its intake is feeble today. After some time Judith emerges
from the kitchen and, flashing across the livingroom, says,
"Come talk to me while I get dressed, Duv." I follow her
to her bedroom and sit down on the bed; she takes her
clothes into the adjoining bathroom, leaving the door open

only an inch or two. The last time I saw her naked she was seven years old. She says, "I'm glad you decided to come."

"So am I."

"You look awfully peaked though."

"Just hungry, Jude."

"I'll fix that in five minutes." Sounds of water running. She says something else; the sink drowns her out. I look idly around the bedroom. A man's white shirt, much too big for Judith, hangs casually from the doorknob of the closet. On the night-table sit two fat textbooky-looking books. *Analytical Neuroendocrinology* and *Studies in the Physiology of Thermoregulation*. Unlikely reading for Judith. Maybe she's been hired to translate them into French. I observe that they're brand new copies, though one book was published in 1964 and the other in 1969. Both by the same author: K. F. Silvestri, M.D., Ph.D.

"You going to medical school these days?" I ask.

"The books, you mean? They're Karl's."

Karl? A new name. Dr. Karl F. Silvestri. I touch her mind lightly and extract his image: a tall hefty sober-faced man, broad shoulders, strong dimpled chin, flowing mane of graying hair. About fifty, I'd guess. Judith digs older men. While I raid her consciousness she tells me about him. Her current "friend," the kid's latest "uncle." He's someone very big at Columbia Medical Center, a real authority on the human body. Including her body, I assume. Newly divorced after a 25-year marriage. Uh-huh: she likes getting them on the rebound. He met her three weeks ago through a mutual friend, a psychoanalyst. They've only seen each other four or five times; he's always busy, committee meetings at this hospital or that, seminars, consultations. It wasn't very long ago that Judith told me she was between men, maybe off men altogether. Evidently not. It must be a serious affair if she's trying to read his books. They look absolutely opaque to me, all charts and statistical tables and heavy Latinate terminology.

She comes out of the bathroom wearing a sleek purple pants-suit and the crystal earrings I gave her for her 29th birthday. When I visit she always tries to register some little sentimental touch to tie us together; tonight it's the earrings. There is a convalescent quality to our friendship nowadays, as we tiptoe gently through the garden where our old hatred lies buried: We embrace, a brother-sister hug. A pleasant perfume. "Hello," she says. "I'm sorry I was such a mess when you walked in."

"It's my fault. I was too early. Anyway, you weren't a mess at all."

She leads me to the livingroom. She carries herself well. Judith is a handsome woman, tall and extremely slender, exotic-looking, with dark hair, dark complexion, sharp cheekbones. The slim sultry type. I suppose she'd be considered very sexy, except that there is something cruel about her thin lips and her quick glistening brown eyes, and that cruelty, which grows more intense in these years of divorce and discontent, turns people off. She's had lovers by the dozens, by the gross, but not much love. You and me, sis, you and me. Chips off the old block.

She sets the table while I fix a drink for her, the usual, Pernod on the rocks. The kid, thank God, has already eaten; I hate having him at the table. He plays with his plastic thingy and favors me with occasional sour glares. Judith and I clink our cocktail glasses together, a stagy gesture. She produces a wintry smile. "Cheers," we say. Cheers.

"Why don't you move back downtown?" she asks. "We could see more of each other."

"It's cheap up there. Do we want to see more of each other?"

"Who else do we have?"

"You have Karl."

"I don't *have* him or anybody. Just my kid and my brother."

I think of the time when I tried to murder her in her bassinet. She doesn't know about that. "Are we really friends, Jude?"

"Now we are. At last."

"We haven't exactly been fond of each other all these years."

"People change, Duv. They grow up. I was dumb, a real shithead, so wrapped up in myself that I couldn't give anything but hate to anybody around me. That's over now. If you don't believe me, look into my head and see."

"You don't want me poking around in there."

"Go ahead," she says. "Take a good look and see if I haven't changed toward you."

"No. I'd rather not." I deal myself another two ounces of rum. The hand shakes a little. "Shouldn't you check the spaghetti sauce? Maybe it's boiling over."

"Let it boil. I haven't finished my drink. Duv, are you still having trouble? With your power, I mean."

"Yes. Still. Worse than ever."

"What do you think is happening?"

I shrug. Insouciant old me. "I'm losing it, that's all. It's like hair, I suppose. A lot of it when you're young, then less and less, and finally none. Fuck it. It never did me any good anyway."

"You don't mean that."

"Show me any good it did me, Jude."

"It made you someone special. It made you unique. When everything else went wrong for you, you could always fall back on that, the knowledge that you could go into minds, that you could see the unseeable, that you could get close to people's souls. A gift from God."

"A useless gift. Except if I'd gone into the sideshow business."

"It made you a richer person. More complex, more interesting. Without it you might have been someone quite ordinary."

"With it I turned out to be someone quite ordinary. A nobody, a zero. Without it I might have been a happy nobody instead of a dismal one."

"You pity yourself a lot, Duv."

"I've got a lot to pity myself for. More Pernod, Jude?"

"Thanks, no. I ought to look after dinner. Will you pour the wine?"

She goes into the kitchen. I do the wine thing; then I carry the salad bowl to the table. Behind me the kid begins to chant derisive nonsense syllables in his weirdly mature baritone. Even in my current state of dulled deceptivity I feel the pressure of the kid's cold hatred against the back of my skull. Judith returns, toting a well-laden tray: spaghetti, garlic bread, cheese. She flashes a warm smile, evidently sincere, as we sit down. We clink wine-glasses. We eat in silence a few minutes. I praise the spaghetti. She says, finally, "Can I do some mindreading on you, Duv?"

"Be my guest."

"You say you're glad the power's going. Is that snowjob directed at me or at yourself? Because you're snowing somebody. You hate the idea of losing it, don't you?"

"A little."

"A lot, Duv."

"All right, a lot. I'm of two minds. I'd like it to vanish completely. Christ, I wish I'd never had it. But on the other hand, if I lose it, who am I? Where's my identity? I'm Selig the Mindreader, right? The Amazing Mental Man. So if I stop being him—you see, Jude?"

"I see. The pain's all over your face. I'm so sorry, Duv."

"For what?"

"That you're losing it."

"You despised my guts for using it on you, didn't you?"

"That's different. That was a long time ago. I know what you must be going through, now. Do you have any idea why you're losing it?"

"No. A function of aging, I guess."

"Is there anything that might be done to stop it from going?"

"I doubt it, Jude. I don't even know why I have the gift in the first place, let alone how to nurture it now. I don't know how it works. It's just something in my head, a genetic fluke, a thing I was born with, like freckles. If your freckles start to fade, can you figure out a way of making them stay, if you want them to stay?"

"You've never let yourself be studied, have you?"

"No."

"Why not?"

"I don't like people poking in my head any more than you do," I say softly. "I don't want to be a case history. I've always kept a low profile. If the world ever found out about me, I'd become a pariah. I'd probably be lynched. Do you know how many people there are to whom I've openly admitted the truth about myself? In my whole life, how many?"

"A dozen."

"Three," I say. "And I wouldn't willingly have told any of them."

"Three?"

"You. I suppose you suspected it all along, but you didn't find out for sure till you were sixteen, remember? Then there's Tom Nyquist, who I don't see any more. And a girl named Kitty, who I don't see any more either."

"What about the tall brunette?"

"Toni? I never explicitly told her. I tried to hide it from her. She found out indirectly. A lot of people may have found out indirectly. But I've only told three. I don't want to be known as a freak. So let it fade. Let it die. Good riddance."

"You want to keep it, though."

"To keep it and lose it both."

"That's a contradiction."

"Do I contradict myself? Very well, then I contradict myself. I am large, I contain multitudes. What can I say, Jude? What can I tell you that's true?"

"Are you in pain?"

"Who isn't in pain?"

She says, "Losing it is almost like becoming impotent, isn't it, Duv? To reach into a mind and find out that you can't connect? You said there was ecstasy in it for you, once. That flood of information, that vicarious experience. And now you can't get it as much, or at all. Your mind can't get it up. Do you see it that way, as a sexual metaphor?"

"Sometimes." I give her more wine. For a few minutes we sit silently, shoveling down the spaghetti, exchanging tentative grins. I almost feel warmth toward her. Forgiveness for all the years when she treated me like a circus attraction. *You sneaky fucker, Duv, stay out of my head or I'll kill you! You voyeur. You peeper. Keep away, man, keep away.* She didn't want me to meet her fiancé. Afraid I'd tell him about her other men, I guess. *I'd like to find you dead in the gutter some day, Duv, with all my secrets rotting inside you.* So long ago. Maybe we love each other a little now, Jude. Just a little, but you love me more than I love you.

"I don't come any more," she says abruptly. "You know, I used to come, practically every time. The original Hot Pants Kid, me. But around five years ago something happened, around the time my marriage was first breaking up. A short circuit down below. I started coming every fifth time, every tenth time. Feeling the ability to respond slip away from me. Lying there waiting for it to happen, and of course that doused it every time. Finally I couldn't come at all. I still can't. Not in three years. I've laid maybe a hundred men since the divorce, give or take five or ten, and not one brought me off, and some of them were studs, real bulls. It's one of the things Karl's going to work on with me. So I know what it's like, Duv. What you must be going through. To lose your best way of making contact with others. To lose contact gradually with yourself. To become a stranger in your own head." She smiles. "Did you know that about me? About the troubles I've been having in bed?"

I hesitate briefly. The icy glare in her eyes gives her away. The aggressiveness. The resentment she feels. Even when she tries to be loving she can't help hating. How fragile our relationship is! We're locked in a kind of marriage, Judith and I, an old burned-out marriage held together with skewers. What the hell, though. "Yes," I tell her. "I knew about it."

"I thought so. You've never stopped probing me." Her smile is all hateful glee now. She's glad I'm losing it. She's relieved. "I'm always wide open to you, Duv."

"Don't worry, you won't be much longer." Oh, you sadistic bitch! Oh, you beautiful ball-buster! And you're all I've got. "How about some more spaghetti, Jude?" Sister. Sister. Sister.

Fourteen

Yahya Lumumba
Humanities 2A, Dr. Katz
November 10, 1976

The "Electra" Theme in Aeschylus,
Sophocles, and Euripides

The use of the "Electra" mofit by Aeschylus, Sophocles, and Euripides is a study in varying dramatic methods and modes of attack. The plot is basically the same in Aeschylus' *Choephori* and the *Electras* of Sophocles and Euripides: Orestes, exiled son of murdered Agamemnon, returns to his native Mycenae, where he discovers his sister Electra. She persuades him to avenge Agamemnon's murder by killing Clytemnestra and Aegisthus, who had slain Agamemnon on his return from Troy. The treatment of the plot varies greatly at the hands of each dramatist.

Aeschylus, unlike his later rivals, held as prime consideration the ethical and religious aspects of Orestes' crime. Characterization and motivation in *The Choephori* are simple to the point of inviting ridicule—as, indeed, can we see when the more worldly-minded Euripides ridicules Aeschylus in the recognition scene of his *Electra*. In Aeschylus' play Orestes appears accompanied by his friend Pylades and places an offering on Agamemnon's tomb: a lock of his hair. They withdraw, and lamenting Electra comes to the tomb. Noticing the lock of hair, she recognizes it as being "like unto those my father's children wear," and decides Orestes has sent it to the tomb as a token of mourning. Orestes then reappears, and identifies himself to Electra. It is this implausible means of identification which was parodied by Euripides.

Orestes reveals that Apollo's oracle had commanded him to avenge Agememnon's murder. In a long poetic passage, Electra steels Orestes' courage, and he goes forth to kill Clytemnestra and Aegisthus. He obtains entrance to the palace by deception, pretending to his mother Clytemnestra that he is a messenger from far-off Phocis, bearing news of Orestes' death. Once inside, he slays Aegisthus, and then, confronting his mother, he accuses her of the murder and kills her.

The play ends with Orestes, maddened by his crime, seeing the Furies coming to pursue him. He takes refuge in the temple of Apollo. The mystic and allegorical sequel, *The Eumenides*, sees Orestes absolved of blame.

Aeschylus, in short, was not overly concerned with the credibility of his play's action. His purpose in the *Oresteia* trilogy was a theological one: to examine the actions of the gods in placing a curse upon a house, a curse stemming from murder and leading to further murder. The keynote of his philosophy is perhaps the line, "'Tis Zeus alone who shows the perfect way of knowledge: He hath ruled, men shall learn wisdom, by affliction schooled." Aeschylus sacrifices dramatic technique, or at least holds it in secondary importance, in order to focus attention on the religious and psychological aspects of the matricide.

The *Electra* of Euripides is virtually at an opposite pole from the concept of Aeschylus; though he uses the same plot, he elaborates and innovates to provide far richer texture. Electra and Orestes stand out in relief in Euripides: Electra a near-mad woman, banished from the court, married to a peasant, craving vengeance; Orestes a coward, sneaking into Mycenae the back way, abjectly stabbing Aegisthus from behind, luring Clytemnestra to her doom by a ruse. Euripides is concerned with dramatic credibility, whereas Aeschylus is not. After the famous parody of the Aeschylean recognition scene, Orestes makes himself known to Electra not by his hair or the size of his foot, but rather by

* * *

Oh God. Oh shit. Shit shit shit. This is deadly. This is no fucking good at all. Could Yahya Lumumba have written any of this crap? Phony from Word One. Why should Yahya Lumumba give a shit about Greek tragedy? Why should I? What's Hecuba to him or he to Hecuba, that he should weep for her? I'll tear this up and start again. I'll write it jivey, man. I'll give it dat ole watermelon rhythm. God help me to think black. But I can't. But I can't. But I can't. Christ, I'd like to throw up. I think I'm getting a fever. Wait. Maybe a joint would help some. Yeah. Let's get high and try again. A lil ole stick of mootah. Get some soul into it, man. Smartass white Jew-bastard, get some soul into it, you hear? Okay, now. There was this cat Agamemnon, he was one big important fucker, you hear, he was The Man, but he got fucked all the same. His old lady Clytemnestra, she was makin' it with this chickenshit muthafuck Aegisthus, and one day she say, Baby, let's waste old Aggie, you and me, and then you gonna be king—gwine be king?—gonna—and we have a high ole time. Aggie, he off in the Nam runnin' the show, but he come home for some R & R and before he know what happenin' they stick him good, right, they really cut him, and that all for *him*. Now there this crazy cunt Electra, dig, she the daughter of ole Aggie, and she get real uptight when they use him up, so she say to her brother, his name Orestes, she say, listen, Orestes, I want you to *get* them two muthafucks, I want you to get them real good. Now, this cat Orestes he been out of town for a while, he don't know the score, but—

Yeah, that's it, man! You're digging it! Now go on to explain about Euripides' use of the *deus ex machina* and the cathartic virtues of Sophocles' realistic dramatic technique. Sure. What a dumb schmuck you are, Selig. What a dumb schmuck.

Fifteen

I tried to be good to Judith, I tried to be kind and loving, but our hatred kept coming between us. I said to myself, She's my kid sister, my only sibling, I must love her more. But you can't will love. You can't conjure it into existence on nothing more than good intentions. Besides, my intentions had never been that good. I saw her as a rival from the word go. I was the firstborn, I was the difficult one, the maladjusted one. I was supposed to be the center of everything. Those were the terms of my contract with God: I must suffer because I am different, but by way of compensation the entire universe will revolve about me. The girlbaby who was brought into the household was intended to be nothing more than a therapeutic aid designed to help me relate better to the human race. That was the deal: she wasn't supposed to have independent reality as a person, she wasn't supposed to have her own needs or make demands or drain away their love. Just a thing, an item of furniture. But I knew better than to believe that. I was ten years old, remember, when they adopted her. Your ten-year-old, he's no fool. I knew that my parents, no longer feeling obliged now to direct all their concern exclusively toward their mysteriously intense and troubled son, would rapidly and with great relief transfer their attention and their love—yes, particularly their love—to the cuddly, uncomplicated infant. She would take my place at the center; I'd become a quirky obsolescent artifact. I couldn't help resenting that. Do you blame me for trying to kill her in her bassinet? On the other hand you can understand the origin of her life-long coldness toward me. I offer no defense at this late date. The cycle of hatred began with me. With me, Jude, with me, with me, with me. You could have broken it with love, though, if you wanted to. You didn't want to.

On a Saturday afternoon in May, 1961, I went out to my parents' house. In those years I didn't go there often, though I lived twenty minutes away by subway. I was outside the family circle, autonomous and remote, and I felt powerful resistance to any kind of reattachment. For one thing I had free-floating hostilities toward my parents: it was their fluky genes, after all, that had sent me into the world this way. And then too there was Judith, shriveling me with her disdain: did I need more of that? So I stayed away from the three of them for weeks, months, at a time, until the melancholy maternal phonecalls became too much for me, until the weight of my guilt overcame my resistances.

I was happy to discover, when I got there, that Judith was still in her bedroom, asleep. At three in the afternoon? Well, my mother said, she was out very late last night on a date.

Judith was sixteen, I imagined her going to a high school
basketball game with some skinny pimply kid and sipping
milkshakes afterwards. Sleep well, sister, sleep on and on.
But of course her absence put me into direct and unshielded
confrontation with my sad depleted parents. My mother, mild
and dim; my father, weary and bitter. All my life they had
steadily grown smaller. They seemed very small now. They
seemed close to the vanishing point.

I had never lived in this apartment. For years Paul and
Martha had struggled with the upkeep of a three-bedroom
place they couldn't afford, simply because it had become
impossible for Judith and me to share the same bedroom
once she was past her infancy. The moment I left for college,
taking a room near campus, they found a smaller and far less
expensive one. Their bedroom was to the right of the entry
foyer, and Judith's down a long hall and past the kitchen, was
to the left; straight ahead was the livingroom, in which my
father sat dreamily leafing through the *Times*. He read nothing but the newspaper these days, though once his mind had
been more active. From him came a dull sludgy emanation of
fatigue. He was making some decent money for the first time
in his life, actually would end up quite prosperous, yet he
had conditioned himself to the poor-man psychology; poor
Paul, you're a pitiful failure, you deserved so much better
from life. I looked at the newspaper through his mind as he
turned the pages. Yesterday Alan Shepard had made his
epochal sub-orbital flight, the first manned venture into space
by the United States. U.S. HURLS MAN 115 MILES INTO
SPACE, cried the banner headline. SHEPHARD WORKS
CONTROLS IN CAPSULE, REPORTS BY RADIO IN
15-MINUTE FLIGHT. I groped for some way to connect
with my father. "What did you think of the space voyage?" I
asked. "Did you listen to the broadcast?" He shrugged. "Who
gives a damn? It's all crazy. A mishigos. A waste of everybody's time and money." ELIZABETH VISITS POPE IN
VATICAN. Fat Pope John, looking like a well-fed rabbi.
JOHNSON TO MEET LEADERS IN ASIA ON U.S. TROOP
USE. He skimmed onward, skipping pages. HELP OF
GOLDBERG ASKED ON ROCKETS. KENNEDY SIGNS
WAGE-FLOOR BILL. Nothing registered on him, not even
KENNEDY TO SEEK INCOME TAX CUTS. He lingered at
the sports pages. A faint flicker of interest. MUD MAKES
CARRY BACK STRONGER FAVORITE FOR 87th KEN-

TUCKY DERBY TODAY. YANKS OPPOSE ANGELS IN OPENER OF 3-GAME SERIES BEFORE 21,000 ON COAST. "Who do you like in the Derby?" I asked. He shook his head. "What do I know about horses?" he said. He was, I realized, already dead, although in fact his heart would beat for another decade. He had stopped responding. The world had defeated him.

I left him to his brooding and made polite talk with my mother: her Hadassah reading group was discussing *To Kill a Mockingbird* next Thursday and she wanted to know if I had read it. I hadn't. What was I doing with myself? Had I seen any good movies? *L'Avventura*, I said. Is that a French film? she asked. Italian, I said. She wanted me to describe the plot. She listened patiently, looking troubled, not following anything. "Who did you go with?" she asked. "Are you seeing any nice girls?" My son the bachelor. Already 26 and not even engaged. I deflected the tiresome question with patient skill born of long experience. Sorry, Martha. I won't give you the grandchildren you're waiting for. You'll have to get them from Judith; it won't be all that long.

"I have to baste the chicken now," she said, and disappeared. I sat with my father for a while, until I couldn't stand that and went down the hall to the john, next to Judith's room. Her door was ajar. I glanced in. Lights off, blinds drawn, but I touched her mind and found that she was awake and thinking of getting up. All right, make a gesture, be friendly, Duvid. It won't cost you anything. I knocked lightly. "Hi, it's me," I said. "Okay if I come in?"

She was sitting up, wearing a frilly white bathrobe over dark-blue pajamas. Yawning, stretching. Her face, usually so taut, was puffy from too much sleep. Out of force of habit I went into her mind, and saw something new and surprising there. My sister's erotic inauguration. The night before. The whole thing: the scurry in the parked car, the rise of excitement, the sudden realization that this was going to be more than an interlude of petting, the panties coming down, the awkward shiftings of position, the fumble with the condom, the moment of ultimate hesitation giving way to total willingness, the hasty inexpert fingers coaxing lubrication out of the virgin crevice, the cautious clumsy poking, the thrust, the surprise of discovering that penetration was accomplished without pain, the pistoning of body against body, the boy's quick explosion, the messy aftermath, the guilt and confusion and disappointment as it ended with Judith still unsatisfied. The drive home, silent, shamefaced. Into the house, tiptoe, hoarsely greeting the vigilant, unsleeping parents. The late-night shower. Inspection and cleansing of the deflowered and slightly swollen vulva. Uneasy sleep, frequently punctured. A long stretch of wakefulness, in which the night's event is considered: she is pleased and relieved to have entered womanhood, but also frightened. Unwillingness to rise and face the world the next day, especially to face Paul and Martha. Judith, your secret is no secret to me.

"How are you?" I asked.

Stagily casual, she drawled, "Sleepy. I was out very late. How come you're here?"

"I drop in to see the family now and then."

"Nice to have seen you."

"That isn't friendly, Jude. Am I that loathsome to you?"

"Why are you bothering me, Duv?"

"I told you, I'm trying to be sociable. You're my only sister, the only one I'll ever have. I thought I'd stick my head in the door and say hello."

"You've done that. So?"

"You might tell me what you've been doing with yourself since the last time I saw you."

"Do you care?"

"If I didn't care, would I ask?"

"Sure," she said. "You don't give a crap about what I've been doing. You don't give a crap about anybody but David Selig, and why pretend otherwise? You don't need to ask me polite questions. It isn't natural coming from you."

"Hey, hold on!" Let's not be dueling so fast, sister. "What gives you the idea that—"

"Do you think of me from one week to the next? I'm just furniture to you. The drippy little sister. The brat. The inconvenience. Have you ever talked to me? About anything? Do you even know the name of the school I go to? I'm a total stranger to you."

"No, you're not."

"What the hell *do* you know about me?"

"Plenty."

"For example."

"Quit it, Jude."

"One example. Just one. One thing about me. For example—"

"For example. All right. For example, I know that you got laid last night."

We were both amazed by that. I stood in shocked silence, not believing that I had allowed those words to pass my lips; and Judith jerked as though electrified, her body stiffening and rearing, her eyes blazing with astonishment. I don't know how long we remained frozen, unable to speak.

"What?" she said finally. "What did you say, Duv?"

"You heard it."

"I heard it but I think I must have dreamed it. Say it again."

"No."

"Why not?"

"Leave me alone, Jude."

"Who told you?"

"Please, Jude—"

"*Who told you?*"

"Nobody," I muttered.

Her smile was terrifyingly triumphant. "You know something? I believe you. I honestly believe you. Nobody told you. You pulled it right out of my mind, didn't you, Duv?"

"I wish I had never come in here."

"Admit it. Why won't you admit it? You see into people's minds, don't you, Duvid? You're some kind of circus freak. I've suspected that a long time. All those little hunches you have, and they always turn out to be right, and the embarrassed phony way you cover up for yourself when you're right. Talking about your 'luck' at guessing things. Sure! Sure, luck! I knew the real scoop. I said to myself, This fucker is reading my mind. But I told myself it was crazy, there aren't any such people, it has to be impossible. Only it's true, isn't it? You don't guess. You look. We're wide open to you and you read us like books. Spying on us. Isn't that so?"

I heard a sound behind me. I jumped, frightened. But it was only Martha, poking her head into Judith's bedroom. A vague, dreamy grin. "Good morning, Judith. Or good afternoon, I should say. Having a nice chat, children? I'm so glad. Don't forget to have breakfast, Judith." And she drifted on her way.

Judith said sharply, "Why didn't you tell her? Describe the whole thing. Who I was with last night, what I did with him, how it felt—"

"Stop it, Jude."

"You didn't answer my other question. You've got this weird power, don't you? *Don't you?*"

"Yes."

"And you've been secretly spying on people all your life."

"Yes. Yes."

"I knew it. I didn't know, but I really did, all along. And it explains so much. Why I always felt dirty when I was a kid and you were around. Why I felt as if anything I did was likely to show up in tomorrow's newspapers. I never had any privacy, even when I was locked in the bathroom. I didn't *feel* private." She shuddered. "I hope I never see you again, Duv. Now that I know what you are. I wish I never *had* seen you. If I ever catch you poking around in my head after this, I'll cut your balls off. Got that? I'll cut your balls off. Now clear out of here so I can get dressed."

I stumbled away. In the bathroom I gripped the cold edge of the sink and leaned close to the mirror to study my flushed, flustered face. I looked stunned and dazed, my features as rigid as though I had had a stroke. *I know that you got laid last night.* Why had I told her that? An accident? The words spilling out of me because she had goaded me past the point of prudence? But I had never let anyone push me into a revelation like that before. There are no accidents, Freud said. There are never any slips of the tongue. Everything's deliberate, on one level or another. I must have said what I did to Judith because I wanted her at last to know the truth about me. But why? Why her? I had already told Nyquist, yes; there could be no risk in that; but I had never admitted it to anyone else. Always taken such great pains to conceal it, eh, Miss Mueller? And now Judith knew. I had given her a weapon with which she could destroy me.

* * *

I had given her a weapon. How strange that she never chose to use it.

Sixteen

Nyquist said, "The real trouble with you, Selig, is that you're a deeply religious man who doesn't happen to believe in

God." Nyquist was always saying things like that, and Selig never could be sure whether he meant them or was just playing verbal games. No matter how deeply Selig penetrated the other man's soul, he never could be sure of anything. Nyquist was too wily, too elusive.

Playing it safe, Selig said nothing. He stood with his back to Nyquist, looking out the window. Snow was falling. The narrow streets below were choked with it; not even the municipal snowplows could get through, and a strange serenity prevailed. High winds whipped the drifts about. Parked cars were disappearing under the white blanket. A few janitors from the apartment houses on the block were out, digging manfully. It had been snowing on and off for three days. Snow was general all over the Northeast. It was falling on every filthy city, on the arid suburbs, falling softly upon the Appalachians and, farther eastward, softly falling into the dark mutinous Atlantic waves. Nothing was moving in New York City. Everything was shut down: office buildings, schools, the concert halls, the theaters. The railroads were out of commission and the highways were blocked. There was no action at the airports. Basketball games were being canceled at Madison Square Garden. Unable to get to work, Selig had waited out most of the blizzard in Nyquist's apartment, spending so much time with him that by now he had come to find his friend's company stifling and oppressive. What earlier had seemed amusing and charming in Nyquist had become abrasive and tricksy. Nyquist's bland self-assurance conveyed itself now as smugness; his casual forays into Selig's mind were no longer affectionate gestures of intimacy, but rather, conscious acts of aggression. His habit of repeating aloud what Selig was thinking was increasingly irritating, and there seemed to be no deterring him from that. Here he was doing it again, plucking a quotation from Selig's head and declaiming it in half-mocking tones: "Ah. How pretty. 'His soul swooned slowly as he heard the snow falling faintly through the universe and faintly falling, like the descent of their last end, upon all the living and the dead.' I like that. What is it, David?"

"James Joyce," said Selig sourly. "'The Dead,' from *Dubliners*. I asked you yesterday not to do that."

"I envy the breadth and depth of your culture. I like to borrow fancy quotations from you."

"Fine. Do you always have to play them back at me?"

Nyquist, gesturing broadly as Selig stepped away from the window, humbly turned his palms outward. "I'm sorry. I forgot you didn't like it."

"You never forget a thing, Tom. You never do anything accidentally." Then, guilty over his peevishness: "Christ, I've had about enough snow!"

"Snow is general," said Nyquist. "It isn't ever going to stop. What are we going to do today?"

"The same as yesterday and the day before, I imagine. Sitting around watching the snowflakes fall and listening to records and getting sloshed."

"How about getting laid?"

"I don't think you're my type," Selig said.

Nyquist flashed an empty smile. "Funny man. I mean finding a couple of ladies marooned somewhere in this building and inviting them to a little party. You don't think there are two available ladies under this roof?"

"We could look, I suppose," Selig said, shrugging. "Is there any more bourbon?"

"I'll get it," Nyquist said.

He brought the bottle over. Nyquist moved with a strange slowness, like a man moving through a dense reluctant atmosphere of mercury or some other viscous fluid. Selig had never seen him hurry. He was heavy without being fat, a thick-shouldered, thick-necked man with a square head, close-cropped yellow hair, a flat wide-flanged nose, and an easy, innocent grin. Very, very Aryan: he was Scandinavian, a Swede perhaps, raised in Finland and transplanted to the United States at the age of 10. He still had the elusive traces of an accent. He said he was 28 and looked a few years older than that to Selig, who had just turned 23. This was February, 1958, in an era when Selig still had the delusion that he was going to make it in the adult world. Eisenhower was President, the stock market had gone to hell, the post-Sputnik emotional slump was troubling everybody even though the first American space satellite had just been orbited, and the latest feminine fashion was the gunny-sack chemise. Selig was living in Brooklyn Heights, on Pierrepont Street, commuting several days a week to the lower Fifth Avenue office of a publishing company for which he was doing freelance copy-editing at $3 an hour. Nyquist lived in the same building, four floors higher.

He was the only other person Selig knew who had the

power. Not only that, having it hadn't crippled him at all.
Nyquist used his gift as simply and naturally as he did his
eyes or his legs, for his own advantage, without apologies and
without guilt. Perhaps he was the least neurotic person Selig
had ever met. By occupation he was a predator, skimming an
income by raiding the minds of others; but, like any jungle
cat, he pounced only when hungry, never for sheer love of
pouncing. He took what he needed, never questioning the
providence that made him so superbly fitted for taking,
yet he did not take more than he needed, and his needs
were moderate. He held no job and apparently never had.
Whenever he wanted money he made the ten-minute subway
ride to Wall Street, sauntered through the gloomy canyons
of the financial district, and rummaged about freely in the
minds of the moneymen cloistered in the lofty boardrooms.
On any given day there was always some major development hatching that would have an impact on the market—a
merger, a stock split, an ore discovery, a favorable earnings
report—and Nyquist had no difficulty learning the essential details. This information he swiftly sold at handsome
but reasonable fees to some twelve or fifteen private
investors who had learned in the happiest possible way that
Nyquist was a reliable tout. Many of the unaccountable
leaks on which quick fortunes had been made in the bull
market of the '50's were his doing. He earned a comfortable living this way, enough to support himself in a congenial style. His apartment was small and agreeable—black
Naugahyde upholstery, Tiffany lamps, Picasso wallpaper, a
well-stocked liquor closet, a superb music system that
emitted a seamless flow of Monteverdi and Palestrina,
Bartok and Stravinsky. He lived a gracious bachelor life,
going out often, making the rounds of his favorite restaurants, all of them obscure and ethnic—Japanese, Pakistani,
Syrian, Greek. His circle of friends was limited but distinguished: painters, writers, musicians, poets, mainly. He
slept with many women, but Selig rarely saw him with the
same one twice.

Like Selig, Nyquist could receive but was unable to send;
he was, however, able to tell when his own mind was being
probed. That was how they had happened to meet. Selig,
newly arrived in the building, had indulged himself in his
hobby, letting his consciousness rove freely from floor to floor
by way of getting acquainted with his neighbors. Bouncing

about, surveying this head and that, finding nothing of any special interest, and then suddenly:

—Tell me where you are.

A crystalline string of words glimmering at the periphery of a sturdy, complacent mind. The statement came through with the immediacy of an explicit message. Yet Selig realized that no act of active transmission had taken place; he had simply found the words lying passively in wait. He made quick reply:

—35 Pierrepont Street.

—No, I know that. I mean, where are you in the building?

—Fourth floor.

—I'm on the eighth. What's your name?

—Selig.

—Nyquist.

The mental contact was stunningly intimate. It was almost a sexual thing, as though he were slicing into a body, not a mind, and he was abashed by the resonant masculinity of the soul he had entered; he felt that there was something not quite permissible about such closeness with another man. But he did not draw back. That rapid interplay of verbal communication across the gap of darkness was a delicious experience, too rewarding to reject. Selig had the momentary illusion of having expanded his powers, of having learned how to send as well as to draw forth the contents of other minds. It was, he knew, only an illusion. He was sending nothing, nor was Nyquist. He and Nyquist were merely picking information out of each other's minds. Each planted phrases for the other to find, which was not quite the same thing, in terms of the situational dynamics, as sending messages to one another. It was a fine and possibly pointless distinction, though; the net effect of the juxtaposition of two wide-open receivers was an efficient send/receive circuit as reliable as a telephone. The marriage of true minds, to which let no impediments be admitted. Tentatively, self-consciously, Selig reached into the lower levels of Nyquist's consciousness, seeking the man as well as the messages, and as he did so he was vaguely aware of disquiet in the depths of his own mind, probably indicating that Nyquist was doing the same to him. For long minutes they explored each other like lovers entwined in the first discovering caresses, although there was nothing loving about Nyquist's touch, which was cool and impersonal. Nevertheless Selig quivered; he felt as if he stood at the edge of an abyss. At last he gently withdrew, as did Nyquist. Then, from the other:

—Come upstairs. I'll meet you by the elevator.

He was bigger than Selig expected, a fullback of a man, his blue eyes uninviting, his smile a purely formal one. He was remote without actually being cold. They went into his apartment: soft lights, unfamiliar music playing, an atmosphere of unostentatious elegance. Nyquist offered him a drink and they talked, keeping out of one another's minds as much as possible. It was a subdued visit, unsentimental, no tears of joy at having come together at last. Nyquist was affable, inaccessible, pleased that Selig had appeared, but not at all delirious with excitement at the discovery of a fellow freak. Possibly it was because he had discovered fellow freaks before. "There are others," he said. "You're the third, fourth, fifth I've met since I came to the States. Let's see: one in Chicago, one in San Francisco, one in Miami, one in Minneapolis. You're the fifth. Two women, three men."

"Are you still in touch with the others?"

"No."

"What happened?"

"We drifted apart," Nyquist said. "What did you expect? That we'd be clannish? Look, we talked, we played games with our minds, we got to know each other, and after a while we got bored. I think two of them are dead now. I don't mind being isolated from the rest of my kind. I don't think of myself as one of a tribe."

"I never met another one," said Selig. "Until today."

"It isn't important. What's important is living your own life. How old were you when you found out you could do it?"

"I don't know. Five, six years old, maybe. And you?"

"I didn't realize I had anything special until I was eleven. I thought everybody could do it. It was only after I came to the States and heard people thinking in a different language that I knew there was something out of the ordinary about my mind."

"What kind of work do you do?" Selig asked.

"As little as I can," said Nyquist. He grinned and thrust his perceptors brusquely into Selig's mind. It seemed like an invitation of sorts; Selig accepted it and pushed forth his own antennae. Roaming the other man's consciousness, he quickly grasped the picture of Nyquist's Wall Street sorties. He saw the entire balanced, rhythmic, unobsessive life of the man.

He was amazed by Nyquist's coolness, his wholeness, his clarity of spirit. How limpid Nyquist's soul was! How unmarred by life! Where did he keep his anguish? Where did he hide his loneliness, his fear, his insecurity? Nyquist, withdrawing, said, "Why do you feel so sorry for yourself?"

"Do I?"

"It's all over your head. What's the problem, Selig? I've looked into you and I don't see the problem, only the pain."

"The problem is that I feel isolated from other human beings."

"Isolated? You? You can get right inside people's heads. You can do something that 99.999% of the human race can't do. They've got to struggle along using words, approximations, semaphore signals, and you go straight to the core of meaning. How can you pretend you're isolated?"

"The information I get is useless," Selig said. "I can't act on it. I might just as well not be reading it in."

"Why?"

"Because it's just voyeurism. I'm spying on them."

"You feel guilty about that?"

"Don't you?"

"I didn't ask for my gift," Nyquist said. "I just happen to have it. Since I have it, I use it. I like it. I like the life I lead. I like myself. Why don't you like yourself, Selig?"

"You tell me."

But Nyquist had nothing to tell him, and when he finished his drink he went back downstairs. His own apartment seemed so strange to him as he re-entered it that he spent a few minutes handling familiar artifacts: his parents' photograph, his little collection of adolescent love-letters, the plastic toy that the psychiatrist had given him years ago. The presence of Nyquist continued to buzz in his mind—a residue of the visit, nothing more, for Selig was certain that Nyquist was not now probing him. He felt so jarred by their meeting, so intruded upon, that he resolved never to see him again, in fact to move somewhere else as soon as possible, to Manhattan, to Philadelphia, to Los Angeles, anywhere that might be beyond Nyquist's reach. All his life he had yearned to meet someone who shared his gift, and now that he had, he felt threatened by it. Nyquist was so much in control of his life that it was terrifying. He'll humiliate me, Selig thought. He'll devour me. But that panic faded. Two days later Nyquist came around to ask him out to dinner. They ate in a nearby

Mexican restaurant and got smashed on Carta Blanca. It still appeared to Selig that Nyquist was toying with him, teasing him, holding him at arm's length and tickling him; but it was all done so amiably that Selig felt no resentment. Nyquist's charm was irresistible, and his strength was worth taking as a model of behavior. Nyquist was like an older brother who had preceded him through this same vale of traumas and had emerged unscathed long ago; now he was jollying Selig into an acceptance of the terms of his existence. The superhuman condition, Nyquist called it.

They became close friends. Two or three times a week they went out together, ate together, drank together. Selig had always imagined that a friendship with someone else of his kind would be uniquely intense, but this was not; after the first week they took their specialness for granted and rarely discussed the gift they shared, nor did they ever congratulate each other on having formed an alliance against the ungifted world around them. They communicated sometimes by words, sometimes by the direct contact of minds; it became an easy, cheerful relationship, strained only when Selig slipped into his habitual brooding mood and Nyquist mocked him for such self-indulgence. Even that was no difficulty between them until the days of the blizzard, when all tensions became exaggerated because they were spending so much time together.

"Hold out your glass," Nyquist said.

He poured an amber splash of bourbon. Selig settled back to drink while Nyquist set about finding girls for them. The project took him five minutes. He scanned the building and turned up a pair of roommates on the fifth floor. "Take a look," he said to Selig. Selig entered Nyquist's mind. Nyquist had attuned himself to the consciousness of one of the girls—sensual, sleepy, kittenish—and was looking through her eyes at the other, a tall gaunt blonde. The doubly refracted mental image nevertheless was quite clear: the blonde had a leggy voluptuousness and fashion-model poise. "That one's mine," Nyquist said. "Now tell me if you like yours." He jumped, Selig following along, to the mind of the blonde. Yes, a fashion model, more intelligent than the other girl, cold, selfish, passionate. From her mind, via Nyquist, came the image of her roommate, sprawled out on a sofa in a pink housecoat: a short plump redhead, breasty, full-faced. "Sure," Selig said. "Why not?" Nyquist, rummaging through minds, found the girls' phone number, called, worked his charm. They came up for drinks. "This awful snowstorm," the blonde said, shuddering. "It can drive you crazy!" The four of them went through a lot of liquor to a tinkling jazz accompaniment: Mingus, MJQ, Chico Hamilton. The redhead was better-looking than Selig expected, not quite so plump or coarse—the double refraction must have introduced some distortions—but she giggled too much, and he found himself disliking her to some degree. Still, there was no backing out now. Eventually, very late in the evening, they coupled off, Nyquist and the blonde in the bedroom, Selig and the redhead in the livingroom. Selig grinned selfconsciously at her when they were finally alone. He had never learned how to suppress that infantile grin, which he knew must reveal a mingling of gawky anticipation and plummeting terror. "Hello," he said. They kissed and his hands went to her breasts, and she pushed herself up against him in an unashamedly hungry way. She seemed a few years older than he was, but most women seemed that way to him. Their clothes dropped away. "I like lean men," she said, and giggled as she pinched his sparse flesh. Her breasts rose to him like pink birds. He caressed her with a virgin's timid intensity. During the months of their friendship Nyquist had occasionally supplied him with his own discarded women, but it was weeks since he had been to bed with anyone, and he was afraid that his abstinence would rush him into an embarrassing calamity. No: the liquor cooled his ardor just enough, and he held himself in check, ploughing her solemnly and energetically with no fears of going off too fast.

About the time he realized the redhead was too drunk to come, Selig felt a tickle in his skull: Nyquist was probing him! This show of curiosity, this voyeurism, seemed an odd diversion for the usually self-contained Nyquist. Spying's *my* trick, Selig thought, and for a moment he was so disturbed by being observed in the act of love that he began to soften. Through conscious effort he reconstituted himself. This has no deep significance, he told himself. Nyquist is wholly amoral and does what he pleases, peeks here and peeks there without regard for propriety, and why should I let his scanning bother me? Recovering, he reached toward Nyquist and reciprocated the probe. Nyquist welcomed him:

—How you doing, Davey?

—Fine. Just fine.

—I got me a hot one here. Take a look.

Selig envied Nyquist's cool detachment. No shame, no guilt, no hangups of any kind. No trace of exhibitionistic pride nor voyeuristic panting, either: it seemed altogether natural to him to exchange such contacts now. Selig, though, could not help feeling queasy as he watched, through closed eyes, Nyquist busily working over the blonde, and watched Nyquist similarly watching him, echoing images of their parallel copulations reverberating dizzily from mind to mind. Nyquist, pausing a moment to detect and isolate Selig's sense of uneasiness, mocked it gently. You're worried that there's some kind of latent gayness in this thing, Nyquist told him. But I think what really scares you is contact, any sort of contact. Right? Wrong, Selig said, but he had felt the point hit home. For five minutes more they monitored each other's minds, until Nyquist decided the time had come to come, and the tempestuous tremors of his nervous system flung Selig, as usual, from his consciousness. Soon after, growing bored with humping the jiggling, sweaty redhead, Selig let his own climax overwhelm him and slumped down, shivering, weary.

Nyquist came into the livingroom half an hour later, the blonde with him, both of them naked. He didn't bother to knock, which surprised the redhead a little; Selig had no way of telling her that Nyquist had known they were finished. Nyquist put some music on and they all sat quietly, Selig and the redhead working on the bourbon, Nyquist and the blonde nipping into the Scotch, and toward dawn, as the snow began to slacken, Selig tentatively suggested a second round of lovemaking with a change of partners. "No," the redhead said. "I'm all fucked out. I want to go to sleep. Some other time, okay?" She fumbled for her clothes. At the door, wobbling and staggering, making a boozy farewell, she let something slip. "I can't help thinking there's something peculiar about you two guys," she said. *In vino veritas.* "You aren't a couple of queers, by any chance, are you?"

Seventeen

I remain on dead center. Becalmed, static, anchored. No, that's a lie, or if not a lie then at the very least a benign misstatement, a faulty cluster of metaphors. I am ebbing. Ebbing all the time. My tide is going out. I am revealed as a bare rocky shore, iron-hard, with trailing streamers of dirty brown seaweed dangling toward the absenting surf. Green crab scuttling about. Yes, I ebb, which is to say I diminish, I attenuate. Do you know, I feel quite calm about it now? Of course my moods fluctuate but

I feel

Quite calm

About it now.

This is the third year since first I began to recede from myself. I think it started in the spring of 1974. Up till then it worked faultlessly, I mean the power, always there when I had occasion to call upon it, always dependable, doing all its customary tricks, serving me in all my dirty needs; and then without warning, without reason, it began dying. Little failures of input. Tiny episodes of psychic impotence. I associate these events with early spring, blackened wisps of late snow still clinging to the streets, and it could not have been '75 nor was it '73, with leads me to place the onset of outgo in the intermediate year. I would be snug and smug inside someone's head, scanning scandals thought to be safely hidden, and suddenly everything would blur and become uncertain. Rather like reading the *Times* and having the text abruptly turn to Joycean dream-gabble between one line and the next, so that a straightforward dreary account of the latest Presidential fact-finding commission's finding of futile facts has metamorphosed into a foggy impenetrable report on old Earwicker's borborygmi. At such times I would falter and pull out in fear. What would you do if you believed you were in bed with your heart's desire and awakened to find yourself screwing a starfish? But these unclarities and distortions were not the worst part: I think the inversions were, the total reversal of signal. Such as picking up a flash of love when what is really being radiated is frosty hatred. Or vice versa. When that happens I want to pound on walls to test reality. From Judith one day I got strong waves of sexual desire, an overpowering incestuous yearning, which cost me a fine dinner as I ran nauseated and retching to the bowl. All an error, all a deception; she was aiming spears at me and I took them for Cupid's arrows, more fool I. Well, after that I got blank spaces, tiny deaths of perception in mid-contact, and after that came mingled inputs, crossed wires, two minds coming in at once and me unable to tell the which from the which. For a time the color appercept dropped out, though that has come back, one of the many false returns. And there were other losses, barely discernible ones but cumulative in their effect. I make lists now of things I once could do that I can no longer. Inventories of the shrinkage. Like a dying man confined to his bed, paralyzed but observant, watching his relatives pilfer his goods. This day the television set has gone, and this day the Thackeray first editions, and this day the spoons, and now they have made off with my Piranesis, and tomorrow it will be the pots and pans, the Venetian blinds, my neckties, and my trousers, and by the next week they will be taking toes, intestines, corneas, testicles, lungs, and nostrils. What will they use my nostrils for? I used to fight back with long walks, cold showers, tennis, massive doses of Vitamin A, and other hopeful, implausible remedies, and more recently I experimented with fasting and pure thoughts, but such struggling now seems to me inappropriate and even blasphemous; these days I strive toward cheerful acceptance of loss, with such success as you may have already perceived. Aeschylus warns me not to kick against the pricks, also Euripides and I believe Pindar, and if I were to check the New Testament I think I would find the injunction there as well, and so I obey, I kick not, even when the pricks are fiercest. I accept, I accept. Do you see that quality of acceptance growing in me? Make no mistake, I am sincere. This morning, at least, I am well on my way to acceptance, as golden autumn sunlight floods my room and expands my tattered soul. I lie here practicing the techniques that will make me invulnerable to the knowledge that it's all fleeing from me. I search for the joy that I know lies buried in the awareness of decline. Grow old along with me! The best is yet to be, The last of life, for which the first was made. Do you believe that? I believe that. I'm getting better at believing all sorts of things. Why, sometimes I've believed as many as six impossible things before breakfast. Good old Browning! How comforting he is:

> Then welcome each rebuff
> That turns earth's smoothness rough,
> Each sting that bids not sit nor stand, but go!

> Be our joys three parts pain!
> Strive, and hold cheap the strain.

Yes. Of course. And be our pains three parts joy, he might have added. Such joy this morning. And it's all fleeing from me, all ebbing. Going out of me from every pore.

*   *   *

Silence is coming over me. I will speak to no one after it's gone. And no one will speak to me.

*   *   *

I stand here over the bowl patiently pissing my power away. Naturally I feel some sorrow over what's happening, I feel regret, I feel—why crap around?—I feel anger and frustration and despair, but also, strangely, I feel shame. My cheeks burn, my eyes will not meet other eyes, I can hardly face my fellow mortals for the shame of it, as if something precious has been entrusted to me and I have failed in my trusteeship. I must say to the world, I've wasted my assets, I've squandered my patrimony, I've let it slip away, going, going, I'm a bankrupt now, a bankrupt. Perhaps this is a family trait, this embarrassment when disaster comes. We Seligs like to tell the world we are orderly people, captains of our souls, and when something external downs us we are abashed. I remember when my parents briefly owned a car, a dark-green 1948 Chevrolet purchased at some absurdly low price in 1950, and we were driving somewhere deep in Queens, perhaps on our way to my grandmother's grave, the annual pilgrimage, and a car emerged from a blind alley and hit us. A schvartze at the wheel, drunk, giddy. Nobody hurt,

but our fender badly crumpled and our grille broken, the
distinctive T-bar that identified the 1948 model hanging
loose. Though the accident was in no way his fault my father
reddened and reddened, transmitting feverish embarrassment, as though he were apologizing to the universe for
having done anything so thoughtless as allowing his car to be
hit. How he apologized to the other driver, too, my grim
bitter father! It's all right, it's all right, accidents can happen,
you mustn't feel upset about it, see, we're all okay! Looka
mah car, man, looka mah car, the other driver kept saying,
evidently aware that he was on to a soft touch, and I feared
my father was going to give him money for the repairs, but my
mother, fearing the same thing, headed him off at the pass. A
week later he was still embarrassed; I popped into his mind
while he was talking with a friend and heard him trying to
pretend my mother had been driving, which was absurd—she
never had a license—and then I felt embarrassed for him. Judith,
too, when her marriage broke up, when she walked out on an
impossible situation, registered enormous grief over the shameful
fact that someone so purposeful and effective in life as Judith
Hannah Selig should have entered into a lousy, murderous
marriage which had to be terminated vulgarly in the divorce
courts. Ego, ego, ego. I the miraculous mindreader, entering
upon a mysterious decline, apologizing for my carelessness. I
have misplaced my gift somewhere. Will you forgive me?

* * *

Good, to forgive;
Best, to forget!
Living, we fret;
Dying, we live.

* * *

Take an imaginary letter, Mr. Selig. Harrumph. Miss Kitty
Holstein, Something West Sixty-something Street, New York
City. Check the address later. Don't bother about the zipcode.
Dear Kitty:
*I know you haven't heard from me in ages but I think now
it's appropriate to try to get in touch with you again.
Thirteen years have passed and a certain maturity must have
come over both of us, I think, healing old wounds and*

*making communication possible. Despite all hard feelings
that may once have existed between us I never lost my
fondness for you, and you remain bright in my mind.*

Speaking of my mind, there's something I ought to tell you.
I no longer do things very well with it. By "things" I mean
the mental thing, the mindreading trick, which of course I
couldn't do on you in any case, but which defined and shaped
my relationship to everybody else in the world. This power
seems to be slipping away from me now. It caused us so much
grief, remember? It was what ultimately split us up, as I tried
to explain in my last letter to you, the one you never
answered. In another year or so—who knows, six months, a
month, a week?—it will be totally gone and I will be just an
ordinary human being, like yourself. I will be a freak no
longer. Perhaps then there will be an opportunity for us to
resume the relationship that was interrupted in 1963 and to
reestablish it on a more realistic footing.

I know I did dumb things then. I pushed you mercilessly. I
refused to accept you for yourself, and tried to make something
else out of you, something freakish, in fact, something just like
myself. I had good reasons in theory for attempting that, I
thought then, but of course they were wrong, they had to be
wrong, and I never saw that until it was too late. To you I
seemed domineering, overpowering, dictatorial—me, mild self-
effacing me! Because I was trying to transform you. And eventually I bored you. Of course you were very young then, you
were—shall I say it?—shallow, unformed, and you resisted me.
But now that we're both adults we might be able to make a go of it.

I hardly know what my life will be like as an ordinary
human being unable to enter minds. Right now I'm floundering,
looking for definitions of myself, looking for structures. I'm
thinking seriously of entering the Roman Catholic Church.
(Good Christ, am I? That's the first I've heard of that! The
stink of incense, the mumble of priests, is that what I want?)
Or perhaps the Episcopalians, I don't know. It's a matter of
affiliating myself with the human race. And also I want to fall
in love again. I want to be part of someone else. I've already
begun tentatively, timidly getting in touch with my sister
Judith again, after a whole lifetime of warfare; we're starting
to relate to each other for the first time, and that's encouraging to me. But I need more: a woman to love, not just
sexually but in all ways. I've really had that only twice in my
life, once with you, once about five years later with a girl

named Toni who wasn't very much like you, and both times this power of mine ruined things, once because I got too close with it, once because I couldn't get close enough. As the power slips away from me, as it dies, perhaps there's a chance for an ordinary human relationship between us at last, of the kind that ordinary human beings have all the time. For I will be ordinary. For I will be very ordinary.

I wonder about you. You're 35 years old now, I think. That sounds very old to me, even though I'm 41. (41 doesn't sound old, somehow!) I still think of you as being 22. You seemed even younger than that: sunny, open, naive. Of course that was my fantasy-image of you; I had nothing to go by but externals, I couldn't do my usual number on your psyche, and so I made up a Kitty who probably wasn't the real Kitty at all. Anyway, so you're 35. I imagine you look younger than that today. Did you marry? Of course you did. A happy marriage? Lots of kids? Are you still married? What's your married name, then, and where do you live, and how can I find you? If you're married, will you be able to see me anyway? Somehow I don't think you'd be a completely faithful wife—does that insult you?—and so there ought to be room in your life for me, as a friend, as a lover. Do you ever see Tom Nyquist? Did you go on seeing him for long, after you and I broke up? Were you bitter toward me for the things I told you about him in that letter? If your marriage has broken up, or if somehow you never married, would you live with me now? Not as a wife, not yet, just as a companion. To help me get through the last phases of what's happening to me? I need help so much. I need love. I know that's a lousy way to go about making a proposition, let alone a proposal, that is, saying, Help me, comfort me, stay with me. I'd rather reach to you in strength than in weakness. But right now I'm weak. There's this globe of silence growing in my head, expanding, expanding, filling my whole skull, creating this big empty place. I'm suffering a slow reality leakage. I can only see the edges of things, not their substance, and now the edges are getting indistinct too. Oh, Christ. Kitty I need you. Kitty how will I find you? Kitty I hardly knew you. Kitty Kitty Kitty

* * *

Twang. The plangent chord. Twing. The breaking string. Twong. The lyre untuned. Twang. Twing. Twong.

* * *

Dear children of God, my sermon this morning will be a
very short one. I wish only that you should ponder and
meditate the deep meaning and mystery of a few lines I
intend to rip off the saintly Tom Eliot, a thoughtful guide for
troubled times. Beloved, I direct you to his *Four Quartets*, to
his paradoxical line, "In my beginning is my end," which he
amplifies some pages later with the comment, "What we call
the beginning is often the end/ And to make an end is to
make a beginning." Some of us are ending right now, dear
children; that is to say, aspects of their lives that once were
central to them are drawing to a close. Is this an end or is it a
beginning? Can the end of one thing not be the beginning of
another? I think so, beloved. I think that the closing of a door
does not preclude the opening of a different door. Of course,
it takes courage to walk through that new door when we do
not know what may lie beyond it, but one who has faith in
Our Lord who died for us, who trusts fully in Him who came
for the salvation of man, need have no fears. Our lives are
pilgrimages toward Him. We may die small deaths every day,
but we are reborn from death to death, until at last we go
into the dark, into the vacant interstellar spaces where He
awaits us, and why should we fear that, if He is there? And
until that time comes let us live our lives without giving way
to the temptation to grieve for ourselves. Remember always
that the world still is full of wonders, that there are always
new quests, that seeming ends are not ends in truth, but only
transitions, stations of the way. Why should we mourn? Why
should we give ourselves over to sorrow, though our lives be
daily subtractions? If we lose *this*, do we also lose *that*? If
sight goes, does love go also? If feeling grows faint, may we
not return to the old feelings and draw comfort from them?
Much of our pain is mere confusion.

Be then of good cheer on this Our Lord's day, beloved, and
spin no snares in which to catch yourselves, nor allow yourselves the self-indulgent sin of misery, and make no false
distinctions between ends and beginnings, but go onward,
ever searching, to new ecstasies, to new communions, to new
worlds, and give no space in your soul to fear, but yield
yourself up to the Peace of Christ and await that which must
come. In the Name of the Father, and of the Son, and of the
Holy Ghost. Amen.

*   *   *

Now comes a dark equinox out of its proper moment. The bleached moon glimmers like a wretched old skull. The leaves shrivel and fall. The fires die down. The dove, wearying, flutters to earth. Darkness spreads. Everything blows away. The purple blood falters in the narrowing veins; the chill impinges on the straining heart; the soul dwindles; even the feet become untrustworthy. Words fail. Our guides admit they are lost. That which has been solid grows transparent. Things pass away. Colors fade. This is a gray time, and I fear it will be grayer still, one of these days. Tenants of the house, thoughts of a dry brain in a dry season.

Eighteen

When Toni moved out of my place on 114th Street I waited two days before I did anything. I assumed she would come back when she calmed down; I figured she'd call, contrite, from some friend's house and say she was sorry she panicked and would I come get her in a cab. Also, in those two days I was in no shape to take any sort of action, because I was still suffering the aftereffects of my vicarious trip; I felt as though someone had seized my head and pulled on it, stretching my neck like a rubber band, letting it finally snap back into place with a sharp *thwock!* that addled my brains. I spent those two days in bed, dozing mostly, occasionally reading, and rushing madly out into the hall every time the telephone rang.

But she didn't come back and she didn't call, and on the Tuesday after the acid trip I started searching for her. I phoned her office first. Teddy, her boss, a bland sweet scholarly man, very gentle, very gay. No, she hadn't been to work this week. No, she hadn't been in touch at all. Was it urgent? Would I like to have her home number? "I'm *calling* from her home number," I said. "She isn't here and I don't know where she's gone. This is David Selig, Teddy." "Oh," he said. Very faintly, with great compassion. "Oh." And I said, "If she happens to call in, will you tell her to get in touch with me?" Next I started to phone her friends, those whose numbers I could find: Alice, Doris, Helen, Pam, Grace. Most of them, I knew, didn't like me. I didn't have to be telepathic to realize that. They thought she was throwing herself away on me, wasting her life with a man without career, prospects, money, ambition, talent, or looks. All five of them told me they hadn't heard from her. Doris, Helen, and Pam sounded sincere. The other two, it seemed to me, were lying. I took a taxi over to Alice's place in the Village and shot a probe upward, *zam!* nine stories into her head, and I learned a lot of things about Alice that I hadn't really wanted to know, but I didn't find out where Toni was. I felt dirty about spying and didn't probe Grace. Instead I called my employer, the writer, whose book Toni was editing, and asked if he'd seen her. Not in weeks, he told me, all ice. Dead end. The trail had run out.

I dithered on Wednesday, wondering what to do, and finally, melodramatically, called the police. Gave a bored desk sergeant her description: tall, thin, long dark hair, brown eyes. No bodies found in Central Park lately? In subway trash cans? The basements of Amsterdam Avenue tenements? No. No. No. Look, buddy, if we hear anything we'll let you know, but it don't sound serious to me. So much for the police. Restless, hopelessly strung out, I walked down to the Great Shanghai for a miserable half-eaten dinner, good food gone to waste. (Children are starving in Europe, Duv. Eat. Eat.) Afterwards, sitting around over the sad scattered remnants of my shrimp with sizzling rice and feeling myself drop deep into bereavement, I scored a cheap pickup in a manner I've always despised: I scanned the various single girls in the big restaurant, of whom there were numerous, looking for one who was lonely, thwarted, vulnerable, sexually permissive, and in generally urgent need of ego reinforcement. It's no trick getting laid if you have a sure way of knowing who's available, but there's not much sport in the chase. She was, this fish in the barrel, a passably attractive married lady in her mid-20's, childless, whose husband, a Columbia instructor, evidently had more interest in his doctoral thesis than in her. He spent every night immured in the stacks of Butler Library doing research, creeping home late, exhausted, irritable, and generally impotent. I took her to my room, couldn't get it up either— that bothered her; she assumed it was a sign of rejection—and spent two tense hours listening to her life story. Ultimately I managed to screw her, and I came almost instantly. Not my finest hour. When I returned from walking her home—110th and Riverside Drive—the phone was ringing. Pam. "I've heard from Toni," she said, and suddenly I was slimy with guilt over my sleazy consolatory infidelity. "She's staying with Bob Larkin at his place over on East 83rd Street."

Jealousy, despair, humiliation, agony.

"Bob who?"

"Larkin. He's that high-bracket interior decorator she always talks about."

"Not to me."

"One of Toni's oldest friends. They're very close. I think he used to date her when she was in high school." A long pause. Then Pam chuckled warmly into my numb silence. "Oh, relax, relax, David! He's *gay*! He's just a kind of father-confessor for her. She goes to him when there's trouble."

"I see."

"You two have broken up, haven't you?"

"I'm not sure. I suppose we have. I don't know."

"Is there anything I can do to help?" This from Pam, who I had always thought regarded me as a destructive influence of whom Toni was well advised to be quit.

"Just give me his phone number," I said.

I phoned. It rang and rang and rang. At last Bob Larkin picked up. Gay, all right, a sweet tenor voice complete with lisp, not very different from the voice of Teddy-at-work. Who teaches them to speak with the homo accent? I asked, "Is Toni there?" A guarded response: "Who's calling, please?" I told him. He asked me to wait, and a minute or so passed while he conferred with her, hand over the mouthpiece. At last he came back and said Toni was there, yes, but she was very tired and resting and didn't want to talk to me right now. "It's urgent," I said. "Please tell her it's urgent." Another muffled conference. Same reply. He suggested vaguely that I call back in two or three days. I started to wheedle, to whine, to beg. In the middle of that unheroic performance the phone abruptly changed hands and Toni said to me, "Why did you call?"

"That ought to be obvious. I want you to come back."

"I can't."

She didn't say *I won't*. She said *I can't*.

I said, "Would you like to tell me why?"

"Not really."

"You didn't even leave a note. Not a word of explanation. You ran out so fast."

"I'm sorry, David."

"It was something you saw in me while you were tripping, wasn't it?"

"Let's not talk about it," she said. "It's over."

"I don't want it to be over."

"I do."

I do. That was like the sound of a great gate clanging shut in my face. But I wasn't going to let her throw home the bolts just yet. I told her she had left some of her things in my room, some books, some clothing. A lie; she had made a clean sweep. But I can be persuasive when I'm cornered, and she began to think it might be true. I offered to bring the stuff over right now. She didn't want me to come. She preferred never to see me again, she told me. Less painful all around, that way. But her voice lacked conviction; it was higher in pitch and much more nasal than it was when she spoke with sincerity. I knew she still loved me, more or less; even after a forest fire, some of the burned snags live on, and green new shoots spring from them. So I told myself. Fool that I was. In any case she couldn't entirely turn me away. Just as she had been unable to refrain from picking up the telephone, now she found it impossible to refuse me access to her. Talking very fast, I bludgeoned her into yielding. All right, she said. Come over. Come over. But you're wasting your time.

It was close to midnight. The summer air was clinging and clammy, with a hint of rain on the way. No stars visible. I hurried crosstown, choked with the vapors of the humid city and the bile of my shattered love. Larkin's apartment was on the nineteenth floor of an immense new terraced white-brick tower, far over on York Avenue. Admitting me, he gave me a tender, compassionate smile, as if to say, You poor bastard, you've been hurt and you're bleeding and now you're going to get ripped open again. He was about 30, a stocky, boyish-faced man with long unruly curly brown hair and large uneven teeth. He radiated warmth and sympathy and kindness. I could understand why Toni ran to him at times like this. "She's in the livingroom," he said. "To the left."

It was a big, impeccable place, somewhat freaky in decor, with jagged blurts of color dancing over the walls, pre-Columbian artifacts in spotlighted showcases, bizarre African masks, chrome-steel furniture—the kind of implausible apartment you see photographed in the Sunday *Times*' magazine section. The livingroom was the core of the spectacle, a vast white-walled room with a long curving window that revealed all the splendors of Queens across the East River. Toni sat at the far end, near the window, on an angular couch, dark blue flecked with gold. She wore old, dowdy clothes that clashed furiously with the splendor around her: a motheaten red sweater that I detested, a short frumpy black skirt, dark hose—and she was slumped down sullenly on her spine, leaning on one elbow, her legs jutting awkwardly forward. It was a posture that made her look bony and ungraceful. A cigarette drooped in her hand and there was a huge pile of butts in the ashtray beside her. Her eyes were bleak. Her long hair was tangled. She didn't move as I walked toward her. Such an aura of hostility came from her that I halted twenty feet away.

"Where's the stuff you were bringing?" she asked.

"There wasn't any. I just said that to have an excuse to see you."

"I figured that."

"What went wrong, Toni?"

"Don't ask. Just don't ask." Her voice had dropped into its lowest register, a bitter husky contralto. "You shouldn't have come here at all."

"If you'd tell me what I did—"

"You tried to hurt me," she said. "You tried to bum-trip me." She stubbed out her cigarette and immediately lit another. Her eyes, somber, and hooded, refused to meet mine. "I realized finally that you were my enemy, that I had to escape from you. So I packed and got out."

"Your enemy? You know that isn't true."

"It was strange," she said. "I didn't understand what was happening, and I've talked to some people who've dropped a lot of acid and they can't understand it either. It was like our minds were linked, David. Like a telepathic channel had opened between us. And all sorts of stuff was pouring from you into me. Hateful stuff. Poisonous stuff. I was thinking your thoughts. Seeing myself as you saw me. Remember, when you said you were tripping too, even though you hadn't had any acid? And then you told me you were, like, reading my mind. That was what scared me. The way our minds seemed to blur together, to overlap. To become one. I never knew acid could do that to people."

This was my cue to tell her that it wasn't only the acid, that it hadn't been some druggy delusion, that what she had felt was the impingement of a special power granted me at birth, a gift, a curse, a freak of nature. But the words congealed in my mouth. They sounded insane to me. How could I confess such stuff? I let the moment pass. Instead I said lamely, "Okay, it was a strange moment for both of us. We were a little out of our heads. But the trip's over. You don't have to hide from me now. Come back, Toni."

"No."

"In a few days, then?"

"No."

"I don't understand this."

"Everything's changed," she said. "I couldn't ever live with you now. You scare me too much. The trip's over, but I look at you and I see demons. I see some kind of thing that's half-bat, half-man, with big rubbery wings and long yellow fangs and—oh, Jesus, David, I can't help any of this! I *still* feel as if our minds are linked. Stuff creeping out of you into my head. I should never have touched the acid." Carelessly she crushed her cigarette and found another. "You make me uncomfortable now. I wish you'd go. It gives me a headache just being this close to you. Please. Please. I'm sorry, David."

I didn't dare look into her mind. I was afraid that what I'd find there would blast and shrivel me. But in those days my power was still so strong that I couldn't help picking up, whether I sought it or not, a generalized low-level mental radiation from everyone I came close to, and what I picked up now from Toni confirmed what she was saying. She hadn't stopped loving me. But the acid, though lysergic and not sulfuric, had scarred and corroded our relationship by opening that terrible gateway between us. It was torment for her to be in the same room with me. No resources of mine could deal with that. I considered strategies, looked for angles of approach, ways to reason with her, to heal her through soft earnest words. No way. No way at all. I ran a dozen trial dialogs in my head and they all ended with Toni begging me to get out of her life. So. The End. She sat there all but motionless, downcast, dark-faced, her wide mouth clapped in pain, her brilliant smile extinguished. She seemed to have aged twenty years. Her odd, exotic desert-princess beauty had wholly fled from her. Suddenly she was more real to me, in her shroud of pain, than ever before. Ablaze with suffering, alive with anguish. And no way for me to reach her. "All right," I said quietly. "I'm sorry too." Over, done with, swiftly, suddenly, no warning, the bullet singing through the air, the grenade rolling treacherously into the tent, the anvil

falling from the placid sky. Done with. Alone again. Not even
any tears. Cry? What shall I cry?

Bob Larkin had tactfully remained outside, in his long
foyer papered with dazzling black and white optical illusions,
during our brief muffled conversation. Again the gentle
sorrowing smile from him as I emerged.

"Thanks for letting me bother you this late," I said.

"No trouble at all. Too bad about you and Toni."

I nodded. "Yes. Too bad."

We faced each other uncertainly, and he moved toward me,
digging his fingers momentarily into the muscle of my arm,
telling me without words to shape up, to ride out the storm,
to get myself together. He was so open that my mind sank
unexpectedly into his, and I saw him plain, his goodness, his
kindness, his sorrow. Out of him an image rose to me, a sharp
encapsulated memory: himself and a sobbing, demolished
Toni, the night before last, lying naked together on his
modish round bed, her head cradled against his muscular
hairy chest, his hands fondling the pale heavy globes of her
breasts. Her body trembling with need. His unwilling drooping
manhood struggling to offer her the consolation of sex. His
gentle spirit at war with itself, flooded with pity and love for
her but dismayed by her disturbing femaleness, those breasts,
that cleft, her softness. You don't have to, Bob, she keeps
saying, you don't have to, you really don't have to, but he
tells her he wants to, it's about time we made it after knowing
each other all these years, it'll cheer you up, Toni, and
anyway a man needs a little variety, right? His heart goes out
to her but his body resists, and their lovemaking, when it
happens, is a hurried, pathetic, fumbled thing, a butting of
troubled reluctant bodies, ending in tears, tremors, shared
distress, and, finally, laughter, a triumph over pain. He kisses
her tears away. She thanks him gravely for his efforts. They
fall into childlike sleep, side by side. How civilized, how
tender. My poor Toni. Goodbye. Goodbye. "I'm glad she
went to you," I said. He walked me to the elevator. What
shall I cry? "If she snaps out of it I'll make sure she calls
you," he told me. I put my hand to his arm as he had to
mine, and gave him the best smile in my repertoire. Goodbye.

Nineteen

This is my cave. Twelve floors high in the Marble Hill Houses, Broadway and 228th Street, formerly a middle-income municipal housing project, now a catch-all for classless and deracinated urban detritus. Two rooms plus bathroom, kitchenette, hallway. Once upon a time you couldn't get into this project unless you were married and had kids. Nowadays a few singles have slipped in, on the grounds that they're destitute. Things change as the city decays; regulations break down. Most of the building's population is Puerto Rican, with a sprinkling of Irish and Italian. In this den of papists a David Selig is a great anomaly. Sometimes he thinks he owes his neighbors a daily lusty rendition of the *Shma Yisroel*, but he doesn't know the words. *Kol Nidre*, perhaps. Or the *Kaddish*. This is the bread of affliction which our forefathers ate in the land of Egypt. He is lucky to have been led out of Egypt into the Promised Land.

Would you like the guided tour of David Selig's cave? Very well. Please come this way. No touching anything, please, and don't park your chewing gum on the furniture. The sensitive, intelligent, amiable, neurotic man who will be your guide is none other than David Selig himself. No tipping allowed. Welcome, folks, welcome to my humble abode. We'll begin our tour in the bathroom. See, this is the tub—that yellow stain in the porcelain was already there when he moved in—this is the crapper, this is the medicine chest. Selig spends a great deal of time in here; it's a room significant to any in-depth understanding of his existence. For example, he sometimes takes two or three showers a day. What is it, do you think, that he's trying to wash away? Leave that toothbrush alone, sonny. All right, come with me. Do you see these posters in the hallway? They are artifacts of the 1960's. This one shows the poet Allen Ginsberg in the costume of Uncle Sam. This one is a crude vulgarization of a subtle topological paradox by the Dutch printmaker M. C. Escher. This one shows a nude young couple making love in the Pacific surf. Eight to ten years ago, hundreds of thousands of young people decorated their rooms with such posters. Selig, although he was not exactly young even then, did the same. He often has followed current fads and modes in an attempt to affiliate himself more firmly with the structures of contemporary existence. I suppose these posters are quite valuable now; he takes them with him from one cheap rooming house to the next.

This room is the bedroom. Dark and narrow, with the low ceiling typical of municipal construction a generation ago. I keep the window closed at all times so that the elevated train, roaring through the adjacent sky late at night, doesn't awaken me. It's hard enough to get some sleep even when things are quiet around you. This is his bed, in which he dreams uneasy dreams, occasionally, even now, involuntarily reading the minds of his neighbors and incorporating their thoughts in his fantasies. On this bed he has fornicated perhaps fifteen women, one or two or occasionally three times each, during the two and a half years of his residence here. Don't look so abashed, young lady! Sex is a healthy human endeavor and it remains an essential aspect of Selig's life, even now in middle age! It may become even more important to him in the years ahead, for sex is, after all, a way of establishing communication with other human beings, and certain other channels of communication appear to be closing for him. Who are these girls? Some of them are not girls; some are women well along in life. He charms them in his diffident way and persuades them to share an hour of joy with him. He rarely invites any of them back, and those whom he does invite back often refuse the invitation, but that's all right. His needs are met. What's that? Fifteen girls in two and a half years isn't very many for a bachelor? Who are you to judge? He finds it sufficient. I assure you, he finds it sufficient. Please don't sit on his bed. It's an old one, bought second-hand at an upstairs bargain basement that the Salvation Army runs in Harlem. I picked it up for a few bucks when I moved out of my last place, a furnished room on St. Nicholas Avenue, and needed some furniture of my own. Some years before that, around 1971, 1972, I had a waterbed, another example of my following of transient fads, but I couldn't ever get used to the swooshing and gurgling and I gave it, finally, to a hip young lady who dug it the most. What else is in the bedroom? Very little of interest, I'm afraid. A chest of drawers containing commonplace clothing. A pair of worn slippers. A cracked mirror: are you superstitious? A lopsided bookcase packed tight with old magazines that he will never look at again—*Partisan Review, Evergreen, Paris Review, New York Review of Books, Encounter,* a mound of trendy literary stuff, plus a few journals of psychoanalysis and psychiatry, which Selig reads sporadically in the hope of increasing his self-knowledge; he always tosses them aside in boredom and disappointment. Let's get out of here. This room must be depressing you. We go past the kitchenette—four-burner stove, half-size refrigerator, formica-topped table—where he assembles very modest breakfasts and lunches (dinner he usually eats out) and enter the main focus of the apartment, the L-shaped blue-walled jam-packed livingroom/study.

Here you can observe the full range of David Selig's intellectual development. This is his record collection, about a hundred well-worn disks, some of them purchased as far back as 1951. (Archaic monophonic records!) Almost entirely classical music, although you will note two intrusive deposits: five or six jazz records dating from 1959 and five or six rock records dating from 1969, both groups acquired in vague, abortive efforts at expanding the horizons of his taste. Otherwise, what you will find here, in the main, is pretty austere stuff, thorny, inaccessible: Schoenberg, late Beethoven, Mahler, Berg, the Bartok quartets, Bach passacaglias. Nothing that you'd be likely to whistle after one hearing. He doesn't know a lot about music, but he knows what he likes; you wouldn't much care for it.

And these are his books, accumulated since the age of ten and hauled lovingly about with him from place to place. The archaeological strata of his reading can readily be isolated and examined. Jules Verne, H. G. Wells, Mark Twain, Dashiell Hammett at the bottom. Sabatini. Kipling. Sir Walter Scott. Van Loon, *The Story of Mankind.* Verrill, *Great Conquerors of South and Central America.* The books of a sober, earnest, alienated little boy. Suddenly, with adolescence, a quantum leap: Orwell, Fitzgerald, Hemingway, Hardy, the easier Faulkner. Look at these rare paperbacks of the 1940's and early 1950's, in odd off-sized formats, with laminated plastic covers! See what you could buy then for only 25¢! Look at the prurient paintings, the garish lettering! These science-fiction books date from, that era too. I gobbled the stuff whole, hoping to find some clues to my own dislocated self's nature in the fantasies of Bradbury, Heinlein, Asimov, Sturgeon, Clarke. Look, here's Stapledon's *Odd John,* here's Beresford's *Hampdenshire Wonder,* here's a whole book called *Outsiders:*

Children of Wonder, full of stories of little superbrats with freaky powers. I've underlined a lot of passages in that last one, usually places where I quarreled with the writers. *Outsiders?* Those writers, gifted as they were, were the outsiders, trying to imagine powers they'd never had; and I, who was on the inside, I the youthful mind-prowler (the book is dated 1954), had bones to pick with them. They stressed the angst of being supernormal, forgot about the ecstasy. Although, thinking about angst vs. ecstasy now, I have to admit they knew whereof they writ. Fellows, I have fewer bones to pick these days. This is rats' alley, where the dead men lost their bones.

Observe how Selig's reading becomes more rarefied as we reach the college years. Joyce, Proust, Mann, Eliot, Pound, the old avant-garde hierarchy. The French period: Zola, Balzac, Montaigne, Celine, Rimbaud, Baudelaire. This thick slug of Dostoevsky occupying half a shelf. Lawrence. Woolf. The mystical era: Augustine, Aquinas, the *Tao Te Ching,* the *Upanishads,* the *Bhagavad-Gita.* The psychological era: Freud, Jung, Alder, Reich, Reik. The philosophical era. The Marxist era. All that Koestler. Back to literature: Conrad, Forster, Beckett. Moving onward toward the fractured '60's: Bellow, Pynchon, Malamud, Mailer, Burroughs, Barth. *Catch-22* and *The Politics of Experience.* Oh, yes, ladies and gentlemen, you are in the presence of a well-read man!

Here we have his files. A treasure-trove of personalia, awaiting a biographer yet unknown. Report cards, always with low marks for conduct. ("David shows little interest in his work and frequently disrupts the class.") Crudely crayoned birthday cards for his mother and father. Old photographs: can this fat freckled boy be the gaunt individual who stands before you now? This man with the high forehead and the forced rigid smile is the late Paul Selig, father of our subject, deceased (*olav hasholom!*) 11 August 1971 of complications following surgery for a perforated ulcer. This gray-haired woman with the hyperthyroid eyes is the late Martha Selig, wife of Paul, mother of David, deceased (*oy, veh, mama!*) 15 March 1973 of mysterious rot of internal organs, probably cancerous. This grim young lady with cold knifeblade face is Judith Hannah Selig, adopted child of P. and M., unloving sister of D. Date on back of photo: July 1963. Judith is therefore 18 years old and in the summertime of her hate for me. How much she looks like Toni in this picture! I never noticed the resemblance before, but they've got the same dusky Yemenite look, the same long black hair. But Toni's eyes were always warm and loving, except right at the very end, and Jude's eyes never held anything for me other than ice, ice, Plutonian ice. Let us continue with the examination of David Selig's private effects. This is his collection of essays and term papers, written during his college years. ("Carew is a courtly and elegant poet, whose work reflects influences both of Jonson's precise classicism and Donne's grotesque fancy—an interesting synthesis. His poems are neatly constructed and sharp of diction; in a poem such as 'Ask me no more where Jove bestows,' he captures Jonson's harmonious austerity perfectly, while in others, such as 'Mediocrity in Love Rejected' or 'Ingrateful Beauty Threatened,' his wit is akin to that of Donne.") How fortunate for D. Selig that he kept all this literary twaddle: here in his later years these papers have become the capital on which he lives, for you know, of course, how the central figure of our investigations earns his livelihood nowadays. What else do we find in these archives? The carbon copies of innumerable letters. Some of them are quite impersonal missives. *Dear President Eisenhower. Dear Pope John. Dear Secretary-General Hammarskjold.* Quite often, once, though rarely in recent years, he launched these letters to far corners of the globe. His fitful unilateral efforts at making contact with a deaf world. His troubled futile attempts at restoring order in a universe plainly tumbling toward the ultimate thermodynamic doom. Shall we look at a few of these documents? *You say, Governor Rockefeller, that "with nuclear weapons multiplying, our security is dependent on the credibility of our willingness to resort to our deterrent. It is our heavy responsibility as public officials and as citizens to save the lives and to protect the health of our people. A lagging civil-defense effort cannot be excused by our conviction that nuclear war is a tragedy and that we must strive by all honorable means to assure peace." Permit me to disagree. Your bomb-shelter program, Governor, is the project of a morally impoverished mind. To divert energy and resources from the search for a lasting peace to this ostrich-in-the-sand scheme is, I think, a foolish and dangerous policy that. . . .* The Governor, by way of replying, sent his thanks and an offprint of the very speech which Selig was protesting. Can one expect more? *Mr. Nixon, your entire campaign is pitched to the theory that America never had it so good under President Eisenhower, and so let's have four more*

*years of the same. To me you sound like Faust, crying out to
the passing moment, Bleibe doch, du bist so schoen! (Am I
too literate for you, Mr. Vice-President?) Please bear in mind
that when Faust utters those words, Mephistopheles arrives
to college his soul. Does it honestly seem to you that this
instant in history is so sweet that you would stop the clocks
forever? Listen to the anguish in the land. Listen to the voices
of Mississippi's Negroes, listen to the cries of the hungry
children of factory workers thrown out of work by a Republican recession, listen to....Dear Mrs. Hemingway: Please
allow me to add my words to the thousands expressing sorrow
at the death of your husband. The bravery he showed in the
face of a life-situation that had become unendurable and
intolerable is indeed an example for those of us who....Dear
Dr. Buber....Dear Professor Toynbee....Dear President
Nehru....Dear Mr. Pound: The whole civilized world re-
joices with you upon your liberation from the cruel and
unnatural confinement which....Dear Lord Russell....Dear
Chairman Khrushchev....Dear M. Malraux....dear....dear
....dear....A* remarkable collection of correspondence, you
must agree. With equally remarkable replies. See, this answer
says, *You may be right,* and this one says, *I am grateful for your
interest,* and this one says, *Of course time does not permit
individual replies to all letters received, but nevertheless please
be assured that your thoughts will receive careful consideration,*
and this one says, *Send this bastard the bedbug letter.*

Unfortunately we do not have the imaginary letters which
he dictates constantly to himself but never sends. *Dear Mr.
Kierkegaard: I agree entirely with your celebrated dictum
equating "the absurd" with "the fact that with God all things
are possible," and declaring, "The absurd is not one of the
factors which can be discriminated within the proper com-
pass of the understanding: it is not identical with the improbable, the unexpected, the unforeseen." In my own experiences
with the absurd....Dear Mr. Shakespeare: How aptly you
put it when you say, "Love is not love Which alters when it
alteration finds, Or bends with the remover to remove." Your
sonnet, however, begs the question: If love is not love, what
then is it, that feeling of closeness which can be so absurdly
and unexpectedly destroyed by a trifle? If you could suggest
some alternate existential mode of relating to others that....*
Since they are transient, the product of vagrant impulses, and
often incomprehensible, we have no satisfactory access to

such communications, which Selig sometimes produces at a rate of hundreds per hour. *Dear Mr. Justice Holmes: In Southern Pacific Co. v. Jensen, 244 U.S. 205, 221 [1917], you ruled, "I recognize without hesitation that judges do and must legislate, but they can do so only interstitially; they are confined from molar to molecular motions." This splendid metaphor is not entirely clear to me, I must confess, and. . . .*

* * *

Dear Mr. Selig:
   The present state of the world and the whole of life is diseased. If I were a doctor and were asked for my advice, I should reply, "Create silence."

Yours very sincerely,
Sören Kierkegaard
(1813–1855)

* * *

And then there are these three folders here, thick beige cardboard. They are not available for public inspection, since they contain letters of a rather more personal kind. Under the terms of our agreement with the David Selig Foundation, I am forbidden to quote, though I may paraphrase. These are his letters to and occasionally from the girls he has loved or has wanted to love. The earliest is dated 1950 and bears the notation at the top in large red letters, NEVER SENT. *Dear Beverly*, it begins, and it is full of embarrassingly graphic sexual imagery. What can you tell us about this Beverly, Selig? Well, she was short and cute and freckled, with big headlights and a sunny disposition, and sat in front of me in my biology class, and had a creepy twin sister, Estelle, who scowled a lot and through some fluke of genetics was as flat as Beverly was bosomy. Maybe that was why she scowled so much. Estelle liked me in her bitter murky way and I think might eventually have slept with me, which would have done my 15-year-old ego a lot of good, but I despised her. She seemed like a blotchy, badly done imitation of Beverly, whom I loved. I used to wander barefoot in Beverly's mind while the teacher, Miss Mueller, droned on about mitosis and chromosomes. She had just yielded her cherry to Victor Schlitz, the big rawboned green-eyed red-haired boy who sat next to her, and I learned a lot about sex from her at one remove, with a 12-hour-time-lag, as she radiated every morning her adventure of the night before with Victor. I wasn't jealous of him. He was handsome and self-confident and deserved her, and I was too shy and insecure to lay anybody anyway, then. So I rode secretly piggyback on their romance and fantasized doing with Beverly the gaudy things Victor was doing with her, until I desperately wanted to get into her myself, but my explorations of her head told me that to her I was just an amusing gnomish child, an oddity, a jester. How then to score? I wrote her this letter describing in vivid sweaty detail everything that she and Victor had been up to, and said, Don't you wonder how I know all this, heh heh heh? The implication being that I'm some kind of superman with the power to penetrate the intimacies of a woman's mind. I figured that would topple her right into my arms in a swoon of awe, but some second thoughts led me to see that she'd either think I was crazy or a peeping tom, and would in either case be wholly turned off me, so I filed the letter away undelivered. My mother found it one night but she didn't dare say anything about it to me, hopelessly blocked as she was on the entire subject of sexuality; she just put it back in my notebook. I picked her thoughts that night and discovered she'd sneaked a look. Was she shocked and disturbed? Yes, she was, but also she felt very proud that her boy was a man at last, writing smutty stuff to pretty girls. My son the pornographer.

Most of the letters in this file date between 1954 and 1968. The most recent was written in the autumn of 1974, after which time Selig began to feel less and less in touch with the rest of the human race and stopped writing letters, except in his head. I don't know how many girls are represented here, but there must have been quite a few. Generally these were all superficial affairs, for Selig, as you know, never married or even had many serious involvements with women. As in the case of Beverly, the ones he loved most deeply he usually never had actual relationships with, though he was capable of pretending he felt love for someone who was in fact a casual pickup. At times he made use of his special gifts knowingly to exploit women sexually, especially about the age of 25. He is not proud of that period. Wouldn't you like to read these letters, you stinking voyeurs? But you won't. You won't get your paws on them. Why have I invited you in here, anyway? Why do I let you peer at my books and my photographs and my unwashed dishes and my stained bathtub? It must be that my sense of self is slipping. Isolation is choking me; the windows are closed but at least I've opened the door. I need you to bolster my grip on reality by looking into my life, by

incorporating parts of it into your own experience, by discovering
that I'm real, I exist, I suffer, I have a past if not a future. So
that you can go away from here saying, Yes, I know David
Selig, actually I know him quite well. But that doesn't mean I
have to show you everything. Hey, here's a letter to Amy!
Amy who relieved me of my festering virginity in the spring
of 1953. Wouldn't you like to know the story of how that
happened? Anybody's first time has an irresistible fascination.
Well, fuck you: I don't feel like discussing it. It isn't much of a
story anyway. I put it in her and I came and she didn't, that's
how it was, and if you want to know the rest, who she was,
how I seduced her, make up the details yourself. Where's
Amy now? Amy's dead. How do you like that? His first lay,
and he's outlived her already. She died in an ᵃuto accident at
the age of 23 and her husband, who knew me vaguely,
phoned me to tell me, since I had once been a friend of hers.
He was still in trauma because the police had made him come
down to identify the body, and she had really been destroyed,
mangled, mutilated. Like something from another planet,
that's how she looked, he told me. Catapulted through the
windshield and into a tree. And I told him, "Amy was the
first girl I ever slept with," and he started consoling me.
He, consoling me, and I had only been trying to be sadistic.
Time passes. Amy's dead and Beverly's a pudgy middle-
aged housewife, I bet. Here's a letter to Jackie Newhouse,
telling her I can't sleep for thinking about her. Jackie Newhouse?
Who's that? Oh, yes. Five feet two and a pair of boobs that
would have made Marilyn Monroe feel topheavy. Sweet.
Dumb. Puckered lips, baby-blue eyes. Jackie had nothing
going for her at all except her bosom, but that was enough for
me, 17 years old and hung up on breasts, God knows why. I
loved her for her mammaries, so globular and conspicuous in
the tight white polo shirts she liked to wear. Summer of 1952.
She loved Frank Sinatra and Perry Como, and had FRANKIE
written in lipstick down the left thigh of her jeans and PERRY
on the right. She also loved her history teacher, whose name,
I think, was Leon Sissinger or Zippinger or something like
that, and she had LEON on her jeans too, from hip to hip. I
kissed her twice but that was all, not even my tongue in her
mouth; she was even more shy than I, terrified that some
hideous male hand would violate the purity of those mighty
knockers. I followed her around, trying not to get into her
head because it depressed me to see how empty it was. How

did it end? Oh, yes: her kid brother Arnie was telling me how he sees her naked at home all the time, and I, desperate for a vicarious glimpse of her bare breasts, plunged into his skull and stole a second-hand peek. I hadn't realized until then how important a bra can be. Unbound, they hung to her plump little belly, two mounds of dangling meat crisscrossed by bulging blue veins. Cured me of my fixation. So long ago, so unreal to me now, Jackie.

Here. Look. Spy on me. My fervid frenzied outpourings of love. Read them all, what do I care? Donna, Elsie, Magda, Mona, Sue, Lois, Karen. Did you think I was sexually deprived? Did you think my lame adolescence sent me stumbling into manhood incapable of finding women? I quarried for my life between their thighs. Dear Connie, what a wild night that was! Dear Chiquita, your perfume still lingers in the air. Dear Elaine, when I woke this morning the taste of you was on my lips. Dear Kitty, I—

Oh, God. Kitty. *Dear Kitty. I have so much to explain to you that I don't know where to begin. You never understood me, and I never understood you, and so the love I had for you was fated to bring us to a bad pass sooner or later. Which it now has. The failures of communication extended all up and down our relationship, but because you were different from any person I had ever known, truly and qualitatively different, I made you the center of my fantasies and could not accept you as you were, but had to keep hammering and hammering and hammering away at you, until—*Oh, God. This one's too painful. What the hell are you doing reading someone else's mail? Don't you have any decency? I can't show you this. The tour's over. Out! Out! Everybody out! For Christ's sake, get *out!*

Twenty

There was always the danger of being found out. He knew he had to be on his guard. This was an era of witch-hunters, when anyone who departed from community norms was ferreted out and burned at the stake. Spies were everywhere, probing for young Selig's secret, fishing for the awful truth about him. Even Miss Mueller, his biology teacher. She was a pudgy little poodle of a woman, about 40, with a glum face and dark arcs under her eyes; like a cryptodyke of some sort she wore her hair cut brutally short, the back of her neck always showing the stubble of a recent shave, and came to class every day in a gray laboratory smock. Miss Mueller was very deep into the realm of extrasensory and occult phenomena. Of course they didn't use phrases like "very deep into" in 1949, when David Selig was in her class, but let the anachronism stand: she was ahead of her time, a hippie born too soon. She really grooved behind the irrational, the unknown. She knew her way around the high-school bio curriculum in her sleep, which was more or less the way she taught it. What turned her on, really, were things like telepathy, clairvoyance, telekinesis, astrology, the whole parapsychological bag. The most slender provocation was enough to nudge her away from the day's assignment, the study of metabolism or the circulatory system or whatever, and onto one of her hobbyhorses. She was the first on her block to own the *I Ching*. She had done time inside orgone boxes. She believed that the Great Pyramid of Gizeh held divine revelations for mankind. She had sought deeper truths by way of Zen, General Semantics, the Bates eyesight exercises, and the readings of Edgar Cayce. (How easily I can extend her quest past the year of my own exposure to her! She must have gone on to dianetics, Velikovsky, Bridey Murphy, and Timothy Leary, and ended up, in her old age, as a lady guru in some Los Angeles eyrie, heavy into psilocybin and peyote. Poor silly gullible pitiful old bitch.)

Naturally she kept up with the research into extrasensory perception that J. B. Rhine was doing down at Duke University. It terrified David whenever she spoke of this. He constantly feared that she was going to give way to the temptation to run some Rhine experiments in class, and would thereby flush him out of hiding. He had read Rhine himself, of course, *The Reach of the Mind* and *New Frontiers of the Mind*, had even peered into the opacities of *The Journal of Parapsychology*, hoping to find something that would explain him to himself, but there was nothing there except statistics and foggy conjecture. Okay, Rhine was no threat to him so long as he went on piddling around in North Carolina. But muddled Miss Mueller might just strip him naked and deliver him to the pyre.

Inevitable, the progression toward disaster. The topic for the week, suddenly, was the human brain, its functions and capabilities. See, this is the cerebrum, this is the cerebellum, this is the medulla oblongata. A child's garden of synapses. Fat-cheeked Norman Heimlich, gunning for a 99, knowing precisely which button to push, put up his hand: "Miss Mueller, do you think it'll ever be possible for people really to read minds, I mean not by tricks or anything but actual mental telepathy?" Oh, the joy of Miss Mueller! Her lumpy face glowing. This was her cue to launch into an animated discussion of ESP, parapsychology, inexplicable phenomena, supernormal modes of communication and perception, the Rhine researches, et cetera, et cetera, a torrent of metaphysical irrelevance. David wanted to hide under his desk. The word "telepathy" made him wince. He already suspected that half the class realized what he was. Now a flash of wild paranoia. Are they looking at me, are they staring and pointing and tapping their heads and nodding? Certainly these were irrational fears. He had surveyed every mind in the class again and again, desperately trying to amuse himself during the arid stretches of boredom, and he knew that his secret was safe. His classmates, plodding young Brooklynites all, would never cotton to the veiled presence of a superman in their midst. They thought he was strange, yes, but had no notion of *how* strange. Would Miss Mueller now blow his cover, though? She was talking about conducting parapsychology experiments in class to demonstrate the potential reach of the human brain. Oh where can I hide?

No escape. She had her cards with her the next day. "These are known as Zener cards," she explained solemnly, holding them up, fanning them out like Wild Bill Hickok about to deal himself a straight flush. David had never actually seen a set of the cards before, yet they were as familiar to him as the deck his parents used in their interminable canasta games. "They were devised about twenty-five years ago at Duke University by Dr. Karl E. Zener and Dr. J. B. Rhine. Another name for them is 'ESP cards.' Who can tell me what 'ESP' means?"

Norman Heimlich's stubby hand waving in the air. "Extrasensory perception, Miss Mueller!"

"Very good, Norman." Absentmindedly she began to shuffle the cards. Her eyes, normally inexpressive, gleamed with a Las Vegas intensity. She said, "The deck consists of 25 cards, divided into five 'suits' or symbols. There are five cards marked with a star, five with a circle, five with a square, five with a pattern of wavy lines, and five with a cross or plus sign. Otherwise they look just like ordinary playing cards." She handed the pack to Barbara Stein, another of her favorites, and told her to copy the five symbols on the blackboard. "The idea is for the subject being examined to look at each card in turn, face down, and try to name the symbol on the other side. The test can be run in many different ways. Sometimes the examiner looks briefly at each card first; that gives the subject a chance to pick the right answer out of the examiner's mind, if he can. Sometimes neither the subject nor the examiner sees the card in advance. Sometimes the subject is allowed to touch the card before he makes his guess. Sometimes he may be blindfolded, and other times he may be permitted to stare at the back of each card. No matter how it's done, though, the basic aim is always the same: for the subject to determine, using extrasensory powers, the design on a card that he can't see. Estelle, suppose the subject has no extrasensory powers at all, but is simply operating on pure guesswork. How many right guesses could we expect him to make, out of the 25 cards?"

Estelle, caught by surprise, reddened and blurted, "Uh—twelve and a half?"

A sour smirk from Miss Mueller, who turned to the brighter, happier twin. "Beverly?"

"Five, Miss Mueller?"

"Correct. You always have one chance out of five of guessing the right suit, so five right calls out of 25 is what luck alone ought to bring. Of course, the results are never that neat. On one run through the deck you might have four correct hits, and then next time six, and then five, and then maybe seven, and then perhaps only three—but the *average*, over a long series of trials, ought to be about five. That is, if pure chance is the only factor operating. Actually, in the Rhine experiments some groups of subjects have averaged 6½ or 7 hits out of 25 over many tests. Rhine believes that this above-average performance can only be explained as ESP. And certain subjects have done much better. There was a man once who called nine straight cards right, two days in a row. Then a few days later he hit 15 straight cards, 21 out of 25. The odds against that are fantastic. How many of you think it could have been nothing but luck?"

About a third of the hands in the class went up. Some of them belonged to dullards who failed to realize that it was shrewd politics to show sympathy for the teacher's pet enthusiasms. Some of them belonged to incorrigible skeptics who disdained such cynical manipulations. One of the hands belonged to David Selig. He was merely trying to don protective coloration.

Miss Mueller said, "Let's run a few tests today. Victor, will you be our first guinea pig? Come to the front of the room."

Grinning nervously, Victor Schlitz shambled forward. He stood stiffly beside Miss Mueller's desk as she cut the cards and cut them again. Then, peering quickly at the top card, she slid it toward him. "Which symbol?" she asked.

"Circle?"

"We'll see. Class, don't say anything." She handed the card to Barbara Stein, telling her to place a checkmark under the proper symbol on the blackboard. Barbara checked the square. Miss Mueller glanced at the next card. *Star*, David thought.

"Waves," Victor said. Barbara checked the star.

"Plus." *Square, dummy!* Square.

"Circle." *Circle*. Circle. A sudden ripple of excitement in the classroom at Victor's hit. Miss Mueller, glaring, called for silence.

"Star." *Waves*. Waves was what Barbara checked.

"Square." *Square*, David agreed. Square. Another ripple, more subdued.

Victor went through the deck. Miss Mueller had kept score: four correct hits. Not even as good as chance. She put him through a second round. Five. All right, Victor: you may be sexy, but a telepath you aren't. Miss Mueller's eyes roved the room. Another subject? Let it not be me, David prayed. God, let it not be me. It wasn't. She summoned Sheldon Feinberg. He hit five the first time, six the second. Respectable, unspectacular. Then Alice Cohen. Four and four. Stony soil, Miss Mueller. David, following each turn of the cards, had hit 25 out of 25 every time, but he was the only one who knew that.

"Next?" Miss Mueller said. David shrank into his seat. How much longer until the dismissal bell? "Norman Heimlich." Norman waddled toward the teacher's desk. She glanced at a card. David, scanning her, picked up the image of a star. Bouncing then to Norman's mind, David was amazed to detect a flicker of an image there, a star perversely rounding its points to form a circle, then reverting to being a star. What was this? Did the odious Heimlich have a shred of the power? "Circle," Norman murmured. But he hit the next one—the waves—and the one after that, the square. He did indeed seem to be picking up emanations, fuzzy and indistinct but emanations all the same, from Miss Mueller's mind. Fat Heimlich had the vestiges of the gift. But only the vestiges; David, scanning his mind and the teacher's, watched the images grow ever more cloudy and vanish altogether by the tenth card, fatigue scattering Norman's feeble strength. He scored a seven, though, the best so far. *The bell,* David prayed. *The bell, the bell, the bell!* Twenty minutes away.

A small mercy. Miss Mueller briskly distributed test paper. She would run the whole class at once. "I'll call numbers from 1 to 25," she said. "As I call each number, write down the symbol you think you see. Ready? *One.*"

David saw a circle. *Waves,* he wrote.

Star. *Square.*

Waves. *Circle.*

Star. *Waves.*

As the test neared its close, it occurred to him that he might be making a tactical error by muffing every call. He told himself to put down two or three right ones, just for camouflage. But it was too late for that. There were only four numbers left; it would look too conspicuous if he hit several of them correctly after missing all the others. He went on missing.

Miss Mueller said, "Now exchange papers with your neighbor and mark his answers. Ready? Number one: circle. Number two: star. Number three: waves. Number four. . . ."

Tensely she called for results. Had anyone scored ten hits or more? No, teacher. Nine? Eight? Seven? Norman Heimlich had seven again. He preened himself: Heimlich the mindreader. David felt disgust at the knowledge that Heimlich had even a crumb of power. Six? Four students had six. Five? Four? Miss Mueller diligently jotted down the results. Any other figures? Sidney Goldblatt began to snicker. "Miss Mueller, how about zero?"

She looked startled. "*Zero?* Was there someone who got all 25 cards *wrong?*"

"David Selig did!"

David Selig wanted to drop through the floor. All eyes were on him. Cruel laughter assailed him. *David Selig got them all wrong.* It was like saying, David Selig wet his pants, David Selig cheated on the exam, David Selig went into the girls' toilet. By trying to conceal himself, he had made himself terribly conspicuous. Miss Mueller, looking stern and oracular, said, "A null score can be quite significant too, class. It might mean extremely strong ESP abilities, rather than the total absence of such powers, as you might think." Oh, God. Extremely strong ESP abilities. She went on, "Rhine talks of phenomena such as 'forward displacement' and 'backward displacement,' in which an unusually powerful ESP force might accidentally focus on one card ahead of the right one, or one card behind it, or even two or three cards away. So the subject would appear to get a below-average result when actually he's hitting perfectly, just off the target! David, let me see your answers."

"I wasn't getting anything, Miss Mueller. I was just putting down my guesses, and I suppose they were all wrong."

"Let me see."

As though marching to the scaffold, he brought her the sheet. She placed it beside her own list and tried to realign it, searching for some correlation, some displacement sequence. But the randomness of his deliberately wrong answers protected him. A forward displacement of one card gave him two hits; a backward displacement of one card gave him three. Nothing significant there. Nevertheless, Miss Mueller would not let go. "I'd like to test you again," she said. "We'll run several kinds of trials. A null score is fascinating." She began to shuffle the deck. God, God, God, where are you? Ah. The bell! Saved by the bell! "Can you stay after class? she asked. In agony, he shook his head. "Got to go to geometry next, Miss Mueller." She relented. Tomorrow, then. We'll run the tests tomorrow. God! He was up all the night in a turmoil of fear, sweating, shivering; about four in the morning he vomited. He hoped his mother would make him stay home from school, but no luck: at half past seven he was aboard the bus. Would Miss Mueller forget about the test? Miss Mueller had not forgotten. The fateful cards were on her desk. There would be no escape. He found himself the center of all attention. All right, Duv, be cleverer this time. "Are you ready to begin?" she asked, tipping up the first card. He saw a plus sign in his mind.

"Square," he said.

He saw a circle. "Waves," he said.

He saw another circle, "Plus," he said.

He saw a star. "Circle," he said.

He saw a square. "Square," he said. *That's one.*

He kept careful count. Four wrong answers, then a right

one. Three wrong answers, another right one. Spacing them with false randomness, he allowed himself five hits on the first test. On the second he had four. On the third, six. On the fourth, four. Am I being too average, he wondered? Should I give her a one-hit run, now? But she was losing interest. "I still can't understand your null score, David," she told him. "But it does seem to me as if you have no ESP ability whatever." He tried to look disappointed. Apologetic, even. Sorry, teach, I ain't got no ESP. Humbly the deficient boy made his way to his seat.

* * *

In one blazing instant of revelation and communion, Miss Mueller, I could have justified your whole lifelong quest for the improbable, the inexplicable, the unknowable, the irrational. The miraculous. But I didn't have the guts to do it. I had to look after my own skin, Miss Mueller. I had to keep a low profile. Will you forgive me? Instead of giving you truth, I faked you out, Miss Mueller, and sent you spinning blindly onward to the tarot, to the signs of the zodiac, to the flying-saucer people, to a thousand surreal vibrations, to a million apocalyptic astral antiworlds, when the touch of my mind against yours might have been enough to heal your madness. One touch from me. In a moment. In the twinkling of an eye.

Twenty-one

These are the days of David's passion, when he writhes a lot on his bed of nails. Let's do it in short takes. It hurts less that way.

* * *

Tuesday. Election Day. For months the clamor of the campaign has fouled the air. The free world is choosing its new maximum leader. The sound-trucks rumble along Broadway, belching slogans. Our next President! The man for all America!

Vote! Vote! Vote! Vote for X! Vote for Y! The hollow words merge and blur and flow. Republocrat. Demican. *Boum*. Why should I vote? I will not vote. I do not vote. I am not plugged in. I am not part of the circuit. Voting is for *them*. Once, in the late autumn of 1968, I think it was, I was standing outside Carnegie Hall, thinking of going over to the paperback bookshop on the other side of the street, when suddenly all traffic halted on 57th and scores of policemen sprang up from the pavement like the dragon's-teeth warriors sown by Cadmus, and a motorcade came rumbling out of the east, and lo! in a dark black limousine rode Richard M. Nixon, President-Elect of the United States of America, waving jovially to the assembled populace. My big chance at last, I thought. I will look into his mind and make myself privy to great secrets of state; I will discover what it is about our leaders that sets them apart from ordinary mortals. And I looked into his mind, and what I found in there I will not tell you, except to say that it was more or less what I should have expected to find. And since that day I have had nothing to do with politics or politicians. Today I stay home from the polls. Let them elect the next President without my help.

* * *

Wednesday. I doodle with Yahya Lumumba's half-finished term paper and other such projects, a few futile lines on each. Getting nowhere. Judith calls. "A party," she says. "You're invited. Everybody'll be there."

"A party? Who? Where? Why? When?"

"Saturday night. Near Columbia. The host is Claude Guermantes. Do you know him? Professor of French Literature." No, the name is not Guermantes. I have changed the name to protect the guilty. "He's one of those charismatic new professors, Young, dynamic, handsome, a friend of Simone de Beauvoir, of Genet. Karl and I are coming. And a lot of others. He always invites the most interesting people."

"Genet? Simone de Beauvoir? Will they be there?"

"No, silly, not them. But it'll be worth your time. Claude gives the best parties of anybody I know. Brilliant combinations of people."

"Sounds like a vampire to me."

"He gives as well as takes, Duv. He specifically asked me to invite you."

"How does he know me at all?"

"Through me," she says. "I've talked of you. He's dying to meet you."

"I don't like parties."

"*Duv*—"

I know that warning tone of voice. I have no stomach for a hassle just now. "All right," I say, sighing. "Saturday night. Give me the address." Why am I so pliable? Why do I let Judith manipulate me? Is this how I build my love for her, through these surrenders?

* * *

Thursday, I do two paragraphs, a.m., for Yahya Lumumba. Very apprehensive about his reaction to the thing I'm writing for him. He might just loathe it. If I ever finish it. I *must* finish it. Never missed a deadline yet. Don't dare to. In the p.m. I walk up to the 230th St. bookstore, needing fresh air and wanting, as usual, to see if anything interesting has come out since my last visit, three days before. Compulsively buy a few paperbacks—an anthology of minor metaphysical poets, Updike's *Rabbit Redux*, and a heavy Levi-Straussian anthropological study, folkways of some Amazonian tribe, that I know I'll *never* get around to reading. A new clerk at the cash register: a girl, 19, 20, pale, blond, white silk blouse, short plaid skirt, impersonal smile. Attractive in a vacant-eyed way. She isn't at all interesting to me, sexually or otherwise, and as I think that I chide myself for putting her down—let nothing human be alien to me—and on a whim I invade her mind as I pay for my books, so that I won't be judging her by superficials. I burrow in easily, deep, down through layer after layer of trivia, mining her without hindrance, getting right to the real stuff. Oh! What a sudden blazing communion, soul to soul! She glows. She streams fire. She come to me with a vividness and a completeness that stun me, so rare has this sort of experience become for me. No dumb pallid mannequin now. I see her full and entire, her dreams, her fantasies, her ambitions, her loves, her soaring ecstasies (last night's gasping copulation and the shame and guilt afterward), a whole churning steaming sizzling human soul. Only once in the last six months have I hit this quality of total contact, only once, that awful day with Yahya Lumumba on the steps of Low Library. And as I remember that searing, numbing experience, something is triggered in me and the same thing happens. A dark curtain falls. I am disconnected. My grip on her consciousness is severed. Silence, that terrible mental silence, rushed to enfold me. I stand there, gaping, stunned, alone again and frightened, and I start to shake and drop my change, and she says to me, worried, "Sir? *Sir?*" in that sweet fluting little-girl voice.

* * *

Friday. Wake up with aches, high fever. Undoubtedly an attack of psychosomatic ague. The angry, embittered mind mercilessly flagellating the defenseless body. Chills followed by hot sweats followed by chills. Empty-gut puking. I feel hollow. Headpiece filled with straw. Alas! Can't work. I scribble a few pseudo-Lumumbesque lines and toss the sheet away. Sick as a dog. Well, a good excuse not to go to that dumb party, anyhow. I read my minor metaphysicals. Some of them not so minor. Traherne, Crashaw, William Cartwright. As for instance, Traherne:

Pure native Powers that Corruption loathe,
   Did, like the fairest Glass
    Or, spotless polished Brass,
Themselves soon in their Object's Image clothe:
   Divine Impressions, when they came,
Did quickly enter and my Soul enflame.
   'Tis not the Object, but the Light,
That maketh Heav'n: 'Tis a clearer Sight.
   Felicity
Appears to none but them that purely see.

Threw up again after that. Not to be interpreted as an expression of criticism. Felt better for a while. I should call Judith. Have her make some chicken soup for me. Oy, veh. Veh is mir.

* * *

Saturday. Without help of chicken soup I recover and decide to go to the party. Veh is mir, in spades. Remember, remember, the sixth of November. Why has David allowed Judith to drag him from his cave? An endless subway ride

downtown; spades full of weekend wine add a special *frisson*
to the ordinary adventure of Manhattan transporation. At last
the familiar Columbia station. I must walk a few blocks,
shivering, not dressed properly for the wintry weather, to the
huge old apartment house at Riverside Drive and 112th St.
where Claude Guermantes is reputed to live. I stand hesitantly
outside. A cold, sour breeze ripping malevolently across the
Hudson at me, bearing the windborne detritus of New Jersey. Dead leaves swirling in the park. Inside, a mahogany
doorman eyes me fishily. "Professor Guermantes?" I say. He
jerks a thumb. "Seventh floor, 7-G." Waving me toward the
elevator. I'm late; it's almost ten o'clock. Upstairs in the
weary Otis, creak creak creak creak, elevator door rolls back,
silkscreen poster in the hallway proclaims the route to
Guermantes' lair. Not that posters are necessary. A high-
decibel roar from the left tells me where the action is. I ring
the bell. Wait. Nothing. Ring again. Too loud for them to
hear me. Oh, to be able to transmit thoughts instead of just
to receive them! I'd announce myself in tones of thunder. Ring
again, more aggressively. Ah! Yes! Door opens. Short dark-
haired girl, undergraduate-looking, wearing a sort of orange sari
that leaves her right breast—small—bare. Nudity a la mode.
Flashes her teeth gaily. "Come in, come in, come in!"

A mob scene. Eighty, ninety, a hundred people, everyone
dressed in Seventies Flamboyant, gathered in groups of eight
to ten, shouting profundities at one another. Those who hold
no highballs are busily passing joints, ritualistic hissing intake
of breath, much coughing, passionate exhaling. Before I have
my coat off someone pops an elaborate ivory-headed pipe in
my mouth. "Super hash," he explains. "Just in from Damascus.
Come on, man, toke up!" I suck smoke willy-nilly and feel an
immediate effect. I blink. "Yeah," my benefactor shouts. "It's
got the power to cloud men's minds, don't it?" In this mob
my mind is already pretty well clouded, however, sans canna-
bis, solely from input overload. My power seems to be
functioning at reasonably high intensity tonight, only without
much differentiation of persons, and I am involuntarily taking
in a thick soup of overlapping transmissions, a chaos of
merging thoughts. Murky stuff. Pipe and passer vanish and I
stumble stonedly forward into a cluttered room lined from
floor to ceiling with crammed bookcases. I catch sight of
Judith just as she catches sight of me, and from her on a
direct line of contact comes her outflow, fiercely vivid at first,

trailing off in moments into mush: *brother, pain, love, fear, shared memories, forgiveness, forgetting, hatred, hostility, murmphness, froomz, zzzhhh, mmmm. Brother. Love. Hate. Zzzhhh.*

"Duv!" she cries. "Oh, here I am, Duvid!"

Judith looks sexy tonight. Her long lithe body is sheathed in a purple satiny wrap, skin-tight, throat-high, plainly showing her breasts and the little bumps of her nipples and the cleft between her buttocks. On her bosom nestles a glittering slab of gold-rimmed jade, intricately carved; her hair, unbound, tumbles gloriously. I feel pride in her beauty. She is flanked by two impressive-looking men. On one side is Dr. Karl F. Silvestri, author of *Studies in the Physiology of Thermoregulation.* He corresponds fairly closely to the image of him that I had plucked from Judith's mind at her apartment a week or two ago, though he is older than I had guessed, at least 55, maybe closer to 60. Bigger, too—perhaps six feet five. I try to envision his huge burly body atop Jude's wiry slender self, pressing down. I can't. He has florid cheeks, a stolid self-satisfied facial expression, tender intelligent eyes. He radiates something avuncular or even paternal toward her. I see why Jude is attracted to him: he is the powerful father-figure that poor beaten Paul Selig never could have been for her. On Judith's other side is a man whom I suspect to be Professor Claude Guermantes; I bounce a quick probe into him and confirm that guess. His mind is quicksilver, a glittering, shimmering pool. He thinks in three or four languages at once. His rampaging energy exhausts me at a single touch. He is about 40, just under six feet tall, muscular, athletic; he wears his elegant sandy hair done in swirling baroque waves, and his short goatee is impeccably clipped. His clothing is so advanced in style that I lack the vocabulary to describe it, being unaware of fashions myself: a kind of mantle of coarse green and gold fabric (linen? muslin?), a scarlet sash, flaring satin trousers, turned-up pointed-toed medieval boots. His dandyish appearance and mannered posture suggest that he might be gay, but he gives off a powerful aura of heterosexuality, and from Judith's stance and fond way of looking at him I begin to realize that he and she must once have been lovers. May still be. I am shy about probing that. My raids on Judith's privacy are too sore a point between us.

"I'd like you to meet my brother David," Judith says.

Silvestri beams. "I've heard so much about you, Mr. Selig."

"Have you really?" (*I've got this freak of a brother, Karl. Would you believe it, he can actually read minds? Your thoughts are as clear as a radio broadcast to him.*) How much has Judith actually revealed about me? I'll try to probe him and see. "And call me David. You're Dr. Silvestri, right?"

"That's right. Karl. I'd prefer Karl."

"I've heard a lot about you from Jude," I say. No go on the probe. My abominable waning gifts; I get only sputtering bits of static, misty scraps of unintelligible thought. His mind is opaque to me. My head starts to throb. "She showed me two of your books. I wish I could understand things like that."

A pleased chuckle from lofty Silvestri. Judith meanwhile has begun to introduce me to Guermantes. He murmurs his delight at making any acquaintance. I half expect him to kiss my cheeks, or maybe my hand. His voice is soft, purring; it carries an accent, but not a French one. Something strange, a mixture, Franco-Italic, maybe, or Franco-Hispanic. Him at least I can probe, even now; somehow his mind, more volatile than Silvestri's, remains within my reach. I slither in and take a look, even while exchanging platitudes about the weather and the recent election. Christ! Casanova Redivivus! He's slept with everything that walks or crawls, masculine feminine neuter, including of course my accessible sister Judith, whom—according to a neatly filed surface memory— he last penetrated just five hours ago, in this very room. His semen now curdles within her. He is obscurely restless over the fact that she never has come with him; he takes it as a failure of his flawless technique. The professor is speculating in a civilized way on the possibilities of nailing me before the night is out. No hope, professor. I will not be added to your Selig collection. He asks me pleasantly about my degrees, "Just one," I say. "A B.A. in '56. I thought about doing graduate work in English literature but never got around to it." He reaches Rimbaud, Verlain, Mallarmé, Baudelaire, Lautréamont, that whole sick crew, and identifies with them spiritually; his classes are full of adoring Barnard girls whose thighs open gladly for him, although in his Rimbaud facet he is not averse to romping with hearty Columbia men on occasions. As he talks to me he fondles Judith's shoulderblades affectionately, proprietorially. Dr. Silvestri appears not to notice, or else not to care. "Your sister," Guermantes murmurs, "she is a marvel, she is an original, a splendor—a *type*,

M'sieu Selig, a *type*." A compliment, in the froggish sense. I poke his mind again and learn that he is writing a novel about a bitter, voluptuous young divorcee and a French intellectual who is an incarnation of the life-force, and expects to make millions from it. He fascinates me: so blatant, so phony, so manipulative, and yet so attractive despite all his transparent failings. He offers me cocktails, highballs, liqueurs, brandies, pot, hash, cocaine, anything I crave. I feel engulfed and escape from him, in some relief, slipping away to pour a little rum.

A girl accosts me at the liquor table. One of Guermantes' students, no more than 20. Coarse black hair tumbling into ringlets; pug nose; fierce perceptive eyes; full fleshy lips. Not beautiful but somehow interesting. Evidently I interest her, too, for she grins at me and says, "Would you like to go home with me?"

"I just got here."

"Later. Later. No hurry. You look like you're fun to fuck."

"Do you say that to everybody you've just met?"

"We haven't even met," she points out. "And no, I don't say it to everybody. To lots, though. What's wrong? Girls can take the initiative these days. Besides, it's leap year. Are you a poet?"

"Not really."

"You look like one. I bet you're sensitive and you suffer a lot." My familiar dopy fantasy, coming to life before my eyes. *Her* eyes are red-rimmed. She's stoned. An acrid smell of sweat rising from her black sweater. Her legs are too short for her torso, her hips too wide, her breasts too heavy. Probably she's got the clap. Is she putting me on? *I bet you're sensitive and you suffer a lot. Are you a poet?* I try to explore her, but it's useless; fatigue is blanking my mind, and the collective shriek of the massed mob of partygoers is drowning out all individual outputs now. "What's your name?" she asks.

"David Selig."

"Lisa Holstein. I'm a senior at Barn—"

"*Holstein?*" The name triggers me. Kitty, Kitty, Kitty! "Is that what you said? Holstein?"

"Holstein, yes, and spare me the cow jokes."

"Do you have a sister named Kitty? Catherine, I guess. Kitty Holstein. About 35 years old. Your sister, maybe your cousin—"

"No. Never heard of her. Someone you know?"

"Used to know," I say. "Kitty Holstein." I pick up my drink and turn away.

"Hey," she calls after me. "Did you think I was kidding? Do you want to go home with me tonight or don't you?"

A black colossus confronts me. Immense Afro nimbus, terrifying jungle face. His clothing a sunburst of clashing colors. *Him*, here? Oh, God. Just who I most need to see. I think guiltily of the unfinished term paper, lame, humpbacked, a no-ass monstrosity, sitting on my desk. What is he doing here? How has Claude Guermantes managed to draw Yahya Lumumba into his orbit? The evening's token black, perhaps. Or the delegate from the world of high-powered sports, summoned here by way of demonstrating our host's intellectual versatility, his eclectic ballsiness. Lumumba stands over me, glowering, coldly examining me from his implausible height like an ebony Zeus. A spectacular black woman has her arm through his, a goddess, a titan, well over six feet tall, skin like polished onyx, eyes like beacons. A stunning couple. They shame us all with their beauty. Lumumba says, finally, "I *know* you, man. I know you from someplace."

"Selig. David Selig."

"Sounds familiar. Where do I know you?"

"Euripides, Sophocles, and Aeschylus."

"What the fuck?" Baffled. Pausing, then. Grinning. "Oh, yeah. Yeah, baby. That fucking term paper. How you coming along on that, man?"

"Coming along."

"You gonna have it Wednesday? Wednesday when it due."

"I'll have it, Mr. Lumumba." *Doin' my best, massa.*

"You better, boy. I counting on you."

"—Tom Nyquist—"

The name leaps suddenly, startlingly, out of the white-noise background hum of party chatter. For an instant it hangs in the smoky air like a dead leaf caught by a lazy October breeze. Who said "Tom Nyquist" just then? Who was it who spoke his name? A pleasant baritone voice, no more than a dozen feet from me. I look for likely owners of that voice. Men all around. You? You? You? No way of telling. Yes, one way. When words are spoken aloud, they reverberate in the mind of the speaker for a short while. (Also in the minds of his hearers, but the reverberations are different in tonality.) I summon my slippery skill and, straining, force needles of inquiry into the nearby consciousnesses, hunting for echoes. The effort is murderously great. The skulls I enter are solid bony domes through whose few crevices I struggle to ram my limp, feeble probes. But I enter. I seek the proper reverberations. *Tom Nyquist? Tom Nyquist?* Who spoke his name? You? You? Ah. There. The echo is almost gone, just a dim hollow clangor at the far end of a cavern. A tall plump man with a comic fringe of blond beard.

"Excuse me," I say. "I didn't mean to eavesdrop, but I heard you mention the name of a very old friend of mine—"

"Oh?"

"—and I couldn't help coming over to ask you about him. Tom Nyquist. He and I were once very close. If you know where he is now, what he's doing—"

"Tom Nyquist?"

"Yes. I'm sure I heard you mention him."

A blank smile. "I'm afraid there's been a mistake. I don't know anyone by that name. Jim? Fred? Can you help?"

"But I'm positive I heard—" The echo. *Boum* in the cave. Was I mistaken? At close range I try to get inside his head, to hunt in his filing system for any knowledge of Nyquist. But I can't function at all, now. They are conferring earnestly. Nyquist? Nyquist? Did anybody hear a Nyquist mentioned? Does anyone know a Nyquist?

One of them suddenly cries: "John Leibnitz!"

"Yes," says the plump one happily. "Maybe that's who you heard me mention. I was talking about John Leibnitz a few moments ago. A mutual friend. In this racket that might very well have sounded like Nyquist to you."

Leibnitz. Nyquist. Leibnitz. Nyquist. *Boum. Boum.* "Quite possibly," I agree. "No doubt that's what happened. Silly of me." John Leibnitz. "Sorry to have bothered you."

Guermantes says, mincing and prancing at my elbow, "You really must audit my class one of these days. This Wednesday afternoon I start Rimbaud and Verlaine, the first of six lectures on them. Do come around. You'll be on campus Wednesday, won't you?"

Wednesday is the day I must deliver Yahya Lumumba's term paper on the Greek tragedians. I'll be on campus, yes. I'd better be. But how does Guermantes know that? Is he getting into my head somehow? What if he has the gift too? And I'm wide open to him, he knows everything, my poor pathetic secret, my daily increment of loss, and there he stands, patronizing me because I'm failing and he's as sharp as I ever was. Then a quick paranoiac flash: not only does he have the gift but perhaps he's some kind of telepathic leech, draining me, bleeding the power right out of my mind and into his. Perhaps he's been tapping me on the sly ever since '74.

I shake these useless idiocies away. "I expect to be around on Wednesday, yes. Perhaps I will drop in."

There is no chance whatever that I will go to hear Claude Guermantes lecture on Rimbaud or Verlaine. If he's got the power, let him put *that* in his pipe and smoke it!

"I'd love it if you came," he tells me. He leans close to me. His androgynous Mediterranean smoothness permits him casually to breach the established American code of male-to-male distancing customs. I smell hair tonic, shaving lotion, deodorant, and other perfumes. A small blessing: not all my senses are dwindling at once. "Your sister," he murmurs. "Marvelous woman! How I love her! She speaks often of you."

"Does she?"

"With great love. Also with great guilt. It seems you and she were estranged for many years."

"That's over now. We're finally becoming friends."

"How wonderful for you both." He gestures with a flick of his eyes. "That doctor. No good for her. Too old, too static. After fifty most men lose the capacity to grow. He'll bore her to death in six months."

"Maybe boredom is what she needs," I reply. "She's had an exciting life. It hasn't made her happy."

"No one ever needs boredom," Guermantes says, and winks.

"Karl and I would love to have you come for dinner next week, Duv. There's so much we three need to talk about."

"I'll see, Jude. I'm not sure about anything about next week yet. I'll call you."

Lisa Holstein. John Leibnitz. I think I need another drink.

* * *

Sunday. Greatly overhung. Hash, rum, wine, pot, God knows what else. And somebody popping amyl nitrite under my nose about two in the morning. That filthy fucking party. I should never have gone. My head, my head, my head.

Where's the typewriter? I've got to get some work done. Let's go, then:

We see, thus, the difference in method of approach of these three tragedians to the same story. Aeschylus' primary concern is theological implications of the crime and the inexorable workings of the gods: Orestes is torn between the command of Apollo to slay his mother and his own fear of matricide, and goes mad as a result. Euripides dwells on the characterization, and takes a less allegorical

No damned good. Save it for later.

Silence between my ears. The echoing black void. I have nothing going for me at all today, nothing. I think it may be completely gone. I can't even pick up the clamor of the spics next door. November is the cruelest month, breeding onions out of the dead mind. I'm living an Eliot poem. I'm turning into words on a page. Shall I sit here feeling sorry for myself? No. No. No. No. I'll fight back. Spiritual exercises designed to restore my power. On your knees, Selig. Bow the head. Concentrate. Transform yourself into a fine needle of thought, a slim telepathic laser-beam, stretching from this room to the vicinity of the lovely star Betelgeuse. Got it? Good. That sharp pure mental beam piercing the universe. Hold it. Hold it firm. No spreading at the edges allowed, man. Good. Now ascend. We are climbing Jacob's ladder. This will be an out-of-the-body experience, Duvid. Up, up and away! Rise through the ceiling, through the roof, through the atmosphere, through the ionosphere, through the stratosphere, through the whatsisphere. Outward. Into the vacant interstellar spaces. O dark dark dark. Cold the sense and lost the motive of action. No, stop that stuff! Only positive thinking is allowed on this trip. Soar! Soar! Toward the little green men of Betelgeuse IX. Reach their minds, Selig. Make contact. Make . . . contact. Soar, you lazy yid-bastard! Why aren't you soaring? *Soar!*

Well?

Nothing. *Nada. Niente.* Nowhere. *Nulla. Nicht.*

Tumbling back to earth. Into the silent funeral. All right, give up, if that's what you want. All right. Rest, for a little while. Rest and then pray, Selig. Pray.

* * *

Monday. The hangover gone. The brain once again receptive. In a glorious burst of creative frenzy I rewrite *The "Electra" Theme in Aeschylus, Sophocles, and Euripides* from gunwale to fetlock, completely recasting it, revoicing it, clarifying and strengthening the ideas while simultaneously catching what I think is just the perfect tone of offhand niggerish hipness. As I hammer out the final words the telephone rings. Nicely timed; I feel sociable now. Who calls? Judith? No. It is Lisa Holstein who calls. "You promised to take me home after the party," she says mournfully, accusingly. "What the hell did you do, sneak away?"

"How did you get my number?"

"From Claude. Professor Guermantes." That sleek devil. He knows everything. "Look, what are you doing right now?"

"Thinking about having a shower. I've been working all morning and I stink like a goat."

"What kind of work do you do?"

"I ghostwrite term papers for Columbia men."

She ponders that a moment. "You sure have a weird head, man. I mean really: what do you do?"

"I just told you."

A long digestive silence. Then: "Okay. I can dig it. You ghostwrite term papers. Look, Dave, go take your shower. How long is it on the subway from 110th Street and Broadway to your place?"

"Maybe forty minutes, if you get a train right away."

"Swell. See you in an hour, then." *Click.*

I shrug. A crazy broad. Dave, she calls me. Nobody calls me Dave. Stripping, I head for the shower, a long leisurely soaping. Afterward, sprawling out in a rare interlude of relaxation, Dave Selig re-reads this morning's labors and finds pleasure in what he has wrought. Let's hope Lumumba does too. Then I pick up the Updike book. I get to page four and the phone rings again. Lisa: she's on the train platform at 225th, wants to know how to get to my apartment. This is more than a joke, now. Why is she pursuing me so single-mindedly? But okay. I can play her game. I give her the instructions. Ten minutes later, a knock on the door. Lisa in thick black sweater, the same sweaty one as Saturday night, and tight blue jeans. A shy grin, strangely out of character for her. "Hi," she says. Making herself comfortable. "When I first saw you, I had this intuitive flash of you: *This guy's got something special. Make it with him.* If there's one thing I've

learned, its that you've got to trust your intuition. I go with
the flow, Dave, I go with the flow." Her sweater is off by now.
Her breasts are heavy and round, with tiny, almost imperceptible nipples. A Jewish star nestles in the deep valley between them. She wanders the room, examining my books, my
records, my photographs. "So tell me," she says. "Now that I'm
here. Was I right? *Is* there anything special about you?"

"There once was."

"What?"

"That's for me to know and you to find out," I say, and
gathering my strength, I ram my mind into hers. It's a brutal
frontal assault, a rape, a true mindfuck. Of course she doesn't
feel a thing. I say, "I used to have a really extraordinary gift.
It's mostly worn off by now, but some of the time I still have
it, and as a matter of fact I'm using it on you right now."

"Far out," she says, and drops her jeans. No underpants.
She will be fat before she's 30. Her thighs are thick, her belly
protrudes. Her pubic hair is oddly dense and widespread,
less a triangle than a sort of diamond, a black diamond
reaching past her loins to her hips, almost. Her buttocks are
deeply dimpled. While I inspect her flesh I savagely ransack
her mind, sparing her no areas of privacy, enjoying my access
while it lasts. I don't need to be polite. I owe her nothing:
she forced herself on me. I check, first, to see if she had been
lying when she said she'd never heard of Kitty. The truth:
Kitty is no kin to her. A meaningless coincidence of sur-
names, is all. "I'm sure you're a poet, Dave," she says as we
entwine and drop onto the unmade bed. "That's an intuition
flash too. Even if you're doing this term paper thing now,
poetry is where you're really at, right?" I run my hands over
her breasts and belly. A sharp odor comes from her skin. She
hasn't washed in three or four days, I bet. No matter. Her
nipples mysteriously emerge, tiny rigid pink nubs. She wrig-
gles. I continue to loot her mind like a Goth plundering the
Forum. She is fully open to me; I delight in this unexpected
return of vigor. Her autobiography assembles itself for me.
Born in Cambridge. Twenty years old. Father a professor.
Mother a professor. One younger brother. Tomboy childhood.
Measles, chicken pox, scarlet fever. Puberty at eleven, lost
her virginity at twelve. Abortion at sixteen. Several Lesbian
adventures. Passionate interest in French decadent poets.
Acid, mescaline, psilocybin, cocaine, even a sniff of smack.
Guermantes gave her that. Guermantes also took her to bed

five or six times. Vivid memories of that. Her mind shows me more of Guermantes that I want to see. He's hung very impressively. Lisa comes through with a tough, aggressive self-image, captain of her soul, master of her fate, etc. Underneath that it's just the opposite, of course; she's scared as hell. Not a bad kid. I feel a little guilty about the casual way I slammed into her head, no regard for her privacy at all. But I have my needs. I continue to prowl her, and meanwhile she goes down on me. I can hardly remember the last time anyone did that. I can hardly remember my last lay, it's been so bad lately. She's an expert fellatrice. I'd like to reciprocate but I can't bring myself to do it; sometimes I'm fastidious and she's not the douching type. Oh, well, leave that stuff for the Guermanteses of this world. I lie there picking her brain and accepting the gift of her mouth. I feel virile, bouncy, cocksure, and why not, getting my kicks from two inputs at once, head and crotch? Without withdrawing from her mind I withdraw, at last, from her lips, turn around, part her thighs, slide deep into her tight narrow-mouthed harbor. Selig the stallion. Selig the stud. "Oooh," she says, flexing her knees. "*Oooh.*" And we begin to play the beast with two backs. Covertly I feed on feedback, tapping into her pleasure-responses and thereby doubling my own; each thrust brings me a factored and deliciously exponential delight. But then a funny thing happens. Although she is nowhere close to coming—an event that I know will disrupt our mental contact when it occurs—the broadcast from her mind is already becoming erratic and indistinct, more noise than signal. The images break up in a pounding of static. What comes through is garbled and distant; I scramble to maintain my hold on her consciousness, but no use, no use, she slips away, moment by moment receding from me, until there is no communion at all. And in that moment of severance my cock suddenly softens and slips out of her. She is jolted by that, caught by surprise. "What brought you down?" she asks. I find it impossible to tell her. I remember Judith asking me, some weeks back, whether I had ever regarded my loss of mental powers as a kind of metaphor of impotence. Sometimes yes, I told her. And now here, for the first time, metaphor blends with reality; the two failures are integrated. He is impotent here and he is impotent there. Poor David. "I guess I got distracted," I tell her. Well, she has her skills; for half an hour she works me over, fingers, lips, tongue, hair, breasts, not getting a rise out of me with anything, in fact turning me off more than ever by her grim purposefulness. "I don't understand it," she says. "You were doing so well. Was there something about me that brought you down?" I reassure her. You were great, baby. Stuff like this sometimes just happens, no one knows why. I tell her, "Let's just rest and maybe I'll come back to life." We rest. Side by side, stroking her skin in an abstract way, I run a few tentative probing efforts. Not a flicker on the telepathic level. Not a flicker. The silence of the tomb. Is this it, the end, right here and now? Is this where it finally burns out? And I am like all the rest of you now. I am condemned to make do with mere words. "I have an idea," she says. "Let's take a shower together. That sometimes peps a guy up." To this I make no objection; it might just work, and in any case she'll smell better afterward. We head for the bathroom. Torrents of brisk cool water.

Success. The ministrations of her soapy hand revive me.

We spring toward the bed. Still stiff, I top her and take her. Gasp gasp gasp, moan moan moan. I can get nothing on the mental band. Suddenly she goes into a funny little spasm, intense but quick, and my own spurt swiftly follows. So much for sex. We curl up together, cuddly in the afterglow. I try again to probe her. Zero. Zee-ro. Is it gone? I think it's really gone. You have been present today at an historic event, young lady. The perishing of a remarkable extrasensory power. Leaving behind this merely mortal husk of mine. Alas.

"I'd love to read some of your poetry, Dave," she says.

*   *   *

Monday night, about seven-thirty. Lisa has left, finally. I go out for dinner, to a nearby pizzeria. I am quite calm. The impact of what has befallen me hasn't really registered yet. How strange that I can be so accepting. At any moment, I know, it's bound to come rushing in on me, crushing me, shattering me; I'll weep, I'll scream, I'll bang my head against walls. But for now I'm surprisingly cool. An oddly posthumous feeling, as of having outlived myself. And a feeling of relief: the suspense is over, the process has completed itself, the dying is done, and I've survived it. Of course I don't expect this mood to last. I've lost something central to my being, and now I await the anguish and the grief and the despair that must surely be due to erupt shortly.

But it seems that my mourning must be postponed. What I thought was all over isn't over yet. I walk into the pizzeria and the counterman gives me his flat cold New York smile of welcome, and I get this, unsolicited, from behind his greasy face: *Hey, here's the fag who always wants extra anchovies.*

Reading him clearly So it's not dead yet! Not quite dead! Only resting a while. Only hiding.

*   *   *

Tuesday. Bitter cold; one of those terrible late-autumn days when every drop of moisture has been squeezed from the air and the sunlight is like knives. I finish two more term papers for delivery tomorrow. I read Updike. Judith calls after lunch. The usual dinner invitation. My usual oblique reply.

"What did you think of Karl?" she asks.

"A very substantial man."

"He wants me to marry him."

"Well?"

"It's too soon. I don't really know him, Duv. I like him, I admire him tremendously, but I don't know whether I love him."

"Then don't rush into anything with him," I say. Her soap-opera hesitations bore me. I don't understand why anybody old enough to know the score ever gets married, anyway. Why should love require a contract? Why put yourself into the clutches of the state and give it power over you? Why invite lawyers to fuck around with your assets? Marriage is for the immature and the insecure and the ignorant. We who see through such institutions should be content to live together without legal coercion, eh, Toni? Eh? I say, "Besides, if you marry him, he'd probably want you to give up Guermantes. I don't think he could dig it."

"You know about me and Claude?"

"Of course."

"You always know everything."

"This was pretty obvious, Jude."

"I thought your power was waning."

"It is, it is, it's waning faster than ever. But this was still pretty obvious. To the naked eye."

"All right. What did you think of him?"

"He's death. He's a killer."

"You misjudged him, Duv."

"I was in his head. I *saw* him, Jude. He isn't human. People are toys to him."

"If you could hear the sound of your own voice now, Duv. The hostility, the outright jealousy—"

"*Jealousy?* Am I that incestuous?"

"You always were," she says. "But let that pass. I really thought you'd enjoy meeting Claude."

"I did. He's fascinating. I think cobras are fascinating too."

"Oh, fuck you, Duv."

"You want me to pretend I liked him?"

"Don't do me any favors." The old icy Judith.

"What's Karl's reaction to Guermantes?"

She pauses. Finally: "Pretty negative. Karl's very conventional, you know. Just as you are."

"Me?"

"Oh, you're so fucking straight, Duv! You're such a puritan! You've been lecturing me on morality all my goddamned life. The very first time I got laid there you were, wagging your finger at me—"

"Why doesn't Karl like him?"

"I don't know. He thinks Claude's sinister. Exploitive." Her voice is suddenly flat and dull. "Maybe he's just jealous. He knows I'm still sleeping with Claude. Oh, Jesus, Duv, why are we fighting again? Why can't we just *talk?*"

"I'm not the one who's fighting. I'm not the one who raised his voice."

"You're challenging me. That's what you always do. You spy on me and then you challenge me and try to put me down."

"Old habits are hard to break, Jude. Really, though: I'm not angry with you."

"You sound so smug!"

"I'm *not* angry. You are. You got angry when you saw that Karl and I agree about your friend Claude. People always get angry when they're told something they don't want to hear. Listen, Jude, do whatever you want. If Guermantes is your trip, go ahead."

"I don't know. I just don't know." An unexpected concession: "Maybe there *is* something sick about my relationship with him." Her flinty self-assurance vanishes abruptly. That's the wonderful thing about her: you get a different Judith every two minutes. Now, softening, thawing, she sounds uncertain of herself. In a moment she'll turn her concern outward, away from her own troubles, toward me. "Will you come to dinner next week? We very much do want to get together with you."

"I'll try."

"I'm worried about you, Duv." Yes, here it comes. "You looked so strung out on Saturday night."

"It's been a pretty rough time for me. But I'll manage." I don't feel like talking about myself. I don't want her pity, because after I get hers, I'll start giving myself mine. "Listen, I'll call you soon, okay?"

"Are you still in so much pain, Duv?"

"I'm adapting. I'm accepting the whole thing. I mean, I'll be okay. Keep in touch, Jude. My best to Karl." And Claude, I add, as I put down the receiver.

* * *

Wednesday morning. Downtown to deliver my latest batch of masterpieces. It's colder even than yesterday, the air clearer, the sun brighter, more remote. How dry the world seems. The humidity is minus sixteen percent, I think. The sort of weather in which I used to function with overwhelming clarity of perception. But I was picking up hardly anything at all on the subway ride down to Columbia, just muzzy little blurts and squeaks, nothing coherent. I can no longer be certain of having the power on any given day, apparently, and this is one of the days off. Unpredictable. That's what you are, you who live in my head: unpredictable. Thrashing about randomly in your death-throes. I go to the usual place and await my clients. They come, they get from me what they have come for, they cross my palm with greenbacks. David Selig, benefactor of undergraduate mankind. I see Yahya Lumumba like a black sequoia making his way across from Butler Library. Why am I trembling? It's the chill in the air, isn't it, the hint of winter, the death of the year. As the basketball star approaches he waves, nods, grins; everyone knows him, everyone calls out to him. I feel a sense of participation in his glory. When the season starts maybe I'll go watch him play.

"You got the paper, man?"

"Right here." I deal it off the stack. "Aeschylus, Sophocles, Euripides. Six pages. That's $21, minus the five you already gave me is $16 you owe me."

"Wait, man." He sits down beside me on the steps. "I got

to read this fucker first, right? How I know you did a righteous job if I don't read it?"

I watch him as he reads. Somehow I expect him to be moving his lips, to be stumbling over the unfamiliar words, but no, his eyes flicker rapidly over the lines. He gnaws his lip. He reads faster and faster, impatiently turning the pages. At length he looks at me and there is death in his eyes.

"This is shit, man," he says. "I mean, this here is just shit. What kind of con you trying to pull?"

"I guarantee you'll get a B+. You don't have to pay me until you get the grade. Anything less than B+ and—"

"No, listen to me. Who talking about grades? I can't turn this fucking thing in *at all*. Look, half this thing is jive-talk, the other half it copied straight out of some book. Crazy shit, that's what. The prof he going to read it, he going to look at me, he going to say, Lumumba, who you think I am? You think I a dummy, Lumumba? You didn't write this crap, he going to say to me. You don't believe Word One of this." Angrily he rises. "Here, I going to read you some of this, man. I show you what you give me." Leafing through the pages, he scowls, spits, shakes his head. "No. Why the hell should I? You know what you up to here, man? You making fun of me, that's what. You playing games with the dumb nigger, man."

"I was trying to make it look plausible that you had written—"

"Crap. You pulling a mindfuck, man. You making up a pile of stinking Jew shit about Europydes and you hoping I get in trouble trying to pass it off as my own stuff."

"That's a lie. I did the best possible job for you, and don't think I didn't sweat plenty. When you hire another man to write a term paper for you, I think you have to be prepared to expect a certain—"

"How long this take you? Fifteen minutes?"

"Eight hours, maybe ten," I say. "You know what I think you're trying to do, Lumumba? You're pulling reverse racism on me. Jew this and Jew that—if you don't like Jews so much, why didn't you get a black to write your paper for you? Why didn't you write it yourself? I did an honest job for you. I don't like hearing it put down as stinking Jew shit. And I tell you that if you turn it in, you'll get a passing grade for sure, you'll probably get a B+ at the very least."

"I gonna get flunked, is what."

"No. No. Maybe you just don't see what I was driving at.

Let me try to explain it to you. If you'll give it to me for a minute so I can read you a couple of things—maybe it'll be clearer if I—" Getting to my feet, I extend a hand toward the paper, but he grins and holds it high above my head. I'd need a ladder to reach it. No use jumping. "Come on, damn it, don't play games with me! Let me have it!" I snap, and he flicks his wrist and the six sheets of paper soar into the wind and go sailing eastward along College Walk. Dying, I watch them go. I clench my fists; an astonishing burst of rage explodes in me. I want to smash in his mocking face. "You shouldn't have done that." I say. "You shouldn't have just thrown it away."

"You owe me my five bucks back, man."

"Hold on, now. I did the work you hired me to do, and—"

"You said you don't charge if the paper's no good. Okay, the paper was shit. No charge. Give me the five."

"You aren't playing fair, Lumumba. You're trying to rip me off."

"Who ripping who off? Who set up that money-back deal anyhow? Me? *You.* What I gonna do for a term paper now? I got to take an incomplete and it your fault. Suppose they make me ineligible for the team because of that. Huh? Huh? What then? Look, man, you make me want to puke. Give me the five."

Is he serious about the refund? I can't tell. The idea of paying him back disgusts me, and it isn't just on account of losing the money. I wish I could read him, but I can't get anything out of him on that level; I'm completely blocked now. I'll bluff. I say, "What is this, slavery turned upside down? I did the work. I don't give a damn what kind of crazy irrational reasons you've got for rejecting it. I'm going to keep the five. At least the five."

"Give me the money, man."

"Go to hell."

I start to walk away. He grabs me—his arm, fully outspread toward me, must be as long as one of my legs—and hauls me toward him. He starts to shake me. My teeth are rattling. His grin is broader than ever, but his eyes are demonic. I wave my fists at him, but, held at arm's length, I can't even touch him. I start to yell. A crowd is gathering. Suddenly there are three or four other men in varsity jackets surrounding us, all black, all gigantic, though not as big as he is. His teammates. Laughing, whooping, cavorting. I am a toy to them. "Hey, man, he bothering you?" one of them asks. "You need help, Yahya?" yells another. "What's the mothafuck honkie doing to you, man?" calls a third. They form a ring and Lumumba thrusts me toward the man on his left, who catches me and flings me onward around the circle. I spin; I stumble; I reel; they never let me fall. Around and around and around. An elbow explodes against my lip. I taste blood. Someone slaps me, and my head rockets backward. Fingers jabbing my ribs. I realize that I'm going to get very badly hurt, that in fact these giants are going to beat me up. A voice I barely recognize as my own offers Lumumba his refund, but no one notices. They continue to whirl me from one to the next. Not slapping now, not jabbing, but punching. Where are the campus police? Help! Help! Pigs to the rescue! But no one comes. I can't catch my breath. I'd like to drop to my knees and huddle against the ground. They're yelling at me, racial epithets, words I barely comprehend, soul-brother jargon that must have been invented last week; I don't know what they're calling me, but I can feel the hatred in every syllable. Help? Help? The world spins wildly. I know now how a basketball would feel, if a basketball could feel. The steady pounding, the blur of unending motion. Please, someone, anyone, help me, stop them. Pain in my chest: a lump of white-hot metal back of my breastbone. I can't see. I can only feel. Where are my feet? I'm falling at last. Look how fast the steps rush toward me. The cold kiss of the stone bruises my cheek. I may already have lost consciousness; how can I tell? There's one comfort, at least. I can't get any further down than this.

Twenty-two

He was ready to fall in love when he met Kitty, overripe and eager for an emotional entanglement. Perhaps that was the whole trouble; what he felt for her was not so much love as simply satisfaction at the idea of being in love. Or perhaps not. He never understood his feelings for Kitty in any orderly way. They had their romance in the summer of 1963, which he remembers as the last summer of hope and good cheer before the long autumn of entropic chaos and philosophical despair descended on western society. Jack Kennedy was running things then, and while things weren't going especially well for him politically, he still managed to give the impression that he was going to get it all together, if not right away then in his inevitable second term. Atmospheric nuclear tests had just been banned. The Washington-to-Moscow hot line was being set up. Secretary of State Rusk announced in August that the South Vietnamese government was rapidly taking control of additional areas of the countryside. The number of Americans killed fighting in Vietnam had not yet reached 100.

Selig, who was 28 years old, had just moved from his Brooklyn Heights apartment to a small place in the West Seventies. He was working as a stockbroker then, of all unlikely things. This was Tom Nyquist's idea. After six years, Nyquist was still his closest and possibly only friend, although the friendship had waned considerably in the last year or two: Nyquist's almost arrogant self-assurance made Selig increasingly more uncomfortable, and he found it desirable to put some distance, psychological and geographical, between himself and the older man. One day Selig had said wistfully that if he could only manage to get a bundle of money together— say, $25,000 or so—he'd go off to a remote island and spend a couple of years writing a novel, a major statement about alienation in contemporary life, something like that. He had never written anything serious and wasn't sure he was sincere about wanting to. He was secretly hoping that Nyquist would simply hand him the money—Nyquist could pick up $25,000 in one afternoon's work, if he felt like it—and say, "Here, chum, go and be creative." But Nyquist didn't do things that way. Instead he said that the easiest way for someone without capital to make a lot of money in a hurry was to take a job as a customer's man in a brokerage firm. The commissions would be decent, enough to live on and something left over, but the real money would come from riding along on all the in-shop maneuvers of the experienced brokers—the short sales, the new-issue purchases, the arbitrage ploys. If you're dedicated enough, Nyquist told him, you can make just about as much as you like. Selig protested that he knew nothing about Wall Street. "I could teach you everything in three days," said Nyquist.

Actually it took less than that. Selig slipped into Nyquist's mind for a quick cram course in financial terminology. Nyquist had all the definitions beautifully arranged: common stocks and preferred, shorts and longs, puts and calls, debentures, convertibles, capital gains, special situations, closed-end versus open-end funds, secondary offerings, specialists and what they do, the over-the-counter market, the Dow-Jones averages, point-and-figure charts, and everything else. Selig memorized all of it. There was a vivid quality about mind-to-mind transferences with Nyquist that made memorizing things easy. The next step was to enroll as a trainee. Every big brokerage firm was looking for beginners—Merrill Lynch, Goodbody, Hayden Stone, Clark Dodge, scads of them. Selig picked one at random and applied. They gave him a stock-market quiz by way of preliminary screening; he knew most of the answers, and those he didn't know he picked up out of the minds of his fellow testees, most of whom had been following the market since childhood. He got a perfect score and was hired. After a brief training period he passed the licensing test, and before long he was a registered representative operating out of a fairly new brokerage office on Broadway near 72nd Street.

He was one of five brokers, all of them fairly young. The clientele was predominantly Jewish and generally geriatric: 75-year-old widows from the huge apartment houses along 72nd Street, and cigar-chomping retired garment manufacturers who lived on West End Avenue and Riverside Drive. Some of them had quite a lot of money, which they invested in the most cautious way possible. Some were practically penniless, but insisted on buying four shares of Con Edison or three shares of Telephone just to have the illusion of prosperity. Since most of the clients were elderly and didn't work, the bulk of dealings at the office were transacted in person rather than by phone, there were always ten or twelve senior citizens schmoozing in front of the stock ticker, and now and then one of them would dodder to the desk of his pet broker and place an order. On Selig's fourth day at work one venerable client suffered a fatal heart attack during a nine-point rally. Nobody seemed surprised or even dismayed, neither the brokers nor the friends of the victim: customers died in the shop about once a month, Selig learned. Kismet. You come to expect your friends to drop dead, once you reach a certain age. He quickly became a favorite, especially among the old ladies; they liked him because he was a nice Jewish boy, and several offered to introduce him to comely granddaughters. These offers he always refused, but politely; he made a point of being courteous and patient with them, of playing grandson. Most of them were ignorant, practically illiterate women, kept in a state of lifelong innocence by their hard-driving, acquisitive, coronary-prone husbands; now, having inherited more money that they could possibly spend, they had no real idea of how to manage it, and were wholly dependent on the nice young broker. Probing their minds, Selig found them almost always to be dim and sadly unformed— how could you live to the age of 75 without ever having had an idea?—but a few of the livelier ladies showed vigorous, passionate peasant rapacity, charming in its way. The men were less agreeable—loaded with dough, yet always on the lookout for more. The vulgarity and ferocity of their ambitions repelled him, and he glanced into their minds no more often than necessary, merely probing to have a better idea of their investment goals so he could serve them as they would be served. A month among such people, he decided, would be sufficient to turn a Rockefeller into a socialist.

Business was steady but unspectacular; once he had acquired his own nucleus of regulars, Selig's commissions ran to about $160 a week, which was more money than he had ever made before, but hardly the kind of income he imagined brokers pulled down. "You're lucky you came here in the spring," one of the other customer's men told him. "In the winter months all the clients go to Florida and we can choke before anybody gives us any business here." As Nyquist had predicted, he was able to turn some pleasant profits by trading for his own account; there were always nice little deals circulating in the office, hot tips with substance behind them. He started with savings of $350 and quickly pyramided his wad to a high four-figure sum, making money on Chrysler and Control Data and RCA and Sunray DX Oil, nimbly trading in and out on rumors of mergers, stock splits, or dynamic earnings gains; but he discovered that Wall Street runs in two directions, and much of his winnings melted away through badly timed trades in Brunswick, Beckman Instruments, and Martin Marietta. He came to see that he was never going to have enough of a stake to go off and write that novel. Possibly just as well: did the world need another amateur novelist? He wondered what he would do next. After three months as a broker he had some money in the bank, but not much, and he was hideously bored.

Luck delivered Kitty to him. She came in one muggy July morning at half past nine. The market hadn't opened yet, most of the customers had fled to the Catskills for the summer, and the only people in the office were Martinson, the manager, Nadel, one of the other customer's men, and Selig. Martinson was going over his totals, Nadel was on the phone to somebody downtown trying to work a complicated finagle in American Photocopy, and Selig, idle, was daydreaming of falling in love with somebody's beautiful granddaughter. Then the door opened and somebody's beautiful granddaughter came in. Not exactly beautiful, maybe, but certainly attractive: a girl in her early twenties, slim and well proportioned, perhaps five feet three or four, with fluffy light-brown hair, blue-green eyes, finely outlined features, a graceful slender figure. She seemed shy, intelligent, somehow innocent, a curious mixture of knowledge and naiveté. She wore a white silk blouse—gold chain lying on the smallish breasts—and an ankle-length brown skirt, offering a hint of excellent legs beneath. No, not a beautiful girl, but certainly pretty. Refreshing to look at. What the hell, Selig wondered, does she want in this temple of Mammon at her age? She's here fifty years too early. Curiosity led him to send a probe drilling into her forehead as she walked toward him. Seeking only surface stuff: name, age, marital status, address, telephone number, purpose of visit—what else?

He got nothing.

That shocked him. It was an incredible experience. Unique. To reach toward a mind and find it absolutely inaccessible, opaque, hidden as if behind an impenetrable wall—he had never had that happen to him before. He got no aura from her at all. She might as well have been a department store's plaster window mannequin, or a mindless robot from another planet. He sat there blinking, trying to account for his failure to make contact. He was so astounded by her total blankness that he forgot to listen to what she was saying to him, and had to ask her to repeat.

"I said, I'd like to open a brokerage account. Are you a broker?"

Sheepish, fumbling, stricken with sudden adolescent clumsiness, he gave her the new-account forms. By this time the other brokers had arrived, but too late: by the rules of the house she was his client. Sitting beside his cluttered desk, she told him of her investment needs while he studied the elegant tapered structure of her high-bridged nose, fought without success against her perplexing and enigmatic mental inaccessibility, and, despite or perhaps because of that inaccessibility, felt himself helplessly falling in love with her.

She was 22, one year out of Radcliffe, came from Long Island, and shared a West End Avenue apartment with two other girls. Unmarried—there had been a long futile love affair ending in a broken engagement not long before, he would discover later. (How strange it was for him not to be discovering everything at once, taking the information as he desired it.) Her background was in mathematics and she worked as a computer programmer, a term which, in 1963, meant very little to him; he wasn't sure whether she designed computers, operated them, or repaired them. Recently she had inherited $6500 from an aunt in Arizona, and her parents, who evidently were stern and formidable advocates of sink-or-swim education, had told her to invest the money on her own, by way of assuming adult responsibilities. So she had gone to her friendly neighborhood brokerage office, a lamb for the shearing, to invest her money. "What do you want?" Selig asked her. "To stash it away in safe blue chips, or to go for a little action, a chance for capital gains?"

"I don't know. I don't know the first thing about the market. I just don't want to do anything silly."

Another broker—Nadel, say—would have given her the Nothing Ventured, Nothing Gained speech, and, advising her to forget about such old and tired concepts as dividends, would have steered her into an action portfolio—Texas Instruments, Collins Radio, Polaroid, stuff like that. Then he would churn her account every few months, switch Polaroid into Xerox, Texas Instruments into Fairchild Camera, Collins into American Motors, American Motors back into Polaroid, running up fancy commissions for himself and, perhaps, making some money for her, or perhaps losing some. Selig had no stomach for such maneuvers. "This is going to sound stodgy," he said, "but let's play it very safe. I'll recommend some decent things that won't ever make you rich but that you won't get hurt on, either. And then you can just put them away and watch them grow, without having to check the market quotations every day to find out if you ought to sell. Because you don't really want to bother worrying about the short-term fluctuations, do you?" This was absolutely not what Martinson had instructed him to tell new clients, but to hell with that. He got her some Jersey Standard, some Telephone, a little IBM, two good electric utilities, and 30 shares of a closed-end fund called Lehman Corporation that a lot of his elderly customers owned. She didn't ask questions, didn't even want to know what a closed-end fund was. "There," he said. "Now you have a portfolio. You're a capitalist." She smiled. It was a shy, half-forced smile, but he thought he detected flirtatiousness in her eyes. It was agony for him not to be able to read her, to be compelled to depend on external signals alone in order to know where he stood with her. But he took the chance. "What are you doing this evening?" he asked. "I get out of here at four o'clock."

She was free, she said. Except that she worked from eleven to six. He arranged to pick her up at her apartment around seven. There was no mistaking the warmth of her smile as she left the office. "You lucky bastard," Nadel said. "What did you do, make a date with her? It violates the SEC rules for customer's men to go around laying the customers."

Selig only laughed. Twenty minutes after the market opened he shorted 200 Molybdenum on the Amex, and covered his sale a point and a half lower at lunchtime. That ought to take care of the cost of dinner, he figured, with some to spare. Nyquist had given him the tip yesterday: Moly's a good short, she's sure to fall out of bed. During the mid-afternoon lull, feeling satisfied with himself, he phoned Nyquist to report on his maneuver. "You covered too soon," Nyquist said immediately. "She'll drop five or six more points this week. The smart money's waiting for that."

"I'm not that greedy. I'll settle for the quick three bills."

"That's no way to get rich."

"I guess I lack the gambling instinct," Selig said. He hesitated. He hadn't really called Nyquist to talk about shorting Molybdenum. I met a girl, he wanted to say, and I have this funny problem with her. I met a girl, I met a girl. Sudden fears held him back. Nyquist's silent passive presence at the other end of the telephone line seemed somehow threatening. He'll laugh at me, Selig thought. He's always laughing at me, quietly, thinking I don't see it. But this is foolishness. He said, "Tom, something strange happened today. A girl came into the office, a very attractive girl. I'm seeing her tonight."

"Congratulations."

"Wait. The thing is, I was entirely unable to read her. I mean, I couldn't even pick up an aura. Blank, absolutely blank. I've never had that with anybody before. Have you?"

"I don't think so."

"A complete blank. I can't understand it. What could account for her having such a strong screen?"

"Maybe you're tired today," Nyquist suggested.

"No. No. I can ready everybody else, same as always. Just not her."

"Does that irritate you?"

"Of course it does."

"Why do you say of course?"

It seemed obvious to Selig. He could tell that Nyquist was baiting him: the voice calm, uninflected, neutral. A game. A way of passing time. He wished he hadn't phoned. Something important seemed to be coming across on the ticker, and the other phone was lighting up. Nadel, grabbing it, shot a fierce look at him: *Come on, man, there's work to do!* Brusquely Selig said, "I'm—well, very interested in her. And it bothers me that I have no way of getting through to her real self."

Nyquist said, "You mean you're annoyed that you can't spy on her."

"I don't like that phrase."

"Whose phrase is it? Not mine. That's how you regard what we do, isn't it? As spying. You feel guilty about spying on people, right? But it seems you also feel upset when you can't spy."

"I suppose," Selig admitted sullenly.

"With this girl you find yourself forced back on the same old clumsy guesswork techniques for dealing with people that the rest of the world is condemned to use all the time, and you don't like that. Yes?"

"You make it sound so evil, Tom."

"What do you want me to say?"

"I don't want you to say anything. I'm just telling you that there's this girl I can't read, that I've never been up against this situation before, that I wonder if you have any theories to account for why she's the way she is."

"I don't," Nyquist said. "Not off the top of my head."

"All right, then. I—"

But Nyquist wasn't finished. "You realize that I have no way of telling whether she's opaque to the telepathic process in general or just opaque to you, David." That possibility had occurred to Selig a moment earlier. He found it deeply disturbing. Nyquist went on smoothly, "Suppose you bring her around one of these days and let me take a look at her. Maybe I'll be able to learn something useful about her that way."

"I'll do that," Selig said without enthusiasm. He knew such a meeting was necessary and inevitable, but the idea of exposing Kitty to Nyquist produced agitation in him. He had no clear understanding of why that should be happening. "One of these days soon," he said. "Look, all the phones are lighting up. I'll be in touch, Tom."

"Give her one for me," said Nyquist.

Twenty-three

David Selig
Selig Studies 101, Prof. Selig
November 10, 1976

Entropy As a Factor in Everyday Life

Entropy is defined in physics as a mathematical expression of the degree to which the energy of a thermodynamic system is so distributed as to be unavailable for conversion into work. In more general metaphorical terms, entropy may be seen as the irreversible tendency of a system, including the universe, toward increasing disorder and inertness. That is to say, things have a way of getting worse and worse all the time, until in the end they get so bad that we lack even the means of knowing how bad they really are.

The great American physicist Josiah Willard Gibbs (1839-1903) was the first to apply the second law of thermodynamics—the law that defines the increasing disorder of energy moving at random within a closed system—to chemistry. It was Gibbs who most firmly enunciated the principle that disorder spontaneously increases as the universe grows older. Among those who extended Gibbs' insights into the realm of philosophy was the brilliant mathematician Norbert Wiener (1894—1964), who declared, in his book *The Human Use of Human Beings*, "As entropy increases, the universe, and all closed systems in the universe, tend naturally to deteriorate and lose their distinctiveness, to move from the least to the most probable state, from a state of organization and differentiation in which distinctions and forms exist, to a state of chaos and sameness. In Gibbs' universe order is least probable, chaos most probable. But while the universe as a whole, if indeed there is a whole universe, tends to run down, there are local enclaves whose direction seems opposed to that of the universe at large and in which there is a limited and temporary tendency for organization to increase. Life finds its home in some of these enclaves."

Thus Wiener hails living things in general and human beings in particular as heroes in the war against entropy—which he equates in another passage with the war against evil: "This random element, this organic incompleteness [that is, the fundamental element of chance in the texture of the universe], is one which without too violent a figure of speech we may consider evil." Human beings, says Wiener, carry on anti-entropic processes. We have sensory receptors. We communicate with one another. We make use of what we learn from one another. Therefore we are something more than mere passive victims of the spontaneous spread of universal chaos. "We, as human beings, are not isolated systems. We take in food, which generates energy, from the outside, and are, as a result, parts of that larger world which contains those sources of our vitality. But even more important is the fact that we take in information through our sense organs, and we act on information received." There is feedback, in other words. Through communication we learn to control our environment, and, he says, "In control and communication we are always fighting nature's tendency to degrade the organized and to destroy the meaningful; the tendency... for entropy to increase." In the very long run entropy must inevitably nail us all; in the short run we can fight back. "We are not yet spectators at the last stages of the world's death."

But what if a human being *turns* himself, inadvertently or by choice, into an isolated system?

A hermit, say. He lives in a dark cave. No information penetrates. He eats mushrooms. They give him just enough energy to keep going, but otherwise he lacks inputs. He's forced back on his own spiritual and mental resources, which he eventually exhausts. Gradually the chaos expands in him, gradually the forces of entropy seize possession of this ganglion, that synapse. He takes in a decreasing amount of sensory data until his surrender to entropy is complete. He ceases to move, to grow, to respire, to function in any way. This condition is known as death.

One doesn't have to hide in a cave. One can make an interior migration, locking oneself away from the life-giving energy sources. Often this is done because it appears that the energy sources are threats to the stability of the self. Indeed, inputs do threaten the self: a push usually will upset equilibrium. However, equilibrium itself is a threat to the self, though this is frequently over-looked. There are married people who strive fiercely to reach equilibrium. They seal themselves off, clinging to one another and shutting out the rest of the universe, making themselves into a two-person closed system from which all vitality is steadily and inexorably expelled by the deadly equilibrium they have established. Two can perish as well as one, if they are sufficiently isolated from everything else. I call this the monogamous fallacy. My sister Judith said she left her husband because she felt herself dying, day by day, while she was living with him. Of course, Judith's a slut.

The sensory shutdown is not always a willed event, naturally. It happens to us whether we like it or not. If we don't climb into the box ourselves, we'll get shoved in anyway. That's what I mean about entropy inevitably nailing us all in the long run. No matter how vital, how vigorous, how world-devouring we are, the inputs dwindle as times go by. Sight, hearing, touch, smell—everything goes, as good old Will S. said, and we end up sans teeth, sans eyes, sans taste, sans everything. Sans everything. Or, as the same clever man also put it, from hour to hour we ripe and ripe, and then from hour to hour we rot and rot, and thereby hangs a tale.

I offer myself as a case in point. What does this man's sad history reveal? An inexplicable diminution of once-remarkable powers. A shrinkage of the inputs. A small death, endured while he still lives. Am I not a casualty of the entropic wars? Do I not now dwindle into stasis and silence before your very eyes? Is my distress not evident and poignant? Who will I be, when I have ceased to be myself? I am dying the heat death. A spontaneous decay. A random twitch of probability undoes me. And I am made into nothingness. I am becoming cinders and ash. I will wait here for the broom to gather me up.

* * *

That's very eloquent, Selig. Take an A. Your writing is clear and forceful and you show an excellent grasp of the underlying philosophical issues. You may go to the head of the class. Do you feel better now?

Twenty-four

It was a crazy idea, Kitty, a dumb fantasy. It could never have worked. I was asking the impossible from you. There was only one conceivable outcome, really: that is, that I would annoy you and bore you and drive you away from me. Well, blame Tom Nyquist. It was his idea. No, blame me. I didn't have to listen to his crazy ideas, did I? Blame me. Blame me.

Axiom: It's a sin against love to try to remake the soul of someone you love, even if you think you'll love her more after you've transformed her into something else.

* * *

Nyquist said, "Maybe she's a mindreader too, and the blockage is a matter of interference, of a clash between your transmissions and hers, canceling out the waves in one direction or in both. So that there's no transmission from her to you and probably none from you to her."

"I doubt that very much," I told him. This was August of 1963, two or three weeks after you and I had met. We weren't living together yet but we had already been to bed a couple of times. "She doesn't have a shred of telepathic ability," I insisted. "She's completely normal. That's the essential thing about her, Tom: she's a completely normal girl."

"Don't be so sure," Nyquist said.

He hadn't met you yet. He wanted to meet you, but I hadn't set anything up. You had never heard his name.

I said, "If there's one thing I know about her, it's that she's a sane, healthy, well-balanced, absolutely normal girl. Therefore she's no mindreader."

"Because mindreaders are insane, unhealthy, and unbalanced. Like you and like me. Q.E.D., eh? Speak for yourself, man."

"The gift tips the spirit," I said. "It darkens the soul."

"Yours, maybe. Not mine."

He was right about that. Telepathy hadn't injured him. Maybe I'd have had the problems I have even if I hadn't been born with the gift. I can't credit all my maladjustments to the presence of one unusual ability; can I? And God knows there are plenty of neurotics around who have never read a mind in their lives.

Syllogism:
Some telepaths are not neurotic.
Some neurotics are not telepaths.
Therefore telepathy and neurosis aren't necessarily related.
Corollary:
You can seem cherry-pie normal and still have the power.

I remained skeptical of this. Nyquist agreed, under pressure, that if you did have the power, you would have probably revealed it to me by now through certain unconscious mannerisms that any telepath would readily recognize; I had detected no such mannerisms. He suggested, though, that you might be a latent telepath—that the gift was there, undeveloped, unfunctional, lurking at the core of your mind and serving somehow to screen your mind from my probing. Just a hypothesis, he said. But it tickled me with temptation. "Suppose she's got this latent power," I said. "Could it be awakened, do you think?"

"Why not?" Nyquist asked.

I was willing to believe it. I had this vision of you awakened to full receptive capacity, able to pick up transmissions as easily and as sharply as Nyquist and I. How intense our love would be, then! We would be wholly open to one another, shorn of all the little pretenses and defenses that keep even the closest of lovers from truly achieving a union of souls. I had already tasted a limited form of that sort of closeness with Tom Nyquist, but of course I had no love for him. I didn't even really *like* him, and so it was a waste, a brutal irony, that our minds could have such intimate contact. But you? If I could only awaken you, Kitty! And why not? I asked Nyquist if he thought it might be possible. Try it and find out, he said. Make experiments. Hold hands, sit together in the dark, put some energy into trying to get across to her. It's worth trying, isn't it? Yes, I said, of course it's worth trying.

You seemed latent in so many other ways, Kitty: a potential human being rather than an actual one. An air of adolescence surrounded you. You seemed much younger than you actually were; if I hadn't known you were a college graduate I would have guessed you were 18 or 19. You hadn't read much outside your fields of interest—mathematics, computers, technology—and, since those weren't my fields of interest, I thought of you as not having read anything at all. You hadn't traveled; your world was limited by the Atlantic and the Mississippi, and the big trip of your life was a summer in Illinois. You hadn't even had much sexual experience: three men, wasn't it, in your 22 years, and only one of those a serious affair? So I saw you as raw material awaiting the sculptor's hand. I would be your Pygmalion.

In September of 1963 you moved in with me. You were spending so much time at my place anyway that you agreed it didn't make sense to keep going back and forth. I felt very married: wet stockings hanging over the showercurtain rod, an extra toothbrush on the shelf, long brown hairs in the sink. The warmth of you beside me in bed every night. My belly against your smooth cool butt, yang and yin. I gave you books to read: poetry, novels, essays. How diligently you devoured them! You read Trilling on the bus going to work and Conrad in the quiet after-dinner hours and Yeats Son a Sunday morning while I was out hunting for the *Times*. But nothing really seemed to stick with you; you had no natural bent for literature; I think you had trouble distinguishing Lord Jim from Lucky Jim, Malcolm Lowry from Malcolm Cowley, James Joyce from Joyce Kilmer. Your fine mind, so easily able to master COBOL and FORTRAN, could not decipher the language of poetry, and you would look up from *The Waste Land*, baffled, to ask some naive high-school-girl question that would leave me irritated for hours. A hopeless case, I sometimes thought. Although on a day when the stock market was closed you took me down to the computer center where you worked and I listened to your explanations of the equipment and your functions as though you were talking so much Sanskrit to me. Different worlds, different kinds of mind. Yet I always had hope of creating a bridge.

At strategically timed moments I spoke elliptically of my interest in extrasensory phenomena.

I made it out to be a hobby of mine, a cool dispassionate study. I was fascinated, I said, by the possibility of attaining true mind-to-mind communication between human beings. I took care not to come on like a fanatic, not to oversell my case; I kept my desperation out of sight. Because I genuinely couldn't read you, it was easier for me to pretend to a scholarly objectivity than it would have been with anyone else. And I had to pretend. My strategy didn't allow for any true confessions. I didn't want to frighten you, Kitty, I didn't want to turn you off by giving you reason to think I was a freak, or, as I probably would have seemed to you, a lunatic. Just a hobby, then. A hobby.

You couldn't bring yourself to believe in ESP. If it can't be measured with a voltmeter or recorded on an electroencephalograph, you said, it isn't real. Be tolerant, I pleaded. There *are* such things as telepathic powers. I know there are. (Be careful, Duv!) I couldn't cite EEG readings—I've never been near an EEG in my life, have no idea whether my power would register. And I had barred myself from conquering your skepticism by calling in some outsider and doing some party-game mindreading on him. But I could offer other arguments. Look at Rhine's results, look at all these series of correct readings of the Zener cards. How can you explain them, if not by ESP? And the evidence for telekinesis, teleportation, clairvoyance—

You remained skeptical, coolly putting down most of the data I cited. Your reasoning was keen and close; there was nothing fuzzy about your mind when it was on its own home territory, the scientific method. Rhine, you said, fudges his results by testing heterogeneous groups, then selecting for further testing only those subjects who show unusual runs of luck, dropping the others from his surveys. And he publishes only the scores that seem to prove his thesis. It's a statistical anomaly, not an extrasensory one, that turns up all those correct guesses of the Zener cards, you insisted. Besides, the experimenter is prejudiced in favor of belief in ESP, and that surely leads to all sorts of unconscious errors of procedure, tiny accesses of unintentional bias that inevitably skew the outcome. Cautiously I invited you to try some experiments with me, letting you set up the procedures to suit yourself. You said okay, mainly, I think, because it was something we could do together, and—this was early October—we were already searching selfconsciously for areas of closeness, your literary education having become a strain for both of us.

We agreed—how subtly I made it seem like your own idea!—to concentrate on transmitting images or ideas to one another. And right at the outset we had a cruelly deceptive success. We assembled some packets of pictures and tried to relay them mentally. I still have, here in the archives, our notes on those experiments:

Pictures Seen By Me	*Your Guess*
1. A rowboat	1. Oak Trees
2. Marigolds in a field	2. Bouquet of roses
3. A kangaroo	3. President Kennedy
4. Twin baby girls	4. A statue
5. The Empire State Building	5. The Pentagon
6. A snow-capped mountain	6. ? image unclear
7. Profile of old man's face	7. A pair of scissors
8. Baseball player at bat	8. A carving knife
9. An elephant	9. A tractor
10. A locomotive	10. An airplane

You had no direct hits. But four out of ten could be considered close associations: marigolds and roses, the Empire State and the Pentagon, elephant and tractor, locomotive and airplane. (Flowers, buildings, heavy-duty equipment, means of transportation.) Enough to give us false hopes of true transmission. Followed by this:

Pictures Seen By You	*My Guess*
1. A butterfly	1. A railway train
2. An octopus	2. Mountains
3. Tropical beach scene	3. Landscape, bright sunlight
4. Young Negro boy	4. An automobile
5. Map of South America	5. Grapevines
6. George Washington Bridge	6. The Washington Monument
7. Bowl of apples and bananas	7. Stock market quotations
8. El Greco's *Toledo*	8. A shelf of books
9. A highway at rush hour	9. A beehive
10. An ICBM	10. Cary Grant

No direct hits for me either. But three close associations, of sorts, out of ten: tropical beach and sunny landscape, George

Washington Bridge and Washington Monument, highway at rush hour and beehive, the common denominators being sunlight, George Washington, and intense tight-packed activity. At least we deceived ourselves into seeing them as close associations rather than coincidences. I confess I was stabbing in the dark at all times, guessing rather than receiving, and I had little faith even then in the quality of our responses. Nevertheless those probably random collisions of images aroused your curiosity: there's something in this stuff, maybe, you began to say. And we went onward.

We varied the conditions for thought transmission. We tried doing it in absolute darkness, one room apart. We tried it with the lights on, holding hands. We tried it during sex: I entered you and held you in my arms and thought hard at you, and you thought hard at me. We tried it drunk. We tried it fasting. We tried it under conditions of sleep-deprivation, forcing ourselves to stay up around the clock in the random hope that minds groggy with fatigue might permit mental impulses to slip through the barriers separating us. We would have tried it under the influence of pot or acid, but no one thought much about pot or acid in '63. We sought in a dozen other ways to open the telepathic conduit. Perhaps you recall the details of them even now; embarrassment drives them from my mind. I know we wrestled with our futile project night after night for more than a month, while your involvement with it swelled and peaked and dwindled again, carrying you through a series of phases from skepticism to cool neutral interest to unmistakable fascination and enthusiasm, then to an awareness of inevitable failure, a sense of the impossibility of our goal, leading then to weariness, to boredom, and to irritation. I realized none of this: I thought you were as dedicated to the work as I was. But it had ceased to be either an experiment or a game; it was, you saw, plainly an obsessive quest, and you asked several times in November if we could quit. All this mindreading, you said, left you with woeful headaches. But I couldn't give up, Kitty. I overrode your objections and insisted we go on. I was hooked, I was impaled, I browbeat you mercilessly into cooperating, I tyrannized you in the name of love, seeing always that telepathic Kitty I would ultimately produce. Every ten days, maybe, some delusive flicker of seeming contact buoyed my idiotic optimism. We *would* break through; we *would* touch each other's minds.

How could I quit now, when we were so close? But we were never close.

Early in November Nyquist gave one of his occasional dinner parties, catered by a Chinatown restaurant he favored. His parties were always brilliant events; to refuse the invitation would have been absurd. So at last I would have to expose you to him. For more than three months I had been more or less deliberately concealing you from him, avoiding the moment of confrontation, out of a cowardice I didn't fully understand. We came late: you were slow getting ready. The party was well under way, fifteen or eighteen people, many of them celebrities, although not to you, for what did you know of poets, composers, novelists? I introduced you to Nyquist. He smiled and murmured a sleek compliment and gave you a bland, impersonal kiss. You seemed shy, almost afraid of him, of his confidence and smoothness. After a moment of patter he went spinning away to answer the doorbell. A little later, as we were handed our first drinks, I planted a thought for him:

—Well? What do you think of her.

But he was too busy with his other guests to probe me, and didn't pick up on my question. I had to seek my own answers in his skull. I inserted myself—he glanced at me across the room, realizing what I was doing—and rummaged for information. Layers of hostly trivia masked his surface levels; he was simultaneously offering drinks, steering a conversation, signaling for the eggrolls to be brought from the kitchen, and inwardly going over the guest list to see who was yet to arrive. But I cut swiftly through that stuff and in a moment found his locus of Kitty-thoughts. At once I acquired the knowledge I wanted and dreaded. He could read you. Yes. To him you were as transparent as anyone else. Only to me were you opaque, for reasons none of us knew. Nyquist had instantly penetrated you, had assessed you, had formed his judgment of you, there for me to examine: he saw you as awkward, immature, naive, but yet also attractive and charming. (That's how he really saw you. I'm not trying, for ulterior reasons of my own, to make him seem more critical of you than he really was. You were very young, you were unsophisticated, and he saw that.) The discovery numbed me. Jealousy curdled me. That I should work so ponderously for so many weeks to reach you, getting nowhere, and he could knife so easily to your depths, Kitty! I was instantly suspi-

cious. Nyquist and his malicious games: was this yet one
more? *Could* he read you? How could I be sure he hadn't
planted a fiction for me? He picked up on that:

—You don't trust me? Of course I'm reading her.

—Maybe yes, maybe no.

—Do you want me to prove it?

—How?

—Watch.

Without interrupting for a moment his role of host, he
entered your mind, while mine remained locked on his. And
so, through him, I had my first and only glimpse of your
inwardness, Kitty, reflected by way of Tom Nyquist. Oh! It
was no glimpse I ever wanted. I saw myself through your
eyes through his mind. Physically I looked, if anything,
better than I imagined I would, my shoulders broader than
they really are, my face leaner, the features more regular. No
doubt that you responded to my body. But the emotional
associations! You saw me as stern father, as grim schoolmaster,
as grumbling tyrant. Read this, read that, improve your
mind, girl! Study hard to be worthy of me! Oh! Oh! And that
flaming core of resentment over our ESP experiments: worse
than useless to you, a monumental bore, an excursion into
insanity, a wearying, grinding drag. Night after night to be
bugged by monomaniacal me. Even our screwing invaded
by the foolish quest for mind-to-mind contact. How sick
you were of me, Kitty! How monstrously dull you thought
me!

An instant of such revelation was more than enough.
Stung, I retreated, pulling away quickly from Nyquist. You
looked at me in a startled way, I recall, as if you knew on
some subliminal level that mental energies were flashing
around the room, revealing the privacies of your soul. You
blinked and your cheeks reddened and you took a hasty
diving gulp of your drink. Nyquist shot me a sardonic smile. I
couldn't meet his eyes. But even then I resisted what he had
showed me. Had I not seen odd refraction effects before in
such relays? Should I not mistrust the accuracy of his picture
of your image of me? Was he not shading and coloring it?
Introducing sly distortions and magnifications? Did I truly
bug you all that much, Kitty, or was he not playfully exagger-
ating mild annoyance into vivid distaste? I chose not to
believe I bored you quite so much. We tend to interpret

events according to the way we prefer to see them. But I vowed to go easier on you in the future.

Later, after we had eaten, I saw you talking animatedly to Nyquist at the far side of the room. You were flirtatious and giddy, as you had been with me that first day at the brokerage office. I imagined you were discussing me and not being complimentary. I tried to pick up the conversation by way of Nyquist, but at my first tentative probe he glared at me.

—Get out of my head, will you?

I obeyed. I heard your laughter, too loud, rising above the hum of conversation. I drifted off to talk to a lithe little Japanese sculptress whose flat tawny chest sprouted untemptingly from a low-cut black sheath, and found her thinking, in French, that she would like me to ask her to go home with me. But I went home with you, Kitty, sitting sullen and graceless beside you on the empty subway train, and when I asked you what you and Nyquist had been discussing you said, "Oh, we were just kidding around. Just having a little fun."

* * *

About two weeks later, on a clear crisp autumn afternoon, President Kennedy was shot in Dallas. The stock market closed early after a calamitous slide and Martinson shut the office down, turing me out, dazed, into the street. I couldn't easily accept the reality of the progression of events. *Someone shot at the President.... Someone shot the President.... Someone shot the President in the head.... The President has been critically wounded.... The President has been rushed to Parkland Hospital.... The President has received the last rites.... The President is dead.* I was never a particularly political person, but this rupture of the commonwealth devastated me. Kennedy was the only presidential candidate I ever voted for who won, and they killed him: the story of my life in one compressed bloody parable. And now there would be a President Johnson. Could I adapt? I cling to zones of stability. When I was 10 years old and Roosevelt died, Roosevelt who had been President all my life, I tested the unfamiliar syllables of *President Truman* on my tongue and rejected them at once, telling myself that I would call him President Roosevelt too, for that was what I was accustomed to calling the President.

That November afternoon I picked up emanations of fear on all sides as I walked fearfully home. Paranoia was general everywhere. People sidled warily, one shoulder in front of the other, ready to bolt. Pale female faces peered between parted curtains in the windows of the towering apartment houses, high above the silent streets. The drivers of cars looked in all directions at intersections, as if expecting the tanks of the storm troopers to come rumbling down Broadway. (At this time of day it was generally believed that the assassination was the first blow in a right-wing putsch.) No one lingered in the open; everyone hurried toward shelter. Anything might happen now. Packs of wolves might burst out of Riverside Drive. Maddened patriots might launch a pogrom. From my apartment—door bolted, windows locked—I tried to phone you at the computer center, thinking you might somehow not have heard the news, or perhaps I just wanted to hear your voice in this traumatic time. The telephone lines were choked. I gave up the attempt after twenty minutes. Then, wandering aimlessly from bedroom to livingroom and back, clutching my transistor, twisting the dial trying to find the one radio station whose newscaster would tell me that he was still alive after all, I detoured into the kitchen and found your note on the table, telling me that you were leaving, that you couldn't stay with me any more. The note was dated 10:30 A.M., before the assassination, in another era. I rushed to the bedroom closet and saw what I had not seen before, that your things were gone. When women leave me, Kitty, they leave suddenly and stealthily, giving no warning.

* * *

Toward evening I telephoned Nyquist. This time the lines were open. "Is Kitty there?" I asked. "Yes," he said. "Just a minute." And put you on. You explained that you were going to live with him for a while, until you got yourself sorted out. He had been very helpful. No, you had no hard feelings toward me, no bitterness at all. It was just that I seemed, well, insensitive, whereas he—he had this instinctive, intuitive grasp of your emotional needs—he was able to get onto your trip, Kitty, and I couldn't manage that. So you had gone to him for comfort and love. Goodbye, you said, and thanks for everything, and I muttered a goodbye and put down the phone. During the night the weather changed, and a weekend of black skies and cold rain saw JFK to his grave. I missed everything—the casket in the rotunda, the brave widow and the gallant children, the murder of Oswald, the funeral procession, all that instant history. Saturday and

Sunday I slept late, got drunk, read six books without absorbing a word. On Monday, the day of national mourning, I wrote you that incoherent letter, Kitty, explaining everything, telling you what I had tried to make out of you and why, confessing my power to you and describing the effects it had had on my life, telling you also about Nyquist, warning you of what he was, that he had the power too, that he could read you and you would have no secrets from him, telling you not to mistake him for a real human being, telling you that he was a machine, self-programmed for maximum self-realization, telling you that the power had made him cold and cruelly strong whereas it had made me weak and jittery, insisting that essentially he was as sick as I, a manipulative man, incapable of giving love, capable only of using. I told you that he would hurt you if you made yourself vulnerable to him. You didn't answer. I never heard from you again, never saw you again, never heard from or saw him again either. Thirteen years. I have no idea what became of either of you. Probably I'll never know. But listen. Listen. I loved you, lady, in my clumsy way. I love you now. And you are lost to me forever.

Twenty-five

He wakes, feeling stiff and sore and numb, in a bleak, dreary hospital ward. Evidently this is St. Luke's, perhaps the emergency room. His lower lip is swollen, his left eye opens only reluctantly, and his nose makes an unfamiliar whistling sound at every intake of air. Did they bring him here on a stretcher after the basketball players finished with him? He has spent relatively little time in hospitals. He wonders if his clothing is stained with dried blood, but when he succeeds in looking down—his neck, oddly rigid, does not want to obey him—he sees only the dingy whiteness of a hospital gown. Each time he breathes, he imagines he can feel the ragged edges of broken ribs scraping together; slipping a hand under the gown, he touches his bare chest and finds that it has not been taped. He does not know whether to be relieved or apprehensive about that.

Carefully he sits up. A tumult of impressions strikes him. The room is crowded and noisy, with beds pushed close together. The beds have curtains but no curtains are drawn. Most of his fellow patients are black, and many of them are in serious condition, surrounded by festoons of equipment. Mutilated by knives? Lacerated by windshields? Friends and relatives, clustering around each bed, gesticulate and argue and berate; the normal tone of voice is a yelping shout. Impassive nurses drift through the room, showing much the same distant concern for the patients as museum guards do for mummies in display cases. No one is paying any attention to Selig except Selig, who returns to the examination of himself. His fingertips explore his cheeks. Without a mirror he cannot tell how battered his face is, but there are many tender places. His left clavicle aches as from a light, glancing karate chop. His right knee radiates throbbings and twinges, as though he twisted it in falling. Still, he feels less pain than might have been anticipated; perhaps they have given him some sort of shot.

His mind is foggy. He is receiving some mental input from those about him in the ward, but everything is garbled, nothing is distinct; he picks up auras but no intelligible verbalizations. Trying to get his bearings, he asks passing nurses three times to tell him the time, for his wristwatch is gone; they go by, ignoring him. Finally a bulky, smiling black woman in a frilly pink dress looks over to him and says, "It's quarter to four, love." In the morning? In the afternoon? Probably the afternoon, he decides. Diagonally across from him, two nurses have begun to erect what perhaps is an intravenous feeding system, with a plastic tube snaking into the nostril of a huge unconscious bandage-swathed black. Selig's own stomach send him no hunger signals. The chemical smell in the hospital air gives him nausea; he can barely salivate. Will they feed him this evening? How long will he be kept here? Who pays? Should he ask that Judith be notified? How badly has he been injured?

An intern enters the ward: a short dark man, concise and fine-boned of body, a Pakistani by the looks of him, moving with bouncy precision. A rumpled and soiled handkerchief jutting from his breast pocket spoils, though, the trig, smart effect of his tight white uniform. Surprisingly, he comes right to Selig. "The X-rays show no breakages," he says without preamble in a firm, unresonant voice. "Therefore your only injuries are minor abrasions, bruises, cuts, and an unimportant concussion. We are ready to authorize your release. Please get up."

"Wait," Selig says feebly. "I just came to. I don't know what's been going on. Who brought me here? How long have I been unconscious? What—"

"I know none of these things. Your discharge has been approved and the hospital has need of this bed. Please. On your feet, now. I have much to do."

"A concussion? Shouldn't I spend the night here, at least, if I had a concussion? Or *did* I spend the night here? What day is today?"

"You were brought in about noon today," says the intern, growing more fretful. "You were treated in the emergency room and given a thorough examination after having been beaten on the steps of Low Library." Once more the command to rise, given wordlessly this time, an imperious glare and a pointing forefinger. Selig probes the intern's mind and finds it accessible, but there is nothing apparent in it except impatience and irritation. Ponderously Selig climbs from the bed. His body seems to be held together with wire. His bones grind and scrape. There is still the sensation of broken rib-ends rubbing in his chest; can the X-ray have been in error? He starts to ask, but too late. The intern, making his rounds, has whirled off to another bed.

They bring him his clothing. He pulls the curtain around his bed and dresses. Yes, bloodstains on his shirt, as he had feared; also on his trousers. A mess. He checks his belongings: everything here, wallet, wristwatch, pocketcomb. What now? Just walk out? Nothing to sign? Selig edges uncertainly toward the door. He actually gets into the corridor unperceived. Then the intern materializes as if from ectoplasm and points to another room across the hall, saying, "You wait in there until the security man comes." Security man? *What* security man?

There are, as he had feared, papers to sign before he is free of the hospital's grasp. Just as he finishes with the red tape, a plump, gray-faced, sixtyish man in the uniform of the campus security force enters the room, puffing slightly, and says, "You Selig?"

He acknowledges that he is.

"The dean wants to see you. You able to walk by yourself or you want me to get you a wheelchair?"

"I'll walk," Selig says.

They go out of the hospital together, up Amsterdam Avenue to the 115th Street campus gate, and into Van Am Quad. The security man stays close beside him, saying nothing. Shortly Selig finds himself waiting outside the office of the Dean of Columbia College. The security man waits with him, arms folded placidly, wrapped in a cocoon of boredom. Selig begins to feel almost as though he is under some sort of arrest. Why is that? An odd thought. What does he have to fear from the dean? He probes the security man's dull mind but can find nothing in it but drifting, wispy masses of fog. He wonders who the dean is, these days. He remembers the deans of his own college era well enough: Lawrence Chamberlain, with the bow ties and the warm smile, was Dean of the College, and Dean McKnight, Nicholas McD. McKnight, a fraternity enthusiast (Sigma Chi?) with a formal, distinctly nineteenth-century manner, was Dean of Students. But that was twenty years ago. Chamberlain and McKnight must have had several successors by now, but he knows nothing about them; he has never been one for reading alumni newsletters.

A voice from within says, "Dean Cushing will see him now."

"Go on in," the security man says.

Cushing? A fine deanly name. Who is he? Selig limps in, awkward from his injuries, bothered by his sore knee. Facing him behind a glistening uncluttered desk sits a wide-shouldered, smooth-cheeked, youthful-looking man, junior-executive model, wearing a conservative dark suit. Selig's first thought is of the mutations worked by the passage of time: he had always looked upon deans as lofty symbols of authority, necessarily elderly or at least of middle years, but here is the Dean of the College and he seems to be a man of Selig's own age. Then he realizes that this dean is not merely an anonymous contemporary of his but actually a classmate, Ted Cushing '56, a campus figure of some repute back then, class president and football star and A-level scholar, whom Selig had known at least in a passing way. It always surprises Selig to be reminded that he is no longer young, that he has lived into a time when his generation has control of the mechanisms of power. "Ted?" he blurts. "Are you dean now, Ted? Christ, I wouldn't have guessed that. When—"

"Sit down, Dave," Cushing says, politely but with no great show of friendliness. "Did you get badly hurt?"

"The hospital says nothing's broken. I feel half ruined, though." As he eases into a chair he indicates the bloodstains on his clothing, the bruises on his face. Talking is an effort; his jaws creak at their hinges. "Hey, Ted, it's been a long time! Must be twenty years since I last saw you. Did you remember my name, or did they identify me from my wallet?"

"We've arranged to pay the hospital costs," Cushing says, not seeming to hear Selig's words. "If there are any further medical expenses, we'll take care of those too. You can have that in writing if you'd like."

"The verbal commitment is fine. And in case you're worrying that I'll press charges, or sue the University, well, I wouldn't do anything like that. Boys will be boys, they let their feelings run away with themselves a little bit, but—"

"We weren't greatly concerned about your pressing charges, Dave," Cushing says quietly. "The real question is whether we're going to press charges against *you*."

"Me? For what? For getting mauled by your basketball players? For damaging their expensive hands with my face?" He essays a painful grin. Cushing's face remains grave. There is a little moment of silence. Selig struggles to interpret Cushing's joke. Finding no rationale for it, he decides to venture a probe. But he runs into a wall. He is suddenly too timid to push, fearful that he will be inable to break through. "I don't understand what you mean," he says finally. "Press charges for what?"

"For these, Dave." For the first time Selig notices the stack of typewritten pages on the dean's desk. Cushing nudges them forward. "Do you recognize them? Here: take a look."

Selig leafs unhappily through them. They are term papers, all of them of his manufacture. *Odysseus as a Symbol of Society. The Novels of Kafka. Aeschylus and the Aristotelian Tragedy. Resignation and Acceptance in the Philosophy of Montaigne. Virgil as Dante's Mentor.* Some of them bear marks: A−, B+, A−, A and marginal comments, mainly favorable. Some are untouched except by smudges and smears; these are the ones he had been about to deliver when he was set upon by Lumumba. With immense care he tidies the stack, aligning the edges of the sheets precisely, and pushes them back toward Cushing. "All right," he says. "You've got me."

"Did you write those?"

"Yes."

"For a fee?"

"Yes."

"That's sad, Dave. That's awfully sad."

"I needed to earn a living. They don't give scholarships to alumni."

"What were you getting paid for these things?"

"Three or four bucks a typed page."

Cushing shakes his head. "You were good, I'll give you credit for that. There must be eight or ten guys working your racket here, but you're easily the best."

"Thank you."

"But you had one dissatisfied customer, at least. We asked Lumumba why he beat you up. He said he hired you to write a term paper for him and you did a lousy job, you ripped him off, and then you wouldn't refund his money. All right, we're dealing with him in our own way, but we have to deal with you, too. We've been trying to find you for a long time, Dave."

"Have you?"

"We've circulated xeroxes of your work through a dozen departments the last couple of semesters, warning people to be on the lookout for your typewriter and your style. There wasn't a great deal of cooperation. A lot of faculty members didn't seem to care whether the term papers they received were phony or not. But we cared, Dave. We cared very much." Cushing leans forward. His eyes, terribly earnest, seek Selig's. Selig looks away. He cannot abide the searching warmth of those eyes. "We started closing in a few weeks ago," Cushing continues. "We rounded up a couple of your clients and threatened them with expulsion. They gave us your name, but they didn't know where you lived, and we had no way of finding you. So we waited. We knew you'd show up again to deliver and solicit. Then we got this report of a disturbance on the steps of Low, basketball players beating somebody up, and we found you with a pile of undelivered papers clutched in your arm, and that was it. You're out of business, Dave."

"I should ask for a lawyer," Selig says. "I shouldn't admit

anything more to you. I should have denied everything when you showed me those papers."

"No need to be so technical about your rights."

"I'll need to be when you take me to court, Ted."

"No," Cushing says. "We aren't going to prosecute, not unless we catch you ghosting more papers. We have no interest in putting you in jail, and in any case I'm not sure that what you've done is a criminal offense. What we really want to do is help you. You're sick, Dave. For a man of your intelligence, of your potential, to have fallen so low, to have ended up faking term papers for college kids—that's sad, Dave, that's awfully sad. We've discussed your case here, Dean Bellini and Dean Tompkins and I, and we've come up with a rehabilitation plan for you. We can find you work on campus, as a research assistant, maybe. There are always doctoral candidates who need assistants, and we have a small fund we could dip into to provide a salary for you, nothing much, but at least as much as you were making on these papers. And we'd admit you to the psychological counseling service here. It wasn't set up for alumni, but I don't see why we need to be inflexible about it, Dave. For myself I have to say that I find it embarrassing that a man of the Class of '56 is in the kind of trouble you're in, and if only out of a spirit of loyalty to our class I want to do everything possible to help you put yourself back together and begin to fulfill the promise that you showed when—"

Cushing rambles on, restating and embellishing his themes, offering pity without censure, promising aid to his suffering classmate. Selig, listening inattentively, discovers that Cushing's mind is beginning to open to him. The wall that earlier had separated their consciousnesses, a product perhaps of Selig's fear and fatigue, has started to dissolve, and Selig is able now to perceive a general image of Cushing's mind, which is energetic, strong, capable, but also conventional and limited, a stolid Republican mind, a prosaic Ivy League mind. Foremost in it is not his concern for Selig but rather his complacent satisfaction with himself: the brightest glow emanates from Cushing's awareness of his happy station in life, ornamented by a suburban split-level, a strapping blonde wife, three handsome children, a shaggy dog, a shining new Lincoln Continental. Pushing a bit deeper, Selig sees that Cushing's show of concern for him is fraudulent. Behind the earnest eyes and the sincere, heartfelt, sympathetic smile lies fierce contempt. Cushing despises him. Cushing thinks he is corrupt, useless, worthless, a disgrace to mankind in general and the Columbia College Class of '56 in particular. Cushing finds him physically as well as morally repugnant, seeing him as unwashed and unclean, possibly syphilitic. Cushing suspects him of being homosexual. Cushing has for him the scorn of the Rotarian for the junkie. It is impossible for Cushing to understand why anyone who has had the benefit of a Columbia education would let himself slide into the degradations Selig has accepted. Selig shrinks from Cushing's disgust. Am I so despicable, he wonders, am I such trash?

His hold on Cushing's mind strengthens and deepens. It ceases to trouble him that Cushing has such contempt for him. Selig drifts into a mode of abstraction in which he no longer identifies himself with the miserable churl Cushing sees. What does Cushing know? Can Cushing penetrate the mind of another? Can Cushing feel the ecstasy of real contact with a fellow human being? And there is ecstasy in it. Godlike he rides passenger in Cushing's mind, sinking past the external defenses, past the petty prides and snobberies, past the self-congratulatory smugness, into the realm of absolute values, into the kingdom of authentic self. Contact! Ecstasy! That stolid Cushing is the outer husk. Here is a Cushing that even Cushing does not know: but Selig does.

Selig has not been so happy in years. Light, golden and serene, floods his soul. An irresistible gaiety possesses him. He runs through misty groves at dawn, feeling the gentle lashing of moist green fern-fronds against his shins. Sunlight pierces the canopy of high foliage, and droplets of dew glitter with a cool inner fire. The birds awaken. Their song is tender and sweet, a distant cheebling, sleepy and soft. He runs through the forest, and he is not alone, for a hand grasps his hand; and he knows that he has never been alone and never will be alone. The forest floor is damp and spongy beneath his bare feet. He runs. He runs. An invisible choir strikes a harmonious note and holds it, holds it, holds it, swelling it in perfect crescendo, until, just as he breaks from the grove and sprints into a sun-bright meadow, that swell of tone fills all the cosmos, reverberating in magical fullness. He throws himself face-forward to the ground, hugging the earth, writhing against the fragrant grassy carpet, flattening his hands against the curve of the planet, and he is aware of the world's inner throbbing. This is ecstasy! This is contact! Other minds

surround his. In whatever direction he moves, he feels their
presence, welcoming him, supporting him, reaching toward
him. Come, they say, join us, join us, be one with us, give up
those tattered shreds of self, let go of all that holds you apart
from us Yes, Selig replies. Yes, I affirm the ecstasy of life. I
affirm the joy of contact. I give myself to you. They touch
him. He touches them. It was for this, he knows, that I
received my gift, my blessing, my power. For this moment of
affirmation and fulfillment. Join us. Join us. Yes! The birds!
The invisible choir! The dew! The meadow! The sun! He
laughs; he rises and breaks into an ecstatic dance; he throws
back his head to sing, he who has never in his life dared to
sing, and the tones that come from him are rich and full,
pure, squarely striking the center of the pitch. Yes! Oh, the
joining, the touching, the union, the oneness! No longer is he
David Selig. He is a part of them, and they are a part of him,
and in that joyous blending he experiences loss of self, he
gives up all that is tired and worn and sour in him, he gives
up his fears and uncertainties, he gives up everything that
has separated himself from himself for so many years. He
breaks through. He is fully open and the immense signal of
the universe rushes freely into him. He receives. He trans-
mits. He absorbs. He radiates. Yes. Yes. Yes. Yes.

He knows this ecstasy will last forever.

But in the moment of that knowledge, he feels it slipping
from him. The choir's glad note diminishes. The sun drops
toward the horizon. The distant sea, retreating, sucks at the
shore. He struggles to hold to the joy, but the more he
struggles the more of it he loses. Hold back the tide? How?
Delay the fall of night? How? How? The birdsongs are faint
now. The air has turned cold. Everything rushes away from
him. He stands alone in the gathering darkness, remembering that ecstasy, recapturing it momentarily, reliving it—for it
is already gone, and must be summoned back through an act
of the will. Gone, yes. It is very quiet, suddenly. He hears
one last sound, a stringed instrument in the distance, a cello,
perhaps, being plucked, pizzicato, a beautiful melancholy
sound. *Twang*. The plangent chord. *Twing*. The breaking
string. *Twong*. The lyre untuned. Twang. Twing. Twong. And
nothing more. Silence envelops him. A terminal silence, it is,
that booms through the caverns of his skull, the silence that
follows the shattering of the cello's strings, the silence that

comes with the death of music. He can hear nothing. He can feel nothing. He is alone. He is alone. He is alone.

He is alone.

"So quiet," he murmurs. "So private. It's—so—private—here."

"Selig?" a deep voice asks. "What's the matter with you, Selig?"

"I'm all right," Selig says. He tries to stand, but nothing has any solidity. He is tumbling through Cushing's desk, through the floor of the office, falling through the planet itself, seeking and not finding a stable platform. "So quiet. The silence, Ted, the silence!" Strong arms seize him. He is aware of several figures bustling about him. Someone is calling for a doctor. Selig shakes his head, protesting that nothing is wrong with him, nothing at all, except for the silence in his head, except for the silence, except for the silence.

Except for the silence.

Twenty-six

Winter is here. Sky and pavement form a seamless, inexorable band of gray. There will be snow soon. For some reason this neighborhood has gone without refuse pickups for three or four days, and bulging plastic sacks of trash are heaped in front of every building, yet there is no odor of garbage in the air. Not even smells can flourish in these temperatures: the cold drains away every stink, every sign of organic reality. Only concrete triumphs here. Silence reigns. Scrawny black and gray cats, motionless, statues of themselves, peer out of alleys. Traffic is light. Walking quickly through the streets from the subway station to Judith's place, I avert my eyes from the faces of the few people I pass. I feel shy and selfconscious among them, like a war veteran who has just been discharged from the rehabilitation center and is still embarrassed about his mutilations. Naturally I'm unable to tell what anybody is thinking; their minds are closed to me now and they go by me wearing shields of impenetrable ice;

but, ironically, I have the illusion that they all have access to *me*. They can look right into me and see me for what I've become. There's David Selig, they must be thinking. How careless he was! What a poor custodian of his gift! He messed up and let it all slip away from him, the dope. I feel guilty for causing them this disappointment. Yet I don't feel as guilty as I thought I might. On some ultimate level I just don't give a damn at all. This is what I am, I tell myself. This is what I now shall be. If you don't like it, tough crap. Try to accept me. If you can't do that, just ignore me.

* * *

"As the truest society approaches always nearer to solitude, so the most excellent speech finally falls into silence. Silence is audible to all men, at all times, and in all places." So said Thoreau, in 1849, in *A Week on the Concord and Merrimack Rivers*. Of course, Thoreau was a misfit and an outsider with very serious neurotic problems. When he was a young man just out of college he fell in love with a girl named Ellen Sewall, but she turned him down, and he never married. I wonder if he ever made it with anybody. Probably not. I can't imagine Thoreau actually balling, can you? Oh, maybe he didn't die a virgin, but I bet his sex life was lousy. Perhaps he didn't even masturbate. Can you visualize him sitting next to that pond and whacking off? I can't. Poor Thoreau. Silence is audible, Henry.

* * *

I imagine, as I near Judith's building, that I meet Toni in the street. I seem to see a tall figure walking toward me from Riverside Drive, hatless, bundled up in a bulky orange coat. When we are half a block apart I recognize her. Strangely, I feel neither excitement nor apprehension over this unexpected reunion; I am quite calm, almost unmoved. At another time I might have crossed the street to avoid a possibly disturbing encounter, but not now: coolly I halt in her path, smile, hold up my hands in greeting. "Toni?" I say. "Don't you know me?"

She studies me, frowns, seems puzzled for a moment. But only a moment.

"David. Hello."

Her face looks more lean, the cheekbones higher and sharper. There are some strands of gray in her hair. In the days when I knew her she had one curious gray lock at her temple, very unusual; now the gray is scattered more randomly through the black. Well, of course she's in her middle thirties now. Not exactly a girl. As old now, in fact, as I was when I first met her. But in fact I know she has hardly changed at all, only matured a little. She seems as beautiful as ever. Yet desire is absent from me. All passion spent, Selig. All passion spent. And she too is mysteriously free of turbulence. I remember our last meeting, the look of pain on her face, her obsessive heap of cigarette butts. Now her expression is amiable and casual. We both have passed through the realm of storms.

"You're looking good," I say. "What is it, eight years, nine?"

I know the answer to that. I'm merely testing her. And she passes the test, saying, "The summer of '68." I'm relieved to see that she hasn't forgotten. I'm still a chapter of her autobiography, then. "How have you been, David?"

"Not bad." The conversational inanities. "What are you doing these days?"

"I'm with Random House now. And you?"

"Freelancing," I say. "Here and there." Is she married? Her gloved hands offer no data. I don't dare ask. I'm incapable of probing. I force a smile and shift my weight from foot to foot. The silence that has come between us suddenly seems unbridgeable. Have we exhausted all feasible topics so soon? Are there no areas of contact left except those too pain-filled to reopen?

She says, "You've changed."

"I'm older. Tireder. Balder."

"It isn't that. You've changed somewhere inside."

"I suppose I have."

"You used to make me feel uncomfortable. I'd get a sort of queasy feeling. I don't any more."

"You mean, after the trip?"

"Before and after both," she says.

"You were always uncomfortable with me?"

"Always. I never knew why. Even when we were really close, I felt—I don't know, on guard, off balance, ill at ease, when I was with you. And that's gone now. It's entirely gone. I wonder why."

"Time heals all wounds," I say. Oracular wisdom.

"I suppose you're right. God, it's cold! Do you think it'll snow?"

"It's bound to, before long."

"I hate the cold weather." She huddles into her coat. I never knew her in cold weather. Spring and summer, then goodbye, get out, goodbye, goodbye. Odd how little I feel for her now. If she invited me up to her apartment I'd probably say, No, thank you, I'm on my way to visit my sister. Of course she's imaginary; that may have something to do with it. But also I'm not getting an aura from her. She's not broadcasting, or rather I'm not receiving. She's only a statue of herself, like the cats in the alleys. Will I be incapable of feeling, now that I'm incapable of receiving? She says, "It's been good to see you, David. Let's get together some time, shall we?"

"By all means. We'll have a drink and talk about old times."

"I'd like that."

"So would I. Very much."

"Take care of yourself, David."

"You too, Toni."

We smile. I give her a little mock-salute of farewell. We move apart; I continue walking west, she hurries up the windy street toward Broadway. I feel a little warmer for having met her. Everything cool, friendly, unemotional between us. Everything dead, in fact. All passion spent. It's been good to see you, David. Let's get together some time, shall we? When I reach the corner I realize I have forgotten to ask for her phone number. Toni? Toni? But she is out of sight. As though she never was there at all.

* * *

It is the little rift within the lute,
That by and by will make the music mute,
And ever widening slowly silence all.

That's Tennyson: *Merlin and Vivien*. You've heard that line about the rift within the lute before, haven't you? But you never knew it was Tennyson. Neither did I. My lute is riven. Twang. Twing. Twong.

Here's another little literary gem:

Every sound shall end in silence, but the silence never dies.

Samuel Miller Hageman wrote that, in 1876, in a poem called *Silence*. Have you ever heard of Samuel Miller Hageman before? I haven't. You were a wise old cat, Sam, whoever you were.

*   *   *

One summer when I was eight or nine—it was before they adopted Judith, anyway—I went with my parents to a resort in the Catskills for a few weeks. There was a daycamp for the kiddies, in which we received instruction in swimming, tennis, softball, arts & crafts, and other activities, thus leaving the older folks free for gin rummy and creative drinking. One afternoon the daycamp staged some boxing matches. I had never worn boxing gloves, and in the free-for-alls of boyhood I had found myself to be an incompetent fighter, so I was unenthusiastic. I watched the first five matches in much dismay. All that hitting! All those bloody noses!

Then it was my turn. My opponent was a boy named Jimmy, a few months younger than I but taller and heavier and much more athletic. I think the counselors matched us deliberately, hoping Jimmy would kill me: I was not their favorite child. I started to shake even before they put the gloves on me. "Round One!" called a counselor, and we approached each other. I distinctly heard Jimmy thinking about hitting me on the chin, and as his glove came toward my face I ducked and hit him in the belly. That made him furious. He proposed now to clobber me on the back of the head, but I saw that coming too and stepped aside and hit him on the neck close to his adam's-apple. He gagged and turned away, half in tears. After a moment he returned to the attack, but I continued to anticipate his moves and he never touched me. For the first time in my life I felt tough, competent, aggressive. As I battered him I looked past the improvised ring and saw my father flushed with pride, and Jimmy's father next to him looking angry and perplexed. End of round one. I was sweating, bouncy, grinning.

Round two: Jimmy came forth determined to knock me to pieces. Swinging wildly, frantically, still going for my head. I kept my head where he couldn't reach it and danced around

to his side and hit him in the belly again, very hard, and
when he folded up I hit him on the nose and he fell down,
crying. The counselor in charge very quickly counted to ten
and raised my hand. "Hey, Joe Louis!" my father yelled.
"Hey, Willie Pep!" The counselor suggested I go over to
Jimmy and help him up and shake his hand. As he got to his
feet I very clearly detected him deciding to butt me in the
teeth with his head, and I pretended to be paying no
attention, except when he charged I stepped coolly to one
side and banged my fists down on his lowered back. That
shattered him. "David cheats!" he moaned. "David *cheats*!"

How they all hated me for my cleverness! What they
interpreted as my cleverness, that is. My sly knack of always
guessing what was going to happen. Well, that wouldn't be a
problem now. They'd all love me. Loving me, they'd beat me
to a pulp.

* * *

Judith answers the door. She wears an old gray sweater and
blue slacks with a hole in the knee. She holds her arms out to
me and I embrace her warmly, pulling her tight against my
body for perhaps half a minute. I hear music from within: the
Siegfried Idyll, I think. Sweet, loving, accepting music.

"Is it snowing yet?" she asks.

"Not yet. Gray and cold, that's all."

"I'll get you a drink. Go into the livingroom."

I stand by the window. A few snowflakes blow by. My
nephew appears and studies me at a distance of thirty feet.
To my amazement he smiles. He says warmly, "Hi, Uncle
David!"

Judith must have put him up to it. Be nice to Uncle David,
she must have said. He isn't feeling well, he's had a lot of
trouble lately. So there the kids stands, being nice to Uncle
David. I don't think he's ever smiled at me before. He didn't
even gurgle and coo at me out of his cradle. Hi, Uncle David.
All right, kid. I can dig it.

"Hell, Pauly. How have you been?"

"Fine," he says. With that his social graces are exhausted;
he does not inquire in return about the state of my health,
but picks up one of his toys and absorbs himself in its
intricacies. Yet his large dark glossy eyes continue to examine

me every few moments, and there does not seem to be any
hostility in his glance.

Wagner ends. I prowl through the record racks, select one,
put it on the turntable. Schoenberg. *Verklaerte Nacht.* Music
of tempestuous anguish followed by calmness and resignation.
The theme of acceptance again. Fine. Fine. The swirling
strings enfold me. Rich, lush chords. Judith appears, bringing
me a glass of rum. She has something mild for herself, sherry
or vermouth. She looks a little peaked but very friendly, very
open.

"Cheers," she says.

"Cheers."

"That's good music you put on. A lot of people won't
believe Schoenberg could be sensuous and tender. Of course,
it's very early Schoenberg."

"Yes," I say. "The romantic juices tend to dry up as you get
older, eh? What have you been up to lately, Jude?"

"Nothing much. A lot of the same old."

"How's Karl?"

"I don't see Karl any more."

"Oh."

"Didn't I tell you that?"

"No," I say. "It's the first I've heard of it."

"I'm not accustomed to needing to *tell* you things, Duv."

"You'd better get accustomed to it. You and Karl—"

"He became very insistent about marrying me. I told him
it was too soon, that I didn't know him well enough, that I
was afraid of structuring my life again when it might possibly
be the wrong structure for me. He was hurt. He began
lecturing me about retreats from involvement and commitment, about self-destructiveness, a lot of stuff like that. I
looked right at him in the middle of it and I flashed on him as
a kind of father-figure; you know, big and pompous and stern,
not a lover but a mentor, a professor, and I didn't want that.
And I started thinking about what he'd be like in another ten
or twelve years. He'd be in his sixties and I'd still be young.
And I realized there was no future for us together. I told him
that as gently as I could. He hasn't called in ten days or so. I
suppose he won't."

"I'm sorry."

"No need to be, Duv. I did the smart thing. I'm sure of it.
Karl was good for me, but it couldn't have been permanent.

My Karl phase. A very healthy phase. The thing is not to let a
phase go on too long after you know it's really over."

"Yes," I say. "Certainly."

"Would you like some more rum?"

"In a little while."

"What about you?" she asks. "Tell me about yourself. How
you're making out, now that—now that—"

"Now that my superman phase is over?"

"Yes," she says. "It's really gone, eh?"

"Really. All gone. No doubt."

"And so, Duv? How has it been for you since it happened?"

* * *

Justice. You hear a lot about justice, God's justice. He
looketh after the righteous. He doeth dirt to the ungodly.
Justice? Where's justice? Where's God, for that matter? Is He
really dead, or merely on vacation, or only absent-minded?
Look at His justice. He sends a flood to Pakistan. Zap, a
million people dead, the adulterer and the virgin both.
Justice? Maybe. Maybe the supposedly innocent victims weren't
so innocent after all. Zap, the dedicated nun at the leprosarium
gets leprosy and her lips fall off overnight. Justice. Zap, the
cathedral that the congregation has been building for the past
two hundred years is reduced to rubble by an earthquake the
day before Easter. Zap. Zap. God laughs in our faces. This is
justice? Where? How? I mean, consider my case. I'm not
trying to wring some pity from you now; I'm being purely
objective. Listen, I didn't *ask* to be a superman. It was
handed to me at the moment of my conception. God's
incomprehensible whim. A whim that defined me, shaped
me, malformed me, dislocated me, and it was unearned,
unasked for, entirely undesired, unless you want to think of
my genetic heritage in terms of somebody else's bad karma,
and crap on that. It was a random twitch. God said, Let this
kid be a superman, and Lo! young Selig was a superman, in
one limited sense of the word. For a time, anyhow. God set
me up for everything that happened: the isolation, the suffering, the loneliness, even the self-pity. Justice? Where? The
Lord giveth, who the hell knoweth why, and the Lord taketh
away. Which He has now done. The power's gone. I'm just
plain folks, even as you and you and you. Don't misunderstand: I accept my fate, I'm completely reconciled to it, I am
NOT asking you to feel sorry for me. I simply want to make a

little sense out of this. Now that the power's gone, who am I?
How do I define myself now? I've lost my special thing, my
power, my wound, my reason for apartness. All I have left
now is the memory of having been different. The scars of it.
What am I supposed to do now? How do I relate to mankind,
now that the difference is gone and I'm still here? *It* died. I
live on. What a strange thing you did to me, God. I'm not
protesting, you understand. I'm just asking things, in a quiet,
reasonable tone of voice. I'm inquiring into the nature of
divine justice. I think Goethe's old harpist had the right slant
on you, God. You lead us forth into life, you let the poor man
fall into guilt, and then you leave him to his misery. For all
guilt is revenged on earth. That's a reasonable complaint. You
have ultimate power, God, but you refuse to take ultimate
responsibility. Is that fair? I think I have a reasonable complaint too. If there's justice, why does so much of life seem
unjust? If you're really on our side, God, why do you hand us
a life of pain? Where's justice for the baby born without eyes?
The baby born with two heads? The baby born with a power
men weren't meant to have? Just asking, God. I accept your
decree, believe me, I bow to your will, because I might as
well—what choice do I have, after all?—but I'm still entitled
to ask. Right?

Hey, God? God? Are you listening, God?

I don't think you are. I don't think you give a crap. God, I
think you've been fucking me.

* * *

Dee-dah-de-doo-dah-dee-da. The music is ending. Celestial harmonies filling the room. Everything merging into
oneness. Snowflakes swirling beyond the windowpane. Right
on Schoenberg. You understood, at least when you were
young. You caught truth and put it on paper. I hear what
you're saying, man. Don't ask questions, you say. Accept.
Only accept, that's the motto. Accept. Accept. Whatever
comes to you, accept.

* * *

Judith says, "Claude Guermantes has invited me to go
skiing with him in Switzerland over Christmas. I can leave
the baby with a friend in Connecticut. But I won't go

if you need me, Duv. Are you okay? Can you manage?"

"Sure I can. I'm not paralyzed, Jude. I haven't lost my
sight. Go to Switzerland, if that's what you want."

"I'll only be gone eight days."

"I'll survive."

"When I come back, I hope you'll move out of that housing
project. You ought to live down here close to me. We should
see more of each other."

"Maybe."

"I might even introduce you to some girlfriends of mine. If
you're interested."

"Wonderful, Jude."

"You don't sound enthusiastic about it."

"Go easy with me," I tell her. "Don't rush me with a
million things. I need time to sort things out."

"All right. It's like a new life, isn't it, Duv?"

"A new life. Yes. A new life, that's what it is, Jude."

* * *

The storm is intense, now. Cars are vanishing under the
first layers of whiteness. At dinner time the radio weather
forecaster talked of an accumulation of eight to ten inches
before morning. Judith has invited me to spend the night
here, in the maid's room. Well, why not? Now of all times,
why should I spurn her? I'll stay. In the morning we'll take
Pauly out to the park, with his sled, into the new snow. It's
really coming down, now. The snow is so beautiful. Covering
everything, cleansing everything, briefly purifying this tired
eroded city and its tired eroded people. I can't take my eyes
from it. My face is close to the window. I hold a brandy
snifter in one hand, but I don't remember to drink from it,
because the snow has caught me in its hypnotic spell.

"*Boo!*" someone cries behind me.

I jump so violently that the cognac leaps from the snifter
and splashes the window. In terror I whirl, crouching, ready
to defend myself; then the instinctive fear subsides and I
laugh. Judith laughs too.

"That's the first time I've every surprised you," she says.
"In 31 years, the first time!"

"You gave me one hell of a jolt."

"I've been standing here for three or four minutes *thinking* things at you. Trying to get a rise out of you, but no, no, you didn't react, you just went on staring at the snow. So I sneaked up and yelled in your ear. You were really startled, Duv. You weren't faking at all."

"Did you think I was lying to you about what had happened to me?"

"No, of course not."

"Then why'd you think I'd be faking?"

"I don't know. I guess I doubted you just a little. I don't any more. Oh, Duv, Duv, I feel so sad for you!"

"Don't," I say. "Please, Jude."

She is crying softly. How strange that is, to watch Judith cry. For love of me, no less. For love of me.

* * *

It's very quiet now.

The world is white outside and gray within. I accept that. I think life will be more peaceful. Silence will become my mother tongue. There will be discoveries and revelations, but no upheavals. Perhaps some color will come back into the world for me, later on. Perhaps.

Living, we fret. Dying, we live. I'll keep that in mind. I'll be of good cheer. Twang. Twing. Twong. Until I die again, hello, hello, hello, hello.

ABOUT THE AUTHOR

Robert Silverberg was born in New York and makes his home in the San Francisco area. He has written several hundred science fiction stories and over seventy science fiction novels, including *Lord Valentine's Castle*, *Majipoor Chronicles*, *Valentine Pontifex*, *Dying Inside*, *Thorns*, *The Book of Skulls*, *Star of Gypsies* and *At Winter's End*. He has won three Hugo awards and five Nebula awards. He is a past president of the Science Fiction Writers of America.

Read the powerful novels of award-winning author

ROBERT SILVERBERG

One of the most brilliant and beloved science fiction authors of our time, Robert Silverberg has been honored with two Hugo awards and four Nebula awards. His stirring combination of vivid imagery, evocative prose, and rousing storytelling promise his audience a reading experience like no other.

☐ VALENTINE PONTIFEX (24494 • $3.95)

☐ LORD VALENTINE'S CASTLE (27436 • $4.50)

☐ MAJIPOOR CHRONICLES (25530 • $3.95)

Prices and availability subject to change without notice.

Read these fine works by Robert Silverberg, on sale now wherever Bantam paperbacks are sold or use the handy coupon below for ordering.

CHERNOBYL
—A novel by Frederik Pohl

"Forty years ago **Chernobyl** would have been far-out science fiction; now it is sober (and sobering) fact. Fred Pohl, one of the great masters of science fiction, would have done a good job of it as SF; he does an even better job of it now. Grim and gripping, with people as people, not caricatures." **—Isaac Asimov**

"Pohl movingly bestows a recognizable human face upon a catastrophe that could have happened anywhere." **—Publishers Weekly**

"A bright marriage of technofiction to disaster . . . As if Tom Clancy's **The Hunt For Red October** has been mated with Arthur Hailey's **Airport.** But Pohl officiates at the wedding with much more skill and style than either Hailey or Clancy . . . It has been months since I last read a popular novel so expertly done." **—Chicago Sun-Times**

"Along with a splendid cast in a gripping and vivid narrative, Pohl presents as balanced and insightful a picture of the USSR as may be found. A pro's pro in top form, tackling an inherently fascinating subject: the combination is irresistable." **—Kirkus Reviews**

Buy **Chernobyl** now, on sale wherever Bantam Spectra books are sold, or use the handy coupon below for ordering:

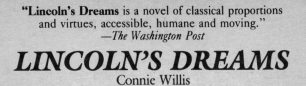